GUILTY ADDICTIONS

GUILTY ADDICTIONS

A Political Mystery

Garrett Wilson

NeWest Press
Edmonton

Canadian Cataloguing in Publication Data
Wilson, Garrett, 1932–
  Guilty addictions

  ISBN 1-896300-09-X

  I. Title.
PS8595.I5833G84 1999   C813'.54   C99-910238-9
PR9199.3.W49845G84 1999

Editor for the Press: Don Kerr
Cover and book design: Brenda Burgess
Cover photograph (legislative buildings) © Copyright 1999 Keith Burgess
Cover photograph (hunter) © Copyright 1999 Chuck Gordon
Back cover photograph © Copyright 1999 Chuck Gordon

NeWest Press acknowledges the support of the Canada Council for the Arts for our publishing program. We also acknowledge the financial support of the Government of Canada through the Book Publishing Industry Development Program (BPIDP) for our publishing activities.

THE CANADA COUNCIL | LE CONSEIL DES ARTS
FOR THE ARTS | DU CANADA
SINCE 1957 | DEPUIS 1957

Canadian Patrimoine
Heritage canadien

Permission to use the quotation from *Better Than Sex: Confessions of a Political Junkie*, copyright 1994 by Hunter S. Thompson, published by Random House, Inc. courtesy Random House, Inc.

This is a work of fiction. Although many of the events described in the story may have occurred at one time or another, all of the characters are imaginary. They bear no relation to people in real life.

Printed and bound in Canada

NeWest Publishers Limited
Suite 201, 8540-109 Street
Edmonton, Alberta T6G 1E6

In spite of the odd blot, Canada and its provinces enjoy political systems that are the envy of the world. To the very many men and women of honour and integrity whose devotion to public service have made this so, this book is humbly dedicated.

—And to Molly

Acknowledgements

Over the five year gestation of this story from its conception in the spring of 1994 I have drawn upon the assistance of many friends. As this is my first venture into the field of fiction, a lot of help was needed.

Linda McKnight of Westwood Creative Concepts in Toronto suffered through the early drafts and provided both encouragement and sound advice.

Aydon Charlton, a very knowledgeable member of the literati, followed with professional critique and friendly suggestion.

Dave Margoshes, a fellow writer, reviewed a developing draft, identified many weaknesses and proferred a solution for each.

Don Kerr, an experienced editor and member of the board of NeWest, spotted some merit through the mist and, as final editor, delivered polish and insightful analysis.

Along the way, others contributed meaningfully: Deputy Chief of Police (Ret'd) Ed Swayze, drew upon his extensive experience as a homicide investigator to evaluate and advise; Bill Armstrong, very old friend and former oil patch executive, gave both technical and literary suggestions; Merrilee Rasmussen, Q.C., my law partner, was generous with encouragement and forbearance; Kim Laycock and Julie Williams uncomplainingly printed and copied draft after draft.

Much of this story was written in two of the most scenic sites in Canada; overlooking the mystic vale of the Miramichi River in New Brunswick, and next to Lake Kagawong, at Perivale, on Manitoulin Island, Ontario. Except for the distraction of the natural beauty, both locations were ideal for a concentrating writer. In New Brunswick, I must recognize the kindness of George and Rox Vanderbeck of Sunny Corner; Peter O'Neill, whose Newcastle law office and sister Sally printed early drafts; and Mario and Sally Di Carlo of Minto, who introduced us to the Miramichi. At Manitoulin, my sister Sheila and brother-in-law Bob McMullan provided accommodation, kindness and editorial assistance.

Jacqueline, my wife and best friend, was present throughout with support and encouragement.

Not everybody is comfortable with the idea that politics is a guilty addiction. But it *is*. They *are* addicts, and they *are* guilty and they *do* lie and cheat and steal—like all junkies. And when they get in a frenzy, they will sacrifice anything and anybody to feed their cruel and stupid habit, and there *is* no cure for it. That is addictive thinking. That is politics—

—Hunter S. Thompson,
Better Than Sex: Confessions of a Political Junkie

ONE

"'Dust unto dust' always strikes me as the sort of phrase Abraham Lincoln might have coined. A simple but eloquent statement of the ethereal quality of life."

Cameron Hunt spoke as much to the open grave as to the younger man standing beside him, then watched sympathetically as Oxford LaCoste turned slowly towards the speaker, needing an almost physical effort to wrench his eyes away from the casket lowering into the earth before him. He resented the interruption. Hunt continued.

"Ben was a fine man, Oxford, a very fine man. But limited by human frailties, as we all are. He did deal with them better than many, but they were there, nonetheless. He would want us to remember him as he was, no more."

The man whose body was descending into the grave had been Oxford's mentor as well as friend, and he was not prepared to have him reduced to mortal terms, even in death. Sullen with sorrow, he now felt anger flooding into him.

Seeing that, Hunt changed course.

"Enough of that for now. I came over to warn you that the premier has his eye on you. My guess is he will have a proposition for you before he leaves town."

"For me? Such as?" Oxford was still angry.

"Ben's constituency, I'm guessing, or . . ."

"WHAT! How could he? Ben's not even . . ." Oxford's anger turned to disgust as he gestured at the open grave.

1

"I know, I know. But politicians think differently than you and me. And this politician is becoming very concerned about his future. Cracks are showing in his temple."

The two lawyers looked across the prairie gravesite to where Premier Harris Halliday and the official party were standing with Ben Forsyth's widow, Ruth. Until five days ago Ben had been the highly respected minister of Provincial Development in Halliday's government. The September day was iron grey and the ever-present wind of southwestern Saskatchewan flung a few early and threatening snowflakes at the topcoats of the official party, isolated by status from the other mourners.

Oxford considered Cameron Hunt's warning, squinting into the wind at the older lawyer, a tall, wide-shouldered man, still erect in spite of his age, with steady almond eyes above a strong wind-chiselled face. As he often did, Oxford thought Hunt completely belonged to the short-grass cattle range that stretched south and west away from them far beyond the horizon. In his early thirties, Oxford was less than half Hunt's age and he felt a quick pang of contrition at having been even slightly irritated with the elder whose wisdom he had learned to admire. If the old country lawyer who had founded the law office Oxford now operated thought something was up with the visiting politicians, it would behoove Oxford to stay alert.

When he had attended previous ceremonies in this cemetery Oxford had thought the site lacking in beauty and dignity. Today he felt it was entirely inadequate to the distinction attained by Ben Forsyth. But he knew the early settlers who had come west seeking land of their own had far too great a desire for what they found to donate it for common graveyard use. Marginal land with little productive or prospective value would do just as well. Western cemeteries are often found at uncomfortable distances from the communities they serve, frequently on hillsides too steep or barren to plow. Human nature, thought Oxford.

Now the promising political and legal career of Ben Forsyth had come to a full stop two miles east of his West Willow home on the exposed and treeless flank of Sunburst Bench. The chilling wind that funnelled down the Willow

River valley cut short the social discourse that followed the interment, the exchange of gossip which was the real reason for the presence of many of the mourners. The crowd that had followed the funeral procession to the graveside ceremony hastened to accept the invitation that had been issued from the pulpit to "join the family at lunch which will be served following the interment." The church basement was too small to accommodate the mourners and the Memorial Hall had been pressed into service.

There Premier Harris Halliday, with coffee balanced in one hand and the other extended, approached Oxford with easy familiarity. No introduction apparently was needed beyond the two previous, and surely forgotten, "How are ya's" at political meetings in West Willow when Ben Forsyth had taken the trouble to bring his young law partner to the attention of the premier.

"Terrible loss, Oxford, terrible loss. To all of us. To the whole province, in fact."

"Yes, sir. We'll miss him greatly." Oxford ended the handshake first, thinking that for such an experienced and successful politician Halliday imparted a distinctly wimpish odour.

"Some of us more than others, though. You for sure. Me, my government, particularly. Ben was doing great things for us." Harris Halliday, for seven years premier of Saskatchewan as head of the Western Democratic Alliance government, was almost totally lacking in physical presence, little of which had to do which his modest stature. In fact, as Oxford noted in his first real conversation with the man, if it were not for the aura of his office he would be so nondescript as to be almost invisible among this gathering of so many tall and burly men of the range.

"Yes, sir." Oxford dutifully supplied a connector to assist the politician.

"Yes, indeed, Ben was engaged in some very important work, very critical work. Vital work. Don't know how we're going to replace him." Halliday seemed to be straining to supply the sincerity he felt the situation required.

"Yes, sir." Again Oxford filled the hole, now feeling that his help was really not needed.

"Ben thought very highly of you, Oxford. Always spoke of you as a very reliable and capable lawyer. Said he'd not have been comfortable going into politics if he'd not had you to take over his law office." Halliday took a sip of his coffee, his eyes on Oxford.

"Nice of you to say that, sir." Now it begins, Oxford thought Cameron Hunt wasn't losing anything to his years yet. He was right on the money again.

"Yes, Val here often heard Ben speak of you. And me too, of course," Halliday added hastily.

"By the way, you do know Val Sisik, my deputy, don't you, Oxford?" Halliday gestured to his right. A tall, lean, and sharp-featured man arrived at the premier's shoulder, bearing a plate of sandwiches and cakes.

"How do you do, sir," Oxford said, putting forth his hand to the man the political writers suggested was the real power behind the Halliday throne.

"Happy to know you, Oxford. The premier is correct. Ben Forsyth frequently expressed his admiration for you. Held you in such high regard that he placed you in charge of his affairs, as I understand it. Yes?" Something in Sisik's speech grated on Oxford; it was as if he was being told he was in the presence of a superior person.

"Well, in a way," Oxford admitted. "Ben's will appoints me an executor of his estate, together with Cameron Hunt. I do regard it as an honour."

"Yes, Ben must have had a great deal of faith in you. I'm sure his confidence is well placed." Sisik smiled paternally.

"Which brings us to an important matter we'd like to discuss with you, Oxford," Halliday took over, swallowing the last of the dainty sandwiches he had been munching while listening to the other two. "We'd like your help in completing a bit of Ben's unfinished business. A rather important assignment."

"I'm afraid I'll be tied up with the law office and Ben's estate for some time," Oxford replied, thinking of Cameron Hunt's suggestion that the premier would be looking to him to take over as the party's local candidate.

"Well, it's as a lawyer that we want to retain you. I'm sure you'll be able to work us in with your other clients.

4

And I think we all know that Ben would have wanted you to step in, on his behalf as well as ours." So Cameron's guess wasn't right, Oxford thought, taking a moment to react to the unexpected proposal. His pause was a mistake.

"Okay, then," Halliday continued, giving Oxford no opportunity to object. "That's settled. You'll come aboard this project. Glad to have you with us, Oxford. I'll enjoy working with you." And Oxford found himself shaking the premier's hand as if to seal a bargain. "Val here will work out the details. I'd better get over to Ruth. She's beginning to look a little upset."

With that Halliday moved smoothly across the polished floor that was more accustomed to dancers than mourners and joined Ruth Forsyth and the small group of her relatives. Oxford LaCoste, watching glumly, realized that he had just experienced how difficult it was to refuse a premier. He wondered what it was he had agreed to.

Dr. Vladimir Sisik took over. Oxford was interested to meet the deputy minister to the premier, a man he knew had a somewhat obscure background and who seemed to encourage the aura of mystery that had developed around him.

Oxford knew that Ben Forsyth had been more than a little curious about Vladimir Sisik when he had first met the imported economist, so curious that he had made some cursory inquires about Sisik's background. Ben had learned that Sisik had appeared from behind the Iron Curtain in the 1960s, claiming to be a graduate of the University of Warsaw. He made his way to England and the London School of Economics where he earned a doctorate in public finance. After a few years lecturing at two or three junior colleges in New England, he surfaced in Newfoundland in the position of economic advisor to the government of Premier Owen Clearshaw.

Clearshaw, determined to force his province forward into economic prosperity, underwrote a number of dangerously speculative economic ventures that he hoped would provide both employment and financial reward. His failure rate was nearly perfect and the Clearshaw government collapsed in scandal and ignominy when the resulting losses nearly destroyed Newfoundland's financial stability.

Sisik's reputation was tarnished, but he emerged from

5

the Newfoundland wreckage in better condition than most members of the defeated administration. Although he had been Clearshaw's economic advisor, he produced a dossier of recommendations and stern warnings he claimed had been ignored by a premier who had become maddened in the pursuit of profit.

Sisik returned to academia where he wrote a treatise in defence of the Newfoundland experiment, privately published under the title, *The Stimulus of Economic Development by Direct Public Investment.* Upon the strength of Sisik's self-declared expertise in the area, Premier Halliday, entering his second term of office, brought him to Saskatchewan and placed him in charge of assessing and selecting potential economic development ventures. Sisik's field of responsibility had so rapidly expanded, and Halliday had so come to depend upon his advice in almost every area, that some members of the Saskatchewan cabinet grumbled that the economist had secured a Rasputin-like hold on the premier. Oxford didn't know Ben's views any more. He hadn't mentioned them to Oxford.

Now, speaking to Oxford LaCoste, Sisik displayed the style that had earned him a take-charge reputation among the bureaucrats in Regina.

"How soon into Regina can you come, Oxford? We'll need to brief you in detail, and most of what you do will be in the city. Two days from now, three? No more. We like to get you started quickly. I'll send a plane for you. Don't waste time driving, at least for now." Sisik spoke quickly and, it seemed to Oxford, urgently. There was a decided accent. Or was it an affectation, Oxford wondered?

"But," the lawyer protested, "I can't get away right now. The office, Ben's affairs. I couldn't."

"The premier said this was an important matter. You heard? Yes? It is. I emphasize that. You understand that we ask for priority over your other work. Once you are familiar with the assignment, you will better understand. Also, I think the level of compensation we intend will accommodate a certain amount of inconvenience." Sisik was speaking sternly now, clearly not accustomed to resistance.

"This is Wednesday. I'll have a plane on the strip out

here at eight o'clock Monday morning. That will give you two days plus the weekend to get things under control here, quite sufficient, I'm sure. Yes?"

Taking compliance for granted, Sisik went on. "You will need to be in Regina three, maybe four days at first. After that, who knows? I expect that you will not take long, perhaps only a week. Maybe two or three. If more time is needed, it will mean that we have a long-life affair and we will then review our arrangements. As to those arrangements. You are engaged by the Executive Council. You will report through me to the premier, no one else. That must be clearly understood. Yes?" The deputy minister paused until Oxford nodded.

"But," Oxford spotted an opening. "What is it I'm expected to do? The premier mentioned a 'project.' What's my function?"

"That detail later. When we meet in Regina," Sisik overrode the question. "Our usual retainer rate is two thousand dollars per diem, plus all reasonable expenses. I think that will be suitable, do you not agree? Yes?"

This time Oxford did more than nod, he stammered, "Of course." In truth, he had never successfully charged as much as half that for a full hard day in court including much late night preparation time. Sisik smiled at the anticipated effect.

"Fine. That's all settled, then. My secretary will call you Friday with the further details. One final thing, however. Your first instructions, counsellor." Oxford's new client was now very serious.

"I know I don't have to mention confidentiality but I wish now to emphasize how important it is in this case. Even the fact of your retainer is to be confidential, to be revealed to no one. And," here Sisik actually put his index finger to Oxford's chest, "any files of the government of Saskatchewan or any of its agencies in the possession of or among the effects of our good friend Ben Forsyth are the property of the government of Saskatchewan. They will be turned over directly to me, unopened, unreviewed, undisturbed. Please indicate that you understand and accept that instruction. Yes?"

Oxford stared at Sisik, certain he was hearing rehearsed lines. More sure of himself now, he replied, "Certainly. Quite clear."

"Good." Sisik relaxed and smiled. "Here is my card. On the back is the number of my cellular phone. That also is confidential. It is reserved for the use of the premier, but he has authorized you to have it also. The telephone is always with me. Call any time, the day or night. Particularly if you should discover any confidential government files that Ben Forsyth might have been keeping, perhaps at his office or at his home down here. See you on Monday. Yes?"

Sisik marched stiff-necked and straight across the hall to Premier Halliday and Ruth Forsyth to whom he bowed, stiffly, from the waist. Like a Prussian count, Oxford thought, watching, and wondered if Sisik had to remember not to click his heels.

A sudden shudder of excitement hit him. This was a big deal. Maybe a really big deal. He had been retained to serve at a very high level. About as high as it gets in Saskatchewan. Oxford grinned in spite of himself, then wiped it off, remembering the solemnity of the situation. Within a few minutes, Patrick Justice, the retired RCMP staff sergeant who served as security advisor to Harris Halliday, summoned their driver, and the premier and his party left for the West Willow air field and their aircraft. A Piper Cheyenne, executive styling within and thinly disguised as an air ambulance, was the $3 million flagship of the Executive Air Service maintained for members of Halliday's government. "'Arris 'Alliday's Air Force," was the derisive description supplied by the opposition party in the Saskatchewan Legislature.

As soon as the official party left the hall, Ruth Forsyth turned back from watching their departure and beckoned imperiously to Oxford. "My turn," he thought disconsolately, as he dutifully walked over to her.

Oxford had little experience with bereaved widows, but this one had already become a burden. Always egotistical, selfish, and full of criticism, Ruth Forsyth had become even more so since her husband's death, blaming the world and everyone around her for her loss. Her constant demands had kept Oxford running since she had returned to West

Willow to take charge of the funeral arrangements. Ruth's consumption of expensive Scotch, long a problem, had risen to an alarming level.

"You'd think they might have stayed a little longer. Ben was his most important minister, after all. Said he had an important delegation waiting for him in Regina. I'll just bet." She was angry as usual and Oxford sympathized with the fleeing Harris Halliday.

"I want you to come by the house this evening, Oxford. Some important matters I want to discuss with you." Ruth had a way of choosing a word for the day, or sometimes several days. Today's word, Oxford noted, was "important."

"Sure, what time would be convenient? How about 7:30?" He had learned not to be around Ruth any later in the day than necessary; she became much too difficult and unpleasant as her whiskey evenings wore on.

"That'll be fine. Looks like everyone will be long gone by then. Lots of important things to do today, it seems." Ruth had always been fastidious about her appearance, but the effects of too little sleep and far too much drink for several days running had defeated even her skill with cosmetics. Oxford had seen that condition too often to feel any sympathy, even on a day such as this, and he quickly made his escape, temporary as it was.

Two

"It will be a smooth flight. Thermals are out of season."
Val Sisik opened the bar on the Cheyenne and poured
a stiff rye and water for Harris Halliday, a Perrier for himself.

The premier accepted gratefully and took a long swallow, grimacing slightly. He did not much enjoy rye whiskey,
preferred scotch, but would not make the admission, much
less switch, even privately. Rye was the drink of choice in
rural Saskatchewan and Harris Halliday carefully tended
his chosen image as a man of the country.

Conscripted to the leadership of the Western Democratic
Alliance almost eight years earlier, Halliday had won two
elections. He would have to call a third in a year or, at the
most, two. The WDA, formed to present "a free enterprise
alternative" to Saskatchewan's powerful socialist party,
was losing its connection with the voters, in spite of an
impressive record of industrial and commercial investment.

Halliday himself maintained a high voter approval rat-
ing, far ahead of his government. The public liked his folksy
ways but no longer accepted him as an apostle of a new
economic order. Halliday's program of public and private
investment and privatization was running out of steam.
Now the WDA premier hefted his drink.

"Much more time with Ruth Forsyth and I'd need something stronger than this. She is some witch. Ben was a hel-
luva great guy. Where did he get her from?"

"They married very early, as I understand," Sisik replied. He had heard the question often, and knew it was not put for information.

"Must have been tough on Ben. Probably lucky they have no kids."

Sisik awaited the real question. It came immediately.

"Will the kid play?" Halliday dropped his voice to be sure that Justice and the two aides sitting forward could not hear.

"He'll play. Two thousand a day opened his eyes like I had hit him with a stock prodder." Sisik enjoyed an occasional lapse into the premier's idiom.

"'Never met a lawyer I liked nor one I couldn't buy,'" Halliday chuckled. "Whoever said that first had it right. Bastards, all of them."

"Except maybe Ben Forsyth," he added after a reflective moment.

And still later, as he looked down upon a late-running combine trailing a plume of dust a mile below, "You come up with that file, you call me right now, day or night, wherever, whatever. Clear?"

"Clear." The deputy minister was accustomed to the premier asserting himself occasionally.

THREE

That evening as he walked homeward along the quiet West Willow streets Oxford LaCoste tried to make sense out of his day, oblivious to the history around him that he usually found so fascinating. Events had rushed at him without time for assimilation.

The retainer from the premier, from the Executive Council actually, Sisik had said, was as yet unexplained. But whatever it was, it might go on a while. Become "a long-life affair," in Sisik's words. What could that mean? Or lead to? And where might it take him?

Out of West Willow, for sure. For good? Maybe? He had often wondered if his attachment to this community was permanent, or merely a way station of his life and career. He liked the town, the land, and its people. So much so that he had steeped himself in their history.

As a place of habitation, Oxford learned, West Willow's origin trailed well back before the time of Christ. The deep, wooded coulees and the clear springs feeding into Willow River were often home to the nomadic tribes wandering the plains on foot following the vast bison herds. By the time the horse, acquired from the Spaniards in New Mexico in the 1500s, reached the northern natives two centuries later, the site had become almost constantly occupied. The last of the aboriginals to seek sanctuary along the Willow River were several thousand of the followers of Sitting Bull fleeing the avenging Long Knives of the United States Cavalry after the Battle of Little Big Horn in 1876. Not long after Sitting Bull and the last of his lodges recrossed the Medicine Line and surrendered to the United States Army in the spring of 1881, Harmon Jasper, a young American trader, struck out east from Cypress Hills to seek his fortune. After five lazy days of riding through the empty countryside, Harmon found himself camped on the west rim of a wide and rolling valley. The next morning, coffee in hand, he watched a brilliant sunrise leap over the east rim and sweep down into the valley. Harmon Jasper rode no further and his Sunburst Ranch was born.

As much a trading post as a ranch, the Sunburst lasted twenty-four years until the founder, struggling to save some of his cattle from the monstrous winter of 1906/1907, was himself trapped in one of the worst of its many blizzards. Spring released the frozen bodies of Harmon and his horse from the drifted over coulee in which they had sought shelter. Marie Jasper, the Metis wife Harmon recruited from one of the last buffalo expeditions out of Red River, assessed her holdings, now stocked only with carcasses, and returned to Manitoba with her two children.

But Harmon Jasper's site selection was confirmed seven years after his death when, with the arrival of steel, the town of West Willow was surveyed on the remains of his Sunburst Ranch.

Now a comfortably prosperous community of three thousand, West Willow had been home to Oxford LaCoste for eight years, since Ben Forsyth had enlisted him to the Hunt and Forsyth law office.

"I want to run for the legislature next year," Ben had said, "and I'm pretty sure I can get elected. If I do, it's your office. If I don't, there's enough here for both of us anyway, and we'll work it out."

Ben Forsyth had been elected easily enough. The Western Democratic Alliance had won all but ten seats in the sixty-five seat legislature. When Premier Halliday took the new member from Willow River into his first cabinet, Ben turned the law firm of Hunt, Forsyth, and LaCoste over to Oxford, moved to Regina and bought a condominium.

Appointed Minister of Wildlife Resources and Lands, Ben served six years in that office until he took over the Provincial Development portfolio a year before his death. As other more senior ministers fell victim to scandal, his demonstrated natural flair for politics and administrative ability had promoted him to the position as the likely heir to Harris Halliday.

Early the previous Saturday morning, Ben Forsyth had died of carbon monoxide poisoning in the garage of his Regina condominium after returning late from an out-of-town political meeting. The death had been judged accidental. He had fallen asleep at the wheel of his still running car.

As Oxford walked slowly through the dark and empty West Willow streets, windstripped leaves from the Northwest Poplars that dominate the boulevards blew and bunched about the curbs. He was deep in thought over the events of the day; some were unexpected, some strange. But he felt undercurrents he could not identify. And some of them stemmed from Ruth Forsyth.

Ruth had been difficult, as Oxford had expected, but the interview had been brief. Ruth's only sister, who had moved in and taken charge of the Forsyth household the day after Ben's death, had been sent packing back to her nearby farm home. Now alone, the widow Forsyth was dedicating the evening and night to some serious drinking, well under way by the time of Oxford's arrival.

Ben Forsyth's widow had one message to impart. She did so quickly and drunkenly, and then consigned her guest back into the night.

"I have told Cameron and now I'll tell you. I'm damn mad that Ben appointed you two as executors. I could handle our affairs just fine, thank you, without your help where it's not wanted. And I'm mad, too, that Ben never told me that he'd done it, or I'd have had a thing or two to say about it, you can be sure.

"But there isn't a damn thing I can do about it now, I know. I've checked." She poured a good shot of Chivas Regal to top up the tumbler beside her. "You and that old Cameron Hunt aren't the only lawyers in the world, you know."

Oxford sat silently through this onslaught. Ben had

14

warned them, when his will had been drawn, that Ruth would be furious if she learned that her husband had not trusted her to handle his financial affairs, but he confessed that he lacked the courage to tell her himself.

"I expect to make a few more wills before I go, anyway," Ben had told Cameron and Oxford, as he signed the will only the year before, "and hopefully Ruth will straighten out and I can depend on her. Then she'll never have to know about what we're doing here today."

That was Ben, all right, Oxford thought. Ben was always loyal, always hopeful that things would work out for the better. Anyone else would have left Ruth years ago, but Ben stuck.

He should have been right about the will. At only forty-seven Ben had no reason to think that will would be going to the courthouse for probate. Just one day after Ben's death, Ruth had demanded a copy of the will, explaining that she wanted to see if it contained any special directions respecting funeral arrangements. Although the reason was superficially plausible, both Oxford and Cameron Hunt had wondered at the timing of the request. But knowing they could not justify refusing, or even delaying, the request, they had meekly complied, expecting that a storm would follow.

Now, having vented her anger at being excluded from the management of her husband's estate, Ruth Forsyth turned to her real concerns.

"So, I'm not going to make a fuss about Ben's will, not even about the fact that he didn't leave everything to me. Those ungrateful brothers of his don't deserve what he gave them, but I'm not going to fight about it." She picked up her glass and startled Oxford with the amount she removed in one swallow.

"But the will says, 'all my personal effects to my said wife,' or something like that, doesn't it, Oxford?"

"Yes. Yes, it does."

"What are 'personal effects,' Oxford?"

"Well, the usual, you know, clothing, jewellery, the like." The lawyer was trying to be careful but was aware that he was not looking sharp.

"And books?"

"And books, in a personal library, yes."

"And files?" Jesus, Oxford thought, someone else is interested in Ben's files. Careful, now.

"Well, personal files, yes. But client files, definitely no. Other files, it would depend."

"Depend on what?" Ruth persisted.

"Well, as a cabinet minister, Ben worked for the government. Files he was working on for the government would belong to the government." Maybe that would do it, Oxford hoped.

"How about files and notes and things, maybe having to do with his government work, that Ben was preparing for his own personal use? Maybe for his memoirs? Maybe a diary?" Ruth had obviously "checked" this area also.

"Well, a personal diary, I guess would be personal. Files and notes, I don't know. There's the problem of confidentiality and ownership of information. Probably it would be a matter of degree." Oxford felt pressed.

"And who would decide that question of degree?" Ruth was like a bulldog, in spite of the Scotch.

"Well, in the first instance, the executors and the beneficiaries. And any third parties involved, such as the government. The court as a last resort, if no agreement could be reached."

"Yeah, fine, Oxford, don't try to lawyer me." Ruth hit her glass hard onto the coffee table. "I lived with one long enough, thank you." She leaned forward theatrically, being careful not to lose her balance.

"Somebody has to look at those files first and decide if they're personal, or not personal, or maybe half and half. I'm going to be that somebody. I want you to give me every damn file of Ben's that you come across, and I want them unopened. I'll give you back those that aren't personal, but I don't want you and Cameron Hunt snooping through Ben's personal stuff deciding what you'll give me and what you won't. Is that clear?"

Oxford recalled that Val Sisik earlier that day had also been very firm about Ben's files. Before he could respond, Ruth was at him again.

"And don't worry about any so-called client files. Ben

hadn't practised law for years, since he was elected. We all know that. So you jus' gimme all of Ben's files, unnerstan'?" The Scotch was beginning to take control.

"I'll talk to Cameron. I know we certainly won't want to poke about in Ben's personal life. I'm sure . . ." Ruth cut him off.

"Jus' do as I'm tellin' you, Oxford, or there'll be trouble. Lotsa trouble. Now get out of here. I'm tired."

And he had left the Forsyth home, a long, modern brick bungalow neatly tucked among old Colorado Blue Spruce. And now, a thoroughly alarmed young lawyer, he crossed the street towards his own home. As Oxford turned into his tiny yard, an oversized English setter jumped happily out of a stuffed chair on the verandah and, tail wagging furiously, greeted his master.

"Hiya, Sam." Oxford bent to embrace the dog and receive a cold nose nuzzling in his ear.

"Come on, time for bed."

Oxford turned out his light and sank back onto the pillow. It had, he reflected, been something of a day.

Whatever the hell Ben Forsyth had been up to was obviously a little out of line for a minister of Provincial Development in the government of the Province of Saskatchewan. But Oxford was excited and sleep was slow to come. However his mission might turn out, it promised to be new and different.

FOUR

Early Saturday afternoon Oxford looked up from his files at the large, imploring brown eyes that had broken his concentration. Sam lifted his head from the arm of the ancient leather chair that was reserved for him in Oxford's office, the eyes now sparkling and the tail banging hopefully and noisily against the cowhide seat.

"You think so, do you Sam?" At those words the dog sprang from his chair and over to the lawyer. With chin on his master's knee, Sam gazed upwards, pleading with the brown eyes and subdued whimpers. Oxford was familiar with the request.

"Okay, okay, Muttley. I think you're right. It *is* a nice day and the season's on. Let's get out of here." Oxford gave in and shoved back from his desk. He had worked long hours, particularly since Ben Forsyth's funeral three days earlier, and his brain craved fresh air and exercise.

Half an an hour later the lawyer and setter were jouncing happily out of town in Oxford's Jeep heading to the irrigation flats ten miles east where the pheasants thrived. Sam sat in the front passenger seat leaning and peering ahead as he watched intently for any feathered creatures that might be gravelling along the shoulder of the road.

Oxford regarded the Jeep as his only major idiosyncrasy. An elderly working model of the CJ line, it had completed a hard tour of duty with an oil well service company before

Oxford, on a sudden impulse, liberated it from a used car lot in Swift Current. Even for a bachelor it was impractical. It carried only two, had ridiculously little cargo room, rode like a stone boat and the powerful Oldsmobile V8 engine someone had transplanted under the hood guzzled fuel like a 747. Oxford had no need whatsoever for the Jeep's power and four wheel drive. But it was fun and he indulged himself around West Willow and driving down to the family homestead he maintained. Occasionally he resorted to its amazing acceleration. It would leap from a sedate 100 kilometres per hour to an eye-popping 160 so quickly as to astound any local hotshot with an expensive pick-up truck who sought to trifle with the decrepit looking Jeep. As a concession to practicality and his professional image, Oxford also owned a Saab 900, "pre-owned" but sparkling.

Sam loved the Jeep and, to Oxford's delight, presided from his seat as if he were the owner and Oxford his chauffeur. The lawyer, the Jeep, and the dog had become a West Willow institution.

Oxford parked the Jeep in a ditch and the two of them moved out on foot. Sam happily coursed through the buck brush along the ditches and into the willow clumps where the birds like to congregate on warm fall afternoons. Oxford followed, keeping to the edge of the brush, his old Winchester twelve gauge in hand, only half his mind on what Sam was doing.

Oxford was not a keen hunter, but he enjoyed the excursions he and Sam took together. The setter's enthusiasm and talent with game birds was delightful to watch and the beauty of the Indian summer days in southwestern Saskatchewan was intoxicating. The shooting was incidental; Oxford thought he would prefer to leave the shotgun hanging on his basement wall except he didn't want to disappoint Sam.

Like all youngsters raised in rural Saskatchewan, Oxford had a basic familiarity with firearms. He had learned to shoot gophers in his father's pasture almost as soon as he could carry the single-shot .22 that stood always behind the door in the farm house back porch. Later he had graduated to the 30-30 carbine that was used to teach the coyotes to respect the farmyard, and particularly the hen house. The Winchester he carried had been his father's and, although Oxford was comfortable with the old shotgun, he had not dedicated himself to becoming more than a barely respectable wing shot.

In fact, Oxford had not fired a gun for years when Ben Forsyth showed up one evening with Sam, a gangly two-month-old setter of the Laverack strain. The breeder had pressed the pup onto him, Ben explained, and he had finally accepted the gift, thinking that it was just the ticket for a young lawyer living alone in West Willow.

"Someone to come home to at night, Oxford," Ben had said. "I'm beginning to worry that you'll turn into one of those slightly strange bachelor types. Not that a dog will entirely prevent that, but he should help."

Oxford had not at first welcomed Sam, particularly since he had no experience in raising a dog. But Henrietta Parr, who supervised Oxford's modest household, agreed with Ben Forsyth and took charge. Once the pup was house trained Oxford's reservations disappeared. He learned how to protect his shoes and other chewables, and he began to enjoy the companionship. Because of Sam he got out and about more, often just for walks together, but Oxford also found himself lacing up his old Adidas again. In university, although not much interested in athletics, he had taken up jogging to restore his brain after long hours in the books. Now he and Sam ran happily together along the quiet road allowances. The pounds that had gathered around Oxford's waistline melted away and his six-foot frame returned to the 175 pounds it had carried when he left law school. Before long the setter found out where Oxford spent his days, invited himself into the law office, charmed Ethel Tremblay, the firm's secretary/manager, and appropriated the old leather chair to himself. Grown into a tall, graceful animal with liver markings on a white background, delicate feathers on his legs and a plume-like tail, Sam was a beautiful specimen of his breed.

Right now Sam was making bird sign. His tail went rigid and he began to stalk slowly forward. A hen pheasant lost her nerve and burst into flight, followed by two more. Then

20

a rooster rose angrily and crossed swiftly between dog and hunter. Oxford had been thinking of Ben Forsyth and was startled. He took a mechanical shot and missed. Sam looked at him.

"Sorry, Sam. Shot three feet behind him. But that's okay. Hank said she didn't want to see any more than two birds tonight and we've lots of time."

Mrs. Henrietta Parr lived across the alley from Oxford. When Burt Parr's heart failed, no longer able to keep up with the demands of their sheep ranch, Hank sold out and brought her invalid husband to West Willow. Burt had lasted only two more years, and the widow, who had the strength and physique of a police matron and had never known a day of indolence in her life, became desperate for something to occupy her time. When Oxford arrived, Hank, as she had been known since her tomboy girlhood, took over. House, laundry, yard, and then Sam all fell under her care. Oxford lived as a carefree bachelor knowing that his home—and dog—were in good hands.

Sam raised another rooster. This one made the mistake of climbing straight up, presenting Oxford with a ridiculously easy shot. His short twinge of shame at having taken advantage of the bird disappeared when Sam proudly delivered it to his hand. Oxford shared the setter's pleasure as he tucked their prize into the game pocket at the back of his jacket.

As he trudged along behind Sam, Oxford's mind worried at the Ben Forsyth mystery presented to him by Harris Halliday, Vladimir Sisik, and Ruth Forsyth. Obviously, they were all anxious to locate whatever it was that Ben had been working on, but why would he be better able to find it than they? If it had to do with politics, and surely it must, they were all far more capable of uncovering Ben's tracks than he.

Oxford had not taken a close interest in Ben Forsyth's work as a cabinet minister, or even his responsibilities as the Member of the Legislative Assembly for West Willow. When Ben had been first elected, Cameron Hunt had called the three of them into session down at the office. Hunt pointed out that Oxford was going to be hard-pressed to handle the work load there, even with some mild assistance from him. If Ben's constituents got the idea that they could get to him through his old law firm, Oxford would be overwhelmed. Not only that, Hunt went on, but a certain class of client would try to curry favour with the new cabinet minister by throwing legal work into his law firm, never mind that he no longer had any financial interest there. That again would be unfair to Oxford, who would have trouble recognizing in time that he might be compromising Ben, at least in the client's mind, and also unfair to Ben, who might be called upon to repay perceived favours he knew nothing about.

The solution that Hunt proposed and they adopted was simple. Abandoning any thoughts of choosing another community in his riding, Ben would place a competently-staffed constituency office in West Willow so Oxford could send any constituent with a governmental problem across the street. And, for the first year at least, Oxford would not accept any work from anyone who had not previously been a client of the firm.

It worked. Hunt's foresight saved both Oxford and Ben a great deal of trouble and embarrassment. And Oxford quickly became adept at identifying the favour-seekers.

But even aside from that forced separation of law and politics, Oxford soon found that he had little connection to Ben Forsyth's new life. In the beginning, Ben had reported enthusiastically on his work and experiences, but before long he became more and more reticent, which suited Oxford exactly. He had discovered that he had no taste for political intrigue, and the stories of backroom wheeling and dealing disgusted him. Oxford was quite satisfied to devote himself to the law office, which kept him busy through long days and most weekends. He watched the ascending political career of Ben Forsyth from a safe distance.

In truth, Oxford soon developed a distaste for the policies and personnel of the Western Democratic Alliance. Although he had never been a political partisan, had never been active in any political party, he had naturally helped in Ben's campaigns. The first election had been exciting and fun. The second much less so, and Oxford noticed that the workers around the WDA campaign committee rooms were somehow different. He mentioned it to Ben, only half in jest.

"Have you noticed that every knuckle-dragger and redneck in this corner of the province is out front in your campaign?" Oxford had asked, trying to smile as he did so.

But Ben had not been amused. "A politician has to take his support where he can find it," he retorted, closing the subject.

And it had stayed closed, as if they both recognized a dangerous area of potential serious disagreement. But Oxford now wondered why he had been so content to turn a blind eye to this side of Ben's life that he found so disagreeable, almost ugly. And keep that eye turned the more obvious it became that Ben was changing—had changed, was no longer the Ben Forsyth he had known.

Oxford had often acknowledged to himself that he had loved Ben Forsyth like a brother. But he had never had a brother. Or a sister either. Had he been fearful of losing the respect and affection of the one human being to whom he was close, so fearful that he shut out all the signals that trouble was closing in? Had he failed Ben Forsyth?

Even though the political columnists were giving high marks to the member from Willow River, and even touting him as the likely successor to Harris Halliday, Ben Forsyth had long since ceased showing any enthusiasm for his work. For at least a year, both Hunt and Oxford had noted that Ben had almost completely stopped speaking about his political life. But neither man had suggested doing anything. They were concerned and available if Ben should ask for help. But he had not asked, nor had he discussed with them any of his problems or plans.

So how am I supposed to find out what he had been up to? Oxford mused. Just then Sam flushed a full covey of pheasants. At least a dozen birds leaped noisily into the air, beating furiously in all directions as Oxford raised his gun, only half-heartedly trying to pick out the roosters from the hens and then not taking a shot at all.

"That's okay, Sam," he said to the obviously disappointed setter. "Hank didn't say we had to bring two. One will do, and it's time we went home."

Driving back to West Willow Oxford wondered again about what would be expected of him in Regina on Monday. His desk was cleared and he was ready for action. Fortunately, he had been booked for little litigation on the fall calendar, and had been able to adjourn almost every item. Time he now had, but for what?

He had spent much of the last three nights in anxious speculation about that. What work had Ben Forsyth, a minister of the Crown, been engaged in that somehow could be carried on by Oxford LaCoste, country lawyer? And why were both Vladimir Sisik and Ruth Forsyth so interested in Ben Forsyth's files? And if there was a connection between those two questions, what was it?

His imagination had not been able to conjure up even one plausible answer and the curiosity and anticipation were growing to serious levels.

Oxford looked over at Sam. Sometimes when bird hunting the setter would develop such a state of anxiety that his teeth would chatter.

I'm not quite that bad yet, Sam. But Monday can't come too soon.

FIVE

"*Courtesy of the Government of Saskatchewan, Vladimir Sisik, Deputy Minister to the Premier,*" read the card in Oxford's hand. It carried the gold crest of the Executive Council. On the back was scrawled, "*See you at noon. We'll have lunch. Val.*"

Oxford had extracted the card from an impressive envelope taped to a box that had just been delivered to his suite on the seventeenth floor of the Flatlander Inn on College Avenue in Regina. The Flatlander was a recent addition to the growing number of edifices throughout Saskatchewan that owed their existence to the Halliday government. Promoted and financed by the Economic Renewal Agency, the Flatlander project had weathered a storm of zoning protest that had not yet completely subsided. The necessary exemptions to locate the hotel in a restricted neighbourhood had been secured from the City of Regina only after some blunt interventions by Val Sisik on the subject of the city's provincial grant entitlements. Oxford had been contemplating the view across Wascana Park and Wascana Lake to the front of the legislative buildings when the bellman wheeled the case to his door.

Oxford LaCoste contemplated the twelve bottles of assorted wines and liquors in the box, added them to the morning's events.

The Executive Air Service had indeed been waiting for

him at the West Willow field at eight o'clock, just over three hours ago. On arrival at the government hangar in Regina, a uniformed driver lifted his bags out of the plane's luggage compartment and delivered Oxford to the Flatlander where he found himself pre-registered to a suite more suitable for a family of eight than a single country lawyer with simple tastes.

Oxford's experience with government clients to date was limited to the Town of West Willow and the Rural Municipality of Willow River, but he strongly doubted that the treatment he was receiving from his new government client was standard procedure. Surely a two thousand dollars a day lawyer would be presumed capable of making his own hotel arrangements and gifts, if any, should show up only after a job very, very successfully done. An expensive suite and a case of liquor and wine. Hardly ordinary.

The concerns Oxford had developed since the funeral of Ben Forsyth deepened, but he easily decided that his wisest course was to keep those concerns to himself for the time being. But stay awake, kid, he told himself. He knew he was a little out of his league here, and might find himself all trussed up with an apple in his mouth before he know what was going on.

He looked again at the case of wine and liquor, bearing the imprints of the Saskatchewan Liquor Board, and thought of the well-stocked bars Ben Forsyth had for the last several years maintained in his homes, both in Regina and West Willow. There had been a never-ending supply that appeared to be unaffected by the ever-increasing siege of Ruth Forsyth. And Ben himself, for that matter.

Oxford answered a knock at his door, a somewhat imperious knock, he thought.

"My secretary has ordered room service for lunch. You like lobster rolls? Yes?" Val Sisik breezed past Oxford and into the suite.

"What's a lobster roll?"

"Like a lobster sandwich. The seafood here is good. An outstanding view from here. At least for Regina, yes? From here you can keep an eye on us, Oxford. Vice versa, of course. You look almost directly at the premier's office, left of the legislature front steps. My office is straight across to the right."

"Thank you very much for the, the . . ." Oxford gestured feebly at the case of liquor.

"Oh, nothing, that. Nothing at all. Perquisites of office. It's nothing. Well, down to business."

Over lunch, Val Sisik outlined the dilemma that had brought about Oxford's retainer.

"Our mutual friend, Ben Forsyth, was assigned the Provincial Development portfolio. About one year. Sean McCarthy had been minister since this government was first elected. This, of course, you know.

"The government had suffered several—too many—bad economic ventures. Poorly planned and costly. Costly in terms of public money and the credibility of this government. Opinion polls tell us this. We could not afford any more losses, on either front. But this you also know, yes?"

Oxford did know something of this. Economic development had been the dominant policy thrust of the Halliday government. Ben Forsyth had been proud of the increased investment in the province, much of it venture capital attracted and stimulated by government participation. But there had been failures. They had been seized upon by the opposition and the press, and the government was on the defensive.

"We can't afford any more losses." Sisik put his hands on the table and leaned forward in emphasis.

"We need a success. A big success. A—what do they call it?—a winner. And we had our winner. When Ben Forsyth died.

"That's where you come in, Mr. LaCoste." As Oxford's mouth opened, Sisik answered the unspoken question.

"Ben Forsyth was in charge."

Oxford subsided, determined not to ask the next obvious question. He would wait Sisik out.

Sisik explained, slowly, almost reluctantly, as if it was difficult for him to reveal any detail of the project Ben had been in charge of.

"You will know of the laser beam, yes? High intensity light beam. Very powerful, very high temperature."

Several months previously, Sisik outlined, the government had been approached with a proposal to acquire a process of extraction that would greatly enhance the value of the province's heavy oil deposits. Simply put, the technique was based upon the laser. When the beam was directed into the oil-bearing formations, its tremendous heat loosened the oil's viscosity, permitting it to flow easily to the lift pumps. If the technique worked, it could be extended as a tertiary recovery system to almost all the western oil fields. Almost seventy per cent of all discovered oil lay beyond the reach of existing technology. Accessing even a fraction of that resource would be of inestimable value.

"Very big potential. Huge. So big it was kept very, very confidential. Not even cabinet were told. The premier made the decision alone. We would acquire the process, if proven, of course, but no one was to be told. Until up and running. As I said, too many failures already. This project was good but risky. No announcement until feasibility fully established. If it didn't prove out, it didn't happen. You understand, yes?

"A lot of money at stake. Fifteen million dollars. All government money, no private investment. It was a big risk. Had to be very private."

Oxford listened in fascination to the hesitant revelation of the intrigue that Ben Forsyth had been involved in. And that he was now being drawn into. Sisik explained that only the premier, Ben, and Sisik himself knew of the decision to acquire the process. Feasibility studies had been carried out by PanSask Petroleum, the government's oil company, but the engineers there knew nothing of the terms of the deal. Gus Walker, Saskatchewan's Agent General in Hong Kong, through whom the proposal had been introduced, was aware only that the offer was being considered, nothing more.

"Premier Halliday entrusted the entire transaction to Ben Forsyth. Ben was competent and very trustworthy. Also, he is—was—a lawyer. No need to involve other lawyers. A simple matter, really. No—what's the word?— hard assets. No land, equipment, that sort of thing. Just patents. Plus disclosure of research and feasibility work done. And we have all that. The technical people at PanSask have run the process, and could continue to do so. If it was ours to run. You understand, yes?"

Sisik suddenly stood as if he was becoming agitated in spite of himself. Gesturing at Oxford, he continued.

"The transaction was almost complete. At least, that's what Ben Forsyth reported to us. As I said, the purchase price was a large sum of money, even for these things—fifteen million dollars. And that money had been advanced to Ben. It was placed in escrow. The closing was to take place in just a few days. The turnover.

"And then," Sisik glared sternly at Oxford. "And then Ben died. And somehow he seems to have taken with him all traces of the transaction. Including the money.

"We are not able to locate Ben's files. No contracts, correspondence, nothing. All we have is a duplicate of the file we had developed before the matter was entrusted to him. Yes. Another copy is made for you." Sisik pointed to a sealed packet he had tossed on a sideboard when he entered the room.

"So there it is," Sisik summed up for a dumbfounded Oxford. "We think—we hope—that Ben Forsyth had perhaps supplied some additional security. Perhaps he maintained his files and financial transaction records in his own personal depositories. You understand, yes? If so, you will come across them while carrying out inventory of his estate. Then all will be well.

"If not so easy, then your retainer will run on for a while.

"You see, Mr. LaCoste, we require your assistance in finding those missing files. And, of course, the money. You understand? Yes?" Val Sisik had fully recovered his composure.

"But," Oxford exploded, "the money. How could fifteen million dollars go missing? Good Lord, you don't carry that kind of money around in a bag. Ben didn't have it in his wallet, did he? Wasn't it at least in some trust or escrow account?"

"A fair question. I told you this transaction was to be handled very quietly. As I said, the funds had been placed in escrow. But under Ben's sole control. Not a simple matter. These were public monies, you understand, yes? Ben had reported he was ready to close. The funds were forwarded to an escrow account in Hong Kong for release when Ben gave final approval.

"The funds left that account not long before Ben's death.

Apparently upon his direction. They were moved to an institution in the Turks and Caicos Islands. The Turks and Caicos is one of the those jurisdictions with banking secrecy. You've heard about numbered bank accounts, I presume?" Sisik concluded dryly.

"But what about the people you were dealing with? Someone was selling this process to you. Where are they?"

"Another fair question. They have disappeared, whereabouts unknown. They, too, were in Hong Kong."

"But, but . . ." Oxford sputtered.

"Please. No more questions for now. Many answers are in the files you now have. Later we will talk more."

Oxford slumped back in his Flatlander easy chair and stared at Vladimir Sisik in open-mouthed horror.

"Yes. It is a problem," Sisik offered. "But let us remember that Ben Forsyth was an honourable man. And a very competent lawyer. Yes? Somewhere there will be a simple explanation for all this. Your work is to find that explanation. You understand. Yes?"

Oxford pulled himself to his feet and walked over to the window where he looked out into the Regina sunshine as if to assure himself that the world he knew was still out there. Thoughts of Ruth Forsyth's interest in her husband's files crossed his mind. He turned to Sisik.

"I wonder if I'm your man. This is all too sophisticated and high-level for me. Cameron Hunt and I have already been through Ben's safety deposit box in West Willow. There was nothing there having anything to do with this. I have Cameron's authorization with me, and this afternoon I'll be checking Ben's box in the Royal Bank at the main branch here. If what you're looking for is there, it's yours right now. If it isn't, I don't know where else to look. As far as I know, Ben wasn't a complicated man and didn't lead a complicated life. He was pretty well off, but his estate doesn't suggest anything out of the ordinary.

"And what I'm doing I'm doing as one of Ben's executors, anyway. There's no need for you to hire me to do it."

"That is understood," Sisik replied. "We have considered the matters you raise. We think there will be little overlap between your work as executor and as our solicitor.

It is more important there be a solicitor-client relationship between us. Remember that confidentiality is of supreme importance. As you now understand. Yes?

"More. As executor, you have authority and reason to be investigating Ben Forsyth's affairs. Cover, is that what they call it? To have any other lawyer doing what we think needs to be done would cause questions. We cannot afford questions. You understand? If you discover the material we need in the safety deposit box this afternoon, fine. Somehow I doubt you will. I fear the mystery will be deeper than that. Ben Forsyth was a more complicated man that we gave him credit for. He seems to taken some pains with—with whatever he has done here. You understand? Yes?" Sisik said this somewhat feebly, Oxford thought.

The two men fell silent. Then Sisik, as Oxford had, walked over to the window and looked across the autumn-leaved Wascana Park to the legislative buildings. After a moment he turned back to Oxford.

"Not to be melodramatic, it should be apparent to you that the fate of this government depends upon a successful resolution of this matter. As the premier told you, Ben would want you, likely no one else, to fix this. If you do, you will have our gratitude. That can be very beneficial. You understand?

"Please consider the alternative. If this affair becomes public—probably sooner than we want—the government will have no choice but to suggest what to some will be the obvious. That Ben Forsyth somehow made off with that money. For his own benefit. Probably in a conspiracy with the vendors of the process. You will understand?"

Lovely, thought Oxford, at first to himself, and then, leaping angrily to his feet, "Lovely. Just lovely. So your problem becomes Ben's problem becomes my problem, just like that. And I hop on my white horse and charge off to everyone's rescue. Hoo boy!" He circled behind his chair, seized its back and glared at Sisik.

"I'm sorry. I thought you would appreciate a realistic appraisal. I think we all need to have everything on the table. There is a great deal at stake for everyone. And before you hold me responsible for your discomfort, please consider that I did not create the facts I have outlined to you. No?" Sisik sat again at their luncheon table, inviting Oxford to do the same.

I need help here, lots of help, Oxford thought, and then came up with a temporizing solution.

"Whatever it is you are asking me to do, and I'm still not sure what that is, has to overlap my duties as one of Ben's executors. But I am only one of two executors. I can't accept these instructions without the knowledge and approval of my co-executor. I have to talk to Cameron Hunt." Oxford very much wanted to talk to Cameron Hunt, and the sooner the better.

Sisik looked thoughtful for a moment before responding. "Yes, I suppose that is so. Unfortunate, but unavoidable. I'll have to ask you to first secure Mr. Hunt's agreement to treat this with equal confidence. Will that be a problem?"

"No. I'm sure it won't be. He has always been very discreet. Extremely so, in fact." Cameron Hunt had been an exasperation to Ben Forsyth, who had a politician's thirst for gossip. "Old clam lips," Ben had often teased the older lawyer, not a whit disrespectfully. Hunt would only smile.

"All right. That's agreed then. When will you speak to Mr. Hunt?"

"Tonight. I'll drive down as soon as I'm finished at the bank. I should be able to come back in tomorrow."

"Why don't I lay on a plane for you? You can go down and back tonight."

"No, I don't want any more of your planes, thank you. I'll have trouble enough explaining to the hangar rats back home what I was doing this morning behaving like a big wheel. I thought we wanted to keep suspicions down?"

"You're right. I'm sorry. I frequently forget about the acute powers of observation and deduction possessed by our rural residents."

"Well, it doesn't take much to notice one of your fancy government aircraft, and folks are quite able to put two and two together, even down at West Willow." Sisik was just another imported urbanite who thinks everyone in rural Saskatchewan is a hick, Oxford thought.

"Yes. Of course. Well, I must go now. We will talk tomorrow." Sisik went to the door. "Oh! But of course you will call me this afternoon if there is anything at all helpful at the Royal Bank? Yes?"

"Certainly," and Oxford closed the door, firmly. Then he returned to the window and the sunshine. He stood unseeing for a long while, numb and full of foreboding.

What the hell, Ben? What the hell, he thought.

What Oxford found later that afternoon in Ben Forsyth's large safety deposit box at the main branch of the Royal Bank he did not fully understand, but he did not think it would fall into the category of helpful.

The guaranteed investment certificates in the safety deposit box had been expected; they filled out the balance of Ben Forsyth's portfolio as already known to his two executors. The same with the title to the Regina condominium.

But the hefty manila envelope was a surprise. It was sealed, and each flap was further secured by the scrawl of Ben's initials that would reveal any surreptitious opening. The face of the envelope bore a message, also in Ben's hand.

PERSONAL AND CONFIDENTIAL.
The contents of this envelope are the personal property of the undersigned. They have no material value. They are private and are to be examined by my executors only in the event of my death. Others will respect their confidentiality during my lifetime.
Benjamin Forsyth.

Oxford read the message several times as if unable to comprehend the simple words, then quickly placed the envelope in his briefcase and returned to the Flatlander. A telephone call to Cameron Hunt confirmed his availability that evening. Another call advised Val Sisik that the safety deposit box had contained nothing of interest.

Then he went down to the car rental agency off the lobby, hired a Pontiac Bonneville and headed for West Willow, a three and a half hour drive into the fall sunset. With a short food stop along the way, he would be at Cameron Hunt's door by eight o'clock.

Six

Foreclosure. To a prairie farmer the word has the ring of doom. Clifton Carlson stared stupidly at the letter from the credit union's lawyers. It very firmly told him that foreclosure proceedings would be initiated in thirty days unless all arrears were paid up and his mortgages returned to good standing

After several minutes of numbness, Clifton put both hands on his huge walnut desk, pushed himself shakily to his feet and looked around as if he was in a strange place. He had never become accustomed to the size of this office, assigned to him as the minister responsible for PanSask Petroleum. He could not shake from his mind an uncomfortable comparison; many people within view of his fifteenth floor windows were raising entire families in houses of smaller dimension.

The office was really part of the empire of William G. Whitaker, the president of PanSask. Whitaker (Wee Willy behind his back) had succeeded in his campaign to have Harris Halliday's cabinet approve his appointment in spite of a complete lack of any experience in the petroleum industry or as a corporate executive beyond serving as head of his brokerage firm's Regina office. Willy's demonstrated talent as a stock broker and, much more importantly, as a Bay Street fund raiser for the WDA, had been deemed to sufficiently qualify him to run the large Crown corporation.

Short of stature and no longer able to disguise his advancing rotundity, Willy's pomposity burst its bounds with his appointment. During the layout of the executive floors of the PanSask Building in downtown Regina, Willy created for himself a more than sumptuous office that consumed eight hundred square feet of building space. But Willy was a skilled self-preservationist and with an eye to warding off accusations of ostentation, so he arranged that the minister's office at the other end of the floor be slightly larger.

Sean McCarthy had kidded Carlson about the office. "It takes a plenty big ego to fill an office like that, Clifto, me boy. You'll grow into it."

But Clifton Carlson's ego had not grown to fit his office. Once or twice, after a strong performance in the legislature, he had felt confidence welling up in him, but it did not last. Even though he was regarded as one of the more effective front bench members of the Halliday government, Clifton never quite silenced the inner voice that said he should never have left his farm along the east shore of Last Mountain Lake.

He looked a confident man. Although his frame was slight, Clifton was almost six feet in height. Yet sometimes he thought the blonde hair and fair skin of his Nordic ancestors made him appear effeminate. As a boy and youth he had never been accepted as an equal by his peers. He lacked athletic ability on the ball diamond and the hockey rink, and his scholastic achievements had not counted as compensation.

The nagging feeling of inadequacy was so omnipresent that to Clifton it became like a physical handicap, something he could shove into the back of his mind until he stumbled or came up short when he reached too far. Then he would again be rudely reminded that he was not quite as good as he should be.

The thought that he should have limited his life to the operation of the family farm was clamouring for attention as he looked at the contents of the "Personal and Confidential" envelope he had just been handed by his secretary in the same late afternoon as Oxford LaCoste drove out of Regina towards West Willow. None of this would ever have happened if he had stayed out of politics, he knew. The stress and publicity of political life had been more than his marriage, shaky but savable, had been able to withstand.

Carol had taken the kids, moved out and hit him with the toughest lawyer she could find. She demanded half of everything, no exceptions, and that included the farm. It made no difference that it had been homesteaded by his grandfather. Because Clifton's parents had not turned it over to him until after his marriage to Carol, that made it vulnerable to her claim.

The values Carol's appraisers put on the farm astonished Clifton. There were only two ways by which he could pay half those values to her. Sell or borrow. To save the farm he borrowed. Mortgaged himself right up to the eyes.

It had been a mistake. Like many western farmers, Clifton found himself jammed between surging interest rates and falling grain prices. The farm could not earn enough to carry the debt load, the more so since Clifton's political responsibilities required him to contract out most of the farm work. His ministerial salary covered maintenance for Carol and the kids with barely enough left over for him. He was seriously in arrears on his loans.

Borrowing from the local credit union had been another mistake, but nowhere else could Clifton find the level of financing he needed. The credit union's board of directors were almost all supporters of the opposition party. He could expect no mercy from them. The letter from the credit union's lawyers meant exactly what it said, he knew. Thirty days!

The mere commencement of foreclosure proceedings would mean the end of his political career, Clifton was sure. Premier Halliday would remove him from cabinet just as soon as the litigation became public. The loss of his salary and expense account as a minister would spin him right into bankruptcy and oblivion.

If only he had thrown Sean McCarthy off the place that day seven—no, eight—years ago. At least said NO! And stuck to it. But it had seemed then to be the reasonable and natural thing to do, to run for the Legislative Assembly. And even Carol had been in favour then. It was not until later that she came to detest political life.

Things had come easily to Clifton. The family farm was well-established and prosperous. After taking a degree in Agriculture at the University of Saskatchewan, he had joined his father, married Carol, his sweetheart since high school, and then taken over the farm when their first child was born. With lucky timing, just before land prices zoomed in the late 1970s, Clifton purchased his uncle's adjoining place and consolidated four sections of productive grain land.

So it had been with politics. His neighbours had approached Clifton to run against an unpopular councillor on the rural municipality and he won easily. When the reeve's position opened up at the next election Clifton faced no serious opposition and became the youngest reeve in the province. Active in the Saskatchewan Association of Rural Municipalities, he came to the attention of the early founders of the Western Democratic Alliance.

He should have stopped there. When Sean McCarthy came looking to him as the WDA candidate he should have turned him down flat.

But who then could have foreseen what lay ahead? His election as an MLA had been as easy as his municipal elections. After just two years, premier Halliday had taken Clifton into his cabinet.

That was when it began to unravel. In the beginning, Carol had rather enjoyed being the wife of the MLA, the social invitations and prominence. Clifton's attendance in Regina during the few weeks the Legislature was in session each spring was a pleasant nuisance. But cabinet minister is full-time. Clifton had to move to Regina. Carol and the kids refused to join him. Soon the marriage failed. Then hard times hit the farming industry. Then . . .

Sitting again at the huge walnut desk in the grand office, Clifton Carlson held his head in his hands and wondered how he could have turned so much opportunity into such a disaster. And how, how, how, could he save himself?

SEVEN

The Hunt residence was not large enough to qualify as stately, but it had about it an air of substance and dignity as befitted its owner. Two-storied, white, black-roofed, it was set well back from the street on a lot that stretched down to the river. A wide verandah across the southern exposure faced the river and connected to Cameron's book lined study where Oxford joined the elderly counsellor.

Cameron Hunt had been born of the range. The Hunt Ranch his father had founded covered much of the grazing lease that had once carried the stock of Harmon Jasper's Sunburst Ranch. In 1940 he hung his saddle on the tack room wall and fitted his lanky frame into the cockpit of a Royal Canadian Air Force Lancaster bomber. A gifted pilot, Hunt flew two tours of duty over occupied Europe.

Hunt's navigator was a lawyer from Halifax. On leave together in London, they visited the Inns of Court, the chambers of the city's trial lawyers, and spent three days prowling around the courtrooms in the Old Bailey.

Back in Canada after the war, Hunt headed to law school with his veteran's credits and returned to West Willow, not as a rancher but as a practising lawyer. He continued to operate the Hunt Ranch, slowly converting it to purebred polled Herefords. Ben Forsyth, also raised on a local ranch, joined the Hunt law office when he came out of law school.

The firm's founder had formally retired to enable Ben to bring in a younger man and free himself for a political career, but he had continued to see a few old clients. Most of the time Hunt could be found among his beloved books and cattle records.

"What's up, Doc? as my grandson would say" Hunt greeted Oxford, smiling at the frown on the younger lawyer's face.

Oxford dropped into the chair Hunt offered, in spite of himself joining in the smile.

"Well, actually, quite a bit, sir. This might take a while."

And it did, Hunt's gaze never leaving Oxford's face during the telling. Nor did he interrupt.

"And now we come to this." Oxford handed Hunt the envelope with Ben Forsyth's handwriting on the face. Cameron Hunt perused Ben's message much as Oxford had when he had first seen it. Then, carefully, as if it deserved delicate treatment, he set the envelope aside.

"Tell me again, Oxford. You say that heavy oil extraction process came to the government's attention just a few months ago?"

"Yes, Sir. That's what I was told."

"You'd noticed, hadn't you, that Ben seemed seriously out of sorts lately?"

"Well, yes, but I didn't see much of him anymore. He wasn't the same Ben he used to be."

"No, he was not. His burden had become heavy. But I had thought he had changed more than a few months ago, about the time he took on this last portfolio. That's about a year back, isn't it?"

"A year Thanksgiving, as I remember it. We were here for dinner that weekend, in fact."

"Exactly. So we were. Drank a toast to Ben on his promotion, didn't we?" Hunt sighed. "Well, this isn't getting on with duty, is it? Better get at it." He reached for a letter opener, slit open the envelope and slid its contents onto a coffee table. A package of documents and correspondence spilled out. Hunt pawed among the material with a lawyer's practised eye.

"Hullo. What's this?" Hunt picked up another envelope,

letter-sized. It was addressed, again in Ben's handwriting, "*To Cameron Hunt and Oxford LaCoste, Personal and Confidential.*"

Hunt held the envelope up to the light. It was opaque. "Well, no stopping now," he said and reached once more for the letter opener. He lifted out several typewritten, folded sheets, examined them and said, "It's Ben, all right. He never could type properly. Still using that old portable electric from the looks of it."

"Dear Cameron and Oxford,

If you are reading this, it will mean that I have left you some serious unfinished business, very serious. I am sorry to involve you in my problems, but, if anybody can understand, it will be you two.

Do you remember the discussion you and I had, Cameron, about the pragmatism of politics, when you convinced me that my naive idealism would serve only to prevent me from accomplishing any of the worthwhile dreams that attracted me to public life? That was when I was wondering if I should continue to be a candidate for the WDA or step aside in favour of someone else who would better fit the party mould.

'Forget the minor injustices and keep your eye on the main chances,' you said. 'Lose five small contests to gain one major victory.' Politics, we agreed, is not for the faint of heart.

Please understand that I don't attempt in any way to shift responsibility for what has happened. You were right seven years ago and your philosophy is still valid today. You were, though, aiming your principles toward a higher plane of political activity than I encountered as the MLA for Willow River and, particularly, as a member of the Halliday cabinet.

It is my foolishness, my tragedy, that I deceived myself (and others, including you) for years instead of squaring up to the problem back when something sensible could have been done about it. What do we call it in the law—'wilful blindness?'—an apt phrase for what has become a collective malady in this province.

It started immediately, the day after, perhaps even the night of, that wonderful election that swept us to power seven years (70 years? 700 years?) ago, with the creation of 'The Transition Team,' a usually normal function to assist with the transfer of power from an outgoing to an incoming government.

In our case, the transition team was merely a cover name for what was really a group of career butchers.

This was the point at which it all began, the point where Ben Forsyth should have stepped forward in protest. I didn't, and I failed you, myself, my province. I failed honour itself.

The so-called transition team, acting in the name of the new WDA government, immediately set up temporary offices in downtown Regina. They created a boiler room, a centre for telephone selling, except that theirs was a different message. I saw it when I visited those offices ten days after the election.

It was taped to each of 8 or 10 telephone-equipped desks. It read, 'You are hereby advised that your services are no longer required by the government of Saskatchewan and that your employment is terminated effective today. This is not to be taken as a comment upon your competence as an employee. Please vacate your office forthwith and advise us where we may further get in touch with you or your solicitor.' That was the entire message, three sentences.

That message was received by several hundred civil servants, most of them career employees whose only offence was that they were seen to adhere to the political philosophy of the government we had dislodged from office.

Seen by whom? you might well ask. It didn't take much to get your name on the lists fed to those telephones. Otherwise responsible members of the business and professional community, WDA supporters, prepared their own tallys, denunciations of the sort that got folks a ride in the tumbrels during the French Revolution. No evidence required, no trial, no protest. Same process here.

The ranchers down home take much more care in selecting the poor performing cattle to be culled from their herds and sent to slaughter.

Over some late night drinks someone wondered if maybe we weren't going too far with those dismissals (that someone, I'm ashamed to admit, was not me), that perhaps we were losing some good people. The response from one of our senior advisors was (and it is still seared into my mind) 'Goddam sperm-gargling Commie-loving pinko faggots.' Everyone laughed happily and that killed the protest, weak as it had been.

Why didn't that tell me that I was a stranger in a strange place? That I didn't belong with the people I was now associating with. Today I can't answer that question, and it haunts me at night.

We were, of course, like frenzied studs, so anxious to get at the levers of power and correct the generation of wrongs carried out by the government we had dislodged. Not one of us had ever served in office before, but that didn't concern us one bit. We had won and we were on a roll.

Premier Halliday set the tone at our first cabinet meeting with the remark, 'Every successful revolution breaks a few legs.'

I was given the Wildlife Resource Department, as you know, a junior portfolio that insulated me from a lot of the rawness of the political action that was going on around me. Oh, sure, I knew of the games that were being played with government tenders and contracts, that the rules were bent right out of shape to enrich our supporters, but a little more 'wilful blindness' kept me unconcerned.

Things got worse, and I knew that too, but it seemed as if we were actually making progress, the province was more prosperous and it was easy to take credit for that. And by now I was part of the team. It's always tough to be the only fault-finder, particularly when things are going well.

To hell with it. The truth is that I had become just as corrupt as those around me. I loved the work and the *life and I was prepared to pay the price of belonging.*

But, oh what a price. I watched the rape of government pension plans to subsidise showcase developments (and make some WDA supporters very wealthy), the creation of an enemies list (just like Richard Nixon's), the fire-sale of government assets to our friends in the name of privatization, the improper use of electronic surveillance equipment, even the securing, on some pretence, of a terminal on CPIC so we could really check out our enemies.

The WDA bagmen levered millions in so-called political donations from companies doing business with the government in complete defiance of the election laws. Much of that money is tucked into secret slush accounts intended to perpetuate themselves for all time.

On and on it went and there seemed to be no limit, even for me.

Until I got the Provincial Development assignment. Then I quickly reached my limit when I saw what had been going on in that department.

Of course I had known of the harebrained schemes Sean McCarthy had got us into, but I thought he had just been stupid, not out and out crooked. But crooked he had been, in a way that would have made Boss Tweed of Tammanny Hall proud. He had become so arrogant that he had stopped bothering to cover his tracks. He left files full of deals that would sicken you. They did, finally, sicken me.

And here they are. This envelope contains the evidence of enough corruption to blow the WDA and the Halliday government straight to hell, where they belong. Me too, I guess.

What was I going to do with this? I'm not sure. Perhaps go public with it, but I'm still searching for another way, some way to correct the abuses and clean up this government without destroying it. Maybe I'm still naive and foolish, but I'm still working on it. It's July as I write this and I've given myself only until the end of the year to make my decision.

I may not be entirely alone. I think there are two or

three members of caucus, maybe more, whose stom-
achs are as full as mine, but it's too early to be sure.

I may have placed myself in some danger with this
material. I hope not. I don't want to believe these peo-
ple could be that sinister. If nothing has been done by
the time you read this, then I turn this material over to
you to decide what action should be taken, if any. I'm
sorry to do this, but I leave the whole thing entirely to
your discretion.

Ben Forsyth

Hunt and Oxford had been reading side by side. When they finished, Oxford stood up shakily and took a couple of deep breaths. "No wonder Ben hadn't been himself lately."

"Yes," Hunt replied, still calm, still regarding the letter. "What's CPIC?" he asked, pointing to the acronym.

"Canadian Police Information Center. It contains a record of every arrest and conviction in the country, plus all the other sorts of info that you would expect the police to want to keep track of."

"And the government, that bunch of, of crooks I guess, has access to this?" Hunt wasn't so calm now.

"Seems so. Sounds sinister, doesn't it."

"It's Orwellian. It's undemocratic. Well," Hunt said after a moment, "let's have a look at Ben's brief."

Together they leafed through the photocopied corre-spondence, memoranda, and notes that Ben had compiled, all stapled into sections, each apparently detailing a sepa-rate transaction. The material would make quick sense to those familiar with the background, but it was all strange to Hunt and Oxford. They would have to read and analyze Ben's files carefully.

"I think we'd better leave this for now," Hunt said. "There's a lot of material here and it's going to take some time to digest. If you like, I'll go through it tomorrow. Best we take some care in learning what we are dealing with. Ben has left us with a heavy decision."

"But what about this?" and Hunt handed Oxford a sin-gle sheet of paper that was unattached to any other file.

Oxford read a copy of a letter from a Regina branch of the

Western Dominion Bank requesting that two safety deposit boxes be cleared as the branch was closing. The letter was addressed to "James Karpan, c/o Office of the Minister, Department of Provincial Development, Legislative Buildings, Regina, Saskatchewan." It was dated the previous January.

"This doesn't seem to have anything to do with the rest of the material, but I don't recollect that Ben had any accounts or whatnot with the Western Dominion. Did he?" Hunt asked.

"Not that I know of, but I suppose I'd best check this out when I'm back in Regina. I suppose Karpan is one of Ben's assistants," Oxford replied.

"Yes, do that. And now let's discuss the other side of the little problem Ben has dropped in our laps," Hunt said. "Obviously, Ruth has some inkling of what Ben was about, and that is why she has made demand for his files. I don't want to speculate on what she might be proposing to do with this material, at least for now, but we have to give some thought to her right to have it.

"Next, we have to consider Dr. Sisik's demand for the same files. Certainly some of this material looks as if it could be claimed by the government as having been removed from their offices without permission.

"And finally, what about the instructions Ben left with us in his letter? He authorized us to do with this as we see fit. Does that override the claims from Ruth? Or the government? Or either or both of them? What are your thoughts?"

"I see another problem," Oxford suggested. "If Ben removed government files without authority, even with the best of motives, hasn't he maybe committed a criminal offence? I'm thinking of the Ottawa civil servant who was charged with breach of trust for sneaking government files out of his office and turning them over to the media. Sure, Ben's no longer around to be charged, but can we assume that no one else was involved, or that the police wouldn't want to know? If this stuff might be evidence of a criminal offence, don't we have some obligation about how to treat it?"

"Yes," Hunt picked up on that line, "but that concern might be magnified if this material contains evidence of criminal conduct by others. Just glancing at it suggests that

Ben had uncovered some unsavoury kickback arrangements the police might very much be interested in."

Hunt thought for a moment, then continued, "So, we fall back on a lawyer's best technique in a difficult situation."

"Which is?"

"Stall. At least until we know more about what we are dealing with. And maybe some development will come along that will make our decision easier.

"It's been a long day. Particularly for you. Let's get some fresh air before we hit the hay." Hunt led the way outside through the darkness and down to the river. A hunter's moon, dappled with the small, narrow leaves fallen from the bordering willow, beckoned to them from the still waters.

They stood silently, watching the reflection. Then Hunt spoke.

"I'm remembering Ben as a boy. When I first met him. In those days Saturday night was shopping time. The town was full of people, wagons, trucks, what have you. It was the weekly social excursion. Ben's folks drove an old one-ton Ford. It was their general purpose vehicle, likely the only one they owned back then. Hauled grain, cattle, took the family to town. Ben was a wide-eyed little face peering up through the windshield of that truck. A trip to town was a big event.

"Then he was at high school here in West Willow. A one-room country school before that. Ben was a hell of a ball player.

"One afternoon Ethel came into my office with a smile on her face and announced that a Mr. Ben Forsyth wondered if he might see me. I chased Ethel down to the Dew Drop Inn for Cokes and Ben and I had a long chat. He was planning on university that fall, Ben said, and was wondering about law as a career. Wanted to know if that was a good idea, would he be suitable. He was plenty nervous, but deadly serious. I was careful to be the same. It might seem strange today, but back then it took a lot of courage for a young fellow like Ben to walk into a law office. And ask to talk to an old timer like me. I'm sure he'd never met me. Knew who I was, of course. As I kinda knew who he was. This was a real small town then. I respected that courage." Hunt paused a moment.

"I think," he went on, "that even then Ben had the ability to capture your attention. He did mine that day, anyway. He made me think of the time during the war when that navigator of mine, Ken Hatfield, dragged me around the Inns of Court in London. Opened my eyes enough that I wound up a lawyer myself.

"We spent a long time together that afternoon, Ben and I. And, of course, he did go on to law school. Likely would have got there without my encouragement. But six years later he's back here, degree in hand, wanting to article with me. Of course I went along." Hunt was silent for a long moment. Oxford, too, was quiet; he felt anything he might say would be an interruption.

"Back again, isn't he, sort of?" Hunt put the question softly, more to the reflection in the river than to Oxford. "No. Rather, he never really left, did he? Even when he was in the cabinet, he was somehow still here. And last week he came back permanently. And tonight, with what he's given us in that envelope, he's sure as hell here." Hunt fell silent again, then spoke in a stronger tone.

"Ben was a quick student. At least for the mechanics of the law. But he could never accept the imperfections of the justice systems. For such a reasonable man he became downright unreasonable on that subject. Refused to agree that, like any system devised and run by humans, justice could be expected to throw up the odd human error.

"Ben did quite a bit of criminal defence work in his early years here, and was good at it. But he gave it up. Found it too stressful. Couldn't sleep when he had a case going. Couldn't sleep if he lost one, if he thought his client was innocent. And he usually believed in his clients." Hunt shook his head, as if in exasperation.

"It was no good arguing with him. I tried explaining that sometimes people are simply victims. And that's true. Sometimes circumstance, or an unusual combination of circumstances, creates a condition where someone gets hurt and you can't put your finger on any one element of real responsibility. There's not always a remedy for the injured party. It's just a wider extension of an act of God.

"But that was never good enough for Ben. He never stopped looking for the better way."

"Ben should have stayed away from politics," Oxford said. "Never mind that he was very good at it."

Hunt stood staring into the river. Then, without turning, "Did Ben ever tell you about the trouble he got into in law school?"

"No," was all the response a surprised Oxford could muster.

"Don't wonder. Didn't tell me either. I heard about it a couple of years after it happened from Harry Rogers. Classmate of mine. Mr. Justice Rogers now, but back then he was practising in Saskatoon and a part-timer on the law faculty.

"Seems that one of Ben's classmates had crossed an influential member of the faculty. Forget what the alleged offence was, but the lad was being denied his final examinations. The dean had meekly supported the decision. It was a serious case of highhanded treatment at the hands of arrogant academics. But it put the young fellow in a hell of a spot. So our Ben stepped in. Got a lawsuit going to force the law college to let his classmate, his first client—unpaid, of course—sit the exams. Named the dean of law and three faculty members in the litigation. Caused a hell of a fuss. Lots of publicity, all embarrassing to the law college.

"The faculty caved in. The exams were written and passed.

"But now Ben was *persona non grata* around the law college. He had been in line to graduate with distinction. That was gone.

"So," Hunt turned and smiled at Oxford. "Ben started early sticking to his principles. And never mind the cost."

"He sure as hell did," Oxford replied, moved by the account. Then, feeling weariness wash over him, "That's it for me. I think I'll head for bed. Goodnight, sir."

"Goodnight, Oxford." Hunt watched as the younger man walked up the long walk to the Pontiac, then turned again to the river and its reflecting moon. And more recollections of Ben Forsyth.

When Ben had sought his advice about a political career, Hunt had been concerned about Ben's ability to accept the limitations he would surely encounter in that world. The justice system, Hunt warned, with all its failings is light years ahead of the best we have been able to achieve with representative democracy. He dug into his library for a copy of Walter Bagehot and read some excerpts to Ben:

> *An influential Member of Parliament . . . has not only to give time and labour, he has also to sacrifice his mind too—at least all the characteristic part of it, that which is original and most his own . . . A man who tries to enter Parliament must be content to utter common thoughts . . . And to some minds there is no necessity more vexing or more intolerable.*

Bagehot wrote about the British House of Commons more than a hundred years ago, Hunt told Ben, but his words certainly fitted the Saskatchewan legislature of today. If you decide to join that league, he warned, be prepared to grit your teeth and learn how to suffer fools, and seem to do so gladly.

Fools, yes. But crooks, no. We did not contemplate crooks, did we Ben?

What a shock for Ben, so dedicated to integrity and justice, to enter the Halliday cabinet and find himself surrounded by corruption, Hunt thought. And turn a blind eye to it and then be forced to acknowledge that he had compromised his own principles. Little wonder that he had been so out of sorts and relying on the anaesthetic of alcohol.

Hunt knew about the use of alcohol as an antidote for fear and pain. He had often flown into combat with men who could not climb into their aircraft without a couple of stiff drinks, a practice tacitly approved by their commanding officers. Most had returned to normal conduct once the ever-present fear of death had been removed from their lives.

But booze also confused the mind, Hunt thought, and wondered if Ben's normally clear thinking had been at all affected by his heavy drinking of the last several months. Not likely, Hunt concluded. He knew Ben Forsyth as a stubborn but stable man of much quiet courage. He would be careful and logical in reaching his decision, and then he would see it through to the end, and damn the torpedoes.

The question now, Hunt knew, was did Cameron Hunt and Oxford LaCoste have the courage to complete Ben Forsyth's undertaking? I'm a little long in the tooth for serious action, Hunt grinned. But maybe teamed with Oxford's youth we can handle this assignment.

Hunt gazed again at the trees and the river in the moonlight and the words of a half-forgotten poem slipped into his mind.

> *The feathers of the willow*
> *Are half of them grown yellow*
> *Above the swelling stream;*
> *And ragged are the bushes*
> *And rusty now the rushes,*
> *And wild the clouded gleam.*

Cameron Hunt shivered, not only from the cold night air, and turned away from the river towards home and bed.

EIGHT

Oxford sat a few moments on his veranda where Sam had been awaiting him. Cameron Hunt had been right. It had been a long day. But his mind was in turmoil and he knew sleep was out of the question.

Inside, he switched on his stereo, plugged in an André Gagnon CD, and settled into his easy-listening arm chair. The Bang and Olefson speakers he had splurged on poured out the smooth piano that he had learned to love during his years in Montreal. He let his mind go loose.

How, he began to wonder, had he, Oxford Francis LaCoste, arrived at such an unusual predicament? All because of a man named Benjamin Forsyth he had never heard of eight years ago?

That a LaCoste even found his way into this part of the world was, Oxford knew, the result of strange and faraway events.

In January, 1944, a cell of the Maquis resistance in Paris was blown to the Gestapo. After a long and dreadful night of torture, six summary executions were carried out at dawn and fourteen year old Yves LaCoste became an orphan. But he was streetwise, and the education gained during four years of life in Paris under the Nazi occupation enabled the boy to survive until the liberation of his city in August.

A bit of carelessness when Yves helped himself to some Canadian Army supplies brought him to the attention of the

Red Cross. Investigation soon uncovered the existence of relatives living in southern Saskatchewan. In the spring of 1945, a tough and belligerent Yves arrived at the doorstep of his father's cousin, Alphonse Fournier, on a half section grain farm buttressed by three sections of Crown grazing lease.

Alphonse, ten years older than Yves' father, had emigrated to Canada when not much older than Yves. He had stopped in Montreal long enough to find a bride, then moved west to take up farming, joining a small French settlement in the light soil area near the American border south of West Willow.

Alphonse and Marie had survived, but not without hardship. Almost established when the Depression hit them, Alphonse was just recovering his financial strength when Yves arrived. Two of their three children had died in infancy, leaving only the daughter, Yvette. Yves, with his strong back and energy, was welcomed.

Yves adapted well to the West and became a dependable arm in the running of Alphonse's mixed cattle and grain operation. Nature took its course, assisted by the remoteness of the Fournier farm, and Yvette and Yves were married.

The Fournier strain were not strong child bearers. Only one child, a boy, survived a number of pregnancies, and five years later Yvette succumbed in childbirth. That infant also was lost.

Yves LaCoste had insisted that his son be given an English name, provoking a heated family debate. Yves insisted that he had been assured upon entering Canada that it was a bilingual country. Perhaps it is, he said, but not here in the West. Even so, he argued, to be given an even chance, the boy should have a balanced name. So Oxford Francis LaCoste was christened. Yves had been unable to think of any name more English than Oxford.

Oxford was considered a delicate child, a fineness of feature, a gift from his mother, speaking of fragility. The boy was protected from the more rigorous work of the farm, the more so when he displayed a disinterest in its vehicles and machinery. His father and grandfather viewed this as a serious aberration. Yet he had excellent reserves of energy.

After the death of his mother, his sixty-year-old grand-mother took charge of Oxford. Every day since leaving Montreal Marie Fournier had quietly hated the farm and the West and her determination that her grandson would not succeed to life as a farmer never wavered.

When Oxford was ten, Alphonse's strength left him and Marie saw her opportunity. She would take her husband back to Montreal where she could better care for him. Naturally, Oxford would go too, where there were better schools and no need to spend two hours a day riding a school bus. To placate Yves, the farm would be turned over to him, subject only to a modest annuity to maintain Alphonse and Marie during the few years remaining to them.

It was done. Yves made little protest. He found the prospect of living alone strangely attractive and when it came about he was entirely comfortable. He became one of the species of western hermits who live in contented isolation, almost as remote from society as a northern trapper, seen only on occasional visits to town for supplies or equipment.

For the first two or three years, Oxford returned during the summers, but his visits became shorter and stopped alto-gether. Although Yves was pleased to see his son, it was obvious that he did not know what to do with him. Oxford saw that he was an interruption to his father's way of life. With little interest in farming and no real friendships in the community, he felt more and more like a stranger in the West. And Oxford found he had no taste whatever for clean-ing the farm's old, wooden grain bins on sweltering August afternoons when the dust hung like fog and so clogged his lungs that he spat black for days. His accuracy with the .22 reduced the gopher population plaguing Yves' pastures, almost the only contribution Oxford felt he made to the farm.

Nor was he comfortable around Yves' machinery. After an incident with the cultivator, Yves never again allowed Oxford to handle the equipment. Summerfallowing one afternoon, a task that numbed his mind as he drove the tractor in minutely decreasing but seemingly never-ending circles around the huge fields, Oxford carelessly allowed the cultivator to entangle with the guy wire of a power pole.

"It's the only pole in the field," Yves pointed out, as he

sadly surveyed the wreckage. It was so. The power line angled across country and only one of its poles stood inside Yves' fence lines. His father's silent conviction of inept stupidity hung darkly over the remainder of Oxford's visit.

Oxford could never explain what caused him to return to Saskatchewan to take his law degree. Alphonse had died while his grandson was completing his secondary schooling and Marie died four years later, shortly after Oxford secured a Bachelor of Arts degree from McGill University. Feeling alone and disconnected, almost on whim he applied to the law school in Saskatoon.

Later Oxford wondered if he had felt a subconscious obligation to his father, and to the West. When he had gone on to university Yves had easily responded to Marie's request that he fund Oxford's continued education. Then, when Marie's death ended his annuity obligation, Yves had written Oxford to say that he would continue to provide an income to him so long as it was useful. Very truthfully, Yves had said he had no use for the money himself. The arrangement enabled Oxford to complete three years of law school without recourse to student loans.

With his law degree and facility in two languages, but unsure of his future, Oxford temporized by accepting a position with the government in Ottawa. There, in August of the year after his graduation, he received the telephone call from West Willow.

Yves LaCoste, who all his life had enjoyed the agility of a cat, had taken one chance too many with a power take off unit, the drive shaft that connects from a farm tractor to its implement. Swathing a field of wheat, he stepped off the tractor to clear the swather without disengaging the power drive. As Yves crossed the uncovered U-joint on the power shaft, it snagged his heavy denim coveralls. Yves leaped like a hooked salmon, but the machinery drew him in. It wound his leg, then his torso, under and around and over the shaft, again and again and again, until not enough substance of either Yves or his clothing remained for the shaft to retain its grip. By the time a passing neighbour was attracted to the equipment stalled in the middle of the field, the tractor had run out of fuel.

It was Ben Forsyth who placed the phone call to Oxford LaCoste in Ottawa. The West Willow detachment of the RCMP had enlisted Ben's help in locating the only known next of kin.

Oxford arranged an extended leave of absence and returned to Saskatchewan to complete the harvest of his father's crops and wind up the farming operation. The cattle went to market after harvest, and the machinery and equipment were sold by auction. Oxford, undecided about what to do with the land, postponed that decision, and was later glad that he had.

He retained Ben Forsyth to help him with the formal requirements of administering his father's estate. The older lawyer's understanding and compassion drew Oxford to him. The younger man had never had a strong sense of family but slowly he realized that now he had no family at all. None. So far as he knew, he had not one relative in the world.

Oxford was not surprised at that fact. He had known since the death of his grandparents that Yves was all he had left. But Yves had been a relatively young man in good health. Oxford had not been prepared to be an orphan.

He was surprised at the effect upon him of that event. It was disturbing. He thought about his friends and acquaintances and found not one without a relative. He was unique in a way he would not have chosen.

Thus it was that when Ben Forsyth suggested that Oxford join his law office, the acceptance was quick and easy. The move to West Willow was somehow like coming home, although he had almost no recollection of the town from his childhood.

The farm he inherited was forty miles from West Willow, too far for normal supply journeys during his early years there. The Fourniers secured their groceries and mail, and shipped their grain, from the closest village on the nearest railway, then a long ten miles away. His memory provided only hazy recollections of two or three boyhood visits to West Willow.

Oxford discovered that the farm itself was now family to him. It had been his grandfather's homestead and his father's life. Ben Forsyth and West Willow provided an opportunity to be close to that last bit of family. Oxford's initial indecision about what to do with the farm turned quickly to firm resolution. He did not sell the land. It became a permanent part of his new life.

He quitclaimed the grazing lease back to the government, an easy decision since he was without cattle and no longer an eligible tenant. The remaining six quarters of cultivated and titled land were rented to a nearby grain farmer who was a skilled and trustworthy operator. The home yard and buildings he reserved to himself. They became Oxford's retreat and sanctuary, his touchstone to his past.

In his years alone Yves LaCoste had not cared for the farmstead. In the style of many western farmers, the buildings of obvious utilitarian value, the machine shed, the workshop, the grain bins, were reasonably well maintained, while the house in particular was run down and gave every evidence of being the residence of an uncaring bachelor. But Oxford, bachelor or not, suddenly found that he did care, and he set about restoring the entire farmstead to a glory it had never really known.

A painting contractor was sent down from West Willow. The outbuildings, barn, machine shed, workshop, hen house, the few of the hated wooden grain bins Oxford deemed worthy of saving, all received matching coats of paint. The cedar shingle roofs were stained black, the walls painted a bright red, all with white trim. The bungalow was white with red trim and black roof. Even the old corrals were straightened up and painted white, although Oxford never intended to use them. The farmstead had never looked so good.

The old place became Oxford's second home. He and the ancient Jeep and later Sam spent most of his free weekends there. He tidied up the house and put in a few modern appliances. He bought a riding mower and trimmed the yard and the grid-road ditch along the front. Then he straightened the three-strand barbed wire fence and painted the posts white.

When he ran out of restoration projects, Oxford began taking a briefcase of difficult files on his weekend visits and was pleased to learn that he was better able to concentrate away from the office.

The few neighbours accepted Oxford warmly, but pretty much left him alone, perceiving that to be what he wanted. It was. He enjoyed their honks and waves as they drove by when he was working in the yard, and appreciated that they did not often stop in to gossip. Oxford's return to his boyhood home gave him a contentment that he did not fully understand but was happy not to question.

The sudden silence announcing the end of the CD snapped Oxford out of his reverie. He stood, stretched, and switched off the stereo.

"So here we are, Sam," he said to the perplexed setter. "Here we are indeed. And that's all the philosophy I can muster just now. Let's hit the sack."

NINE

The trouble with living west of Regina, Oxford thought for the umpteenth time over the years, was that one was always driving to the city in the mornings and back in the evenings, almost never the other way around. That meant you squinted into the sun on both trips, not a small discomfort considering the intensity of the Saskatchewan sun.

He had left West Willow early without bothering to check his office, wanting to think about Ben Forsyth's letter with a mind clear of any of the smaller concerns that might be lurking on his desk. Besides, he had been away only one day, nothing serious should have developed, and, in any event, Ethel Tremblay, the office manager/secretary who had more seniority in the Hunt, Forsyth, and LaCoste law offices than even Ben Forsyth, could handle any emergency. Ethel had arranged that her son and his wife would deliver Oxford's Saab to Regina tomorrow, relieving him of the rental car.

Ben's file had been left for Cameron Hunt to dissect and digest, as he had offered. Oxford, they had agreed, would return to Regina to look for files and documents at Ben's ministerial offices and the small office he had maintained in his condominium home. Also, he would check the safety deposit boxes at the Western Dominion Bank mentioned in the letter to James Karpan. When both had completed their tasks, they would meet again to consider where they were and where they should go.

Oxford's mind turned to his relationship with Ben Forsyth, whose unfinished business he was about. Oxford knew that law students frequently idolize the senior lawyers under whom they serve their articles, and wondered, not for the first time, if that was the explanation for the extremely high regard in which he had always held Ben Forsyth. When he accepted Ben's offer to join the firm in West Willow, all was conditional upon his serving a one year period of articles, a sort of internship, and successfully sitting the Saskatchewan bar examinations. Only then would he become qualified as a practising lawyer.

Not that either Ben or Oxford considered that there was any risk in the undertaking. As Ben put it, failing the bar examination was roughly equivalent to being caught *in flagrante delicto* with a sheep. But the process had to be endured. It was designed to equip the fledgling lawyer with practical experience to go with the academic training he had acquired in law school.

As Oxford quickly learned, the program was essential. His law degree was comparable to an understanding of the theory of flight, academic knowledge of limited practical use when seated for the first time in the cockpit of an aircraft with takeoff clearance.

Ben Forsyth, with assistance from Cameron Hunt, gently led Oxford through the mysteries of the legal world, particularly the requirements of the land titles and judicial systems. "It just looks magical," Ben insisted, "but it's really quite logical. Do nothing until you understand what you are doing. Question, study, and examine. Then it will make sense."

And soon enough it did make sense. And Oxford discovered that he had a natural bent for marrying his academic training to the practical problems of the firm's clients.

From the senior Cameron Hunt, Oxford learned the philosophy of dealing with clients whose expectations were often excessive.

"Nothing improves the pedigree of a cow more than crossing it with a locomotive, or, more lately, a truck, as in this case," Hunt explained one afternoon as he handed Oxford a claim file.

West Willow, with neither court-house nor land titles office, usually transacted business with those offices by mail. To familiarize Oxford with the systems, the judges, the staff, and other lawyers, Ben frequently sent him off to search titles and conduct court motions in Swift Current and even as far as Regina. It was not economical, but it was excellent training for the lawyer-to-be and Oxford was very appreciative.

The provincial court held weekly sessions in West Willow, its circuit riding judges driving down from Swift Current or other larger centres to hear motor vehicle and criminal charges developed by the local detachment of the RCMP. Ben indoctrinated Oxford into the quirks of these lower level jurists, some of whom delighted in exploiting any evidence of timidity or uncertainty displayed by tyro attorneys who appeared before them. Oxford learned to tailor his presentations according to the prejudices of the judicial personality of the day, including the one judge who was famously and consistently tardy for his own courts because, while en route, he could not resist stopping to gather beer bottles from the roadside.

Ben Forsyth's tutelage was not only compassionate and professional, but friendly and often carried on over drinks in the back of the office after hours. But Ben was not above playing a practical joke on his fledgling law student, taking advantage of Oxford's lack of mechanical aptitude and unfamiliarity with modern farm equipment. A memorandum appeared on Oxford's desk.

"Our client had some repairs to his combine performed at the West Willow John Deere agency. They installed a counterbinder on the wheat flattener with a squarehead hydrostatic coupler, using a universal bushing degreaser. Apparently the mechanics left only 5 1/4 inches of clearance between the kernel rotor and the straw-feed regulator.

"Is this actionable negligence? Let me have an opinion by the end of the week."

Oxford struggled with this for most of a day until he twigged to the giggles of the secretaries.

The year passed quickly and Oxford developed the attachment of the student for the master that has been common since the time of Plato. But Oxford's admiration for Ben Forsyth did not stop growing after he was admitted to the bar and had been formally introduced to the Court of Queen's Bench by Ben. In spite of the nagging concern about Ben's involvement with the WDA and the Halliday government, he was sure that Ben Forsyth was the finest man he would ever be privileged to know. Now Oxford wondered if that high regard would make it impossible for him to view objectively the problems Ben had left behind.

The story Hunt had told the night before of how Ben had risked his career almost before it began by the action against the dean of law and three faculty members illustrated Ben Forsyth completely in character. Garbed in principle, sword in hand.

Oxford had no doubt that even an older and wiser Ben Forsyth was still capable of pulling the temple down around him. And it seemed from what he had passed over to his two law partners that that was exactly what he had intended on doing.

Back in his Flatlander suite, Oxford called Dorothy Crane, executive secretary to the minister of Provincial Development, and arranged to meet in Ben's office in the legislative building early the next morning. Ben's two ministerial offices, Dorothy advised, were being maintained in an untouched condition on orders of the premier's office pending examination and release by Mr. LaCoste on behalf of Mr. Forsyth's executors.

No appointment of a new minister of Provincial Development was expected for some time, Dorothy reported, and the premier was serving as acting minister for the time being.

Oxford walked from the Flatlander through the leaf-strewn Regina streets, across the one square block of green space called Victoria Park, and into the small area of the city that is still known as "Downtown." There he entered the glitzy premises of the Western Dominion Bank, all glass and stainless steel, and inquired about the safety deposit boxes at the branch it had once maintained on Albert Street, not far from the legislative building.

That branch had been closed six months earlier, Oxford learned. He displayed his professional card and the letter found in Ben's file, and was referred to a manager.

"Oh, yes. Some problem about that, I believe. Let me check that out and get back to you. Will you be in town long? Where are you staying?"

That evening Oxford received a telephone call in his suite. The caller identified himself as Inspector Adam Jakes of the Regina Police Service. "I'm just downstairs. Might I come up for a moment?"

The policeman clearly intended to dominate the discussion and he came quickly to his point.

"You inquired about certain safety deposit boxes at the Western Dominion Bank today. What is the nature of your interest?"

Oxford was startled. What the hell is this about? he started to say, then thought better of it. He remembered he did have some experience with police. Play it straight.

"I'm one of the executors of the late Benjamin Forsyth. It's part of my duty to identify all of Mr. Forsyth's assets. I was following up on a letter found among Ben—Mr. Forsyth's effects. It seemed to suggest that his estate might have some interest in a safety deposit box at the bank. So, naturally, I made inquiries," he continued with some deliberate formality. "Perfectly normal. So, what seems to be the problem?" Oxford decided to ask a question or two of his own.

"The bank received no reply to that letter," the Inspector replied after a moment's consideration, "and, when the time came to close the branch, decided to open those last two boxes so the contents could be transferred and the building turned over. They called us. In the course of our investigation we interviewed Mr. Forsyth. It was his office the letter was directed to. He denied any knowledge of the boxes or their contents. He was very positive that he had no ownership of those contents. Or any interest in them."

"Well, I'm sure that's good enough for us," Oxford

replied, then continued with another question of his own. "What was in them?"

"Sorry. Classified." The inspector was all cop on that one.

"Then who is James Karpan? and where is he?"

Jakes looked at Oxford long and carefully before he replied.

"There is no James Karpan. It was a pseudonym. He does not exist."

The two sat and looked at each other as if considering their next moves. The inspector, tall, well-built but not heavy, ruddy-faced with a military mustache, looked all the world like a British officer, but his speech, though articulate, said clearly that he had nothing of the sort in his make-up. Casually dressed, he was confident but thoughtful.

"Did you know Mr. Forsyth well?" the inspector moved first.

"Yes. We were very good friends." Something is coming, Oxford thought.

And it did come. Jakes had a strong interest in Ben Forsyth. What had been his emotional condition lately? How was his marriage? Any financial difficulties? Had he been involved in any activity that might have placed him in danger? Politicians occasionally make enemies. Did Ben Forsyth have enemies?

Oxford became concerned. "Are you questioning the manner of Ben's death? I understood it was clearly accidental."

"No. Not really. But we like to follow a routine in these cases," Jakes replied, somewhat airily, Oxford thought.

Again the policeman gazed thoughtfully at Oxford as if his experience and intuition told him that the lawyer did hold some information that he would like to have. He got up to leave. "You'll call me if anything comes to mind, won't you?"

"Of course," Oxford replied mechanically.

"Perhaps we can be of assistance to each other," Jakes persisted, then stepped out the door. "Good night."

Now what the hell was that all about, Oxford wondered as he closed the door behind the policeman and turned back into his suite. He had certainly touched a nerve with his innocent inquiry at the bank.

Ben Forsyth had made it very plain in his letter to

Cameron Hunt and Oxford that he had been living in a corrupt world, but Oxford had carelessly assumed that Ben the Puritan was overstating things a bit. Now he wondered. We just touched things around the edges and a cop jumped out at us.

What had been in those safety deposit boxes to cause such a reaction? And who was hiding behind the name James Karpan?

Why had Ben kept that letter to Karpan in the envelope with the other material? Without any explanation? He must have known how sensitive it would be. Had he been so overwrought that he just forgot such an explosive item? Had there been some purpose in the way he left the letter for Hunt and Oxford?

Oxford slept very poorly.

TEN

Most of the cabinet ministers in the Saskatchewan government maintain two offices, one where their department is headquartered, usually in a Regina office building, and one in the legislative buildings which they use during sessions of the legislature. It becomes a matter of personal preference as to which becomes the primary office, and which the secondary. Ben Forsyth had preferred to work in the legislative buildings.

As Oxford walked up the front steps of the "marble palace," as the beautiful building is sometimes described, he turned and looked back across the flower gardens, now empty and waiting for winter, over Wascana Lake, its shallow, muddy depths masked beneath a deep azure surface, brilliant in the fall sunshine. Sisik had been right. Standing on the top step, Oxford could see that with a good set of binoculars he could look right into his suite in the Flatlander.

"There's no one here but us," Dorothy Crane said, as she handed Oxford a coffee and led him into the private office in the minister's suite. They sat in the chairs used when the minister received small delegations.

Dorothy had been as close to Ben as he had been, Oxford knew, and must feel his loss just as keenly. Both of them owed much of their position in life to the kindness of Ben Forsyth.

Dorothy had worked with Ben from the time of his first

election, in fact had been the office manager in his committee rooms in West Willow. There, with the opportunity and encouragement provided by the candidate, she first discovered that she had ability and talent. Pregnant and hastily married at twenty to the son of a local farmer, she had no previous experience with which to question his constantly stated opinion that she was just a third-rate housewife. With new found self-esteem and confidence, Dorothy shed her complaining husband and, with her six-year-old daughter, followed Ben Forsyth to Regina and a job in the minister's office. Three years later she had advanced to the senior position, loved her work, and held the same high regard for Ben Forsyth as did Oxford.

This was a new and improved version of the Dorothy Crane Oxford had known at West Willow who now sat easily across from him in the minister's suite. Taller than he remembered, perhaps due to her fashionable high-heeled shoes, and more slender, she wore a smart navy suit and was altogether an unusually attractive and self-possessed young woman. He had seen her from time to time over the years, of course, but usually on informal occasions when her attire and deportment had not been quite as striking as he found it this morning. It took a moment for Oxford to register the fact that she was speaking to him.

"What's this all about, Oxford? Why all the high-level concern and mystery? The circuits are smoking on the jungle telegraph around this place."

"There seems to be a lot of interest in some confidential files of Ben's that have somehow gone missing," he replied.

Dorothy's eyebrows arched and her mouth pursed. "What confidential files? Can you be a bit more specific?"

Dorothy sounded just a little protective, Oxford thought.

"I guess there wouldn't be any point in not levelling with you, would there? Would Ben have had any files you didn't know about?"

"No, I don't think he did. But that doesn't mean I know where they all are now. Ben kept some files away from the office." They were fencing, Oxford saw, and, on a flash of impulse, decided that he could fully trust Dorothy, *had* to trust her.

"You know that Cameron Hunt and I are Ben's executors, don't you?"

Dorothy nodded in quiet reply.

"Well, Ben has tossed us a real hot potato." And Oxford described Ben's envelope and its contents. The reaction was calmer than he expected.

"So that's what he did with it," she said, obviously relieved, when Oxford finished. "He had me package all that material together. Then he said he 'would take it from there.' I didn't quite know what he meant by that, but I was worried silly that it was going to be something drastic.

"Ben was terribly upset when we came into this office—when he began to find out what had been going on here. You know how honest Ben was. Well, Sean McCarthy wasn't—isn't. Some of the deals that had been cooked in this place would curl your hair. McCarthy's people had accidentally left behind a large set of personal files. I found them. And I snooped, of course. They were on some very smelly affairs. When I showed them to Ben he had me quickly make a copy of the works. I did, and put the originals back as if we'd never seen them. Wasn't long before McCarthy's executive assistant was back here for them, looking very worried. They were right where they had been left. I put on a good act of not having even noticed them.

"Then Ben went through the files himself, made a selection. Then he added a few he had dug up somewhere else. I guess you and Mr. Hunt now have the result. What are you going to do with it?" Dorothy looked directly at Oxford.

"We don't know. Haven't decided. Do you think Ben would have gone public with it?"

"Yes. Absolutely. He was very angry. Said he'd already overlooked a lot of the stuff that had been going on around this government. That he didn't approve of. When he uncovered this can of worms he was really upset. He was mad at himself. For not having spoken out sooner. I mean, he felt he had betrayed his own principles."

They sat in silence for a moment. Oxford thought about his conversation with Adam Jakes, some of the questions the police-officer had posed. As he lifted his gaze, their eyes met; Dorothy had been looking at him pensively.

"Dorothy, do you think anyone else might have known that Ben had those files, that he was planning something serious?"

"I've worried about that. Epecially since that awful Val Sisik was in here the morning after Ben's death. He was searching through Ben's files. Even the computers. It's impossible to keep a secret in this building. I'm sure Sean McCarthy was aware that Ben was upset about some of his deals. But I don't think he knows we copied his files. I hope he doesn't. But he might not even give a damn. He's really arrogant. And he's very tight with the premier.

"Why do you ask?" she added with a quick glance of concern.

"For the same reason you're worried, I guess." Oxford declined to go further.

"How about Ruth?" he asked. "Would she know about any of this?"

"Not a chance. Ben had given up confiding in her, even about little things. No way would he have trusted her on something like this. No way."

"Dorothy," he said, "there was another file, wasn't there. One having to do with a heavy oil extraction process?"

Dorothy looked at him for a long serious moment. "How would one of Ben's executors know anything about that?"

"I can't tell you how I know about it. Just that it's very important that we find that file."

"Why?" Dorothy was still the loyal, protective secretary. Like a faithful dog sitting on its master's grave, Oxford thought.

"Because," Oxford began, fully intending to explain, when Dorothy held up her hand, then put a finger to her lips, signalling silence.

"I'm expected at the other office," she said, getting quickly to her feet. "I'm sorry. I have to go. What about lunch? Where are you staying?"

"The Flatlander."

"Fine. I'll pick you up there. The front door at twelve sharp? Come, I'll walk out with you."

And she did, smiled at Oxford at the security station

inside the front door, and turned and left him. He drove back to his hotel and spent the rest of the morning burning with curiosity.

At noon, Oxford stepped into the red Camry as it pulled up to him, turned and demanded, "What the hell is this all about?" The navy skirt rode well above the knees and his eyes were drawn to the shapely leg on the accelerator.

Dorothy didn't answer until her car turned the corner and pointed north on Albert Street. Again she put her finger to her lips, but spoke, "I'm sorry. I just had a number of unexpected things come up this morning. Why not let me tell you all about it over lunch?"

Oxford subsided into silence until a waiter ushered them into the back booth of a quiet pasta restaurant in northwest Regina. He was mildly surprised at the aplomb with which she directed her choice of location.

"This is about as far as you can get from the legislative buildings and still be in Regina," Dorothy smiled as they settled in. "It suddenly occurred to me that one of the antics of this government that most upset Ben was its use of bugs. Electronic eavesdropping, I think they call it. And why wouldn't they put one of their damn bugs in Ben's office if they were concerned about what was going on there? And my car, too, while they were at it."

"Bug the office of one of their own ministers?" Oxford asked in disbelief.

"Yup. Wouldn't cause them a second thought, particularly since said minister isn't around any more. Wouldn't bother them much if he was, though."

"Who is 'they' in this scenario?"

"Sean McCarthy and his henchperson, Patrick Justice. They run a slimy espionage system all through this government."

"On whose instructions?" Oxford persisted.

"Their own," Dorothy replied. "Those two have been operating as an independent authority for some time now. They claim to have the approval of the premier. But I don't think they do, at least until after the fact. Everyone knows Halliday's afraid to challenge McCarthy. They've given up questioning what he does. Let's hope I'm wrong, but when you started talking about that heavy oil file, I got shivers up my back." She rolled her shoulders, grimaced, and continued.

"I mean that was one very big deal. It had Ben so upset that he forgot about everything else. Including that other package we talked about."

"What was he upset about?" Oxford asked.

"I don't know. The file came to him from the premier directly. I guess Halliday didn't want Sean McCarthy anywhere near this deal, wanted it handled competently. Probably honestly, too. Ben was pleased to take it on.

"The negotiations started last spring. Everything was going along fine. Ben went over to Hong Kong at the end of June. Made the banking arrangements. Met with the other side. He was being very meticulous, as always. I thought the deal was due to close a couple of weeks ago." Dorothy paused, looked searchingly at Oxford, then reached a decision and carried on.

"One morning Ben came into the office, his eyes staring out of his head. He was apoplectic, but silent. Completely silent. Wouldn't say a word. Stomped around the office, stared out the window. Stomped around some more. It was scary. Then he called me in. He was furious. Controlled, but furious. Told me to put every word of all the files having anything to do with the heavy oil deal on computer disks. I was to do it myself. I was to let no one know it was being done. I was to give the disks to him as soon as I was finished. No explanation. No questions allowed." Again Dorothy stopped, then took a breath and continued.

"So, of course, I did. Practically all the technical data we had was already on discs. I just needed to pick up the correspondence, contracts and the like. A lot of that was still in our hard drives. I was able to use the scanner for most of what wasn't, and it didn't take long.

"When I reported back to Ben with the package of discs, he had two more instructions for me. I was to delete any trace of the files from the computers, the hard drives, leaving only the discs. Then I was to shred the files themselves." She was twisting her napkin now, and tension made her voice husky.

"Naturally I thought he had cracked up. I thought the

strain he had been under had gotten to him. When I started to protest, Ben became very serious, very calm, very deliberate.

"'Dorothy,' he said to me, 'I know this sounds strange. But I know exactly what I am doing and it is the most important thing I will ever do in my life. Now please do exactly as I ask.'"

By now she had put a glass of water to her lips and was speaking into it, her eyes downcast.

"So, of course, I did. And I never heard the file mentioned again until this morning." Dorothy looked up at Oxford. She was finished.

"What happened to the discs?" Oxford asked.

"Don't know. Ben took them out of the office and I never saw them again."

"What do they look like?"

"Well, you know what a so-called floppy computer disc looks like, about four inches square. I used more discs than I needed. Four, I think. Even so all of them together wouldn't take up much more room than a cigarette package. You could store the Encyclopaedia Britannica in less space."

Dorothy paused while the waiter brought their orders. She shook her head to decline the proffered pepper grinder. Oxford accepted.

"By the way, that weekend Ben died, one of the hotshots from the premier's office was in our offices checking our computers. Was that what they were looking for?" Dorothy asked.

"Probably. How do you know that?"

"A friend on the cleaning staff. I told you there are no secrets around there."

"But no one has mentioned to you that they would like the heavy oil file?"

"No one but you. Now that you mention it, that is strange, isn't it?" Dorothy poked listlessly at her chef's salad, then turned to Oxford, tears glistening in her eyes. Then she reached and put her hand on his.

"Oxford," her voice broke, "what was our Ben up to?"

In reply Oxford could only shake his head sadly, "I wish I knew." But he squeezed her hand gently before it was withdrawn. They concentrated on their pasta.

After a moment Dorothy looked up and spoke. "There's someone in PanSask you could talk to. A geophysicist, I think. He had something to do with evaluating the laser recovery process. He was over to see Ben a few times. On that and other deals. I got the idea he was under-impressed by this government. Name is Howard Gordon."

"Can you fix me up with an appointment?"

"I think so. I'm sure, yes. I'll set it up."

Later that afternoon, after Dorothy dropped him off, Oxford sat in his suite in the Flatlander Inn, looked across Wascana Park and Lake at the legislative buildings, then impulsively walked across College Avenue into the park and picked a bench in the sunshine overlooking the lake. He pondered the question Dorothy had raised over lunch, "What had Ben Forsyth been up to?"

What contribution could he could bring to the search for an answer to that question? And Oxford wondered, where did his loyalties lie? The quick review of Ben's confidential file on Monday night in Cameron Hunt's home, bolstered by Dorothy's comments today, proclaimed loudly and clearly that Saskatchewan was burdened by a corrupt and venal government and that Ben Forsyth, Oxford's role model and mentor, had been embarked upon a mission that could bring down that government, a mission interrupted by Ben's death.

But that very same government had retained him as its lawyer and was now his client, a client to whom he must give all of his loyalty. The ethics of his profession demanded no less.

Yet his commission, his retainer, his instructions were to recover the files and funds relating to the heavy oil transaction, nothing more. Although Vladimir Sisik had commanded that Oxford turn over all files belonging to the government, that command was really only a request directed to Oxford as one of Ben's executors. As such it was not related to the retainer and was certainly ineffective. Even the deputy minister to the premier had no authority over the duly appointed executors of a deceased cabinet minister.

Or did he?

Oxford's bench was on the lake front directly across

from the legislative building, a favourite route of Regina's joggers. Two or three had padded past him without his notice, but now his senses alerted to another runner approaching. This time he turned to look.

A young woman. Very attractive, Oxford quickly noted. His attention was captured by the easy grace of her running. As a sometime jogger himself, Oxford was impressed with the lightness of her movement. Tall and lithe, her long legs flashed towards him with the smoothness of a ballerina. As she crossed in front of him, she smiled so warmly and naturally that Oxford was stunned and unable to work his facial muscles in response until she was past. Watching her, he noted that her hair, gathered casually in an elastic, did not bounce but flowed behind with a undulating movement that heightened the elegance of her passage. She was not running so much as gliding. And then she disappeared, down the curve of the path behind a grove of spruce.

Oxford sat as if overcome by paralysis, his senses jumbled. A message shot through his mind, telling him to leap to his feet and run after her. Then it was gone. The image of the girl's smile hung before him like that of the Cheshire cat, then faded away.

A wave of melancholy washed over him, astonishing him with the suddenness of its attack. He felt himself overwhelmed with loneliness, an emotion he had not known since childhood. "Am I losing it?" he asked himself.

Women had never played a major role in Oxford's life. At university in Montreal and Saskatoon he had drifted in and out of relationships with bohemian casualness. None had provided any sense of commitment. At West Willow, his position in the small community denied him such casual encounters. He enjoyed the odd weekend arrangement but had not met anyone he might think of in a permanent way. It was a matter of small consequence. Until now. An unpleasant memory from his university days intruded. Again. As it too often did. Oxford had been the master of ceremonies at the annual law school banquet. Two male members of his class had enrolled in a course entitled "*The Evolution of Law and Feminism*," causing some consternation and delight. At the conclusion of dinner, Oxford included in his humorous remarks the announcement, "The members of the Law and Feminism class will now clear the tables while the gentlemen retire to the drawing room for brandy and cigars."

The riot was instantaneous. Two female faculty members leaped to their feet and stamped out of the banquet, followed by a number of woman undergraduates. The next morning they protested loudly to the dean and demanded Oxford's expulsion. Only grovelling apologies had saved Oxford's year.

The incident left a sour taste in Oxford's mouth. For a long time he wondered if it had soured his whole attitude towards women. He could not comprehend how so much offense could be taken where none at all had been intended.

He looked down the path after the runner. My God, he thought, it must be wonderful to share life with a girl like that. The loneliness attacked again. He felt wretched. Oxford shook himself and stood. And thought of Dorothy Crane. An image of Dorothy floated into his mind, much like the one the jogger had left with him. Then came a strange feeling of tenderness.

ELEVEN

 Oxford returned to the Flatlander and seized one of the three telephones in his suite.

"Prociuk and Rossom. May I help you?"

"Chris Rossom, please."

"May I tell him who is calling?"

Oxford hesitated, then complied. His teeth always gritted when he heard that question. He was sure that if he introduced that affectation in his West Willow office his phone would stop ringing within a week. Either that or the earthy responses from his no-nonsense clients would drive his staff into the street.

"Oxford. Are you in town?" Chris Rossom's voice melted the irritation that had been rising in his caller.

"Yep. I am. And I'm in a drink buying mood. Are you free after work?"

"Almost. Nearly. Yes. Now I am. Where shall we meet?"

"Flatlander Lounge. No. Hold it. I just remembered I have some booze here in my suite. I'm in 1702. As close to now as you can get here."

"I'll never admit it but I'll cancel this one item and be there by 4:30."

"Great. See you then."

Oxford put down the phone. He felt better already. He and Chris Rossom had lived together as bachelor undergraduates at the University of Saskatchewan until Sally King had come into Chris' life. Although Oxford moved out in favour of Sally, there had been no dislocated feelings and the three continued as close friends. Nothing had changed that, Oxford knew, although he had been moved two more degrees outward since the births of Kara and Robin.

With family responsibilities upon him by the time he graduated from law school, Chris had been elated to land one of the secure and well-paid positions in the provincial department of the Attorney-General. He had long dreamed of a career as a lawyer for the Crown, the most prestigious client of all. But after just five years, although it cost a serious drop in income that he and Sally could ill afford, he jumped at the chance to join a young but developing firm that now consisted of five lawyers.

Chris had never spoken of his reasons for leaving the government, explaining only that things had not turned out as he had expected. Oxford sensed that his friend had run afoul of something ugly, something that he preferred not to talk about, and he had been careful not to pry.

Chris Rossom hefted the bottle of expensive single malt Scotch and squinted at Oxford.

"You could never tell the difference between bad booze and worse. How did you get this?" Then, seeing Val Sisik's card on the case of liquor, "Oh! I see. Of course. Well, it's a good thing you have me and a few other discriminating friends to balance this other variety. Let's get at it."

The lawyer poured the whiskey over ice, slid down into a settee, cocked one foot over the other on the top of the coffee table, waved the glass expansively and spoke.

"Here's to the practice of law in West Willow, Sask. Sure beats the hell out of the racket here in Regina."

As Chris Rossom took a large swallow of Scotch, his host didn't respond and he quickly abandoned humour. He put his feet back on the floor, leaned forward and asked, "What's going on, Oxford? What's it all about? Sally and I have been concerned about you since we heard of Ben Forsyth's death. Can we help?"

Oxford stared into his Scotch for a moment and made a mental adjustment, balancing the need to unload his problems before his old friend with the need to maintain the confidentiality his client was entitled to—and demanded. Never before with Chris, whose discretion he trusted, had he felt this concern. It is not unusual for lawyers to occasionally take each other into confidence, sharing their difficulties, including those of their clients, when faced with problem situations and wanting another perspective. Lawyers with partners do that all the time, the entire firm being bound by the requirements of solicitor and client privilege. Lawyers in solo practice, like Oxford, often miss that luxury and Oxford had often come to Chris Rossom for help in working through thorny problems. He had never been disappointed in the quality of his friend's judgement, nor ever been concerned about his total discretion.

But this time seemed different and Oxford began to edit his intended account, feeling uncomfortable, and made the more so by Chris Rossom's quizzical look as he waited.

"Ben Forsyth was pretty much your favorite human being, wasn't he?" Chris asked finally, hoping to get Oxford started.

"Just about," Oxford admitted, "although I wouldn't want to get into ranking, at least not in present company. I think I'm adjusting to Ben's death, tough as that is", he continued. "That's not what's bothering me, it's some of the problems he left behind."

"I see," said Chris, then, as if admitting he had not seen it at all, "how do you mean?"

"Some of the work Ben was doing for the government, unfinished work, has come to Cameron Hunt and me as his executors. Causes us some real concern. Me particularly. Mr. Hunt, as you know, is a pretty unflappable guy. Comes from driving bombers into the teeth of anti-aircraft guns, I think."

Oxford was stalling. Chris waited for the continuation.

"Ben the lawyer and Ben the politician were coming into conflict with each other and he passed that conflict to us. We can't decide how to handle it."

"I can certainly believe that," Chris said, trying to make it easier for his struggling friend. "Many of us have wondered for years how Ben Forsyth was able to continue as a member of the Halliday government, known locally as Ali

Baba and Friends. He had principles. The rest couldn't spell the word."

"Was it that obvious?" Oxford asked.

"Sure, to the so-called elite in Regina, anyway. This town seethes with gossip about the government. Who has clout, who hasn't. What deals are cooking and who is cooking them and how does one get in on the action. This is a government town and almost nothing of consequence happens here without government participation. Certainly nothing involving money. Hell, you can't even run a decent charitable fund raiser here without the blessing of the Halliday gang because without it the movers and shakers won't lift a finger.

"It's always been like this, more or less, no matter what the stripe of the government," Rossom continued, obviously into a favorite theme, "but since the Western Democratic Alliance took over it's been more, a great deal more. The scene here is not unlike what it must have been around one of the corrupt courts of the Middle Ages. Who's in favour with the king today and what did he have for breakfast?

"It's so bad," and now the lawyer sprang to his feet, "that even the slippery contractors won't bid a government project because they know the fix is in somewhere and if they're not on the inside there's no point in going through the motions. Around this town today, if you're not on the inside you are very definitely on the outside. Neutrality has become an offence. I can tell you stories. Sorry, I didn't mean to get carried away. Maybe I'll just have a little more of this single malt and settle down." Chris tilted the Scotch into his glass.

"It's just that Ben Forsyth didn't belong with that bunch. He was a class act and he was giving some colour of integrity to a government that didn't—doesn't—deserve it. All right, I'll shut up." And Chris Rossom settled back into his chair.

"No, please don't," Oxford protested. "I need to know all this. Ben never talked politics with us, so all I know is what I've picked up from the media, and I've not paid much attention even to that. Ben was very disturbed the last few months," Oxford explained. "He had been working too hard and drinking too much. We didn't know why then, but now we think it was because he had become at odds with the government."

"Why didn't he just quit? Throw in the towel? Resign? Go back home and practise law with you and leave this bunch to drown?" Chris asked.

"Don't know for sure. I think he felt he had waited too long, that he had become compromised. Maybe he felt he owed it to himself, and others, to do something about the problem." Oxford said.

"Do something? Like what?" Chris was now very alert.

"I think . . . I know I don't need to say this, Chris, but this is very much just between the two of us—I believe Ben was thinking of exposing some of the raw deals pulled by his government."

"Jesus H. Christ. Blow the whistle on these dudes? From inside? Holy penitentiary, Batman, do you have any idea what that would mean?" Chris was on his feet again.

"Just a little, I guess, after listening to you a moment ago. Presumably it would mean the end of the Halliday government, which I suppose is what Ben had in mind," Oxford replied.

"Oh, it would mean that, for sure. But that would be just a side effect. Christ, the fallout would be nuclear. There would be judicial inquiries, criminal investigations, prosecutions, prominent citizens in the slammer, you name it. Hell, the judicial system would probably be overloaded for years." Chris was excited.

"But," Chris stopped and stared at Oxford, "Ben's gone. So there'll be no exposure and none of this will happen. Isn't that right?"

"Well . . . now you see the problem," Oxford said, reaching for the Scotch. "How's your drink?"

Chris Rossom held out his glass, staring at Oxford. Then he began to speak, slowly and carefully.

"Let me see if I understand this. I think you're telling me that you have Ben's evidence. That he left it to you somehow. That you're thinking of using it as he might have."

Chris moved over to the window, looked over the park to the legislative building and continued, "That means that you'll become the whistle-blower. You instead of the Honourable Ben Forsyth, minister of Provincial Development, now deceased. In the place and stead of, as we lawyers would say. Then all the shit and abuse that would have come down around the late Ben Forsyth will now be directed at you, solely. Am I right so far?" he asked, turning around.

"Let's assume you are. Carry on."

"Yeah, let's assume that," Chris said dryly, "and let's us assume a few other events, the reasonable and probable consequences, again as we lawyers would say, of such a disclosure on your part.

"The people who have so far benefited, profited if you prefer, from the conduct of this government, are not the nicest people in Saskatchewan. They're not going to take kindly to the notion that some Johnny-come-lately do-good-er is proposing to expose their game and make them cough up their loot. They'll become very mean indeed. They'll think bad thoughts about you. Some of those thoughts may come to action." Chris swirled the Scotch in his glass.

"I've read of a saying they use down in Latin America. You know—in those banana republics we used to deride for their corruption until we became almost as bad ourselves. Well, when the revolution finally comes and the new good guys want to root out the old crooks, they look for the "unusually wealthy people." Folks who didn't have any money before but who suddenly have a lot probably got it corruptly.

"Think about that a moment," Chris said. "The phrase says it all. And it applies here. The people here who have been snorting at the Halliday trough are not ORFs, although some of those have done very well, too."

"What's an ORF?" Oxford interjected.

"Old Regina Family. Two generations is old, which, at that, is usually long enough to have achieved some respectability. No, the people who will be right pissed off at Oxford LaCoste, boy windmill-tilter, will have no compunction about observing the niceties when they find themselves threatened. I'm trying to tell you that I see a lot of very real danger for you if you were to attack this government and its friends. It's obvious from what I said earlier that I'd love to see them brought to justice, but I'm also pretty fond of you, my old friend." Chris Rossom sipped his Scotch, looked at Oxford, and continued.

"Having given you all that on the down side, if there is anything I can do to help, please let me. I don't know what you have, or what you might do with it, and probably I shouldn't. But whatever you do, count me with you." He raised his glass in salute, then took a serious swallow.

The two lawyers looked into their drinks.

"Thanks, Chris, for that offer and all the background. That's going to be really helpful, more than I can fully explain now. And I won't be bashful about asking for help. Right now I've got Cameron Hunt holding my hand, and that's good, but I don't think he would understand the world you just described. I may be in over my head before I know it. I guess that means that maybe I am now," he said, grinning for the first time.

"On a different subject," Oxford continued, "what do you know about offshore banking, numbered accounts in the Caribbean Islands, and all that? That's a little out of our line down in West Willow."

"It's a little out of my line too," Chris replied, with a suddenly furrowed brow that told Oxford that his friend did not at all believe that this was an entirely different subject, but more likely close to the reason for the expensive suite they were sitting in. "But it's very much in my partner Herb Prociuk's line. In fact, he has developed a bit of a specialty in what they call asset protection trusts. That's a nice euphemism for the technique of hiding your loot behind a numbered bank account in one of those so-called offshore jurisdictions that welcome that sort of money. They used to be called tax havens, now they've gone a step further. Herb has attracted several clients of the sort we've been talking about and who are busy squirrelling their nuts away in case of a hard winter. Or, in case a bigger squirrel comes along.

"Don't sniff, Oxford. You know lawyers can't choose their clients. Or at least aren't supposed to. Besides, these are currently very respectable citizens of this here town. What do you need to know?"

"I don't know, yet. I suppose it would be naive to ask if it's possible to track that kind of money?"

"Pretty much impossible, I'm sure, although I think that varies a little bit depending on which country the money is in. Would you like me to ask Herb, anonymously of course?"

"Yes, do that, please. Ask him specifically about the Turks and Caicos Islands."

"Ha! The place that wanted to become part of Canada a few years ago, our Hawaii. Don't know why we didn't go along with that. Whoever turned them down doesn't spend too many winters in Saskatchewan. Sure, I'll ask Herb, quietly." Chris stood up again.

"And now, how about coming over for dinner while you're in town? I told Sally I was coming over here. She promises to put spaghetti and that famous meat sauce of hers on the menu if that will still attract you. She'll be disappointed if you can't make it. So will Robin and Kara."

"That's a deal. I have go back down to West Willow tomorrow, but I was thinking of coming right back in, anyway. Now I am for sure. I can't pass up Sally's meat sauce. It's been too long since I saw the kids. How are they doing?"

"Great. Two Tasmanian devils. They'll be wild to see Uncle Ox. Be ready with a bedtime story."

"That I can handle," and Oxford grinned again.

The two friends shook hands with, Oxford was sure, much more than usual warmth. As he turned back into the suite after seeing Chris to the elevator, the loneliness was gone and he felt full of confidence and strength.

Why is that, he wondered. Because all he had learned was that his problems were far larger than he had imagined.

TWELVE

The door opened easily to the key Ruth Forsyth had given him, but Oxford was slow to enter. Although he had visited the Regina condominium once or twice with Ben, he felt very much a stranger here. Already he wished he had come in daylight. Reminding himself that he was only here to look for any files in Ben's home office having to do with the heavy oil deal, he stepped into the foyer.

The office, or den as Ben had called it, was as far as he had ever been before, and Oxford knew it was just to his left. But as he switched on lights he saw the entrance to the garage to the right and could not resist opening the door and going through.

Ben and Ruth Forsyth had purchased the condo just a few weeks after Ben's cabinet appointment. Ben had thought it a little tony, but Ruth insisted that they required a Regina home in keeping with their new station in life.

The garage Oxford was standing in fronted onto the street, behind a large concrete driveway and parking pad. Two separate doors opened into what was really a two and half car garage, what with the storage area for bicycles and barbecue and the like. Across the garage from the door Oxford had come through, another door opened onto the patio in back.

It was here that Ben Forsyth had died, slumped behind the wheel of his black Chrysler, government issue for its ministers.

Now that he knew the problems Ben had been wrestling with in the months before his death, Oxford wondered why the man had continued to work so hard on his departmental and political responsibilities? Why did he give a damn for the day to day obligations on top of everything else? After all, he had been considering bringing down the government and destroying the Western Democratic Alliance party itself.

Ruth Forsyth had told Oxford how Ben had reached such a state of continuing exhaustion that when he returned home late at night he had developed the habit of catnapping in his car before dragging himself off to bed. Frequently, hearing him drive in, she had come down to the garage, shaken him awake and made him come to his bed. But all too often Ruth herself had been too deep in whiskey slumber to hear her husband's return.

According to newspaper and television reports, and accounts attributed to Ruth, she had not heard Ben return on his last night on earth. He had been speaking at a WDA meeting in Yorkton, had stayed too late and had not left until close to midnight. It is a good two hour drive from Yorkton to Regina, so it was almost 2:00 in the morning when Ben pulled into his garage. Oxford suspected that Ben might have had one or two post-meeting drinks before leaving Yorkton.

Ruth stated that about five o'clock she was awakened by an insistent sound invading her sleep. Noticing that Ben's bed was empty, she raced down to the garage, threw open the door and recoiled at the stench of exhaust fumes. Ben was still in his car and the engine was running. He had fallen asleep without turning off his ignition.

Ruth punched the buttons opening the outside garage doors and dialled 911. A police cruiser was the first to arrive. A constable turned off the ignition but it was too late. Ben was pronounced dead upon arrival at the Plains Hospital at 5:30 A.M.

Ben Forsyth had died right where he was now standing, Oxford noted uncomfortably. What an unnecessary death. What a tragic loss to the people of Saskatchewan. Oxford shuddered, took hold of himself, marched out of the garage, across the foyer and into the tiny office.

Ben's office. His desk and chair. His reference books. His pemmican pounder paper-weight, almost the only thing he brought from his office at West Willow. An eerie feeling came over Oxford as he looked about and then sat in Ben's chair.

Ruth certainly had made first review of the files here, he knew. There would be no surprises like those in the safety deposit boxes. The angry widow had made sure not to overlook any "personal effects."

After half an hour, Oxford had recovered all that remained in Ben Forsyth's home office that had any relevance to his problem. Just two files containing appraisals of the tremendous potential locked in Saskatchewan's heavy oil deposits. Nothing about the laser extraction process. He added the files to the few he had secured from Vladimir Sisik and reviewed all the information he had acquired thus far. Then he pulled a pad of foolscap to him, and began to make notes.

1. *Saskatchewan has one of the world's largest concentrations of heavy oil. Worth billions. Problem: the oil (called heavy because it's so glutinous) is maxi expensive to recover. Plus refine. Most methods able to lift only a fraction of available oil to the surface.*

2. *Thus, the laser technique. The tremendous heat of the laser beam reduces the heavy oil to a fluid that flows easily through the pumps.*

3. *But using the laser on light oil deposits has real potential. Modern recovery methods able to capture only thirty per cent (less than one-third!) of all the light crude discovered in all fields in Western Canada. Billions (plus) of barrels identified but beyond reach. If laser can tap even a fraction, value beyond imagination. Thus, Halliday's interest.*

4. *The laser process offered to Halliday government by Josef Rafael. Last spring he approached Gus Walker (Sask. Agent General in Hong Kong, former WDA MLA) with proposal. Rafael aware of Sask. heavy oil deposits. Knew a good recovery process would be valuable here.*

5. *Josef Rafael an Israeli and one of inventors of laser process. Developed at Technicon University in Haifa (by Jewish Russian emigres who brought it with them). Process cleared experimental stage—ready for field conditions. Sask. heavy oil fields best suited to the process.*

6. *Exclusive rights to laser. Price = $15 million. (Rafael says only development cost). $$$ payable after feasibility studies successful.*

7. *Rafael sure laser adaptable to Athabaska tar sands. If so, riches of Croesus.*

8. *Gus Walker promptly forwarded the proposal to Harris Halliday who asked Vladimir Sisik to perform an evaluation.*

9. *Sisik found the process feasible. Potential to make the Halliday government a player on the world petroleum market. Enormous political benefits— if successful.*

10. *But Sisik warned that failure would be disaster electorally. Because of damage to government's image by economic fiascos promoted by Sean McCarthy. (Sisik very critical of McCarthy— impulsive, imprudent.)*

11. *Situation called for two requirements— (a) McCarthy could not be trusted with acquisition. (b) Total secrecy necessary until success could be announced. If failure, all information to be suppressed until after election.*

12. *Enlisted dependable Ben Forsyth to handle the deal. Need to know restricted to Halliday, Sisik, and Ben.*

13. *Evaluation of process given to technicals at PanSask Petroleum. but they not otherwise included in transaction. Gus Walker dealt out of any further involvement.*

14. *Funding a problem. To maintain secrecy, financing came from five different gov't accounts (including PanSask).*

Oxford leaned back and reflected on what he had learned about financing the laser purchase. He thought the methods Halliday and Sisik used were pseudo-legal at best. After all, public monies of the magnitude of fifteen million dollars are subject to the financial controls of the legislature. But Ben went along. Why? Oxford turned again to his notes.

15. *Ben to Hong Kong in June. Met with Josef Rafael. Set up escrow account for fund transfer. When feasibility cleared.*

16. *Feasibility studies took longer than estimated. Premier and Sisik anxious to close. Told Ben to reduce due diligence. Ben finally agreed. Said political responsibility was premier's.*

17. *Ben finally ready to close. Told premier and Sisik feasibility okay. Fund transfer to take place in three or four days.*

But within a week Ben was dead. Vladimir Sisik immediately checked on the status of the laser deal and was shocked to learn that it had not closed when Ben had said it would. He found that the fifteen million dollars had been moved from Regina to the escrow account in Hong Kong, as Ben had reported. But several days before his death Ben cancelled the closing and transferred the funds to a numbered account in the London & Belfast Bank in the Turks and Caicos Islands. There the trail stopped. All attempts to reach Josef Rafael had failed. All Ben's files had disappeared. Your problem, Mr. LaCoste.

An alarm exploded Oxford's thoughts. He was instantly alert but needed several long seconds to identify the noise and its source. The doorbell. It was only a few feet away and had sounded like a klaxon. Keerist! He got to his feet and answered. A pleasant looking man dressed in blue jeans and jacket stood on the step.

"I'm sorry if I'm interrupting. I thought maybe Ruth was here. I'm Tom Randall. Two doors down. Friends of Ben and Ruth. I, we, were away when, when Ben died. I was raking the yard and saw the lights. You know." He stood silent.

Oxford held out his hand. "Oxford LaCoste. Ben's law partner. Just looking through a few things. No, Ruth isn't here, but won't you come in for a moment?"

It was the right thing to say. Randall accepted almost eagerly. Oxford drew him into the small office. His visitor seemed anxious to talk.

"Enjoyed a few nightcaps with Ben in here. He was a great guy, eh? Troubles lately, though. Ruth was a problem, we all knew that, eh? But this was something more. He wasn't his old self, y'know?"

"That's right," Oxford agreed, sensing that he should encourage Randall. "He seemed to have something serious on his mind. We noticed that down in West Willow. Must have been more obvious here."

"Sure was. Ben was working too hard, eh? Too many late nights. Drinking pretty heavy, too, y'know? Usually he left that to Ruth. Sorry! Maybe I'm out of line."

"No. That's okay. We know about that. It was a tough situation."

"Yeah! It got to be kinda lonely for Ruth, eh? Ben was away a lot. Neighbours didn't come around much any more because she was likely to be plastered, y'know? Any time of the day or night. That just made it worse."

Randall looked cautiously at Oxford as if seeking clearance. Then he spoke in a "just-between-us-two" tone. "Ruth seemed to have made a new friend lately, though, eh? Just the last few weeks. A black Mercedes here the odd time, y'know? Late, usually around midnight. When Ben was away.

"I run a produce import firm. Weird hours. Usually pull in here about eleven o'clock or midnight, y'know? Bit of a night owl, eh? Like Ben. Why we got to be such good friends, I guess. So, I'd see that Merc from time to time. Not a lot. Wondered about it, but nothing more.

"Until we heard about Ben's death. We were away, y'know. Left the very night it happened, as it turned out. Two weeks in Acapulco, eh? Charter flight. One of those red-eye specials that never run on time. Supposed to leave here at 1:30 A.M. Didn't even make it into Regina 'till after three in the friggin' morning.

"So we didn't leave home until after 2:00. When the cab took us past this place I noticed the Merc in the driveway again, eh? Only this time it was backed in. Like it was ready for a getaway, y'know? But I wasn't paying much attention. I was so damn tired. Getting too old for those all-nighters.

"Didn't hear about Ben's death until we got home. Then I remembered the Merc. Don't suppose it means anything. But I thought I should mention it to somebody, y'know? How's Ruth doing?"

"Not bad," Oxford assured him. "She has some family down home. They're keeping an eye on her. She'll be all right." He had some questions for Randall, but the neighbour had little to add and seemed anxious to leave now that he had delivered his one message.

"Give our best to Ruth," and he scuttled back up the quiet street.

Now what the hell was that all about? Oxford wondered. He stood on the front step and gazed at the Forsyth drive-way. Who was Ruth's friend? And why that car? It would have been here about the time Ben returned home that night. Better mention this to Inspector Jakes.

Oxford turned back into Ben's office, sat again in Ben's swivel chair and raised his eyes. There, over Ben's desk, hung the physical proof of his professional attainments. Bachelor of Arts, University of Saskatchewan; Bachelor of Laws, University of Saskatchewan; certificate of enrollment in the Law Society of Saskatchewan; appointment as One of Her Majesty's Counsel, Learned in the Law.

Ben Forsyth had been proud of his professional status, Oxford knew. He could not imagine any circumstances under which Ben would bring dishonour to himself or his profession.

Sure, there were crooked lawyers, and Oxford knew a few of them. In fact, he wondered if there any longer was a higher standard of honesty in the legal profession than in the population at large, or if there ever had been, although he was inclined to think that Cameron Hunt's generation of lawyers had been cut from finer cloth.

The Ben Forsyth Oxford knew did not have a crooked

bone in his body, lawyer or no lawyer. So how did he allow himself to be sucked into the WDA quagmire?

And, Ben, what did you do with the fifteen million dollars? And why?

Then darker thoughts intruded. Oxford stood, walked again into the garage and stared at the spot where Ben Forsyth had died. Did what happened here have something to do with that missing fifteen million dollars?

What did happen here? Who was Ruth's friend? What was that black Mercedes doing here? And how, Oxford asked himself as he returned the condominium to darkness and walked out to his car, am I going to find the answers to those questions?

THIRTEEN

The Assiniboia Club, Western Canada's oldest men's club, occupies a dignified three-story building a block east of the Hotel Saskatchewan. For years it had served as the unofficial seat of the province's government. Ministers of both Liberal and Conservative administrations reached as many decisions over drinks and dinner in the club as they did in the cabinet room of the legislative building. The practice ended in 1944. Members of the CCF government of T. C. Douglas did not seek membership. Nor would they have been welcome. The members of the august club were in shock at the election of the first socialist government in North America.

But politics continued to be the staple subject of conversation in the Assiniboia Club. And would be again this evening.

Stu Drake, deep in contemplation, swung his drink in circles on the side table, almost unaware that he held it in his hand. He was seated in his favourite private dining room, number twelve on the second floor of the club. He had arrived well ahead of his guests, partly because the stock markets closed early in the afternoon, Regina time, and partly because he wanted time to think.

His subject was politics, specifically the Western Democratic Alliance and the government of Premier Harris Halliday. Stu Drake, the third generation owner of Drake &

McKay, the only independent brokerage firm remaining in Saskatchewan, held a unique, and increasingly uncomfortable, position of responsibility respecting the WDA.

Stu held no party office, never had, but was the generally acknowledged founder, the inventor, of the WDA. In the beginning that had been a prideful thing, but of late the conduct of the WDA Government had become a matter of embarrassment. The reputation of Stu Drake, successful community leader, was suffering. Stu was acutely aware that it was only a matter of time before today's half-humourous jibes became tomorrow's loss of business for Drake & McKay.

It had all begun on a serene Saturday afternoon in July at Stu's summer place at B-Say-Tah Point. The Drake deck overlooking Echo Lake was a favourite summer watering hole, and many of those present that afternoon were regulars with cottages of their own along the Qu'Appelle Valley, an hour's drive northeast of Regina. Stu had issued a few select invitations and more than a dozen men, all financially successful and prominent in their fields, surrounded the Drake bar that afternoon. Not many years later, the number who would claim to have been among this early group would have capsized Stu's large cantilevered deck into the lake.

Stu had first enlisted Andy Lawson, of Lawson Plumbing Supply, and Perry Klein, whose KleinKo Construction was Regina's largest contractor. The three then selected the invited group of businessmen, insurance brokers, lawyers, accountants, large farmers, and cattlemen. They had been careful to include a few prominent members of both the Conservative and Liberal parties, but most of the guests carried no political identity other than a common loathing of the socialist government that three weeks earlier had won re-election to another four years in office in Regina. The air over Stu's deck turned blue with the invective of political postmortem.

After a reasonable session of bitching, Stu called for attention.

"I suppose you're wondering why I called this meeting," he said, grinning. "Well, it is a meeting. And I'm going to be right up front." Stu turned serious.

"We have a political problem in this province. A big one. Something needs to be done about it, and I think you're the people who can do it.

"It's my guess that everyone here lost his vote last month. Again. And the socialists won the election handily with not much more than forty per cent of the vote. Have another healthy majority. The third one in a row.

"The other two parties, the Liberals and the Tories, split the other sixty per cent between them. Hardly elected enough members to mount an effective opposition." Stu reached for his gin and tonic, in a tall, frosted glass, and gestured with it as a lecturer would use a pointer.

"This isn't new. And it isn't rocket science. You all know the numbers as well as I do.

"Because we continue to split the free enterprise vote this way we keep on electing the socialists. Every time we try to all get behind either the Liberals or the Conservatives, we don't quite make it. Yes, sure, we succeeded twenty years ago with Ross Thatcher, but we only hung together for two elections. We proved we know how to do it, but we can't stop squabbling among ourselves.

"And that," Stu stated forcefully, "is because both the Liberals and the Tories run their parties here as wings of their federal parties. Neither will give up the field here to the other for fear of being shut out in the federal elections. They're both more interested in Ottawa than they are in Saskatchewan.

"Which leaves us with just one option. We need a new party, one we can all feel at home in. Where the Libs and the Tories can work together and leave their scrapping to the federal election. And finally get rid of those goddam socialists."

Stu Drake was an effective salesman. He had pitched a lot of stock issues in his day.

"Again this isn't new," Stu continued. "We've talked about this before. But it's always been too tough for us. Starting a political party from scratch is a big deal. This is a big province with a lot of miles in it. You need a leader, money, organization, policy. Mostly a leader. Someone to push the thing. It never got off the ground.

"But today's a little different," Stu announced with pride in his voice. "We have someone who can kickstart this idea. You'll meet him in a moment. Andy Lawson and Perry Klein and I have spent some time with him, and we think we can make some things happen."

The names of Andy Lawson and Perry Klein drew approval from the listeners. Lawson Plumbing Supply had outlets in three provinces and KleinKo Construction had tentacles that reached all over Western Canada.

"We were particularly interested in Andy's assessment. You all know how Andy built his business. All alone out on the road with a truck full of manufacturer's samples setting up a dealer network. Not everyone knows how to do that. Andy does. A successful political leader has to be able to do that. Andy thinks our guy is up to it."

Andy Lawson waved his beer in acknowledgement and approval.

"So," Stu gestured sternly with his drink. "So, Andy, Perry, and I scratched up fifty thousand for openers. We think our guy's that good. If you agree, we'd like you to match that. That's less than five thousand per and I know that won't hurt anyone here. If our guy is any good, he can raise enough to keep himself going. If he isn't, well, maybe someone else is. But, for Christ's sake, let's do something other than sit around and eat plank steak and bitch.

"Here he is. Decide for yourselves. Gentlemen, let me introduce Lloyd Grange. He'll give you the rest of the details." At Stu's words, a man who had been standing unobtrusively in the living room stepped through the patio doors and out onto the deck.

All confidence and smile, Lloyd Grange shook Stu's hand, then stepped easily onto a chair. It was his moment, he knew it, and he quickly made the most of it.

Grange was almost too pretty to be a man's man. Two inches over six feet and broad shouldered, blond and blue-eyed with even white teeth, he looked like Hollywood's choice for the heroic running back who won the big game. But his voice, deep, with a hint of harshness, commanded instant respect.

And he knew how to play a crowd. Waiting until he had

their complete attention, Grange began softly, outlining his background. Raised on a family farm at Yorkton, he had taken a degree in business administration at the University of Manitoba, then worked with the Winnipeg Grain Exchange before setting up his own management consulting firm. Most recently he had organized the very successful PanAmerican Games in Winnipeg. The death of his father had brought him back to Saskatchewan.

Then Grange turned to politics. He had decided to devote himself to the defeat of the socialist administration that had for so long stifled progress in his home province. He had been forced to leave Saskatchewan to find a career and a future and he didn't want his children to have to do the same. He was convinced that the real majority in Saskatchewan shared his convictions.

Lloyd Grange knew his audience and he played their music. He was the pied piper come at the right time. As the gins and tonic and the white rums and Coke went down with the sun, and the wives and the steaks arrived, Lloyd Grange sold himself.

"Ain't he a helldamner?" Andy Lawson said to a corner of the group over coffee later. They agreed.

"What are we going to do for policy, Andy? A program? A political party has to stand for something," someone asked.

"Policy's the least of our worries," Andy replied. "What we need is some velocity, and this guy will give us lots of that. If we can develop enough velocity, the policy will look after itself."

"Your young man is very impressive," Clara Drake said after she and Stu had seen the last of their guests away. "And very attractive. The girls were very taken with him. Me, too."

"Yes," Stu replied. "I wonder if that might not be his blind spot. But he's certainly a mover. He'll flash across this province like a comet. I just hope he doesn't flame out like one."

Lloyd Grange performed exactly as Stu Drake had predicted. He made two tours around Saskatchewan, pulled together a steering committee of well-connected people, arranged the formation of the Western Democratic Alliance as a contender on the Saskatchewan political scene, and at the founding convention the following spring had himself elected as interim leader. Then he went back out on the road allowances looking for candidates. And he found them. Good ones.

The public utterances of Lloyd Grange, Leader of the Western Democratic Alliance, were at first a little embarrassing to some of his early supporters. Saskatchewan, he said, was "strangling under the iron heel of socialism," "Communism first entered Canada in the guise of the Post Office." "A little bit of socialism is like a little bit of pregnancy; it's hard to stop." On the political spectrum, he placed himself "somewhere to the right of Genghis Khan." Saskatchewan, Grange promised, would burst with prosperity and opportunity when it threw aside the "heavy yoke of socialism."

But the WDA organizers chortled. Grange "resonated" with the public, particularly in rural Saskatchewan. His crowds and support swelled.

No one was more surprised than Stu Drake at how quickly it all happened. Two years after its formation, the WDA won a by-election and a toehold in the Saskatchewan Legislature. At the general election a year later the new party seized more seats than either the Liberals and Conservatives. Lloyd Grange, elected among the WDA MLAs and confirmed as party leader, became the Leader of the Opposition.

Then the defections began. Two Liberal MLAs, anxious to get in on the ground floor of a political movement with a future, crossed the floor of the legislature to sit with the WDA. One of them took with him the entire provincial membership list of the Liberal Party, a gift that ensured him a cabinet position if the WDA ever achieved government.

The Liberal leader stormed in protest at his loss. "Good riddance," he yelled. "The IQ level of both my caucus and the WDA caucus just doubled."

But more defections followed, from both the Liberals and the Conservatives. With so much momentum behind it the WDA became a government in waiting, with a general election little more than a year away.

And then it happened, the flame-out that Stu Drake had first foreseen but had then forgotten in the headiness of success.

It began with the growing rumour that Lloyd Grange's extraordinary energy had taken him into a few too many bedrooms, sometimes with wives of prominent WDA supporters. Then the party treasurer called for an audit into WDA finances. There was a suspicion of missing donations.

Afterward, even Stu Drake admitted that he could never have contemplated such a classic case of instant and catastrophic political ruin.

The RCMP pulled over a car racing towards the American border. Behind the wheel was an intoxicated Lloyd Grange. Also in the car were a briefcase containing more than two hundred thousand dollars in WDA political funds and an unregistered revolver. And the attractive sixteen year old Grange family baby-sitter. The WDA leader was unable to satisfactorily explain just why he was in possession of any of the three items.

After consultations with his lawyers and WDA officials, Grange saw the wisdom in negotiating a plea bargain to the criminal charges in return for a light sentence, resigned his office and his seat in the legislature, and left the province. The affair was over quickly.

The WDA, leaderless, adrift and in shock, was rescued by Sean McCarthy, one of its early MLAs. Acting as house leader, he first rallied the troops in the legislature, then convinced a rancher named Harris Halliday that the chaos in the WDA was a God-given opportunity for him. An early leadership convention confirmed McCarthy's choice, Gus Walker gave up his seat in favour of Halliday, and, after the formality of a by-election and the passage of a few months, Lloyd Grange was forgotten and the WDA had regained its momentum.

Harris Halliday, of the famed Halliday Hereford Ranch, was an immediate hit with the voters of rural Saskatchewan. He took his political theme from former United States President Jimmy Carter. "Why Not The Best," he declaimed. "There's so much more we can be." He softened the Grange stridency; the WDA became more positive. The approval ratings soared.

Then the bouncing ball of politics hopped over to Harris Halliday and the WDA. Another defector, this time from the governing socialists, exposed an unholy backroom deal. The government, hoping to maintain the split in the opposition vote and save itself from the charging WDA, had agreed to prop up the Liberal Party. Funds and election expertise were promised to the hapless Liberals to ensure that they would place vote-splitting candidates in selected constituencies.

The WDA at first were stunned by their good fortune. Then Sean McCarthy seized both the opportunity and the moral high ground. Piously, he sadly bemoaned the depths to which the old-line parties had sunk in their pursuit of power. Careful not to antagonize the demoralized Liberals, WDA organizers intensified their seduction of long-time party supporters. The Liberal leader, humiliated by another exposure of his inability to surmount the steep learning curve of Saskatchewan politics, was unable to staunch the haemorrhage. The Liberal Party, the most successful and enduring in the province's history, prepared to slip silently beneath the turbulent political waves.

Publicly, McCarthy was kind and saddened at the Liberal's demise. Privately, he was crude and vicious in condemnation of the Liberal leader, a medical doctor who had arrogantly assumed that no previous training or experience was required to joust in the Saskatchewan political arena.

"He squats to piss," McCarthy declared, dismissing his vanquished opponent.

At the general election eighteen months later, Halliday and the WDA overwhelmed the long-serving socialists with a landslide victory. All that Stu Drake had hoped and planned for had come to pass.

"Having a directors meeting, Stu?" Perry Klein asked as he and Andy Lawson stepped into number twelve.

"No," Stu smiled in return, "just working up a small conspiracy. Want to join?"

Big Andy chuckled. "Not so sure. That last one was maybe enough for me. Maybe too much."

"That's what I want to talk about," Stu said, no longer

smiling. "Things may be getting out of hand across the swamp." And he gestured towards Wascana Lake and the legislative buildings. "I'm running into some pretty serious stuff. Hearing worse."

"Huh!" Perry Klein snorted. "Try it in my industry. Contractors are a pretty grown-up bunch. We've been around, seen a lot. We're not good-goody-two-shoes. We're used to making a contribution here and there. It all goes into the cost of project. But this WDA bunch have got a lot of us pretty upset. Too many hands out. Some of us are starting to think that people are going to wind up in jail. No one likes that."

"Same thing in my line," Big Andy rumbled. "I hear lots of talk. Every job with some government involvement, someone is on the take. Even if it's just getting financing from that Renewal Agency. It's like a banana republic. Damn disgrace."

"I thought we should talk about that," Stu said. "This government's fiscal paper has made a lot of investment dealers very wealthy, but Halliday's crew is starting to behave like drunken sailors. The spending has gone through the roof. The financial community thinks the province's credit is about used up."

"Yah!" said Big Andy. "None of those WDA MLAs have any business experience. Never even ran a peanut stand. And most of them aren't too bright, either."

"Andy, you know intellect isn't a requirement for politics," Perry Klein said. "It isn't exactly one of the learned professions."

"Yah! I know. Just smart enough to learn how to play the game but dumb enough to think it's important."

"I think that was said about football," Perry laughed.

"It fits politics," Andy declared. "Particularly this WDA bunch. All misfits and unemployables."

"Okay! Okay! you two," Stu took over. "Maybe we don't have the highest calibre of government members. Sure, there are a few rusty nails in there, but they're not all bad. But that's not the real problem. They don't seem to have any sense of purpose. Other than lining their pockets and getting re-elected, that is."

"I'm afraid that's it, Stu," Perry agreed sadly. He inspected his empty glass and then looked up at the other two.

"Power is their only program."

They called for fresh drinks and the dinner menu. On into the evening they searched for ways to rescue the political mission they had launched with so much hope and promise.

FOURTEEN

 Oxford was munching on croissant and coffee, the Flatlander continental room service breakfast, when his phone rang.

"Good morning, Oxford, it's Dorothy Crane. I have an appointment for you to see Howard Gordon at PanSask at ten o'clock this morning. It turns out this is his last day there, so I hope you can make it. Sorry to call so early. By the way, I'm using a line in another office. We're clear."

"Already up and at 'em, thanks. Sure, I can make it. I'll let you know how I make out."

"There's something more, Oxford. I checked Ben's appointment book. He was over to see Gordon just three days before he was so upset about the matter you and I talked about. When he gave me those strange instructions."

Howard Gordon was obviously a no-nonsense type. A stocky, barrel-chested man with brushcut blonde hair, he came out and introduced himself the moment he heard Oxford announcing his arrival to the receptionist. His office had a spare, Spartan appearance, not entirely due, Oxford was sure, to the fact that its occupant was packing up for departure.

"Yep. On my way back to Oklahoma. This was my first experience with the world of politics and it'll be my last. I'm an oilman, pure and simple, and I'll remember that in the future.

"Dorothy Crane gave you a warm introduction. Says you're an old friend and associate of Ben Forsyth. Ben was the only straight shooting politician I met in the whole year I spent up here. What can I do to help you?"

Time again for frankness Oxford knew, so he went as far as he could in explanation. As one of Ben's executors, he was concerned about some loose ends on a transaction involving the acquisition of a laser beam heavy oil recovery process. Could Mr. Gordon shed any light on Ben's involvement?

"Sure, I don't mind telling you as much as I know about that, which is maybe more than a little bit. Bunch of damned nonsense, really. Felt that way when I first looked into the notion. Became convinced the more we examined it.

"But I'm a geophysicist by training and not supposed to know anything about that kind of technical engineering. So I was shunted aside from the feasibility studies. That was okay with me when I figured the whole idea was nothing but a political boondoggle. It was smoke and mirrors. I mean that literally. The concept called for manoeuvering the laser beam around underground by the use of mirrors. The idea being that the laser would generate enough heat to loosen the viscosity of the oil and let it flow.

"The problem is this—even if the technique is workable, the heat creates so much smoke and steam that the laser, which is really just an intense light beam, becomes so impeded it's inefficient. It's a self-defeating process. I know the laboratory types here say they can make it work. They can't. Trying to please their masters. Damned dishonest puppies. Told Ben Forsyth that. Didn't listen." Gordon impressed Oxford as a man of firm opinions who didn't care if his advice was accepted or rejected.

"Did you have anything to do with the people who developed the process?" Oxford ventured.

"No, never met them. No contact." Gordon was firm on that. "One thing, though, that might interest you. Seemed to interest Ben Forsyth," Gordon said, and went on. "I was down in Tulsa a few weeks ago lining up the job I'm going back to. Met an old friend who's been banging around the Middle East the last twenty years or so, everything from

Oman to Saudi Arabia, even Libya. Over a drink I mentioned this crazy laser deal we were looking at up here.

"He laughed like hell. Said that the promoters behind that had been trying to peddle it all around the Mediterranean for two or three years. Hadn't been able to find anyone who'd believe for a moment it could work. They were down to looking for someone who'd just take it on as an R and D project. Couldn't give it away.

"Said the last time he'd seen them was at the big trade show in Rome last winter. They were still looking for a sponsor." Gordon looked at Oxford as if deciding to carry on, then did so.

"When I came back here everyone was still hot for the silly deal, so I decided to stick my nose in a little. Don't usually do that. I checked to see if anyone from here had been at the Rome show. Sure enough, Premier Halliday and, what's his name, his deputy—Sisik, that's it, had been over in Europe on another one of those trade promotion tours this government's so famous for. Yep, they checked in on Rome.

"It was none of my business, but it looked to me as if this government was going to buy that laser scheme. I didn't have any idea what they were planning to pay for it, but almost anything was likely to be too much.

"Still, it was only money and none of my business. But Ben Forsyth seemed to be the point man on the deal and I liked Ben. I thought he might like to know my little story and I called him. He came right over the next morning," Gordon said with the authority of one who had just checked his facts. "I told it to him pretty much as I've told it to you. It seemed to upset him. He asked me to keep it between ourselves, and I did. Until now. Is that of any help to you?" The oilman looked squarely at Oxford, his jaw forward as if in stubborn defiance of the fools around him.

"An immense help, thank you," Oxford had to concentrate to avoid stammering. "That will help us with several of our concerns. Thank you for telling me. Thank you for telling Ben."

"Glad to hear that. Ben Forsyth was a fine man. My flight out of here leaves in a few hours. Here's my card if you need me."

Howard Gordon was a lucky strike, Oxford thought. Threw a whole new light on the laser deal. How would Cameron Hunt assess this information?

FIFTEEN

"Seems like our Ben was being set up to be the patsy—is that the word?—in the piece." Cameron Hunt ladled a steak the size of a legal brief onto Oxford's plate. Hunt's wife, Vivian, was visiting a grandchild and Hunt always took her absence as an opportunity to catch up on his red meat consumption. Like many cattlemen, he believed meat was meant to be eaten, and in quantity.

"There's enough cholesterol here to support a cardiac clinic," Oxford observed, smiling. "But that's not to be taken as a complaint."

"Nonsense. That's just a myth those quacks peddle to keep their medical labs busy so they can spend their winters in Maui. Eat up. You're just a growing boy." Hunt tucked into his steak, equally as large as Oxford's. "I went four and a half years without even seeing a steak. If I live to be a hundred, I'll never catch up.

"Your man Gordon sounds like quite a fellow. Quite a thing for him to extend himself for Ben as he did, and a bit dangerous, too, I expect, even though he was leaving in any event. Confidentiality is an essential trait in the oil industry and his reputation could have taken something of a beating." Hunt admired a forkful of Hereford.

Oxford had returned to the Hunt residence in West Willow and, while his host barbecued the huge steaks, brought him up to date, concluding with an account of his conversation with Howard Gordon.

"Probably nothing a lawyer dislikes more than to find out, usually too late, that his client has told him only that part of the story that he thought the lawyer needed to know, usually the self-serving part. By the time the lawyer discovers that he was operating on only partial information, he has worked out arrangements that make both him and the client look like perfect fools. Then, of course, it's all the lawyer's fault." Hunt paused to recharge their glasses with a full-bodied red wine, another feature of his dining that expanded in Vivian's absence, then continued.

"Sounds to me as if Ben discovered at the eleventh hour, thanks to Mr. Gordon, that his principals, Premier Halliday and Mr. Sisik, knew more about the laser transaction than he did. And that the price was wildly exorbitant. And, further, since he was the only negotiator and in sole control of the funds, he was in an excellent position to be held fully responsible if the acquisition turned out to be improvident, the patsy, as it were." Hunt returned to his steak.

After dinner, Hunt and Oxford moved to the study with another of the old lawyer's bachelor luxuries, cowboy coffee, boiled in the pot as if percolators, filters, and drip machines had never been invented. Hunt loved the bite of it, he said. Oxford could take it or leave it, but again he marvelled at his host's constitution. In spite of his age, the huge meal, and enough caffeine to jolt a steer, Hunt would enjoy his usual peaceful sleep.

Hunt picked up the file Ben Forsyth had left to his two executors. "I've been through this very carefully," he said. "Ben has indeed left us with a problem.

"After reading this material I can understand why Ben wasn't sure what he was going to do with it. There's a lot of file here. Must be a couple of hundred pages. With enough evidence to bring down the Halliday government and destroy the WDA as a political force in this province. Besides putting a few prominent people in jail.

"Dorothy Crane told you that most of this came out of files Sean McCarthy accidentally left behind when he vacated his offices in favour of Ben. It's amazing that all this could represent just one politician's illicit activity . McCarthy's a one-man gang. There are other ministers implicated, but I hope and pray this isn't a representative sample.

"It's graft. Nothing more. Nothing less. The man seems to be obsessed with garnering as much loot as he can using the power of his office. Sometimes he's cunning; sometimes just crude. Listen.

"McCarthy has retained so-called public relations services at an exorbitant monthly rate. There are contracts here calling for twenty-five thousand dollars a month, payable whether or not any work is performed. The favoured firms are remitting ten thousand dollars a month into a Caribbean bank account controlled by McCarthy. Crude but lucrative.

"A simple refinement calls for a third party in the transaction. Like this. Jezzica Mines, the uranium developers, needed a waiver of an environmental impact assessment for their project at Wonder Lake. They retained Steve Briggs as a consultant. Remember him? Defeated WDA candidate. No other known qualifications. Briggs did his job, though. McCarthy granted the waiver. Don't know what Briggs was paid, but McCarthy now owns a marvellous condominium in Scottsdale, Arizona. Made a great deal on it. It's worth about two hundred and fifty thousand dollars U.S. and our man picked it up for half that. From whom? None other than Steve Briggs.

"Quite a bit of that third party arrangement in this package. Corporations have learned that the way to this government's heart is to retain the right consultant, or lawyer. McCarthy has been passing out advice as to who would be the right such person. Those so chosen are remembering their benefactor very handsomely. McCarthy actually tracks their deposits to his accounts and doesn't hesitate to shake them up if they miss a payment.

"For brazenness this man is an Olympian. He has placed three members of his rural constituency executive on the payroll of the government bus company. None of them have ever showed up for work. And how could they? Not one of them lives on a bus route. They just pick their cheques up at the post office twice a month and keep good care of McCarthy's voters."

Hunt paused to refill their wine glasses. His complexion was reddening now. Oxford wondered if it was the wine or building indignation.

"Just two more examples, Oxford, and I'll quit, although I could go on for quite a while. There's enough here to keep us all night. I think you should read this stuff yourself, when you have time.

"One of the more sophisticated schemes involves that hotel you're staying in, the Flatlander. McCarthy arranged the financing for that project from the public pension funds administered by his government. Four per cent. A fraction of the market rate. And then had his department lease three floors at a rental twice what comparable space brings anywhere else in Regina. For twenty-five years, an unheard-of term. McCarthy's take? A nice packet of stock in the mother corporation. It's listed on the Vancouver exchange. Shares are being held for him in another name.

"And, finally, the most disgraceful scheme of them all, one operating right on the floor of the Legislative Assembly. A number of WDA MLAs have created dummy corporations whose sole purpose is to supply them with false invoicing for supposedly reimbursable expenses. Those invoices are paid by the Legislative Assembly to the corporations. The funds are then converted to cash and returned to the individual MLAs. Envelopes full of cash are regularly placed in the desks of those MLAs, as I said, right on the very floor of the Assembly. That venal conduct defiles every tradition of parliamentary government. I can't express my disgust vehemently enough." Hunt put down his notes and went out to the kitchen, returning with his coffee pot. Oxford declined.

"Amazing that McCarthy left all this evidence lying about. Seems that he had a confidential staffer who kept track of each deal. So many of them someone had to. But enough of McCarthy. There's more, dealing with the WDA itself." Hunt shoved aside two thick files and pulled another to him.

"Here's the WDA 'slush fund.' This one, however, is so large as to strain that definition." Hunt shook his head sadly.

"The WDA have been using what they think is a loophole in the legislation prohibiting anonymous political donations. They take the money into so-called 'trust funds.' They've been squeezing funds out of firms doing business with their government, a special form of kickback. This money is paid anonymously under the guise of campaign contributions, but it isn't reported on the WDA election financing returns. Yet it is available for the use of the WDA, particularly its dirty tricks department. Those activities, of course, by their very nature need to be funded with secret money.

"Believe it or not, the WDA has more than three million dollars sitting in a so-called trust account. Anonymous money. Unaccountable money. The worst kind of money any political party can possess.

"Just one example of what this kind of money can do and has done. The mayor of Saskatoon is a vocal opponent of the Halliday government. Using those secret funds, a WDA operative created a scurrilous, untrue, and defamatory pamphlet accusing the mayor of illicit sexual activities. It was placed on the windshields of a large number of cars parked around Saskatoon. Anonymous. No identification. No responsibility. Exactly the sort of thing our election legislation tries to prevent.

"Like you, I'm sure," Hunt resumed, " I've been giving a lot of thought to what our obligations are with respect to this material. What point of view have you come to?" he asked.

"I've tried to avoid reaching any decision before hearing what you've just told me. I had been leaning to the view that the government was entitled to the return of its files, as unsavoury as they might be. But this is worse than I expected," Oxford admitted. "And do these files belong to the government or Sean McCarthy? What do you think?"

"Probably a bit of both. Ben's collection ranges from the merely dishonourable to the clearly criminal," Hunt replied. "With respect to the former, I don't think we'd be faulted for returning the material. But that portion that identifies criminal conduct is, I think, in a different category and probably should be disclosed to the police. Now I'm concerned about whether we should attempt to divide Ben's files, or treat them as all one way or the other. Any thoughts on that?"

"My immediate reaction is to avoid division," Oxford replied. "That would put us in an uncomfortable role. But let's not forget about Ruth. I'm sure she would feel entitled to the whole package, but certainly she would demand anything we didn't feel needed to go to the police." Oxford had, in fact, himself forgotten about Ruth the last few days, and now suffered a shiver of discomfort as he brought her back to the forefront of his mind.

"Shouldn't we be making a bit of a report to Ruth soon, by the way?" Oxford asked. "If only to keep peace in the family, so to speak?"

"You're right," Hunt agreed. "Easier for me to do than you. I'll pop over and see her tomorrow. Tell her as little as possible, but keep her mollified. She told you she'd already taken legal advice. We don't need someone barging in here with a lot of questions we can't even answer to ourselves. But what do we do about the police side of this thing? Do you agree that at least some of this material must go to the police? And if so, when?"

"Yes, to the first question, but I'd like to temporize on the second. Stall, I think you called it." Oxford felt very much out of his depth. Although he appreciated being treated as a full partner by Hunt, he also wished the older lawyer would be more assertive, supply more leadership, or take some of the weight off his shoulders. Oxford thought of one way forward.

"I'm going back in to Regina in the morning. How about I discuss our problem with Inspector Jakes? I know that sounds funny, talking to the police about going to the police, but I think I trust him. I know he can't talk off the record, but he might be able to let us know how much interest they have in these files. For all we know, it might be something they already have." That sounded a little thin and desperate, Oxford knew.

"That might be a good idea, but it's putting one foot across the Rubicon, you know. I guess we will be giving him at least some of this material in any event. We're just concerned about when and how." Oxford suddenly felt that he had been steered straight into the corral Hunt wanted him in. More assertive, indeed. He grinned to himself.

Oxford LaCoste walked again through the darkened streets of West Willow contemplating the activities of his late friend, Ben Forsyth. He now knew something of what Ben had been about, at least with respect to his political concerns as a member of the Halliday government. But what had he done after his conversation with Howard Gordon?

It had quickly occurred to Oxford, after leaving Gordon's office, that Ben might have got right on the phone to Hong Kong to check out Josef Rafael. But Dorothy had not been able to dig anything of interest out of the telephone logs at the office. Nothing out of the ordinary at all.

Ben had, however, made an unscheduled trip to Calgary the day after speaking to Gordon, over in the morning, back that night. He had told Dorothy that he was merely checking some market features with a couple of consultants before locking up the laser transaction. He wanted to be sure the potential was as strong as represented, or some such reason, Dorothy remembered.

But it was two days later that Ben stormed into the office and demanded that Dorothy pull all the files on the laser acquisition. Dorothy had not considered that there was any connection between Calgary and Ben's state of mind two days later, but Oxford now wondered.

He tried to put himself in Ben's shoes. What would he do if confronted with the situation Ben faced after leaving Howard Gordon's office?

Oxford turned in at his gate and hoped that he would sleep as well as he knew Cameron Hunt would.

Sixteen

On the drive back to Regina, Oxford reviewed the political perspective Cameron Hunt had given him the night before. After completing their review of Ben Forsyth's files, the old lawyer had poured them each a nightcap. Oxford recognized the signal that Hunt wanted to settle back and philosophize.

Oxford always enjoyed these sessions with the old lawyer who had long experience as a keen observer of the Saskatchewan political scene. Ben Forsyth's election had so piqued Oxford's interest that he had become something of a student of the political history of the province. His acquired knowledge enabled him to participate in Hunt's occasional dissertations on the subject, to the added enjoyment of them both.

The Western Democratic Alliance and its government, Hunt observed, had not only taken Saskatchewan politics to a new low but had done so by redefining patronage, that seemingly indispensable bugbear of democratic politics. All previous governments had engaged in the practice, to greater and lesser degree, but always with a view to perpetuating themselves in office. Party support was rewarded and solidified with jobs, contracts, whatever was at the disposal of the government of the day. Seldom, however, were such spoils of enough value to enrich any one individual. The skilful use of patronage dictated that the plums be spread about as widely as possible to maximize the political gratitude.

As for the members of the dispensing government, it was enough that they be continued in office. No further reward was expected.

Until the arrival of the WDA, political service and personal wealth were almost considered to be mutually exclusive in Saskatchewan, Hunt claimed. With one exception, no premier and no cabinet minister had ever been publicly accused of lining his own pockets in office. And none were much improved financially by political service. In fact, they were more likely to be impoverished. A number were, including a couple of premiers. Remember that there were no legislative pensions until recent times.

Oxford agreed with Hunt's thesis. He had read the accounts of the inquiry commission that investigated the excesses of the Liberal Party and government of the late 1920s under Premier James Gardiner. Known as the "Gardiner Machine" because of its supposedly ruthless use of patronage, no evidence was found that Gardiner or any of his ministers had personally profited.

Hunt told Oxford that Gardiner, who served more than twenty years as federal minister of Agriculture, former premier Charles Dunning who went on to be minister of Finance in Ottawa, and Prime Minister John Diefenbaker, all left modest estates and no evidence of ill-gotten wealth in spite of their years in positions of great power.

Oxford knew from his reading that Premiers Ross Thatcher and Allan Blakeney, and their ministers, served without scandal. True, certain businesses, most notably advertising agencies and the more political law firms, flourished under one government and withered under another, but no one became noticeably wealthy during those times.

It was a little known fact, Hunt told Oxford, that before legislative pensions were established, W. J. Patterson, who succeeded Gardiner as premier and served more than eight years, and later did a term as lieutenant governor, was so close to poverty after he left office that the Saskatchewan Legislature granted him a small pension so that he could live out his last days in dignity.

Hunt related that, until Clarence Fines, Provincial Treasurer in the CCF government of T. C. Douglas in the

1940s and 1950s, no Saskatchewan politician was thought to have done unusually well while in office. But although Fines retired to apparent affluence in Florida, no one really knew whether his success was due to taking improper advantage of his office or merely skilful and legitimate investing.

According to Hunt, the WDA under Harris Halliday approached office with attitudes never before seen in Saskatchewan public affairs. Attitudes he said were similar to those of the marauding Khans of Mongolia—to the victors belong the spoils. A new financial elite was being created consisting of the Halliday government and those close to it. Chris Rossom's "unusually wealthy people."

"This corruption can be attributed directly to the manner in which the WDA came into existence," Hunt explained. "They're a coalition of supposed free enterprise entrepreneurs without any real political philosophy beyond a determination to seize power, to kick the socialists out of office. When they succeeded, they found themselves without any principles to guide them in working the levers of government. They've been trying to keep themselves in tune with the will of the people by extensive polling, and by tailoring their policy and programs to fit the public mood. But this has made them like a dog chasing its own tail. Turning ever inwards, they'll eventually consume themselves. But not before they wreak havoc with the public institutions of the province. Particularly the treasury."

Oxford wondered about all that as he turned east onto the TransCanada Highway. Perhaps his lack of interest in current political activity had been a disadvantage. Probably it was, for a lawyer at least. One who works with laws should be more concerned about how they come into existence. But Oxford had for years relied upon a bit of philosophy he had borrowed from someone, Bismarck maybe. How did it go? Lovers of sausage and laws should avoid being present during their making. Probably it was treaties rather than laws, but same principle.

Ben Forsyth had not imparted to Oxford much of the political wisdom he was acquiring as a member of the Halliday cabinet. A time or two when they were together he had questioned Ben about controversial events in the news, but Ben had made it clear, both that he was subject to cabinet confidentiality, and that he preferred to leave his political career in Regina. Would Ben now agree with Hunt's thesis about the WDA? Oxford suspected he would.

His lack of interest in things political had quickly become a thing of the past, Oxford realized. He was now playing catch-up, trying to duplicate the thinking, the very advanced thinking, of Ben Forsyth so that he could identify what the hell Ben had been about in his last days.

The country mouse has been tossed willy-nilly onto the city fast track, he mused. And there will be no going back to what was. So, shape up, kid. Too much mush in your brain anyway.

SEVENTEEN

Clifton Carlson stopped the pick-up on Look Out Butte, a rounded hill just east of his home place, somewhat grandly named by his grandfather. From here there was a clear view over the buildings and across his land down to Last Mountain Lake, five miles to the west but appearing much closer. The distant water, a long slender finger stretching to the horizons north and south, shimmered in the late afternoon sun.

He had stopped here many times in his lifetime. First as a very small boy in the company of his father and grandfather. Then with his father. Then with Carol. And now, alone.

Here with the eager ears of a child he had learned the history of this farm, the good years, the bad years. The crop of 1915 that had frozen in June, recovered, stooled out, and matured into a huge bumper with wartime prices that built the large red brick house that still dominated the other buildings, even the hip-roofed barn. The Dirty Thirties, when the dust and thistle blew and the land was almost lost to the rapacious mortgage companies from down east, a place that his boyish mind pictured as distant and evil.

Here, too, he had learned something of the politics of Saskatchewan. His family's hatred of the Liberals. Their disgust with the failures of the Conservatives. The reluctant, almost furtive, attraction to the economic panacea offered by the CCF under Douglas, and, later, the experiment with the Social Credit importation from Alberta.

Now he thought of his own record with this land, some good, mostly now bad. The first year he had cropped the land he bought from Uncle Lars had been a triumph. Lars, a stubborn man, had refused to adopt modern farming practices and sneered at the new-fangled notions his nephew brought home from college. Clifton had taken soil samples, fertilized to shore up the identified deficiencies and hit a bonanza, his own 1915. Lars came out from retirement in town to witness the sixty bushel yields from his tired land and left in shaken silence.

On the whole, Clifton thought, he had done well. One big mistake, though, was probably going to put him under. The farm could not carry the load of debt he had taken on to settle out with Carol. Perhaps, if the good times had continued for a few more years. But why had he naively assumed that they would? Truth was the divorce had been so stressful that he had not been thinking clearly. Maybe, too, he had let too much ego displace common sense. Too determined to avoid the humiliation of breaking up the farm.

Same thing with politics. Done well there, too. Except for the one big mistake that had taken him too far. But things had certainly started well.

Clifton had been thrilled to receive the invitation from Stu Drake. He had never met Drake but certainly knew who he was. Drake was the most prominent businessman and community leader in Regina. The long-serving president of the Saskatchewan Roughriders, Drake was regarded as the benefactor who kept football in Saskatchewan.

"Having a few people out to the lake Sunday, week after next. Some quality folks from around the province. People like you who take an interest in what's happening around them. I think you'll know mostly everyone there. Sure hope you can join us."

Clifton attended, all right. Carol saw to that. The Drake summer place at B-Say-Tah Point, on Echo Lake, an hour's drive northeast of Regina, was almost legendary.

His inclusion in that now-famous afternoon had led Clifton into some exhilarating backroom experiences during the formation of the Western Democratic Alliance. The early WDA founders had truly believed they were changing the world for the better.

He had been a part of all that. Maybe it had been a little intoxicating, too. And addictive. Clifton searched again for an explanation of why he had so easily succumbed to Sean McCarthy's blandishments and accepted the WDA nomination in the Long Lake riding.

Hindsight! Only with hindsight could he place the mistake at that point, he told himself, for what, the hundredth time? He could have turned down Halliday's offer of a cabinet post. That was where he should have said no. But what politician ever refuses a cabinet post?

Clifton looked again down at the farmstead. Memories welled up. He saw his grandfather and grandmother sitting in their rockers on the broad verandah they so loved during their last years. He saw his mother happily fussing about her flower garden, snipping sweetpeas, cooing to her roses. His father in his shop determined to devise the perfect cultivator. Carol and their children tossing feed to the leghorn chickens.

He was going to lose this place, Clifton knew that. He was going to fail his legacy. Unless a miracle saved him. Or something.

Or something. Clifton thought again of the lawyer in Regina who had approached him with a proposition. His client would be very appreciative of advance notice of the precise location of the large petro-chemical plant being proposed west of Moose Jaw. So appreciative that said client would be pleased to deposit two hundred and fifty thousand dollars to the minister's account, very discreetly, anywhere in the world.

That was enough, more than enough, to solve his problem. But Clifton's inner voice told him that only total disaster awaited down that road. Yet he knew that a harsh fate stared him in the face right now. And other colleagues in the Halliday cabinet were playing with that fire, he knew, and they had not been burned. At least not yet.

Clifton banged his fist against the steering wheel and started the pick-up. There had to be another way. There *would* be another way.

He drove down to the farmstead.

EIGHTEEN

It was Oxford's first visit to the Regina Police Station. He had defended a few cases in Regina, but his clients had all been introduced to the criminal justice system by the RCMP. He found the modern, two-story building just east of the downtown area of the city. He stopped at the front steps and read the brass plaque commemorating the famous Market Square Riot of 1935, a violent confrontation between RCMP and city police and a group of unemployed men trekking their grievances to the government in Ottawa.

After he spoke to the constable at reception, who summonsed Inspector Jakes, Oxford wandered over to view the collection of native art hanging on the walls of the spacious lobby.

"There are two schools of thought about this exhibition," Adam Jakes startled Oxford, who had not heard him arrive at his shoulder. "One is that it's a sincere contribution to cross-cultural understanding in our community. The other is that it's mere tokenism."

"And where do you stand?" Oxford asked with a smile.

"Firmly in the middle. I believe it is unavoidably both. Purity of motive is hard to achieve. There's a larger display on the upper levels. Would you like to see them?"

"Maybe I'll come back and do that another time. Can we talk?" Oxford asked.

"Certainly. Come on back to my office."

Oxford followed the policeman a surprising distance back into the labyrinth of the building. Obviously the inspector's office was not intended for much use by members of the public.

"We don't get to put much individuality into these offices," Jakes said as he closed the door. "They are ours only while on duty, then they belong to the next shift." He correctly guessed that Oxford was struck by the plainness of the inspector's quarters. "The best I can do," he gestured to the two chairs across from his desk.

"Just fine, thanks," Oxford sat and decided to get right into things. "We have come across files of Ben Forsyth's that we, Cameron Hunt and I, think might be of some interest to you. The problem is, we're not sure we're at liberty to release them to you. But we do think you ought to know about them." And Oxford gave Jakes a summary description of the contents of Ben's envelope. Jakes listened intently and without interruption. Oxford was pleased that the policeman made no notes.

"What did Mr. Forsyth intend to do with that material?" Jakes asked when Oxford finished.

"We think to force the resignation of the Halliday government, at least. Perhaps to initiate a criminal investigation as well." Oxford was disappointed at the lack of reaction from the policeman.

Jakes looked steadily at Oxford for a moment. "Either course of action would have been severely unpopular with some very powerful people. Any chance anyone knew of those intentions?"

"We don't think so, yet there's a lot of interest in recovering Ben's files. But we think that's because of some very sensitive negotiations he was conducting for the government," Oxford replied, then added, "Those files seem to be missing."

The inspector nodded, as if he knew that it would be useless to inquire into that subject.

"At our earlier meeting," Jakes said, "I asked you if Mr. Forsyth had any known enemies."

"I didn't know of these files at that time," Oxford

replied, and then went on, "Yes, and I asked you if there was some question about Ben's death. Is there?"

"We'd be very interested in looking at Mr. Forsyth's material dealing with the fraudulent scheme at the Legislative Assembly." Jakes ducked Oxford's question.

Oxford said nothing. He saw no point in asking for elaboration.

"Maybe I should tell you what was in the safety deposit boxes you were inquiring about," Jakes said finally. "They contained almost 500 very neatly parcelled one thousand dollar bills." In spite of himself, the policeman smiled at the effect of that statement upon the young lawyer. Oxford's mouth fell open in astonishment.

"The scheme you describe that operated at the Legislative Assembly just might provide an explanation of the source of those funds," Jakes suggested.

"But, but . . ." Oxford was sputtering. He stopped and started again, "Karpan, James Karpan, the man who had the boxes. I know you told me he doesn't exist, but who opened those boxes under that name? Surely you can find out."

"Well, so far we haven't been able to. And, needless to say, no one has come forward to claim ownership of those monies, nor has anyone we have interviewed admitted to any knowledge of what might have been in those boxes. We haven't yet revealed what the contents were. That's not to say we're completely without suspicions, however."

"You said before that you talked about this to Ben Forsyth. Yes?"

"Yes. He convinced me very quickly that he knew nothing of the boxes or their contents. According to the bank records, no one had entered the boxes since Mr. Forsyth had taken over the Provincial Development department, where Mr. James Karpan was supposedly employed."

"Did you tell Ben what was in the boxes?"

"No, but I went farther with him than with any of the other government officials we spoke to. I think he understood that we were talking about illicit funds. Not too difficult to make that assumption, of course. People normally keep valuables in safety deposit boxes, and money is the most common item of value," Jakes explained dryly. "The amount, however, might exceed the average person's guess."

"Can't you trace one thousand dollar bills?" Oxford asked, "Can't the banks tell you who bought them, and when, and where?"

"Negative. Could at one time, but no longer. Inflation seems to have overtaken the old controls. We do know where some of them came from, however."

Jakes stopped there. Seeing that there would be no more information forthcoming on that subject, Oxford returned to the question that Jakes had sidestepped.

"Is there some concern about Ben's death being accidental?"

"Not necessarily. Death by carbon monoxide poisoning frequently raises some questions. I think I explained that we like to follow a routine in these matters."

Oxford was not satisfied by the response. "Is there anything more you can tell me about that?"

"No, not really, not at this time, anyway. We're not treating it as a homicide. We're just . . . following a routine, as I said."

"I ran into something that might interest you." And Oxford told Jakes about his conversation with Tom Randall. This time the policeman took notes.

When Oxford completed his account, Jakes made a few more notes, then looked up.

"Part of our . . . routine, is to interview the neighbourhood. The Randalls were away, as he told you. They're on our callback list. Perhaps we're a little slack. Should have caught up to them by now. Thanks for this."

"What about that Mercedes? Who was that?"

Jakes did not respond for a moment. "I don't think we know. But we will know. Probably unimportant. These things usually are. But we'll check." Jakes closed that subject and returned to another.

"We would really like to review the material Mr. Forsyth left you," he said.

"Yes," Oxford replied, "I think you should see it. I'll speak to Mr. Hunt. I'm sure we'll work something out. I'll call you."

"Anytime, please. Here is my card. My office can reach me at any hour, but I've put my home number on the back, as well. If anything happens, please call me." Jakes stood and put out his hand, "I appreciate your coming in."

Oxford was deep in thought as he walked slowly back to the visitors' parking stalls. He had dealt with a number of police officers in his years of practice, but he had never met one as cool and articulate as Adam Jakes. He thought Jakes was very likely an unusually effective investigator.

Somewhere beneath the inspector's last words Oxford was sure he had heard a warning. "If anything happens." Like what? Oxford shrugged. He was due for dinner at the Rossom's tonight and he had just enough time to pick up a couple of gifts for Robin and Kara. Better get Sally some flowers, too, he thought, smiling as he thought of the pride she took in her meat sauce, which actually was very ordinary. Tonight he would again insist it was world class.

Nineteen

After two bedtime stories, each once repeated, Sally relieved Oxford from demands for more. "I'll see these munchkins asleep. Besides, you and Chris need a chance to talk."

Chris, perched in front of the television, quickly punched it into blackness.

"Have a bit of a report for you from Herb Prociuk. Not likely very helpful. Herb tells me that the Turks and Caicos are one of several Caribbean tax haven jurisdictions that have enacted strict secrecy legislation. And it's one of the toughest. Disclosure of information about the clients of banks is actually prohibited, not just discouraged," Chris continued.

"Next to impossible to get any information about a numbered account. But I gather only the unsophisticated settle for just an everyday garden variety numbered account. Herb says he sets up his trusts so that the numbered account is held by the trustee, usually some local trust company on the islands. That way the bank holding the account doesn't even have any record of who put up the money, much less who's entitled to it. Creditors trying to get at those trusts have a devil of a time. Even if they can find them in the first place.

"We assume, Herb and I, that Interpol will have some way of digging out the source of funds in those numbered accounts. But the average citizen is out of luck. Even Interpol would probably have trouble digging through one of those trusts. That what you needed to know?" he concluded.

"I guess so, although it's not quite what I wanted to hear. It's helpful because it forces me to concentrate on the front end of my transaction, rather than the back."

"I guess I won't ask what that means," Chris said. "But Oxford, I've been doing a lot of thinking since we talked the other afternoon about those files Ben left you. I'm really concerned about the heat you'll come under if you disclose that material.

"It would have been one thing if Ben had exposed the government. He originated the material and as a member of the cabinet he would have been speaking with authority, if not always first person knowledge. You, unfortunately, would be in the position of messenger, and a number of them have been shot over the years," Chris said.

"But wouldn't I, we, Cameron Hunt and I, just turn the whole mess over to the police and let them handle it?" Oxford asked.

"Yes, sure, but that doesn't fully insulate either of you from perceived responsibility as the source of the complaint. The thinking of this government will be that, if they can destroy your credibility, they will have effectively handled the problem.

"Keep in mind that those files are just a lot of paper. Paper without authentication. Anyone can run off accusatory material. To make it evidence, give it weight and believability, we look at the source. Destroy the source, destroy the paper. That's too simple, but you know what I mean. If they claim your stuff is just political slime, what do you do? How do you prove your case?"

He's right, Oxford thought. I haven't given enough thought to authenticating Ben's files. Only because I knew Ben, know he would have only solid stuff. But if I'm called on that, how do I prove it? Another thought hit. A big one. Holy Christ! Dorothy! She pulled most of this evidence together herself. Right out of Sean McCarthy's files. She can authenticate it if anyone can. But at what risk? I can't drag her into danger. He looked across at Chris, who was still speaking.

"The criminal justice system in this here province might just not be up to a problem of this sort. Oxford, how come you never asked why I left the Attorney-General's department?"

"Simply because I thought that, if you wanted me to know, you'd tell me. Should I ask?"

"Doesn't matter. Now's the time for me to tell you—and thanks for your thoughtfulness. I arrived in the department about the same time that the WDA was elected, so at first I didn't notice anything going on. And there wasn't that much change from the established order of running things. But we quickly learned that the turkeys who had been elected as WDA members thought they had won the right to decide who would and wouldn't be prosecuted in this fair province along with their right to run everything else. Needless to say, that meant that they and their friends were to be 'hands off.'

"Us noble prosecutors, of course, would have nothing to do with that and business carried on as usual. Without fear or favour. Remember our first WDA Attorney-General, Derrick Mason? Well, Derrick was an old-time lawyer who understood the need for non-political justice, and he protected the department. But the pressure became too strong for Derrick. After three years, Halliday bought him off with a juicy posting to London as Saskatchewan's Agent General. Then we got the current goon, Clayton Vandenboesch. He's a true brown shirt who intended to take personal charge of all prosecutions. He fancies himself an American district attorney type but actually he's just a not-too-bright thug who managed to qualify as a lawyer.

"Still, it was difficult to get the prosecutors to roll over and do what they were told. So we had the Night of the Knives, which you'll remember. Seven senior prosecutors from all over the province were fired, "selective early retirement," it was called, all in the name of economy and government downsizing, of course.

"That did the trick. There isn't a lot of market for used Crown prosecutors, you know, and people with fifteen and twenty years service, closing in on their pensions, are pretty vulnerable in the face of strong-arm tactics like that. Some pretty smelly decisions started happening in the department.

"Then we had a few hirings, quietly, of course, and each new body just seemed to have an uncle who was a WDA MLA, or some such qualification rather than any demonstrated legal ability. I began to wonder about my career choice.

"Next came the Big Rock Park affair. Remember it? Sure, but most of what I'll now tell you never seeped into the press. All that was reported was that two government bureaucrats were accused of taking bribes and fired. "Not enough evidence for a prosecution" was the line.

"The real story was that the two employees were the fall guys for a neat little WDA scam to privatize a chunk of the park and sell it to their friends for a pittance. Money changed hands, all right, but it all went into the pockets of the minister of Recreation. A prosecution would have been embarrassing to the WDA, so none took place. 'Not enough evidence,' as I said. It stank. There was plenty of evidence, enough to put the minister and two of his friends away for a couple of years.

"I was lucky not to have been on the file, but I was close to it, so close that I could see what was happening. That's when I decided to cut and run while I still could. That was a good decision. Since then things in the department have gotten steadily worse. Maybe the WDA can't quite get away with murder yet, but I wouldn't bet on it.

"What will happen when you expose the WDA corruption? They have a neat little technique that'll fit nicely. They'll turn it over to the RCMP for investigation. Sounds like just the right thing to do, doesn't it? It is, except that the Attorney-General will see to it that only one poor cop is put on the file, and maybe not even full time for him. The investigation will take forever. A year from now it's forgotten. And the WDA has another election under their belt.

"They have a variation on that technique. Same beginning, only this time the AG asks for a report in about six weeks. By then the investigation is just beginning. So it's simple for the department lawyers to give an opinion that there's not enough evidence for a prosecution. File is closed." Chris stood and stretched.

"So why do I tell you this now? I should have laid all this on you long ago, but now you really need to know. Because, my friend, as I've already said, the WDA won't take kindly to you coming out with an exposure of their corruption. And you can't count on the support of the criminal justice system, at least to the extent it can be controlled by the Attorney-General and his lackeys, and that's a bunch. If they can find a way to turn this back on you, they will, depend on it." Chris walked over and put his hands on Oxford's shoulders.

"But remember my offer. If you decide to go for this, please count me in," and he squeezed Oxford's shoulders before turning away and returning to his seat.

"What about the opposition?" Oxford asked. "What if I just turn these files over to them?"

"That would play right into the WDA's hands. Toss Bre'r Rabbit into the briar patch. Politicize the whole affair. And the WDA are nothing if not master politicians. They'd probably turn it all over to some legislative committee and use their comfortable majority to cover up the whole mess. A tried and true formula. Sure, it would get some exposure along the way, but in the end it would come to nothing. Nope! Can't recommend that.

"By the way, Oxford. There's a dude in the premier's office you should watch out for, Patrick Justice. Security Advisor, or some such title. He's particularly sleazy. Ex-RCMP. Kicked out, so the story goes. Liked to beat up on prisoners. Usually native. There were a lot of them. Always 'resisting arrest' or 'attempting escape' or some such. Finally one died and the force tossed him out. A bad one."

"Haven't met him yet."

"Well, I hope you don't. But if you do, count your fingers after you shake hands with him." It was nearly midnight when Oxford returned to the Flatlander, yawning and ready for sleep. His message light was blinking.

"Please call Ethel Tremblay at West Willow immediately. Urgent. Call no matter how late", the message centre advised.

Ethel Tremblay had been the principal and frequently only secretary of the Hunt, Forsyth, and LaCoste law offices for thirty-five years. At home she was the administrative arm of the registered seed farm she and her husband operated ten miles north of West Willow. Ethel was a solid, unflappable woman but tonight she was a sobbing wreck when Oxford reached her. She was at the West Willow hospital.

Cameron Hunt had been savagely beaten by an intruder in his home. He was in critical condition and was in intensive care, Ethel reported. The house had been ransacked. Vivian Hunt had been contacted and was on her way home.

"The doctors don't think he can make it, Oxford. He's in terrible shape and he's not a young man. They're afraid to move him, or they'd send him in to Regina," Ethel was gasping as she struggled for control.

Oxford ran to the elevator and headed down to his car. As he swung west from Albert Street onto the TransCanada Highway he remembered the warning Adam Jakes had given him, "if anything happens." Well, something sure as hell had happened.

TWENTY

At 4:30 in the morning, Oxford found Ethel Tremblay huddled on a settee in a waiting lounge of the hospital, a cup of cold, black coffee clutched forgotten in her hand. She had obviously not slept, but the tears were gone, replaced by haggard dejection.

"It's almost all over, Oxford. He hasn't regained consciousness and his pulse is slowly fading. If he wasn't so tough, he wouldn't have made it this far."

"When did it happen?" Oxford asked.

"We don't know for sure. The neighbours found him at eleven o'clock, just by luck, or he'd have lain there all night. When they let their dog out he went over to Hunt's and started barking, wouldn't come home. The dog was on the back step, fussing at the open door. He and Mr. Hunt were great friends. Mr. Hunt used to . . ." Ethel stopped herself.

"He was terribly hurt, Oxford, barely breathing when they found him. I don't know how this could happen. Why would anyone want to harm Mr. Hunt? What would anyone want in his house? We don't have any criminals in West Willow, not this sort of thing."

"How did they get in?" Oxford asked the question as much to steady Ethel as for his own information.

"Who knows? Probably just walked in the door. Vivian couldn't get Mr. Hunt to lock doors. Said he hadn't been brought up that way, didn't believe in it, didn't think it was necessary. Or they could have knocked and he would have let them in. Let anyone in, he was so trusting." Ethel started to sniffle.

"Can I see him?"

"Yes, but there isn't much to see, he's so wrapped up. He's back this way." Ethel stood to lead the way.

Ethel was right, Oxford saw, as he gazed at the mummy-like Cameron Hunt. And she was right to suggest that the old lawyer would not recover. It was just a matter of time, he was sure, and very little of that.

Sixty times the man pilots his bomber through enemy fire, then dies in his own home at the hands of an unknown enemy. Could I have prevented this if I had been more alert to what Adam Jakes was trying to tell me? And Chris Rossom? Probably not, considering the proud and stubborn courage of Cameron Hunt. But I would feel much better if I had tried.

Ethel and Oxford were catnapping in the lounge when the news came. Vivian Hunt and her daughter were with them, having arrived not long after Oxford.

It was over. It was just before eight in the morning.

An hour later, Oxford sat in the kitchen of his small home, more exhausted and dejected than ever before in his life. He knew he was too numb to feel the grief that would come, but the guilt was pressing in upon him.

Oxford stared at the card Adam Jakes had given him. "Call me if anything happens," he had said. Well it had happened.

Their forensic people would be in the Hunt residence for some time, the RCMP had explained. They would let them know when it would be clear for the family to reenter their home. It would be unlikely that anything of value survived. Ben's files would be gone, Oxford knew that.

Impulsively, Oxford dialled Adam Jakes' home number. He wondered, did an inspector of police have Saturdays off?

"Jakes here." This one did.

Oxford reported. Jakes was sympathetic, but full of business. After a rapid series of questions, few of which Oxford could intelligently respond to, Jakes said, "I'm coming down. It's not our jurisdiction, of course, but I'll be there this afternoon."

Oxford hung up, feeling very much relieved. He had avoided thinking about it, but he knew that he had become very lonely, that the problems left by Ben Forsyth to his two executors, Cameron Hunt and Oxford LaCoste, had now come down to him alone. He did not like the feeling. He needed Inspector Jakes.

Oxford was sleeping like a drugged man when his telephone jangled him semi-awake. "Oxford, glad I caught you. It's Myron Cooper."

His turgid mind struggled to complete the identification, then finally told him—Cooper—yes—the credit union—manager.

"Sure, Myron. How are you?"

"Fine. Look, hell of a thing about Mr. Hunt. I'm sorry. He was a wonderful man." Cooper said.

"Yes, he was. A terrible loss." Oxford agreed, now sufficiently awake to wonder why Cooper was calling.

"Look Oxford, I'm sorry to bother you, but Mr. Hunt left something here for you yesterday. A package. He asked me to put it in safekeeping for you. I don't know how important it is, but we close at three o'clock on Saturdays, you know. I could bring it over, I suppose." Cooper said.

"No, Myron, that's fine. I'll come down and pick it up. Be there in plenty of time. And Myron, thanks, it was good of you to call." Oxford was suddenly alert enough to remember to try to appear calm and only mildly interested.

Why the credit union, Oxford wondered, as he faced stiffly into the shower. His entire system felt gritty, but he knew it was all under the surface where it would not wash out. Cameron Hunt had not believed in credit unions and refused to do business with them. Oxford was not a customer either, although he maintained pleasant relations with the staff and did some work with them. Strange, however, for Hunt to ask a favour of them. He drove downtown, picked up the package, and headed for his office.

The offices of Hunt, Forsyth, and LaCoste occupied an elderly, yellow brick single-story building on main street that had been built as a general store during West Willow's early prosperity. When Cameron Hunt had converted the building to a law office, he had deliberately included a few Dickensian touches reminiscent of the chambers of the English barristers at the Inns of Court he remembered so fondly. His beloved books sat upon rows of oak shelving behind protective glass doors, much like china cabinets.

Oxford opened the heavy brass-trimmed oak door and hesitated at the chill, the feeling of strangeness that hit him as he entered. He ignored the metaphor of death that came to his mind, marched to his office near the back, shoved aside the correspondence Ethel Tremblay had laid out for him, and opened Cameron Hunt's package. He knew it contained Ben's files. The size and heft were the same as when he had first retrieved them from Ben's safety deposit box. But he had to be sure.

The files were there. On top was a letter, in Cameron Hunt's hand.

Dear Oxford,

I went over to see Ruth this morning as we dis-cussed, on the pretext of reviewing the state of Ben's investments. Things were going so well that I chanced inquiring, subtly I thought, about how Ben had been getting along with the Halliday government. Ruth demanded to know where I might have got the idea that there was anything wrong at all. I tried responding that politics is a difficult world, but there was no stop-ping her.

She accused me of having found something among Ben's papers that would make me think there were problems between him and the premier. I tried my best to deny that, but you know how poor a liar I am. She repeated her demand for all Ben's personal papers and became quite aggressive.

I sensed that I made a serious mistake. After worry-ing about the matter for several hours, I decided it would be wise to put Ben's files out of my possession until we can make a decision about their final disposi-tion. I thought our office, or even our customary bank, would be too obvious a repository, so I settled upon the credit union.

I hope this is nothing more than the overreaction of a silly old man.

Cameron

P.S. I've also been thinking about Ben after his conversation with your Mr. Gordon. My bet is that Ben would hire a lawyer at that point.

C H

Oxford stared stupidly at Cameron Hunt's note. My God, he thought, Ben Forsyth will consign himself to permanent purgatory when he learns that Cameron Hunt was killed over his damned files, if that is what happened, and it probably did. A tremendous shudder ran through him, he gasped, then was overcome with sobbing. He put his head into his hands and cried like a broken-hearted child.

When he recovered, Oxford slowly got to his feet, feeling drained and weak. He glared at the files Ben Forsyth had created as if they were poisoned, then picked them up and walked out to the filing cabinets. Pulling a drawer at random, he stuck the files in the first spot his hand reached and slammed the drawer closed. Was there any significance, he wondered as he turned away, in the fact that he had accidentally chosen the Ms to hide the material? Dial M for Murder.

Oxford was sleeping deeply on the leather couch Cameron Hunt had installed in the back office for the purpose of naps when the office telephone pulled him awake. He stumbled to the nearest handset. "Hello," he muttered, suddenly wondering why he had bothered to answer at all.

"Good. I knew you were in here somewhere. Come and get me." It was Adam Jakes.

"What do you mean? Where are you?" Oxford's brain was slow.

"Out front."

Oxford walked to the front door and was startled by the sight of the police-officer returning the receptionist's phone to its cradle and scratching a happy Sam behind the ear.

"Your car is out front, the door is unlocked, your dog is here, seemed reasonable that you were here too. Best way

134

to find you, I thought," Jakes smiled. "You look like you've been ridden hard and put away wet."

"Yes," Oxford replied, "but I think I'm okay now. Here, I have something for you to read while I finish waking up." He recovered the files and Hunt's note, took Jakes into his office and left him.

In the office washroom Oxford's ablutions restored him a bit. The empty feeling he attributed to the emotional release, although he wasn't sure. He was not an emotional guy, Oxford reflected, but maybe this is a little too much.

"I've spent most of the afternoon with the RCMP," Jakes said, putting down Ben's files as Oxford returned. "They were kind enough to share their investigation. Municipal cops, like me, get a great deal more experience with breaking and entering than the RCMP. It's our bread and butter, so to speak, so I think I might have been helpful to them.

"This was no ordinary B and E. It was sophisticated, made to look clumsy. Lab tests will tell whether the door was unlocked or if the lock was picked. No matter, the door was marked up to make it appear as if it had been jimmied, with a bar, which it wasn't.

"The house was ransacked as if in search for valuables. That again was an attempt at disguising the real purpose. The beds were undisturbed. The first place thieves look for jewellery and the like is under a mattress, because, believe it or not, a great number of people store those items there. Valuables are not usually found in kitchens. This kitchen was torn apart. Same with the files in the study. There are more examples. The freezers, for instance. People rarely keep money or jewellery in a deep freeze, but they will put documents there. These freezers were ransacked," Jakes said, sounding very much like a lecturer at a police college.

"Same with the murder. Made to make it look as if the intruder had been surprised at his work and had beaten Mr. Hunt indiscriminately. Not so. The blows were intended to kill, and did. Only the man's superior condition allowed him to survive a few hours. The battering was a superficial cover-up." Jakes concluded his assessment of the crime scene and picked up Ben Forsyth's files.

"Probably there was a double purpose to this event, to

recover these files and to silence all knowledge of their contents. The first purpose failed, since we have the files. The second partially failed because you also are known to be aware of this material. Which means you may be in considerable danger." The two men looked at each other without expression.

"I'd already come to that conclusion," Oxford said with a dry throat. In truth he had avoided putting it to himself quite so bluntly.

"Good," said Jakes, "we need to talk about that. But let me mention a few other features first. It would appear from Mr. Hunt's note to you that, excluding unusual coincidence, Ruth Forsyth is implicated in his death. It would follow, it seems to me," Jakes went on, "that she might well be implicated in the death of her husband, also."

"But," Oxford exclaimed, "I thought Ben's death was accidental. Why would Ruth want to do away with him anyway?"

"Death by carbon monoxide poisoning almost always leaves a question or two, as I think I've already said. As to your second question, I don't know," Jakes replied. "But don't forget the funds in the safety deposit boxes. A great deal of murder has taken place for much less than five hundred thousand dollars. Until those funds are fully explained, they remain as a powerful motive for crime.

"Now, what about this postscript in Mr. Hunt's note?" Jakes asked. "Why would Mr. Forsyth feel the need to retain a lawyer?"

"That . . . that's a reference to an unrelated matter. One I'm not at liberty to discuss," Oxford replied, feeling a little foolish.

"Unrelated to this affair that seems to have your life in some danger?"

"Yes, at least as far as I know," Oxford said, suddenly wondering if that was really so.

"One would want to be quite certain, wouldn't one?" Jakes pointed out, somewhat acidly.

"It's a matter of solicitor and client privilege, I'm afraid. And I'm under very explicit instructions as to confidentiality."

"In my experience there's a crook on at least one end of

every case of solicitor and client privilege. Is there one here?" Jakes was smiling, but his tone said he was not amused.

"Hey! Don't be so hard on us. If you cops had your way, you'd repeal the presumption of innocence."

"Might be a good idea at that," Jakes said, clearly unhappy. "Well, let's set that aside for now. Who do you think might be behind all this? Any suggestions?"

"Not really. It would have to be someone who knew that Ben had put those files together. I've no idea who that might be. Seems that Ruth knew, but she couldn't have killed Mr. Hunt."

"But who did she tell? Seems reasonable to assume that it would have to be someone close to the Halliday government, anxious to protect it. Why would Mrs. Forsyth want to get between her husband and the government?" Jakes asked.

"Can't answer that. Ben was miserable with Ruth's drinking, but we all thought she was as happy as a clam. No money problems, good position in life, and a husband who let her drink all she wanted. Doesn't sound reasonable that she would be working against Ben's interests."

"One never knows," Jakes spread his hands in a philosophical gesture of futility.

Jakes turned the conversation back to the question of Oxford's safety. He thought that the real concern of whoever was behind the attack on Cameron Hunt would be the files, the evidence. If they could secure them without making an attempt on Oxford's life, so much the better. Certainly, they would not want to risk another killing and miss the files again. Jakes proposed taking them into safekeeping. He would not turn his investigators loose on them just yet, although he would like to check out the fraudulent scheme at the Legislative Assembly as the likely source of the five hundred thousand dollars.

"Okay," Oxford agreed. "I have to park those files somewhere and you should be a good safe place. But just for safekeeping. No investigation and no copies. And since I'm not sure yet that I should be doing this, let's keep this between ourselves."

As to his personal safety, Oxford answered Jakes' questions. Yes, he lived alone, except for Sam, who had just demonstrated that he wasn't much of an alarm system. He did have a garage but seldom used it. No, he did not have an alarm on his car. No, he did not have a phone in his car, nor did he carry a cellular. Usually he did not let anyone know when he would be driving to or from Regina, and he was almost always alone on those trips.

Jakes could not promise much security for Oxford, but he did elicit the lawyer's promise to keep the policeman fully advised of his whereabouts and travel plans at all times.

As he was leaving, Jakes returned to Hunt's postscript. "I still don't understand how Mr. Forsyth's possible need for a lawyer can be a matter of solicitor and client privilege for you," he told Oxford. "I'd like you to consider that carefully. Perhaps you need a lawyer, yourself," the policeman suggested, smiling, but not at all in jest. Jakes left Oxford with his thoughts.

Perhaps I do at that, Oxford thought. The notion grew. That would be one way of bringing some additional thinking to his situation. Cameron Hunt was not replaceable, but it would be nice to have some help.

Oxford looked around his offices. Hunt, Forsyth, and LaCoste. A month ago all three had been alive. Now two of them were gone.

God! he felt lonely.

TWENTY-ONE

The residents of West Willow are of two minds on the subject of the Jasper House. Some insist it must have been built by Harmon Jasper himself and think it is long overdue for a good fire. Others take pride in the authentic relic of days of greater glory when the town was a prominent cattle shipping point. No one disputes that the old weather-stained yellow brick hotel has character. Standing at the intersection of Railway Avenue and Main Street, the two standard names to be found in every western railway town, the Jasper House still towers two stories above its neighbours. Across the street the train station that once supplied the hotel with guests now serves as the West Willow Museum.

Nowhere is the atmosphere of the Jasper House more prominent than in the Antelope Room, which clings to its reputation as West Willow's pre-eminent dining facility by adhering to its motto—"plain food, well cooked, and plenty of it." The walls are hung with old photographs of the early ranching days, cattle drives, horse breaking, grizzled cattlemen, and branding. Next to the entrance hangs a large slab of pine with the charred images of the old brands of the region, several still in use. Many a cattle deal had been sealed with a handshake beneath the high, pressed-tin ceiling. A few still are.

The Antelope Room was home away from home for

Oxford LaCoste. He revelled in its meat and potato menu. In spite of the day's emotional turmoil he was famished. As he crossed the large lobby of the Jasper House heading for the dining room he had in mind The Ranchman, a sixteen ounce T-bone steak with gobs of mashed potatoes and gravy.

Oxford entered the Antelope Room, the conversation with Adam Jakes buzzing in his head, and stopped in his tracks.

Dorothy Crane was seated at the corner table. She was alone, and busy with the menu.

Dorothy! Hey! How about that? What a break. She sure is a sight for sore eyes.

Then a sobering thought hit. He had let Jakes assume that Ruth Forsyth was the sole source of information putting Cameron Hunt in possession of Ben's files and had completely overlooked his conversation with Dorothy when she had been concerned about electronic surveillance in her office. Oxford had acknowledged in her office that he and Cameron had the files. If Jakes was right that anyone with knowledge of those files was in danger, that included Dorothy. Oxford went over to her table.

"What brings you back to West Willow?" Oxford asked, happily accepting the invitation to join her for dinner. He was pleased, too, to note that Dorothy was again smartly dressed, this time in designer jeans and a long-sleeved white shirt with the collar casually tucked up.

"Hillary. My daughter. She's visiting her father this weekend. Usually she comes down on the Friday bus, but a school football game last night interfered. Since it's Thanksgiving weekend, I agreed to drive her down this morning and decided to stay over and see a few friends. I don't get back here much anymore.

"But, Oxford," she exclaimed, "what a terrible thing with Cameron Hunt. Do they have any idea who did it?"

"I don't think so, but I'd like to talk to you about that."

"Whatever does that mean?" Dorothy asked, her eyes widening.

So Oxford told her. He was impressed with her calm absorption as she received the account of all that had happened since their lunch just a few days earlier in a week that had ended in murder. Dorothy was quick to see the danger.

"Oxford, we could be next." She seized his hand. "This is serious. We have to do something."

"Look," he replied, wanting to play down the danger, "it's not a good situation but I don't think anyone has us on their list."

"Don't underestimate these people, Oxford. They're quite capable of murder. They will do anything to protect their power."

"Who do you mean? Specifically, that is?" Oxford asked, surprised by her directness and vehemence.

"Those close to Halliday. McCarthy. Justice. Two or three others. Not so much Halliday himself, but he will overlook any conduct, accept any explanation, if it's put to him as being in his interest." Dorothy was very firm in response.

"Dorothy, Inspector Jakes and I jumped to the conclusion that it was from Ruth Forsyth that someone learned that Mr. Hunt had Ben's files. But it suddenly occurred to me when I saw you sitting here that perhaps our conversation in your office had been overheard, as you feared. We talked about those files there before you stopped us."

"Oh, I think we were being listened to, all right. The next morning all my files were moved to the premier's office. They gave the plausible explanation that, since he was the acting minister of Provincial Development, it would be more convenient to have the files in his office. Maybe. But all the background material I collected for Ben is gone, along with all the rest of the sorry story."

"How does that leave you?"

"Isolated, I think," Dorothy replied. "I don't really have a job anymore. I'm just answering a telephone. I don't think I have a future around this government. But I'd like to stay alive. Should I be worrying, Oxford?"

"God! I hope not. But Adam Jakes made me promise that I'd keep him fully advised on my whereabouts and travel plans. Would you mind doing the same thing for me? I think we should keep our heads together on this until it blows over. Maybe you and Jakes are right, we should treat this seriously." Oxford surprised himself with his firmness. Where did he get off making a request like that?

Dorothy looked at Oxford for a moment before replying, "I think I'd feel better doing that. In fact, I know I would."

"I'm going to pick up a cell phone as soon as I can. How about I pick up two? Something that will fit in your purse?" Oxford asked.

"Good idea. Now how about some of that saskatoon pie? And perhaps a glass of wine?"

Oxford perked up. For some reason he felt a whole lot better.

TWENTY-TWO

When the insistence of his bedside telephone dragged him awake on Sunday morning, Oxford's first thought was to do violence to the instrument. The urge subsided as he picked up the handset and saw by his digital alarm that it was ten o'clock. Lots of people with normal lives would be up and around by this time, he told himself.

"Oxford, sorry if I wakened you, but I know I have to catch you before you get out and about." It was Chris Rossom.

"It's okay. I was just telling myself that normal people might be up by now. Good morning."

"Oxford, we heard about Cameron Hunt on the news last night. Sally and I are really upset. So we wonder how you are. What a hell of a thing."

"Yes, it is a hell of a thing. The phone call was waiting when I got home from your place the other night. Drove straight down. He died not long after I got here. Never recovered."

"How are you holding up?"

"I'm okay now. Rocked me pretty badly, though. Came apart a little bit yesterday, I'm afraid. Guess I'm okay now."

"I shouldn't wonder," Chris said, then, "Oxford, I hate to ask, but does this have anything to do with what we were talking about?"

"I'm afraid it does, or at least we think so. Chris, I think I need a lawyer. Can I retain you?"

"What the hell for? Never mind. Of course."

"Maybe in two capacities. As the surviving executor of Ben's estate, for sure. I think personally, too. I have a problem of solicitor client privilege I need help with," Oxford explained.

"Sounds like you're living in interesting times, as the old Chinese curse says. When can we get together?"

"I think not until next week, what with Cameron's funeral and all. I'll be in touch as soon as I can."

"Okay, whenever. Good luck, Oxford."

He heard the two loud knocks that Hank Parr employed to announce her arrival in his kitchen and went out to meet her. Sam was on his back, feet waving happily in the air as Hank scratched his chest. She looked up.

"This good-for-nothing watchdog was actually earning his keep the other night. Kicked up a hell of a row. So much so that I came out to see what was going on. Just in time to see a car pull out down the alley. Somebody had been looking at your place."

"Oh-oh! What night?"

"Friday. Well, sometime after midnight. You know what I mean. I was still watching that damn television. Same night of Cameron Hunt's trouble, if that's what you're thinking."

"Yes. I guess I was thinking that. You tell the police?"

"No. Should I?"

"Probably. I'll let them know. They'll likely come around to talk to you."

"Won't do them much good. Didn't see much but tail-lights turning onto the street."

"Well, sometimes even that can be important."

"So? Well, tell them to come around then. Maybe this mutt is worth his grub, after all. Might have saved us a big cleaning job." Hank fondled Sam's ears.

Should he call Inspector Jakes with this little item? Oxford wondered, then thought better of it. It would keep until later. They had already concluded that he was in some danger. Maybe he should wear a sign saying, I don't have the damn files.

On Monday morning, Thanksgiving, Oxford sat in his office trying to organize the work that was piling up and calculate how much worse things were going to be as a result of Cameron Hunt's death. As Ben Forsyth's surviving executor he would now have to pick up all the responsibilities Hunt had assumed for the two of them. That meant having to deal with Ruth Forsyth. He could not delegate that to Chris Rossom, as much as he might like to.

The phone rang. It was Val Sisik. "I thought I might catch you at your desk," he said. "A terrible thing, Oxford, terrible. The premier sends his condolences. We all do. If there's anything at all we can do . . . " Sisik was a bit unctuous, Oxford thought, as he made the obligatory response.

"We know this will make matters more difficult, yes? You have a, a full plate? But we need to discuss the work you are doing for us. When will you return to Regina?"

Oxford felt a flash of resentment. Christ! The man is only interested in his problems. He concentrated on retaining his composure. Time to assert some independence.

"I'm afraid I won't be able to come in until the first of next week."

There was a long pause. "These are important matters, Oxford. Too important to wait. Yes? Please do better." Sisik spoke sternly.

"I'm sorry. Mr. Hunt's funeral is Wednesday. His death complicates things for me here. I need what there is of this week to clear my decks. If it's possible, I'll try to get in Friday. But I doubt it." He could easily do that, Oxford knew. Why was he being so difficult?

There was another long pause. "Call me the moment you get in. We will discuss." Sisik abruptly rang off.

As Sisik hung up the phone he looked across his office at Patrick Justice. "Not until the first of next week, he says. How much does that complicate things?"

"Probably none. We're stalled. At dead ends everywhere," Justice replied. "Will the folks at PanSask start getting edgy?"

"They'll do as they're told." Sisik was unconcerned about PanSask. "Still nothing on Rafael?"

"Nothing more yet. He hopped over to Singapore and disappeared. He hasn't shown up in Tel Aviv, or at least his office swears he hasn't. I admit they don't sound worried enough to make me happy, but what can I do? It's hard to dig up information over there unless you go to the authorities, and you won't let me do that." Justice explained.

"I've about given up on the idea of the LaCoste kid coming up with anything for us, by the way," he said. "Why don't you just cut him loose?"

"He is another line out there, yes?" Sisik replied. "Something will break open there soon. Ben Forsyth couldn't make fifteen million dollars disappear—nor Rafael—not without help. Forsyth did not steal it. Was not that kind. Young Oxford will stumble onto something soon. And he will tell us. We complicate matters for him. With those files Ben Forsyth left him. Yes?

"Have you spoken with your contacts? On the force?" Sisik added. "What file do they have on Hunt's murder?"

"Nothing. They're looking for an unknown intruder. Can't even get a make on how he was travelling. No one saw a strange vehicle that night at all. I know those guys, they'll get nowhere."

"What about Forsyth's files? They could become a bigger problem than he left us on the laser deal. If they become public, yes? Can we confirm that LaCoste has them?" he asked.

"Don't know how, short of asking him. But I think we'd better assume he does have 'em. They're not in his hotel room. I took a good look when I put the bug in. I wish we'd done that right in the beginning, like I wanted to."

"Perhaps, perhaps," Sisik said. "You're just a little too quick with your toys sometimes. They cause problems too, yes?"

"Maybe. But we need a lead on where LaCoste might have those files. For sure, after what happened to Hunt he isn't going to keep them around his house. Or office. He knows someone is after them. He'll take precautions. He isn't legally stupid."

"No. Don't underestimate him. He has talked to the police."

"What! When? What cops?"

"An Inspector Jakes of the Regina force was in West Willow Saturday. He spent some time in the law office with our Mr. LaCoste. So our West Willow informant reports."

"Christ! These small towns. What the hell would Jakes be doing down there? It's not his jurisdiction. He's a smart and very straight cop. Now we really have a problem."

"Same problem. Yes, a bit more acute, but no change in target. Apply yourself," Sisik lectured. "And about the remainder of McCarthy's files that we brought up? Have they been purged?" he asked.

"Yeah, but I had to shred one hell of a lot. The guy has no discretion at all. He kept everything. And he has his hand in a lot of cookie jars. I expect enough got away to put him away for a lot of years, and a few others too. Why would he do that, or worse still, leave it behind? Is he crazy?"

"Sean McCarthy is an idiot savant. A brilliant politician. Yes. Very alert to what is dangerous for others but lacking awareness to avoid the same dangers himself. Even with many liabilities, our Mr. McCarthy has been a great asset to this government in many ways, yes? Particularly in his handling of the civil service."

"How so?" Justice wanted to know.

"By the climate of terror he has created. Keeping our bureaucrats in constant fear of losing their jobs has done wonders for their productivity, yes? But Sean is his own worst enemy. To paraphrase Adam Smith, 'He has an overweening conceit of his own abilities and an absurd presumption in his own good fortune.' Mind you," he explained, "Smith spoke of market speculators, but the description fits McCarthy very well."

"Who's Adam Smith?"

"He was the first right-winger."

"Well, you'd better keep an eye on this right-winger. He's trouble with a capital T," Justice warned.

"Oh yes, we're forewarned now. We have put two keepers in his office. Cannot completely prevent his little peccadillos, but can make sure his tracks are covered. Yes? Now find that mess of his that got away."

TWENTY-THREE

 On Tuesday afternoon Ethel Tremblay came in to Oxford's office, looking puzzled.

"There's a fellow named Paul Godfrey on the phone. From Vancouver. He's been asking me a bunch of questions about Ben. I finally told him he ought to talk to you. He sounds a little excited," she said. Oxford picked up the phone.

"Mr. LaCoste, my name is Paul Godfrey. I'm with McRae, Gordon, and Lee here in Vancouver. I'm an old friend of Ben Forsyth. We were classmates. We were doing some work for Ben, some rather delicate work. I was out of the country, in our Taiwan office, and just learned, only the other day, of Ben's death. Tragic. I understand you are, were, whatever, an associate of Ben's?" Ethel was right, the words were tumbling over the phone.

"I guess you could say that. I took over Ben's law firm. We were very good friends."

"So I understood from your secretary," Godfrey was suddenly calm and under control. "May I ask who is looking after Ben's affairs?"

"I am his executor, the surviving executor. The other executor was murdered on Friday night." Oxford said that matter-of-factly.

"My God!" The control just as suddenly left Godfrey. "Murdered?" He paused, searching for words. "I'm truly sorry," was the best he could do.

"I take it that Mrs. Forsyth is not named an executrix?" he asked carefully.

"No. Only as an alternative to the first two, now me."

"Mr. LaCoste, I don't know how to say this, and I'm hesitant to say much over the phone, but I think you and I need to talk, and as soon as possible. About some of the work we were doing for Ben. Would it be possible for us to get together, perhaps later this week?" Godfrey asked, then went on.

"I'm sorry. You're in Saskatchewan and I'm in Vancouver. I don't mean to suggest that you come out here. I'll certainly come to Regina, or West Willow, if you like, but I was wondering about Calgary. I'll be in our offices there on Thursday and Friday and I can stay over the weekend."

"I think I can make that work," Oxford replied. "Calgary's not a long drive from here."

"Yes, I know. I was raised in Swift Current. From there west everyone is half Albertan. I was hoping that would be convenient. When do you think you can make it?"

"Friday afternoon. I'll drive over in the morning. Be in your offices at two o'clock."

"Great. See you then." Godfrey, Oxford thought, sounded relieved.

TWENTY-FOUR

Those who knew Sean McCarthy well knew that a harsh upbringing helped explain the unusual energy that he brought to the Saskatchewan political arena. The first eighteen years of McCarthy's life were spent in near-brutal manual labour on a marginal bush farm in northern Saskatchewan.

In 1945 Brendan McCarthy, having survived five years as a member of the South Saskatchewan Regiment, and more encounters with the Provost Corps than the enemy, threw off his uniform and became a farmer. With his veteran's credits, a wife and two children, and Sean on the way, he undertook to scrabble some productive acreage away from the forest fringe along the Carrot River in northeastern Saskatchewan. He succeeded, barely, but in his later years wondered if the gain had been worth the struggle.

The rest of the McCarthy family was in no doubt whatsoever on that question. Sean's mother and two older brothers detested every acre, every foot, of the farm that had been won by their toil and sacrifice. All of them, one by one, finally escaped their desperate homestead until Brendan McCarthy, alone and bitter, was forced to sell his hard-won land and move to town and the wet canteen in the Legion Hall.

Sean McCarthy never mentioned his boyhood on that farm, not even when stump-speaking to a farming audience. The years of deprivation, poverty, and shame were, even in the glory of his manhood and success, still too painful to recall.

His schoolmates remembered the over-sized boy in the under-sized clothing at the back of the school bus, hiding his embarrassment with noisy shouting. In class Sean was bright but sought an unobtrusive role where his hand-me-downs would not draw attention. Socially, the family was almost invisible, rarely appearing at community events. At sports days, almost compulsory for children, the McCarthys seldom showed. That Brendan McCarthy was a martinet who drove his family like beasts of burden was no secret to their neighbours.

Sean managed to secure a high school education before escaping from his father's farm and harsh discipline. Working summers driving heavy road construction machinery, he spent two winters securing a diploma in vocational agriculture at the University of Saskatchewan, and came away realizing that he had not really tasted the wine of higher education. But now he became a young man in a hurry, anxious to succeed, determined above all else to be poor no more.

A job as an agricultural fertilizer salesman was the right beginning. Some basic training in direct sales techniques and public relations exposed an extraordinary natural talent. Touring his huge rural marketing district, Sean McCarthy discovered he had a photographic memory, not only for the names and faces of the many men and women he met, but also for the personal details that went with each face. At every subsequent encounter he not only recognized by name but knew exactly where and when they had last spoken and easily picked up the conversation where it had broken off. It was a rare and great talent, the equal of James Farley, Franklin Roosevelt's postmaster general who addressed more than 50,000 Americans by their first names. It is the dream of every politician.

More than six feet in height, broad and burly, red-headed, with huge Irish ears, Sean, on first impression was clumsy and slow-witted. But the observer soon noticed that the big man's movements were not only full of power but swift and smooth, almost graceful, and that his mind was keen and alert.

It was natural that Sean would come to the attention of Lloyd Grange, searching for candidates for the Western Democratic Alliance, and that he would welcome the overture. Sean had no difficulty in capturing the WDA nomination in his district, and his tremendous personal popularity carried him easily through the election. He was among the vanguard of WDA MLAS who sat in opposition in the Saskatchewan Legislature.

Again, it was the right beginning. Sean McCarthy soon displayed an instinctive knack for political strategy and became a powerful figure in the caucus and the backrooms of the WDA. When Lloyd Grange self-destructed, it was Sean McCarthy who pulled together the shocked troops of the WDA, convinced them that Harrison Halliday was the leader the party needed to win the government, and then convinced Halliday to accept the challenge. With the scent of success in his nostrils, Sean McCarthy was not to be denied his goal. It was McCarthy more than anyone who put together the campaign strategy that brought the to power in Saskatchewan.

McCarthy had, of course, been able to choose his own portfolio in the Halliday cabinet, and had picked Provincial Development, which seemed a modest choice at the time. But the ambitious farm boy who was determined to be poor no more knew what he was about. The department he wanted was the one that gave him quick entry to the world of business. McCarthy had read about Willy Sutton, a lifelong bank robber, who, when asked at the end of his long career why he had robbed banks, answered with devastating simplicity: "Because that's where the money is."

Sean McCarthy determined that he, too, would keep his eye on where the money was.

As minister of Provincial Development, McCarthy quickly engaged the Halliday government in a policy of public investment in high-risk economic initiatives under the slogan "Public/Private Partnership." The entrepreneurs who flocked to his door quickly learned that a piece of the action for Sean McCarthy was essential if their proposals for government assistance were to have any success.

After successes in the early WDA years, McCarthy lost

his touch. As many of the ventures he supported failed, exposing questionable merit and judgement, the Halliday government became embroiled in controversy. McCarthy's stature in the caucus and the party rendered him immune to serious criticism, even when rumours of his personal financial gain began to seep into the public. But in cabinet his political capital finally began to diminish. His fellow ministers, more aware than others of McCarthy's dangerous conduct, began to protest. Halliday, finally and reluctantly, removed his flamboyant minister from his favourite portfolio and placed him in another where the opportunities would be less tempting.

Sean accepted the apparent demotion with equanimity. In fact, recognizing the political problem he had become, he had recommended the change. He had no political ambition beyond the position he had already achieved. Status, whether political or social, had no interest for him. What he craved now was wealth, and he needed only that amount of power that made possible his continued acquisition of assets. He knew that with the skills and connections he had developed he could continue to prosper in any portfolio, so long as the Halliday government survived. After that, he knew he would be on his own, and he wanted to be well-prepared, and fully capitalized, for that eventual day. He would, he swore, be poor no more.

What McCarthy could not and would not accept was the destruction of his credibility in the business community that looked to him as its point of entry to the Halliday government. Without that he knew there would be no hidden participating interests, no commissions tucked neatly into offshore bank accounts, no insider stock tips. His political power would be in his own eyes worthless if his access to illicit gain dried up.

So, when Val Sisik lectured McCarthy on the subject of the imprudent maintenance of incriminating files and strongly advised him to change his ways, Sean meekly agreed, but was unconcerned. But when the contacts he assiduously cultivated in the premier's office told him in private that Ben Forsyth had made a collection of McCarthy's files for the purpose of destroying him and the Halliday government, Sean reacted like a she-wolf whose cubs were under attack.

McCarthy had carefully built a public image as an entirely affable and easy-going man since his days as a salesman, but he possessed the ruthlessness of a pirate. On the march to power all resistance, even within the WDA, was put down without hesitation. As a powerful minister of the Crown he became his father's son. On first taking power, he headed a purge of the civil service supposedly intended to ensure loyalty and efficiency but which destroyed morale and productivity. Thereafter, McCarthy would dismiss an employee on a whim, as if to amuse himself with the display of his own power and to maintain a suitable level of fear among his subordinates.

Faced with the problem of his own files being turned against him, Sean McCarthy would experience no compunction when choosing a solution.

McCarthy fully believed the information about Ben Forsyth. He had long disliked and distrusted his fellow minister, sneering at him as a goody-goody two shoes. It was just like Forsyth to pull a trick like this, he thought as he worked the problem through in his mind; good thing he is dead. His informant gave no clue as to the present whereabouts of the files, but Sean McCarthy knew where to start looking. And who to have conduct the search.

When more information was available, it would come to him immediately. McCarthy had good sources and paid them well. Adele Haynes and Patrick Justice in the premier's office were two of his best.

Twenty-five

Oxford stood again beside an open grave in the West Willow cemetery. From its steadily shrinking membership, the local Legion had mustered just enough veterans for a colour party in honour of their comrade, Squadron Leader Cameron Dexter Hunt, DFC. Stiffly, but with great dignity, they had each in turn placed a poppy on the casket, saluted, turned and marched back into rank. Their leader had intoned Laurence Binyon's salute to fallen veterans,

> *At the going down of the sun*
> *and in the morning*
> *We will remember them.*

Now, from the speakers of a ghetto blaster, the taped but haunting bugle notes of "The Last Post" rang down the valley and echoed through the hills. The Canadian flag, ceremoniously folded, reposed at the centre of the casket. On the flag Vivian Hunt had placed the Distinguished Flying Cross that had been awarded to her husband in a 1944 ceremony at Buckingham Palace.

His eyes closed against the tears, his fists clenched tightly as he stood at parade attention, Oxford felt grief flowing through his entire system. He had accepted Ben Forsyth's death as a tragic loss, a careless accident, but one of those events that just seem to happen. Cameron Hunt's death was different. Murder, and preventable, if they'd taken more care. And Oxford LaCoste could not escape some responsibility for that unnecessary death. That made his pain more intense. I know I can never make it up to you, old-timer. But I'd like to redeem myself a little bit.

As the last bugle note died away, Oxford opened his eyes and looked over the mourners. Fewer than before, they were also different, more grayheaded, more simply clothed. Today there were no visiting dignitaries. These were men and women of the land, Cameron Hunt's people.

As Oxford turned to leave, his mind turned to the thought that had come to him in the night. He was alone again. Ben Forsyth and Cameron Hunt had become his family in the eight years since his father died and he had returned to the West. Now he was an orphan again.

Twenty-six

Adele Haynes was the number one secretary in Premier Halliday's front office. Smart, experienced, toughened by a bitter divorce and alert to the realities of life, she was the gatekeeper to the premier's inner sanctum. Adele picked up her phone as the receptionist rang a call through.

"Good morning, Cliff. What can I do for you?"

"'Morning, Ad. I need a few minutes with the boss. No briefing. It's personal. And a bit urgent," Clifton Carlson explained.

"Just a moment while I check his schedule, Cliff," she said, not needing to check anything, but wanting time to mentally review whether the minister's request presented any special problem. She decided it did not.

"How about this afternoon, Cliff? Tiffin time. Five o'clock."

Over drinks in the premier's office late that afternoon, Clifton confessed his impending financial collapse. After long consideration, he had decided this was his only hope, that somehow Harris Halliday could push a button and bail him out.

"So, there it is," Clifton ended his explanation. "I'll have to resign, of course, and I'm sorry for the embarrassment it will cause you. Trouble is," he went on, playing his hole card and hoping it was an ace, "losing the cabinet position will probably cost me my seat. I'm hanging on to a pretty thin majority as it is."

"Yes. You had a bit of a squeaker last time, didn't you," Halliday agreed. "What was it? Couple of hundred votes?"

"One hundred eighty-eight to be exact. That's tough country out there."

"Must be," Halliday mused, recognizing very well what Carlson was up to. Every night the premier did the mental arithmetic that told him he needed every seat he could find if his government was to win re-election. Carlson's seat was one he counted on.

"How do you see yourself getting out from under all that debt?" Halliday asked.

"Refinance," Clifford replied. "I need to extend my loans and hopefully get a bit of a break on interest. Problem is, I'm out of security, maxed out."

"Seems to me I've read somewhere that you can't borrow your way out of debt," Halliday said dryly. "A lot of farmers out there are trying it. It's not working for them, either."

"I know. And if wheat prices don't turn around, I'll go down too. Like so many others. But if things do pick up, and I'm already out of business . . . " Clifton shrugged and left his remark unfinished.

"How do you see me helping?" Halliday asked.

"Well, I know it would be too touchy for the government to give me one of those subsidized agro-loans you invented. But I thought maybe the Party . . . "

"The Party!" Halliday interjected, "What could the Party do?"

"Well, I really don't know. But I hear stories about a couple of special funds. I thought maybe a low-interest personal loan might be possible. Something to get the credit union off my back."

"Special funds? What special funds? I don't know about any special funds," Halliday said, his voice rising, a little too deliberately, Clifton thought.

"I don't either. But, as I said, I hear things," Clifton replied. Then, "There is the caucus account, of course. I think it's getting pretty fat with those advertising allowances all our MLAs assigned in there. And I'm sure we haven't spent half of all the research grants we get."

"I don't have anything to do with running either the Party or the caucus, as you know," Halliday said firmly, "and I doubt there is anything that either could do for you that won't cause more trouble than you're in now.

"But," the premier said, putting his glass down and rising to his feet, "I appreciate you letting me know about the problem. I'll work on this. If I can come up with something, I'll let you know. But don't count on it happening."

"I won't. And thanks," Clifton said as he too stood and turned to leave, careful not to show his rising hopes. His pitch had sold, he was sure. Halliday needed his Long Lake riding and would bail out his minister to save it.

TWENTY-SEVEN

The premises of McRae, Gordon, and Lee in Calgary's Bankers' Hall were as lavish as Oxford expected from a law firm with offices in four cities in Canada and five overseas. They were offices of the sort that country lawyers like him saw only in the posed portraits of legal publications. Oxford had checked the Canadian Law List and confirmed that Paul Godfrey was a ranking partner, but the office Oxford was invited into was somewhat sparse. As if sensing his visitor's curiosity, Godfrey explained.

"I'm just a transient here. This is one of the offices we keep for visiting partners. My home digs are in Vancouver."

Slight of frame, with narrow features, jet black hair and spectacled intense eyes, Godfrey looked more like a bean counter than a lawyer, Oxford thought. But Godfrey was clearly sincere in his expressions of sympathy at the loss of Ben Forsyth and so obviously had been a good friend of Ben's that Oxford quickly concluded that he was in trustworthy company.

"I'm embarrassed to ask, but may I have a look at your letters probate in Ben's estate?" Godfrey asked.

"Sure. I brought the original so you can make your own copies," and Oxford handed over the court order appointing Cameron Hunt and Oxford LaCoste executors of the Last Will and Testament of Benjamin Forsyth, copy attached.

"Judicial Centre of Swift Current," Godfrey mused, "my

home town, I think I mentioned on the phone," as he rang in a secretary to make photocopies. "Thanks," he said to Oxford, "our file will need to be covered off with a copy of this.

"Although we both came from the same corner of Saskatchewan," Godfrey continued, "Ben and I didn't meet until we got to law school. Then we became best buddies. We had always hoped to practise together, but Ben had a job waiting for him in his home town and I got an offer from Calgary and that was that.

"When Ben called me last month I hadn't heard from him in over a year. I knew he was a member of the Saskatchewan cabinet, of course, but we didn't keep in touch in a regular way. He wanted to see me right away, seemed very anxious. I was in Vancouver but luckily was due to come over to Calgary the next day. So he came over, too, and we met here. Ben had a problem with a deal he was handling for the provincial government, he said, and part of the problem was in Hong Kong. He knew we have offices there and thought we could help," Godfrey explained.

"It might make it easier if I mentioned that I know about the heavy oil extraction process Ben was working on," Oxford interjected. "In fact, I've been trying to run down what happened."

"You're right. That does make it easier. We're a little nervous here about our position on this. It's not entirely clear who we owe an obligation of confidentiality to. Although Ben was our client, we know the money wasn't his," Godfrey replied. "I had serious misgivings when Ben asked us to handle this for him, but we eventually went along."

"Some potentially smelly aspects of his deal had begun to surface, and he was in position to be tagged with responsibility if it went sour. He wanted to sequester the whole transaction, including the purchase money, until he had a chance to check it all out. Just take everything right out of circulation, so to speak. Ben had heard of asset protection trusts, didn't know much about them, but thought the name described what he wanted to do. He wanted to make the fifteen million dollars purchase price disappear into protective custody until things cleared up. He would look after tucking away everything else having to do with the transaction.

"That's where we got edgy." Godfrey paused, then continued. "Helping Ben hide fifteen million dollars that he admitted belonged to the government of Saskatchewan didn't pass the smell test at first. But, as Ben pointed out, the money was already under his control and he was ensuring that it would be protected to the government, which was an improvement on the present situation. So, because it was Ben, I went along. Felt better about it when we got a report back from Hong Kong, but I'll come to that.

"We do a lot of overseas trust work and we set up a coded trust for Ben. Used the Windward Islands Trust Company in the Turks and Caicos as trustee with the government of Saskatchewan as beneficiary, time and method of payout as directed by Ben Forsyth or his designate, or executor, upon production of the codes. As I'm sure you do, too, Oxford, lawyers always use that stock phrase, 'or his executors, etc.' to cover off the event of death. It's a just in case thing, without any real contemplation that it will ever be needed. Particularly when Ben didn't think he would need to keep these arrangements in place for more than a few weeks.

"But," Godfrey spread his hands philosophically, "once in a while we get reminded of the reason we do these things this way. Ben's gone, so is Cameron Hunt, and you're the executor, it says here," said Godfrey tapping the letters probate his secretary had returned to his desk.

"So, you have the direction over a fifteen million dollar trust in the Caribbean. Money's not yours, of course, but the say-so about how and when it's paid out is. You'll need the codes, of course, but I assume Ben has left them where you can find them."

Oxford's jaw went slack and he looked dumbly across the desk at Godfrey. He felt a sense of relief tinged with annoyance. Thank God the money's safe and so is Ben's reputation. But what the hell, Ben? I loved you. Did you have any idea of what you were doing to me? How much more can there be to all this?

"To say I'm a bit surprised would be serious understatement," Oxford sputtered. "I knew Ben had made some strange moves with that money, but I didn't expect to find it on my doorstep, so to speak."

"Can't blame you. It *is* a unique situation, a bit weird, to use the current idiom.

"But," he went on, "let me tell you about the Hong Kong report. Perhaps it will make you feel a bit better, as it did me at the time. Ben asked us to check out his opposite number, the vendor of the process, a bird in Hong Kong by the name of Josef Rafael. That was no problem. Rafael was quite easy to find, in fact still at the address Ben gave us. He was working out of a temporary office, and our resident partner there had a chat with him the next day.

"When our man in Hong Kong explained that he was representing Ben Forsyth and had been instructed to ask some serious questions about the proposed deal, Rafael was unusually cooperative, considering what he told us," Godfrey said.

"Rafael had initially approached Premier Halliday about taking over his extraction process. They met at a trade show in Rome. Halliday seemed interested and Rafael explained that he needed six million dollars up front to recoup his group's investment plus a participating interest. The premier arranged for Rafael to meet the next day with his deputy, Sisik, I think is the name. The next day Rafael and Sisik met and Sisik quickly set the terms of a deal. The up front price would be fifteen million dollars, not six million, but the extra nine million dollars would be paid out as directed by Sisik."

Godfrey paused and took off his glasses. To Oxford it seemed a warm gesture, as if Godfrey wanted to reduce the embarrassment level.

"This is where Rafael's story became very strange indeed," the other lawyer continued. "Sisik explained that the nine million dollars would be funding another venture, that western democratic governments sometimes needed to carry out their responsibilities very unobtrusively to avoid public exposure that might defeat their programs. Sisik instructed Rafael to take his proposal to the Saskatchewan government representative in Hong Kong. 'To initiate discussions at the appropriate level,' or some such gobbleygook. Rafael would make no reference to the discussions already held with Premier Halliday and Sisik or the deal would not proceed. Sisik was very firm about that.

"Rafael said he wasn't suspicious and agreed to the deal. At the time, he said, it seemed reasonable to him. Although later he began to wonder where the nine million dollars was really going, he didn't ask any questions and carried on. The deal was a make or break for him.

"Our firm takes pride in its ability to provide service internationally, but it isn't often that we produce results as quickly as we did for Ben Forsyth. It was only two days after we had met here in Calgary that I was able to phone him with that report from Hong Kong.

"He was furious at first," Godfrey said, "but then he seemed almost pleased. Armed with that information from Rafael, he expected he would be able to straighten things out in Regina more quickly than he had thought, whatever that meant.

"Ben requested that our man visit Rafael again. To tell him that serious questions were being asked about his deal, particularly the nine million dollars. That a scandal was brewing. If Rafael wanted to salvage the deal, that is, his six million dollar deal, perhaps he'd like to take a vacation, become unavailable for a while. If Rafael would cooperate and lie low for a while, it might be possible to hold everything together.

"Rafael agreed. He was very concerned that there might be scandal, yet he was anxious to hang on to his sale. He said he would be pleased to drop out of sight for a while. Would contact our man quietly sometime later to see if the coast was clear.

"With that accomplished, Ben instructed us to protect the purchase monies, so-called anyway. The whole fifteen million dollars. So, the next week we moved the funds from Hong Kong to the Turks and Caicos. Through another institution for extra security, and then to Windward Islands Trust Company, completed the paperwork, and closed the file for further instructions.

"Then I come back from a trip to our Taiwan office to learn about Ben, and here we are." Paul Godfrey was finished.

TWENTY-EIGHT

Oxford gave himself the weekend off. After calling Chris Rossom and arranging to see him first thing Monday morning, he drove to Banff for some quiet contemplation.

Oxford had been introduced to Banff by Ben Forsyth, who had demanded that Oxford learn to ski. He needed a skiing partner more than a law partner, Ben insisted, since Ruth would no longer risk the slopes. Oxford was sentenced to a week at the ski school at Sunshine Village and discovered that although his natural ability was limited his capacity to enjoy the mountains was not.

From then on the two lawyers regularly spent at least two weekends a winter at Lake Louise where they found an interesting variety of intermediate runs and the best scenery in the Rockies.

Although their abilities were about equal, Oxford was cautious while Ben was often almost reckless as he continually challenged himself. Oxford teased him that, like pilots, there were old skiers and bold skiers, but no old, bold skiers. But Ben was incorrigible. He powered through the moguls on brute strength, punishing himself just to prove he could do it. Oxford declined. His love was carving through the undisturbed early morning powder, delighting in the hiss of his skis and the speeding wind upon his face.

The pair usually managed to stay at the Chateau. They both loved the castle-like halls and the ornate dining room where they spent many a long evening deep in discussion.

They had really enjoyed each other's company, Oxford thought, remembering their last visit in early April. Would he come alone this winter? He thought not.

Wandering the between season streets of the too touristy Banff, Oxford wondered at the boldness of Ben Forsyth in seizing control of the laser transaction. Certainly, if a scam had been in the making, it had been pre-empted by his action. But what had Ben planned to do next? Cameron Hunt had been right. Ben did hire a lawyer after his talk with Howard Gordon, not for advice about what to do to protect himself but for assistance in carrying out a course of action upon which he had already decided.

Obviously, in Ben's mind the nine million dollar mark up on the Rafael deal tied in with the files he had put together on the corrupt Halliday administration. He must have had a confrontation in mind. With Halliday himself? With McCarthy? With others? When and how? Ben had told Paul Godfrey that Rafael's story would actually bring things to a head more quickly. What had Ben been planning?

And what would Oxford LaCoste do about it if he did have the answers to those questions? Did he intend to carry out Ben Forsyth's plans? Would he bring down the Halliday government? And what risk would that involve? How much danger to Oxford LaCoste?

On Sunday, Oxford pondered that question during the long drive to Regina, a trip he always enjoyed. He knew that many regard the terrain between Calgary and Regina as equivalent to the view from the Trans-Siberian Railway, but to Oxford the flat fields and rolling pastures were beauty indeed. He was a true westerner.

Oxford's mind turned to a Sunday afternoon more than a year after his father's death. He had been performing some minor renovations in the old farmhouse when he discovered a roll of documents in a large, cracked vase at the back of a dusty cupboard. He sat down and read a yellowed clipping from a 1947 issue of *Le Monde* telling of the posthumous award of the Legion d'Honneur to his grandfather, Marcel

LaCoste, in recognition of his sacrifices on behalf of the French resistance, the Maquis. The award citation itself was also in the roll. And a long letter to Yves LaCoste from someone who had served in the Maquis with Marcel and had survived. The letter spoke passionately of the dedication and courage of Marcel and his wife, Claire. Oxford re-examined the vase and found the medal itself lying on the bottom.

He had sat for the rest of that afternoon, reading and rereading and creating an image of the bravery and skill of his grandparents Marcel and Claire LaCoste, and the care and cunning that had enabled them for so long to escape detection by the Gestapo. And finally the treachery of a collaborator who had delivered the two and their colleagues to the long night of torture that ended with their summary execution at dawn by firing squad.

Yves LaCoste had never mentioned a word of all this to his son. Neither had Alphonse or Marie Fournier. Why not? Perhaps Yves had managed to keep it from Alphonse and Marie. But why would he? And why would he hide from his only son, only child, the exploits and honour of his own parents?

Yves had spoken very little of his early life in Paris. Occasionally, when Oxford was very young, his father had recounted adventures from his own boyhood in the quiet pre-war years. But from the war time, from his experiences during the Nazi Occupation, nothing. And of his own parents, nothing that would give the slightest suspicion of the remarkable events Oxford uncovered that quiet country afternoon.

Prominent among the many contributions Marcel and Claire had made to the work of the resistance had been the publication of an underground newspaper. In its pages they countered the German propaganda with news items from the transmissions of the British Broadcasting Corporation reporting the successes of the Allied Forces. They carried editorials counselling their countrymen not to accept the defeat of their nation.

To stiffen the will of their readers, they quoted the heroes of France.

Napoleon—*"To live in defeat is to die every day."*
Marshall Foch—*"A people is conquered only when it accepts defeat."*
Clemenceau—*"In war as in peace, the last word is to those who never surrender."*

Their work was dangerous and it cost them their lives. But, *Le Monde* said, *"they were a beacon of hope to their fellow Parisians during the dark days of the Occupation."*

Oxford had never told anyone, not even Ben Forsyth, about what he discovered in the farmhouse cupboard. Over the years since, he had wondered what the bravery and sacrifice of his grandparents might mean to his own life. Now, as he drove across the treeless plains, a thought nagged at him; would he find in the example of Marcel and Claire what his response must be to the problem left to him by Ben Forsyth?

To Oxford the approach to Regina from the west at sunset was enchanting. Built upon a flat glacial lake bed, without the character granted by a river, or even a natural lake, the city looked from a distance like a child's blocks piled upon a floor. But in the glory of a western sunset it often shimmered like a mirage. A number of the downtown office towers, sheathed in tinted glass, reflected the sun's setting rays, reminding him of minarets in the illustrated copy of *Arabian Nights* he had enjoyed as a child.

Oxford checked back into his waiting suite at the Flatlander. What the hell, he thought, why not?

TWENTY-NINE

The woman raised up on one elbow, then swung herself over the supine man so that her still-hardened nipples grazed his chest. She traced a fingertip across his brow and down the bridge of his nose.

"So, when do we leave, darling?" she asked.

With an effort he refrained from wincing as her whiskey breath flooded his nostrils. Instead, he smiled.

"Soon, now. Things are starting to sort themselves out. Our problem will be solved before long," he replied. "Let us not hurry. Would it seem to be decent for you to be leaving so soon?"

"Fuck decency. I don't give a damn for anyone here. Besides, we're not coming back, anyway. Remember?" She tapped his forehead with her finger. "We're going to sail the seven seas, see the pyramids at dawn, snorkel the Great Barrier Reef. We're going to live, live, live. Oh! darling. I can hardly wait," she exclaimed.

"Of course. But we don't want to create suspicions." He slid out from underneath her and reached for his clothing.

She watched him dress in silence, then spoke, in a caustic tone.

"Oh, I'll be patient, all right. But just don't get any ideas that you don't need me anymore. We're in this together, all the way."

"Don't worry," he smiled at her. "It will be as we

169

planned. It has so far, yes?" And he put a finger to her lips.

As he left he wondered which cruise liners were the most susceptible to drunks falling overboard. Not the sort of thing they would print in their brochures, he knew.

THIRTY

"Ready for me?" Sean McCarthy poked his head around the heavy oak door that opened onto the office of Premier Harris Halliday.

"Sure. Come in, Sean," Halliday said from his desk. "Thanks for coming over."

"Problem?" McCarthy asked.

"Quite a few, in fact," Halliday replied dryly. "But one I think you might be able to help with right now."

"Shoot."

Harris Halliday outlined the situation facing Clifton Carlson, Energy minister and member for Long Lake. "We're going to need that riding, Sean," he concluded. "Maybe Carlson can't hold on to it anyway, but it's gone for sure if he goes in the tank. We need to prop him up. I want you to dig into one of those little funds I don't know anything about and give him a lifesaver." It was a neutral statement, somehow neither command nor request.

McCarthy turned ninety degrees away from Halliday and peered out the window over Wascana Lake. He needed to hide his reaction. Jesus, he thought, where did we find these losers? Carlson has been a minister almost from the beginning. He has had the energy portfolio for more than three years. All those hungry oil companies, grateful for any little royalty break or concession. And he's broke? Keerist!

"How much?" McCarthy turned back to the premier.

"He thought fifty thousand will do it. But check that out. We need to keep him afloat until after the election. I'm still shooting for June. So, eight months, give or take. Then he can sink."

"Any preferences about where the money comes from?" McCarthy wanted to see Halliday squirm a bit. The premier liked to insist that he knew nothing about the seamier side of politics, the financing of party activities and campaigns, but McCarthy more than anyone else knew that to be a fiction. Although the Party campaign accounts were controlled in strict secrecy by Mick Starky, the Regina businessman who served as party treasurer and chief fundraiser, Mick gave regular reports to Halliday, who was after all the Party leader. McCarthy knew Mick had few scruples, but he might complain about tapping Party funds for a loan to just one of their sixty-odd candidates.

"I told you I don't know how you people handle these things," Halliday retorted. "Phone Mick. Carlson suggested there might be enough in the caucus account to cover this."

McCarthy's eyebrows lifted at the suggestion that caucus funds could be resorted to in this way. The government and opposition members received grants for the operation of their offices at the legislature. Expenses such as secretaries, telephones, and research were provided for on a formula based on the number of MLAs elected. Reimbursement for approved advertising and publicity was also available. The WDA members had created a network of dummy companies to develop fictitious expenses which they then billed to the legislature. Much of the money secured in this way was converted into cash and slipped back to the WDA MLAs, but the rest was channelled into the WDA caucus account. It now had a surplus of several hundred thousand dollars.

"There might be, at that," McCarthy mused. "But Karl Bramwell is caucus chair now and he takes himself seriously. He won't act on my say-so. He'll want to hear it from you."

"That's okay. If that's the way you decide to play this, tell Karl to call me. I'll approve it. But then I'll forget everything about it. Understood?" Halliday was suddenly firm.

"Of course."

McCarthy smiled as he left the premier's office. He

thought it childish of Halliday to attempt to stay above the murky dealings of the WDA. But the premier's determined remoteness made it wonderfully easy for Sean McCarthy to take control of that part of WDA politics for which he had such a natural affinity.

Karl Bramwell did not like him, Sean McCarthy knew, but Karl would never question instructions from the premier. Besides, he had a hole card he had been waiting for the right opportunity to use. Bramwell would fall in line. It would be simple. It would be just as easy to tap Karl for one hundred thousand as for the fifty poor Carlson needed and pocket the difference. Not a bad day's work, McCarthy smiled.

In the reception area McCarthy winked at Adele Haynes who caught the signal instantly and a moment later followed out into the corridor. Dimly lit and hidden from sight behind the marble wall above the grand staircase, that corridor outside the premier's office and the cabinet room had seen many a quick political deal. Today McCarthy's hand brushed Adele's unobtrusively at thigh level and, with a practised movement, she folded her fingers over the five one hundred dollar bills thus transferred.

"Things are cooking, Ad. Anything I should know?" McCarthy asked.

"Don't think so, Sean. Cliff Carlson was over yesterday. Something personal. Not much else."

"Yeah. I just got filled in on that. Little Cliffy's in over his head. Karl Bramwell should be calling tomorrow. Let me know, will you?"

"Sure. No problem, Sean. Take care." And she stepped back into the premier's suite.

"You too, Ad." Sean McCarthy whistled as he strolled out to the rotunda of the legislative building. He paused at the marble well designed in replication of Napoleon's tomb at Les Invalides.

It's all in the timing, eh, Nap? And in grabbing the opportunities when they come along. If you'd been born fifty years earlier or later, the world would never have heard of you. But you lived at a time when your talents took you to the top. Me, too, McCarthy grinned. Then he slapped the railing as he wheeled and strode down the corridor to his own offices.

THIRTY-ONE

 "And so there we are," Oxford said to Chris Rossom, as he finished relating the story he had been told by Paul Godfrey.

"Now do you agree that I need a lawyer?"

They were seated in Chris Rossom's law office. Oxford thought wistfully about his own office, and wondered if he would ever return to the normal life he had been enjoying before all this descended upon him.

"Did you tell Godfrey that you were acting on instructions from the Government of Saskatchewan?" Chris asked.

"No. I was there solely as Ben's executor. The fact that I act for the government is in itself confidential. Sisik made that very clear."

"Right," Chris thought for a moment, and then went on. "You were hired to find the fifteen million bucks. You, as executor of Ben Forsyth's estate, now have that information. If you don't transfer that info to yourself as solicitor to the government, and hand it over to your client, we have a tiny conflict of interest, don't we?"

"I can see that far myself," Oxford replied dryly.

"Easy. I'm just trying to work this through. Although it looks suspiciously like someone had grand larceny in mind with that nine million, dollars it would be pretty tough to bring charges without the missing Josef Rafael in the witness stand," Chris said.

"Godfrey said Rafael would report in to their Hong Kong office before long," Oxford replied. "He'll be available."

"Fine. Let's put him in the witness box, then. And then it's his testimony against the word of the premier and his deputy. Pretty strong stuff. Who do you think a jury would believe?" Chris asked, then ignored his own question and continued with another.

"Is there no documentation anywhere about what was supposed to happen with that nine million dollars?"

"None that we know of," Oxford replied. "Rafael was expecting instructions to come from Sisik about the time the deal closed."

"You mean Sisik was going to trust this hotshot stranger with nine million bucks?" Chris was incredulous.

"Seems so. But Rafael was in love with his invention and it needed a lot of work and money to perfect. And there was the matter of his participating interest which would disappear if he double-crossed Sisik. He seems a bit naive to even have agreed to the deal in the first place. Makes it likely that Sisik thought he could control Rafael. And," Oxford added, "Sisik strikes me as far too smart to leave any incriminating documents lying around."

"Okay. Assume all that. Then there's no documentation on the deal. Do we have a strong prima facie case of criminal conduct that might override your duty to disclose to your client? Ben would have made a great witness. Now you release the material. It goes to court. You're the witness. Credible, not as good as Ben, but good. And Dorothy. Yes, Dorothy too. She knows a good bit about the deal. In addition to having found the other stuff," Chris concluded.

"But first shouldn't we be discussing criminal conduct with the police, Adam Jakes in particular? He knows a little bit about this whole mess, although nothing yet about the missing fifteen million dollars. Would I be in breach of my instructions as to confidentiality by telling Adam Jakes about my conversation with Paul Godfrey? I'm seeing him this afternoon."

"I hope no more so than by discussing it with me," Chris replied.

"I have someone I'd like you to meet, by the way," Chris

said. "Someone I think you should talk to before you decide what you're going to do with those other files you have. Can we meet in the lounge at the Hotel Saskatchewan at five?"

"Sure," Oxford said, "Who is it?"

"Tad Osborne. Local news hound. A real character. Knows everything that goes on in this town. His paper won't print a lot of his exposés, which makes Tad very frothy indeed. Bit of a boozer, so we need to get to him at the front end of his evening. He's a regular at the Sask."

"Tad Osborne," Oxford mused. "Seems to me Ben mentioned him a time or two. I think they knew each other."

"Likely. Everybody knows Tad. And he knows everybody. You'll like him. See you after work." Chris ushered Oxford out.

Back at the Flatlander, Oxford called Dorothy Crane's office, only to be told, "She's not in today. She's at home."

Wondering what that meant, Oxford called Dorothy's home. He found out.

"Someone burgled my apartment, Oxford. But, if that wasn't bad enough, they vandalized the place. Trashed it, Hillary says. I'm sick. And also damn good and angry." Dorothy sounded angry. And a little frightened.

Oxford offered his help.

"No, thanks, Oxford. It's under control now. It happened Saturday night. We found it when we came home late. The insurance man was here this morning. I've arranged for some men to come and haul away the ruined furniture this afternoon. I've some shopping to do," Dorothy said.

"I was going to suggest lunch, but maybe dinner would be a better idea," Oxford offered.

"Now that is helpful. A great idea. Hillary has a game tonight. Can you pick me up? Is 6:30 all right?" Dorothy sounded pleased.

"Sure. It's a deal."

"Oxford . . . " Dorothy paused. "I've been wondering. Do you think there could be a connection? Between my break-in and . . . ?"

"Don't know. We'll talk about that. I have some things to tell you." Oxford hung up. Cameron, he thought. Dorothy, and now me?

Adam Jakes had agreed to see Oxford at three o'clock. The inspector listened intently as Oxford related all he knew of the laser transaction and the missing fifteen million dollars, including everything he had learned from Paul Godfrey.

"So, I hope you'll understand why I wasn't free to discuss this earlier. And why I think I should tell you about it now," Oxford concluded. "I have a conflict of interest here if I don't pass the information on the whereabouts of the fifteen million dollars to my client, the government. I'm hoping you can see a legitimate reason why that information should be withheld, at least for now."

"What good will it do them?" Jakes asked.

Oxford stared at Jakes, wondering what he meant.

"Where are the codes?" Jakes asked.

Oxford shrugged. "Search me."

"Without the codes they can't get at the money," Jakes said. "It's still as safe as Ben Forsyth intended it to be. They probably can't even confirm that the money is where you say it is."

"I'm not sure I understand," Oxford said.

"We don't get a lot of experience of this sort of thing in Regina," Jakes explained, "but I don't think that Windward Islands Trust Company will give even you the time of day without those codes. They won't even admit that an account exists. And you are Ben Forsyth's executor and entitled to direct the trust. Anyone else won't get in the door."

"Not even if I show up with copies of the trust documents? I have those," Oxford said.

"Do they mention fifteen million dollars?" Jakes asked.

"Now that you mention it, no they don't. I see," Oxford said, feeling a little foolish. "No codes, no dough. Mr. Sisik already knows the fifteen million dollars went into a numbered account in the Turks and Caicos. Now he'll know for sure only which institution now has the money. Not much closer to solving his problem."

"Exactly," Jakes said.

"I agree with your assessment, by the way," the inspector continued. "I think we can safely assume that there was a major fraud in the works, particularly in light of a number of other things we know have been taking place lately. But just now we're a little short of evidence. Too short, I think, to ask you to compromise your legal obligations.

"However, I might suggest a little discreet editing of your report," Jakes smiled. "Would it be necessary to include the reference to the nine million dollar mark up in the purchase price? Just leave it as a fifteen million dollar deal? I defer to you. You're the lawyer."

"I'm going to take that risk. I have the feeling I'm going to be taking a few more risks before long, and this one looks pretty small in comparison. Besides, just at the moment, I don't have a very warm feeling about my two instructing clients, Mr. Halliday and Mr. Sisik. I know that doesn't change my duty to them, but I have a conscience, too, you know." Oxford surprised himself with the heat of his reply.

"Well, I never doubted that. Then we can agree, can we, that the two-price arrangement will stay with us for the time being?" he asked. Oxford nodded.

"To change the subject, your friend Dorothy Crane had a bit of trouble over the weekend."

"Yes. I know. I spoke to her this morning. Is there a connection?" Oxford asked.

"Her apartment received treatment similar to the Hunt house in West Willow, only this time some of the furniture was sliced open. Different style and I think different people. But, probably same objective. You should advise her to be very careful," Jakes replied.

"I've given her a cell phone. I'll stay in close touch with her," Oxford said.

"I suggest the two of you avoid quiet places. Don't make yourselves vulnerable."

THIRTY-TWO

From Inspector Jakes' office Oxford drove directly to the Hotel Saskatchewan to review his situation and await Chris Rossom and Tad Osborne. The hotel, originally built as one of the chain of grand hotels maintained by the Canadian Pacific Railway, was cast off by the CPR when it was unable to meet the competition of the modern motor hotels offering parkades, swimming pools, and waterslides. Never as grand as the Empress in Victoria, or the Frontenac in Quebec City, the Saskatchewan stood well above the crowd in Regina, where it was still known as "The Hotel."

When Chris arrived he found Oxford settled into a corner of the Monarch Lounge and took the opportunity to provide a description of their guest, due any minute.

"He's a real character, Oxford, but a straight shooter and a hell of a newsman. I got to know him when I was prosecuting, and I make a point of having a drink with him once in a while just so I know what's going on around town.

"He's a third generation journalist. You've heard of Timothy Osborne, 'Black Tim,' the old rascal who put together a small newspaper empire here back in the twenties. Tad's grandfather. He ran his papers as organs of the Liberal Party, which was why he did so well. But that was accepted in those days.

"Tad's father was more moderate and respectable. And less successful. But he kept the papers alive until he finally sold out. Couldn't compete with the chain that runs all our dailies, so he joined it. Tad thinks his old man got rid of the papers to keep them out of his hands, and he's probably at least partly right.

"But it was part of the deal that Tad have a job for life on the *Daily Clarion* here in town. And that's likely why Tad is still with us. He's bitter. Has a running feud with his editors and publisher. Gets so heated at times that the other reporters wonder how Tad keeps his job, deal or no deal. But no one questions the quality of his work. He's of the old school. Thorough and fearless and not very modest. He's good and he'll tell you so himself. Works hard and drinks just as hard. Only in his mid-fifties but looks like a pensioner.

"You might want to consider letting him break the story if you decide to go with those files Ben Forsyth left you," Chris suggested. "You'll have to get plenty of public exposure before you can expect any action out of the Department of Justice. If you drop those files in there without media attention, they'll just sink out of sight.

"Tad Osborne will know how to handle a hot potato like this. He's the old-fashioned kind of newshound, the kind with ink in his veins. Here he is now." Chris waved to a searching arrival.

"Can you fucking imagine?" Tad Osborne said as he flung himself into a seat at their table. "That half-educated twit, that rapacious captain of industry who owns more newspapers than anyone in Canada, who fancies himself as God's gift to the publishing industry, has just issued another of his *bon mots*. Another edict of the chairman. This time the asshole has made himself a laughing-stock in every newspaper office in the fucking world."

Tad paused to take a deep swallow of the Guinness that a well-trained waiter had placed before him. His ancient Harris Tweed jacket gave evidence of many a spill. "This time," he ranted, bushy eyebrows flaring over flashing brown eyes, "this time he's gone over the edge. This time, if you'll believe it, he has announced that 'one of the greatest myths of the newspaper industry is that journalists are essential to producing a newspaper.'" Tad enunciated the quotation in very sonorous tones.

"Well," Tad continued, somewhat calmer, "at least the facade has been torn away. Now at least we know what we are about. Keep a few advertising and subscription salesmen and some make-up people. Fire everyone else. Who the fuck needs news content and editorial opinion anyway. Tad Osborne."

With that he stuck his hand at Oxford and said, "Oxford LaCoste, I presume."

"You bet," Oxford replied, delighted at the performance, "happy to know you."

"Chris tells me you are the successor to Ben Forsyth."

"Yes. In more ways than one, it seems," Oxford replied.

"Ah! Perhaps we should talk about that," Osborne said alertly. "I'd like to think that Ben and I were good friends. We spent some time together. Trusted each other. Drank some very good single malt Scotch. Ben had a very discriminating palate."

"Yes. Ben spoke of you. You two must have got along well."

Tad Osborne's features, once handsome, spoke of a life too well lived. Small but well proportioned, he seethed with compressed energy. His vitality, Oxford noted, was still in good supply as the reporter continued.

"Ben was very much out of place in the Halliday government. That we could all see. I told him that a few times. Said he was like a dove in a flock of crows. Lately I got the impression that he was beginning to agree with me," Osborne said.

Oxford nodded in agreement.

"Tad," Chris said, "I know you have strong feelings about the Halliday government, but your paper seems very non-critical. It certainly supports all their so-called economic initiatives."

"Jesus. Now you've gone and done it," Osborne almost exploded. "Set me off on that topic. That colourless, cowardly rag I work for is a fucking disgrace as a newspaper. It's called monopoly, me lad, although the answer's not quite as simple as that. This is a one newspaper town, so the policy is to keep the advertisers happy and publish as cheaply as possible. Investigative reporting is expensive

181

and too frequently all you come up with is stories embarrassing to the advertisers, or at least the power elite in this town, which is really the same thing.

"The activities of the Halliday gang have become so blatant that any cub reporter could dig up a juicy exposé on his second day on the job. But just try it. I've handed in some dandy stuff about the kickback schemes going on over the lake. All killed," Osborne's eyes were flashing. "Sure. They'll run stuff about some poor city councillor who took one too many junkets at city expense, or hammer some minister for putting his wife and kids on the government aircraft, but anything serious, forget it." Osborne was waving his Guinness now.

"The *Washington Post* this rag is not. Watergate could happen in Regina and the *Clarion* would find some fucking rationalization for not covering it. Not in the public interest. Since when do newspapers become the arbiters of the public interest? Our duty to the public interest is the pursuit of truth." Osborne noticed that his voice had risen so that he was attracting attention. He leaned forward and in lower tones continued.

"It's shameful. Listen. I had the goods on that Beaver River project, the one the government has gone on the line for to the tune of hundreds of millions. The risk level on that deal is out of sight and I had proof, a copy of the independent consultants' report done for the underwriting—the one that was cancelled because of that risk. The government had to bail the deal out with even more dough." Osborne leaned further forward and began to tap the table with his forefinger, emphasizing his words.

"I convinced the paper to go with my story. It was solid. Somehow Sean McCarthy got wind of what was happening and had a little chat with our darling publisher. Not in the public interest to do the story. Deal was a little fragile just now, but only temporary, of course. Exposure might collapse the project. Cost the taxpayer all that money. Etcetera, etcetera, etcetera. End of story. End of *my* story.

"And that, my friends, is as true as I fucking sit here," Osborne said, leaning back.

"Time for an Osborne Special," he said to the waiter.

"What's an Osborne Special?" Oxford asked, wanting time to think about what he had just heard.

"Usually that's a secret so that people can't count my drinks, but it's a deal I make with the bartender when I come in. If it's a drinking day, it's a double Glenfiddich. If it's not, it's non-alcoholic. Today it's double Glenfiddich," Osborne explained. "Would you like one?"

Oxford smiled and passed.

"What about the TV stations?" Chris asked.

"Well, they do a better job than we do, I hate to admit," Osborne said. " But they haven't the staff to get into the heavy stuff. And there's no permanence to their stories. With them it's a ninety second wonder. And the radio stations, hell! They read the *Clarion* for their news."

"Is that true what you said about Watergate?" Oxford asked. "If it was that serious, if you had solid evidence of corruption reaching right into the premier's office, would your paper ignore it?"

Osborne looked at Oxford for a moment, as if in thought, then said slowly, "if it was that big a story, big enough to capture national attention, maybe not. Because then the option is to take it to one of the few eastern papers that aren't part of our little publishing group. If they'll pick it up, then the local rag has no choice but to go along. But it would have to be very big. And very solid. Not much that happens in Saskatchewan is considered news east of Winnipeg. And libel chill is very goddam real, let me tell you," Osborne concluded.

Oxford considered this in silence. Chris said nothing. Osborne watched for a moment, then asked, "Is there maybe something we should be discussing?"

"Yes," said Oxford, suddenly determined. "Yes, there sure as hell is."

Oxford looked at Chris who opened his mouth, thought better of it and reached for his Scotch.

"I have that kind of a story," Oxford said. "Most of it consists of files put together by Ben Forsyth. He was going to blow the whistle on the Halliday government, but didn't live to do it. Now I'm going to fill in for him. At least I think I am," he added, with a small note of doubt.

"Sweet Jesus! And Hallelujah! Ben finally turned on them. Isn't that just too fucking beautiful for words." Osborne seized his Special. Then, over the rim of his glass, he spoke slowly.

"That could be risky, you know."

"Yes. I do know that," Oxford replied simply.

"Okay. At your service. I'm your man. Sounds like a reporter's dream of a lifetime. Where do we start?"

"Don't know. The police are involved. I've been in touch with Adam Jakes. Probably we should coordinate anything we do with him. I'll talk to him tomorrow," Oxford replied.

"Here's my Osborne card. All my numbers are there. Call me anytime. Meanwhile, I'll give some thought about how to play this. How about lunch? Tomorrow? No, day after, Wednesday. Here." And Tad pointed to the dining room.

"Done. See you then," Oxford said, getting to his feet and putting out his hand. "Now, if you'll excuse me, I have a date."

"You what?" Chris exclaimed. "This is bigger news than we've been talking about. You have a date? Who's the lucky lady?"

"Up yours," Oxford said, smiling. "I'm having dinner with Dorothy Crane. See you tomorrow."

THIRTY-THREE

His message light was blinking as Oxford returned to his Flatlander suite. Val Sisik. Since it was after six, as he returned the call Oxford hoped Sisik would be gone for the day. No luck.

"You're working late," Oxford said when Sisik answered.

"Not really. I have call forwarding to my cell," Sisik replied, then went on, not at all pleasantly, Oxford noted. "You're in town. I was expecting a report from you today. When will I receive it?"

"I was plugged today," Oxford replied, surprised at his own firmness. "But I can make it tomorrow."

"Fine. Nine o'clock. My office," Sisik commanded.

"Sure. That'll work. How do I find you?" Oxford asked.

"Premier's suite. Up the stairs to the second floor, turn left twice. The door on the north wall straight past the elevator. It has a small brass plaque." Sisik rang off.

Things are turning a bit nasty, Oxford thought as he hung up the phone. Well, maybe I can play at that, too, he muttered grimly, surprised at himself.

THIRTY-FOUR

 Oxford had discovered Memories, a downtown restaurant of modest decor but with a famous menu. He pridefully noted that Dorothy in a black sheath turned a few heads as they were escorted to their window seat overlooking Victoria Avenue.

Over rack of lamb they discussed her break-in and his trip to Calgary. Nothing much of value had been taken from the apartment, but a great deal of damage had been done. It seemed all too likely that whoever had broken in had been looking for something in particular.

Learning of Ben's visit to Paul Godfrey closed the puzzle for Dorothy.

"That's what he was doing there. He wasn't checking market potential at all. And Mr. Godfrey's report about what they found from Josef Rafael was what sent Ben into a rage. But why did he hide all that from me?" she asked plaintively. "He used to confide in me completely."

"Probably he was trying to protect you. He could tell that things were getting pretty sticky. Particularly after he decided upon his course of action. Whatever that was," Oxford suggested.

"I guess you're right," Dorothy agreed. And, after a moment, "and I'm glad. And grateful. This is all too much for me."

Oxford decided to include Dorothy in those aware of the

nine million dollar mark up on the Rafael transaction. She was not surprised.

"That's their *modus operandi*, isn't that what they call it? Just the numbers are a little bigger. Sure, they had a scam in mind. No wonder Ben was so upset. He was livid," she said.

"Do you think Halliday knows about it? Is in on it?" Oxford asked.

"Hard to say. But, yes, would be my guess. I don't think even Sisik would have the nerve to try to pull that off under Halliday's nose without cutting him in on the deal."

"What about those codes? They seem to be critical. Any idea where Ben might have stashed them?" he asked.

"Not a clue. Same place as he put the computer disks I gave him, I suppose. Are the codes just numbers on a piece of paper?"

"Seems so. They could be memorized pretty easily, but one would want to have the backup somewhere. Like your pin number, only longer," Oxford said.

"Ben had a very good memory for numbers," Dorothy observed. "He carried an incredible lot of telephone numbers in his head." Then she asked, "Does Sisik know about this yet?"

"Not yet. I'm going to see him in the morning."

"That will really make him determined to find where Ben hid that stuff. Oh! Oxford. This is getting too serious." Dorothy put her hands on the table and sat up straighter.

"I'm frightened, Oxford," she said, "just plain scared. I know there are so many burglaries here that Regina is now B and E City, as Hillary calls it. I read in the papers that there are so many break-ins here that the insurance companies are thinking of getting out of the business. I know I shouldn't feel singled out, but I do. I can't shake the feeling that those horrible people, McCarthy, Justice, that whole bunch, are behind this. And I'd rather have a burglar than them," Dorothy said.

"You see, Hillary might well have been there when this happened, and what then?" she asked. "It was only a last minute thing that she decided to come with me to Little Theatre. They're looking for those files of Ben's and they must think I have them. Will they come again? What am I going to do, Oxford? I'm so worried. I hope I can look after myself, but what about Hillary? She doesn't deserve this." A tear welled in Dorothy's eye.

"Do you think I should ask for police protection? I think I should," she declared suddenly.

"Why would they come back? There was nothing at your place. You should be okay, Dorothy. They might try me next, but I'm going to turn those files over to the police—and to the press. That should stop McCarthy and company from trying to recover them. It will be just too damn late. And I'm going to do that just as soon as I can. Tomorrow, or Wednesday at the latest."

"That will bring a lot of pressure on you, won't it?" Dorothy asked.

"It has to be done. We can't give the files back to them, can we?" he smiled at her.

"No. I guess we can't do that. But, you be careful, too, Oxford," Dorothy said, reaching over and squeezing his hand.

"Oxford, there's something else I've been thinking about," she said, very serious again. "When Ben came back from the goose hunt out at the Halliday ranch last month, he said something that I didn't pay any attention to at the time. But now, maybe, I wonder if it doesn't mean something.

"He said, 'if I'm not around, Oxford should go goose hunting with Reuben,'" Dorothy recalled. "Do you think he meant something by that?"

"Who's Reuben?"

"Reuben Halliday, Harris' older brother. He runs the ranch."

"What's the context? What else was Ben talking about?" Oxford persisted.

"Nothing special. He used to shoot out there every year, usually twice, sometimes more often. When he came back, I asked him how the hunt went. He said it was great, as usual, and then made that remark.

"The 'if I'm not around' part has started looking a little more significant since his death," she added.

"Worth thinking about," was all Oxford could offer, as he handed his credit card to the waiter.

At the coat check, as he held her coat, Dorothy suddenly turned and gave Oxford a hug, then put her hand to his cheek. "Thank you, Oxford. And be careful."

It was a friendly gesture, but Oxford's temperature shot up and his body thrilled. Whew! He watched with new interest as he followed her graceful stride to the door.

THIRTY-FIVE

The Lear jet flashed smoothly down Regina Airport's Runway Twelve and lifted easily into the sky. It made a left turn and by the time it crossed over the IPSCO steel mill a mile north of the city was already passing through 12,000 feet.

Like a scalded cat, thought Sean McCarthy, the Lear's only passenger, thrilled by the plane's speed and performance. Someday I'll have one of these, he promised himself. And maybe sooner than later.

McCarthy was no stranger to executive jets. Many of the corporations courting the Saskatchewan government made their aircraft available to the senior minister. In fact, McCarthy had flown in a number of corporate aircraft and as an intending purchaser had made comparisons of their features. He had settled on the Lear as his favourite. This Lear belonged to ArDan Construction Inc. of Edmonton, the company that had won the contract for the massive hydroelectric project on the Saskatchewan River. The plane was carrying the minister responsible to some sensitive discussions with a view to renegotiating several aspects of that contract.

"May I get you anything, Mr. McCarthy?" asked the attractive hostess. Except for the two pilots up front, she was the only other occupant of the aircraft.

McCarthy ordered a Scotch. It pleased him that ArDan

had provided the hostess, a special touch. When the drink was delivered, he ran his hand up the woman's leg beneath her dress to the curve of her buttock and smiled at her. She made no move to evade his touch and McCarthy wondered if he should change his plan to return to Regina that evening. He made no secret of his appetite for women and guessed that this one had been briefed to accommodate him.

McCarthy smiled to himself. His reputation as a womanizer had extended to the point that he was suspected of having seduced one or two of the young girls who served as pages on the floor of the legislature, delivering messages to the members and running errands. During the last session, as McCarthy leafed through his papers searching for a statistic, one of the opposition back-benchers broke up the House by loudly asking, "What page is McCarthy on now?"

His mind returned to business. ArDan wanted to replace the fixed price for materials on the hydro project with cost-plus provisions. It would add millions to the project cost but McCarthy knew that ArDan would seriously sweeten the contribution they had already made to his Bahamian bank account. There would be an uproar when the opposition found out about the contract change, but McCarthy could handle that. He had already worked out a plausible explanation. These opportunities would not be around for ever, McCarthy knew. It was harvest time.

As he did almost daily, McCarthy ran the mental calculations on his holdings, adding in the number he was sure ArDan would agree to. It was an impressive total, enough to keep the wolf away, but not yet enough to support a Lear jet and a few other ambitions.

The trouble was so much of it was speculative. He had hidden stock in a dozen venture companies. If only one or two made it big, he would be over the top. That mineral play in Chile was the one he prayed for. His interest there was very substantial, and had cost him nothing personally. He had merely granted a few environmental waivers to the mother corporation's mine in northern Saskatchewan.

That idiot Dean, Billy Dean. McCarthy's thoughts became ugly as they turned to his special assistant and the two safety deposit boxes that had fallen into the hands of the police.

It had been a neat arrangement. Although the WDA party fundraisers kept a vigilant eye out for anyone doing business with the government, and forced a sort of tithing into the party accounts, that had not prevented McCarthy from running his own small program. His political staff solicited contributions to the minister's constituency association from all supplicants seeking approvals. Those contributions far exceeded anything needed to run a respectable campaign in McCarthy's rural riding of Pheasant Hills.

It had been Billy Dean's job to run the surplus contributions through a bank account in the name of the riding association but kept in Regina where the local executive knew nothing about it. Dean converted the funds into thousand dollar bills. Every once in a while, when he felt he had too many bills on hand, Dean tucked them into the safety deposit boxes.

Certainly, McCarthy had approved putting the boxes into an assumed name. He did not want his name, or that of his assistant, on them. James Karpan was a good choice.

But Dean forgot to give the bank a forwarding address for James Karpan when they moved out of the Provincial Development offices. And neither of them had been aware that the Western Dominion Bank had decided to close its Albert Street branch. The next thing McCarthy knew that damn cop, Jakes, was around asking questions. Karpan? James Karpan? Never heard of him. Safety deposit boxes? Don't know what you're talking about.

Sweet Jesus! Half a million in nice, cold cash gone like smoke. It had taken seven years to build that stash and McCarthy knew he would not have another seven years to replace it. But this deal with ArDan would make up for his loss. More than make up for it, if he kept his wits about him. The hostess would have to wait.

That young lawyer, what's his name? LaCoste. Ben Forsyth's buddy. Snooping around. Another goddam problem to look after. Never liked that Forsyth. Sanctimonious son of a bitch, even though he was good for the party. Forsyth is gone now, but he left trouble. Well, there's a solution for every problem.

"Seat belt time, Mr. McCarthy. We're dropping in to

Edmonton Municipal now." It was the co-pilot, come back to deliver the message personally.

Sean McCarthy looked at his watch. Just about the hour flat. This was certainly the way to travel.

Thirty-six

Judy Lester was blond and voluptuous and not at all dumb. She handled her duties as the premier's receptionist very adroitly. But she did provoke a lot of ribald comment and gossip that the bachelor Harris Halliday seemed to enjoy.

At one of the WDA cabinet retreats to Cypress Hills, Sean McCarthy went straight to the point. Smiling over his Scotch, he addressed the premier.

"Harris, I sure hope you're fucking that Judy Lester."

"Why?" was the startled response.

"Because everyone sure thinks you are."

Halliday simpered and the observers were never able to reach a consensus on where the truth might lie.

Judy Lester quickly sized up Oxford as he stepped into the premier's suite. She straightened her shoulders, thrusting her impressive bosom forward, and smiled invitingly.

"Mr. LaCoste? Mr. Sisik is waiting for you in the premier's office. This way please," and she stepped forward to usher Oxford into the inner sanctum of Harris Halliday. Judy was disappointed to see that her visitor was so impressed with the offices as to be oblivious to her practised movements.

The office normally occupied by Premier Harris Halliday was suitably impressive, Oxford thought. Large windows east and north overlooking the grounds and the flower beds, now black and waiting for winter. Walls panelled with classical brocade tapestry, finished with oak, above a sumptuous carpet, all spoke of tradition and power. Oxford knew that every one of the premiers of Saskatchewan had governed from here.

Val Sisik was seated behind the large desk opposite the fireplace, his back to the east window. "The premier is holidaying at his ranch for a few days," Sisik said, but offered no other explanation as to why this entitled him to the premier's office in his absence.

After an initial appraisal of Oxford, Patrick Justice stood at the north windows, looking out over the dark gardens and the still-blue Wascana Lake towards the Flatlander. Sisik did not introduce the premier's security advisor whom Oxford noted as wide shouldered and tall, but with a thickening middle that gave him an overall beefy appearance. Straw-coloured hair over eyes that bothered Oxford until he concluded that they were set too close together.

"What do you have for us?" Sisik asked, somewhat imperiously Oxford thought.

"Well, I do have something to report," Oxford said, and delivered the edited version of his Paul Godfrey interview that he had been rehearsing in his mind since awakening early that morning.

"I have copies of the trust documents Mr. Godfrey gave me," Oxford said, as he handed them to Sisik. "I note, however, that they make no mention of amounts. They merely create an open account for the receipt of whatever deposits might come in."

And, Oxford added, striving for a little drama, "I have no codes nor any idea where they might be located."

Sisik had listened intently to Oxford's report. Now he leafed quickly through the documents, paused for a moment, then looked intently at Oxford.

"And that's it?" he asked, with a note of doubt in his voice.

"That's it." Oxford met the deputy's eyes without flinching.

Sisik continued to stare at Oxford, forcing a contest that Oxford found surprisingly easy to handle.

"Do you mean to say," Sisik spoke at last, "that as the surviving executor of Ben Forsyth you are authorized to deal with these funds? But without the codes you are unable to do so?"

"That's as I understand it," Oxford replied.

"You have tested that advice, yes? You have spoken to Windward Trust?"

"No," Oxford admitted.

Again his inquisitor stared at Oxford.

Finally, Sisik stood up. "Fine. We knew the funds had been directed to the Turks and Caicos. Now we know for certain what bank has them and under what arrangements. But not how much or how we can recover them. Not much progress, yes?"

"And," he asked, turning to stare Oxford down, "no explanation as to why Ben Forsyth did this, why all this trouble?"

"None that I've been able to find, sir," Oxford replied, with what he hoped was just the right note of obsequiousness. After all, it was vital that he be believed.

"I see. Presumably Ben had some depository that you have not yet located. Yes?" Sisik didn't believe him.

"I guess that's it, but I don't know where else to look."

"I instructed initially that you keep a sharp lookout for other files Ben Forsyth might have had in his possession. Files bearing upon his work as a minister of this government. What have you to report on that front?" Sisik demanded on a new tack, again fixing Oxford with his intense glare.

Pat Justice left his post by the window and moved over to the premier's desk so that he had a clear view of Oxford's countenance. Now the reason for the security advisor's presence and the use of Halliday's office became fully apparent to Oxford. Sisik had brought to bear all the intimidation he could muster to force Oxford to disgorge any information he might attempt to withhold. I'm under suspicion, Oxford thought.

To Sisik he replied, "I have found nothing of any interest. In fact, I've really encountered no files at all." Then he added, "Mrs. Forsyth has requested all Ben's personal files, but he must have kept them all in their home in Regina here. If so, she will now have them."

Sisik continued to stare at him for a moment, then barked a series of questions that Oxford thought sounded like a script. As the lawyer responded to each one, his distaste for Sisik and Justice grew but so did his confidence. I'm lying through my teeth, he thought, and doing pretty well at it.

Suddenly Sisik's tone lightened. "Well, so be it," he said. "Keep at it, Oxford. Something will soon turn up. You've done good work, so far.

"By the way, Oxford. Ben Forsyth was very cautious. Appointed two lawyers as his executors. One is gone. You are left. What provision if both are gone?"

"Authority passes to Mrs. Forsyth. Pretty standard." Oxford deadpanned his answer, but wondered if the question was meant to intimidate him.

"I see," Sisik mused, as if he didn't see at all. "Premier Halliday is hosting a goose hunt at his ranch. End of season. He has asked me to extend an invitation to you, yes? To join his small party. Ben Forsyth was a frequent guest. The premier thought it would be appropriate if you substituted for Ben. You can do so?"

The switch was too sudden for Oxford. He needed time on this one. Suddenly he remembered Ben's words to Dorothy. "If I'm not around, Oxford should go goose hunting with Rueben." Full ahead slow, boy.

"I think I'd like to do that, if I can get away. All right if I let you know as soon as I can? In a day or two?"

"Certainly. Five o'clock Friday. At the ranch. In time for dinner. Provide your own transportation. You'll be assigned one of the guest houses. All day shooting is on now, so the hunt will run all day Saturday. Dinner Saturday night, too. Optional if you'd like to stay overnight for a ranch breakfast Sunday before leaving. Call Thursday. Yes?" And Oxford was dismissed.

"Why did you do that?" Justice fumed after Oxford had left. "Invite him to that shoot? Why do you want him underfoot?"

"What did you think of his performance?" Sisik asked, ignoring Justice's question.

"He's hiding something. No doubt of it," replied Justice.

"Exactly. And become a little antagonistic, yes? We don't need that. He's supposed to be on our side. So, perhaps a little honey. Or good Scotch. And your western good old boy camaraderie. Time for some Halliday charm, yes? Turn on some charm yourself. Stop acting like a police-officer," Sisik lectured.

"I am a cop, for Christ's sake," Justice retorted, "and, if you'd let me do things my way, we'd have had our answers a long time ago.

"Somebody did Dorothy Crane's apartment over the weekend," Justice continued, then stopped.

"Is that all you know?" an exasperated Sisik asked after a moment.

"I just reviewed the tapes from our friend's room at the Flatlander this morning. Otherwise, I wouldn't know anything about it. I've only had time to make a fast phone call on it. The place was torn apart. Nothing much taken. Obviously someone was looking for something."

"Who then?" Sisik asked.

"Well, they didn't leave a calling card, so I'll give you one guess."

"Who?" Sisik demanded.

"Sean McCarthy. Who else?"

"What! Why him? How do you know?" Sisik was perturbed.

"Who else?" Justice repeated. "He has pretty good listening posts around here. He always seems to know as much as we do. Really, he's overdue to have heard that Ben Forsyth had left some pretty nasty stuff on him. And our Sean is a pretty direct boy."

"But McCarthy's too bright to try something like that himself. Who does that kind of work for him?" Sisik asked.

"Oh, Sean has made connection with some of the local talent. Some boys who will do anything for a buck. And the future considerations Sean promises them. Sean treats them very well. They're not whiz kids, but they think Sean's big-time and they'll try almost anything he wants," Justice explained.

"Good Lord!" Sisik exclaimed. "We can't have that loose

cannon rumbling around the deck. God knows what he'll do."

"Well," Justice replied, "I don't know what you're going to do about it. Sean will be Sean. I sure wouldn't recommend another father to son chat."

"No, that won't work," Sisik agreed, "but think of something that will. And meanwhile, about that girl, Crane. She's still sitting in Forsyth's office? Yes? Get her out of here. In fact, get her out of town. She's trouble. She knows too much."

"What do you want me to do?"

"Transfer her. Prince Albert. LaRonge maybe. Far. Can she refuse?"

"Not likely. She needs the job. Has a kid. No husband."

"Then transfer her. Immediate. Make it attractive. But immediate. Yes?"

"Okay, okay. Consider it done."

THIRTY-SEVEN

Sean McCarthy stepped out of Karl Bramwell's office and closed the door gently behind him. He stopped momentarily with the door at his back, pursed his lips in a silent whistle then broke into a self-satisfied smile and strode down the corridor.

McCarthy had, he knew, just escalated Bramwell's dislike of him to the level of pure hatred, but that was unavoidable and of little consequence. His main purpose had been achieved. Bramwell had made no fuss and had cut the one hundred thousand dollar cheque from the caucus account as McCarthy had requested, claiming that he was following the premier's instructions.

As McCarthy had expected, Bramwell had not believed him when he explained that the premier wanted to be kept clear of the transaction and particularly did not want to know the numbers involved. McCarthy knew that before the caucus chairman would write any such cheque he would call Halliday to confirm the request and would do so the moment McCarthy left his office.

That was when McCarthy played his card. Bramwell, normally a stolid and upright man, occasionally displayed a severe weakness for the grape. Some weeks before, in a Regina restaurant, after many drinks too many, the chairman of the WDA caucus had made a lewd and shocking proposal to a young waitress. The waitress complained to her

200

manager and the scene became ugly. Bramwell and his party had been requested to leave the premises. The next day a hungover but sober Bramwell had sent an emissary to apologize and smooth the ruffled feathers. He had thought the matter hushed up and forgotten, but Ace Kozak's listening posts had picked it up and Ace had passed the item on to Sean McCarthy. For future considerations, Ace had put it.

McCarthy had known immediately that he would one day use the story to good advantage, but had not thought it would become so valuable, and so soon. He had not needed to draw Karl Bramwell a picture.

"By the way, I had dinner down at The Kitchen the other night. I hear you're a bit of a regular there. Great food, eh? And really good service. And the waitresses. Great tits and legs."

That was all it took. Bramwell's eyes filled with fear of exposure, ridicule, and political death. McCarthy watched the resistance wilt and wither. Without another word the caucus chairman called in his secretary and directed her to prepare the cheque.

Sean McCarthy patted his breast pocket, his lips pursed again, and this time the whistle was audible the entire length of the legislative corridor.

THIRTY-EIGHT

Val Sisik stared at the wall full of original oil paintings, his hands clasped behind his back so tightly that his fingers were numb. He was furious. So angry that the art before him swam out of focus. He knew what was there. Luthi, Sapp, Henderson. All Saskatchewan artists. The best the nouveau riche lawyers could find to decorate their boardroom.

Sisik was not a man accustomed to waiting on others and he had counted each one of the twenty minutes since the law firm receptionist had shown him into the room to await the pleasure of the senior partner.

"Mr. Bradley will be right with you," she had said, but Sisik knew better. Vincent Bradley was one of the most arrogant men he had ever met and keeping others waiting upon him was his deliberate style, his method of establishing psychological superiority. There would be no exception for the deputy minister to the premier.

Sisik had never been able to understand why Harris Halliday held such a high regard for Vincent Bradley. The lawyer was now a prominent member of the WDA but he was a Johnny-come-lately, one of the many who saw the merit of the party's program only after its success was assured. Bradley's law firm was large but not particularly well regarded for the calibre of its legal work. Sisik knew that the firm's success was due to an unholy alliance between Bradley and

Sean McCarthy. An alliance that had thrown so much government work to Bradley that his firm had grown in just a few years to be one of the largest in Saskatchewan.

Sisik knew also that Bradley and his partners considered their business and professional conduct to be above reproach, but they took every unscrupulous advantage they could rationalize in some way. Their swank offices carried a ridiculously low rental. To the partnership this was merely an appropriate inducement to a tenant so prestigious as to attract others to their building. In truth, the rental concession was a payoff from the building developer for the political influence Bradley exercised to bring in a number of lucrative government leases.

Bradley had wangled an appointment as chairman of the Economic Renewal Agency, a position that gave him enormous influence over the acceptance or rejection of the many credit applications that came before his board. Applicants quickly learned that becoming clients of Bradley's firm assured approval of their financing proposals. And the lawyer saw no conflict of interest whatsoever in representing both the borrower and the lender in processing the security requirements of the loan. His fees to both were scandalous.

Suddenly, Bradley, accompanied by two junior lawyers and a secretary, swarmed into the conference room as he barked instructions to each of them that could easily have been imparted in his own office an hour later. As his minions departed, the lawyer turned to Sisik.

"Yes, Val, what can I do for you?"

Sisik, noting the absence of either apology or explanation, spoke, in the icy tone that caused cabinet ministers to tremble, "I believe we have . . . had . . . an appointment to discuss those documents I had couriered over to you this morning. At the premier's suggestion, I might add."

Sisik's words had no effect on Bradley. "Oh, yes. Those trust agreements. I had our people run over them. They're really not very well done—not up to our standard—but I suppose they'll work. What about them?"

Sisik gritted his teeth and carried on. "Since the death of Ben Forsyth, who has the direction over that trust?"

"His executors, whoever that might be. We would have appointed an alternate in the documents, but these pass the authority to the executors in the event of Forsyth's death."

"There is also the matter of codes. How necessary are they?" Sisik asked.

"Essential. As a matter of fact we tested that. We don't use Windward Trust, but they seem to be a quite satisfactory institution. We took the liberty of calling them," Bradley said, and then waited, forcing Sisik to make the request.

"And . . . ?" Sisik's tone was menacing.

"Wouldn't give us a thing," Bradley was oblivious to Sisik's anger. "Went so far as to say we were calling on behalf of the Government of Saskatchewan. Didn't impress them at all. They said that they were sure we would expect them to honour the established procedures. Wouldn't even admit that the trust existed, although, of course, that was implied."

"Without the codes there is no access to the trust? Are there no alternatives?" Sisik asked.

"Really only one. If it can be established that the trust was put in place to protect the proceeds of crime, or is part of a criminal transaction . . . " Bradley left his response unfinished.

"I see," Sisik mused, then, "well, that doesn't help, of course," and he stood up to leave. "Thank you."

"Fine. Please give my regards to Harris." Bradley did not acknowledge titles.

THIRTY-NINE

"Jesus! What a crusade. And it hasn't even started yet. But I've got more respect around that crummy paper than I've ever had. And just because I crammed your story down their throats." Tad Osborne threw himself into a chair opposite Oxford.

"I need some plasma. Ordered a double sunblossom on the way in."

"What's a sunblossom?" Oxford was curious.

"Oh! That's a neat little concoction of vodka, tonic, soda, and orange juice. Used to be the standard eye-opener before journalists turned into a bunch of wimpish sippers of mineral water. A sunblossom kick-starts the brain wonderfully.

"I sinned somewhat last night," Tad explained. "Got a wee bit carried away down at the Press Club. Tuned up a couple of WDA flacks who wandered in with their monstrous expense accounts. Looking to give us the daily spin on their insipid handouts, they were. I seem to remember telling them they'd soon be peddling their resumes on the upper reaches of the Orinoco."

"Cripes! Was that a good idea?" Oxford was concerned.

"No. Not a bit. But wonderful fucking fun. Wish you'd been there. Hah!" Tad inhaled half his sunblossom, then smiled blissfully.

"But this is dangerous stuff. You know that. You told me yourself. What the hell . . . ?" Oxford was cut off.

"I know. I know. But what can happen now? I got the go-ahead on the story yesterday afternoon. The *Clarion* will run it as soon as I hand it in. And that will be very damn soon after you get me those files. It's a big eight-wheeler comin' down the track, Oxford. Whooeee!" Then Tad went serious.

"This isn't Watergate only because this isn't Washington D.C., the capital of the world's most powerful nation. But it's our Watergate. It's the biggest political story ever to hit Saskatchewan. And just as Watergate did in Richard Nixon, this story will be the end of Harris Halliday. And a lot of people around him.

"You ever hear of Tammany Hall and a fellow by the name of Boss Tweed?" Tad asked.

"Just barely," Oxford replied. "Ben Forsyth mentioned him. I gather he was a big-time political crook."

"Big time, indeed. Very big time. Operated in New York City more than a hundred years ago. 1860s and 70s. Set the standard, so to speak. Clipped the city treasury for more than thirty million dollars in just one three year period. Thirty million mid-1800s dollars. No idea what that would represent today. His career total was over two hundred million dollars.

"Tammany was the Democratic political machine in New York. Tweed was The Boss. They owned the mayor, the governor, the judges, the prosecutors, the police, you name it. They stole brazenly. Phony invoices for work never done and goods never delivered. Build a courthouse for three million dollars but charge twelve million. Yes. That huge a mark up. Buy land cheap and sell it to the city for millions. Crude. Very crude." Tad leaned into his lecture.

"How did they get away with it? Where was the valiant press? Where was the public outrage? Hah! Where, you ask?" he demanded, poking a finger at Oxford, who had asked nothing, but listened, spellbound.

"All muzzled. Muzzled with money. Same principles being used by the WDA today. Different place. Different people. Same game.

"Tweed bought the New York press with advertising and printing contracts. The owners wouldn't let the editors

206

and newshounds touch Tweed. Some got fired for trying. Even the great Horace Greeley was shackled. Tweed bought public respectability the same way. The elite of the city, the great leaders of the community, were cut in on the action. Tweed kept their property taxes low so long as they stayed in line.

"When things got too hot, Tweed appointed six of those great community leaders as a committee to investigate the city's books. The chairman was the famous John Jacob Astor, then pretty much the world's richest man. Remember? He later went down with the Titanic. But that bunch of citizens above reproach reported that they had personally examined the accounts and found everything absolutely correct. Not a dime missing. Jesus!" Tad stopped to finish his sunblossom.

"Truth was that millions were missing, and they bloody well knew it. Self-interest makes crooks out of a lot of normally decent folks." Tad waved to their waiter.

While they waited for their order, Tad carried on. "How does the Boss Tweed formula compare with what's going on here today? Well, look. Instead of John Jacob Astor take a peek at Glenn Stanton. He touts himself as the self-made prince of private enterprise. His pre-fab plant, AllWest Industries, is one of the biggest employers around Regina. He's also the WDA toady who fronts their Free Free Enterprise political action group. It's supposedly non-partisan but it parrots nothing but WDA tripe.

"Guess who uses his WDA brownie points to con this government into guaranteeing AllWest's debt? Five million dollars to date. That's very hush-hush. Confidentiality agreement. Can't have it known that the spokesman of stand alone capitalism is being propped up by the provincial treasury, now can we?

"Tweed's techniques are in full play here in Saskatchewan today," he went on. "The very people who should be defending us against the WDA pirates are sharing in the loot in some way.

"For example. Where's the Regina Board of Trade? Those stalwart defenders of prudent fiscal management and low taxation? What do you hear from them as Halliday and company pile deficit on top of deficit? Our per capita public debt is now the second highest in Canada, more than fifteen thousand dollars for every man, woman, and child in Saskatchewan. Not a peep from the Board of Trade. As long as it's done in the name of free enterprise—even public bankruptcy is okay." Tad was waving his knife. Oxford couldn't decide if Tad was lecturing a class or conducting a symphony.

"Lawyers and accountants? Don't count. Sorry, Oxford, but your profession gave up its principles years ago, probably when the law schools started drowning us in lawyers we didn't need, don't want. And I'm not sure that accountants ever had any principles, political ones, anyway.

"Doesn't matter. They all snort into the political trough of the day with elbows sharp as switch blades. Whatever the WDA wants to do is fine with them so long as they get lots of government work and charge their ridiculous fees. There'll never be a word of protest against this government from the shysters and the bean counters. They've become nothing better than camp followers.

"And the so-called investigative journalists? There are several neat little ways the WDA has of keeping the newshounds off their ass. Make sure their kids in university have summer jobs. Lots of junkets for the political writers, subsidized to the point that the editors can't refuse the itty bitty cost the paper picks up to make it look clean. Trips to New York to see how our financial geniuses deal with the gnomes of Wall Street. Hah! That's a laugh.

"My friends in the press gallery have been bought and paid for in a dozen little ways. Here's just one. At the end of every legislative session, there's a traditional blow-out in the gallery, attended by all the reporters and the MLAs. Plus all the political staff from all the caucus offices. And anybody else who's thirsty.

"Well, there was the one little blast that got carried away. Just a couple of years ago. Some of our more profound observers of the Saskatchewan political scene decided a water fight with fire hoses seemed like a good idea. By the time the fun was over, the legislative building needed a forty thousand dollar reno job.

"Did you ever hear or read one little word about that from our brave soldiers of the fourth estate? Of course not. Because the WDA quietly picked up all the cost of the repairs. Not a word was said about asking the culprits to pay for their own fun. Hell of a deal for McCarthy and his gang. Bought the whole press gallery for forty grand. Ever since that little caper the guys and dolls covering the legislature have been legally blind to any WDA transgression. They'll be blind for a long time to come. Statute of limitations is six years." Their waiter returned with their lunch. Tad put down his knife. The performance was over.

"When can we get started?" Tad asked.

"I think tomorrow. Adam Jakes is still out of town, but due back later this afternoon. I want to talk to him first. I'll call you as soon as I do."

"Here's to us," Tad said, raising his coffee in a toast. "The brave twosome. Not quite Woodward and Bernstein. But, what the hell. Best we can do. Get those files to me. We'll give everyone something to think about." Tad Osborne stood and put his hand out to Oxford. They shook hands warmly.

Oxford strolled the few blocks to the Flatlander, hands in pockets, head down, full of thought. Tad Osborne had left him with plenty to think about. Although he was determined to carry out his commitment to expose Ben Forsyth's files, his mind churned with concerns. The explosive results could take any number of nasty turns. New possibilities flooded into his mind faster than he could consider them.

Perhaps it was a good thing that Adam Jakes was out of town. Oxford felt a strong need to prepare himself mentally for the ordeal to come. He had been like one charged with a mighty mission but with his feet set in concrete. Anxious to launch his attack on Halliday and company, he was stymied until he could recover Ben's files from Adam Jakes. Although that should only be a few more hours, tomorrow morning at the latest, he had been impatient. Now he thought the delay might be a blessing.

As Oxford entered the Flatlander lobby, wondering what to do with the empty afternoon in front of him, a sudden thought struck. He did not want to spend any more time than necessary in this sleazy place after hearing Tad Osborne's descriptions. In the elevator, he pushed the button for the parking garage. Less than an hour later he was dropping down into the Qu'appelle Valley between Echo and Pasqua Lakes. He had decided upon a colour tour. Even though many of the leaves were gone, the waters sparkled in the brilliant fall sunshine. He crossed the valley floor into the Standing Buffalo Indian Reserve, turned east along the north shore of Echo Lake, across the neck of land that held the town of Fort Qu'Appelle, and followed the road that led him along Mission Lake to the village of Lebret. Here he felt pulled as if magnetically into the parking lot of an old stone church with a prominent steeple. *Sacred Heart Church*, he read. Formerly *La Mission Qu'Appelle—1865*. 1865 was modern times in Quebec, but not in Saskatchewan where recorded history was then just beginning. The cornerstone displayed the Roman numerals MCMXXV. Oxford struggled for a moment before identifying 1925 as the year of construction of the current building. He walked into the adjacent cemetery and read some of the century old granite crosses, several so weathered that the names and dates were almost obliterated.

Oxford, although born and raised Catholic, had never been particularly devout. His father, Yves, had attended mass only to please Marie and Alphonse, first his employers and then his in-laws. Yves had not bothered with the church from the day he had been left alone on the farm. In Montreal, Oxford had dutifully accompanied Marie and Alphonse to mass but had enjoyed his freedom during the summers spent with his father.

At law school in Saskatoon, his already modest faith had quickly withered before the fierce storms of undergraduate logic. His loss, when Oxford finally noticed it, caused only a pang, quickly forgotten.

Now, as he stood in the ancient churchyard he was strangely disturbed. He turned away from the church and the lake. A primitive path, marked with the stations of the cross, wended up a steep hill of the north valley slope. At the top, a large metal cross overlooked the entire valley. It beckoned.

Oxford walked across the road that had brought him

here, and began the climb. As he passed the stations, the lessons of his long ago catechism returned.

When Oxford reached the thirteenth station, he paused only for breath, then turned and mounted a wooden stairway that took him even higher, to the very edge of the valley rim and the large cross that had drawn him. Then he turned to the view below. Mission Lake before him and to the west was a golden shimmer against the late afternoon sun. At the far edge of Mission, Fort Qu'Appelle stood in silhouette against Echo Lake. To the east, Katepwa Lake lay darkly blue in the deepening haze. No boat scarred the sheen of the lakes; the season was over. Oxford's Saab was a toy next to the tiny church.

After a few moments, Oxford chose a spot on the cusp of the hill, crushed the dry and prickly grass beneath his shoes, then sat comfortably. And reflected. Where the hell was he in all this?

Everything that he had learned in the few weeks since Ben Forsyth's death jumbled through his mind, stirred by Tad Osborne's passion. How had the WDA government, as corrupt as it was, come into being? How could Harris Halliday, by all accounts a decent man when conscripted to politics, allow so much evil to flourish all about him? Was the premier of Saskatchewan really part of a scheme to defraud his own government of nine million dollars?

Dorothy Crane had told Oxford that when she and Ben Forsyth first arrived in Regina with the WDA—"two wide-eyed innocents from the country"—Ben had been very open about what went on in cabinet. In those early years Premier Halliday had been very much the captive of a few of the powerful WDA operatives led by Sean McCarthy. In fact, on a few remarkable occasions, the premier had been sent out of cabinet meetings when his protestations had caused difficulties for McCarthy and his group. The first minister sent packing by his own subordinates who were supposedly dependent upon his good will for their very appointments.

In later years, Dorothy said, Halliday had become more assertive, particularly after his second election win. And with the arrival of Vladimir Sisik the premier's office began to wield real authority, although it was questionable as to how much of that emanated directly from Harris Halliday. In any event, Sean McCarthy continued to operate much as he pleased.

Dorothy thought that the premier, his own moral principles desensitized by the graft all around him, finally had become quite capable of making his own grab for loot. She had no trouble believing that a large part of the nine million dollar mark up on the laser purchase was intended for the pockets of Harris Halliday.

Tad Osborne believed the media carried a large share of responsibility for the WDA government. They had so relentlessly exposed every flaw in the background of anyone entering public life that political service was no longer regarded as an honourable vocation. Politics no longer attracted the best and brightest. Anyone with the slightest blemish ran a heavy risk of public humiliation.

"How many accomplished people—achievers—the kind you'd want running your government, have a perfect record?" Tad had demanded. "Smoked a joint in college? Sorry. You're unfit for high public office. It's humanly impossible to avoid all conduct that might look a little stupid later. Abraham Lincoln said it well. He noticed that people without vices were also usually without virtues.

"The media has chased out our good candidates. The field is left to bland do-nothings and the otherwise unemployables for whom politics is a far better deal than they can get anywhere else. So, we get the WDA."

Tad's exaggeration did not fit Ben Forsyth, Oxford knew. Nor Harris Halliday. They and others with accomplished careers had been attracted to politics for the right reasons. But somehow they had been sucked into the swamp of corruption by those around them, those who did fit Tad's description.

Tad Osborne made Oxford nervous. He was just too damn gung ho, too much 'full speed ahead and damn the torpedoes.' There would be torpedoes. Chris Rossom had convinced him of that. But Oxford now agreed with Chris that, without Tad to detonate the publicity, it would be nearly futile for him to try blowing Ben Forsyth's whistle on the Halliday government.

So he needed Tad Osborne. And would have to put up with Tad's ebullience and the risks it created. Hopefully, there would be no more stupidity. Christ! Tad's tantrum at the Press Club was a serious mistake. Good thing the balloon is going up this week. If Chris is right, any damn thing could happen if this story leaked out prematurely.

Oxford wondered if he could stand up to the heat when it came. He knew that he had never been in a tight corner, never had to test his courage, never really tasted danger. Nothing like Marcel and Claire in their years under the Gestapo.

Oxford shivered. The sun was sinking. Although he still sat in sunshine, it was no longer warm. Below him the light had left the Qu'Appelle Valley and the blue haze deepened into darkness. The shadow line began to rise toward Oxford, up the path he had climbed, seeming to pause at each station of the cross before enveloping it and moving to the next.

Oxford's eyes turned down and into the valley where the old church stood bathed in shadows. A memory struck him like a stone.

Driving alone through rural Quebec one Saturday evening he had come upon a church much like this one. A mass was beginning. He was drawn in, where he was astonished to notice a casket before the altar. He must have blundered into a funeral. But it was prayers.

The priest was explaining. The casket contained the remains of a parishioner, a good friend whose funeral would be on the morrow. It was a blessing she could be with us tonight.

"One day we will all come to this," the priest continued. "In this church or another like this one. In a casket much like this. But very likely we will have little to say about our casket. How grand it shall be. Where and when it shall rest. No! Those decisions—those choices—will be made by others after our passing. *'For our days of choosing are now!'*" the priest thundered.

As the power of the long ago words returned to him, Oxford's mind and vision suddenly cleared. He saw the damned legal niceties for what they were. The supposed conflict of interest. The question of where his loyalties belonged. Could he act on the information he held, or did it belong to his client, the government? What duty did he owe Ben Forsyth? Cameron Hunt? Oxford LaCoste?

FUCK IT! He started as the profanity, unusual for him, burst forth. Then it continued. Fuck conflict of interest! Fuck Val Sisik, Premier Halliday, all of them! Fuck the Law Society! They can stick their license up their ass if it comes to that. Fuck Oxford LaCoste if he hasn't got the balls to step up to the plate. This is your decision, young Oxford. Your call. Your life afterwards. Your time of choosing. So fucking well choose right!

The catharsis was over as suddenly as it had begun. And he knew the power of the command of self.

He looked down the dusking valley and his shoulders raised as the burden of indecision lifted from him. It was his day of choosing and he had chosen.

Oxford stepped down the wooden stairs, surprised at his determination as he contemplated the undertaking before him. It was unlike him, he thought, but welcome. The answer had come to him. He stopped momentarily. Then he smiled. In spite of his pretended decision and firmness, he had been harbouring doubts. Now they were gone. Good, now on with it.

At his car Oxford suddenly decided to treat himself to a decent dinner, another rarity. Sally Rossom had spoken of a wonderful restaurant in Wolsley, a restored fine residence, La Parisienne. It lay not many miles further east. He pointed the Saab east. Perhaps the menu would fit the name.

FORTY

Oxford closed the door to his suite and leaned back against it, weary after his long afternoon and too large a dinner at La Parisienne. Across the room his message light beckoned. Inspector Jakes. Finally back in town, Oxford first thought.

But surely Adam Jakes was not returning telephone calls at nine o'clock at night? Oxford wondered, noting the time of the message as he dialled the inspector's direct line.

"Can you come down to my office right away? I'll send a car if you like." Jakes was all business.

Oxford had not seen the Regina Police Station at night before, and wondered if the buzz of activity was normal. This time a plainclothes officer came for Oxford and ushered him back to Jakes' office. The inspector was on the phone but waved Oxford to a seat. When he hung up, Jakes got up and closed the door. Oh-oh! This is different, Oxford noted.

"Sorry to trouble you so late, but we've a bit of an event on our hands," Jakes began. Oxford smiled and waved the inconvenience away.

"Tad Osborne was murdered tonight," Jakes stated. Oxford started out of his chair, mouth agape and eyes staring. Frozen in shock, he did not respond.

"We're checking everyone who had been in recent contact with the deceased," Jakes said formally, "and we find you on that list." He consulted some notes. "As recently as lunch today, in fact."

Oxford's mind was spinning out of control. He wanted to put his foot out against the wall and steady it.

"I only met him the other day. After I left here—you." Oxford was sure he was stammering. "Am I under suspicion?" he blurted.

"I hardly think so," Jakes replied, more gently now. "But we hope you can help us. The first few hours of a homicide investigation are critical. May I ask what your business was with Mr. Osborne?"

"I spoke to him about doing a story on those files you have. I had decided to turn them over to him. I called you yesterday to clear it with you. Your office said you were out of town. Same thing today," Oxford explained, the spinning now almost stopped. Cripes, he thought, I'm supposed to be a lawyer and this guy scared me right out of my wits. No wonder my clients fold under police questioning.

"Who else knew that?" Jakes continued the questioning.

"Chris Rossom. Dorothy Crane. No one else."

"Are you positive?" Jakes pressed.

"Positive that no one else learned of it from me," Oxford assured him. "No! Wait. Tad told his editors. Yesterday, he said."

Jakes considered this for a moment. "We have already checked his computer at the *Clarion*. He had some rough notes, just unconnected thoughts really, on the story he was planning. But it would be enough to alert anyone close to the Halliday government."

"Oh! My God!" Oxford blurted.

"Let's not jump to conclusions. Had Osborne told you his plans for the rest of the day? Did you speak to him again this afternoon or evening?"

"No. I was waiting to get in touch with you. Would have if I'd been able to," Oxford explained.

"Yes. I was away. Sorry." Jakes apologized.

"Guess it doesn't matter now." Oxford was calming down. "What happened?"

"Mr. Osborne had been seated alone at his usual table in the lounge at the Hotel Saskatchewan when he received a phone call. We have established that the call came from a phone booth. It was made about 5:30 P.M. He left almost immediately after. We have not yet located anyone who saw him alive after that. His body was discovered shortly after 7:00 P.M. on a little-used sideroad a few miles east of the city. The body was nude to the waist. His jacket and shirt were thrown in the ditch. His hands had been bound. Cigarette burns on the torso and two crushed fingers, apparently with pliers left at the scene. A strong suggestion of torture," he continued.

"Although we don't have any medical report yet, death seems to have been caused by a severe knife wound in the region of the heart. It appears that the event was interrupted by the approaching headlights of the car that discovered the body. A vehicle was seen leaving the scene in a hurry." Jakes was finished. He looked at Oxford.

Oxford felt his emotions drain into a puddle at his feet. He was devastated and could barely speak. "Those damn files," he croaked.

"Perhaps. Maybe even probably. Until now we had no hypothesis at all. Although a colourful man, even abrasive, Mr. Osborne had no serious enemies we are aware of," Jakes said.

"But," Oxford sputtered, "we only met yesterday. How would anyone find out so quickly?"

"Did he say anything else about the story project? Anyone he might have talked to about it?" Jakes asked.

"Just his editors. Yesterday afternoon. He said they had cleared it to run." An awful thought struck Oxford like a hammer.

"I killed him," he said. "I killed him with those files. Just like I killed Cameron Hunt with them."

"No! You did not," Jakes said sharply. "You didn't kill Cameron Hunt and you didn't kill Tad Osborne. Pull yourself together. You're needed. Now more than ever. Go back to your hotel and go to bed. You need some rest and I have work to do. I'll call you tomorrow when things calm down a bit around here," and Jakes stood up.

Oxford leaped to his feet. "Good Christ," he exclaimed, in an unusual burst of profanity. "Dorothy. She might be next. Why didn't we think of that?" he demanded of Jakes.

"Actually, you're likely next, if you're looking for priorities on your file theory. But, yes, I'd suggest she take some extra care," Jakes temporized.

"I don't care about me. I don't want any more death on my conscience, thank you. May I borrow your phone? Thank you." Oxford was back in control of himself. Very much so.

"Dorothy? Oxford. Something's happened. No time for explanation right now. Put on your dressing gown, whatever, I'm coming over. We'll talk when I get there." Oxford hung up and turned to Jakes.

"We have quite a few things to talk about tomorrow. I'll be at this number or the Flatlander. And I've got this cell phone." And Oxford scribbled the numbers of Dorothy Crane's apartment and his cell phone on the inspector's pad, and was gone, leaving Adam Jakes looking slightly abashed.

Dorothy shuddered in horror as Oxford related an expurgated version of the death of Tad Osborne. She sat quietly, perched in an armchair with the purchase label still attached, her feet drawn under her, make-up removed, housecoat chin high. Oxford thought he had never seen anything more touching.

"So," he concluded, "I don't know what happens now. Hopefully we'll find out tomorrow."

Dorothy's brown eyes gazed steadily at Oxford as if she was digesting his information and considering a decision. "I mentioned police protection the other night. What about that?" she asked. "Obviously you and I are in considerable danger. And what about Hillary? She doesn't even know about all this. But she's right in the middle of it."

"Maybe that's a good idea. But I doubt there's anything Jakes can do about it tonight. It's too late. Likely he couldn't find people without pulling them off other details. I doubt he could do that without clearance." Oxford had no idea if that was so, but it sounded plausible. "So, you'll have to make do with me for tonight," he said, with a smile that he hoped projected confidence. "If you'll dig up a blanket and a pillow, I'm going to camp on that couch tonight. I'm not leaving you alone."

The result startled and pleased him as Dorothy's eyes widened and then she threw her arms around him in a tight but brief hug. "Thank you, Oxford. I'll feel so much better with you here." This time he hugged her back, his hands around the small of her back, pulling her to him.

"I can do better with that couch," she said after a moment. "That's a fold-out. It'll just take me a moment to make it up."

In the night, Oxford was sure he sensed Dorothy straightening his covers and brushing a kiss over his ear. He was almost certain he had not dreamed it.

FORTY-ONE

When Adam Jakes called the next morning, they were sitting over coffee, uncertain what to do next. Dorothy had booked off work until further notice. With misgivings, she had allowed Hillary to go to school.

Jakes accepted Oxford's invitation and drove over to join them. He claimed he had been able to snatch some sleep, but he looked weary.

"There's not much more to report," he said. "We have some promising stuff at the crime lab, but we'll have to wait for results. Everything else is tamped down for the moment. We confirmed that Mr. Osborne's meeting with his editors took place. The response was positive. The paper was going to carry the story. Subject, of course, to it meeting the usual journalistic standards." Jakes repeated this last bit somewhat dryly. And, of course, subject to appropriate verification," this he underlined with lifted eyebrows.

"All that is standard, I'm sure," Jakes continued. "So much so that I wonder why it was necessary to emphasize it. Doing so might have increased our problem."

"How so?" Oxford asked.

"Well," Jakes replied, "if those conditions were told to someone else, in the manner they were described to me, it would be almost an invitation, at least a suggestion, that the story could be prevented by seizing the evidence. Of course," he said, and this caustically, "no one who took part in the meeting with Tad Osborne has said a word about it to anyone else. But maybe I've just heard too much 'I didn't do it' in my time."

"How many were at the meeting?" Oxford asked.

"Three, in addition to Tad Osborne," Jakes replied.

"Do you mean," Dorothy asked, "that there is a possibility that someone at the *Clarion*, one of those men, might have let someone at the government know that story was coming? Someone like Sean McCarthy or Patrick Justice?"

"It's a possibility we'd be foolish not to consider," Jakes replied.

"There's another possibility," Oxford announced. "Tad got carried away at the Press Club—the night before his death. He told me about it. He told a couple of government press officers they'd be looking for new jobs a long way from here once his story ran. I'm sorry, Adam. I should have remembered that last night. I guess I was too upset."

"That's okay. No harm done. Glad you remembered now. We'll check that out."

"But that's awful," Dorothy exclaimed. "That's a sentence of death for Oxford if McCarthy or Justice know he has those files. I know those men. They'll stop at nothing to protect themselves."

"It was a sentence of death for Tad Osborne if that's what happened," Oxford observed.

"I'm not saying it did, but we had best keep the possibility in mind," Jakes said.

"But, if we have that concern," it suddenly occurred to Oxford, "who else at the paper can we trust with the files? Sure, we can make copies, but what good does that do if the writer is protecting the government? The story will be so watered down as to be useless."

"I noted that the *Clarion* editors didn't offer to put another writer on the story," Jakes said. "It was as if the matter had been closed by Osborne's death. I'm sure there are other writers there who would love to have the story, but none with enough courage to threaten to take the story to the *Globe and Mail* if it didn't receive proper coverage."

"What do we do, then?" Dorothy asked.

"Wait. At least for now," Jakes replied. "Whoever it is who wants those files doesn't have them yet. And it seems they're not likely to stop until they do. So, since there's not much else we can do, we wait and watch until they move."

Oxford and Dorothy considered this for a moment, then Oxford spoke for them.

"We've been concerned about Dorothy's safety, since her apartment was ransacked. And especially since Tad Osborne last night. Whoever it is out there obviously thinks she might have the files. Shouldn't she have some protection? And Hillary, her daughter?"

Jakes looked calmly at the two of them.

"After what happened to Tad Osborne last night, I think it's a safe assumption that whoever carried out that interrogation found out exactly what he wanted to know. Unless Tad was an unusually strong man. Even then I doubt he'd have considered the information worth dying to protect. So they know who has the files. Our friend Oxford here. In fact," Jakes continued, "it would probably draw unwelcome attention to Dorothy if we assigned a police-officer to sit on her doorstep. Wouldn't that signal that there was something other than Dorothy we were concerned about?"

There was a moment's reflection on this. Then Dorothy sprang to her feet, suddenly angry.

"But what about Oxford? You're saying they know he has the files. You're leaving him exposed. Like bait." She waved a finger at Adam Jakes. "Just like one of those goats they tether out to attract the tiger. You can't *do* that."

"Well, not quite," Jakes replied. "The goat gets dragged out to the stake quite against his will. We are not making Oxford's situation any worse. We're just admitting that at the moment we can't make it any better. What else do you see we can do?"

"Get rid of the files," Dorothy exclaimed. "For a start. Then advertise that in some way. To do nothing is a stupid option."

Oxford and Jakes looked at each other, then Oxford spoke. "I've already done that, Dorothy. Adam has the files. Has had them for a week. We just haven't told anyone that yet. And I'm not sure we should now, either."

"Why not?" she persisted. "Why get yourself killed?"

"I don't think it's that simple. Chris Rossom convinced me that it's not just the files. Hell, for all they know we could have made so many copies by now they'd never run them all down. It's somebody behind the files to give them credibility. Ben had that credibility. Probably I do too, acting in his place, so to speak. So, just dumping the files doesn't quite take the heat off me, I'm afraid. Different if Tad had been able to run his story. Then it would be too late. Or mostly so. Once the story is out in the public, there's not much point in shooting the messenger. Gets too dangerous, too."

"Do you agree?" Dorothy demanded of Jakes.

"Pretty much. Once the story runs, it's too late to suppress it. Should remove motive."

"Then let's get another reporter. Now. Today."

"I'm going to," Oxford said. "And this time it's the Globe and Mail."

"They don't have anybody here, Oxford," Dorothy said. "Their stringer out of Winnipeg covers this town."

"Okay, then. Winnipeg it is. I'll call today. How much time do we have, Adam?"

Jakes shrugged. "Hard to say. But some. I expect Tad Osborne's death will cause some considerable consternation. And, hopefully, confusion. I don't think it was intended that he die. I'd be surprised if any more serious moves were made for a while. The heat's on, as they say."

"Business as usual, then, until I can locate another reporter with balls. But there's another matter. I've been invited to a goose hunt at the Halliday ranch this weekend," Oxford announced. "I'm to let them know today if I'm going to accept. What do I do?" he asked Jakes.

"Who issued the invitation?" Jakes always went for the details, Oxford noted.

"Val Sisik," he replied, then added the detail without waiting to be questioned. "Tuesday morning when I reported on the fifteen million dollar trust. We met in the premier's office, by the way."

"Oh, yes. We need to talk about that," Jakes said, "but carry on with this for now. Where do you meet? Who will be in the party?"

Oxford supplied all he had been told by Sisik.

"But there's another element. An important one. Dorothy, please tell Adam about that strange comment of Ben's."

She turned to Jakes. "Ben went shooting at the premier's ranch last month. He often did. It was the season opening, I think. When he came back, he said something like 'If I'm not around, Oxford should go goose hunting with Reuben.' That's the premier's brother," she added quickly, seeing Jakes' question coming.

"I didn't pay any attention to it at the time, but it came back to me the other day. With Ben's death, I thought maybe it had some significance," she said.

"Interesting," was all Jakes said. He turned to Oxford.

"Are you a goose hunter?" he asked.

Oxford explained that he was not much of a hunter of anything. He did own a pretty good shotgun, and did do some pheasant and upland bird shooting along the Willow River and its coulees, but nothing else. He had never hunted geese.

Jakes weighed some pros and cons before Oxford and Dorothy. Most goose hunting is done from pits, he explained, holes dug or drilled into the ground so that the hunter can make himself as invisible as possible to wary geese attracted to the decoys. With proper conduct, it is a very safe sport. But shotguns, particularly with heavy loads of powder and shot, are very lethal weapons. And in a situation where everyone has a shotgun, accidents can happen. Every few years, the inspector said, some goose hunter was killed, usually when he leaped up in his pit in front of a companion taking aim at a low flying bird.

Obviously, it would be a very dangerous situation for Oxford to place himself in, but it was preposterous to think that anyone would be planning to do harm to him in the presence of the premier of the province, Jakes suggested.

"No! It's not," Dorothy interjected vehemently. "It's just how these people would think. They'd think that was just good cover. You don't know them like I do."

Jakes looked at Dorothy for a moment, then said, "You might be right, at that." He turned to Oxford.

"Well, what do you think?"

"I think I'm going. That comment of Ben's seems to make it worth the risk. I don't know why I'm being asked, but I can't find out if I don't go."

"Oxford, you can't. It's too dangerous." Dorothy was determined.

"I'll be careful. Somehow we have to find out what the hell is going on around us." "Besides," he said to Dorothy with a smile, "I hope I'm a bit smarter than your average goat. I'll call you tomorrow. I'd better get going now. Got some travelling to do."

Back at the Flatlander Oxford bought a *Globe and Mail* at the newstand. In his room he looked up the Winnipeg bureau, called and left his number. Half an hour later his call was returned. Jane Lindsay. How could she help?

Oxford explained, perhaps too circumspectly he thought as he detected doubt in her responses, then went further. "It's an exposé of the Halliday government. Fully documented. It's one very big story. Tad Osborne of the *Clarion* was going to run it. He was killed last night, we think to stop the story."

That did it. Jane Lindsay wanted the story. She would move heaven and earth, but she couldn't possibly get to Regina before Monday. Would that be soon enough?

"It will have to do," Oxford replied. Then he thought about the goose hunt. He had to get down to West Willow tonight and over to the Halliday ranch tomorrow afternoon. "Yes. That will work just fine. Call me here when you get in."

FORTY-TWO

Vladamir Sisik was in a cold fury, barely controlled.
"What are you able to tell me?" The question was
directed at Patrick Justice.

"Very little more," Justice replied. "My sources at the
station say that our friend Mr. LaCoste was called down for
questioning last night, but didn't stay long. He didn't return
to his room, so there is nothing on the tape after his callback to the police last night. That's current to early this
morning when I cleared the tapes. Tad Osborne, Oxford
LaCoste, and a local lawyer by the name of Chris Rossom
were seen having drinks in the Hotel Saskatchewan
Monday afternoon. That was Osborne's watering hole.

"You know that Osborne and LaCoste were planning a
story. They spoke by phone Tuesday. That's on our tape. They
were to meet for lunch yesterday. As far as I know they did."

"And who was stupid enough to kill the reporter?" Sisik
asked.

"I'd guess some of McCarthy's friends. It seems it was-
n't intentional. Just some heavy questioning that got interrupted," Justice replied.

Sisik pounded his fists together and cursed long and
eloquently in a language unknown to Justice. Then he
stared at Justice for a long moment.

"LaCoste lied to us about those damn files, as we suspected. He also lied to us about the codes, yes?"

"Seems reasonable. But maybe not. Fifty-fifty," Justice said, then asked, "Why would LaCoste hold out the codes on us?"

Sisik ignored that question and asked another of his own. "What will McCarthy try next?"

Justice looked at him for a moment, then said, "I see. If McCarthy's goons make the same mistake with LaCoste as they did with Osborne the codes to that fifteen million dollars go up in smoke. Probably forever. If LaCoste has them."

"Exactly. Now find me a solution," Sisik hissed.

FORTY-THREE

 "Oxford! I'm so glad you called." Dorothy sounded sincerely pleased.

"Said I would," he replied woodenly, then recovered. "I'm glad too. How're you doing. Everything okay?"

"No! Not okay. Definitely not. Oxford, I've been fired. Letter came by courier this afternoon. They've offered me a position in Prince Albert. In the Lands Branch. I'm supposed to report next week."

"Can they do that?"

"'Fraid so. As a minister's secretary I'm an order-in-council appointment. They can terminate me at any time. Usually they try to find another position in the public service. This means they really want me out of here. They'll know I can't move to Prince Albert. Not with Hillary in school here. I told you I was just marking time. Now I'm not. Damn."

"What happens if you don't go?" Oxford didn't quite understand.

"That's it. Finito. My present appointment is terminated next week. The job in P.A. is just a sop. It's a serious downgrade, although they are offering to protect my salary. And pay moving expenses. But if they wanted me around they'd find me something here in Regina. I'm unemployed. Know of anybody who'd like a reasonably competent secretary with lots of political experience? Ha!" She was bitter.

"Maybe. But not offhand. Hey, Dorothy, we'll find some-

228

thing. Don't panic. I'll be back in Regina Sunday. I'm seeing the reporter Monday morning. We'll work on this together. How about dinner?"

"Sure. With pleasure. This time on me. And I'm alone. I told Hillary to stay put down in West Willow for another couple of days. I've lots of time now to show you I do know how to cook. Oxford, I'm sorry to lay my troubles on you. You've plenty on your mind right now. You got ahold of the *Globe and Mail* then."

"Gal named Jane Lindsay. She's plenty interested. I'll call you Sunday when I know more about my travel times. And, no apology necessary. I want to help. Take care."

"*You* take care, Oxford. Watch those people. They're every bit as bad as I said they are. I don't want anything to happen to you. And, Oxford . . . thanks. I feel so much better just having talked to you. G'night."

"Night." Oxford sat staring at the phone for several moments. Dorothy. It had not before occurred to him how tough life as a single mom must be. Losing a job could be the end of the world. He'd find her another job. Chris Rossom would probably jump at the chance to have someone as competent as Dorothy in his office.

What about his own office? Hadn't Ethel Tremblay said something about wanting to hang it up before long? Would Dorothy consider moving back to West Willow?

Was this opportunity in disguise?

FORTY-FOUR

Nestor "Ace" Kozak sat at his usual table. The Fireside Lounge, in a hotel just a few blocks down the street from the Saskatchewan, was the darkest bar in Regina and privy to a good deal of covert conversation. Ace transacted much of his business here.

Ace's main line of work was euphemistically called bill collecting. He was the last resort of a number of otherwise respectable businessmen, and others, some of whom did not bother to attempt more conventional methods. Ace had developed a deserved reputation for squeezing money out of hopeless situations, without regard for the niceties of actual liability. Even bankruptcy did not deter Ace. Although he had never actually smashed a kneecap, he had convinced many that they would be a long time in recovery unless they conjured up some cash. No one officially complained, anxious to avoid a repeat visit to a number of interesting pressure points Ace had drawn to their attention.

But Ace was no narrow specialist. His line of work was constantly expanding as more opportunity came his way. Having learned the value of information, he maintained a network of listening posts throughout Regina. He paid special attention to barmaids and cocktail waitresses with good ears. Ace was aware that some introductions qualified for payment under the heading of finders' fees.

Early experiences with the Regina police had taught Ace

the futility of small-time crime. Breaking and entering would now be undertaken only on retainer. But his skills were still sharp.

Ace had not yet pulled off the big score, but he was confident he was getting closer. The client he was expecting tonight came with a lot of promise and potential.

Sean McCarthy eased his big frame into the booth opposite Ace. Sean was not happy. "What happened?" he demanded, even before he sat down.

"Well, you know Artie. He likes his work a little too much, and he got carried away. If that fucking car hadn't come along, it would have been okay."

"I don't know Artie. I've never met him, and I never will," McCarthy sternly reminded his listener.

"What did you learn?" he asked.

"He didn't have any files. He was waiting to get them from the lawyer. They were going to meet the next day. Thought he'd get them then."

"And the lawyer still has them?"

"Seems so." Ace shrugged.

"Do we know where?"

"No." McCarthy's anger was making Ace nervous. His left hand tightened around the glass it had been fondling.

McCarthy looked at his companion for a long moment, then said, "I think you should take a holiday, a long one. Take Artie with you. Drive down to Vegas.

"This was a complete fuck-up," McCarthy continued, his fury now spilling out. "I give you a simple little assignment—just get me some information—and you turn it into murder. I didn't tell you to kill Osborne—just squeeze him a little. You should pay me for all the trouble you created, but I want you out of town. I'll look after this myself from here. Go."

With that, McCarthy picked up the large ashtray, then put it down with several bills underneath, stood and strode out of the bar.

After a moment, Ace palmed the bills, noting the one thousand dollar denomination as he swiftly moved them under the table where he counted them with a practised thumb. There were ten.

231

Then he reached into his jacket pocket, switched off the voice activated Sony recorder and disconnected the microphone jack. He unclipped the tiny mike from just inside his left cuff and pulled the cord through the sleeve. Ace patted the recorder inside his pocket, looked after the departed Sean McCarthy and smiled. His ship had just come in. That recording would keep him on easy street for the rest of Sean McCarthy's life.

FORTY-FIVE

Oxford was a jumble of emotions as he set out for the Halliday ranch. Volunteering for the expected danger of the goose hunt was, he knew, very much out of his character. Although he felt compelled to go, he suspected his real reason was to avoid being convicted of cowardice in his own mind.

He had never been the macho type, looking for ways to strut his manhood. But he felt Cameron Hunt and Ben Forsyth watching him from a far distance, and knew that if he turned away from the challenge he would be betraying them.

Then there were his grandparents, Marcel and Claire. How would he have handled the dangers of living under the Nazi occupation? Faced with such everyday bloody reality could he, as they did, actually defy and attack the awesome power of Hitler's war machine?

Is heroism an inherited trait or just an accident of circumstance? If it is a matter of genes, Oxford was sure he was the skip generation of the LaCoste line. Maybe, he thought, it's just an addiction. He had read of people addicted to the rush of adrenaline. Would a daily dose of danger lead to the craving for more?

Whatever. Oxford noticed that as he neared the Halliday ranch his mission took on a different flavour than it had a few days ago back in Regina. Here it was not quite so academic. A lot easier to taste, he thought, as he felt the dryness in his mouth.

He had chosen the old Jeep for the occasion. Deliberately, as another declaration of independence. Sam was brokenhearted when Oxford and the Jeep, complete with shotgun and hunting gear, left West Willow without him.

Adam Jakes and Oxford had gone over the goose hunt proposal two or three times before deciding that it was an acceptable risk. They finally concluded that, on balance, the chances of uncovering something helpful outweighed the likely dangers. But Jakes had left the final decision to Oxford, making sure he understood the risks.

The murder of Tad Osborne had been the largest factor, both pro and con, in their debate. As Jakes said, that event proved that there was very real danger afoot, but it was dangerous for Oxford wherever he was—West Willow, Regina, or goose hunt. The balance tipped when Jakes opined, for reasons he did not make clear to Oxford, that there was a strong likelihood Oxford's excursion would shake loose new and useful information.

Oxford had pushed Jakes with more questions about Ben Forsyth's death, but the inspector was reticent. What about that black Mercedes? What about Ruth? And her so-called friend? What had they been up to the night Ben died? Something directly tied to the death? Or some illicit activity that diverted Ruth's attention from the problem in the garage?

It seemed unbelievable to Oxford that Ruth could have deliberately contributed to her husband's death. But Cameron Hunt's note rankled. After she became suspicious Hunt had the files, someone came looking for them.

Jakes had responded to Oxford's inquisitiveness with the stock line that his men were pursuing several lines of investigation.

When Oxford telephoned Sisik to accept the invitation, he learned he would be joining the premier, his brother Reuben, Sisik, Patrick Justice, and Sean McCarthy. Jakes had smiled when told that McCarthy would be in the group. That seemed to settle the question for him. He told Oxford that they might as well have all their ducks on the same pond.

Once the decision to go was made, Jakes moved onto planning. He intended to give Oxford as much support and protection as he could. Jakes and some of his men would position themselves in the vicinity of the Halliday ranch. Oxford was to carry his cell phone, even while hunting, and he memorized the number of a phone Jakes would have with him.

"But is there coverage out there?" Oxford had asked. Jakes grinned as he explained that he had checked that out. The first rural area in the province to receive cellular coverage from the government telephone corporation had included the premier's ranch. Purely coincidental, Jakes observed, but wonderfully convenient for us.

As Oxford approached the ranch and his trepidation increased, he thought of Cameron Hunt's career as a bomber pilot. I'm not even sure that anyone is going to shoot at me, he admitted, and I'm nervous. Hunt went out sixty times knowing full well that a lot of very big guns wanted to shoot him out of the sky.

And Marcel and Claire LaCoste. They lived every moment day and night for years in constant danger of the ugly fate that finally did claim them. But their wits and cool heads had saved them often.

The letter from Marcel's colleague in the Maquis had described one narrow escape. Marcel had been holed up in a small hotel owned by a supporter of the Resistance when a lookout dashed in with word that the Gestapo were coming. Without enough time for flight, the proprietor took Marcel to the dining room. He pleaded a shortage of tables to a group of Wehrmacht officers and secured their permission to seat Marcel with them. When the Gestapo burst into the hotel, their only possible suspect was a French civilian calmly reading the menu surrounded by officers of the German army.

Compared to that kind of danger this is a tea party, Oxford told himself, so stop being a wimp. He turned his mind to the pleasant side of his mission.

He was looking forward to visiting the Halliday ranch. Since his return to West Willow, Oxford had become interested in the early ranching history of the region and the

Halliday brand was one of the oldest. It reached back before the turn of the century when Rube Halliday, grandfather of the current owners, arrived with cattle he had driven from Wyoming. Running for miles along the north shore of the South Saskatchewan River in the western sector of the province, the Halliday ranch was a modern and fully self-sufficient cow-calf operation with a strong sideline in grain production.

Oxford's historical interest had been sparked by the story of Harmon Jasper and his Sunburst Ranch. That led him to investigate the other large cattle spreads that had moved onto the open range of southwest Saskatchewan in the early years. He was intrigued by their romantic names, the Turkey Track, the T-Down Bar, the 76, the Matador. The Matador, Oxford knew, had occupied more than 130,000 acres next to Rube Halliday until it was broken up in the 1920s.

A number of ranchers were clients of Hunt, Forsyth, and LaCoste and Oxford shamelessly inveigled invitations to visit them. He found that each spread displayed the free souled personality of their founders melded to the choice of site, usually a deep, wooded coulee with ample spring-water. None of them resembled the Cartwright Ponderosa. Oxford loved them all.

Oxford had heard descriptions of the Halliday spread. As the decline in the population of rural Saskatchewan turned several nearby communities into ghost towns, the Hallidays had gathered up a number of small houses and moved them to the ranch. Converted into guest cottages along either side of the main drive leading to the ranchhouse, their addition to the other numerous buildings of the Halliday head-quarters gave the whole the appearance of a small village.

The current Hallidays, Rueben and Harris, had turned the ranch into a model of purebred Hereford cattle and cereal grain production. Big, burly Rueben, the elder, was the unquestioned decision maker. The much slighter Harris, in spite of his office and a superior academic education, deferred to his imposing brother. Rueben was the hands-on cattleman, Harris the technologist. The premier had begun his career as a bureaucrat. With degrees in agricultural economics, he spent several years in Ottawa before returning to the ranch to institute a program of scientific performance testing.

Halliday Herefords were very much in demand. Their annual ranch production sale was a price and trend-setter for the industry.

Sean McCarthy's enlistment of Harris Halliday for the leadership of the WDA had been inspired choice. The WDA's natural constituency was rural Saskatchewan, and Harris Halliday was accepted so readily the Party's pollsters had trouble believing his approval ratings.

Oxford arrived as instructed at five o'clock and was met by a pleasant woman who introduced herself as Beth Halliday, Reuben's wife. Following her directions, Oxford parked in front of a small cottage at the end of the row. Drinks would be served in the ranchhouse at 5:30, Beth told him. Dress entirely casual.

Reuben Halliday was tending bar beside a huge field-stone fireplace. Oxford noted sharply creased khaki trousers above snakeskin western boots, a navy blue shirt with a leather vest. Auburn hair greying at the temples. Bushy eyebrows over twinkling eyes. A gnarled and calloused hand grasped the last guest.

"You must be Oxford. Glad you could make it. What can I get you?"

Val Sisik and Harris Halliday, standing before the fire, nodded welcome, the premier waving cheerily. Patrick Justice and Sean McCarthy, deep in conversation in the far corner of the large living room, looked up as Oxford entered then turned quickly away, causing a quick suspicion. Were they talking about him? All were dressed in elegant casuals. Too elegant, Oxford thought. Like the cover on an L.L. Bean catalogue. Models draped around the hunting lodge.

Reuben handed Oxford his Scotch and soda and, carrying a tumbler of Scotch that would have required two of Oxford's hands to hold, came around the bar to join him.

"Ben Forsyth thought very highly of you. Ben was a fine man and a good friend of mine. Welcome to our home," he said.

The warmth and sincerity seemed out of character for

the big man and at first Oxford was startled. "Thank you," he replied, then, thinking more was required, added, "I'm honoured to be a substitute for Ben. He was my very good friend, too."

Rueben nodded approval and changed the subject. "Your first goose hunt?"

"I'm afraid so," Oxford confessed. "I've never shot anything bigger than a cock pheasant, and not a lot of them."

"Well, they can take some hitting, too," Reuben said. "But this is a very different kind of shooting. I'll show you the ropes. This is Toby," he said, as a large tawny dog left his place in front of the fire and came over to inspect Oxford. "A Chesapeake. About the only breed big and strong enough to handle these late season honkers."

"Oxford. So glad you could make it." Harris Halliday joined them, followed by Sean McCarthy.

The premier introduced Oxford and McCarthy. "Sure pleased to finally meet you, Oxford. I've certainly heard many good things about you."

I'll just bet, Oxford muttered to himself as he responded with banalities. If Dorothy is right, this man would have my guts for guitar strings just as quickly as he now shakes hands.

But McCarthy's big Irish face showed no trace of malice or guile, just twinkling eyes and a warm smile.

Premier Halliday took Oxford gently by the elbow and led him aside. "I really am glad you could join us. You've had a lot of responsibility shoved on you lately. Without warning. And without much chance for recreation. You need a break."

"Thank you, sir. I very much appreciate the invitation."

"Not at all. Not at all. I'm happy to be able to share a bit of our sanity saver with you. I've learned how important it is to step aside from stress. This ranch restores my soul. And nothing does it quicker than a goose hunt. Makes it easy to concentrate your attention away from your responsibilities. Flushes the mind. You'll see. Relax. Enjoy yourself. You're part of the team, you know. We're counting on you. Have to look after you. Come along. I think I hear dinner being served." Oxford followed meekly after the premier, his spirits charged and his mind whirling with pleasure and exhilaration.

The hunt supper was strictly a male event. Although Oxford heard Beth Halliday issuing instructions in the kitchen, the meal was served by a silent man dressed in chef whites. Basic ranch steak and potatoes accompanied by a rich goose stew, very much a novelty for Oxford.

The discussion was goose hunting only. Much of it, Oxford soon noticed, was prompted by Reuben as a gentle instruction to the newcomer. But he wondered also if perhaps there was not a taboo prohibiting the topics of business and politics. Neither was mentioned. Reuben Halliday spoke with an eloquence and breadth of knowledge that surprised Oxford.

"Never mind horse racing," Reuben said. "This is really the sport of kings. Certainly the Canada Goose is the king of birds. James Michener described them in his book *Chesapeake* as 'One of the great birds of the world,' but that was understatement. They are big, strong, beautiful and very, very smart. And romantic. Their migrations are great adventures and signals of the seasons. And those migrations are miracles of navigation and endurance. Geese have been seen by airline pilots flying at 25,000 feet. They're remarkable."

Reuben went on to describe the waterfowl flyway that ran north and south through western Saskatchewan. "It's a funnel. The birds that are raised in the Northwest Territories far east and west of us follow this route. Millions of geese and ducks come through here every fall. We're smack in the middle of the flyway. We've been shooting geese here since the Hallidays first arrived. It's the greatest sight and sound show in the world. The geese raft on the river and come out to the fields to feed. Thousands of birds stretched across the sky and the air filled with their calling. When I can't get in my pit anymore, I'll want someone to take me out there in my wheelchair."

Harris Halliday took over. "This western flyway really is one of the great wonders of the world. And it's a very valuable resource. Waterfowl hunting is one of our top tourism dollar earners. It's a little known fact that one quarter of all the waterfowl in North America are raised here in Saskatchewan. That, plus the flyway bringing through most of the birds raised in the Arctic, makes for a lot of birds.

"The anti-hunting groups don't understand this," the premier went on. "I don't think they want to. The goose population is growing every year. Hunting pressure has almost nothing to do with it. In all Saskatchewan we now shoot more geese than ducks. That was unbelievable just a few years ago."

"I can believe goose hunting pumps a lot of dollars into our economy," Sean McCarthy said. "The average hunter doesn't have all the support services of the Halliday ranch. Hotels, meals, fuel, guides, contracting pit digging, decoys, you name it. It all adds up to a pretty expensive sport.

"By the way," McCarthy went on. "I dropped into the hotel in town on the way out here. Some friends of mine are bunked in there. The place looks like a guerilla encampment. Guns all over hell and everyone dressed in camouflage clothing. And signs posted everywhere: *'Please don't use our towels to clean your guns.'* That place is making money this month."

"You bet it is," Reuben laughed. "And Edie charges five dollars a bird for cleaning. She does a hell of a business this time of year. Has an assembly line with three or four assistants. Several hundred dollars a day. And she's not the only one cleaning birds."

"And the premier is right about the tourist dollars," McCarthy said. "The streets in town are filled with American vehicles. Fancy, expensive outfits from Iowa, Minnesota, Nebraska, you name it. Big spenders."

"You bet they are," Harris Halliday agreed. "They leave a ton of dough here. And they're very, very welcome. Hunters have become a much maligned and abused fraternity. In the so-called polite society, I see people wince and look down their noses at me when I mention I'm a hunter. But not around here. Here not only the folks in town but even the farmers whose land is shot over wave and smile at the visiting hunters.

"But, you know," he went on, "we have a developing problem with the snow geese. There are so many of them now that they are crowding out the others. And I've read that they are destroying the habitat in their Arctic breeding grounds. But they're so flighty they're hard to hunt. And they're not very tasty. Somehow we have to increase the hunting pressure on them for their own protection. But that'll be hard to sell to the so-called environmentalists, the 'all hunting is awful' bunch."

Big Reuben Halliday was obviously enjoying both his meal and the discussion. He seemed as enthusiastic as a youngster. Very much like Cameron Hunt, Oxford thought, as he listened and observed his dinner companions. And the comforting notion grew on him that Reuben Halliday was cut of the same cloth as Hunt and could be counted on if needed. Oxford felt less alone and exposed than when he had first arrived.

"To Ben Forsyth, his memory." Reuben suddenly raised his wineglass in a toast.

"Ben was here on opening day," Reuben said to Oxford. "I don't think he missed an opening day in the last five years, probably longer. He loved to see these geese. Shooting had become incidental to Ben. That was Ben's last hunt, but he made the most of it. Sort of as if he knew," he said thoughtfully.

The arrangements for tomorrow's shoot were all in place, Reuben explained. A tractor-mounted thirty-six-inch auger had drilled six pits in a field where the geese had been feeding all week. The pits were chest deep and furnished with five gallon buckets for seats; when seated, the shooter's head would be just below ground level. A cover, a light frame of two layers of chicken wire interlaced with straw, would disguise the hunter's presence and permit vision through the straw.

The pits were placed about eight feet apart in a line across the anticipated wind direction. The hunters would face downwind with the decoys behind them so that the birds, landing into the wind, would pass over the pits before reaching the decoys.

They would be up early and in the field an hour before first light. It would take time to set up the decoys and make final preparations. They would place "only a few dozen or so" decoys, Reuben told them. He did not hold with those hunters who set out several hundred. The decoys had to go up in the morning this time of year, or they would become covered with frost. Shining in the morning sun, they would spook the wary birds.

The shoot would go all day. Early season goose hunting is restricted to mornings only, but after mid-October all day shooting is permitted, supposedly to encourage the birds to migrate. The geese leave the river to feed twice daily, in the morning and again in the afternoon, as they stock up for their long journey south. But they were very experienced now, shy of decoys and any unusual features, such as pits that were not well concealed and carelessly exposed hunters.

"So, keep your heads down and don't move," Reuben was very firm. "I'm calling the shoot. That means that no one moves a whisker until I say so. When I yell 'shoot,' you jump up and give 'em hell, but not a second before. These are big birds and they'll look like B-29s when they come in over you. You'll think you can hit 'em with a stick, but you'll be surprised how hard it is to bring them down. Some of those babies will weigh fifteen pounds, or even more.

"The birds are cautious now, and they'll circle and circle. I'll try and tell you where the birds are coming from, but I won't always be able to," he said. If any birds get behind us, I'll tell you what to do then.

"And shoot up only," Reuben was firm again. "No one but the end shooters can take low flyers or cripples out to the sides. And I'll tell them when.

"We do a lot of goose hunting on this ranch and a lot of our guests are inexperienced hunters. We've never had an accident and I don't ever want to have one. Do as I say and there'll be no problem." Reuben was very definite on this.

"We'll wake you in the morning with a pot of hot coffee. Breakfast in here," and Reuben stood up. The evening was over, but he accompanied Oxford back to his cabin. It was on the way to his house, Rueben said, pointing out a bungalow set well apart from the main buildings. As they strolled through the crisp night air, Rueben spoke again of Ben Forsyth's last hunt.

"We had drilled the pits on the south fence line of that barley field, just west of that bunch of bins. It's a great location for opening day before the birds become decoy shy. From that spot you can just see through the breaks to the river and every flock coming up spots our decoys first.

"We limited out early, before nine I'm sure. The rest of us were back here having coffee and more breakfast when Ben slipped out, borrowed my half ton and disappeared until almost noon. When he came back he said he had gone back out to the pits to watch the birds fly. They kept pouring out of the river all morning and he loved just to watch them. A great guy.

"Funny thing. When I went out later to fill the pits because we wanted to cultivate and fertilize that field real soon, Ben had filled in his pit with a spade. Strange thing to do, knowing we'd be out there with the equipment.

"By the way," Reuben asked, turning to Oxford. "Have you found Ben's shotgun? He used to leave it here all season, but he must have taken it with him after opening day. It's not here. His special goose gun and the only one I ever saw like it. Had it factory ordered. An Ithaca over-and-under with three-inch chambers and both barrels full choke.

"Right kind of gun for the pits. Don't have to worry about it jamming up with dust and dirt like those fancy autoloaders and even some pumps. You have a look through Ben's effects and find that gun and hang on to it. Good night, Oxford."

Adam Jakes, clad in black and looking very dangerous, was sitting in the small living room when Oxford entered his cottage. Although all the shades were closed, he instructed Oxford to turn on only the small reading light in the bedroom.

The Inspector and his party were camped in a motor home in an abandoned farmyard nearby. They were masquerading as goose hunters. Two of his men were out digging pits. "The old fashioned way. With spades and by headlights. It's very hard work," Jakes smiled.

In response to Oxford's quizzical look at his garb, Jakes explained that he had not always been an inspector and he hoped he not forgotten all his SWAT training. Oxford dutifully replayed the evening's conversation while the Inspector listened with his usual concentration. Jakes requested a repeat of Reuben's description of Ben Forsyth's last hunt. But, "interesting," was all he said.

Then Jakes turned to the next day and reviewed the precautions Oxford was to take. "It's more difficult when you're not sure where the danger might come from. In spite of what Dorothy Crane says, I find it hard to believe that anyone in that group you will be with can really be a threat. But we'd best assume the worst. I figure Sean McCarthy as our most likely problem, but we can't overlook Justice, or even Sisik.

"Naturally, you'll avoid vulnerable situations as much as possible. Watch that you don't get in front of them while they're carrying a gun," he instructed. "You can't avoid being in a pit next to one of them, but even that won't be so bad if you're not in an end pit with no one behind you. To be brutally frank, anyone wanting to shoot you would be afraid of spilling some shot into the next man in line. But it's not likely Reuben will put you on the end because of your inexperience. If it does happen, make sure you stay down until you know your neighbour is on his feet with his gun pointed in the air where it should be.

"You know," Jakes said, very seriously, "this might not be worth the risk. We've maybe already learned all we're going to learn. You could get the flu overnight," he suggested.

"Nope." Oxford shook his head. "We've been through this," he replied firmly.

"Well, then, be careful and keep that cell phone handy. If anything really strange develops, I'm only a few miles away," and Jakes slid into the night.

As Oxford's eyes closed in sleep, they suddenly burst open and his head came off the pillow. "Already learned," Jakes had said. What the hell had they learned? Oxford wondered. But sleep dragged him back down.

FORTY-SIX

 "Let me see if I have this straight," Sean McCarthy said. "You told me in there LaCoste has an appointment with a *Globe and Mail* reporter Monday morning? About those files he has that Forsyth put together?"

"That's it," Patrick Justice replied. They stood on the tiny veranda of the cottage Rueben Halliday had assigned to McCarthy.

"Well, I won't ask how you know. But you do know? For sure?"

"I know."

"And what's this bit about the cop?"

"LaCoste has been visiting with Adam Jakes of the Regina force. Inspector. Smart and straight."

"But what about? If he's going to give the files to the media, why's he talking to the cops?"

"Don't know that. But it could be the same thing. Those files are pretty hot."

"Not so hot. Just a bunch of paper. Might amount to nothing. Particularly since Forsyth isn't around to back them up."

"Make a hell of a story, though."

"Yeah. Damn media'll feed on anything. See you in the morning."

"Yeah."

FORTY-SEVEN

 "Coffee, sir. Breakfast in fifteen minutes." Oxford blinked into the light as the Halliday cook set a coffee butler and mug on the night table.

Over breakfast of bacon, scrambled eggs, and Texas toast, Oxford wondered if the group was more subdued than the night before. *Is that tension I feel in the air, or is it just my nerves?*

"Okay. Let's go," Reuben commanded. "Oxford, you ride with me."

Reuben steered his half ton out of the ranch yard and into the fields as the others followed. Without a steering wheel for support, Oxford had trouble keeping his seat as the big rancher bounced across his lands with no regard for the rough terrain. "Where's Toby?" he asked.

"Won't need him this morning. Just be in the road. We'll bring him out later if we lose any sinkers. Here we are," Reuben said, swinging his truck ninety degrees as he stopped in a strip of stubble. "Barley," Reuben explained. Oxford, who could see nothing that looked any different from other fields they had crossed, dutifully stepped out.

"Watch out for the pits," Rueben warned. "You can hurt yourself if you stumble into one in the dark." Oxford saw, to one side of the headlights, the line of black holes disappearing into the darkness. The two following trucks spread their headlights in support of Reuben's.

"Give a hand with these decoys," Reuben instructed, and Oxford hastened to obey. The truck boxes were piled with large, dark shapes and great net bags that he soon found were filled with detachable heads. The size of the molded plastic decoys astounded Oxford. They were several times larger than any goose he had ever seen.

"Yeah. A bit big aren't they?" Reuben chuckled. "For years we used decoys that were as lifelike as we could get them. Then someone discovered that oversized decoys worked better. Hell, they've even got one so large the hunter sits inside it. No pit. I don't approve of them, but I like these if only because it takes fewer of them."

Oxford quickly noticed that Reuben insisted on placing the decoys according to some mysterious pattern, and restricted himself to hauling the bundles from the trucks. Once the bodies were set in place, they all worked at attaching the heads, some down in feeding position, some upright, as if watching for danger. When the shotguns were uncased and ammunition bags and thermoses removed, ranch hands who had driven out with them removed the vehicles.

Reuben directed each hunter to a pit and they stowed their ammunition under their bucket seats. Jakes had guessed correctly; Oxford was pointed to a centre pit beside Rueben. Harris Halliday was on Oxford's other side and Sean McCarthy had the end. Sisik and Patrick Justice took the two pits on the other side of Reuben.

When all was in readiness, they cupped cold hands around a last cup of coffee dispensed from the thermoses and watched the flaming paintworks of the dawn spread upwards over the broken clouds. Some mallard ducks whizzed through the darkness, startling them with the wail of their vibrating aileron feathers. Reuben explained that the Canadas would not move until full daylight. They could hear the subdued chatter of rafting geese drifting to them on the wind from the distant river. Reuben, standing stock still, all senses alert, reminded Oxford of Sam on point. There was little conversation; each of them was entranced by the beauty of the moment.

Oxford scrolled back through his memory. The last time

he had watched a western sunrise had been during one of his boyhood visitations to the farm. He had forgotten, or never noticed, the soft suddenness of the sun's arrival over the flat prairies. After the creeping fire of the dawn across the high sky, he was surprised at how soon daylight reached the earth, swiftly lighting the frosted barley stubble.

The detail of the pits they would occupy was now disclosed. He could see how the auger had spun the soil off the blade around the holes, creating gentle slopes, like old and worn volcanos. The fresh dirt was disguised under a scattering of straw, blending the pit cover with the surrounding barley stubble.

As they waited, Reuben showed Oxford the barley kernels in the field that had escaped the harvesting process, leaving a feast for the transient geese. First, the crop had been cut and left to ripen in heavy swaths for almost two weeks. This cost a certain loss that could be aggravated by the weather. Then the swaths were picked up by the combines, a process that caused more shelling and loss. And, finally, the combines themselves were far from entirely efficient, throwing over the back with the chaff another load of kernels that escaped the internal threshing cylinders. Altogether, it added up to a cornucopia for the gleaning geese.

"And they're welcome to it. We'd just as soon not have it in the field if we can't have it in the bin," Reuben explained. "Barley is one of their favourite foods, by the way. They really go for some of the new specialty crops, like lentils and peas. But there's very little of that around here and our geese are still happy with barley.

"Here we go," Reuben suddenly announced, and they clambered into their pits. Then Oxford could hear the signal himself. The chatter of the geese became louder and more excited. A few flights appeared above the horizon, then skeins of birds were moving across the entire bowl of sky, their calling filling the morning with sound.

Suddenly a dozen large birds swept towards them, wings set and feet placed forward for landing. Oxford stared transfixed at the swiftly oncoming shapes as Rueben yelled, "SHOOT!" All guns but one roared and four geese crumpled and fell heavily among the decoys.

"Somebody shot my goose," Sean McCarthy blared with obvious good humour.

"You mean that one heading back to the river?" Harris Halliday laughed. "The one without a feather missing?"

"Get them turned over," Rueben commanded. Patrick Justice climbed quickly out of his pit, placed the downed geese among the decoys in as upright position as possible, and scampered back underground.

"Speckled bellies," Rueben said to no one in particular, then turned to Oxford and explained. "White fronted geese. Different variety. Different call. That's why we call them laughers. Or squeakers. Not as big as Canadas. They tend to fly earlier than the honkers. Have to turn them belly down or they'll spook other birds."

A noisy vee of geese winged over them, high and out of the range of their shotguns. Most of the birds were white with black wing-tips, but some were very dark.

"Snow geese," Rueben told Oxford. "The dark ones are blues. A sub-species. Most of the geese you see up there right now are snows," he said, pointing at the huge skeins crossing the sky. "They do their own thing. Won't come in to our decoys. Damned nuisance. Seem to drive the other birds away. Would be okay if they were better tasting. You've heard about the recipe for snow geese? Stuff them with a large rock, roast for two days. Then throw away the goose and eat the rock. Or marinate them about that long."

After that the Canadas behaved as Reuben had predicted. They were cautious and wary of the decoys, but Reuben was a maestro with his calling and a number of flocks ventured within range. The geese were flying in bunches of ten or fifteen birds with the odd flight of twenty or more. Twice flocks of nearly a hundred swept over their decoys, not stopping and just out of range. But their calling in passage was an impressive and exhilarating din.

Oxford's inexperience showed. His youthful reflexes were good, but not knowing what to anticipate made him slow in getting off his shots. And he found the geese even larger than Reuben had promised. Moving deceptively fast as they swept overhead, their late season plumage was difficult for the lead shot to penetrate.

At first Oxford was chary. He followed Adam Jakes' advice and was the last one to stand when Reuben gave the command to shoot. But soon he felt comfortable and safe between the two Hallidays and began to enjoy himself. Before the morning was over Oxford felt certain that at least two of the fourteen Canadas they had bagged had fallen to his old Winchester.

When the action slowed, the hunters lounged upright, quickly retreating beneath their pit covers when an incoming flight was sighted. All positions, Oxford soon discovered, were cold and uncomfortable.

"All the comforts of home," Reuben had said as he showed Oxford his pit and explained how to throw the pit cover back when he rose to shoot. But it became a frosty, dull morning with a moderately strong wind and after a couple of hours Oxford's cramped joints began to ache, his eyes were caked with the grit blowing into his pit, and he felt the cold seeping into his bones. He examined the soil structure of the Halliday ranch, the thin topsoil blending into blueish clay. This is nothing but a vertical grave, he thought, and shuddered.

But when a flight of geese swung towards their decoys, calling in response to Reuben, Oxford's discomfort disappeared.

To Oxford the straw laced screen that served as his pit cover might as well have been solid plywood. By straining his eyes and his upper spine he was barely able to see bits of sky in front and halfway above his pit. But the geese attracted to their decoy spread all seemed to circle behind them, or out beyond the end pits, well beyond his field of vision. When they did appear, it was only split seconds before Reuben's command, "SHOOT." To Oxford it seemed that the birds had swept past and out of range long before he could clear away the pit cover, raise his gun to his shoulder and look for a target.

It helped to be in the pit next to Reuben. Between his periodic calling, the huntmaster muttered a low monotone of description of incoming flights. "Small bunch at ten o'clock. They're going around. Looking good. Stay down. Two o'clock now. They're coming in. Setting their wings. Get ready. Come, babies, come on. SHOOT!"

At eleven o'clock Reuben declared the morning hunt over as ranch hands arrived with vehicles. The party repaired to the ranch house for lunch. There would be time for a quick nap, also, Reuben stated. Well short of their limit of five birds each, they would return to the pits in the afternoon.

"One of the advantages of hunting so close to home," Reuben explained to Oxford as they rode back to the head-quarters. "Makes it very civilized."

The Halliday ranch, Reuben said, maintained a fully equipped field kitchen, a modern day chuck wagon, which saw service during round-up and harvest. "Sometimes we put on the dog a bit and bring the kitchen out to the pits," he said. "But this late in the season it's a little too cold. We need to warm up or the rest of the day won't be very enjoyable."

Lunch was substantial. Walleye chowder (from the river, Reuben stated) and a marvellous beef stew served with hot biscuits, followed by rhubarb pie and ice cream. The easy camaraderie of the evening before continued as they re-ran the morning's hunt. Even the usually stiff and formal Sisik showed delight in the banter.

"That big Canada nearly gave you a fat head, Sean," he chuckled.

"Fat! My ass. Would have ripped it right off me shoulders if I hadn't seen it just in time. Came down like a rock. Would've felt like one, too."

"Happens from time to time," Rueben said. "Never heard of anyone getting seriously injured. But getting hit by a falling goose can take all the fun out of a morning."

Oxford thought Reuben's attempts at joviality and enthusiasm seemed a little strained and forced.

The promised nap came easily when Oxford returned to his cottage for the permitted half hour before the hunt resumed. Still somewhat sluggish during the drive back to the field in the afternoon, he quickly came to full alert upon arrival at the pits. Sean McCarthy had a proposition he outlined to Rueben. It involved a change in shooting positions.

McCarthy claimed to have been impressed with Oxford's shooting. "He's really very fast and very good, Reuben, particularly for a first timer. I think you should give him that outside pit I'm in, if only for the experience. Harris, you move into Oxford's pit and I'll help him cover the end."

Oxford protested as much as he dared without appearing to be alarmed. The change was made. Harris Halliday dutifully moved over and Rueben tacitly agreed. The premier, Oxford noted, seemed accustomed to taking direction from McCarthy.

As Oxford moved his cartridge bag and shotgun, his mind went into overdrive. He was now in the situation Jakes had warned against, in an end pit. There was no one behind to deter someone in the next pit who might want to take a shot at him. And in the next pit was Sean McCarthy, the man Adam Jakes had rated most likely to be trouble.

Oxford felt an adrenalin rush as he settled himself into the end pit. Well, he thought, at least we'll see what we came to see. Wits on red alert, please. Oxford's eyes turned irresistibly to the next pit. McCarthy was happily whistling as he tidied up the straw around his pit opening.

The flights were slow in the afternoon. An hour went by without Reuben calling any within range. Time was on his side, Oxford decided. His taut nerves relaxed and he began to feel some confidence. But he stayed entirely down in his pit, leaving the watching and the banter to the others as they lounged upright.

Suddenly, Reuben whistled, warning that a flock was approaching. Then he began to call and Oxford knew the birds had swung in towards the decoys.

"SHOOT," the big rancher yelled, but not until the firing stopped did Oxford slowly poke his head up. Only two birds were down.

"What's the matter, Oxford? They went right over you."

"Sorry, Reuben. I was asleep. Too much lunch, I guess."

"Hell, that happens," Reuben chuckled.

Almost no flights were in the sky now. The wind was picking up and the cold was really beginning to bite. Oxford, now standing in his pit watching with the others, noticed some peeking at watches. The hunt, he could feel, would be over soon. And with nothing proven.

Just what had he expected to prove anyway? If Adam

Jakes' suspicions were valid, the well armed man only a few feet away, Sean McCarthy, was capable of murder. And he was the intended victim. Oxford shook his head at the absurdity. Had he intended to prove out the theory by having his own head shot off?

Or was there another way? A thought germinated. A ridiculous idea. Oxford giggled. Then he reconsidered. What the hell, why not? Sometimes the simplest notions are the best. Like Grandfather Marcel dining with the Germans.

The dull grey sky was empty and beginning to darken. Not a bird in sight anywhere. The next flight would have to be it. If there was going to be an it. There might not be another opportunity.

Finally, Reuben pointed toward the river. A long dark line was lifting and falling as it fought into the wind. Oxford looked again at McCarthy. The big politician appeared to be intent only on the approaching geese.

"Looks good," Reuben said a few moments later as the birds stayed on course towards them. "Down."

Oxford sank into his pit and carefully pulled his cover over his head. He removed his camouflage cap and placed it over the end of his gun barrel. And waited, tensed for Reuben's command. It came.

"SHOOT," and Oxford pushed his gun upwards against his pit cover, lifting it violently. He was rewarded.

"BOOM!" His shotgun was torn from Oxford's grasp and his pit filled with a cloud of dust and dirt as the blast from Sean McCarthy's twelve gauge smashed across the earth just above his head.

"GOOD CHRIST! What the hell happened?" Reuben demanded.

"My gun snagged as I was getting up," McCarthy explained.

Reuben ignored McCarthy as he leaped out of his pit and over to Oxford's. He looked down at a thoroughly frightened young lawyer spitting dirt from his mouth and peering back up out of eyes rimmed with dust and topsoil.

"I'm . . . oh . . . oh okay," Oxford stammered. He took the hand Reuben proffered and was lifted lightly out of the pit.

"Are you sure?" Reuben asked, examining Oxford.

Then, satisfied, he reached down and picked up Oxford's Winchester, the barrel scarred by lead from McCarthy's gun. Reuben examined the shotgun, then looked at McCarthy, standing uneasily beside him.

"What the hell do you mean, you snagged your gun? What was it doing pointed over here?" the rancher gestured angrily at Oxford's pit.

"If you'd been holding your gun the way you should've been, this couldn't possibly have happened, even if you did snag your trigger, which is also impossible. Snag it on what? You've got your shooting hand alongside your trigger guard," Reuben stormed.

"My foot was asleep. I stumbled when I stood up," McCarthy tried to explain. Reuben turned away from him in disgust.

"I'm terribly sorry, Oxford," McCarthy mumbled, head bowed like a schoolboy dragged before the principal. "I've been using guns all my life. I . . . I . . . I really don't know what happened. Are you sure you're okay?"

Oxford just nodded.

"Have that gun looked at before you use it again," Reuben told Oxford. "That barrel might have been knocked out of plumb." Reuben walked over a few paces, picked up Oxford's cap, inspected it, and quietly handed it back. Oxford glanced at it, then crammed it into his pocket. The cap looked like it had been chewed by mice over a long winter. Reuben turned and glared at the other three, standing like open-mouthed school boys.

"Well, let's get out of here. That's it for this year. Hell of a way to end it," he said, glaring at McCarthy. Reuben would be slow to forget this incident and he clearly intended to see that McCarthy never did.

"Get us some transportation, Harris," Reuben commanded. "The boys won't be coming to pick us up for another hour otherwise," and he stomped out among the decoys and began to dismantle them, furiously throwing bodies to one side and heads to the other.

Harris Halliday held out his hand to Val Sisik, who promptly produced his cell phone. The premier dialled the ranch headquarters and ordered up a couple of vehicles.

Oxford went off to help with the decoys. As they worked together, Reuben suddenly asked, "How come you had your cap over the end of your barrel, Oxford?"

"The wind was blowing dirt into my pit. I wanted to keep it out of the barrel. When you hollered, I didn't have time to take it off," Oxford replied. Reuben squinted at him, eyes old and wise under the bushy eyebrows. Although nothing more was said, Oxford knew that his explanation had been judged just as unacceptable as McCarthy's.

Oxford considered what he had learned from his experiment. It seemed a hell of a lot of risk just to establish that Dorothy was right. These people were capable of murder, at least Sean McCarthy is. As for the others, they had reacted with about the right amount of alarm and solicitude. Oxford had spotted no clue in the demeanour of Premier Halliday, Val Sisik or Patrick Justice.

He wondered what Adam Jakes would make of it.

FORTY-EIGHT

Reuben had told Oxford that before the advent of the power auger goose pits had been dug by hand, with long handled spades, picks, and bar chisels. Each hunter was responsible for his own pit. That, Reuben said, ensured a certain level of physical conditioning among the goose hunting fraternity.

Out in the late night dark on a western field of the Halliday ranch, Oxford leaned on his long handled spade, wiped his brow, and thought that pit digging might be an overlooked Olympic training program. And the hole that was giving him so much exercise had not long ago been previously excavated. He shuddered to think of having to dig through the undisturbed clay hardpan that lay below the topsoil. It had the consistency of concrete.

The lack of adequate lighting was another hardship. The high-miler ranch half ton Oxford had borrowed from Reuben Halliday had decent headlights, but they did not reach down into the hole where he was digging.

Just the same, Oxford had made good progress in re-excavating the goose pit that Ben Forsyth had occupied in September. He had recovered a shotgun, an over and under, encrusted with rust and soil. It was lying in front of the headlights. Beside the shotgun was a metal detector.

Oxford was more than knee deep into the old pit, and so engaged in clearing the loosened soil from beneath his feet that he was taken entirely by surprise when the two men approached on foot out of the darkness.

"Well done, young Oxford," Val Sisik said dryly. "Some progress at last, I see. At our rates, though, I don't think we recognize overtime."

Oxford looked up at Sisik and Patrick Justice, who casually held a large semi-automatic pistol. Sure that Oxford had seen his weapon, Justice dropped it in his pocket and picked up the shotgun. He turned it over in the headlights.

"A shotgun. Good one, too. An over and under. And a metal detector." he observed. "What do you know?"

Oxford sat on the edge of his hole and wiped the back of his hand across his brow. Weariness and defeat washed over him. "How did you find out?" he asked weakly.

Sisik was scornful. "Observation, young Oxford. Simple observation. You chose not to leave the ranch tonight. When everyone else did. Why not? So, when we left after dinner tonight we waited. And watched. While you come out here with that metal detector and dig this hole. What do you expect to find here, young Oxford? Forsyth's files that you've been lying to us about, or the codes to the Caribbean trust?" Sisik demanded.

"Just the codes. I've put the files away for my own protection. But I haven't been able to find the codes to the trust. I just know why Ben set it up."

"And why was that?" Sisik wanted to know.

"Because he found out about that extra nine million that you and the premier were cutting out of the deal for yourselves," Oxford replied. Sitting in his hole in the headlights looking up at Sisik and Justice, he felt very threatened.

"And that upset Honest Ben Forsyth, did it?" Sisik asked.

"He was furious that you and Premier Halliday would steal that money, and that you would use him to pull it off," Oxford replied, angry now, in spite of his fear.

"Well, now, steal is a strong word. Appropriate might be better," Sisik smiled, very pleased with himself.

"How did you convince the premier to go along with such a crooked deal?"

"One half of nine million dollars is a powerful inducement, Young Oxford. Tucked safely away in overseas accounts. Beyond the reach of the tax man. Makes life after defeat quite palatable. Yes? Now, of course, the figure is fifteen million dollars. Now there is no need to recognize the interest of the vendor. Niceties are done with."

"Where are the files?" Justice interjected.

"Well," Oxford hesitated, "as I said, I put them away for my protection."

"And what does that mean?" Sisik demanded, very much in charge.

"After what happened to Cameron Hunt and Tad Osborne, I thought I should take some precautions," Oxford said.

"Such as?" Sisik demanded, losing his patience.

"The usual. 'To be delivered to the police in the event of my death,'" Oxford replied. And then to his own surprise he blurted out, "why did you have to kill Cameron Hunt? And Tad Osborne?"

"Shut up!" Justice said, but Sisik cut him off.

"Sometimes sacrifices have to be made in the protection of larger interests, young Oxford," he said. "Your Cameron Hunt became a regrettable casualty of Mr. Justice's enthusiasm for his work. As for Mr. Osborne, I can only suggest that he must have stepped in someone else's way."

"You killed Cameron Hunt?" Oxford accused Justice.

Justice stared at Sisik. His mouth opened but no words came out. Then he turned to Oxford. "My friend has a big mouth," he snarled.

"One can never achieve the perfect world," Sisik continued, unconcerned. "One must remain fluid, able to amend one's plans to fit changing circumstances. Yes. Just as here and now." Oxford looked blank at this.

"You wonder what I mean?" Sisik was again pleased with himself. "The recovery of the codes renders it far less important that we also intercept Mr. Forsyth's collection of files. Access to that trust reduces my concern for the fate of the Halliday government to the level of supreme indifference. So, our Mr. Forsyth left buried treasure, did he? And did he leave a map for you also?"

"No. Just a message. That I should come here goose hunting. And then Rueben told me about Ben's last shoot and his missing shotgun. So I thought I should check his pit. Rueben told me where to look. With the metal detector it was easy."

"Where did you get it? The detector?"

"Rueben had one on the ranch. The shotgun is a big piece of metal. It was easy to find."

"Our Mr. Forsyth was clever. More clever than I thought."

"Did you kill him too? Was that your car at his house that night?"

"What? What car?" Sisik stuttered.

"A neighbour told me. He saw it on the way to the airport. A black Mercedes. It was your car, wasn't it? You killed Ben Forsyth."

"Shut up!" Justice commanded. "Don't answer him."

"Oh, it no longer matters. Young Oxford here will not be repeating this conversation to anyone. Kill Ben Forsyth? I wonder. Did I kill your good friend ? Or merely assist him to depart an unhappy life?" Sisik's tone suddenly changed.

"Now get digging, Mr. LaCoste. And take care not to damage that package when you reach it. You too have become expendable."

"What does that mean?"

"There is much disturbed ground in this region. Thanks to all these foolish hunters. No one will notice one more hole. Recently filled. With a nosy lawyer underneath. Now dig."

"You . . . you'd kill me? Why? What have I done?"

"Too much knowledge, my young friend, is not a good thing. Now, unless you'd like Mr. Justice here to use your knees for target practice, dig up that package. Perhaps we can find another use for you."

Oxford bent to his spade. As he tossed the soil at their feet, Sisik and Justice moved back towards the truck. Suddenly a telephone rang. It was Sisik's cellular. It rang again as he removed it from his pocket.

"For Christ's sake, turn that damn thing off," Justice growled as Sisik put the phone to his ear. Justice reached to take it from him.

"HOLD IT, Justice," Adam Jakes commanded from the back of the half ton. "Don't think of making even one little

259

move. Sergeant Sheard here will help you with that nasty pistol."

"DROP IT, Justice," a new voice demanded, as a lithe figure in RCMP uniform, service pistol in hand, dropped out of the back of the half ton, behind the still startled pair. "I never thought much of you when you were wearing the uniform, and I'm thinking nothing of you now. DROP IT!"

The automatic slid from Patrick Justice's fingers into the summerfallow at his feet. Without further instruction, he folded his fingers over his head.

"And you do the same thing with your damn fool phone, Sisik. Get your hands up," Adam Jakes was angry now.

"Get out of that hole, Oxford, and over here." The speed with which the lawyer complied belied his earlier weariness. "Now signal our friends, please," Jakes requested.

Oxford turned the pick-up's headlights on and off twice. Two sets of headlights flashed on half a mile to the west, beside a poplar bluff. Five minutes later two RCMP cruisers pulled into the scene. Two uniformed members and two Regina Police Service constables dressed in hunting clothes joined the group.

As handcuffs were applied to Sisik and Justice, Adam Jakes turned to Oxford. "You okay?" he asked, concern showing in his face.

"Fine," Oxford replied, then added. "A little jittery, I guess. But okay."

"I shouldn't wonder at the jittery part," the inspector said. "You've had a hell of a stressful day. This last little bit would be traumatic. We'll keep an eye on you to see that you come down all right. If you start to feel strange, let us know."

"Adam," one of the constables in hunting gear called from the back of the truck. "Can we shut down these recorders now?"

"Yes," Jakes replied. "Secure everything. And take that wire off Oxford here." Still dressed in black, he moved in front of Sisik and Justice.

"Strange, isn't it, Justice," he said, "that nobody ever thinks that anything of much importance is ever in the back of an old farm half ton? Just a couple of fuel drums and old tarps.

And you the security advisor to the premier. Tsk, tsk, tsk."

"Who are you? What's all this about?" Sisik blustered. "We're here attempting to recover property of the Government of Saskatchewan. What are you trying to do?"

"I am Inspector Adam Jakes of the Regina Police Service," Jakes said, flashing his identification in Sisik's face, "as Mr. Justice here well knows."

"You, Vladimir Sisik," Jakes intoned, "are under arrest for the murder of Benjamin Forsyth, and as an accomplice to the murder of Cameron Hunt."

"You, Patrick Justice," Jakes turned to the security advisor, "are under arrest for the murder of Cameron Hunt."

"Further investigations are underway and you can expect more charges in due course, particularly with respect to an attempt to defraud the Saskatchewan Government of nine million dollars," Jakes concluded.

"Aren't you going to read us our rights, Jakes?" Justice snarled.

"I certainly am," Jakes replied, and proceeded to formally advise each of their right to remain silent, to secure counsel, all to ensure compliance with the requirements of the law.

"This is preposterous," Sisik stammered. "You don't know who I am or what you're doing. You have nothing."

"Shut up, Vladimir," Justice said quietly. "He just read you your rights. Be quiet and listen. You've already talked too damn much."

"You shut up, you incompetent fool," Sisik shouted. "But for your bungling we wouldn't be here." He turned to Jakes.

"What do you mean, I'm charged with Ben Forsyth's murder. His death was an accident. I had nothing to do with it."

"Dr. Sisik, allow me to inform you," Jakes replied, borrowing the deputy minister's ponderous turn of phrase. "Mrs. Ruth Forsyth has been in police custody for several hours. She also is charged with her husband's murder. Ruth Forsyth has confirmed the theory of our investigation. Ben Forsyth died of carbon monoxide inhalation, all right. But that carbon monoxide did not come from his own car. It was piped into the Forsyth garage from another vehicle. Your vehicle, Dr. Sisik. Parked just outside.

"Mr. Justice," Jakes turned to the other. "Do you require any detail on how you accomplished the murder of Cameron Hunt?"

"Fuck you, Jakes."

"Fine," Jakes smiled, unaffected by the profanity, and bent to pick up the cell phone from where it lay at Sisik's feet. "We'll need your phone, Dr. Sisik, an important piece of evidence. Nice of you to keep it with you at all times. Provided a necessary diversion. We'll find another one for you when you get to cells. You might want to consult counsel." Jakes turned to his men.

"I guess we can fill Ben's hole in again," he instructed. "For the last time.

"You see, Dr. Sisik, we were a little ahead of you. We excavated here last night and recovered Mr. Forsyth's little package. In excellent shape. All carefully sealed in plastic. The codes you were looking for. Plus the computer discs and the original memos from you and Premier Halliday directing Mr. Forsyth to complete the purchase of the laser process. At a price of fifteen million dollars. A great piece of evidence, don't you think? When you knew the real cost was only six million. And the taxpayers will be glad to get their money back."

FORTY-NINE

Oxford stood in front of the fireplace in the Halliday ranch house, staring into the flames, his hand cupped around a large coffee mug. He had stirred the fire back to life and the birch logs he had added were burning brightly. He was lost in thought. Adam Jakes stood apart, listening intently to his cell phone.

Reuben Halliday strode heavily into the room and poured himself a mug of coffee. Then he went to a sideboard and produced a bottle of Scotch. "This coffee needs a stick in it," he said, proffering the Scotch to Oxford. Wordlessly he held his mug out in acceptance. Adam Jakes shook his head as Reuben waved the bottle in his direction.

Reuben joined Oxford at the fire for a moment, then, with a weary sigh, turned and faced Jakes.

"Harris refuses to discuss it. He says it is degrading to the office of premier to reply to questions of graft and murder. All he'll say is that he knows nothing about any of this, had no idea what Sisik and Justice were up to, had no part in any of it. I just don't know," Reuben said, shaking his head. Weariness, or deep sadness, washed over his features.

"I've always worried about Harris," he went on as if speaking only to himself. "He has so much, so many gifts, but he has never been satisfied or happy. All his achievements, even becoming premier, lost their taste right away. When he was a kid no toy could keep his interest for more than five minutes. He always needed more. Still does.

"I wish I could say that my kid brother couldn't have touched any of this, but I don't know. I just don't know. I suppose we'll all find out in time. How was Ben killed?" Reuben asked, shaking himself as if out of a reverie.

"Well, carbon monoxide was the cause of death all right," Oxford replied, "but it was supplied by Dr. Sisik. And Ruth. They piped exhaust from Sisik's car outside on the driveway into the garage."

"The technique was crude but effective," Jakes said, joining them. "Sisik provided Mrs. Forsyth with a short length of hard plastic pipe, the plumbing variety. She inserted it at the edge of the garage door. When the door closed, the sleeve at the bottom still provided a good seal and no one would notice the pipe in the darkness.

"The trap started with the family barbecue. Mrs. Forsyth faked a late dinner and built a large briquette fire about midnight. Then she wheeled the barbecue into the garage where it sat for a couple of hours spewing CO. When Mr. Forsyth drove into the garage just before 2:00 A.M. the place was already quite dangerous.

"He followed his usual habit of opening the front windows on his car to equalize temperatures, quite normal but deadly that night. Worse, he allowed himself to take a nap, a bad habit he had developed and one that was known to his wife. But he did turn off his car engine.

"Mrs. Forsyth was waiting. When she was sure he had fallen asleep in his car as they hoped, she dialled Dr. Sisik on his cell phone. He was lurking in the neighbourhood and quickly drove to the Forsyth garage. He backed his large Mercedes up to the garage door, attached a piece of flexible hose to his exhaust and the pipe under the door, and left his engine running. That exhaust added to the barbecue fumes killed Ben Forsyth quite quickly. He didn't have a chance.

"After an hour or so, Sisik held his breath, stepped quickly into the garage from the house and turned on the ignition in Mr. Forsyth's car. Then he removed his pipe and hose and drove off. Mrs. Forsyth waited a bit and then called us.

"It was not very sophisticated and it was extremely risky. The whole operation was exposed for more than two hours while Sisik's car was running outside the Forsyth garage. But, at that time of the night it was very unlikely anyone would notice. And the very simplicity of the scheme made it almost successful."

"But," Rueben asked, "why be so clumsy? Take all that risk? Ben's car must have had a remote starter on it. Why not just fire it up from outside the garage and let it go at that?"

"Car does have a remote," Jakes replied. "But, like most of them, it goes off like a stick of dynamite. Would have wakened Ben up. According to Mrs. Forsyth, Sisik did consider the remote, but a test convinced him it was too noisy."

"But," Rueben persisted, "why would Ruth Forsyth want to do away with Ben? He was everything to her."

"Her alcoholism had progressed to the point where she had begun to blame it and everything wrong in her life on her husband," Jakes explained. "She was easy prey to Sisik. He seduced her, encouraged her in her resentments, and promised her a new life full of romance and adventure. He convinced her that Mr. Forsyth had become disloyal to the Halliday team, subversive, in fact. The husband stood in the way of the lovers' wonderful future, an old scenario, but a real one. She willingly cooperated."

"Ben unwittingly set the stage for his own death," Oxford said. "He had told Sisik that the fifteen million dollar purchase price for the laser had been turned over. Removing Ben at that point would not only cover their tracks on that deal but prevent him from exposing the files he had put together on McCarthy and the whole government."

"How did you put all this together?" Reuben asked.

"It was our theory from the beginning," Jakes replied. "Routinely we checked the gas tank on Mr. Forsyth's car. It was almost full, within a gallon of full. That meant it hadn't been running as long as he had been home and hadn't supplied the carbon monoxide that killed him. That car will consume about a gallon an hour on idle. And obviously the tank had recently been filled.

"We checked the local gas stations. Mr. Forsyth had filled up on the way home that night. The night attendant told us he often did that. He noticed also that Mr. Forsyth seemed unusually tired. 'Wiped,' he called it. The signature on the credit card slip confirmed that. It was just a scrawl."

"Yes," Reuben interjected, "that would be Ben. The careful country man fuelling up last thing at night so he'd be ready to go first thing in the morning."

"I guess so," Jakes agreed, then continued. "With that evidence we checked the calls from the Forsyth telephone and found one to Dr. Sisik's cell phone. From that point on we were sure what had happened, but we were unable to prove much. The technicals found evidence on the garage door consistent with the pipe having been in place, but not much more. Sisik's car hadn't left any identifiable traces on the concrete driveway. We had noticed that the barbecue was still warm, a little strange at that hour. A suspicious circumstance, but little more.

"When Oxford here discovered a neighbour who had seen a car matching Sisik's, we were closer, but still without enough for a conviction. In my view. But with the admissions Oxford secured for us tonight on our tapes, we'll have enough. Besides, we now have a confession. From Mrs. Forsyth.

"We approached her this afternoon. When we decided to go ahead with Oxford's dramatic performance. Confronted with our theory—and the evidence backing it up—particularly the neighbour's observation of Sisik's car—she willingly confessed.

"How is she?" Oxford asked, concerned.

"Apparently quite a bit better since she got all this off her chest. But she'll need a lot of professional help," Jakes replied.

"That . . . performance is the word, all right . . . tonight. Was it really necessary?" Rueben asked. "It was risky as hell. Bad enough this afternoon in the pits. I'd never have allowed Oxford to move into that end pit if you'd told me that McCarthy was dangerous. But, Oxford, what you pulled off tonight was above and beyond any call of duty."

"Maybe," Oxford replied. "But the police didn't have anything to tie Patrick Justice to Cameron Hunt's murder. Or enough. And even Ben's case had some loose ends. I wasn't going to let Justice get away with killing Cameron. When Adam raised the idea of recreating the finding of Ben's cache I couldn't back away. I'm worried that even now they don't have enough to convict him. He didn't admit a hell of a lot."

"True," Jakes agreed. "But I think we'll get a lot of help from Vladimir Sisik. When he assesses the case we have against him, I think he'll want to cooperate. Doesn't strike me as the kind of man who'll do time while his underling walks. Justice went down to West Willow on Sisik's orders.

"He was to recover Mr. Forsyth's files after Mrs. Forsyth told Sisik where they were. We think Justice at first tied Mr. Hunt up while he searched the house. Likely in disguise. When he couldn't find anything, he became brutal trying to extract information. Then he killed to protect himself. He certainly must have thought Mr. Hunt was dead when he left the house.

"The RCMP do have some circumstantial evidence. Some identification of Justice's car. And some soil samples that put it in West Willow. Not completely naked. But not much of a case until Oxford stepped forward."

"I think I need another one of these," Rueben announced, and strode over to the coffee butler and Scotch on the bar. Oxford considered a moment, then joined Rueben. Jakes declined again.

"How are you now?" Rueben asked Oxford.

"Okay, I think. Maybe a little weak in the knees."

"I shouldn't wonder. Someone said, maybe Churchill, that it's the greatest feeling in the world to be shot at and missed. But I can go without the experience," Rueben said, then turned to Jakes.

"And Sean McCarthy? What about him?"

"I'm just told," Jakes replied, gesturing with his cell phone, "that Mr. McCarthy hasn't yet returned to his home in Regina. We have a car and a warrant waiting there."

"Hell! He's had lots of time to get home," Rueben said. "He left here as soon as we got in from the pits. Wouldn't even stay for dinner. Said he was too embarrassed to stay around. Should have been home hours ago."

"*If* he went home," Oxford observed. "He must be up to

something. He's a pretty cunning guy. Wouldn't he know the jig is up?"

"Don't see how," Jakes replied. "As I told you, he likely knows about your date with the *Globe and Mail* on Monday. Our specialists found the bug in your room at the Flatlander. Broadcasting to a tape recorder in the next room. But he shouldn't know we've tied him to Tad Osborne's murder."

"How have you done that?" Reuben asked in surprise. "Is there no end to this mess?"

"There is a bit of it, at that," Jakes replied. "I can tell you that knowing who likely killed Mr. Osborne made it a lot easier for us. There are only a few people in Regina who operate as rent-a-crooks. We found at the scene an instrument known in the trade as a pick, used for picking locks. That identified some likely suspects, people who are never without their tools. Some shoeprints in the soft shoulder of the road gave us a match to a person known to us. A partial fingerprint on the pliers accidentally left behind points to the likely presence of another.

"It was enough to bargain for more. Without being specific, we now have a witness who ties Mr. McCarthy into the homicide. We recovered an unusual piece of electronic evidence. A tape recording of a conversation with Mr. McCarthy. Foolishly intended for extortion, but powerful corroboration.

"It seems that this was a clumsy attempt at extracting information about the whereabouts of the Forsyth files. Although murder wasn't intended, it was an almost certain result since the perpetrators made no attempt to disguise themselves.

"At any rate, Mr. McCarthy is charged with second degree murder. But I can't imagine that he's aware of that."

"It's been a hell of a twenty-four hours," Rueben said. "When you got me out of bed last night I confess I thought you were stretching things a bit with that story about Ben having hidden evidence in his pit. Obviously you weren't. We did well to find that old pit as easily as we did in the dark. By the way, how come you had a metal detector with you?"

"There seemed to be a chance we'd be looking for things here. Useful item. Had quite a few other toys along, too.

"After we dug up the package Mr. Forsyth had buried, I considered pulling Oxford out of the hunt," Jakes said. "But that would have alerted Sisik and Justice and we wouldn't have been able to set them up as we did. These things are usually a calculated risk. We were lucky."

"Maybe a little more involved than luck," Rueben observed. "What a hell of a thing!" he exclaimed. "A cabinet minister about to be arrested and charged with murder. I'm sure that's never happened before in this province, if anywhere else in Canada. And a deputy minister to the premier, too. And another official as well.

"But why did Ben hide that stuff the way he did? How did he ever expect anyone to find it? If he wasn't around, that is?" Rueben asked.

"Apparently he had left instructions for Cameron Hunt and me," Oxford replied. "A cryptic message that only we would have understood. But Ruth found the note and destroyed it because it was addressed to us as Ben's executors. She was mad as hell that Ben appointed us."

"She has told us that she threw several papers addressed to Mr. Hunt and Oxford into the fire. In a fit of anger. We can only assume that directions to dig up his goose pit were included," Jakes said.

"Makes it pretty lucky that we found it at all," Rueben shook his head.

"Yes. Some luck. And a lot of help," Jakes replied. "Thanks for all your's. We couldn't have nailed Dr. Sisik and Justice as we did without you. I know this must be very difficult for you."

"Yes. I confess it's not pleasant. Well, I guess that's it," Rueben said, getting to his feet and stretching. "That's enough for one night. For me, at least. It's late. I'm going to bed. I hope you'll be sensible enough to stay the night. Breakfast starts at six so you can have an early start if you need to."

FIFTY

Sean McCarthy turned off the Lewvan Expressway onto Thirteenth Avenue north of the Regina airport and onto the lot occupied by Prairie U-Drive. He parked his Lincoln Continental at the back of the building where it was not visible from the street and picked up the keys of the three-year-old Ford Windstar from behind its front wheel. Jim Blair, one of the last independents in the car rental industry, had responded to the deputy premier's telephoned request. McCarthy had expected Blair would be helpful. The WDA was Prairie U-Drive's largest account and making a vehicle available late on a Saturday night was a small thing to ask.

McCarthy was headed out of town and out of the country. Just where he had not yet decided; that could wait. Tomorrow he would drive down to Carlyle where a loyal friend hangared a Piper Apache. A quick flip from there across the border to Minot and he would catch the Northwest flight to Denver. From Denver anywhere was possible. He was leaning towards Chile, but there would be time to think about that.

After the incident at the goose hunt McCarthy had decided upon another of the foreign trade missions he had made famous. He had covered the world since becoming a cabinet minister and another overseas trip would surprise no one. How long he would stay out of circulation would depend on the fallout from LaCoste's interview with the *Globe and Mail* on Monday, how the story played. But he had no intention of being hounded by the media. Or, for that matter, the police, if it came to that. Best wait and see just how much LaCoste had, how much Forsyth had left him. Might blow over or it might turn real bad.

He had not come this close to his goal to lose now. If there was one promise he had made to himself that he was determined to keep it was to be poor no more. His money-grubbing days were over. For all time. Anyone who tried to separate him from his winnings was in for a very rough time. He might have to trim back a bit but that would be all. Most of those winnings were already safely tucked away out of the country, beyond reach. If he had to make a one-way trip out of Saskatchewan, so be it. He could live in Australia. Or Europe. Or the Caribbean. Or wherever.

But first he had to get to his office in the legislative building, pick up his stash of cash, his passport, a change of clothes and his ever-ready travel bag. And a few hours sleep. McCarthy did some quick arithmetic. Even after the hefty payment to that damn fool Ace Kozak there should still be on the high side of thirty-five thousand dollars in cash in his office safe. Plus a number of securities, almost all in bearer form. The fifty thousand dollars he had carved out of the caucus loan to Clifton Carlson was still sitting in his chequing account, accessible by his two thousand dollars a day bank card, a special limit granted by his friendly bank. It would be enough to carry him a long way.

And he would be careful. In case anyone was looking for him. Justice had said that LaCoste had been in touch with the police. McCarthy couldn't believe that they could make him on anything, but he'd take some just-in-case precautions. Ditching the Continental was elementary. Same with avoiding his house. No one would pay any attention to the Windstar in the parking lot at the legislature and he had a key to one of the back doors. In tonight, out tomorrow, quietly. The security people at the front wouldn't know he had even been around.

FIFTY-ONE

The leave-taking at the Halliday ranch Sunday morning had been almost emotional. Both Rueben and Beth Halliday, as well as Oxford, were still moved by the dramatic events of the day before. Rueben had held Oxford's hand just a bit longer than usual and the invitation 'Please come again. Come any time.' had been warm and sincere. Harris Halliday had not appeared. Nor had he been mentioned. Avoided, Oxford thought, like an unpleasant subject.

Now Oxford and the old Jeep were Regina bound and he was lighthearted and joyful. Before turning in late last night he had called Dorothy and reported all the happenings. She was delighted to learn he was safe and anxious to have him deliver all the details in person. Oxford had planned to return the Jeep to West Willow and change out of his rough clothing before driving in to Regina, but Dorothy wouldn't hear of it. So he had said 'to hell with appearances' and agreed. He had a suit and a couple of shirts at the Flatlander that would see him through Monday and then he would be out of there. Taking the Jeep into the city would be fun.

Dorothy was going to clean out her desk at the office Sunday morning but would be back at her apartment by the time Oxford arrived in Regina. There was a football game. The Roughriders were at Vancouver. They had made the final for a change. Munchies and maybe a beer had been mentioned. Oxford wasn't much of a football fan, but he was eagerly looking forward to the afternoon.

His cell phone rang. Dorothy. She was excited and breathless, whispering.

"Oxford. Oh! I'm so glad I caught you. He's here."

"Who? Where?"

"Sean McCarthy. Here. At the legislative building. I'm sure of it."

"Where are you?"

"In my office. With the door locked. And the lights out. After I'd been here a while, I got to thinking about him. Then for some reason I felt drawn down to his office. A strange feeling. Finally, I went down. Just to have a look. His office is a floor below. On the bottom level. Around here his place is called the Fuhrerbunker. The WDA use it to drink and play cards. He's in there. I know it. The lights are on and I saw a shadow moving. I never ran so fast in my life as I did coming back up here. What should we do? Oh! Oxford, I'm so scared. Where are you? How soon will you be here."

"Hell! I'm just at Morse. More than a fast hour and a half. I'll call Adam Jakes. Call you back. Turn the phone bell down and sit tight. Don't worry. He can't be up to anything." Oxford wished he believed his last statement.

Jakes was at home. Oxford reported.

"We'll check it out immediately. We've been keeping an eye on the building but his car hasn't showed up. Security hasn't reported anything. He must be moving carefully. Tell Dorothy to sit tight. Until I tell her the coast is clear. I'll be back." Jakes was efficient with words.

Oxford relayed Jakes' words to Dorothy. She was still a little frightened, but fully under control. There was nothing more he could do but drive like hell and hope there was no radar about. The Sunday traffic was light.

The Jeep was fast but its steering was erratic, requiring strong attention from the driver. As the speedometer crept past 150 k.p.h. the steering straightened out but Oxford thought it was because of a form of levitation that overtook the vehicle. It seemed to become partly airborne. He had no business driving the ancient machine at this speed, he knew, but he did not relent.

273

Why was he so anxious, so worried? There was likely no problem in the first place and there was nothing he could do about it in the second. Dorothy! She had become very important to him. Quietly, surreptitiously she had taken a large place in his emotions. Then, a thought. Had Dorothy been this concerned yesterday? About him? Yes. It seems she was.

His cell phone rang. He released the accelerator as he took one hand off the wheel to open the phone and put it to his ear.

"Slow down. We don't want you spread all over the landscape out there." It was Adam Jakes.

"I have. I mean, I am. What's going on."

"Dorothy was right. We think McCarthy is in his office. He has a rented van in the parking lot. Probably used a back door to get into the building. Avoided security. We expect him to leave soon and we're waiting for him. It has been decided—at the policy level—that it would be inappropriate to arrest a minister of the Crown in the legislative building. Even though he doesn't have immunity. The word sacrilege was mentioned. Besides, there'll be less likelihood of resistance outside. We're not sure if he's armed or not.

"I've sent a man in to be with Dorothy. She's all right. Please don't phone until this operation is complete. She'll call you when it is. Relax. And slow down."

"How'd you know I was speeding?"

"Weren't you?"

"Yes."

"Who wouldn't? Relax. It's going to be all right."

FIFTY-TWO

Sean McCarthy stepped out the back door of the legislative building, travel bag over his shoulder and attaché case in hand. He paid no attention to the service van standing next to the building. Two workers in coveralls were busy at the open side door of the van. McCarthy headed to the Windstar in the parking lot a hundred feet away.

"Sean McCarthy!"

The deputy premier turned to the voice. The two workers had fallen in behind him and now stood one to each side. A third figure, the speaker, stepped lightly from the service van and strode rapidly forward. He held out a plastic photo identification card.

"Sean McCarthy, I am Inspector Adam Jakes of the Regina Police Service. I have information charging you as a party to the murder of Taddeus Osborne. And another charging you with the attempted murder of Oxford LaCoste. You are under arrest."

McCarthy stood in shock, hardly aware that his travel bag and attaché case were being removed. He stiffened as he felt his arms being drawn behind him, then submitted as the handcuffs were applied.

"This is bullshit! What the hell do you think you're trying to pull off? You know who I am. You can't do this."

"Yes, Mr. McCarthy, we know who you are. I must

inform you that you have the right to remain silent." Jakes intoned the litany of required advice about the right to counsel. Then, "This way, please." And Jakes opened the back door of the police cruiser that pulled in beside them.

It was over.

FIFTY-THREE

 "Hold on a minute, Adam." Oxford, phone to his ear, picked up the remote control and thumbed off the mute button.

"It's up. It's . . . it's through the uprights. The field goal is good and the Roughriders increase their lead—24 to 14— over the Lions. With three minutes remaining." The television switched to the sideline camera focussed on the jubilation at the Rider bench. Oxford hit the mute button again and spoke into the phone.

"Twenty-four to 14. Three minutes left. They should be able to hang on now. No, I won't bet on it. Thanks, Adam. See you tomorrow." He cradled the phone and leaned back.

Oxford was stretched out in a large easy chair, his feet on a cassock, Dorothy fitted in beside him. They were very happy. She put a finger to his lips.

"Quick now. Fill me in."

"He says we should all be very grateful to your sixth sense. If you hadn't spotted McCarthy in his office, there's every chance he'd have made it out of the country. He had a plane lined up and was heading for the States. Had enough cash and securities with him to last a long time."

"Couldn't they have brought him back? Extradite him?"

"Depends where he got to. He wasn't stopping in the States. We don't have extradition treaties everywhere. Even where we do, it's a long, messy process. This way is better, a lot better. We know right where he is."

Dorothy shuddered, then snuggled in a little tighter. "Yes. A lot better. It's nice to be able to relax. 'Specially like this." After a moment, she asked, "Oxford, speaking of cash, what does Adam say about those safety deposit boxes full of the stuff? Five hundred thousand dollars, you said."

"He's sure it's McCarthy's. Hasn't nailed it down yet. But whoever put the money there was obviously working for McCarthy when he was in your offices."

"Yes. I've been thinking. McCarthy had a special assistant for a long time. Name was Dean, Billy Dean. Smarmy type. Not liked. He left suddenly, not long after McCarthy changed portfolios. I'll bet he knows something. Last I heard he was working for the government in Edmonton."

"We'll have to ask Adam if he knows about him. By the way, he needs to take statements from us. Suggests we come down tomorrow. After we're finished with the *Globe and Mail.*"

"You sure you want me along when you talk to that reporter?"

"Yup! Real sure. Two reasons. First reason. You provide a lot of credibility to this story, my possession of Ben's files. After all, you put them together in the first place. What we call chain of evidence. Second reason. I want you around all the time, as much as possible, for as long as possible."

"Mmmm. I sure like that second reason." And she turned to him.

NEWS FLASH

REGINA—Saskatchewan Premier Harris Halliday died Sunday night in a single vehicle accident. The premier's car flew off the TransCanada Highway overpass at Belle Plaine, west of Regina, into the path of an approaching freight train.

Death was instantaneous according to police. The premier was the sole occupant of the vehicle.

According to family sources, the premier was returning to Regina from his ranch in western Saskatchewan to deal with problems facing his government following the arrest of three senior members of his administration.

Police speculate that the premier might have fallen asleep at the wheel.

FIGHT
OR
DIE

FIGHT OR DIE

A Gunn Brothers Thriller

JAMES HILTON

TITAN BOOKS

Fight or Die
Print edition ISBN: 9781783294886
E-book edition ISBN: 9781783294893

Published by Titan Books
A division of Titan Publishing Group Ltd
144 Southwark Street, London SE1 0UP

First edition: June 2017
10 9 8 7 6 5 4 3 2 1

Names, places and incidents are either products of the author's imagination or used fictitiously. Any resemblance to actual persons, living or dead (except for satirical purposes), is entirely coincidental.

A CIP catalogue record for this title is available from the British Library.

Printed in the USA.

For Rita and Arthur Ogle, forever lights in the night sky.

1

The arrival of the three men sent a shiver crawling down Pamela Duke's back. They were all dressed in a similar fashion, urban combat fatigues with mirrored sunglasses, and moved as a single unit into the cool interior of the bar. Groups of men strutting into the building certainly wasn't unusual—normally they were tourists trawling for fun—but she recognised the trio of Locos. They were expected but nonetheless frightening.

Pamela nodded a greeting and offered the eternal barmaid question to cover her nervousness: "What can I get you guys?"

The first man to reach the bar removed his sunglasses, folded them and placed them on the lacquered wooden counter. "You know what we want, *chica*."

Pamela blanched at the word; it sounded obscene coming from his lips. She straightened, standing her ground. "I've already told your boss: I'm not interested in selling the club to him, or to anyone else."

The other two men stared on impassively, eyeing the bar's few customers through their shades. They moved over to a young man and woman sitting at one of the interior tables.

The young couple had been having a late breakfast, but now, as the men stood over them, they stopped eating and looked up.

The young man returned the stare of the two heavies. "*Hola!*"

Pamela watched as the closest Loco bent at the waist and with slow deliberation, let a large glob of saliva drop onto the man's food.

"You f…!" The young man started up from his seat. His girlfriend grabbed his arm and pulled him back.

"I'm not scared of this dickhead," the boyfriend insisted.

The Loco sneered and moved aside the hem of his shirt to reveal the ribbed hilt of a combat knife. He tapped the pommel with one finger.

The young woman emitted a brief squeal and pulled the young man away from the table. "Come on, Billy. We're going."

As the young couple scurried out into the relative safety of the bright Mediterranean morning, the two men joined their leader at the bar.

"You animals," said Pamela. "You think putting the frighteners on a couple of kids is gonna make me pack up and go home? I've lived in Spain for fifteen years and I've worked way too hard building *my* business to hand it over to a second-rate outfit of donkey fuckers like you!"

"Mrs Duke, where is your husband?" asked the leader. His voice was thick with a southern Spanish accent. "I think I should be talking to the man of the house."

"You know he's away at the trade market. He always goes on Monday and Thursday mornings. Isn't it funny how you only ever come when he's not here? Seeing as your boss has tried to put a stop on our deliveries, you should know better."

"This is your last chance to get a fair price, Mrs Duke. If I have to come back again, I will let my boys off their leash and that will be a sight you do not want to see."

"Fair price? Yeah, right. You should leave now." Quills of anger bristled through Pamela like a static charge.

The Loco who had spat in the tourist's food folded his arms across his chest. The sneer that crept across his face equalled the contempt in his voice, and when he spoke his English was smooth and flawless. "I hardly think a cripple like your husband would be of any comfort anyway. One false leg and half blind—he's a fucking joke!"

"My husband's worth ten of you. He lost his leg serving his country, not by scaring hard-working people out of their homes and businesses."

The leader shot a hand forward and seized a handful of hair. Pamela let out an involuntary yelp as she was yanked forward, her face inches from his. She could feel his breath on her skin, smell the stale stench of tobacco.

"My name is Vincenzo Ortega. I have killed six people and if you don't play the game, you and your crippled husband will be numbers seven and eight." Ortega's hand moved under his open shirt to his armpit, touching the hilt of a knife. "Do you know what the Japanese quick draw is? You draw and cut a throat in less than a second. And I'm finished with the diplomatic approach."

Pamela staggered back, her hips banging against the

shelf behind her, rattling bottles as Ortega shoved her away. Ortega turned and barked a command in Spanish. "Donal, Aspanu, leave our mark."

The two other Locos began kicking over tables and chairs, laughing at the destruction. The few customers remaining made for the door. Pamela yelled at them to stop, but this only seemed to spur their rampage. Bottles smashed as Donal launched a stool over Pamela's head. The heady aroma of rum and whisky filled the air. Pamela carefully brushed slivers of glass from her hair, staring at Ortega with a wild mix of emotions. "You bastards!"

Ortega stared back at her. No emotion showed in his face save for the slightest hint of a smile. The smile was cold and devoid of humour.

Pamela felt a heat rising up her neck and face. "Tell them to stop."

"It's too late for that now, *chica*." Ortega placed a cigarette between his lips. He cast a quick look over his shoulder and barked out a command to one of his men. "*Aspanu, rasgón abajo de la bandera!*"

Aspanu grinned and moved to the Union Flag that adorned the wall facing the bar, embellished with the legend WELCOME TO THE WORLD-FAMOUS WOO HOO CLUB! He reached for a Teflon-coated blade and began ripping into the delicate fabric with obvious joy. "Piece of shit!"

Donal continued to overturn tables and chairs, scattering plates and condiments over the floor. In a few short minutes, the usually pristine establishment that operated as a café by day and a bustling club by night looked like Hurricane Jose had paid a flying visit.

When they were done all three men approached Pamela. Aspanu took his knife and stabbed it down into a stack of menus on the bar, a mere inch from Pamela's fingers. She instinctively shrieked and snatched her hand back. The three men laughed.

Ortega gave Pamela a smile, spreading his hands in an open gesture. "Do we keep going or…?"

Pamela was a strong-willed woman. A lot of army wives get that way. They have as much upheaval in their lives as the soldiers they are married to. A single tear blossomed at the corner of her eye. Not wanting to give the intruders the satisfaction of seeing her wipe it away, she pushed her hair back into a ponytail, shedding the last splinters of broken glass. The tear soaked into her sleeve as she raised her arms.

"Tell your boss to make a serious offer and maybe we'll think about it."

"Too late for that now, *chica*. That boat has sailed. Now you'll take what you get." Ortega's sneer could have curdled milk.

"All of our life savings are in this place!" she said desperately.

"Call it… market fluctuation." Ortega's smoker's voice was sandpaper to her ears. "We'll be back at six so you and your husband can sign over the deeds. If you're not here, we will burn this place down and start over with a new one of our own—"

"Jeez, Daisy, I'd sack your contractor; he's made a real pig's ear of the refurb." A new, deeper voice carried from the doorway of the bar, the American accent thick and unmistakable.

The three Locos turned to see a large silhouette blocking the sun. Ortega spat a warning. "Fuck off. The bar is closed."

The large figure took a step inside. "But I thought the Woo Hoo was always open for a good time. *Woo Hoo!*" The new arrival finished off his sentence with jazz hands.

Ortega nodded towards the stranger and Aspanu stalked forward, blade at the ready. Ortega returned his attention to Pamela. She was smiling.

Aspanu cut the air near the big man's face and then pointed to the door.

There was a soft sound as if the newcomer had made a lazy clap of his hands. Then Aspanu was laid out full stretch on the ground and the interloper was inspecting the man's knife as if he'd just won a prize at a fairground booth. Donal started towards the man. "*Usted es muerto!*"

Pamela stared at Ortega. "You'd better leave now." And then to the newcomer, "Clay, don't kill them. Okay?"

Ortega's gaze flickered between the stranger and Pamela. He eased away from the bar, and his hand stole towards his knife.

Clay cocked his head to one side and addressed Pamela directly. "Are these bozos for real, Daisy?" He raised an eyebrow at Donal, who was approaching, ready to attack. "Now, who are you supposed to be? Tommy the Toreador? The rodeo clown?"

Donal hesitated for a couple of seconds then started forward again. He got almost nose-to-nose with Clay. Clay put on his best worried look, taking a step back. Then he answered with a lunge, driving Aspanu's blade deep into Donal's thigh muscle. Donal let out an ear-splitting shriek and fell writhing to the floor, his own knife forgotten.

Pamela tapped the left side of her chest as Ortega lurched

towards Clay to indicate that he was carrying a weapon. He gave a single nod in response. Clay had disposed of two enforcers in less than fifteen seconds but she knew Ortega was no easy mark—the man exuded a sense of promised violence.

Clay walked casually towards Ortega, his thumbs hooked into his belt. As he stepped over Donal, he tapped his heel sharply on the protruding knife handle, driving the blade deeper into his leg. The fallen gangster howled with renewed vigour. With what appeared to be an afterthought, Clay back-heeled him in the side of the head, silencing him.

"Three desperados to one woman. That hardly seems like fair odds now, does it?"

2

Ortega had spent two years in one of Spain's toughest prisons, where he'd been in the company of many vicious men. He'd also been in enough street fights to recognise a dangerous prospect when he saw one. He studied the big American with practised eyes, made subtle calculations behind his unwavering façade. The man was about six-five, maybe more. His accent unmistakable. Powerful-looking with enough scars on his face to give him a sinister edge. Well over two hundred pounds. Big arms and shoulders. But he wasn't slow: two experienced Locos had gone down in a few seconds. This Clay could be *real* trouble.

Got to take him out!

Ortega set himself.

Do it now!

But then the big man did something unexpected. He started to walk away. "You know what? This is none of my business; go ahead and do what you were gonna do. I'm going for a beer further down the road."

Ortega looked at the big man's back as he stalked away. No way was this American pig leaving here in one piece. He snatched at his knife and lurched after Clay. With deadly intent, he aimed for the kidney and slammed his blade forward—but all he hit was air.

The big man wasn't there. He'd turned in a subtle pivot and now had Ortega's arm caught at the wrist and wrapped up at the elbow. Ortega had been in a few arm-locks in his time but this was unlike anything he'd experienced before. When a cop had you in a hold they were trying to restrain you. This was *very* different.

Pain erupted in his arm, a sudden heat like boiling water in the joint of his elbow. The two men locked eyes in a battle of wills. Ortega strained against the hold.

The big man braced his arms and chest in one severe movement and Ortega felt his elbow joint first hyper-extend and then dislocate fully in a mind-numbing separation of bone and sinew. Ortega felt his legs begin to give way beneath him as his knife clattered to the floor.

"Well I guess you won't be signing any deeds after all," said Clay.

Ortega found his voice, but all he could emit was a high-pitched series of gasping curses.

The woman's—Pamela's—voice rang out from behind the bar. "You know you're right, *Mr Vincenzo Ortega*. My husband isn't a match for you anymore, but you'll find that good men have good friends and Clay here is one of the best. Tell your boss that we're not interested and won't be railroaded. Any more shit like today and *he'll* be the one out of business. For good."

"You piece of shi—" Ortega's response was cut short by an elbow to his face. A quick spin by Clay coupled with a few running steps and Ortega found himself crashing out into the street.

Seconds later Donal and Aspanu were dumped unceremoniously by his side. Clay glowered down at the fallen gangsters. "You'd better listen to the lady. If you come back again, I'll be mighty upset. These are decent people. Bring crap like this here again and you'll pay dearly; unlike the easy ride you got today."

Ortega began to vow retribution but discovered that his mouth didn't work. *That fucker had broken his jaw!* He struggled to his feet, both dislocated arm and shattered jaw sending a barrage of pain through his nervous system.

The big man pointed to the knife embedded in Donal's blood-soaked thigh. "Hey, you might want to get that looked at."

Aspanu had regained consciousness and was looking around, blinking rapidly, clearly trying to make sense of the situation. A fierce grunt and head nodding from Ortega sent him scurrying towards a black Mercedes parked kerbside. Aspanu unlocked the car and then helped Ortega into the passenger seat. Donal, still bleeding profusely and glassy-eyed, was hauled up and pushed without ceremony onto the back seats. The Mercedes then sped away, causing an oncoming car to swerve out of its path.

Pamela slipped her arms around Clay's chest and hugged him close. "Thank you so much. I don't know what would've happened if you hadn't arrived. Those Locos are a bunch of bastards. I hope that's enough to put them off coming back."

"You know I'd never shine you along, Pamela. I don't think we've seen the last of them at all. But it's like we said on the phone last week: you either make a stand and fight for what's yours or you pack up and go."

Pamela looked up into Clay's blue eyes. "I know, I know. But it's not me I'm worried about. It's Larry. I couldn't stand the thought of anything happening to him. But you know how stubborn and proud he is. He'd still square off with them and get himself killed in the process."

Clay nodded in agreement. "Yeah, I know. Larry was one of the best snipers the Brits had, but with no rifle and no leg..." he sucked a sharp intake of breath through his teeth. "Not much chance."

"What do you think will happen now?" asked Pamela. She exhaled, suddenly tired. She had talked long and hard with Larry about moving back to England when the first British ex-pats had given in to the Locos' intimidation, but both had decided that they'd be damned if they were going to be muscled out of their home and livelihood. And besides, what was there to go back to in the UK? The country was going to the dogs faster than you could say Brexit. No, they would stay and brave the storm.

"They'll almost certainly come back with more men. We need to be ready. You need to do as I ask."

"Okay, Clay. That's why you're here. I guess you're in charge." She wiped away her tears and punched Clay on the arm, scolding him gently, "And how many times have I told you not to call me Daisy? That shit sticks you know, soon everyone will call me it!"

Clay laughed and pushed her to arm's length. "But you look like her and Larry likes it!"

"Never mind what Larry likes. I'm in charge and don't forget it." It was familiar banter and it made her feel much better.

Clay Gunn, family friend and sometimes lodger of the Dukes, ushered her back inside. "Come on, Mrs *Pamela* Duke, I'll help you straighten up the place before Larry gets back. If he sees this, he'll be on eBay looking for a rifle before lunchtime."

3

Danny Gunn was parched. A cool drink was his first priority as he alighted from the budget flight into the moderate-sized airport. Three and a half hours in what amounted to little more than a chicken coop with wings had left him feeling uncharacteristically grouchy. He'd always thought that the old army transport planes were bad, but Air España had developed cattle-class travel to a new low.

Almería airport certainly wasn't the biggest or best in Spain, but at least its modest footfall allowed Danny to proceed quickly on his way. After clearing passport control, which comprised of one uniformed officer who looked like he'd been pumped full of formaldehyde before his shift, Danny was waved on into baggage collection with barely a cursory glance at his passport.

His baggage consisted of a dark-grey holdall and a small carry-on rucksack. A quick stop at the first shop available and Danny purchased a litre bottle of spring water. A few minutes later, just as he was sipping the last dregs from the bottle, Clay appeared at his side.

"Well hello, wee one!"

"You're late." Danny poked his older sibling's chest with the plastic bottle.

"Hooey, I've never been late in my life. The only thing I'll be late for is my funeral. They'll have to come and look for me for that one." Clay's deep Texas drawl caused a passer-by to raise his eyebrows.

"And stop calling me wee one," Danny griped.

The two men drew a few bemused glances as they hugged enthusiastically. Danny didn't care, at ease with their affection. The Gunn brothers then made their way towards the exit. The modest crowds of tourists seemed to instinctively give them a wide berth. Danny nodded at the elderly couple who had sat in the seats adjacent to his on the flight. He received little in the way of response.

"It's real good to see you again, little brother," said Clay. "Thanks for coming over so quick."

Danny smiled. "Always happy to spend quality time with my big bro, even if it is on a job. Email and texting doesn't do it for me. If it's not face to face it doesn't count for much."

"Ay-men to that," agreed Clay. He punched Danny's shoulder affectionately.

"Careful, ya big ape. I may need to use that arm in the next day or so."

Strangers and new acquaintances often had trouble reconciling the fact that the two men were full brothers. Clay was very obviously American, with his strong Texan accent. In contrast, Danny spoke with a Scottish brogue, a result of both brothers being raised on opposite sides of the Atlantic during their formative years.

Danny was six years younger than Clay, stood a modest five-nine and his swimmer's build was never going to win him a Mr Universe title. He typified what his old sergeant major had called a "wiry bastard". The kind of body structure that could run all day, take a kicking and keep on ticking.

Something the brothers did share was their fiercely intelligent eyes, which could convey a universe of emotion with a glance. Fury, cunning, warmth, wrath... all were there like a deck of cards waiting to be shuffled by a skilled dealer.

After exiting the arrivals lounge they walked briskly to Clay's rental car, a Toyota Avensis, and joined the sparse traffic leaving the airport.

"So how's your Spanish?" Clay asked.

"Better than my German, worse than my English," Danny replied. He grinned at his brother. "At least I can speak more than five words."

"I know, I know. It's one of those things I always mean to do."

Danny laughed. "You live in a house with three Spanish speakers! How have you managed *not* to learn it?"

"I know. But Celine and Salma were both born in Texas and Sebastian speaks perfectly good English."

"Methinks the Texan protesteth too much."

"What's Spanish for blow it out your ass?"

"*Soplar el culo...*"

"No one likes a smart alec."

Danny grinned and waved a pacifying hand. "So how far is the town?"

Clay pointed in a general north-easterly direction.

"Not far. Half an hour's drive maybe."

Danny had been sure to do some research once he'd received Clay's call. The resort town of Ultima Felicidad had been purpose-built less than ten years earlier. A Spanish official had visited Cancun in Mexico, and thought to reproduce that winning formula once back in his homeland. Like Cancun, the new town had been erected from the ground up with the express purpose of tourism in mind. Señor Covaz of the Spanish Tourist Board convinced some very influential investors to his way of thinking and the resort of Ultima Felicidad was born. Known more commonly as Ultima the resort had promised "ultimate happiness" for visitors and locals alike. The reality of the town fell somewhere short of the real-estate posters.

The resort was situated on a picturesque stretch of the Spanish coastline, nestled midway between the Costa Blanca and the Costa Del Sol. An ideal location. The real wrinkle in the Ultima promise arose when non-Spanish parties started buying up the property in ever increasing frequency. Then came the near fatal financial meltdown of the Spanish economy. Once amiable neighbouring businesses became bitter competition, each and every euro earned vital to their survival. However, the main problem in Ultima wasn't with tourists or rival businesses but with a very different class of people.

In Italy they would have been called Mafia, but here they operated as smaller independent groups with no real family lineage. Over the previous thirty years Spain had become easy pickings for a mix of multi-national criminals. Italian, Eastern European, British, African and even South American gangsters were now known to operate within and through its borders. Each group vied for increased power and prestige as they conducted their various illicit enterprises.

Despite his reason for visiting, his first sight of the town made Danny smile. Ultima shimmered with thousands of glittering fairy lights, which decorated each cultivated palm tree. Diagonal strands wound their way around the tree trunks that lined the roadside in perfect equidistant plots. The town itself was picturesque, each building designed in a Spanish/Mexican style that exuded conviviality. Pueblo shop fronts blended perfectly with steel and smoked glass hotel façades due to the clever use of colour and continuity of styling throughout the entire resort.

"What do you think, Danny?"

"It's great. I can see why Larry and Pamela put their money into this place when they did. I was expecting a town something like Torremolinos or Salou. You know, old fishing villages that had grown into cheap and cheerful resorts, but this place looks more like a Hollywood movie set. *Miami Vice 2025.*"

"Well it was a real gamble for the likes of them. The town could've come to nothing or just struggled along as another so-so destination. Plenty of ordinary folks put their money in at the start and it's largely down to their hard work and investment that this place is what it is today. Now the shit-heels want to scalp it all away. All the big hotel chains are here but it's the smaller businesses that give the town real flavour. Places like the Woo Hoo."

"Yeah. I can understand why the gangs want their claws into this. This place must be a gold mine during the summer. I've seen people murdered in their beds for a lot less than Ultima."

"With the amount of money to be made here, the

organised gangs will resort to bloody murder to protect their interests. I think we're sitting on a powder keg."

"Aye, I know what you mean," Danny said.

"It's been building for years. Lots of foreigners, but especially Brits, have been buying businesses and homes in Spain. At first everything was great, a mini property boom. Then as time went on, more and more British owners were having their homes repossessed by the Spanish authorities or real-estate companies on various bogus technicalities. The Brits were given a legal run-around when they tried to contest the repossessions."

Danny nodded in understanding. Quite a few of these stories had hit the tabloids as even famous British celebrities were conned out of their homes and businesses.

"Then it got even worse. The protection rackets were first. Now there's syndicate gangs muscling the ex-pats into selling their businesses at ludicrously reduced prices. Ten cents on the dollar kind of shit. If the business owners don't concede, then the *threats* of violence quickly turn to action."

None of this was news to Danny but he let Clay spell it out, enjoying listening to his brother's drawl. Danny's question was purely rhetorical. "I presume that going to the police or government is a non-starter?"

Clay shook his head. "Nah, half the guys that are railroading the owners are the ones in office that endorsed the sales in the first place. As for the cops... well, the hierarchy blocks any real investigation. Most of the street cops are okay, but you know what it's like. At the higher levels of the police and government, they all piss in the same pot."

"So it's the same old shit, different country." Danny

closed his eyes for a long moment. "So who's the main man in our case?"

"I still haven't got the head honcho's name but the gang is a local outfit called the Locos. They've been targeting the British pubs and clubs along this stretch of coast. These boys are a real mix-up. Most of them are Spanish, but I've heard there's a few Africans and hajis among them too. I've only been here a couple of days so intel's still a bit light. Larry and Daisy are trying to get a group of the Brits together for a meeting. We'll get more facts then."

"Great," replied Danny, recognising the slow burn of adrenalin in his stomach as he contemplated the possible outcome of this situation. *Yep, this could explode into death and destruction in a heartbeat. Happy days.*

"So how heavy have they come on to Larry and Pamela?"

"Well they've been working on Pam the most. They know that if they put the frighteners on the wife bad enough, she'll usually talk the husband into selling up." Clay steered the Toyota round a gentle bend in the road. The driver's seat was wracked down to its lowest position but Clay's hair still brushed the roof.

"So how handy are these Loco boys then? Tough guys or wannabes?"

"A bit of both. Like most gangs they mostly trade on their reputation. They trashed the Woo Hoo and had a go at me yesterday."

"How many came at you?"

"Three, but the numb-nuts came one at a time. Not the brightest."

Danny shook his head. Knowing how capable Clay was

with his fists, he couldn't help but feel that the Locos had made a big mistake. Clay responded with a look that silently conveyed: *I know—stupid or what!*

"Any skills?"

"The first two, no. But the ringleader had presence. He knew how to handle himself. I had to draw him into attacking me by giving him my back. He wasn't your typical blade-waver."

Danny nodded. Any knife-man worth his salt would never advertise his weapon. With a skilled knife-fighter, you usually only got to see the knife *after* he'd stuck it between your ribs. As Clay slowed the Toyota to a stop in an enclosed parking bay Danny asked, "Any names?"

"The ringleader from the Woo Hoo is called Ortega. As I said, we should pick up some more details when you meet the rest of the local Brits."

"Okay," Danny said. "How long will you be over in Portugal for?"

Clay considered. "Two days maybe, three tops. I've got to sort out a couple of things at the house. You know, legal stuff. Then I'll pick up some supplies on the way back here."

"No problem, Clay. I'll take up the slack while you're gone."

Clay nodded in affirmation. "Larry and Daisy are good friends."

"Is this it?" Danny motioned to the back doors of the building.

"Yep, sure is. The Woo Hoo Club. Larry does a good pint here; you'll like it. Come on, Larry and Daisy are dying to see you again."

Danny smiled. He hadn't seen the couple for over five years and although they were really Clay's friends he'd liked both of them immensely. Pamela had a great sense of humour and a throaty laugh, always doing all the actions while telling a story. She used to toss her hair around like a mad thing while doing an impression of seventies rocker Suzi Quatro. Larry Duke was one of those old-fashioned soldiers that still looked like he was under parade ground inspection; never a hair out of place and creases in his trousers that you could cut bread with.

Good people. Friends.

The type worth protecting.

4

"The textbooks of the world will tell you different, but neon was designed to hide the plain, the ugly and the worn out," Danny said, reading from an article on his iPad. "If you've ever visited Las Vegas in daylight hours you'll understand. By day, drab weathered walls show the dirt, vomit stains and the worst of society's skidmarks—but when the sun goes down and the rainbow spectrum of flashing neon kicks into life, the same bland tableau is transformed into an exotic menagerie of sights, sounds and possibilities. A twenty-dollar hooker in daylight hours can be enough to make a dog tuck its tail and run, but in the dark under the glamour of the blue neon strobe, the same streetwalker can appear as tempting as Beyoncé's little sister."

"I guess that guy doesn't write for the local tourist office?"

Danny laughed and turned the screen towards Pamela. "I suspect not. That's the beauty and the curse of the Internet. Everyone's a critic."

Fortunately, Ultima Felicidad *was* still beautiful when the sun was at its zenith, looking down on its devoted worshippers on the streets and beaches below.

Danny sipped a Diet Coke at one of the dozen or so chrome tables arranged outside at the front entrance of the Woo Hoo. By day, the club served a variety of food and drink, both in the air-conditioned interior and al fresco on the street front terrace.

Larry emerged from the bar and joined him at the table. Pamela had a Coke flavoured with a shot of vanilla essence and Larry touted a bottle of San Miguel that seemed to be perspiring in the late-morning heat. A dog with a shaggy brown-and-white coat limped along behind him as if aping his disability. Danny smiled and held out the back of his hand. The dog pressed a nose that was cold and wet hard against his skin, snuffling the new scent. He appeared to be a collie-cross. What Danny referred to as a "Heinz 57" due to the varieties in the genetic mix. He preferred mixed mongrels to most pedigree breeds.

"Hey, boy, how you doing?" Danny proceeded to ruffle the fur behind the mutt's ear. The dog scooted closer, pressing against his legs.

Pamela leaned over and gently tugged on his curled tail. The dog looked between the two sources of affection.

"What's he called?" asked Danny.

"Jacks," she replied. "Short for One-Eyed Jacks."

The dog turned fully to look at Danny. Jacks was missing his left eye, part of one ear and his left front paw.

"Poor little mite. What happened to him?" Danny continued to pat his head.

"Some idiot ran over him on a quad bike. Squished him up pretty good. Larry found him lying on the path down to the beach. We thought he was a goner at first but when we realised he wasn't dead we took him to the vet. Damn fleabag cost us a shitload of money but you're worth it, aren't you, boy?"

Jacks placed his disfigured leg on Pamela's thigh.

"Well, I agree. He's great." Danny turned his thoughts to more serious matters. "Clay gave me the story on the way over from the airport, but I need to ask a few more questions... you okay with that?"

"Sure, Danny, fire away." As he sat down, Larry tucked his artificial leg under the table.

"I know they're trying to muscle you into selling the club," said Danny, nodding at the sculptured doorway. "But I need to know as much detail about this Loco outfit as possible."

Over the next hour Danny asked for full details on the club's takings, number of staff and their addresses, how many customers on an average week, delivery schedules, suppliers, fire exits and rear access. Pamela seemed exhausted by the litany.

"Why do you need to know all this stuff? You won't have to go looking for these guys. I'm pretty sure they'll come back. Clay said as much too."

"I probably don't need to know half this stuff, but the more I know, the less the Locos can surprise me with."

"Tactical knowledge is king!" Larry nodded in agreement. "I wish it was like it was in the old days. I could just perch up on the roof and ventilate the lot of them."

Pamela squeezed her husband's hand. Danny couldn't

fail to notice the moment. Deep emotions ran just below the surface. Larry pursed his lips, his eyes downcast. His leg made a metallic clang as it struck the base of the table as he shifted position. Jacks raised his head briefly from the full sprawl he'd adopted beneath the table.

"Now, about the Locos, tell me again how many have been to the club in total?" asked Danny.

"About six or seven different faces, usually in threes. The backup changes, but Ortega always leads the way," said Pamela.

Danny blew a snort of air out of his nose. "He's probably a captain."

Larry flushed red. "I'm gonna kill those toss-pots next time they come at us. They waited 'til I was out and tried the bully boy act with Pamela. It's a good job that Clay was on hand or it could have all gone south quick-time."

Pamela tenderly laid a hand on top of Larry's and this calmed him somewhat. Danny could see how much they loved each other. It was obvious that Pamela would do anything to look after her husband and Larry would undoubtedly die trying to protect her in return.

"So Clay is going to be away for the next few days?" asked Larry.

"Aye, he said he was really sorry about leaving just as the job was getting interesting, but he's got some stuff on the home front in Portugal that he can't let slide. I think there's a lot of legal papers that need signing. He's buying some more land next to his first plot. Don't worry, I can hold the fort until he gets back. He'll bring some toys back with him— equipment that I couldn't carry on the plane."

Larry smiled. He knew the kind of toys that the Gunn

brothers played with; not the kind you got with your Happy Meal that was for sure. "This crap with the Locos has been escalating. As soon as I told him what was going on Clay hopped into his car and came straight down here."

"Aye, that sounds like Clay."

"What's his place in Portugal like?"

Danny laughed. "Well, it was a building site last time I was there, but that's quite a while ago. I'm sure he'll have the roof on by now."

"Don't count on it… You know how Clay likes his time outdoors, he'll probably leave the roof off just so he can look at the night sky from his bed," Pamela jested.

"Nah, he's a big fanny really. Clay's idea of a wild night is having English mustard on his hot dog," said Larry. Like most soldiers, he couldn't offer a straight compliment to a friend without a side order of crap to go with it.

Danny laughed, and One-Eyed Jacks looked up again at the sound, cocking his head to one side.

"Look," said Danny, "when these Locos come back, I want you two to get into the kitchen as quick as you can. The staff too." Larry started to protest but Danny cut him off. "It's not about being tough; it's about being smart. If I go down, you've got more chance to protect Pamela back there. I presume you've still got a shotgun around here somewhere?"

"I've got one at home." Larry's face was grim.

"Bring it in… but take things easy. We all know that shooting the place up is the last thing we want. That would be worst-case scenario. Plus, the Spanish cops are all armed as standard; you don't want those guys storming in all guns blazing as well."

"Yeah, I know what you mean," agreed Larry. He puffed out his cheeks. "Got to pay a visit to the little boys' room." He rose and walked inside the club.

Pamela rubbed both hands over her face. She stared at Danny for a few seconds before speaking. "You know, when this crap first started I considered throwing in the towel, going back to England, but then I look at Larry. He's dreamed of having his own bar since our early days together. Thirty years of savings and all of his compensation from the army is tied up in this place. It became my dream too, something we could build together."

"I understand."

"The club means so much to me but nothing in the world would be worth losing Larry for. I came so close already with that bastard landmine."

Danny nodded, his face solemn in agreement.

"Do you want another drink?" asked Larry as he returned to the table.

"No, I'm good thanks," said Danny. He inched back his chair. "I'm going out to walk the area. I'll be gone for at least a couple of hours. You've got my number. The slightest hint of trouble and you buzz me, okay?"

When neither of them responded he said, "The slightest hint of trouble, okay?"

"Okay," agreed Larry and Pamela simultaneously.

"Do you need anything?" asked Larry.

"Nah, I'm good to go. Just want to get the lay of the land. You never know when you might find yourself in one of those back streets. It kind of helps if you know where the hell you are."

Danny rose and started to walk down the street, noting its width and available cover points if a firefight did transpire. At the moment he was at a disadvantage with the bearings of an aimless tourist, but he could fix that. Jacks sprang up to follow and had to be called back twice by Pamela. Danny smiled at the dog's enthusiasm and held up a hand in way of a temporary farewell.

When Danny was out of earshot, Pamela turned to Larry. "What do you think about Danny?"

Larry leaned forward in his seat. "I know he isn't as big or scary-looking as Clay, but that fella is as mean as a tiger with his balls in a gin trap. Since he left the army he's made a living as a 'fixer'. Clay says he's one of those guys you can call on when your back is pressed so hard against the wall you've got mortar in your arse crack."

"Is that on his business card?"

Larry gave a sincere nod. "Maybe it should be."

Pamela watched as Danny turned down a back alley some two hundred metres away. Jacks too watched with his one good eye, huffed once, then settled back into the comparative cool beneath the table.

5

Danny walked with a casual gait as he traversed the alleyways and junctions in a half-mile radius around the Woo Hoo Club, committing as much detail to memory as possible.

Ultima Felicidad had been modelled on an American-style street grid, with each street lying parallel to each other on a north/south bearing and the opposite streets lying on an east/west pattern. This formed neat blocks of buildings that helped give Ultima its stylised yet uniform look, with no building over five storeys high—no doubt to restrict the hotel chains. The streets had been named in the American format also, with First Street and Second Street lying north/south, and the east/west streets named after famous Spanish celebrities and historical figures.

Danny found himself on the junction of Twenty-Third and Banderas. The architecture of the buildings was very similar to the rest of Ultima, but Banderas seemed to play host to a collection of garages, car showrooms and auto spray shops. In marked contrast, the shops and stores on Twenty-Third seemed to be more concerned with designer fashion boutiques and sunglasses. On Thirtieth and Conde, named for the famous bullfighter, Javier Conde, Danny found a home improvement store. Twenty minutes later he paid the cashier and left with two large bags stuffed with a very eclectic range of items.

He was about to cross the narrow street when a loose convoy of bikers rumbled past. Danny stepped quickly back to the kerb. Nice bikes. Big and powerful, a few with custom paint jobs. The riders all sported the same granite expression and gang colours. Tough guys. One of the bikers gave him an exaggerated look of disdain, sitting astride a chopper that was painted a midnight blue. Instead of the usual chrome, the frame was finished in what appeared to be burnished bronze.

Danny kept a Kawasaki 650 in a lockup back in England, but it was a poor relation to these machines that rumbled so loudly they caused the shop windows to vibrate as they passed by. Further down the road a young couple had to jump sideways to avoid a bike that nearly clipped them. The woman managed to lose one of her shoes as she made the mad dash to avoid being run over. When the young man gave the biker the finger, three of the riders slowed and revved the engines in unison. The noise was deafening. The startled couple ducked inside the nearest shop as one of the bikers drew what looked like a steel pipe from his handlebars and pointed the weapon in their direction.

Danny leaned against a shop front, shaking his head at the moronic display and watched the bikers trace their way the full length of the street. He gazed at the colourful gang patch that adorned the back of every one of the bikers' jackets. He filed it away with the rest of the day's details and slowly wound his way back through the grid towards the Dukes' club. *Time*, he thought, *to get things in motion*.

6

The Woo Hoo had steadily filled up during the traditional siesta time. It's a curious fact that the British don't siesta very well, perhaps seeing themselves as being built from hardier stuff than their continental cousins. Danny liked the idea of some quiet downtime each day—if not spent sleeping fully, then dozing with a half-read book for company. But the good-natured festivities that the Woo Hoo promoted during the daylight hours made sleep impossible.

Danny sat in an alcove that afforded a clear view of the club's main entrance. Music pumped from the inset speakers that were tucked invisibly into the alcove seating. Jacks lay at his feet, slumbering, seemingly oblivious to the noise.

The club's day trade consisted of mainly older British ex-patriots that had taken up residence in or around the resort of Ultima. In line with the older crowd's tastes, the music playing was an eclectic mix of sixties, seventies and eighties. Silver-haired and tanned to the colour of a walnut seemed to be the required look for the daytime patrons of the Woo Hoo.

Danny recognised a few minor celebrities in the crowd.

One owned a famous nightclub of his own in London and as usual he had a girl at least forty years his junior hanging on his every word. Opposite sat a comedian who had been big in the nineties, but had lost his star quality due to his overfondness of the whisky bottle and his reputation of being impossible to work with during his "wet seasons". The ageing entertainer had the Woo Hoo crowd in the palm of his hand: half of the club was listening intently to the tale he was recounting about his wild nights of partying with U2 and the female cast of a well-known soap opera.

Danny smiled to himself; a big fish in a little pond. But there was no malice to his judgement. He understood why fading stars came to places like Ultima or Marbella or Miami. They'd struggled all of their professional lives to be somebody and wanted to hang on to the laughs and applause for as long as possible.

No harm, no foul.

And of course having these "celebs" as regulars didn't hurt the Woo Hoo's takings. Tourists came here by the coachload on the chance of seeing an ex-James Bond or another old star sipping a strawberry daiquiri. Larry Duke didn't deny the rumours that Sean Connery himself was part-owner of the club; he just tapped his nose to regular enquirers and replied, "That's between me and Sean."

Of course Connery had never put a penny into the club, but the punters had already made up their minds, preferring to spin stories of how they'd spent their holiday rubbing shoulders with the stars. Larry was never going to let the truth get in the way of a story or a good business opportunity.

The afternoon passed without event. As the sun began to

set, the older crowd drifted away and the Woo Hoo slowly awakened. Pamela escorted Jacks upstairs where he spent his time during the evening trade. Three-legged dogs and drunken partygoers; never the twain should meet.

A myriad of neon lights pulsated in perfect synchronised timing with the beat of the music. The effect was almost hypnotic. Danny wasn't a big fan of nightclubs— too many people—but the atmosphere in the Woo Hoo Club was undeniably great. The sight of young women dressed in what amounted to little more than underwear and skin-tight Lycra bodysuits did nothing to upset Danny's sensibilities either. But always his attention crept back to the main entrance.

The club employed three uniformed doormen at night, but they were there more for effect than any real action. Larry had copied the routine from the upmarket clubs in Los Angeles that had door staff checking for names on a "guest list". The list was a fake of course, but every now and then the doormen would ask each other, "Is it tonight that Posh and Becks are coming?" just loud enough for the revellers to hear. The name-dropping always sent a ripple of excitement through the crowd awaiting entry. It didn't matter that the stars never arrived; the promise was what the Woo Hoo sold. Pamela had even employed lookalikes to breeze into the club. Clubbers went home on those nights swearing that they'd partied with Tom Cruise or Johnny Depp. Woo Hoo!

As the night drew to a close, Danny was grateful that he hadn't had to do more than learn the lay of the land. But he knew it wouldn't last.

7

Vincenzo Ortega sat with his broken right arm in a cast. A rainbow of dark purple bruises shadowed the murder in his eyes like a highwayman's mask. His jaw had been wired in the emergency room at Magdalena Hospital in Almería City. He could now only speak in the manner of a novice ventriloquist.

His two backup men, Aspanu and Donal, were sitting in silence at the rear of the spacious terrace. After the curses that their boss had spewed at Ortega they dared not even make eye contact. The boss had a habit of "shooting the messenger" and all of his underlings knew that the best course of action was to keep your head down during one of his furious rants.

Antoni Barcelo was a physically imposing figure. His broad sloping forehead was framed with a shock of coal-black hair that was swept back off his face in a retro "Elvis" style. The back of his hair was grown past collar length but was still slicked and neat. Appearance was important to Barcelo; he spent a fortune on grooming products and counted a masseuse and skincare specialist among his retained staff. He also wore a Savile Row suit almost every day regardless of the Mediterranean heat.

Today he wore a slate-grey blazer with matching trousers, a white silk shirt and white leather loafers. His face clashed with his wardrobe, however, due to the fact that he was so angry he'd turned a dark crimson. His guttural Spanish rattled like gunfire. "*One* man did this to you? Three of you couldn't handle one tourist? You spend the day in the hospital and I only hear about it now?"

"Boss, I was messed up," Ortega tried to explain. "I just needed some time to get my head straight."

"Why, so you could come up with a line of crap to spin me?" demanded Barcelo. "One damned tourist?"

Ortega struggled through his explanation. "This guy knew what he was doing. I think the Dukes have hired some muscle of their own."

"Well? What the hell do I pay you spineless cretins for? You're supposed to sort out problems like this. Do I need to go down there and break him myself?"

"No, boss, we were just caught off guard. What do you want us to do next? Petrol bomb the place?"

"No. Not yet. That would just cost me more. Send a couple of scouts down to the bar and watch out for this hired help. See if there are any more protectors—I want to know numbers. Let's see if they *are* professionals before I send any more of you imbeciles to get your asses kicked."

Ortega knew Barcelo was a dangerous man but that his boss could be generally relied on to be objective when dealing with outside threats. Rumour had it he'd learned a valuable lesson during a three-year stretch in the notorious Zuera prison as a young man in his twenties. Another inmate had baited him about his pretty-boy looks, offering him a role as a stand-in wife. Antoni had charged in furiously, swinging his fists. The more experienced inmate had dodged his blows and reciprocated with three stabs with a homemade knife. During his four weeks in the prison infirmary Barcelo had vowed never to be shanked again by rushing in without knowing the capability of his enemy.

"Vin, pick out three from your team and send them down there to watch the place. Nobody is to move on them until I have spoken, is that clear?"

Ortega nodded and motioned for his two men to leave with him.

"And, you two!" Barcelo pointed at both Donal and Aspanu. "If you fail me again, you better move to Australia so I don't see you *ever* again."

The two injured men nodded energetically and scuttled after Ortega. Donal favoured his good leg, trying to avoid putting pressure on the sutures in his thigh.

An hour or so later, three Locos sat in a parked car watching the entrance to the Woo Hoo Club. It was getting dark and the evening crowd was beginning to fill the streets. Ortega had described the big guy who'd taken him, Donal and Aspanu down, but as yet the watchers hadn't seen such a man.

"Maybe I should go in and have a closer look," offered Juba Akengala, the only black man in the trio. Juba was Nigerian by birth but had drifted across Africa to wherever there was a head to crack for money. He was very capable with a machete, wielding it with deadly efficiency. His features were narrow and defined but not unattractive. Unlike the other Locos in their urban camouflage, he was dressed smartly in loose denim jeans, a dark-yellow shirt with a distinctive crocodile logo and a pair of new Timberland boots. "I've never been in the club before, so they won't know who I am."

His two companions looked back at him, then the elder of the three, Vasquez, spoke. "Okay, go in, but just keep yourself to yourself. Try to find the big guy Ortega mentioned and if you see him, check if he has any friends with him. Be careful."

Inside the club Danny glanced up from a cocktail menu that he had propped on the table. A tall black man had just entered and strode casually over to the main bar. Danny watched him for a moment or two and then went back to scanning the club with his peripheral vision. Twenty minutes later Danny registered the same man leaving—just another guy on the lookout for a cold beer.

Danny rolled his neck around to relieve the stiffness there. He decided to exercise in the morning; he needed to burn off some energy before the meeting with the other British business owners the following evening. He glanced at his watch; another three hours to closing time. He was confident that the presence of the bustling evening crowd in the club would dissuade any retribution from the Locos. As Danny settled back into his seat his attention was caught by a silver-haired man giving a very poor attempt at the Robot. Danny smiled and shook his head. *You're never too old to make an arse of yourself,* he thought.

8

After a short but restful night's sleep, Danny arose and looked out of the window at the resplendent Spanish sunrise. Taking a deep breath, he closed his eyes and enjoyed the sensation of the sun on his face.

He had remained on watch for all of the previous night's trade, blending in with the revellers. When the last of the clubbers had staggered homeward, Danny had climbed the stairs to the makeshift bedroom that Pamela had prepared for him. Jacks had immediately cozied up to him and had to be called twice before leaving him be.

A camp bed, a small wooden cabinet and a bedside lamp were the sum total of the room's furnishings but he didn't require many creature comforts. His laptop and iPad sat next to the lamp. Danny glanced at his watch; the luminous dial showed 07.30. Using the club's bathroom facilities, he shaved and showered to parade ground standards. Old habits.

Larry and Pamela lived a couple of miles away from the club in a modest villa, so while Clay was travelling Danny had the club premises to himself. He padded down the stairs, taking note of any creaky steps. The walls of the club were enhanced by the clever use of mirrors, which made the main room look much larger than it actually was. Danny sized up the dance floor to be about twenty by twenty feet. Sixteen tables filled the area near the front door and plush booths occupied the outer walls and alcoves. Chrome tables and chairs were stacked neatly to one side of the doorway, ready to be placed outside once the club was open for the day trade.

He closed his eyes and stood motionless at the kitchen entrance. He tried to scan the room with all of his senses in unison. Soft background noise filtered in from the street outside. The rumble of passing traffic. An occasional car horn. The air inside the room was warm and still. No air-con unit had yet been employed.

All quiet.

No perceivable threat.

Confident he was truly alone, Danny moved to the centre of the dance floor. A musty combination of old food smells and the sweat of a thousand dancers echoed in a fragrant bouquet that would never be bottled or sold by Givenchy.

As with most trained fighters Danny had learned a variety of kata—set sequences of attack and defence executed against imaginary opponents. He flowed smoothly through a less used sequence known as *Tegatana Shodan*. The training form was the first in a set using all of the various types and angles of knife-hand strikes. The kata employed fast pivots and turns to negate the attacking force, double blocks and parries, single and double strikes, simultaneous attack and defence and most unusually for kata, pre-emptive attacks.

As he worked through the form several times without

pause, Danny visualised his opponents as very real attackers. This was the secret of kata; making it real in your mind.

He broke an imaginary chokehold by pivoting and sweeping the arms downward, then a knife hand crushed a trachea. He pivoted a quarter turn to dodge a kick to his groin and swept the kick up and out with his left arm as his right slammed into a mastoid muscle under the ear. He slipped inside a visualised right hook and blasted the attacker with a "five swords" combination—five fully focused hand strikes in less than one second.

He paused, relaxing. Beads of sweat trickled down his face as he settled his breathing.

He was at peace again.

After Danny had completed his morning exercises, he took another quick shower and set about finding some breakfast. Larry's instructions had been "eat anything in the kitchen you want"—dangerous words to an ex-squaddie.

After a minute of peering into the dry store and a walk into a small refrigerated room, Danny decided on a large bowl of multi-coloured cereal rings and a mammoth portion of grapefruit segments, a fruit that he'd loved from early childhood visits to his uncle's hotel near Loch Lomond. He consumed the food while a pot of coffee hissed and gurgled its way to capacity. Three mugs of java later and Danny was ready for the day ahead. He was just washing up when the soft scraping of a key turning in a lock made him pause; he adopted a slight crouch automatically, then relaxed when he heard female voices.

He emerged from the kitchen to find Pamela and two staff members entering through the front door.

"Morning. How are you feeling today?" asked Pamela.

"Up and at it, Pamela," Danny replied. "Is Larry with you?"

"Yeah, he's just parking the van around the back."

Right on cue, Larry appeared with a rattle of keys at the back door. He walked towards Danny with his uneven gait.

The two men exchanged greetings in a slightly awkward manner, so Danny decided to be upfront. "Look, Larry, Pamela, thanks again for putting your trust in me. I know the club means everything to you, so I'll do anything I can to help protect it. Thanks for letting me lodge here as well."

Larry seemed lost for words for a long moment. "Nah, Danny, it's me and Pam that are thankful. Thankful there are still good men like you and Clay that give a damn about helping a broken old soldier and his wife."

Danny could see a hint of embarrassment flit across his face. "Look, Larry, I know an old warhorse like you could send these desperados scuttling for the hills. But I need a piece of the action too, you know."

"Oh, don't worry. I suspect you'll have more than a few skulls to crack before this thing is over with."

"Glad to hear it," Danny declared.

Pamela and the two staff members joined the old soldiers. "Danny Gunn, this is Julie and Hernandez. Julie helps cover the front during day shift and Hernandez is our chef."

Julie flashed Danny a smile, which he gladly returned. Hernandez added, "Just call me Dez; everybody else does."

"Nice to meet you, Dez."

Danny held Julie's gaze for a long moment as the group talked. She was very easy on the eye. Her long brown hair was tied back into a neat ponytail, and her eyes were a curious mix of green and grey, very similar to his own. Her teeth were very white and perfectly straight, setting off her light tan and long legs. No ring on her finger. Danny liked everything about her. Her hand was soft and warm in his as they shook hello. Danny caught Pamela's knowing smile.

A few more pleasantries were exchanged before the two staff and Pamela busied themselves with preparations for the forthcoming day's trade.

"At least last night was quiet," Danny said to Larry. "How long have the Locos been after your club?"

"Best part of a month now, but it came to a head the other day. It was lucky that Clay was in town. Look, I couldn't say it in front of Pamela, but I know that I'm no match for these fuckers. That's why I called Clay for help." He tapped his prosthetic limb against a barstool. "I'm not much cop if I have to move fast any more, and if the Guardia knew how crap my eyesight is they'd take my driving licence off me faster than you could say *adiós amigo*."

"Clay counts you and Pamela amongst his nearest and dearest, so the same goes for me. Don't worry, this will all be over with very soon."

Larry rubbed a hand across his clean-shaven face. "Well, it's appreciated. You know we haven't talked about money yet. We don't expect you to risk your neck free of charge. What's the going rate for this kind of job these days?"

"I usually roll for five hundred a day, but this may not be a quick fix. I'll tell you what. I'm having an end-of-season sale... let's call it a grand for the week. If it's still going after that we'll sit down again and talk things through. But you know I'm not here for the money. Clay called on me and it's a closer-to-home job for him, so likewise for me."

Larry smiled, his eyes crinkling into deep fissures at the corners. He gestured over to a booth at the rear of the club. As both men sat he glanced around even though the club was empty. He leaned forward, a half smile creeping across his face. "Are all the stories Clay tells about you true?"

Danny shrugged. "Clay likes to add a little spice to his stories—especially if a beer is helping it along."

"Is it true about the boat off the African coast?"

"What did he say about it?"

"That you and three others boarded a ship that Somali pirates had taken. You slotted sixteen hostiles and sailed the ship back to port in Madagascar."

"It wasn't quite sixteen but, aye, that's about right."

"What about the petrol tanker in Morocco?"

Danny nodded silently.

Larry hesitated for a beat, then asked, "Did you really drop a car battery on someone from the roof of a building?"

"Aye, that was in Africa as well. The shit-heel was part of a death squad that was terrorising the local villagers. He had men dotted around in the surrounding houses. I had to take him out quiet."

"So you dropped a battery on his head?"

"Well it was a lot quieter than 'blatting' him with my '80."

"Guess so." Larry continued, "But what about the guy in the abattoir? That must be made up right?"

"That depends. What did my all too vocal brother tell you about that?" The smile dropped from Danny's face. Danny was going to have words with Clay when he got back from his road trip. If the powers that be ever linked him to any of these *wet* jobs he would be looking at the inside of a cell for the rest of his natural existence.

Larry lowered his voice to barely above a whisper. "He said that you *'might have'* pushed a paedophile through an industrial meat grinder."

Danny swore under his breath. "He raped, tortured and killed four kids and walked out of court on some botched police procedure. He's nobody the world will ever miss."

Then Danny relaxed and his eyes regained their usual happy glint. The men looked at each other; a silent understanding assured Larry that this was indeed the right man for the job. Something Danny had known all along.

9

Danny settled himself in and watched the first of the day's customers drift in. The club continued to steadily fill during the day. All ages, shapes and sizes frequented the Woo Hoo. Maybe it was the hearty portions of food served up by Dez, or maybe because of the genuinely friendly welcome afforded to its visitors, but the club was never short of people putting green in the cash register.

Danny watched a group of six close by, chatting and munching their way through the "belly buster" all-day breakfast. They were obviously three couples, friends on holiday.

No threat.

Then something registered, akin to a déjà vu moment. The same man was sat at the bar. The black guy, the same rangy build in a similar bright T-shirt, sitting in the same seat as yesterday—with the same too-casual look on his face. Everything about the man was completely relaxed apart from his eyes, which were roving around the club's customers with the focus of a cat creeping up on an unwary bird.

Danny moved his centre of balance forward to facilitate a rapid forward dash if required. The small hairs on the back of his neck prickled in preparation. Knowing to trust the uneasy sensation was a basic requisite for a combat soldier, often proving the difference between life and death. The feeling that warned of an unseen sniper on a roof or a blade-wielding killer about to attack. Born from the same instinct that fuelled a detective's "hunch", the warrior's gut feeling was as essential as a knife or sidearm.

Danny tucked his right leg beneath him and eased his frame forward so he barely touched his seat. There were way too many customers in the bar for his liking: way too much scope for collateral damage if the big man at the bar let loose.

The man downed the dregs of his drink, stood up and sauntered out the front door. Danny made to follow but found his way blocked by a woman whose pallor betrayed the quantity of vodka she'd consumed with her lunch. "Hey there, you wanna join us for a drink?"

Sidestepping the woman, Danny watched the man exit the club.

"Hey, you leaving? What's your hurry? Come and sit with us. My friend Tracey thinks you're cute."

Danny glanced at the woman. "I'm kinda busy."

The woman pursed her lips in mild annoyance. "Maybe later then?"

Danny gave a polite smile but continued to the front door. He looked to the right, the same direction the man had taken, but he couldn't see him. The man could have climbed into any one of a dozen cars parked on the street but the reflections from the sun in the many windscreens prevented a clear view inside.

Danny rubbed the back of his hand across his chin. He could check the street, peering into each vehicle as he passed but knew that he stood a chance of walking into an ambush.

He stepped back inside the club. If the guy was trouble, he would be back.

10

As soon as he was out of direct view Juba jogged back to the waiting car. "I told you. I knew I was right!"

"Right about what?" sneered Vasquez. Juba was handy in a fight but had aspirations above his station. Aspanu, although from Madrid like Vasquez and Ortega, was a lazy idiot who got off on beating his wife in front of others to show his machismo. He was only here as far as Vasquez was concerned, because he'd recognise the man who'd put him down so easily.

"The man at the back of the bar, he was there yesterday, same seat—not watching but seeing everything. He's a hired hand."

"How do you know he's not just another dickless tourist out for his morning coffee, eh?" asked Aspanu from the back seat.

"Because it is my job to know such things!"

"Was it the same guy that sucker-punched me? Big as a dinosaur. Face all scarred up?"

"No. But he watches." Juba pointed two forked fingers

at Aspanu to emphasise the point. "He sees."

Vasquez picked out his cell phone from a jacket pocket and rang his employer for instructions. After a few moments the call ended and he turned to Juba. "We watch and wait, follow him if he comes out. If he doesn't, we're going to hit the club just after closing tonight."

Juba gave a triumphant grin, which Vasquez didn't return. Aspanu continued to pick dirt from under his fingernails with a lock knife. "Great. I get to sit in a hot car all day with you two. This just gets better and better."

"If you had done your job in the first place we wouldn't be sitting out here at all," Vasquez growled. "Now shut up and keep your eyes open for the big Yank that you let do a flamenco on your ass."

11

The afternoon passed without further event. Danny had eaten a late lunch in the kitchen courtesy of Dez. Damn that boy could cook! A brief and flirtatious conversation with Julie had rounded lunch off nicely. He'd established that she didn't have a boyfriend (or girlfriend—he knew it didn't pay to assume anything these days) and that came as good news. Maybe, he thought, they'd be able to go for a drink when this thing was over.

Sated and ready for the evening, Danny bid a fond *hasta luego* to Pam and Larry. Again, he was fairly sure that the club would remain safe while full of customers. He glanced at his watch. Nearly seven. It was finally time to meet with the British business owners.

He followed the instructions given to him by Pamela. Larry had offered him the use of their van but Danny had declined the offer, preferring to walk and get more of a feel for the town. He found the desired address with relative ease due to Ultima's blocked grid layout.

He looked up at the wide four-storey apartment building.

As with the rest of the property in Ultima, it was finished to a high standard. It reminded him of some of the more recent waterfront properties in London's Canary Wharf. The stylish smoked-glass windows and doors combined with white faux marble to give the building real character. A low perimeter wall topped with a decorative iron spiked fence served to enclose a neat manicured lawn and gardens. Although illuminated only by spotlights mounted on the building, the lawn looked as green and pristine as a golf course.

Danny glanced at the address that Pam had supplied him with: *Apt. 198A, Santiago Road. (23rd Street).* The apartment in question was owned by a British couple, Philip and Sally Winrow. The rest of the British residents had agreed to meet him there at eight-thirty.

The Dukes had remained at the club as two of their evening barmaids had called in sick earlier that day. It seemed that even the locals fell foul of "Spanish tummy" once in a while.

No problem, the rest of the ex-pats knew to expect him.

Danny entered the cool of the main lobby. A row of mail slots adorned the wall to his right. Above each slot was a printed name and apartment number. He traced a finger from slot to slot and found the Winrows' listing.

As he trotted up the stairs, taking two at a time, he could hear televisions, voices and droning music filtering through the walls. A cackling laugh echoed down from a higher floor. Someone was playing "Love Me Do" way too loud. He liked The Beatles as much as the next man but too loud is too loud. He found the Winrows' apartment and rapped on the door with calloused knuckles.

The door was opened by a petite blond wearing a pink T-shirt that Danny decided must have been sprayed on. The shirt declared the legend SALLY'S SALON… THE ULTIMA ULTIMATE!

"I guess you'd be Sally then?" deduced Gunn.

"And you must be Danny." Sally was young, and tanned to a shade that would become an antique piece of furniture. Her platinum-blond hair contrasted a little too sharply with her skin tone. "Come on in." Her voice had a strong Essex accent.

As Danny entered, a thick layer of cigarette smoke drifted towards the open door. The open-plan living space was sleek and modern and filled with a motley crew of British ex-pats talking in small groups. Danny received a few furtive looks as he entered. He sensed a nervous energy in the room.

One of the men separated from the crowd and approached. He was tall and slim, his goatee trimmed into pencil-thin lines that traced sharp angles on his bony face. He was dressed casually in a T-shirt and shorts, both light blue in colour.

"Is this him? Is this the one we've been waiting for?" He extended his hand. "We've all been looking forward to meeting you."

"And you are?" Danny asked as they shook hands.

"Oh, sorry, mate, I forget my manners. My name's Phil Winrow. Sally's my wife. I run the Midnight Mood Bar down on Second and Iglesias. Larry tells me you're a man that can solve problems."

Danny nodded. "I may be able to help, but I'll need you all to sit down, be quiet and tell your stories in an orderly manner."

"Bloody hell." Phil glanced at Sally, then back to Danny. "You don't waste any time do you!"

"Time is against us. Once the Locos find out you've brought in outside help, they'll have to put the pressure on you guys. They won't go without a fight, that's for sure."

Sally addressed the gathering. "Everybody, this is Danny—he's here to help us. Oh, and his brother as well, but he's not here tonight. If you can all sit down and we'll take turns talking to him."

Danny walked forward as all eyes in the room fell upon him. He could see doubt and disappointment on some of the faces; probably expecting some Stallone clone in his Rambo costume. If Clay had been here he was sure the reaction would have been a very different one.

"I'm Danny. I'm here to help, but there are a few things I've got to make clear to you all. I'm not here as a bouncer or a bodyguard in any of your businesses. I'm here at the behest of Larry and Pamela Duke, whom I'm sure most of you know. They own the Woo Hoo." He paused and scanned the sea of faces. Most were overweight and blotchy from too much food and not enough sunscreen. A chair squeaked on the tiled floor. Someone coughed.

"What I need from you all tonight is anything you can tell me about the Locos. Any names that you know would be useful. Let's start with you." Danny pointed to an older couple sitting to his far right.

The man introduced himself simply as Steve. He was big and bald and his eyes twitched as he spoke. The woman next to him remained silent but nodded along with his every word. He owned a small café near the beach called The Pit Stop, and had experienced visits very similar to the Dukes. As he talked, the heads around him bobbed in agreement and mutual concern.

"We had a fire last year. Now we pay two hundred euros a week to make sure we don't have another one. Two hundred bloody euros!"

"Same gang? The Locos?" asked Danny.

"Yeah, same ones."

The subsequent stories were much the same, but Danny processed the crowd systematically, drawing out information and clarifying details where needed. At times the chatter became animated as the anger in the room threatened to take on a sentience of its own. He allowed them to blow off some steam but moved the conversation on with a few curt words.

After all the business owners had given their stories, Danny glanced at his watch. Time was getting on but he had collated a much more detailed sketch about the outfit he was going up against. He pocketed his small notebook and drained the bottle of San Miguel beer that he'd nursed through the evening.

The crowd of Brits vacated the Winrows' apartment slowly in small groups of twos and threes. Some chatted amiably while others still gave Danny dubious looks as they said their goodbyes. They'd talked through their fears and concerns for nearly two hours and as they returned to their targeted businesses and homes the mood was understandably sombre.

Danny hadn't given any false promises and hadn't tried to whip them up into defending their businesses. These people weren't soldiers, but publicans, caterers and shopkeepers. Everyday people caught in a dire position. In a few previous situations that Danny had helped with, it *had* been necessary to instil a militia mentality into the group, but this was different. A war zone tended to wipe out the very premises that you were trying to preserve. No, a different strategy was needed with this one.

"Thanks for coming, Danny," said Phil Winrow, closing the door behind the last visitor. "Look, I know a couple of boys from London. They might be able to lend a hand." His voice dropped to a whisper. "They did a few armed robberies back in England. They're a couple of hard nuts."

"Why didn't they come tonight?"

"Ah, well, they've caused some trouble of their own in a few of the bars."

Danny shook his head. "I think I'll pass. The last thing we need right now is loose cannons."

"All right, you know best," Phil agreed.

Danny turned to Sally. "I'm stopping at the Woo Hoo if you need to reach me in a hurry. What's your phone number?"

Sally plucked her phone from her pocket. She held out the display so Danny could key in her number.

"Got it. Call me if you think of anything else," said Danny.

"We will." Sally kissed Danny on the cheek and hugged him like they were old friends. Danny was thankful Phil settled for a handshake and a manly clap on the shoulder.

Danny turned in the doorway just as he was leaving and glanced back at the couple. They looked good together in a working-class Ken and Barbie sort of way. He'd never been close to settling down. Had he missed out? They seemed so suited to each other, so in tune. Common logic professed that you never missed what you'd never had but Danny was undecided.

Instead of following the rest of the crowd out—and risk getting buttonholed by one of the business owners—Danny climbed up two flights of stairs and found a bench on the rooftop garden, which Sally had told him about earlier in the evening in one of the rare breaks between questionings. She'd said it was where she went to be on her own and watch the stars at night. It was as nice as she had described it. Sculptured topiary displays gave off abstract silhouettes. The small planters of multi-coloured flowers were arranged in a geometric grid that resembled the streets below.

Danny rubbed his eyes. They still stung from the cigarette smoke in the apartment. His clothes stank of it. He cupped his hands in front of his nose. Yep, those smelled too.

He looked out over the town, at the million pinpricks of light that looked like an inverted firmament. The traffic was light; Larry had explained earlier that most of the locals used the low-cost electric buses that trundled almost silently along the main streets. Of course there were still plenty of cars to be seen, but only a fraction of those found in most resort towns.

Yeah, it certainly was nice in Ultima, but again Danny found himself wondering how it would appear to him by the end of the game. Moving to one of the curved benches, he took out his notebook, angled it to one side in order to catch the light, and read through what he'd written.

Antoni Barcelo—leader
Vincenzo Ortega—soldier. Captain?
20-25 active soldiers?
Usually use knives but some of the soldiers have used shotguns and pistols to threaten. Always travel in groups of 3 or 4.
Known businesses taken over:
The Hot Pink Club

Merryweather Tavern
Ultima Fotoshop
Felicidad Fashions
Jerry's Spanish Fried Chicken
The Black Panther Club
El Sid's Bar & Grill

Danny keyed the second number on his speed dial. After a few seconds Larry's gruff voice answered. "Hello."

"It's Danny. Everything quiet with you?"

"Yeah, they only come calling in the morning when there are fewer witnesses."

"That's good. I've just finished the meeting at the Winrows' apartment."

"How'd it go?"

"Well, I know a bit more about the fuckwits we're up against. It seems there's plenty of them to contend with."

"Yeah, one or two. So what's your plan of action?"

None present at the meeting had known where the gangsters called home. Phil had mentioned that Barcelo had a villa and estate up the coast, but was unable to give any specifics. But Danny knew that they would return to the Woo Hoo eventually. There was more than money at stake now. They had lost face.

"I'll be back at the club in a wee while."

"Okay then. Watch your back out there," offered Larry.

"Always."

Danny put away the notepad and phone then closed his eyes and let his mind relax. He'd found that during his long hours spent on night patrol that this relaxed state of mind was nearly as good as sleep. He breathed in the aroma from the unknown flowers. They were very pleasant. A nice alternative to cordite, smoke and blood.

He was making his way down the staircase when he stopped at the sound of hushed but angry Spanish voices echoing from below.

12

"Something must be going on. We followed the guy from the club here, and two hours later half the Brits in town come marching out of the same building."

"But where's the one we were following?" asked a different voice.

"He must still be up there. Juba was right—he must be a qualified man."

Danny descended silently and risked a furtive glance onto the landing below. Five men were standing in the corridor: three Spaniards, a black man who stood head and shoulders over his companions, and a man who looked Middle Eastern to Danny's eyes. All wore the grey urban camouflage that the Locos were known for. The Arab held a straight-bladed knife along the side of his thigh. The rest appeared unarmed.

Danny was about to make a stealthy exit when the five men approached the door to the Winrows' apartment. One of the Spaniards raised his hand to knock at the door. Danny cleared his throat loudly, then feigned an expression of both surprise and fear as the Locos swung around at the noise.

All five men sprinted towards Danny, whose only option was back up the stairs. Adrenalin flooded into his system, causing a slight numbness in his hands and face. He'd felt the same sensation countless times before. He knew not to fight the fear; instead, he used it, turned it to something more productive.

"Don't kill him, we need him to talk first," shouted one of the five.

On the next landing up, Danny's survival instinct kicked in, hyper alert to anything that could be used as a weapon. The doorways to each apartment were arranged in an alternating pattern. The first door on his left faced a blank wall then the next door on his right was located some twelve feet down the corridor, no doubt designed so that the occupants wouldn't need to look at or talk to their neighbours while opening their front doors.

A child's discarded bucket and spade lay next to one of the first doors, sand still clinging to the plastic. Danny snatched up the spade and raced back towards the stairwell door.

The first Loco was just starting to emerge as Danny crashed into it, utilising all of his weight and momentum. He heard a strangled yelp and the gangster was sent careening backwards into those behind. At least two of the unseen Locos lost their footing and tumbled back down the concrete steps. Their harsh curses told of a painful landing.

On the landing, Danny wedged the blade of the toy shovel under the door with a sharp kick. He knew it wouldn't hold for long but it might buy him precious seconds. The old military axioms flashed into his mind: *Divide and conquer. Search and destroy.* He set off at full tilt and covered the fifty yards of hallway in a respectable time. At the end of the corridor, a door was marked with a yellow sign that displayed a mop and bucket. Danny tried the door, and it opened with the faint squeal of a rusty hinge. Danny grabbed a couple of items from the shelves then started down the staircase at the opposite side of the building.

The door he'd wedged moments earlier clattered loudly as it was kicked open. He judged by the heavy footsteps and raised voices that at least three of the five were still in pursuit. Knowing never to rely on luck, Danny presumed the other two men, maybe more, were still in the fight, probably moving along the floor below him to cut off his escape.

Danny spent a couple of tense seconds opening the plastic bottle he'd procured. *Damn child safety lids.* Working as quickly as possible, he tore a cleaning cloth into two strips, emptied the contents of the bottle over the fabric, then tightly wound the strips of soaking fabric around his hands, tucking the free ends into his palms. The acrid smell filled the enclosed passageway.

The three hoodlums rounded the corner, their faces masks of fury. Looking surprised to see Danny poised and waiting, they faltered for a brief moment, but then surged forward as one.

Danny skipped to the right, causing the three men to bunch together in the narrow hallway. The closest grabbed at him but a snappy straight punch sent the man rocking on his heels. The Loco started to regain his balance then clasped both hands to his face and screamed, *"Mis ojos!"*

Danny grinned; the old bleach trick worked wonders.

The two other men closed in. The Arab had his knife out, and another—one of the Spaniards—snapped out a telescopic baton and lunged forward to attack.

Gunn had been beaten with riot batons a few years back and knew how nasty they could be in close quarters. He ducked low and barrelled in to meet the attack. The baton cut the air a mere inch above his head. The Spaniard was rammed back into the knife-man and all three fighters went down in a tangle of thrashing limbs. Danny tried to stamp down on the hand holding the knife but missed. He grabbed at the Spaniard's face with his left hand then delivered a series of punches to both men. The baton-man succumbed to the bleach in his eyes and dropped his weapon. Danny was quick to snatch it up. A hard slap with the telescopic steel and the guy's nose found a new position on his face. A shot in the throat with the back of Gunn's elbow landed the Spaniard in a semi-foetal position. His mouth worked like a fish out of water as he struggled to breathe.

Lurching up from the floor, the Arab tried to stab at Danny's legs but two quick strikes, forehand and backhand to the jaw with the baton, put him out of the picture. A final whip across the side of his head made sure he stayed down.

Three down… how many more to go? He'd seen five in the hallway but were there more elsewhere?

At least they're trying to capture me, not kill me, he thought. This gave him a distinct advantage against the superior numbers.

Danny picked up the fallen knife, and then with a cold detachment stabbed both of the men through the tops of their feet. This brought fresh howls of agony from the downed gangsters. Not fatal wounds, but they wouldn't be giving chase any time soon.

He strode over to the first Loco he'd dropped and pressed

the steel baton to the hoodlum's face, raising his chin. Tears streamed from the man's reddened eyes, both of which had begun to bruise and swell.

"Who sent you here? Barcelo?" He cracked the man's collarbone with the baton to get his full attention. "Where does he live? Eh? Out with it, ya wee shite."

The Loco was just emitting a pained mewling sound so Danny tried again.

"*Mis ojos.*"

"Stings a bit doesn't it," replied Danny. He looked down at the gangster's mottled face. Not a pretty sight. "You're a waste of friggin' skin." The Loco scuttled butt-first away from Danny, yelling loudly for help. "And you try to be nice to some folks…" A hammer strike with the base of the baton knocked the blinded Loco cold. A single rivulet of blood trickled from the man's scalp, tracing a path down his slack features.

A door opened in the hallway and a resident poked his head out, his mouth hanging open. He glanced at the three injured gangsters and the man standing over them, bloodied knife and baton in hand. The door slammed shut quicker than it had opened.

Time to move. Another disabling foot-job then Danny was up and running again. He tucked the knife into his belt. Better to have a free hand than to over-rely on weapons.

Juba had recovered from his spill down the stairs and hit the first speed dial button on his cell phone. Barcelo's drawling voice greeted him.

"Boss, we've followed the man from the Woo Hoo Club to

a building on Second and Santiago. There was some kind of meeting with the British and now the man is trying to escape."

"Bring him to the warehouse when you've got him," Barcelo commanded, as if capture was a foregone conclusion. "Alive, so we can have a little chit-chat!"

"This man might be a little slippery to catch."

"There are five of you, yes? You better catch him." Then, as an afterthought, "I have men nearby. I'll send a few more down to you to be sure; I don't want this one getting away."

"Okay."

"Oh, and, Juba…"

"Yes, boss?"

"Five hundred to the man that takes him down."

Juba grinned; he could do a lot with five hundred euros right now. The boss had said he had to be taken alive, but hadn't said anything about him still being able to walk. Barcelo was a man who rewarded both loyalty and obedience, neither of which Juba had a problem with. He was making five times what he used to make in Africa and the chances of being killed were much lower. Juba looked down impassively at the smaller Spanish man that had taken the brunt of the impact from the door. Someone else could clean that up.

13

Danny wasn't quite ready to make his getaway. He discarded the drying bleach wraps from his hands and thought momentarily about going back to the Winrows' apartment but decided against it; he was better off on the move and he didn't want to put the couple in unnecessary danger.

He glanced out from the corner stairwell window, which gave him a clear view down onto the street below. A white minivan screeched to a halt outside the main entrance to the apartment building. Another half-dozen Locos piled out in a disorderly rush.

They looked like they were ready to fight.

Danny didn't like to disappoint. He grinned and ducked back into the corridor. From his vantage point, he could see the tall black man—he now realised it was the same man he'd spotted at the club earlier—standing in the street gesturing to his left and right. The corners of Danny's mouth twitched into the briefest of smiles. He'd been right about him after all. Danny figured he was directing the backup team to both sets of stairs in an effort to cut off his escape. If the situation was reversed Danny would have done the same. With both groups climbing the stairs at the same pace, on each floor they would make visual contact and then move on to the next.

He got to the third-floor hallway and adapted his plans, snatching something from the window ledge. As he moved, he heard the group of Locos pounding up the stairs just behind him. He picked up a little speed as he moved towards the sound of voices and pounding feet, snatching a potted cactus from a small veranda outside number 309.

As the first Loco bounded into the hallway, Danny met him with a kick to the stomach and followed through by thrusting the cactus hard into his face. Cactus barbs were embedded into the man's cheek, and he howled. Another kick, this time to the back of his knee joint, sent him crashing to the ground.

The second Loco appeared, this one sporting a mane of peroxide-white hair, and grabbed for Danny's throat.

Gunn dodged back just out of range and caught the man by his extended hand. A sharp rotation of his wrist snapped his locked fingers back on themselves to breaking point. The man dropped to his knees in an effort to escape the terrible pressure in his hand, just in time to receive a knee full in the face.

But credit to Señor Peroxide, it took three more knee blasts and a shot with the baton to put him down completely. Danny knew one big difference between real fights and the movies; not all the bad guys will fall down unconscious after one high kick.

A door opened and a teenage girl stepped into the hallway as Gunn hit Peroxide a final time. Her eyes went wide and she stopped talking into the cell phone that was pressed to her ear. She staggered back into the apartment and slammed the door. Danny could hear her calling for her father in a voice laced with panic. Maybe it was time to leave before a Loco caught him with a lucky shot or any of the residents got caught in the crossfire.

14

Juba watched the team split into two groups and race into the building. He considered following them but decided to wait at the front.

He had learned the skills of a hunter a long time ago. When you were preying on a wild beast, you could use your energy stalking it or you could send in lesser men, the beaters, to flush it out of the bush and be ready to take it down.

Juba touched a hand to his lip, which he'd split during his tumble down the stairs. The painful throb only added to his eagerness to lay hands on this hired man; it would be a pleasure extracting information from him. He would have been much happier if he'd brought along a shotgun or his Ruger 9mm. That would have saved a lot of this running around but Barcelo didn't like the boys waving guns about—he believed they were for killing, not displaying. Maybe he was right.

Danny waited in the hallway for the next party of Locos to clump their way up the staircase. He lifted the telescopic baton with his right hand and held the knife along his left forearm in a reverse grip, ready. He crept towards the stairwell door knowing that this was an optimum location to engage the enemy. The narrow doorway forced them to bottleneck, which meant there was less chance of them surrounding him. More voices drifted up the stairs, betraying the direction they were coming from.

Danny crouched to the side of the door and tried to calm his breathing to its resting rate. He exploded into action as the first of the gangsters opened the door.

The baton cracked into unprotected shins with bone-splintering force and a wide-shouldered Spaniard went down with a howl, clutching at his legs. This left his head unprotected, and Gunn whipped the steel cudgel across the back of his skull. The blow resounded with a satisfying crack.

The second man lurched at Danny as he began to rise from his crouch. The guy was on him in a second, pushing Danny into the wall. Instead of trying to force him back, Gunn gave ground, dropping back to one knee. He jabbed the knife into the soft cavity behind the man's knee and pushed down hard into the structure of the joint. The blade wedged deep between the two large bones, instantly immobilising the leg. The Loco dropped like a sack of wet washing and his face began to contort into a parody of a kabuki mask.

The third gangster proved wily. He backed off from Danny and snapped out a baton of his own.

Danny inched forward in a semi-crouch and dropped his knee across the neck of kabuki-guy, putting a crushing pressure on the carotid arteries. The remaining Loco lunged in with a slashing blow to Gunn's face, followed with a kick and a wild flurry of strikes—any one of which could have ended it for Danny if they had landed cleanly.

This was the most skilled fighter Gunn had faced from the Locos. He was fast but he knew not to charge in blind or hesitate for too long either; the fine line for any fighter. He had a wrestler's build and a face to match… a real bone-crusher type. His flattened nose told of countless fistfights, and the deep scars around his face told of more than one encounter with an unfriendly blade.

Danny blocked with his own baton, each strike sending a shockwave reverberating down into his hand. Both men exchanged blows. Danny's thigh stung from a whip just above the knee, which would have cracked his kneecap if timed a split second earlier. Bone-crusher winced from a palm heel to the ear and a numbing slash across the fingers. Danny feinted left then another diagonal whip sent the steel club tumbling from bone-crusher's broken hand. The man cursed, clutching the damaged hand to his chest.

"*Espero que no tocas el piano.*" Danny doubted that the man had *ever* played the piano but grinned at the resulting look of hatred on his face. Danny skipped back over the two fallen Locos.

As bone-crusher started to advance again, Gunn reversed his direction and blasted into him, aimed a headbutt full into his face and scored a direct hit to the bridge of the nose. A noise akin to a coconut being cracked against a wall resounded down the corridor but the Loco remained on his feet. A knee to the face, a baton strike to the head and another open palm to the ear followed but still he rolled with Danny's blows and scored with a raking headbutt of his own. A kidney punch staggered Gunn and he almost went down on his knees. The heavyset brawler was still proving very dangerous, despite his broken hand, as he seized his chance and surged forward. He caught Gunn in a tight grip from behind, throwing his injured arm around Danny's waist and the other around his throat. The intense pressure on his torso forced the air from Danny's lungs but he was unable to escape.

Danny knew if any more Locos arrived now he'd be finished. This fight had lasted way too long at the twenty or thirty seconds mark. He dropped the baton, knowing it was useless at this range. Danny then grabbed at the arm around his throat and focused all of his strength into bone-crusher's fingers. The hands were slippery with sweat but he managed to secure a tight hold. The gangster's arm felt like a steel band around his neck. Danny twisted his wrist in a tight arc. Two of bone-crusher's fingers snapped back further than they were designed to and the grip was broken. Sucking in a welcome breath, he felt his vision swim momentarily as his equilibrium sought to right itself.

Gunn pivoted, fully reversing their positions, so now he could apply his own counter-choke from behind. Gunn's knotted arms bit deep into bone-crusher's neck, cutting off both oxygen and blood supply to his brain. But Danny knew to wrap his hands in deep to prevent his own fingers being prised and broken. Squatting as he applied the hold, Danny then levered the man backwards so only his toes were touching the ground.

Bone-crusher tried to claw the choke away but with both hands now broken and Danny pulling him off his feet, the attempts were brave but futile. He tried to throw Danny over his shoulder but Gunn again blocked the move by dropping his weight and stamping his heel hard against the back of bone-crusher's knee. The brawler finally slumped to the ground, limbs completely slack, but Gunn kept the sleeper hold tight a few more seconds just to make sure. When he did release the hold the man dropped face down like a corpse.

Time to go.

Danny moved more cautiously; if he encountered another of bone-crusher's ilk he might not make it out. He trotted silently down the stairs and emerged onto the ground floor. He paused to spit out a mouthful of blood and saliva and wipe his eyes clear of sweat, then peered out of the entrance doors. He spotted another Loco sitting with his back to him on a low wall, smoking a cigarette. A ribbon of thin smoke wafted up and over his head. He was dressed head to toe in the required urban camouflage but stood out like a Buddhist monk in a bordello. Danny scowled; whoever thought that vibrant greys and blues provided camouflage needed a slap with a sock full of gravel.

Danny slipped off his belt as he closed silently on the gangster. One quick motion and the leather strap ensnared the man's neck. Gunn pulled sharply and the garrotted Loco was snatched backwards over the low wall. He landed on the back of his skull and shoulders with a telling *crack* and Danny didn't need to employ his raised fist to finish him off. The young man pawed once at the air then lay still. The glowing ember of his cigarette emitted a weak shower of sparks as it landed on the ground next to him.

Danny pulled his belt free and walked away.

15

Juba watched the lone man walk out into the evening air, making sure that he was hidden by the bulk of the minivan. The target seemed to be fastening his belt back around his waist. Juba clicked his tongue in satisfaction. The hired man had gotten past the rest of the Locos. He started towards his target with violent resolve, curling his fingers around the blade that was tucked discreetly in the small of his back. He favoured the "Black Bear" combat knife. He was just as comfortable with a machete but the smaller knife was easier to carry and conceal. The knife was finely crafted and Juba was especially fond of its sub-hilt feature that eradicated any chance of his hand coming into contact with the blade. The eight-inch blade was long enough to fully impale if a killing stroke was required, but just as devastating if used in a slashing attack.

Then Juba reconsidered; it would be too easy to gut this man in the heat of the moment, and where would that leave him with the boss? Barcelo had given clear orders that he wanted to interrogate this newcomer. He released the knife with a snort of derision and reached back into his vehicle.

Danny reached the small topiary gardens that surrounded the apartment building. The decorative iron railing gave the whole front façade a Spanish-colonial feel that looked even more alluring in the failing evening light. He glanced up at the apartment block, wondering how many of the residents had called the police. He smiled as he thought of the bodies he'd left littered around the stairwells. The Guardia Civil, the cops, would have their hands full for a while trying to make sense of that tableau. More than one Loco would spend the night handcuffed to a hospital bed—

Danny turned to see the large black man thundering towards him with what looked like a long black walking stick in his hand. Gunn recognised it as an African knobkerrie. Generations of Zulu warriors had used these fighting sticks to great effect and the running man looked like he was adept in its use.

The club whistled towards Danny's unprotected head.

Gunn felt the iron-hard cane brush his face as he turned into the attack. He went in low and felt the strength of the man slam into his frame. Danny pivoted in a half circle, catching his antagonist in a classic ju-jitsu manoeuvre known as the "full shoulder throw". With the African's clubbing arm captured, Gunn pitched the top half of his body forward and catapulted him head over heels into the iron railings.

The gangster's long legs folded over the decorative spikes, leaving him hanging upside down, impaled by the legs and screaming in pain.

Danny glared down at what he hoped was the last of this

crew. He stooped and picked up the club, then brought the weighted end down across the underside of the man's chin. A sickening crunch told of a broken jaw.

Danny nodded, then turned and made for the street at a jog. He could hear the approaching wail of police sirens. No matter, he would be long gone by the time the Guardia Civil arrived. A block later he realised he was still carrying the fighting stick. Seeing no convenient trash cans nearby, he dropped it into a storm drain. He rolled his neck to relieve the building tension there. A tightness was beginning under his left eye. *Great*, he thought, *I'll look like Rocky in the morning*. "Yo, Adrian, I did it," he whispered to himself.

16

Antoni Barcelo sat behind his solid-teak desk. The leather of the high-backed executive's chair creaked in response to his slightest movement. A flat-screen computer monitor blinked through pictures of almost naked supermodels yet he paid it no attention. Sipping red wine from an ornate crystal goblet, he viewed his bloodied congregation with unblinking shark-like eyes. His team relayed the details of the night's unsuccessful encounter. As he listened, he swirled the full-bodied Rioja in slow concentric circles.

Six Locos stood in a semicircle like errant schoolboys summoned to the headmaster's study. None dared hold his gaze directly. The beaten underlings shifted nervously as the boss sidled around to the front of his desk. The clock on his desk emitted a low warble and the digital display briefly illuminated to announce the turning of another hour. *Bleep-bleep.* 23.00.

"You..." Barcelo singled out one of the group at random. "Tell me again how one piece of shit Brit not only got away from nearly a dozen of you, but managed to fuck most of you up as well?!"

The man winced as he stammered the beginning of his defence. His eyes were dappled with bruises and he still couldn't open them fully due to the corrosive effect of bleach.

"It... it was like Juba said. This guy must be a pro—a qualified man," he offered, blinking one eye then the other in rapid succession.

"Juba? Juba is lying crippled in hospital; it will be weeks before he's walking again. Don't mention Juba to me again!"

"But, boss—"

Barcelo launched his considerable frame at his man. The leader outweighed his underling by at least fifty pounds and he pounded him down onto the marble floor with ease. The Loco waved his hands in front of his face in a weak defence, but Barcelo clubbed his face with punch after punch. The man's nose exploded in a shower of crimson.

The other Locos stared on aghast. All had heard of the boss's notorious temper but few in the room had borne witness to its full savagery. Finally, one of the men took a half-step closer. "Boss, you're going to kill him."

Barcelo stopped and turned his head to inspect the speaker. Blood dripped from his raised fist. Beneath him, the man's face was unrecognisable, but the small bubbles of blood that popped around his nose and mouth indicated that he was still breathing.

Barcelo gripped the desk and levered himself back to a standing position. His cream-coloured jacket now resembled an early Jackson Pollock. "Get him out of here and down to the hospital. He can keep Juba and the other idiots company."

Two of the group lifted the fallen man from the blood-spattered marble. A gelatinous rasping escaped from the man's lungs as he was hoisted upright. The two men carried him out of the room without further comment.

The remaining gangsters bunched together in front of the desk. "So what's the next plan of action, boss?" asked one of the three.

"Well, if this man came from the Woo Hoo Club, it stands to reason that they are the ones who hired him. Don't forget that the guy that messed Ortega up was in the Woo Hoo as well." Barcelo sat on the edge of his desk. He took another sip of wine. He gave a single nod. "I think that the Dukes better have up-to-date fire insurance, because by tomorrow morning it'll be ash."

"You want us to burn the club down?"

"No, I'm praying for a kitchen mishap of epic proportions!" spat Barcelo. "Yes, I want you to burn the fucking club down. That will send a message to the other foreigners. Show them what happens when they try to get clever. Hit it half an hour after closing. Make sure that this simple thing does not go wrong. The next time I want to hear about these Brits is when they're scurrying home with their tails between their legs."

"Who do you want to lead?" asked one of the men.

Barcelo considered this for long moments. Vincenzo was one of his best but he was still recuperating at home, arm broken and his jaw wired shut. Juba had showed real promise but had gotten himself done like a shish kebab by the second hired man.

Who to send?

It was child's play to toss a petrol bomb, but it should also have been child's play for a full squad of men to bring back one man in a simple snatch and grab.

"Get Babi Garcia on the phone. Tell him I've got a special event I need him to look after. One of you will drive him by the club, and he can go back tonight and put this thing to bed."

17

Babi Garcia, like many in his select line of work, was a man of stark contradictions. Born and raised a strict Catholic like most Spaniards of his generation, he attended Mass and read the scriptures regularly. He also attended confession, although the material he confessed was subjected to more selective creativity than a politician claiming expenses. While he confessed to the odd lustful thought or taking someone's parking space (and was duly granted absolution) he chose never to mention the murders, assaults, the robberies or the rapes that he had subjected on other members of God's flock. While priests were forbidden to speak of anything imparted in the confessional, he was never going to pressure-test that maxim.

Garcia looked up from his work, his attention caught by his cell phone vibrating. Annoyed at being disturbed at the late hour, Babi glanced at the caller display. He picked up. "*Hola.*"

Antoni Barcelo's baritone voice cut into his ear as if he were standing shoulder to shoulder. He listened to the head of the Locos spit concise details down the phone.

An interesting job offer.

"Okay, I'll meet you in two hours," Babi agreed. He ended the call and turned back to the matter in hand. A cold smile crept across Garcia's face.

The man lay curled on the floor, completely naked upon a large square of black polythene sheeting. His hands were secured tight behind his back with silver duct tape. His ankles were similarly bound. His genitals had shrivelled to resemble a vol-au-vent nestled in a mess of curly black hair. A clear plastic bag partially filled with urine was fastened over his head and held in place with more tape. It sloshed around the man's face as he thrashed. The apple-sized bruise that decorated the centre of the man's chest was red and angry.

Garcia dropped to one knee and jabbed a single extended knuckle into the centre of the bruise. He knew that the nerve cluster, crushed against the flat bones of the sternum, would send darts of raw agony lancing through his victim's body. As expected, the bound man bucked against the pain. The knuckle strike was one of the simplest yet most effective torture methods ever used.

After glancing at the time displayed on his phone, Babi stepped over the man's supine form and stamped his foot deep into his unprotected stomach. The man, already close to death, emitted a strangled scream of pain, but only succeeded in swallowing a mouthful of urine and stale air. Garcia dropped to his knees, straddling his victim like a willing lover. The nameless man's eyes bulged as the breath rattled in his throat.

Garcia watched intently. This was the part he loved the best: seeing the last sparks of defiance fade from their eyes as they realised that this was *the* moment. No reprieve, no stay of execution. The end. And they'd never even know Garcia's identity or his reason for committing murder.

In fact, the very act of murder was reason enough; to pick up a lone tourist in one of Ultima's trendy bars, take them home and torture them to death. Garcia did not discriminate between the sexes, did not consider himself either gay or straight, as that implied there was a degree of emotion in his couplings. His sexual encounters were just another expression of his bestial nature. No love required, none wanted or ever given. Any sexual partner unlucky enough to fall for his tough-guy charm was sure to be subjected to several hours of sadistic ravaging. Some of these encounters ended with the slow strangulation of his partner. Babi especially liked *bagging* his victims, watching them thrash and fight, desperate for that one last breath.

Unlike many of his ilk, Babi had been raised in a stable, loving environment. No abusive father, no dominating mother, no broken home, no bullying sibling or any of the other textbook justifications. But were any psychiatrist ever to examine him, they would quickly conclude that Babi Garcia was undoubtedly a sociopath. That didn't bother him. No regrets and no remorse. Maybe someday scientists would identify a killer gene that would explain why Garcia existed. Until that day, Garcia knew that he would continue down the devil's path for the reason he'd been doing it for the past twenty years: because he could.

Only one man in all those years had come close to catching him. Pierre Loup had been looking for his younger brother who had vanished while on holiday in the bustling Costa del Sol. The younger Loup had ended his days as one of Babi's victims and the Frenchman (thankfully acting alone, brave but stupid) had tracked Garcia down by some impressive amateur-detective skills.

Pierre had tried to ingratiate himself with Garcia in order to determine if Babi was indeed behind his brother's disappearance. But Garcia had cultivated a real talent for perceiving danger, a survivor's skill. Playing the Frenchman at his own game, he invited Pierre out on his boat on the premise of a day of fishing for shark.

Pierre ended up as the live bait, unprepared for the sudden onslaught by the smiling Spaniard. Garcia had slashed him open from breastbone to groin while offering him a beer, then tied a line around his wrist and dumped him into the dark azure waters of the Mediterranean. Within ten minutes the sharks arrived and after the rope snapped taut a dozen or so times, Babi reeled the bloody cable back aboard and set off home.

The man on the floor had stopped twitching. Garcia looked down on the corpse with disdain. Getting rid of the bodies was no fun. Another run out to sea, he supposed, but it kept the sharks well fed and he was all for animal conservation. Gripping the polythene sheet, he folded it tight over the man's chest and under his arm and buttocks. He rolled the body several times then tucked the loose ends of plastic by folding them back over the head and feet. Several strips of duct tape held the loose flaps in place and secure. He would dump the body later, after he'd finished the Barcelo job. That sounded more fun.

There was nothing like a spot of arson to liven up a quiet night.

18

Danny entered the Woo Hoo Club by the back door and tried to make it upstairs without being seen. No luck. Pamela had been moving bottles of vodka from the storeroom to the main bar and despite his protests she fussed over him like a maiden aunt. She produced a bag of ice and proceeded to press it painfully onto the swelling under his left eye.

"Pam, I'm okay, really. Not to sound like a cliché, but you should see the other guys."

"Oh, but look at your face. Danny, if you want to leave we'll understand."

"Leave? No way. Things are just getting started. I told you this would escalate just by me and Clay being here. The Locos, they won't just roll over and go away. Things may get worse before this is over."

Pam nodded but persisted in pressing the bag of ice to his face.

"I hurt quite a few of them tonight and if I was in charge of the Locos, I would hit this place hard and fast to get my own back. They'll be coming tonight or tomorrow at the latest. As soon as you lock up I need you, Larry and the rest of the staff out as soon as possible. If they come, I can't be watching out for all of you."

Pam chewed her bottom lip but nodded in agreement. "Okay, if you say so."

"Did Larry bring his shotgun in yet?"

"Yeah, he's got it under the bar, just below the cash register. It's wrapped in newspaper so it doesn't spook the staff, although they all know what's going on with the Locos."

"Good. How many shells has he got?"

"A full box," Larry interjected from the kitchen doorway. "I take it by your face that you met some of our local dignitaries."

"Aye, it was quite a welcome committee. They didn't much care for my style of introduction though."

"Just make sure you sleep with one eye open. These fuckers won't take it lying down, they'll be out for blood now," warned Larry.

"I was just saying the same thing to Pam. When you leave tonight make sure you're not being followed and if you think you are, get yourselves over to the police station as fast as possible."

"The cops aren't interested in us, you know that."

"Aye, I know, but the Locos won't try and roll you over in the station now will they? At least it will keep you both safe. Same goes for the staff: Dez, Julie and the others. Make sure they are keeping an eye out for trouble."

Larry nodded but his jaw was set in challenge. Danny held his gaze.

"No heroics, Larry. Your only duty is to keep you and yours safe. Let me worry about the rest of it. Okay?"

Larry flexed his hands and the muscles in his jaw bunched as he looked from side to side. Pam reached and laid a hand on his shoulder. "Okay," he said.

Danny climbed the stairs to his room. After first changing his clothes, which were spattered with both bleach and blood, Danny pressed the bag of ice tight against the knuckles of his left hand. Even after many years of training in various martial arts he knew it was still all too easy to damage the small bones of the hand in a real fight. He flexed his fingers, made a tight fist then flexed again. Nothing broken, not today.

He examined the items he'd bought at the home improvement store the previous day, which were now spread across the bed, floor and windowsill. Then he set to finishing the work he had begun that afternoon.

An hour or so later Larry poked his head into the bedroom. Danny looked up from the soldering iron, surrounded by dishes of coloured powders, liquids, lengths of wire and an assortment of small hand tools.

"Dad never bought me a chemistry set when I was a kid," said Danny as he motioned to the makeshift workshop.

The acrid smell made Larry recoil. He waved a hand and retreated down the stairs. "I don't want to know."

Danny worked on, assembling and constructing. He knew the shit storm was due on a westerly wind. He looked at the range of completed items that now lay on the bed and hoped it would be enough.

The rest of the shift was akin to an endurance test for Danny. He loitered near the kitchen door, scanning the drunken crowd for any threat. The clock above the bar seemed to run in slow motion but finally reached closing time. Revellers staggered out into the night air, some with clearly amorous intent, others talking the usual drunken nonsense to each other.

Finally, the club was quiet.

As soon as he heard the music cease, Danny joined both Pamela and Larry at the front doors. Two young men dressed as Batman and Robin were half a dozen drinks past drunk and were weaving their way slowly up the centre of the road, clinging to each other for support. Robin had lost one shoe and Batman's mask was perched on top of his head like a semi-deflated balloon.

Danny laughed. "They don't look so super now."

Pamela smiled as she threw the bolt on the front door. "Holy cocktail overdose, Batman!"

Danny ushered the Dukes and their staff out of the back door. "Remember what I said: any sign of trouble and you hightail it to the cops."

"Be careful, Danny. Look after it for us; it's all we've got," said Pamela. She cast a look back into the club, clearly uncomfortable with leaving dozens of dirty glasses stacked on the bar.

"Don't worry, lass, the Woo Hoo's in good hands."

Larry rested a hand on Danny's shoulder. "You've got first watch then, soldier."

"Sounds like a plan," replied Danny.

"We'll see you in the morning."

Danny watched the couple drive away. The bar staff and Dez the cook followed. Julie loitered for another few minutes after the others had departed, chatting about nothing in particular. When she eventually climbed into her car at his insistence she sounded a double toot of the horn and gave him a finger wave as she vacated the parking lot.

Danny waited a few moments, inhaled slow and deep, then went back inside the club. A couple of trips later and choice items from his bed were arranged on the bar near the dirty glasses. He poured himself a Diet Coke and unlocked the front door, letting the cool night air waft in.

19

Babi Garcia didn't do contract work for many people. Not many people had need of his particular skill set and he was selective in whom he worked for. Barcelo was one of the few exceptions. Babi had disposed of two of Barcelo's rivals for him three years previously, two gypsy brothers who had tried to muscle in on some of the Locos' protection rackets. The brothers had put the pressure on the owner of a jewellery shop in the old town of Vera. When they had returned for their money, they had met Garcia instead of the goldsmith. Garcia put two bullets in each of the young men's faces without ceremony and then they all took the long trip out to feed the fishes.

Barcelo had paid him very well and didn't ask a single question after the event, caring only that it had been taken care of. Garcia appreciated the trust and offered his help on any future problems that required his direct response. He had *helped* several times since.

One of the Locos had been sent with him to point out the club. The boy—Kino—was barely eighteen but Babi didn't object. He was supposed to be a good driver. *Maybe once the club is ashes*, mused Garcia, *I could have some fun with him.*

"You stay in the car when we get there."

The young gangster lifted his chin. "I'm not scared to get my hands dirty."

"You'll do as you're told. Keep the engine running and be ready to drive. If you mess this up, you might even live to regret it."

Kino pointed. "That's it there. The Woo Hoo Club."

"Good, now slowly does it. Park up across from the front door. Keep the engine running."

Garcia slipped out of the car as soon as it had rolled to a gentle stop and opened the tailgate. He picked out one of six petrol bombs from the beer crate inside, clicked open his Zippo lighter and sparked it into life. The primed rag caught the flame immediately. He had mixed the incendiary bombs himself, getting the mix of petrol, laundry detergent and sand just right. Garcia gazed at the growing flame in admiration and threw the Molotov cocktail overhand at the front window. It traced a graceful flaming rainbow through the night air.

But the petrol bomb never reached the window; instead a man appeared at the doorway, cricket bat in hand, and with one swing propelled the bottle down the street. The bat had what looked like a thick layer of bar towels duct-taped around it. The bottle smashed upon impact and flames spread out across the road in a violent burst of orange.

Garcia realised he was both amused and angry at the same time. Who *was* this guy? He picked up another bottle. He grinned as he sparked the second bomb into life. *Time to make this a little more interesting.* Across the street the man with the bat moved gently from side to side, ready for the pitch.

"Catch!" Garcia launched the bottle, aiming directly at the interloper.

Dodging to one side, the man batted the bottle underhand and sent it back in an arc towards Garcia. It clattered along the street at a shallow angle, the bottle remaining intact, trailing a stream of petrol as it tumbled. The Spaniard kicked it further down the road with a snort of disdain and barked a rapid curse.

A flash of raw anger erupted as Kino appeared at his side. "Let me help!"

"Stay out of my fucking way," Garcia hissed through clenched teeth. "He belongs to me."

20

Danny inhaled, shifted his weight, feet spread wide, and readied himself for the next missile. He breathed out slow and easy. This was a game he'd played years ago with a bunch of bored specialists from the Special Boat Squadron. A lot of those guys had been adrenalin junkies and their off-duty games included blindfold shooting and tyre surfing—crazy, but great fun. Danny remembered sitting in an old truck tyre that was being towed behind a speeding car and hanging on for as long as possible. Other pastimes enjoyed by the SBS included Houdini-like escapology and the much loved Molotov baseball.

Danny had enjoyed the reckless fun of some of the games but never thought that they'd prove to be battleworthy. As he deflected the third bottle with the aid of a fast lunge to his right, he gave a defiant scowl as the bottle erupted in an incandescent starfish along the side of the gangsters' car. The younger man scrambled away from the flames, cursing.

Although Gunn's grasp of Spanish was good—especially compared to Clay's—it still left a lot to be desired when it came to the more colloquial curses. But the expression on the face of the young Loco spoke across the linguistic divide.

The furious boy, who looked to be in his late teens at best, drew a small-calibre pistol from the waistband of his urban-camo trousers. Danny glanced at the sidearm. A cheap piece of Russian crap, only really useful if it was pressed up against flesh point blank.

Another petrol bomb streaked through the air, its tail blazing like a comet. Keeping one eye on the gunman, Gunn barely deflected the fourth bomb and it exploded in a pool of fire a mere six feet away.

The young Loco inched forward with his pistol extended, his gun held sideways in the style of an American gangbanger. Then he pulled the trigger.

Gunn dodged sideways as the pistol emitted its trademark tin-can bark. The shot went wide and a small puff of white adobe was all it scored as it impacted into the wall behind. The young boy continued to pull the trigger as fast as he could manage. Another four shots whined through the air. None came within two feet of Gunn.

"You're one piss-poor pistolero," said Danny.

The young man gawked down at the handgun as he pulled the trigger without result. *Empty.*

"Get back." The bomber shook his head as he regarded the boy with a baleful glare. He barked, "The donkey knows more than you."

But the boy had already scuttled back to relative safety behind the car. The bomber walked forward, his face a mix of self-confidence bordering on smugness and deep-seated anger, the two remaining petrol bombs in hand. He addressed

Gunn in fluent English. "You can just walk away you know. This is your last chance to leave."

"What, leave when we haven't finished our game?" asked Danny as he waved the cricket bat defiantly.

"So let us finish it!"

"Come on then."

"My name is Babi Garcia. Scream it as you die!"

"My name's Jackson Commando. Shove it up your arse."

The bomber curled his lip in a brief smile. He set one of the bottles down on the ground and went to light the other.

Danny knew he planned to sling both bombs simultaneously. He charged. The bomber—Garcia—glanced up and faltered.

He sparked the lighter.

Danny raised the bat.

Garcia touched the petrol-soaked rag, the blue flame springing to life.

Danny closed in.

Garcia drew back his arm to throw the bomb point blank.

Danny launched the bat like a Viking casting an axe.

Garcia ducked the projectile but lost the impetus of his own throw.

Gunn slammed into him, knocking the Molotov cocktail from his hand with a sharp blow to the nerves on the underside of his wrist. He rammed Garcia's back against the side of the car and thrust a fist into his face. But this Garcia was clearly not one of Barcelo's rank-and-file Locos. He rolled back from the shot to the face and used the solidity of the car as a springboard to mount his counter. Danny tucked his chin low as Garcia clamped his hands onto his throat.

21

Garcia spun Danny in a tight arc. Danny's head slammed against the roof of the car, once, twice. On the third attempt, Danny managed to pitch Garcia head first towards the ground. Both men landed heavily alongside the car, air forced from their lungs. Garcia thrashed underneath Gunn, still very much in the fight.

Danny hammered the gangster with the heel of his right hand. Three rapid shots to the jaw sent the Spaniard's head against the asphalt.

Garcia retaliated by twisting and biting down on the hand that circled his throat, and the pain forced Gunn to relinquish his chokehold. Garcia slammed him sideways against the car again. Danny caught a painful boot in the ribs and realised the younger gangster had re-entered the affray. A quick elbow to the testicles sent the Loco back to ringside.

Garcia didn't waste the brief moment of respite and grabbed for a concealed knife. The blade was short and wide. Only the speed of Danny's reflexes prevented the blade penetrating his chest more than the quarter of an inch it did.

Gunn wrapped up Garcia's knife arm in an entangled arm lock and pushed the stiffened fingers of his free hand deep into his throat. Garcia gagged.

Then something dreadful occurred; the younger Loco snatched up one of the remaining petrol bombs with the rag still burning and bowled it towards both skirmishers.

Gunn had been in situations of abject horror before but that didn't prevent the world from going into freeze frame. Micro-seconds flashed through his mind like a strobe light.

Petrol bomb...

Shit.

Fire...

Shit.

Burned to death...

Shit.

Psycho with the knife...

Shit.

"Kino!" screamed Garcia, who had clearly also registered the prospect of a fiery death. He swung his leg in a wild kick and sent the bottle skittering back out of range. Both men resumed their struggle for dominance.

Gunn was well versed in combat ju-jitsu but rarely went to the ground by choice. All it took was an unseen attacker to run in and catch you unaware and the fight (and your life) could be over. Danny felt lucky that out of the two gangsters only Garcia was a competent fighter, but the younger one— Kino—was certainly persistent. He grabbed the discarded cricket bat from the road and waded in with wild abandon.

Gunn could only tuck his head low in way of defence. Even though he had padded the bat so as not to break the petrol bombs on impact, it was still an effective bludgeon. Sparks of purple pain exploded across his vision as the bat hit the back of his skull.

Danny reversed his position by rolling sideways, taking Garcia with him.

As Kino tried another swing with the bat, Gunn hooked one of his feet behind the boy's ankle and kicked out at his knee with the other. He flopped onto the road, howling in pain, all thoughts of fighting hopefully forgotten.

Danny felt the Spaniard's muscles coil as he renewed his efforts to free himself and drive the blade into Danny's chest. He realised Babi Garcia was grinning with the wild relish of a man berserk.

But Gunn had the advantage of training. He rolled fully onto his back and ensnared Garcia's torso tight between his thighs. He then crossed his ankles for maximum leverage and squeezed with all of his might. The effect was much the same as a wrestler's bear hug, but given that the legs are approximately four times stronger than the arms, the effect on the internal organs is horribly effective.

Garcia responded to the body-crush like most people do: he arched his back like a centipede caught in the cruel glare of a child's magnifying glass. As the paralysing effect of the hold took effect, Gunn slammed his right palm with as much force as he could muster into Garcia's unprotected ear. The Spaniard tumbled off him into an ungainly heap next to Kino.

A stamp kick into the side of Garcia's face made sure the man stayed down.

Danny rose to his feet. He clenched his jaw tight and pushed against his teeth with his hand as hard as possible.

None of his teeth moved, his jaw wasn't broken, just hurting like hell from the slaps with the cricket bat. He rolled his neck and looked down with considered contempt at the two losers.

He picked up the one remaining petrol bomb that had survived the fight untouched.

"Well, boys, I'll give you an A for effort, but a C for aptitude. Must do better," Gunn said. The rag gave no resistance as he pulled it free from the neck of the bottle. Then he splashed the petroleum over the two prostrate bodies like an angry priest casting out demons during an exorcism. "Let's see how you like it."

Kino howled in fear, his eyes wide like a rabbit in a snare.

Garcia remained defiant, spitting out liquid. "English piece of shit."

"See that's where you're wrong. I'm not English at all. I'm a Scotsman and proud of it. Mind, this has got nothing to do with you being Spanish and me British; more to do with you being a bunch of trouble-making arseholes. Big difference. I've met fuckers like you the world over. Being a fuckwit is an equal opportunities employer."

"You're all the same to me."

"Well, take that thought with you to hell," remarked Gunn as he produced a lighter from a pocket. He cast a glance around for spectators. There were none. A grim smile flickered across his face. The street scene was something akin to an apocalyptic tableau from the mind of Dante. Pools of flame burned with desperate ambition to spread their destructive capacity, but the cooling pavement offered little in the way of combustible materials. Danny turned his gaze back to the two fallen men, one shuddering in unequivocal terror, the other actually sneering as if daring Gunn to deliver the promised immolation.

The men were saved, not by any act of compassion, but by the blaring sirens of the approaching emergency vehicles.

Gunn and Garcia continued to lock stares. Neither man wanted to leave the encounter unfinished, but neither wanted any police involvement either. Danny gave a curt nod. "I'll finish up with you later."

"Next time it will be different," Garcia replied.

Gunn could see the first hints of red and blue lights reflected in the windows further down the street. The police were only moments away. He pointed a finger at Garcia, turned, snatched up the cricket bat and ran inside the club. He locked the door behind him then checked it was secure.

Garcia pulled Kino to his feet, ignoring the yelps of pain from the younger man. "Can you drive?"

Kino nodded, his eyes wide.

"Then fucking drive," ordered Garcia.

Kino slammed the car into gear, sped out into the street and slewed around the first corner. His wheels sent up a burst of sparks as he clipped the kerb. The car zig-zagged at each subsequent junction, right turn, left turn, so in a few minutes they were many blocks over from the burning crime scene. By the time he braked to a jarring stop, the flames that had decorated the side of the Mercedes had burned themselves out. The paint job was ruined. He looked at Garcia, the whites of his eyes stark against the soft dashboard lights. "Shit, what are we gonna tell the boss?"

"You leave the talking to me," offered Garcia. "First we better get you cleaned up. How's your leg?"

"My knee hurts like a bastard."

"Don't drive back to the boss's villa just yet. My place is just a couple of miles away. We'll get you patched up and get our story straight before we talk to Barcelo."

"But we were supposed to call him as soon as the job was done."

"And tell him what?" Garcia crossed his eyes and spoke in the manner of a simpleton. "Hey, boss, we just got our clocks cleaned and had to run for cover with our asses on fire, how about a bonus?"

"What will he do?"

"To me? Nothing... but to you? I don't even want to think about it."

Kino gulped in dire understanding. "Where do you live?"

Garcia smiled. "Take the next right."

Fifteen minutes later Garcia called Barcelo.

"Is it done?"

"No, it is not. There was a problem. The hired help was waiting for us."

"So? I told you to burn the club down and kill the Brit and the American if they were there."

"The Yank wasn't there, only the Brit. He is a tricky bastard that one. I will need a second shot at him," said Garcia.

"Is the club still standing?"

"Yes. Things did not go as planned..." Garcia gave an abridged version of events to his employer. He could hear Barcelo swearing and the sound of objects crashing around the room.

"One other thing... that bastard Brit killed young Kino

in a most horrible way. I'll explain more when I see you later this morning."

"Tell me now," demanded Barcelo.

"He crushed the boy's neck, but... it didn't kill him straight away. He choked to death slowly. I tried to help but his throat had been stamped on."

The line went quiet but he knew Barcelo was still there. Garcia looked down at Kino's splayed corpse. The boy's throat had indeed been crushed beyond repair. Garcia brushed the flattened cartilage with his toes. He then pressed his heel under Kino's chin as he enjoyed the quiet tension of the call.

Finally, Barcelo spoke and the message was music to Garcia's ears.

Minutes later Danny peered at the two police cars and the fire engine from behind the club's bar. The four policemen—Guardia Civil—were chatting between themselves and seemed to be taking turns to point at the pools of fire and scratch their heads in puzzlement. Two of the fire crew extinguished the flames in seconds.

After about ten minutes of shoulder shrugging and random gesticulations, one of the policemen made a rudimentary attempt at rattling a few of the surrounding doors. Another one of the cops stared straight up into the night sky as if aliens with arsonist tendencies might be to blame.

The first hints of dawn were creeping over the horizon by the time the street was finally silent again. Danny climbed the stairs back to his makeshift bedroom and flopped down onto the camp bed.

He stared at the ceiling.

Damn, was he really going to set those two alight? He had been on the receiving end of flames in times past and knew it ranked high on the worst possible deaths list. An act of evil to be sure. The only way he could square it off in his mind was that they had tried to do it to him first.

Was that reason enough?

Danny exhaled slow and easy, answering his own question. "Aye."

He was asleep before the bedsprings stopped squeaking.

22

The sight that greeted the Dukes made them stop in their tracks. Danny's eyes were dark with bruises and two horizontal scratches were etched deep into his chin.

"Danny?" Pam started towards him, her nursing instinct awakened again.

"Hey, I'm all right. Just a few more bruises that's all; hazards of the job."

"What happened?"

Danny led the couple outside and pointed out the scorch marks from the previous night. A few minutes of recounting had them up to speed on developments. A couple of passing pedestrians stopped to look at the scene so Gunn walked the couple back to the front door.

"What's your insurance like on the club?"

"We're fully covered for most accidents, fire and theft," Larry replied.

"Bump it up this morning, even if you have to pay quite a bit extra. Get the compensation rate raised as high as possible."

"Danny, are we going to lose the club?" asked Pamela. She reached for Larry.

"Clay and I will do our damn best to make sure not, but the game is cranking up now. The Locos have tried to grab me and burn down your club and failed on both counts. They'll make their next move a big one. These gangs are like wild animals; if they show any weakness, the other gangs around here would sense that weakness and move in. I've been looking online this morning—there's quite a few gangs operating in this area; some of them are nasty bastards as well. The two main threats to the Locos are the Rogue Angels and the Colombians."

"Great. That's just what we need, more gangs." Pamela shook her head, her mouth turned down at the corners. The three sat at one of the tables near the front doors.

"Colombians? Like South American Colombians, here in Spain?" asked Pamela. "Really?"

"Aye, they've got tentacles everywhere. The Colombians arrived over forty years ago, with soldiers from both North and South America and they're the most organised of all of the gangs in Spain without a doubt. They operate like a criminal secret service. Spain is an ideal location to conduct business for them, with the relaxed drug laws and easily manipulated legal system."

Larry smiled a tight-lipped smile. "Colombians, eh? I like their coffee."

"Most regular people in Spain don't even realise they're here apparently. They run their pipelines slick and quiet, beyond the reach of the American Drug Enforcement Administration."

Pamela returned to the table with three mugs. "Not Colombian but it's good coffee all the same."

Danny sipped at the bitter brew. He nodded his thanks. "But the guys that caught my attention are a biker gang: the Rogue Angels. I saw them in town the other day."

"I've seen them around as well. Bunch of tough-looking bastards," said Larry. "They seem to have shown up out of the blue in the last month or so."

"I googled them this morning. They're a French gang, mostly from around Marseilles. They've been in the news quite a bit. Lots of violence. A turf war made the headlines a couple of years back. The Rogues went up against another outfit from Marseilles. Sixteen of the rival gang, the Red Wolves, were found murdered in their clubhouse. The bodies had been mutilated and then burned. They sent a very clear message to all the other gangs. They've been in the news quite a bit since too. Their reputation follows them wherever they set up camp."

"And they're French?" asked Pamela. "What are they doing down here?"

Danny took another sip of coffee. "A French undercover cop was murdered. The Marseilles police knew the Rogues were behind the killing and hounded the gang at every corner. A few of the bikers met with *accidents* of their own. I think they learned the hard way that killing cops is really bad for business. So now they roll from town to town, freighting guns, drugs and flesh into whichever marketplace is the highest bidder at the time."

"Great," said Pamela flatly. "So how the hell can these bikers be of any help to us? Are you going to hire them as backup?"

"No, that's not my style. I like to handle things in-house. It's all about trust and who you can rely on."

"What then?"

"Trust me, Pam, it's better if you don't know the details. Let me do what I do. I'll keep you informed if I need to."

"Oh, I see, it's on a need-to-know basis, right?" She shook her head. "You can take the man out of the army but you can't take the army out of the man."

"Come on, it's not like that." Danny put a hand on her shoulder. "You know how it is. If the police come around asking questions, it's better if you don't know what I've been up to. Politicians call it plausible deniability."

"Okay, okay, I get it. Just be—"

"I'm always careful. *Careful* is my middle name."

"That's funny, Clay said it was Valentine. Like the saint," Larry cut in. He smiled wryly.

Danny shook his head. His absent sibling could be a real pain in the arse sometimes. Nothing was sacred. Danny's school years had been bad enough, living as an army brat, getting moved from country to country. As soon as you'd finally made some friends, you were on the move again. Then came the taunting. As soon as the other kids discovered his middle name, he would receive all sorts of tacky Valentine's Day gifts, usually defaced with crude messages from the other boys in the school. Love hearts with an oversized penis drawn on, that kind of thing. He still gritted his teeth each time February fourteenth rolled around. How any woman found a cheap teddy bear with a red heart emblazoned on its chest romantic was still a mystery to him.

"Look, why don't you two sit back out in the sun while

we get ready for the day? Julie and Dez will be here in a few minutes," said Pam.

Danny paid a little more attention when Julie was mentioned.

"You sure?" asked Larry.

"Yeah, I'm sure. You just get in my way."

"Sheesh, nice to be wanted."

Pamela leaned over and kissed Larry full on the lips. "You know I love you, you're just a crap table setter."

"Fine, have it your way. Now bring me one of your finest ales, wench. And make it quick!" Larry adopted a hilarious haughty tone.

"Strictly orange juice or coffee this early on in the day. You know what Dr Simmons said."

"Dr Simmons: bane of my life," Larry whispered from the side of his mouth. "Tried to get me into yoga. I ask you…"

But Danny wasn't really listening. Instead his mind was moving through scenarios, cause and effect, retribution and revenge. Each action committed had a number of probable outcomes, like moves on a chessboard. He visualised various options much like a safe cracker plays with the dial of the combination mechanism. *Click, click, click.* The pieces started to fall into place. The Locos, the Rogue Angels; light the blue touchpaper and stand well back…

Larry was still talking, heedless of his companion zoning out. "…and so I told him, there's nothing wrong with my heart, it's the rest of me that's buggered."

A large blue cylindrical truck rumbled past the club. The sewage tanker looked out of place in the picturesque street. Danny supposed that many of the surrounding rural houses and villas weren't connected to the main network of sewers and had septic tanks that needed to be emptied regularly. It was an ugly truck that kept the rest of the town safe, sanitary and beautiful; the way of the world.

Danny smiled as *click*, the safe door in his mind opened.

23

The sun was reaching its zenith as Danny watched Clay reverse his vehicle into the parking zone at the rear of the club. High overhead, a gull traced a wide circle, gave one shrill caw and moved out to sea.

Clay switched off the engine and clambered out. He groaned loudly as he stretched. "Hello, wee one."

"Hiya, Clay." Danny then slipped into his best Sean Connery voice. "Well, you're a shite for shore eyes."

The Gunn brothers shared a quick embrace.

Clay pointed at Danny's bruises and scrapes. "Been having fun while I've been away?"

"Oh, you know me, making friends and influencing people. I'll tell you all about it later over a cold one."

"Sounds good to me."

"So are you all sorted on the home front?" asked Danny.

"More or less; I'll explain over another of those cold ones you just promised."

"Did you bring your toys?"

"You betcha, and I think you'll like what I brought for you."

"Okay then, so what did you get from Boy-Toys R Us?"

Clay opened the trunk of his car. "Lookie-lookie."

"Shiny," declared the younger Gunn, admiring a selection that included an AK-47 rifle, an old British L1A1 self-loading rifle, a pair of Beretta 92 pistols and a dozen or so packages wrapped and duct-taped in brown greaseproof paper.

"Have you tested all of the kit?"

"Of course I have," Clay grunted. Both men knew better than to go into any live-fire situation with untested kit. The last thing you needed when the shit started flying was a dud firearm.

"So what's in the parcels?"

"Some nice 'go-faster kit' I picked up as well. Night-vision goggles, camo nets, a red-dot sight for one of the Berettas, some other stuff…"

Danny rummaged through the packages. "Is that a stinger?" he asked, as he came to a compacted row of steel spikes that resembled the ridges of an alligator's back. The stinger was designed to be spread across any road surface; the razor-sharp spikes would shred the tyres of any vehicle that drove over them. It effectively brought many police chases to an abrupt stop when deployed.

"Aye, I borrowed it from a friend a while back."

"Why the hell did you borrow a stinger?"

"Ah, there were a few idiots tearing the town up in their cars. I was going to put a stop to it."

"With a stinger?"

Clay shrugged. "Those *Fast and Furious* wannabes were rankling me a-piece. Real pains in the ass."

"So what happened?" asked Danny.

"I never needed the stinger. Two of the dopes ran into

each other head on. Wrote the cars off in one easy move. Both ended up in ER. I haven't seen them since."

"So all's well that ends well."

"I reckon so."

Danny lifted the edge of a blanket to reveal a box of HG 85 grenades. "Shit, Clay, you did well to lay hands on these."

Clay gave a naughty-boy laugh. To the uninformed the simple grey spheres gave no clue to the destructive power they held within. Danny knew from personal experience that they were devastating at the correct range.

"Let's hope we don't have to use them."

"Park that," said Clay, miming an explosion with his outstretched fingers. "Let's hope we *do* get to use them!"

"What are you two deviants laughing about?" Larry poked his head out of the back door of the club. He grinned as he spotted the trunk full of ordnance. "Man, an old SLR, from back when kit was properly made. I never agreed with the change over to the SA80, it always felt like a toy in your hands."

"All in the name of progress, Larry," remarked Clay.

"At least you felt like you were holding a real weapon with the old black gat. The SA80 always felt like a GI Joe toy," scoffed Larry. "It was just like the rest of the eighties; gaudy and done in poor taste."

"I quite like it, feels much like our M4. Kinda short and stubby but gets the job done," Clay offered.

"No taste," said Larry. "Still, that's 'cause you Americans can't shoot for shit anyway."

Danny seized his chance to join in. "It's all that *Rambo* spray and pray malarkey; it knocks their eyes off kilter."

"To hell with the pair of you, Rangers lead the way. Booyah!"

For a moment all troubles were forgotten; just three old soldiers shooting the shit.

Danny looked around the parking lot making sure there were no unexpected observers as Larry hefted the SLR, his hands instantly finding the natural grip. The years seemed to fall away from his face and for a moment Larry Duke had the full bearing of a combat soldier again. The SLR fitted into the curve of his shoulder with the comfort of an old lover rediscovered. He pressed his cheek against the nonslip pebble-grain stock and looked down the iron sights of the rifle.

"So did they have the SLR during the Boer War? Isn't that the last war you fought in?" asked Clay.

Larry kept the rifle hugged close. "I was one of the best snipers that the Royal Fusiliers had."

Danny nodded his respect. He knew that Larry had eight confirmed kills to his name. In the world of video game mentality, eight kills may not sound much, but Danny knew that any soldier that had switched off a target carried that kill forever.

Clay held out his hand. "Come on, gramps, before you hurt yourself."

Larry handed over the weapon. "Pah, I've seen more action than you've seen women. Still, that wouldn't take much beating, you ugly Yankee bugger."

"Do you two want some time alone or can we get back to business?" asked Danny.

Clay and Larry exchanged grins.

"Did you have any trouble getting the kit over the border from Portugal?" asked Danny.

"Nah, I picked most of it up from a pal who lives just over on the Spanish side in Huelva on the Costa de la Luz.

I'm telling you, Ron's got a garage so full of kit, he could supply a small African country and still have some left over. He's far enough away that none of the local assholes will get wind of gringos arming up."

All three men knew how easy it was to obtain firearms in Spain. The country had a long history of gun running, brought to the fore during the Spanish Civil War. Despite the decades since, many of the old service weapons were still tucked away in civilian homes. The only limitation was the depth of your pockets.

A voice from the kitchen caused the trio to turn as one. "Well, I see the good, the bad and the ugly are back together."

"Hiya, Daisy, come an' give me a kiss," demanded Clay as Larry placed the SLR back into the vehicle.

"I'd rather kiss a donkey's arse than you, you big lout."

"Hey, I think I've got a couple of DVDs along those lines."

"Wouldn't surprise me." Pamela shook her head in mock disgust, but she gave him an affectionate hug in way of compensation. Clay stooped and planted a kiss on her cheek. Pamela play-punched him on the shoulder. "And what have I told you about that 'Daisy Duke' crap?"

Clay just flashed a boyish grin and winked at her.

"Come inside. I'll ask Dez to fix you some food and Sally is on her way over with some news."

"Sally?" asked Clay.

"Sally Winrow from Sally's Salon, I presume?" asked Danny.

"The one and the same. Well remembered."

"I've got a good mind for details." Danny tapped the side of his head.

Pamela gave him a dubious look. "I suppose the fact that she's young and blond and beautiful has got nothing to do with her sticking in there?"

"Blond? Beautiful? Can't say I noticed."

Clay locked the car. "I've never met her but I like her already."

"Men! You're all the same."

"Nah, some of us are worse," said Clay.

The three men followed Pamela inside the club. The smell of bacon and coffee greeted them. Clay rubbed his hands together. "Hey, something smells mighty good. I've lived on pre-packed sandwiches for the last few days. Some real food wouldn't hurt right now."

"Dez, can you do these three vagrants a late breakfast apiece? Grilled not fried for Larry."

Dez looked up briefly then he went straight back to cooking and singing along to the radio. "Sure, Pam, three specials coming right up."

Danny was about to tell him that he'd already eaten then reconsidered. A full English breakfast was one of the simple pleasures in life, even for lunch. Besides, most soldiers had a basic rule of thumb during a conflict: eat, sleep and shit whenever you can, because you may not get the chance to do any again for god knows how long.

"Grilled for me too," said Danny.

"Any ways up," said Clay.

Minutes later three large servings were brought to their table. The three friends emptied their plates with gusto.

Danny shook his head as Clay emitted a loud burp into his cupped hands.

"Nice…" said Julie as she removed the plates.

"Oh jeez, I'm sorry, miss," shrugged Clay with a sheepish expression.

Danny gave a tight smile at his brother's embarrassment. In the presence of men Clay was as rough and ready as any of his Texas kin, but he always tried to be a gentleman around the ladies. "It could have been a lot worse."

Clay folded the paper napkin onto his empty plate but said nothing.

Julie bumped Danny with her hip and gave a soft wink as she collected his plate. "Nice?"

"Very." Danny held her gaze. "The food wasn't bad either."

Julie pursed her lips as if to blow him a kiss then turned on her heel and moved back to the kitchen. Danny admired her dark-brown hair. Slim waist, long legs and she smelled faintly of strawberries. She went back about her business and Danny couldn't help more furtive glances as she leaned over the tables to serve customers their meals. Nice girl… nice curves.

The door to the club opened and Sally and a young man Danny didn't recognise entered. "That's Sally," Danny said to Clay, pointing at the newcomers. The Gunn brothers stood up as she approached the table.

"Hello again," Sally said to Danny.

"Hello, you."

"There was a lot of commotion at the flats just after you left the other night. I think you left just in time."

Danny pointed at the bruises on his face. "Not quite."

"That was you?" Sally looked genuinely surprised. "But the neighbours said that a dozen men were injured in a big fight."

Danny shrugged modestly. "Doesn't take a blowtorch to start a forest fire."

Clay coughed quietly.

"Sally, I'd like you to meet my brother, Clay."

"Hello, Clay." She gave him that same wide smile as she had given upon first meeting Danny, then, "You don't look like brothers."

"Nah, I got lucky, I nabbed all the best features before he was even thought of."

Sally looked at him, her face blank in non-comprehension as she took in the totally different accent. A couple of seconds later she laughed and wiggled a finger at the older Gunn.

Sally introduced her companion. "Guys, this is my nephew, Adam."

Adam looked to be around twenty. His body shape told of too many burgers and an allergy to exercise. When he smiled it appeared that God had tucked a few too many teeth into his mouth. His hair was best described as tufty. To top off his good looks quota, his eyes were slightly misaligned. He had that "mad scientist" look about him and Danny wondered if that old-time actor Jack Elam had ever taken vacations in these here parts.

Adam was an excitable chap, his words coming out on fast forward. "Are you really the Gunn brothers?"

"In the flesh," said Danny.

"And that's your real name?" Adam's eyes seemed to part company even more when he was babbling. He made twin finger pistols. "Gun? Like in *pow pow pow*? *Rat-a-tat-tat*?"

Both brothers struggled with his speech due to a mangled Spanish/Essex accent and his frantic delivery.

Danny gave a slow nod in way of answer.

Sally stood behind her nephew and placed her manicured hands on his shoulders. "Adam works for EPS, the delivery company, and he's got some information for you. Just take your time, Adam," then with a sly smile, "they don't speak English very well."

Adam looked at her, puzzled.

Sally dead-panned the brothers. "Well, one's a Jock Mac-Tavish and the other's a Yankee Doodle Dandy."

Adam grinned. "Well I was out on my route yesterday and on my PM run I dropped off five parcels to a villa about twenty-five miles north of here." Adam moved his hands in front of his ample torso as if carrying the loads. "Three next day and two outsize."

The brothers exchanged a look.

"Go on," said Danny.

"Well, while I was dropping off, a carload of Locos parked up and walked past me into the kitchen at the back of the villa. Just about knocked me over."

Sally nodded; she'd obviously heard the details already. She patted down a tuft of his flyaway hair.

"Sure they were Locos?"

"They all had that same grey camouflage gear on. One of them pushed me out of the way. He said I was blocking out the sun."

"Okay," said Danny.

Adam stared at Danny's bruises with something akin to admiration; his mouth hung slightly open as he inspected the older man's face, unabashed. "Then the owner of the villa came to sign for the outsize parcels. His name is Antoni

Barcelo. The Locos all called him the boss… well, '*jefe*' as they passed him. Aunt Sally told me you were going up against the gang so I thought it might be useful."

"Damned right," Danny said. "Well done, Adam, you've just saved us a lot of work trying to trace this guy. I take it you brought his details with you?"

Adam produced a buff folder from under his arm. "I did a little digging around on the Internet last night. It's amazing what you can find out about people."

"Indeed," said Danny.

He spread the contents out on the table, arranging them in a neat collage. The first of the printouts showed Barcelo's name and address. One of the documents was a photocopy of the EPS delivery note. Another showed an estate agent's folio picture of the villa dated a few years earlier. Another sheet from the same company website showed an overhead view of the sprawling property. The price tag of the villa elicited a soft whistle from Danny. "And they say crime doesn't pay."

Coordinates were printed in bold handwriting along the bottom edge of another page.

"Google Earth?" asked Danny.

"Yeah, you gotta love it."

"Is this definitely the same house?"

"Yeah, we use GPS co-ords in the vans now, so I googled them and the address."

Both Gunn brothers huddled over the aerial shot of the villa and its grounds.

"Very nice, looks like the White House," shared Clay. He tapped a calloused finger on the picture. "But the realtor might have to take a new picture when we're finished remodelling it."

"This is great, Adam, now, what else do you remember about the place?" asked Danny.

"Like what?"

"Did you notice any CCTV on the way in?"

"Yeah, he's got a few cameras dotted around. There was a big one at the front gate, and definitely one next to the back door. I wasn't at the front of the house so I'm not sure what they've got installed there."

"Okay, you're doing great. What about dogs?"

"I didn't see any but there was a warning sign at the front gate as well. *Cuidado con el perro*; beware of the dog."

"You speak fluent Spanish?" asked Danny.

"Of course, I grew up here. I've been here since I was eleven years old."

"In Ultima?"

"No, I've been here two years. I grew up over at Alcoy, near Alicante."

"Okay, anything else?"

"There was a little hut just inside the main gate, like a security cabin, but there wasn't anybody in it when I was there. They just buzzed me in from the main house."

Danny pointed back to the aerial photograph. "How high is this perimeter wall?"

Adam gazed at Clay as if measuring the wall against the tallest man in the room. His eyes came to rest about six inches above Clay's head. "Uhm, maybe about seven feet?"

The questions continued for half an hour more. Danny pressed him for details. Adam smiled as he answered each one. His face bore an expression similar to when a fan meets a movie hero in the flesh. His expression began to trouble the younger Gunn brother.

Adam slumped in his chair and declared, "Man, I feel like I've been interrogated by the CIA."

Sally patted his hand. "Oh, Adam, don't be so melodramatic."

"No, no, I'm not complaining. It's exciting, like I'm in one of those spy movies. *Mission Impossible* and all that." He pointed two fingers to simulate a gun.

Clay glowered at the younger man. "It's nothing like that. If it goes wrong in real life, that's it. No cut, no second chances."

Adam recoiled as if he'd been slapped. "I... I know. I just want to help. I see what the criminals, what the gangs, do around here. I just want to be part of something good, something worthwhile."

"You've done more than enough already. What you've given us is great, now you've got to get back to your daily routine. Just keep your eyes open and report anything you think might be useful. Can you do that?"

"Kind of like undercover surveillance?"

Danny sighed. The kid was proving hard work. "Yes... kind of, but only as part of your normal day. Absolutely no heroics—do you understand? Don't do anything that will get you noticed. Am I clear?"

Adam nodded.

"You better listen. I'll kick your ass big time if I catch you messing around. Remember these Locos are for real. They'll gut you and leave you lying for the crows to pick at," Clay rumbled. He did not lift his eyes from the pictures.

"I get it, I get it." Adam waved his hands placatingly.

The group shared a drink at the bar before parting. Sally gave each one of the men an enthusiastic hug, then linked arms with her nephew and said goodbye.

Once they had pulled away in their car, Clay turned to Danny. "Shit, I'd hate to see him full of coffee; he made my ears hurt. I think we need to video him and play him back half speed."

"I know, but he brought us some good intel."

"Hmm, I guess so," Clay grinned. He bumped his knuckles into Danny's ribs. "I think Sally was into you."

Danny fixed him with a sour look. "She's married."

"And?"

"That's it. She's married... end of."

Clay shrugged and wrinkled his nose.

"We're not all womanisers like you, y'know," said Danny. He knew Clay had struggled with his conscience for many years following the untimely death of his wife. Diana had been killed in a hit and run. The driver had never been identified. As sole inheritor of Diana's considerable estate, Clay had become a very eligible Texas bachelor, yet he had declined many offers. Danny teased him from time to time as if he did lead a hedonistic lifestyle.

Clay raised his eyebrows. "Ah, little brother, wise in so many ways, yet a numb-nut in so many others."

"Who said that? Socrates?"

"Dickens, I think."

"Profound."

"Indeed."

"Come on, we've still got a lot of work to do."

"Roger that, wee one, let's get our asses in gear."

"Stop calling me wee one."

Clay shot him a grin.

Danny gathered up the documents Adam had supplied and the brothers walked to the rear of the club. As Julie passed a brief smile was exchanged. Larry gave them a perfunctory nod as they climbed the stairs to Danny's room.

Bedsprings creaked in protest as Clay sat on the bed. Danny picked up his laptop and accessed Google Earth. Seconds later a satellite view of Ultima appeared on screen. He scrolled the map upwards and zoomed until he located the villa. Then he glanced at the three option menus on offer: map, hybrid and terrain. "I'll print off the route from here to the villa. I'll need to link to Pam's printer downstairs."

"Okay. You've been busy I see," said Clay, pointing to the various items arranged along the windowsill.

"I thought a few party favours might come in handy."

After figuring out the identification details for the printer, Danny printed off a series of maps, photographs and plans, all showing the Barcelo's main villa building and surrounding landscape. A quick trip down the stairs and back followed. The various views included topographical detail of the surrounding coastline, a road map of the immediate area and a hybrid view of the grounds that afforded an overlaid combination of road and satellite view.

The villa was a huge affair. It was situated on a narrow peninsula and the perimeter wall arrested all direct access from land. The villa grounds formed a rough V shape, or more correctly an inverted triangle. The building itself was unusual in shape. The main edifice was circular, with a series of interconnected buildings that formed twin Ls to either side. Viewed from above it resembled a swastika with the north and south arms removed. An expansive pool and sun terrace paved with terracotta tiles faced out to sea at the rear of the villa. A narrow stretch of private beach lay at the bottom of a steep wooden staircase.

"The nearest neighbour is about three miles away. That's good; no bystanders if we have to go in heavy."

Clay nodded and selected another picture. "This hill overlooks the whole place. Should be a good spot to set up camp."

"I don't disagree, but I want to try some sideline tactics before we go near that place all heavy-handed. I want to give them something to think about other than us, keep them occupied and off balance."

"What you got in mind?"

Danny outlined his plans and Clay grinned again. "I knew I kept you around for a reason, wee one. See, I like to fuck with the opposition, but you, you take it to the next level. When do we start?"

"As soon as the sun goes down and the punters come out to play."

"I'll bring in some of the kit from the car. We can strip and clean while we're waiting."

24

Hours later, all of the weapons that Clay had brought lay on the camp bed. He loved the distinctive gun-oil smell the rifles and handguns gave off. The AK47 had seen better days but after several checks he was sure it was still fully functional. That was one of the AK's many strengths; it was produced cheaply but it was built to last, a real workhorse weapon. The weapon could fire up to six hundred rounds per minute on full auto fire, and it only took one of those rounds to kill. *God bless Mr Kalashnikov. Seventy million users couldn't be wrong.*

Clay rolled a tapered 7.62 round between his fingers. "What d'you think we'll do when we're too old to play this game?"

Danny shrugged. "Don't know, grow old disgracefully I suppose."

"I'm thinking about starting an adventure business in Portugal. Split my time between there and the States."

Danny worked the slide on one of the Beretta pistols. "What do you mean by adventure?"

"Be a soldier for a day, play at commandos. Let the tourists ride in an armoured car, shoot some blanks, maybe try a killing house with paintball guns, that kind of thing. That was one of the things I had to go and sort out. I've bought a chunk of land a few miles away from my house. It'll be ideal ground if I decide to go ahead with it. There'd be a good job for you as well. I'd need someone to manage it whenever I was back home."

"Sounds like a good idea."

"Well it's easy money and we don't have to get any more of these." Clay rubbed a finger across the scar that emerged from his hairline down onto his forehead. Of all the scars on his face it was the one he was most self-conscious about.

"What about your place in Texas?"

"The house is in safe hands. I let Salma and Sebastian live there rent free while I'm out of the country. They tend the house and the gardens anyway, so everything's square."

Danny nodded. Clay was grateful he didn't say more. Danny occasionally mocked him for having a housekeeper and gardener, even though he knew they were good people. Their daughter, Celine, now a feisty sixteen-year-old, was a budding maths genius with a great future ahead of her. Clay would make sure of that.

Clay had decided it was prudent to stay away from the States for a while after the trouble he and Danny had encountered the previous year. They had rescued a British journalist from the clutches of a mercenary team with orders to terminate her. Death and destruction had followed the brothers from the Nevada desert all the way to the Florida Keys. The resulting federal investigation had led to months of legal wrangling that convinced the Gunns to head to Europe until things died down.

Clay had purchased the property in Portugal. A *fixer-upper* he had called it. Danny had asked why he hadn't just bought one of the many top-end villas available in the Algarve. With the millions he had inherited from Diana's company, money certainly was not a problem, but Clay had wanted something to occupy his time and attention.

"I've got a contract with Odin Corp coming up in a couple of months. But after that... maybe?" replied Danny.

Clay sighed. "I've said it more than once, when are you gonna leave all that behind? We've both done our time in uniform. There's enough trouble in the world without marching into the middle of war zones for a damned private outfit."

Danny gave a non-committal shrug. "I'll know when it's time to put my boots away for good. Just not yet. Besides it's good money. I make a lot more as a PMC than I ever did as a green jacket."

Clay couldn't argue against that. He knew the world of private military contractors could be a lucrative one. "Well, when you are finished with it you know there will always be a place for you with me, either in Portugal or at home with me in Texas."

"I know and I appreciate the offer. Anyway, if you're done with the mayhem, what the hell are we doing here?"

The corners of Clay's mouth twitched into a smile before he answered. "That's different. This is helping out friends in need."

"But will still probably add to our scar collection before we're done."

Clay let the subject drop. He again rolled the 7.62 round in his hand. The feel of the bullet was perhaps a little too comfortable. Maybe Danny was right after all.

Clay had long since left the service of the Rangers yet all these years later he felt a welcome tingle as he palmed the ammunition.

25

As the three friends sat at one of the club's rear booths conversation shifted to the athletic superiority between American football and rugby players. Clay argued the validity of body armour and helmets while Larry cast unsubtle doubts on the manliness of the NFL players. Shaking his head, Danny opted out of the old debate.

Clay looked across the table as he tried to garner Danny's support. He spotted the messenger long before his gaze was reciprocated. Clay's expression never faltered and he announced deadpan, "Incoming."

Adam half waddled, half jogged over to the booth. Sweat was beaded on his brow. "Hi, guys. I've got something for you."

Clay motioned for Adam to sit.

"I've been busy all day but I come bearing gifts." He plopped a small sports bag onto the table. Two inches of stomach showed in a gap between his shirt and the waistband of his jeans.

"Miss Sally not with you?" asked Clay, rubbing his hands together. He'd been looking forward to ribbing Danny some more.

Adam looked back the way he'd come. "Er, no, just me."

"Show us what you've brought," advised Danny.

Adam delved into the bag and produced a small plastic box. "Ta-da!"

The men looked down at the contraption. The small rectangular box was fashioned from black plastic. It had a small amount of circuitry visible between its base and lid, which sat open like a feeding clam. Two rows of copper-coloured needles decorated either end of the box like minuscule teeth.

"Hey, you built a better mousetrap," Clay quipped.

"What is it?" asked Danny.

"It works like a cable splicer. You clip it onto an ADSL cable or a video feed cable and the box transmits the web data or video feed to your computer. I thought we might be able to keep tabs on Barcelo and his men with it. You'll be able to see everything he sees, either on his camera system or on any computers in the house. The system is self-aligning so it will piggyback any bandwidth that is used from the villa. He'll never know we're watching him. It operates on a black line code. I can insert a polymorphic virus that'll leave his system in shreds."

Clay raised his eyebrows. "That all sounds super techie. Will it work?"

Adam nodded then gave Clay a wink. "Oh yeah. It works."

Danny inspected the gizmo.

"I just need to install this software onto your laptop. It'll only take a minute or two. I've got the same program on my iPad." Adam produced a thumbdrive from the bag. The drive was embellished by the cartoon image of a grinning monkey.

"How do you know I've got a laptop?" asked Danny.

"Why would you not have one?" Adam's face was an example of perplexity as he stared back. "Everybody's got one haven't they?"

"Not everybody," said Larry.

Adam continued undaunted. "I've got a laptop, a desktop PC, an Android tablet, a PS4 system and an iPad."

"Can any of those make you dinner or get you laid?" Clay shook his head in the negative.

"Oh and my iPhone." Adam counted off his collection on raised fingers. "And I'm thinking about a Fitbit or iWatch."

After a beleaguered sigh Danny said, "I'll go get it."

As Danny trotted up the stairs to retrieve the computer Adam plopped himself down next to Larry. He gave Clay a toothy grin. "What were you guys talking about when I came in? Spy stuff?"

"No, we were arguing the toss between Peyton Manning and... oh never mind."

Adam stared at Clay.

"We were talking about rocket launchers and samurai swords."

"Wow. It must be great to be you guys," said Adam.

"Oh it is," said Larry. "I get to lie in to seven every morning and then I get to hump boxes of beer in and out of my van for two hours."

"No, I meant with the missions you must have been on."

Clay sighed. "Again with the missions? Adam, we're not spies. We've been soldiers, but most of a soldier's life is taken up getting shouted at by assholes, doing the most mundane tasks ever devised by man and waiting for something halfway interesting to happen."

Undaunted, a mischievous grin stretched Adam's features into new directions. "I know you and Danny are supposed to be good at the old head bashing but you can't be a bona fide hero unless you've got the J.B. factor."

Clay shook his head, his weathered features almost drooping at the boy's logic. "Okay, I know I'll regret this, but I'll ask... J.B. factor?"

"Yeah, all of the best tough guys have the initials J.B."

"Like?" Clay asked with another barely disguised sigh.

"James Bond, Jason Bourne, Jack Bauer, Jack Bristow, Jonas Blane..." He popped up a finger as he recounted the names.

Larry raised his eyebrows. "Who's Jack Bristow?"

"Jack Bristow... from *Alias*. With Jennifer Garner? It's a classic, early J.J. Abrams. I've got the complete box set on Blu-ray if you want to borrow it."

"Hmm..." Clay gave Adam a hound dog look. "I think you've way too much time on your hands."

It didn't dissuade Adam from continuing on his original thread. "Or you can just be called Jack, that's good too."

"You can stop now," advised Clay. The kid was getting on his nerves. Next to him Larry groaned in annoyance.

"Jack Bauer, Jack Bristow, Jack Reacher, Repairman Jack, Jack Sparrow..."

Clay decided to play him at his own game. "Jumpin' Jack Flash, Jack Daniels, Jack and the beanstalk, Jack 'n' Jill, Jack Shit, New Jack City, Jack Kerouac."

"Now you're just being silly," mumbled Adam. "I was just saying it would be cool to blow things up and shoot some bad guys."

"Bollocks," spat Larry. Clay knew he remembered all too well what explosions and bullets did to the fragile bodies of men.

Adam held an imaginary pistol in his hands, his face twisted into the most serious expression he could muster. "But…"

"But nothing," snapped Larry. "I hope you never see it."

"Easy." Clay lowered Adam's hands to the table. He knew Larry was very touchy when it came to the realities of war. Losing limbs and being pushed out of the army you were serving tended to taint your world view. Clay gave a slow blink of recognition and understanding to Larry. As if to illustrate his feelings, Larry's prosthetic limb clanged as it met the metal leg of the table.

Danny's return helped restore flow back to the conversation. He opened the laptop and turned it to face Adam. "Hey, if you break it, you bought it."

"You might know about guns and judo and stuff, but I know how to do just about anything with a computer that you can imagine." Coming from most people that would sound like a line of bullshit. Clay didn't doubt Adam.

Resuming his excited grin, he inserted the thumbdrive into a port and the machine whirred into life. Adam moved his digits over the keyboard with a fluid grace that eluded the rest of his body. As he typed in coded commands he touched each of his large teeth with his tongue in turn. He emitted a groan of almost post-coital satisfaction. "And we're done."

Danny nodded. "So after the box is clipped onto a cable, how far does the signal reach?"

"Up to half a mile or so."

"Is there any way you can use this to freeze the signal?"

"What, like jam the cameras?"

"Exactly like."

"Er… no, but I could design something to do that over the next few days."

"At least start thinking about how you would do it. Don't worry if you can't. If it comes to that I'll just cut the cables when I get close enough." Danny made scissors of his fingers.

"So the only problem now is how to get to the cable in the first place," mused Clay.

"No problem, I'm scheduled to go back there tomorrow," said Adam. "I've got a couple more parcels for him. I'll see if I can hack into the cable then."

"Just remember that these guys are dangerous. If you get caught, you're in the shit big-time. Not only is our chance at a surprise attack compromised but you'll be for the body bag," Danny warned.

Adam looked at each of the three men in turn. "Don't worry, I won't get caught. I'm sure there was a cable that ran alongside the back door. I'll hack that one if I can. Then any time you're close to his villa you can spy on him. Once we're in I can get deeper into his network and hack in remotely from home."

Clay turned to Danny who shrugged, and seeing no further objection, flicked back to Adam. "Okay, so what do we owe you for the box and the program?"

"Owe? Nothing. I'm just glad to be of help."

"Well, it's much appreciated," Clay said. "Adam, do you know who the most important man in the army is?"

Adam counted his teeth with the tip of his tongue again. "The general?"

"No, not the general. It's the quartermaster. The guy who

makes sure that the soldiers get the kit they need for the job in hand, so you're like our quartermaster."

"Really?" Adam's breathing quickened a little.

Clay decided to chip in. "You do realise that the quartermaster brings me breakfast in bed, right?"

This brought forth another of Adam's goofy smiles and one of his eyes did that sideways shift again. "I hope you like Pop Tarts, 'cause that's all I can cook."

"Pop Tarts? Jeez, no. You're sacked. I can't eat those things. They're Satan's own creation." Clay screwed up his face.

"I just about live on them," admitted Adam.

"I've got another favour to ask of you," said Danny.

"Anything."

"I want you to look for a couple of old second-hand cars. I need them to be good runners but it doesn't matter what they look like. Do you know anywhere that sells them?"

Adam drummed his fingers on the table. "There's a car market outside of Almería every Friday. I could go down there and see what's up for grabs."

"Great, you can spend up to four hundred euros on each, the bigger and heavier the better."

"Okay."

"Do you know much about cars?"

"Well, I drive for a living don't I?"

"Not quite the same, but okay."

"I know enough not to bring you a couple of junk piles that'll conk out on you when you need them most."

"Well, I think you understand the situation." Danny reached for his wallet.

"I'll get that," said Clay as he counted out the bills.

"Here's a straight thousand; spend it wisely."

Adam slipped the money into his shirt pocket. "The auction isn't for another couple of days, what do you want me to do until then?"

"Well, that program to freeze the cameras for one thing. Also, I want you to go home and think about what kind of car or truck is best for speed and ruggedness. They'll need to take a few knocks and stay on the road," said Danny.

Adam nodded slowly in deep contemplation.

"Okay, you're dismissed, soldier. Vamoose. And be damn careful tomorrow," said Clay.

Adam blinked a couple of times then gave a half smile. "You can count on me."

The three old soldiers nodded as one and Adam scuttled out into the late-afternoon sunlight.

"That should keep him occupied for a while," said Danny, blowing out his cheeks.

"Nice move, wee one," agreed Clay.

"He seems like a nice kid but he'd be hanging around our necks if we let him."

"He's got some gizmos though. He knows his way around a computer, no doubts there," said Larry. "I wouldn't have a clue."

"Aye, Adam's program might come in handy. If we can get into Barcelo's computer, we might pick up something useful and cause some havoc while we're in there."

"So what's next?" asked Larry.

"Field trip," offered Clay.

"To where?"

"Well, now we know where the villa is we're gonna take

a friendly look-see. Get the lay of the land," said Danny.

Larry lowered his voice. "I wish I was going with you."

"You rest easy on this one." Clay nodded at his old friend. "You know, we could just go in fast and heavy tonight, put a rocket through the front door and take them all out."

"It may well come to that but I think we should try some friendly persuasion first," said Danny.

"Ah, friendly persuasion, that's what it says on my business card," said Clay.

Danny gave a furtive wink to Larry. "When did you change it from Big Texan Butt Muncher?"

26

Clay eased the Toyota through the sparse traffic heading out of the town and followed the narrow coastal road north. Soon the jubilant tourists, blinking neon lights and background music gave way to the natural calm of the country. From the two-lane main road they detoured into countryside and followed a course for several miles that ran parallel to the coastal drop off. Most of the coast north of Ultima was comprised of steep gradients and minor cliffs before meeting the Mediterranean. Barcelo's villa occupied sole position on an elongated peninsula reminiscent of an old Spanish *castillo*.

Clay glanced at Danny, smiling at the way the dashboard lights illuminated his face as he scanned the road ahead. The sat-nav guided them along the road with regular prompts, the emotionless voice little more than a drone. An oldies station played quietly as they drove. Sinatra sung of how he'd done it his way, then went on to extol the virtues of New York, New York. As a change of pace, The Prodigy gave permission to *smack my bitch up* as they covered the last mile to Barcelo's secluded estate. Clay killed the headlights and the music as the soft glow from the villa lights warned of their proximity.

Amber lights in the form of antique lanterns showed the location of the villa clearly. Even in the fading dusk of early evening, the sprawling estate was impressive. The decorative lamps were fixed atop the perimeter wall and gave the estate an old colonial village look. The villa itself was clearly visible as they crested a hill and viewed the property from an elevated position.

Clay allowed the car to roll to a gentle stop. The engine idled quietly and he powered off the radio so no ambient light showed from the vehicle. They lowered the windows and allowed the night sounds to drift in. Indistinct noise travelled from the villa to their vantage point. Just muffled tones; too faint to be identified.

Satisfied that there was no immediate danger, Clay turned off the engine. Sickly sweet aromas were carried in on the gentle breeze.

Clay leaned forward and interlaced his fingers over the top of the steering wheel. The steering column protested slightly as he settled his weight.

Both men examined the path ahead in silent contemplation. The road continued for another five hundred metres then terminated at the main gates of the villa; only one road in and out. This held both advantages and disadvantages in an assault situation.

Clay reached for the rubber-coated Leica binoculars wedged on the dashboard. Not military-grade kit per se, but more than adequate for the task in hand. A silent nod and the brothers slid out into the approaching darkness. Both were dressed in dark outfits; black canvas trousers and shirts. Each had a matching Beretta 92 pistol tucked into their belt. The rest of the heavier weaponry was secured in the trunk.

Both adopted a stealthy crouch as they moved, old habits kicking in through instinct and training. They followed the rise of the hill and then dropped to one knee. The stump of an old tree offered a natural hiding place from which to study the peninsula.

Clay allowed his eyes to drift out of focus and his night vision to kick in. He then surveyed the villa in a slow and steady sweep from left to right. The light from the central windows was a calm shade of orange, the colour of an early autumn sunset. Two cars were parked in front of the glass-fronted body of the villa. Both looked like top-of-the-range Mercedes, one convertible and the other a saloon.

He panned right again and concentrated on the main gateway. Seconds later the glowing ember of a cigarette betrayed the guard sitting in the security hut directly behind the gate. Clay smiled and almost sympathised with the watchman—almost. He'd spent countless mind-numbing nights on sentry duty in his earlier years in the service. At least this bozo had the Mediterranean climate for company.

From his position, Clay could only view the front and eastern wing of the villa. He tapped Danny on the shoulder and signalled his intention. Clay moved slowly up the bluff, taking care not to reveal himself to any chance observers below. Danny remained stationary and vigilant, silently providing backup in the unlikely event of an ambush by the Locos.

The thirty-yard crawl up the hill provided Clay with an unobstructed view of the expansive sun terrace. The pool was illuminated by an underwater lighting system that gave off an aquatic-green hue. Three bikini-clad women moved slowly around in the light-dappled water. One of the girls swam topless. Clay was more interested in the six men dotted around the pool edge. One group of four, obviously talking amongst themselves and another two seated at the top of the steps that gave access to the beach below. The two stairway guardians sat at an oblique angle to each other, almost in the fashion of a Victorian loveseat. One faced in towards the house and pool, the other out to the undulating ocean.

Clay adjusted the focus on the binoculars and scanned the men at the gate. A shotgun leaned against the wall next to the man with the pool view. It looked like a pump-action, maybe a Mossberg or an Ithaca. The watchman seemed way more interested in the pool activities than the weapon or his guard duty.

The second guard appeared a little more vigilant. Periodically, he rose from his seat, glanced down the wooden steps and after satisfying himself that all was quiet, sat back into his upright sun lounger. He cradled a more compact assault shotgun with a shortened barrel, pistol grip and folding stock—maybe an Italian SPAS-12 or the like, certainly a deadly weapon when used correctly.

Clay scanned back to the group of four. The men stood in a loose U-shaped formation. The guy that caught Clay's attention was a bear of a man. Wide back and shoulders, thick black hair, swept high and back like Elvis: Barcelo.

The other three men nodded as Barcelo stabbed the air with his fingers. Clay guessed he was probably telling of all the unspeakable acts of violence he was going to perpetrate upon the British transgressors. He focused on the other three.

One had his right arm in a sling. He was slim-built and maybe fifty years old; he looked mean and dangerous. Suddenly Clay recognised the Loco, and smiled when he remembered how the man's arm had come to be injured.

The other two looked young and athletic and both wore muscle vests over their urban camo trousers. He could see the definition of their arms even at a distance. Their ripped muscles looked like tiger stripes in the deck lights. Big men hyped on steroids. There would be many more like them.

Clay watched for another fifteen minutes, then crawled back to Danny's position. He could feel the coarse sand and scrub grass shift subtly underfoot as he retraced his path.

Danny took the binoculars and traced his way to the spot vacated by Clay. Exactly fifteen minutes later, Danny appeared silently at his brother's side. Both moved back to the vehicle and climbed inside.

Talking in hushed tones, Danny said, "Looks good. Big house, lots of cover points on the way in."

Clay nodded. He drummed his fingers on the dashboard, barely making a sound. For the next ten minutes they compared their observations of the villa and various possible strategies for the breach and siege of the property.

"We could end this now by putting a couple of rounds through the back of Barcelo's head. You could make that shot with the SLR."

Danny considered the proposal. "Aye, not a bad idea."

"Hold the phone, we've got movement at the front of the villa," said Clay.

Barcelo and one of the ripped guys slid into the convertible. The other muscled Loco and the man with his arm in a sling took the Mercedes saloon and followed behind.

The headlights on both cars illuminated the driveway in front of the villa. The gates began to swing open. The guard at the gate emerged from the hut and gave a brief wave as the vehicles passed him.

As the vehicles sped towards their position the brothers climbed from the car and drew their pistols. The Toyota was parked well back from the road and was just another shadow on the hillside. Clay moved to the front of the vehicle while Danny crouched at the rear. Both pistols followed the progress of the two cars. Clay released his breath slowly as both speeding Mercedes zipped by without pause. He opened the car door and slid in.

"Well now, let's see where the boys are going tonight." Clay turned the ignition key and the engine sprang into life as Danny climbed into the passenger seat.

Clay made a quick three-point turn and set off in pursuit. The taillights of the two cars were twin red dots in the distance. Clay pressed down steadily on the accelerator pedal and resisted the urge to switch the headlights back on. He didn't want to alert the men to their presence. The road ahead was a single lane until it got to the first intersection. Ahead, the Mercedes reached the main road and turned towards Ultima.

"Slow and steady gets the job done," said Danny.

Clay gave a single nod in agreement as he flicked on the lights as they too reached the junction. The traffic was sparse and he stayed three cars behind the gangsters.

The lights of Ultima beckoned.

27

Ortega sipped his bottle of Coke through a straw and leaned against the saloon's window. He'd been eating and drinking everything via a straw since his encounter with the big Yank at the Woo Hoo Club. Having his jaw wired was proving both humiliating and painful. Although the double dose of OxyContin took the edge off the pain the pills gave him a serious case of dry mouth. He also winced every time he forgot himself and tried to talk normally. The muscles in the side of his jaw ached and his teeth felt like each one had been hit with a ball-peen hammer. Keeping his face neutral, not showing any outward discomfort, was the real challenge. He rested his arm, now cast from biceps to wrist, tight against his abdomen.

He was determined still to perform his role as a captain even with his injuries. Ortega had been with Barcelo for many years and was acutely aware of how quickly a capable man could rise through the ranks. Young men like the one who had taken his position in the driving seat of Barcelo's convertible ahead, thanks to his broken arm. Santo was young, strong and vicious. Men like him were ambitious and always looking for an opportunity to move a step up the ladder. Ortega was resolute to remain active and not lose his seniority in the organisation. He motioned his own driver to park up behind the convertible.

The four men exited the cars and walked towards their destination. There was a long line of customers waiting to enter the nightclub. Half-naked girls sipped coloured concoctions from test-tube style glasses, while men vied for their attention. "*Mujerzuelas e idiotas*" (which translated meant "sluts and idiots") was Ortega's stock phrase when describing the tourists. He followed his boss past the partygoers, a look of disdain firmly etched into his features. The doormen nodded respectfully to Barcelo and his men as they entered.

Clay's Toyota rolled to a gentle stop on the opposite street corner from the club. As they climbed out of the vehicle, Danny could feel the bass of the music thumping in his chest. He gave a cursory glance to the crowds and nodded at the club logo. "This is on my list. The Hot Pink is one of the businesses they've taken already; it used to belong to a guy from Plymouth."

"So I guess it won't matter if we knock over a drink or two while we're inside."

"No, I don't suppose it will." Danny gave his brother a slight smile. "But we're not exactly dressed for a place like this."

"I'm not sure they'll be looking at us with that amount of bare ass on display. Anyway, my belt is DKNY."

"I just need to grab a couple of things." Danny opened the trunk, retrieved four cardboard tubes, each slightly larger than a permanent marker pen, and slipped them into his pockets. He discarded his black canvas jacket. He knew anyone wearing a jacket would likely be searched by the doormen. The only drugs they would allow to be sold inside were their own. He tapped the Beretta, setting it next to the other weapons. "It might upset the bouncers."

"You want me to follow you in or wait out here?"

"Give me ten minutes inside. That should be long enough to scope the place and see what's going on."

Clay gave Danny the flat-eye. "Great. I'll watch the coats."

The queue of thirty-plus bodies moved quickly into the nightclub. The doormen seemed like they knew their job. They were polite but businesslike, keeping the line orderly but without appearing militant. Danny joined the back of the line next to three girls, one of whom sported a tussle of thick black hair and a leather waistcoat. The embellished back panel of the vest declared Cthulhu lives! Below, a many-tentacled creature stared with a malevolent gaze.

Danny smiled and leaned towards the girl. He had read just about everything the old horror writer had ever penned. "I guess you're a fellow Lovecraft fan then?"

"You read H.P.L.?" she asked with reverence. She gave him the once-over and despite his bruises seemed to like what she saw.

"As often as possible." He extended his hand. "Hi, I'm Danny."

"Gloria." She introduced her friends as well. They smiled and gave him finger waves in the air. They seemed to find this hilarious, bursting into peals of laughter.

"So, you girls just on holiday or do you live here?" Danny could smell the alcohol on their breath. Not drunk but they seemed to be firmly in the happy zone.

"Just on holiday. We all go to the same uni. We just wanted to get away for a little break in the sun before final exams." Gloria's lipstick looked to be a dark shade of purple. Kind of a goth look. Danny smiled to himself; did they even call them goths anymore?

Gloria scrutinised his features without a hint of discomfort. "I have to ask. What happened to your face?"

"Ah, some idiot knocked me off my bike. It looks worse than it is. Has it ruined my good looks?"

"Nah, you've still got it going on," she flirted back.

Danny chatted, paid the cover charge for the three girls as well as himself and was inside six minutes later. The door staff never gave him a second glance.

Danny promised to catch up with Gloria later. Tossing back her mane of dark curls she smiled and gave him a wink. Danny had never attended university, moving from a string of secondary schools straight to the armed forces at age sixteen. Looking at the three students, he thought he might have missed out.

The club was filled to capacity. Someone wearing a neon headband tooted a whistle continuously as he punched the air with his hands. Danny raised an eyebrow; maybe that was what you did these days if you couldn't dance?

He moved around the edge of the wide dance floor, just another face in the crowd. He was sure that he was at least twenty-five years senior to the oldest of the dancers. The club was larger than the Woo Hoo by a wide margin. While not quite on the scale of some of the big-name clubs he'd visited in Ibiza, it was still an impressive sight. On the opposite wall several fifty-inch screens showed live pictures of the clubbers dancing and cavorting below. Danny could not see the video cameras but made a mental note that they were there.

Reaching down in response to the vibration in his pocket, he cupped the cell phone tight to his ear. "I'm in."

Within thirty seconds he spotted Barcelo's entourage moving through the club. As he passed the circular main bar, Barcelo held up two fingers to the Lycra-clad server and pointed to a doorway at the opposite side of the room. The female bartender gave Barcelo an enthusiastic thumbs-up and immediately moved to prepare the drinks.

The Locos seemed to be in no hurry. Barcelo stopped to talk to a gaunt-looking man dressed in a shirt and tie. The man nodded several times and pointed to the rear of the club. The two drivers looked like they were enjoying the spectacle of writhing flesh on the dance floor, mimicking the gyrations of the dancers. Only the guy with his arm in the sling looked unimpressed. He had a face like he'd ingested battery acid. Danny was sure that he was not one of the men he had tangled with at the apartments. Arm in a sling, face like a pit bull. Probably the guy that Clay had rumbled at the Woo Hoo: Ortega.

As he followed, the pounding music continued the assault on his eardrums. Danny liked techno (or whatever they called its latest incarnation these days), with its repeating and hypnotic beat, but when it caused ripples in your skin, it was maybe a touch *too* loud. Four lithe women danced on raised platforms, with only neon-glow tubing and bikini bottoms to cover their modesty, keeping the beat while seemingly impervious to the volume.

The Locos entered a door marked *Private*, guarded by another bouncer dressed in black trousers and a white dress shirt. The bridge of his nose was flat and wide; the guy looked like he'd fought more than a few boxing matches.

Danny bobbed his head to the music as he considered his options. The corner of his mouth twitched into a smile. He cupped the phone tight to his mouth. "Clay, I need a diversion at the front door. Two minutes. The bigger the better."

28

"Sure thing. Your wish is my command."

Inside the car, Clay listened to the music reverberating from the phone. He knew that Danny would leave the connection open. It was an old trick but a useful one. He removed the pistol from his waistband and placed it beneath the car seat. He got out of the vehicle and, with arms loosely crossed, he leaned on the roof of the Toyota and studied the club doormen.

Clay counted off two minutes in his head, then moved towards the club. He leaned slightly to one side and exaggerated his steps. Not the first time he'd played drunk.

The two doormen eyed him with apparent disdain. He'd bypassed the entire queue and was trying to slip his bulk between the advertising podium and the main entrance.

The larger of the two doormen moved to intercept him. He spoke in heavily accented English. "Hey, you can't come in that way. There's a line. Get to the back of it."

Clay slurred his words. "An asshole says *qué*?"

The bouncer shook his head. "*Qué*?"

Clay repeated the joke.

"*Qué?*"

"Exactly."

Laughing, one of the bystanders explained it to the doorman.

"Get lost before I rearrange your face for you," said the doorman. The second bouncer stepped forward in support. Both men looked like they could do the business.

Clay carried on, one eye half closed. "One drink?"

The bouncer pushed a meaty hand against Clay's chest. He looked like he lived on steroids and protein shakes. One of those men whose shoulders meet his ears; no neck to speak of. His dark hair was cropped close to his skull and a vein stood out on his left temple. Only his pencil-thin Errol Flynn moustache and plucked eyebrows sullied his tough-guy image.

Clay allowed himself to be pushed back a step, his arms windmilling. "Whoa, easy, dude. I nearly fell over."

The second bouncer mumbled something unpleasant about his foot and Clay's genitals.

Clay gave them both a lopsided grin. "Say, have you guys heard the old story about the Three Billy Goats Gruff?"

Errol curled his lip, the moustache moving like a caterpillar.

Clay slapped his open palm onto the podium. The sound was akin to a pistol shot. "There was a troll, a mean sonofabitch, that lived under a bridge, see, and whenever anyone tried to cross the bridge, the troll would jump up and threaten to eat them. Well now, there were also three goats who lived nearby. First the youngest goat tried to cross, but the troll scared him off."

Errol shook his head and glanced at the line of customers.

"Then the second goat tried to cross the bridge, but the troll scared him away too. Then the oldest Billy Goat Gruff went to cross the bridge. When the troll appeared he told the monster that he wasn't scared of him and butted the troll right off the bridge and into the river." Clay clapped his hands together and began laughing like it was the funniest story ever.

Errol shook his head. "You crazy American shit. Fuck off and stop wasting my time."

"You don't get it do you? See you're the troll and—" Clay headbutted Errol full in the face. "I'm the goat. Pah, it's no fun when you have to explain it."

The second bouncer hastily flicked a switch on the podium even as Errol fell to the ground. Then he launched himself at Clay.

Inside the club, Danny watched three bouncers respond to the alert call from the front entrance. They moved swiftly, pushing their way through the throng of partygoers. The boxer moved quickly too as he received the alarm call over his comms-unit. Danny knew that his brother would keep them all gainfully occupied for the next few minutes. As soon as the private door was left unguarded, Danny slipped into the room beyond.

The music was muffled by the thickness of the door. Danny took a deep breath. The air was much cooler back here. He could hear yelling from his phone. He smiled as he heard Clay's deep voice followed by the unmistakable sound of impact. "That's one for you." *Slap!* "And one for you." *Crack!*

Danny turned the volume to a lower setting. Clay

sounded like he was having a ball. Danny looked around his new surroundings. He had expected storerooms, maybe an office, but he was surprised to find himself in a corridor lined with six doors, three on either side. He pushed one open and grimaced. It didn't take a genius to deduce this must be where the rich and shameless came for extra services. He'd seen similar setups in a few strip clubs, though it was more unusual in a regular dance club. The décor of each room was identical, dark pink walls with soft vinyl seats spread along two walls. A series of large mirrors took up most of the third wall and ceiling.

The six rooms all proved empty apart from room number four. The door stood slightly open and as he passed by, Danny saw a mop of auburn hair bobbing with a steady tempo in a man's lap. The woman had a tattoo of a coiling serpent that traced the length of her spine. The serpent's tail disappeared beneath a pair of purple hot pants. The guy had his eyes closed, his head tilted towards the ceiling.

Danny moved on down the corridor, and round a corner. Beyond were more doors. He pushed open the first, and looked inside. A table was set with four glasses and two bottles of spirits, one vodka and one whisky.

"Now where have you fuckers got to?" Danny whispered.

A loud slap and a yell of pain pointed him in the right direction. Another doorway lay off to his left. Danny edged up to the door, angling himself to the side of the circular window set in it. Inside he saw stark white tiles and chrome racking. Crates of Cruzcampo, San Miguel, Heineken and Smirnoff were stacked from floor to ceiling.

He ducked under the window and moved to the other

side of the doorway. The new angle revealed that the storeroom was divided by a steel mesh fence that ran from floor to ceiling. It looked to be a secure lock-up that would be more in keeping with a warehouse than a club storeroom. Then he understood; this side of the room contained a very different kind of stock.

A group of seven women huddled in front of Barcelo. One of them had a bright-red mark on her cheek, obviously the recipient of the slap. The other three Locos stood with their backs to the door. A sensation like ice water rapidly spread into the pit of Danny's stomach.

The oldest of the women must have been no more than twenty but most looked closer to fifteen. All of them had the same skinny, long-faced look to them. One of them was speaking in a language Danny didn't understand, but the accent sounded Eastern European to his ears. It made a kind of screwed-up sense to him. Due to radical changes within the Eastern bloc countries, more and more women were lured west by the promise of a better life. It was a harsh reality check when they reached their destination. Instead of the honest job that had been promised, some women ended up in the hands of criminal syndicates.

Cowering behind the woman who'd been slapped was a child. Her baggy T-shirt and jeans couldn't hide the fact she was pre-pubescent. Her dark-rimmed eyes were filled with tears. She was repeating the same silent words over and over: maybe a prayer for help, maybe the woman's name. She gripped the woman's waist with both arms.

If Danny had brought his pistol, the solution would have been four rapid shots. One round to the back of each

Loco's head, then another set of four just to be sure. He had a Buck Bantam knife discreetly tucked into the inside of his waistband but no firearm. There was a very strong chance that at least the two drivers would be armed, probably all four. Not acceptable odds. Gunn was never one to take a knife to a gunfight.

The sound of another harsh slap followed by the collective wail from the women made Danny's lip curl in anger. Forcing himself not to kick the door open and charge in, he retraced his steps to the cubicles. He entered room number two and found what he was looking for within seconds.

29

The plastic cover of the air vent ripped away from the wall with a shower of flaked plaster but little noise. Inhaling the luxurious chilled air as it swept over him, Danny pulled one of the slim tubes from his pocket. The cardboard roll contained a mix of four simple powders. Ground sugar, baking soda, potassium nitrate and coloured dye powder. He'd found the first three in the kitchen of the Woo Hoo. The potassium nitrate was the meat-curing compound more commonly known as saltpetre. Dez the cook had told him he rubbed it into pork loin just as his mother had taught him. The black dye he had purchased along with various other items at the home improvement store.

Mixed together into a paste and allowed to dry, they made a crude but very effective smoke bomb. The fuse was a shoelace soaked in petrol. The mixture he'd prepared had an intense sixty-second burn time. Long enough. He lit the fuse and rolled the tube deep into the open vent. The acrid plumes of smoke were swept into the air-conditioning system.

He moved to the three opposite rooms and repeated the

action. Within seconds streams of black smoke were pumping back through the vents into each adjacent room. Danny hit the fire alarm near the door that led back into the club. The couple from room four came out at a run. The hooker was first out and wasted no time on Danny. The guy followed, bent at the waist, still trying to button up his pants. As he passed he looked at Danny with wide eyes.

"Coitus interruptus?" asked Danny.

"Shit! I want my money back," said the john.

Danny quickly checked that the phone was still connected and gave a brief smile as he heard more howls of pain and loud curses in Spanish. Clay was keeping them entertained out front.

Time to move.

Even as he slipped back into the main nightclub, Danny heard the shouts of alarm go up. The thick smoke gusted into the club and achieved the desired response. Cries of "Fire!" soon rang out. Danny followed the crowds into the street. ·

Outside, the bouncers had stopped trying to corner Clay who had been using the wooden podium as a battering ram. If the music had seemed loud it was nothing against the ear-splitting shrill of the fire alarm. A wide-eyed dancer, nearly naked, crossed her arms across her breasts as she declared, *"El servicio de incendios esta viniendo!"*

And the fire service was indeed on its way.

Danny pushed his way through the milling crowd. He passed the bleeding doormen, now ushering the Hot Pink patrons into the street. When he glanced over to the Toyota, Clay gave him a jovial wave from the front seat.

"Did someone have the toaster set too high?"

Danny spoke into the phone. "Something like that. I'll be over in a minute."

The crowds parted as two fire engines arrived, their sirens at full pitch, adding to the cacophony of noise. No chance of sleep for anyone within a quarter of a mile. The fire crews surged out of the vehicles. Several girls crowded around the firemen while their friends used their phones to take pictures. The firemen didn't seem too upset about the attention either. One of the older men spoke briefly with the bouncers and then entered the club followed by three of his team.

Clay was chewing on a Valor chocolate bar when Danny returned to the Toyota. "The fire teams are speedy around here, I'll give them that," Danny said. "You okay?"

"Yeah," Clay replied. "This is the best candy bar I've ever tasted. Spanish chocolate. Who knew?"

"I meant after your tussle with the goon squad."

Clay just waved the chocolate in the air. "Friggin' amateurs. A real bouncer from back home like Buffalo Joe would eat these guys for breakfast."

"I'll take that as a yes."

Clay swallowed. "What did you see in there?"

"They had a back room full of young girls. I'm guessing skin trade. They were all just kids really. This lot are evil bastards, so whatever happens to them now is just karma."

"They come out yet?" asked Clay. "I haven't seen them."

"Not out this way."

"Well maybe these guys will have something to say about it." Clay pointed to the car now parking next to the fire engine. Two Guardia Civil troopers climbed out and began to move the crowd back from the club. They looked mean and businesslike. Unlike the firemen, the cops received no wolf whistles or offers of marriage.

Five minutes later a firefighter emerged from the doorway holding one of the smoke bombs. The canister was spent. He shook his head and after a brief conversation, walked back inside with the police officers.

"Exit stage right." Danny pointed to Barcelo and his driver. They were hurrying back to the convertible Mercedes. The two other Locos were close behind, heading for the saloon. "Elvis has left the building. You can bet he won't want to be around to answer questions if the cops find those girls."

"Oh, he won't be going anywhere in the next half hour," offered Clay.

"Why not?"

"It seems that someone stuck a knife into his tyres. It's shocking, the blatant disregard some people have for the property of others."

"Cryin' shame."

"I know. Man, I can hardly eat, I'm so upset. I'm thinking about sending him a condolence card; maybe something with puppies on."

"Gee, Clay, you're so thoughtful."

"I know. Sometimes I amaze myself."

One of the police officers emerged from the club, a handkerchief pressed over the lower half of his face. He motioned to one of the men who'd fought with Clay and started speaking. The doorman began waving his hands in apparent denial and the cop stepped forward and grabbed him by the collar. The bouncer looked around the crowd and pointed reluctantly over at the two parked Mercedes.

The second officer appeared and was busy talking into his radio.

"I guess they may have found the girls after all," said Danny.

The policeman stiff-armed the doorman and stalked over to Barcelo. The officer looked like he recognised the boss and wasn't impressed. As he moved, his hand hovered close to his service pistol.

"Well, that cop doesn't look like he's a friend of the Locos," said Danny.

"Nice to know there are still good police on the job."

"There're good men all over, just in shorter supply these days."

The cop had cornered Barcelo and his driver and was now barking questions at them both. The driver tried to object but was forced to raise his hands and sat back against the side of the car in defeat. Barcelo was talking fast and shaking his head, all the while pointing at the ruined tyres. His face increasingly reddened as he realised that the cop was less than concerned about the vehicles.

A police riot van arrived within a few minutes. The Guardia Civil looked like they meant business as they moved the crowd back without much in the way of courtesy. After a few minutes of jostling the dancers away from the club entrance, a pair of cops entered the club once more and re-emerged minutes later with the group of young women that Danny had seen earlier. One cop led the way at the front of the group while the other acted like a sheepdog at the rear, hustling them forward. However, the cops hadn't anticipated that as soon as the girls were outside they would all set off running in different directions. The cop at the rear had the youngest of the girls in his arms and held her tight. The trooper at the front of the line turned on his heel and quickly grabbed one of the other women but the majority were off down the street at a pace that would have made Usain Bolt nod in appreciation.

Danny and Clay shared a smile. The girls were free, at least for a little while.

"Well damn it. It's just getting worse and worse for Spanish Elvis over there."

"Yeah, I can feel the tears startin' to come," laughed Clay. He produced another of the chocolate bars and began eating.

"Hey, I think Elvis *is* about to leave the building." Danny pointed at Barcelo and the three other Locos who were being escorted by the first cop on the scene towards the waiting police van. The look on Barcelo's face was one of unbridled fury.

"That should keep him occupied for the night. The Spanish cops are stubborn bastards and they don't kowtow to the lawyers like they have to in the States. I'm sure he'll be in the lock-up for at least a couple of days while they try to sort out the case with those girls."

Clay looked at the child cradled in the cop's arms. Her dark eyes were wide with fear. His stomach soured at the thought of her intended fate. "It's the same all over the world. Same shit, different country."

"At least she's safe tonight," said Danny, his gaze never leaving Barcelo.

"Ay-men to that, little brother."

"I should have just waited for those fuckers when the smoke started to blow. I could probably have taken all four with my knife. Left them bleeding out on the stockroom floor."

Clay popped another chunk of chocolate into his mouth. "Nah, you played it right, for now. I think you may have blood on your blade before this is done."

"Those fuckers have it coming."

"And ay-men to that too."

30

Only once the police had left did Clay steer his vehicle away from the Hot Pink Club.

Danny used the map app on his cell phone and directed Clay to the desired location a ten-minute drive from town. The perimeter roads around Ultima were almost deserted and they reached their destination without any problems. Clay positioned the car on a corner angle to avoid being spotted from the nearest two sides of the building.

Danny slid out of the vehicle. "The club should be quiet by the time we get back, but just in case, you go first and let me know the coast is clear."

Clay ticked a finger to his forehead in a short salute and drove back the way they had come.

Danny let his eyes rove along the outline of the building ahead. He moved again only after satisfying himself there were no CCTV cameras and no security guard on patrol. A padlock secured the main gates to the yard; he'd have to pick it, a simple procedure that he'd learned many years earlier on the streets of Belfast. He removed the compact shim set from a slit in his belt. A quick inspection of the padlock was followed by a few tentative tugs on the mechanism. There was a bit of play in the lock. He looked first at the pick and tension bar but decided to try a thumb shim. After bending the narrow aluminium strip into a curve he slipped the edge of the blade into the top of the lock. It required a couple of readjustments for the blade to slip between the shackle and the housing. The padlock opened with a distinctive click.

"Open sesame," Danny whispered. He fed the chain free of the gate and after entering, pulled the gate closed behind him. A series of three dull spotlights cast meagre illumination over the entrance to a large utility shed. Ultima Felicidad Desotoro was emblazoned both on the shed and the four dark-blue tankers that were parked neatly in a row.

Danny pounded his hand on the body of the tanker closest to the gate. He moved to the next one. Another blow brought a hollower retort. He repeated the same action on the two remaining vehicles. Satisfied, he returned to the first truck. He tried the driver's door and it swung open with the quiet squeak of a hinge.

Easy money, he thought. Daring to hope, he lowered the sun visor. A wad of papers fastened with a rubber band decorated the visor but no keys dropped into his lap. *Well, that would have been too easy.*

Danny reached again for his shim set. This time he selected a lever that had been ground down from a small optician's screwdriver. After inserting the blade of the tool into the keyhole, he knocked the handle of the screwdriver deep into the cylindrical lock. A sharp twist and the ignition responded.

The rumble of the diesel engine seemed way too loud

for Danny's liking but he knew there were very few people nearby to hear it. He nosed the gates open with the truck and drove back into town.

The parking lot to the side of the Hot Pink Club was quiet with only a half-dozen worse-for-wear stragglers still visible. Danny spotted Clay's Toyota parked up. He rang his brother.

"Keep an eye out while I get this done?" Danny asked.

"Go ahead, Danny boy, I've got your six."

Danny moved to the rear of the tanker and attached the corrugated hose to the wide drainage tap. He dragged the hose to the first Mercedes, rolled down the window and fitted the hose through the gap. Finally, Danny turned the tap on. After a few minutes, he moved quickly to the convertible, dragging the hose with him.

"Better get a step on there." Clay's voice was tinny through the phone.

Like extras from a zombie movie, a few revellers shambled closer to see what was going on.

"That's the second one nearly done. Just another minute or so should do it," said Danny.

"I'd love to see their faces when they come back," Clay chuckled.

"Yeah, it's the gift that keeps on giving."

"That's one gift I wouldn't want to unwrap at Christmas."

Danny chuckled as he finished the task in hand. "Yeah, it smells worse than you do after a night on tequila and tacos."

"Is that any way to speak to your ride home?"

"That's me done. Let's make like good shepherds and get the flock out of here."

"Who said that? Moses?"

"Bo Peep."

"Dumbass." Clay laughed at the terrible joke.

Danny climbed into the cab of the sewage tanker and followed Clay back into the night.

31

The vintage Triumph Bonneville rumbled like a disgruntled bear as the engine idled. The rider of the bike, Jean Vartain, nodded to his two companions then shut off the engine. He swung his leg over the seat and dismounted. After removing his amber-coloured helmet, which matched the petrol tank on the bike, he balanced it carefully on the handlebars. The Triumph was not the fastest thing on the road but it was a pleasure to ride. The custom paint job was a work of art. The rich amber streaks extended from the tank down to blend in perfectly with the leather seat straps. The chrome work glittered as it reflected the storefront lights.

The three men converged at the front door then moved into the grocery store as one unit. The young man behind the counter looked up and paused. He'd been right in the middle of filling a shelf with bottles of brandy. "We're just about to close…" he said uneasily.

Two of the bikers levelled sawn-off shotguns: one a double barrel, the other a pump-action model. Vartain stepped forward, reading the name embroidered on the young man's shirt. "You know who we are… Alonzo?"

"Yes…" Alonzo raised his hands in surrender as he stared at the two shotguns. Vartain knew that the distinctive patch on his jacket left little doubt as to their identity. Most biker gangs wore their colours emblazoned across the back but the Rogue Angels' skeletal motif stretched from the back of the jackets and a bony claw continued over the left shoulder and down over their hearts.

Vartain spoke again. His command was delivered as a harsh bark. "Open the register."

Alonzo nodded and pressed a digit to the screen. The till drawer opened with a brief rattle. One of the Rogues stepped forward, swung his legs over the counter and scooped the notes from the drawer. He fanned the meagre stack between his fingers. "Hundred and forty euros. Any more in the back?"

Alonzo shook his head. "That is all we have."

A new voice cut into the conversation. "Get the hell out of my store. Leave him alone."

Vartain turned and looked at the interloper with scorn. An older man with tufts of grey spiky hair had emerged from the rear of the shop brandishing an aluminium baseball bat. The two gunmen turned as one and raised the shotguns to their shoulders. Vartain smiled and motioned for them to lower their weapons.

Vartain tilted his head to one side then walked towards the man with the bat. "You really want to try that shit, old man?"

The shopkeeper raised his bat higher in defiance. "I know who you are and I'm not afraid of you. There's no way you're taking my money."

"Well, have it your way." Jean Vartain took another step closer.

The old man shot an angry glance at Alonzo and then with a yell, swung the bat. Vartain danced back on the balls of his feet. The aluminium club cut through the air and slammed into a shelf, scattering cans down the aisle. Still moving, Vartain pivoted and slammed his right foot into the shopkeeper's mid-section. The bat clattered to the floor as the older man doubled over. A strangled wheeze escaped his throat as he reached again for the bat.

Vartain kicked the weapon away and in one balletic motion, swept his leg high into the air and let his heel drop onto the base of the old man's skull. The shopkeeper dropped face first to the ground.

"No! Don't!" Alonzo yelled out. "Uncle!"

One of the gunmen stepped close and slammed the butt of his weapon into Alonzo's jaw. He too went to the floor.

Vartain called to him. "Hey, boy. What are you going to say when the cops ask you who did this?" Alonzo said nothing. Vartain walked over and tapped him in the face with the toe of his boot. "Hey, boy. I asked you a question."

"I... I did not see who did it." The words came between sobs.

"No. You say, *no cops.* Nothing happened here," said Vartain.

"No cops. Nothing happened here," sobbed Alonzo.

"Clever boy," said Vartain. "See you next week. And tell the old guy, no heroics next time. If you do call the police, I will burn this place to the ground. You understand?"

Alonzo nodded.

Vartain twirled one finger in the air. "Let's go."

32

Danny had gleaned some sketchy details about the biker gang known as the Rogue Angels from Sally and Phil Winrow during the meeting at their apartment. The Rogues tended to move around every few months but were easily found due to the four Winnebagos that served as their mobile homes. Sally and many of the other Brits had known where the Rogues were parked up. The locals knew too and tended to avoid the vicinity like a plague zone.

From the cab of the tanker, he saw Clay's Toyota indicate and pull in behind a copse of sad-looking trees. Danny drew the tanker up behind and got out. Further up the track were four massive Winnebagos, arranged in a loose semicircle at the end of the road; each sported a custom paint job. There was a modest-sized bar less than fifty yards away.

Valentino's bar was a single-storey affair built from breezeblocks and sported a red metallic roof. Tables and chairs were arranged at the front and side of the main doors, which stood wide open. Only one man was sat at the tables. He was face down and looked like he was asleep. His jacket bore the Rogues' distinctive colours. Music thumped from the building into the night. Nearly two dozen bikes formed a neat line, parked alongside the rear of the bar.

Danny got out of the tanker and walked over to where Clay was hoisting himself out of the Toyota. The big Texan nodded towards the Rogues' camp. "I'll say one thing for them, they've got style. Look at those road-blockers." Clay had often enjoyed extended road trips in his own Winnebago in the States, before it had been destroyed the previous year. "We'll need to be sharp here. I expect these guys will be locked and loaded. Even the cops tend to avoid these buckaroos."

Danny moved to the rear of Clay's car and selected a couple of items from the trunk.

"You sure about this, bro?" Clay said. "This could blow up in our faces. This is throwing a lot of gasoline on the fire."

Danny shared a conspiratorial wink. "Don't worry, this will work in our favour."

"But what if it spills into the streets?" asked Clay, ever the voice of reason.

Danny gave Clay an unwavering look. "It's already in the streets. You know that they tried to burn out the Woo Hoo. The Locos are bad news and so are these fuck-nuts. Maybe it's time we introduced them to each other."

Clay, apparently satisfied, shrugged in acceptance. "Then let's get to it then."

"Watch my back. I'll just be a minute or two." Danny shook the can he was holding.

Clay didn't need to work the slide on his Beretta. He knew there was a round chambered already. "Go."

Moving fast and silent, Danny reached the first Winnebago

in seconds. He was a blur of motion as he added his own contribution to the custom artwork on the exterior of the vehicle. Then, using the saw blade from his Gerber multi-tool, he sliced the air valves free on each tire. A frantic hissing ensued and the vehicle listed to one side. He repeated his actions on the next two Winnebagos, leaving the fourth undamaged. All the while music thumped from inside the bar.

Clay's voice whispered from the phone in Danny's shirt pocket. "Still all clear."

"Good. This is the risky bit."

Danny uncoiled a length of extra-thick paracord from his pocket. Dropping to one knee, he tied one end around the rear bumper of the last Winnebago. Then, moving like a sidewinder snake, he flitted between each of the parked bikes, feeding the cord through the wheels and handlebars. There was a mixture of chopper styles and more conventional road bikes. Each bike looked pristine and well cared for. As he reached the limit of the cord he tied it off in a double reef knot around the handlebars of a Kawasaki Vulcan 850. An ornate version of the Rogues' gang patch was fixed as an ornament between the handlebars of the Kawasaki. Danny wrenched it free from its fixings, then slipped it into a pocket.

"You've got incoming. The guy from the front tables is on his feet and heading your way." Clay's voice was as cold as a winter wind. "You want me to take him out?"

Danny pivoted, crouching low to the ground, and registered the approaching man. "No. I've got him."

The man was clad in dark-grey denims and a thick leather jacket bearing the wrap-around design of the Rogue Angels. His head was almost bald but he sported a thick goatee beard and carried a bottle of Havana Club in his left hand. The bottle was nearly empty. The Rogue stopped up short as Danny stepped directly into his path. "*Qui êtes-vous?*"

Danny gave a shark-like smile. He replied in Spanish. "Never mind who the fuck I am. This is a message from the Locos."

The biker took a step forward, raised the bottle of rum and swung it like a club. Danny, instead of backing off, sprang into the air and slammed his forehead into the Rogue's face. As the man crumpled to the ground, Danny followed him down, legs astride his waist, and planted another headbutt into his nose. The Rogue was left spreadeagled, a trickle of blood tracing its way down the side of his face.

Clay's voice sprang from the phone. "Shit. White men *can* jump."

Danny left the unconscious man where he lay and clambered into the last Winnebago. The keys were in the ignition. "These guys are making this too easy. Clay, drive back the way we came. Wait a half mile down the road and watch for me in your rear view."

The engine roared as Danny pressed the gas pedal to the floor. He repeated this several times more, each time longer and louder than the first. He watched as the Rogues began to emerge from the bar. He heard the collective howl as he slipped the RV into gear and began to speed away. The sound of the bikes tipping and crashing into each other brought screams of outrage. Danny kept it floored and the bikes were dragged along the hard surface of the road. Sparks flashed in the darkness and several unidentified pieces of motorcycle snapped off and spun away along the road. In his rear view,

Danny saw one of the bikers waving a revolver at the rear of the stolen vehicle, then running to one of the remaining RVs. It took the bikers only moments to realise that the other vehicles had been disabled. A loud scream of anger told him that they had seen his artistic handiwork: each Winnebago was now decorated with a large L.

The paracord finally snapped and the bikes were left scattered for a hundred yards down the road.

33

Barcelo stood on the street in front of the police station, regarding the passing vehicles with barely concealed agitation. The municipal police building sat on the south-eastern outskirts of Ultima, well away from the main tourist strip, and his ride home was taking a lot longer than anticipated. He started towards the approaching car driven by Babi Garcia before it even reached the kerb and pulled at the door handle twice before he heard the locks disengage from inside.

"Where's your driver?" asked Garcia.

Barcelo hooked a thumb in the direction of the station. "The assholes are keeping them in a while longer."

"Who's in there?"

"Ortega and two of the boys."

"Why did they let you out?" asked Garcia as Barcelo settled his bulk into the seat.

"They kept trying to tie me to the girls and the club. Ha, good luck with that," said Barcelo.

"The club's in one of your guy's names?"

"Of course. There's nothing on paper to link me. I kept telling them that I was just out for a drink with a couple of friends."

"And they believed you?" asked Garcia.

"Not for a minute, but they had nothing they could use as proof to hold me so I sat and drank something they told me was coffee and protested my innocence."

"So why are they holding Ortega and the others?"

"A couple of the cops were getting heavy-handed so the boys showed their displeasure." Barcelo gave a lopsided grin. "It'll come to nothing. The cops will have to release them soon enough."

The cop who had arrested him appeared on the steps in front of the station and Barcelo gave him a friendly wave as the car moved into the morning traffic. The sun was cresting a new day, shining its brilliance across the picturesque beachfront that was officially termed Ultima Felicidad Abad, but known to locals and visitors alike simply as the Bay. Garcia slipped on a pair of shades as he drove.

Barcelo recounted the night's troubles to Babi Garcia who listened with genuine interest. "Was it the British guy from the Woo Hoo?" asked Garcia. "I definitely want another shot at that one."

The boss shook his head in the negative. "I don't think so. Some weird shit going on at the club though. Smoke billowing everywhere. Whoever was behind it cost me a lot of money last night. I lost a whole shipment of girls."

"Expensive?"

"Some were underage—they would have brought a high price. Two had already been paid for. I'll have to return the money."

"So what next?"

Barcelo worked his jaw as if chewing a strip of leather. "Take me back to my car at the Hot Pink. I'll get one of the guys to fix my tyres and then we'll drive back to the villa. I'll get the men together and figure this shit out. Somebody will pay with their blood, I promise you that."

"You want to call your guy now so he can meet us there?" said Garcia.

Barcelo nodded and used his cell phone to make the brief call.

Garcia looked at his boss. "I've got a score to settle with that Brit but once I've finished with him I'm free to pick up any other jobs you have in mind."

Barcelo nodded in agreement. He had yet to see the troublesome Brit or the American from the Woo Hoo in person. It seemed to him that these idiots sprang up like fleas on a dog if you let them spread. Time to get rid of them once and for all.

Garcia steered into the parking lot of the Hot Pink Club. Barcelo heaved his bulk out of the car and walked towards his beloved Mercedes, fishing the keys from his pocket. The smell made him stop short.

"What the hell!"

Garcia appeared at Barcelo's side as he stared into the interior of the vehicle. Someone had filled the Mercedes with sewage. Only the head rests of the seats were visible.

Barcelo kicked out, his boot slamming into the car door.

Holding his nose, Garcia spoke through a wide grin. "I guess you may require a lift home then?"

"You think that's funny?" Barcelo demanded.

Stepping away from the ruined vehicle, Garcia waved

his hand in front of his face. "You're the closest thing I have to a friend, but that doesn't stop me finding humour in the misfortune of others."

"Babi..." Barcelo growled. He lifted his chin as he registered Garcia's hand moving smoothly to his belt, towards his pistol. Both men stood motionless for long seconds, neither willing to break the deadlock. Finally, he spat out, "Are you going to help or stand around and laugh at me?"

"Like I said earlier, just let me know what you want from me."

"I want you to find whoever did this and either bury them or better still bring them to me and I'll kill them myself."

Garcia pointed to the Mercedes convertible, which was full of the same brown odious sludge. "I think they've left a calling card." He plucked a metallic object from the windscreen of the second car and handed it to Barcelo, who examined it. The screaming skull flanked by black crow's wings had been featured on the news over previous weeks linked to various violent incidents. "I know who these fuckers are. Rogue Angels. French pieces of shit bikers."

"You know where to find them?" growled Barcelo.

Garcia nodded and pointed north. "They hang out ten, fifteen miles out. They've got big camper vans, and bikes. Quite a few of them."

"How many men do you need?"

"I'd rather scope them out on my own."

"Why? You need a backup man."

"Like the last one? The boy who got himself killed?"

"Yeah." Barcelo fumed again. "That guy needs to be

opened slowly with a rusty blade but we'll get back to him soon. He's just one man."

"Two men. There's the big American at the Woo Hoo as well."

"Yeah. Two." Barcelo scowled at the ruined vehicles. "But these Rogue Angels are a bigger threat. We need to take them down first."

"That could work too," Garcia agreed. "Breaking big bad biker boys sounds like a lot of fun. Then I can turn my sights back on the Brit. I've got something special in mind for him."

"I still want you to take someone with you."

"If you insist," grumbled Garcia. "But this will cost you extra."

"You were hired to get rid of the Brit." Barcelo's temper flared to a new height. "Not only did you fail in that task, but you dumped a dead body on my kitchen table."

The tone of Garcia's voice changed subtly. "The boy was reckless and the Brit caught him good. This is what happens when you send a boy to do a man's job."

Again the two men locked gazes, then Barcelo gave a nod of begrudging agreement. This was why he liked having Garcia around on occasion. He wasn't like the rest of the yes-men. He wasn't afraid to speak his mind. But he was proving to be a real pain in the backside when he was right. "Okay. Now, drive me home."

34

Sitting in the rear office of the Woo Hoo, Larry and Pamela Duke looked bemused as Clay related the previous evening's events. Jacks padded happily between them, clearly enjoying having his ears and the top of his head scratched by everyone he passed.

"So let me get this right, you smoke-bombed his club, he lost a truckload of girls, he was carted off by the cops—" Larry counted off on his fingers.

Pamela finished his statement. "And you filled his cars full of shit!"

Larry began to laugh. "And you managed to piss off a whole gang of bikers as well."

"With a bit of luck the Rogues and the Locos will soon be knocking the living crap out of each other. That'll keep them occupied at the very least," said Danny as he sipped on a chilled Cruzcampo beer.

"How do you know the bikers won't just up sticks and leave?" asked Pamela.

"Nah, Danny trashed those rides real good," Clay said.

"They'll be frothing at the mouth to get back at someone. Those boys looked as mad as mad can be. We left their Winnebago a couple of miles down the road. It may need a valet and a respray before they're happy with it again."

"But how will they figure it was the Locos?" asked Pamela, frowning.

"Because Danny boy here monogrammed his works of art on the sides of the Winnebagos. Then we scooted back to the club and Danny left a Rogues crest on Barcelo's car."

Pamela held her face in both hands. "You know, Danny, for someone who looks as nice as you, you're a real Tasmanian devil in disguise."

"Why would you say that?" deadpanned Clay. "He looks nice? In which alternate universe? He's got a face like the asshole end of a haggis."

"Shut it, Yankee boy, or I'll teach you the Texas Two Step like it should be done." Danny mimicked his version of the Ali shuffle and snapped two lightning-fast jabs to within an inch of Clay's nose.

Clay jerked his head back. "Ya little shit. Speed isn't everything you know."

Danny continued with a fair impression of his boxing hero. "Ain't nobody faster than the master of disaster. Clay's gonna come out smokin', and I ain't gonna be jokin'. His eyes are gonna be meetin' when I'm finished givin' my beatin'."

Clay stood up and flexed his muscles. "You better sit down or I'll kick you so hard your lungs will pop out your ass."

"Who said that? Socrates?" Danny held his guard.

"Chuck Norris."

"Ah, profound…"

The levity was interrupted by the warbling ringtone of Larry's phone. He glanced at the caller display before answering. As he listened he shook his head, rubbing his hand across his face in obvious distress. The conversation was brief and Larry ended by promising to see the caller soon.

"Those dirty bastard bikers you've just been on about ransacked old man Torres's shop last night." Larry shook his head again. "They kicked the living daylights out of the old guy. Frightened young Alonzo half to death as well. They're both in hospital; Alonzo isn't so bad but Torres is in a bad way."

Pamela looked shocked. "Old Papa Torres has got cancer. He's struggling just to keep his grocery store open. What the hell sort of people are these?"

Danny spoke slow and quiet. "The kind that's going to get what's coming to them. Big time."

"Ay-men to that," added Clay. "Like Danny said, with a bit of luck the bikers and the Locos will knock the living crap out of each other for us. But we'll make sure and finish the job."

Clay looked at Danny. His eyes had changed somehow. A subtle change, but it was there. The look was one of promised violence; Clay had seen it many times before.

Danny leaned towards Clay. "I'm going to grab a few hours of shut-eye. I want to be fresh for tonight."

"Go for it, bro. I'll hold the fort down here, then we can swap over." Clay rubbed his stomach as he gave Pamela a beseeching look. "Any chance of a bite to eat before I lay my head on the saddlebags? I'm kinda hungry."

"You're always hungry. The Texas economy is probably on the slide since you've been over here." Pamela punched his arm playfully.

Clay shrugged sheepishly. "I can go elsewhere. I don't want to be a burden."

Larry leaned forward and adjusted his prosthetic leg. "While you and Danny are under our roof you have free run of the place. Eat and drink as much as you want. Don't give it a second thought. Dez will rustle up anything you want."

"Coolo mondo." Clay stood to his full height and stretched. "I'll go and have a word with him then."

As Clay sauntered off in search of sustenance he was followed by Jacks, his tail wagging. Pamela watched them leave.

Danny broke her moment of reflection. "I know what you're thinking. Aren't dinosaurs supposed to be extinct."

Pamela shook her head. "For a guy so big he moves like a tiger. Kind of smooth and casual. I've seen professional wrestlers close up and Clay looks as big and dangerous as any of them. Only you could get away with calling him a dinosaur."

"He's a pain-in-the-saur-ass."

Pamela laughed. "You remind me of my own brothers back in England. Rough and ready, but good people."

"How do you know the old guy who got beat up?" asked Danny.

"Papa Torres?" Pamela asked. "We've known him for years, since we first started coming over here on holiday. Most of the Spanish locals are great, easy to get along with as long as you learn a bit of Spanish out of courtesy. Some of the older locals don't speak much English, but at the end of the day we're in their country. Papa really helped us find our feet when we first bought the club. He showed us the best places to buy our supplies, all the little but important things. He introduced us to Dez, who turned out to be the best cook in the whole town. Papa's a tough guy, but the cancer has hit him hard. He should know better than to fight."

Larry sat forward quickly. "What is he supposed to do? Just let them come in and make a fool out of him? Fuck that. I would have done the same."

Pamela's cheeks flushed red. "And get yourself smashed up or killed in the process. What good would that do? What then?"

"I was just saying."

Danny interjected to calm the rising tension. "So what's happened to the old guy?"

Larry gave out a long sigh. "Like I said, he's been taken to hospital. They're keeping him in for a while. Young Alonzo took a smack in the face as well. One of the bikers clocked him as they were leaving. Bastards." Larry gave out a long sigh. "I better go and let Dez know. They're old friends too. Friggin' biker arseholes dishing out the pain to an old man."

"Don't worry," Danny reassured. "We'll pay it back tenfold."

35

Barcelo stood in front of his desk and commanded the gaze of every man before him. They numbered just short of forty. Ortega and the two drivers had arrived back at the villa minutes earlier and sat at the front of the gathering. Many in the room sported cuts, bruises and other injuries. The more senior members sat while the younger soldiers stood behind them.

When Barcelo finally spoke his voice was uncharacteristically quiet. This sent a ripple of unease through the ranks. His men were used to his outbursts and knew to keep their heads down, but this was different. A chill seemed to emanate across the room.

"Who are we?"

The men in the room exchanged glances.

"Who are we?" he asked again.

"We are the Locos, boss," replied one of the soldiers.

"The Locos? The Locos?"

"Yes, boss. The Locos."

"And why do people call us that?"

"Because they think we're crazy."

Barcelo nodded his head slowly. "Do people fear us? Do they respect us?"

"Yes, boss. Fear and respect."

Barcelo pointed at the soldier who had answered him. "Step forward." The soldier clenched his jaw but did as requested. "And what do you think of me?"

"I fear and respect you," the man said, without hesitation.

Barcelo closed his eyes. He gave the man a slow nod and motioned for him to step back. "But what do others think of us? If we are feared and respected would foreign pieces of shit have the balls to tear you up? Would we have French motherfuckers riding into our town and robbing businesses on our doorstep? Taking money from our pockets and food from our mouths? Ruining my cars, my property?"

Ortega hissed his question through wired teeth. "So what's the plan? We hit the Rogues tonight?"

"No. We hit them *now*!" Barcelo opened his eyes. "I want every able man in this room armed and ready to roll in the next half hour. Bring everything you've got. Back here in half an hour!"

The Locos left the villa in a nervous rush. A few did not own guns but knew there would be enough to go around. Despite Barcelo's general dislike of everyday firearm use he knew some of the soldiers had amassed their own personal armouries over the years.

When the soldiers had dispersed, only Barcelo, Ortega and Garcia remained. Barcelo addressed his captain first. "Ortega, you up to this?"

Ortega drew a pistol from his hip and rested it on top of his cast. "I can still shoot just fine with my left."

"And you?"

Garcia sniffed at the question. "You keep paying me and I'll skin every last biker."

"Good."

"I'll be back in a little while. I want to pick up some toys before we go play," said Garcia.

Barcelo waved him away. "Go get your bag of tricks."

As soon as Garcia left the room Ortega spoke. "I don't trust Garcia as far as I can spit. That man would stick a knife in your back just as quick as the one you sent him to kill. And he would wear a smile while he did it."

"I know what he is, but he stays on the payroll for now. At times like this it's handy to have a psychopath to hand."

"Well, you're right on both counts. He's as odd as a two-legged goat and makes Norman Bates look normal." Ortega tapped his fingers to the side of his head.

Barcelo growled. "Loco, you might say?"

36

Vartain palmed a full magazine into his pistol, taking comfort from the metallic ratcheting sound. The bastards that wrecked his bikes would pay dearly. Those gangster wannabes, the Locos, were in for a shock. They were used to dealing with drunken tourists and timid shopkeepers. How would they fare when faced with road warriors ready for battle?

He shouted across the bar so all of his men would hear him. "Tool up. I want to know where these shit-heels hang out and I want them buried."

This brought a roar of agreement from the Rogues. One of the gang, his nose thick and swollen, stood next to Vartain. The tall guy now sported two black eyes and looked like an angry panda, but the shotgun he waved was a pump-action and no joke. "I want the little bastard who clocked me."

Another roar of agreement.

"And ruined half our rides." The roar that went up at the mention of the damaged bikes was like that of a barbarian horde.

Vartain had no particular dislike for the Spanish, disliking most races equally, although the English and Russians were below shit on the ground in his book. Both thought they were superior to everyone else. But these Locos had it coming, and from what he had heard about them, they were a ragtag bunch: blacks, whites and mulattos all in the same outfit. Vartain didn't care much for the blacks either. Paris was overrun with them.

"You," said Vartain, pointing at the two closest bikers. "Go into town, knock the heads of a few shopkeepers and get them to tell you where these Loco dick-pullers hang out. Call me as soon as you have anything. The rest of us will meet you there. We'll hit them back before they expect it."

The two scouts armed themselves and the taller of the two grinned maliciously as he cut the air with a machete. "Won't take long. Be ready."

Vartain holstered the revolver and looked back at the rest of his men. They looked ready. The scouts had just left but Vartain glanced down at his phone as if willing it to ring. With a deep inhalation he forced himself to relax; he rolled his shoulders, tensed and relaxed his hands. He had felt like this many times; it was the burning anticipation of the fight to come and part of him relished the feeling. As a younger man in Marseilles he had studied the French kick-boxing style of savate. It was a rough sport that employed many devastating kicks and punches. Vartain had never become a champion but had won a lot more bouts than he had lost. Savate had been developed by the roughest sailors and stevedores in Europe and it could be deadly when used in its raw combat form. He looked forward to putting his savate, his boot, into the Locos.

"How many vehicles have we still got on the road?" he asked.

"Nine," said one of the older bikers, fat and grey and mean-looking. "The three big vans, one pick-up truck and five bikes. We had to change tyres on the camper vans but it's done now."

Vartain scowled again. How many thousands' worth of damage had been caused? Most of the bikes were custom works of art like the RVs. Ruined at the hands of some dip-shit outfit in a holiday resort. His hands again strayed to the two guns at his waist, the Ruger LCR revolver and his Ruger LC9, old friends that never let him down. He liked the LC9 pistol as it was designed as a concealed carry weapon and sat comfortably in the small of his back. The stubby revolver was perfect for putting down a target for good. A couple of .357 rounds tended to do the job nicely.

"Get them all ready to roll. I want two men per bike, one rider and one shooter. The rest in the pick-up and RVs. When we find out where they are, we hit them hard and we make sure they know why."

The Rogues busied themselves feeding shells into shotguns, drinking liquor and sharing promises of violence. An hour slipped by, then another. One man sat in a corner, sharpening a serrated combat knife. The blade was as long as his forearm.

Vartain's cell phone warbled. "About time." He answered with a perfunctory, "What?"

A slow approximation of a smile crept across his face like an evening shadow. He clicked his fingers twice to get the attention of his men, then moved a raised finger in a tight circle. "Let's go!"

The Rogues moved as one towards the exit. Weapons were

held at the ready even before they knew their destination. One of the bikers kicked a table over on his way past, sending empty bottles and glasses crashing to the floor. The bar staff just kept their heads down, avoiding eye contact and saying nothing, as they had for the previous week.

Engines roared to life as the bikers clambered on to their vehicles. Vartain's Triumph Bonneville had survived with only cosmetic damage. The mirrors had been mangled but the handlebars, wheels and engine were still intact. He powered his bike to the front of the makeshift convoy and waved the rest of his men forward.

37

Danny opened his eyes to see his big brother standing over him.

"All quiet?" asked Danny.

"As the Western Front," replied Clay. "Just came to wake you up."

Danny swung his legs to the floor, stood and stretched. Then he bent at the waist and while keeping his legs locked straight, placed his palms flat on the floor. After holding the stretch for a few seconds he slowly returned to standing.

Danny gave Clay a smile. "Not the nicest wake-up call I've ever had." Clay opened his mouth—no doubt to launch into a well-rehearsed tirade of mock insults—when Julie appeared at the door.

"Hey, you're up," she said.

Clay tipped a non-existent hat. "Hi. Clay Gunn."

"Julie Keen. I work downstairs."

"Pleased to meet you, Julie," said Clay. "I'm trying to peg your accent. Manchester?"

"Close. Huddersfield. Not a million miles away." She

smiled briefly at Clay who towered over her. "I… just wanted to catch up with Danny for a few minutes."

"Hey, I know where I'm not wanted. I'll leave you to it."

Julie flushed a little and stepped aside to let the big man leave. She didn't speak until she heard Clay's footsteps halfway down the stairs. "I worried about you all last night."

"It was pretty busy," Danny replied, adding a little velvet into his voice. "But I'm fine."

"Good. You know…" She paused, then seemed to find her courage. "I've got a couple of days off work next week." She closed the bedroom door behind her. "I thought if you were free…"

Danny pulled her close, his lips finding hers. She smelled of coffee and lemons. She didn't get to finish her thought.

Downstairs, Clay passed an easy half hour with Larry. The old soldier recounted happier times spent with his regiment, telling the exploits of his squaddies without once making the story about himself. Clay too had many stories from his time in the Rangers but was happier listening to his old friend.

Larry was halfway through a tale involving a Komodo dragon, an improvised fishing rod and a can of Spam when Danny joined them. Clay first checked that Julie wasn't nearby then leaned towards his brother. "You're looking pleased with yourself."

Danny raised his eyebrows. "Oh, you know, just making new friends and influencing people."

"Huh?" Larry looked bewildered for a moment.

Clay blew him a kiss. "Julie, darling."

"Ah. Nice one." Larry gave his nod of approval. "Be careful. She's a lovely girl but falls for all the wrong fellas."

Clay chuckled. "Well that's a match dot com right there. They don't get much more wrong than Danny boy."

"Shut it." Danny raised a fist playfully.

"Sigmund Freud could have founded a whole new school of thought if he'd looked into Danny's brain pan. It's part Bruce Lee, part Machiavelli, part Daffy Duck."

"You're too kind."

Danny leaned in and tapped Larry on the shoulder. "You know they classified Clay's brain as solitary confinement."

Larry took the bait. "Why?"

"It's comprised of a single cell."

Clay's response was as flat as a ruined tyre. "Oh, please call a doctor. I think my sides are going to split."

Larry's phone rang. "Hello?"

As he listened his expression changed to one of concern. "How long ago? Okay, thanks."

"What?" asked Clay.

"The bikers are on the move. They all just stormed out of the bar they've been hanging around. Armed to the teeth by all accounts."

"Who called you?" asked Danny.

"The barmaid at Valentino's. She's good friends with Pamela. Married to a Spanish guy who works there as well. Do you think they took the bait?"

"If they're coming out in force, yes. They're either gunning for the Locos or for us. I'm betting on the Locos. They've no way of knowing about me or Clay." Danny sat back and pursed his lips. "If the Rogues know where

Barcelo's villa is, there's a good chance that's where they'll be heading. What do you think, big bro, shall we saddle up and join the party?"

"I like parties," Clay nodded. "Do you think there'll be chips and dip?"

"You never know. Come on then, let's lock and load. See if we can't mix it up a wee bit."

"I wish I was coming with you guys. I'd love a chance to put the hurt on a couple of those bastards," said Larry.

Clay squeezed his friend's shoulder. "Don't worry, *compadre*, we'll bring you back a couple of scalps. You've got us on speed dial if anyone should show up here, right?"

Larry tapped his phone. "Yeah, I got your number."

"Come on, time to rock and roll." Danny nodded his respect to the old soldier then again at Clay. "After you. Rangers lead the way, right?"

38

Vartain pulled over to the side of the road as they reached the turn-off to Barcelo's villa. He waited until the other vehicles had parked alongside him before he spoke. "Normally we would scope out the joint fully before we hit it, but I want this finished as soon as possible."

One of the two scouts who had been tasked with locating the Locos' headquarters pointed down the road. "There's a high wall around the house and a main gate. We need to get through that before we can hit them."

Vartain nodded to the oversized RVs. "If we need to I'll smash right through with one of those."

The scout looked at the Winnebago as if it was a ridiculous idea but this only drew a scathing look from Vartain. "Let me do the thinking. You just be ready to put these mongrels down."

The scout began to reply, "I was born r—" but Vartain had already turned away. The revving of the Triumph's engine drowned out any further conversation. Keeping his bike close to the right border of the road Vartain waved over his shoulder. The convoy split to allow the biggest of the RVs to lead the way. The line of vehicles quickly crept forward like a swarm of angry cockroaches.

After less than a quarter mile the driver of the leading vehicle slammed on his brakes and one of the bikes rear-ended the Winnebago, toppling both rider and pillion to the ground.

Vartain sped forward to see what the hold-up was.

Another procession of vehicles was speeding up the narrow road straight towards them—the Locos!

Vartain snatched the pistol from his belt. "They're coming. Lay them out!"

The Locos' convoy consisted of several low-slung pick-up trucks and six large SUVs. As Vartain shouted his command, three men with automatic rifles lurched into view from behind the cab of the leading truck. Ribbons of fire sprang from the stubby black rifles. Vartain wrenched his bike sideways, the rear tyre skidding momentarily as it lost purchase and his pistol bucked in his hand as he returned fire. The shots went wild as he fought to control the bike and shoot simultaneously. Realising the folly of his actions, Vartain gripped the handlebars and slewed his bike away from the kill zone. He could hear the bullets tear through the outer skin of the big RVs.

The Locos quickly moved their vehicles into a tight V formation, effectively sealing the road. Men in urban camouflage sprang from the vehicles and surged forward, ducking low as they came, using the vehicles as cover. Then the world seemed to explode as both sides opened fire.

The windscreen of the leading RV was shattered as a Loco sprang into view and worked the pump on his shotgun. The driver of the RV gunned the engine and raced forward, crushing the man against the stationary pick-up truck. The shotgun bucked once more before the Loco's ribcage and spine were crushed. The twelve-gauge obliterated the face of the Winnebago driver in a crimson explosion. The three men in the back of the pick-up were sent tumbling; two of the three Locos landed in a sprawl on the road whilst the third slammed face first into the roof of the cab then went down on his back in the truck, his weapon sending countless rounds into the sky as he clamped down on the trigger.

Vartain watched the first of his men die and exploded with rage. With a roar he emptied his pistol into one of the Locos who had fallen from the truck. The man slumped face down, three bullet holes decorating his back. As another Loco sprang from cover and started to shoot, Vartain threw himself clear from his bike but a bullet had already found the calf of his right leg. Twisting even as he landed, he drew his revolver and sighted on the Loco. The Ruger spat once and the gangster pin wheeled to the ground as the .357 slug punched through his chest.

Vartain used his fallen bike as cover as he looked for his men. Many had also taken cover, using the vehicles as shields while they exchanged sporadic fire with the Locos. Most of the shots were hitting nothing but air. Someone was screaming from behind the Locos' vehicular barricade. Vartain grinned in satisfaction as a man lurched into view. It was the screamer. The man clutched the bloody remains of his left hand to his chest, only his thumb and forefinger intact.

One of the Rogues dived down next to his leader. The man raised his shotgun over the bulk of the bike and with a boom knocked the screamer off his feet. No more screaming.

Vartain smiled despite the returning fire sending sparks into the air as it impacted the engine block of his bike.

The impacts lessened as the Locos chose new targets. Vartain scooted to one side and risked poking his head from cover. Two of the mounted bikers had looped back around from the rear of the convoy and broken through the Locos line of defence. The bikers were now acting like cavalry. They kept on the move, attacking the Spaniards as they tore back and forward between the blockades.

The Locos were now forced to fight on two fronts. For a few desperate moments some of them stopped shooting, frozen in indecision, until a bear of a man strode forward. He ignored the bullets zipping past his head and roared a command: "Fight, you bastards!"

39

Barcelo stared aghast as one of his men went down in a spray of red mist. His men were beginning to falter; the constant exchange of fire began to abate. He knew if they did not hit back hard and fast all would be lost. He lurched from his vantage point and strode forward. He put a single bullet into the body of the closest of the Rogues. The biker folded at the waist and pitched to the ground. He turned to his men. "Fight, you bastards!"

The crack of pistols, boom of shotguns and sporadic rattling of rifle fire again tore the air between the two groups. As Barcelo stalked forward, picking his targets accurately, Ortega covered his back.

A biker dropped to one knee less than twenty feet away and Ortega snapped off a shot. The bullet caught the Rogue Angel high on his left side, then Barcelo put a bullet of his own into the biker's throat. The Rogue dropped his weapon and clutched at his neck. Streams of crimson pumped between his fingers. Ortega shot him again and the biker stayed down.

Both men moved as one, efficient and deadly. Another Loco appeared at their side, then another. Within a minute they had created an effective skirmish line and began pressing the Rogues back. Then the ammunition began to run out.

As each man's weapon ran dry they scooted back, seeking cover. The same began to happen with the Rogues. Shots became more infrequent but also more carefully chosen. More men fell in the final minute than in the first.

Barcelo, still furious and defiant, strode forward. Posing like Christ the Redeemer, his empty pistol dangling from one finger, he shouted, "Now what? Is that it?"

Men on both sides rummaged through pockets, hoping for a spare clip.

A wolfish-looking man emerged from behind his bike. He looked at both gangs before remarking in broken Spanish, "Well this is awkward."

"So now what?" Barcelo handed his spent pistol to Ortega. "Sticks and knives?"

"If that's what it takes," replied the biker, his voice returning the disdain delivered by Barcelo. "Are you the leader?"

"I am."

"Your name?"

"Barcelo. Yours?"

"Vartain."

Several men on both sides drew knives from their belts. More than one machete was waved in threat.

Barcelo took a step closer to his adversary. He looked the biker up and down and curled his lip, unimpressed. "You man enough for the old way? One-on-one, hand-to-hand?"

Vartain rolled his neck, then stretched his chest by swinging his elbows back sharply. He grinned, confident. "Just you and me, old man? Sure. Winner takes all."

"Winner takes all. I win, your boys fuck off back to wherever you came from."

Vartain allowed himself another smile. "And when I win?"

Barcelo opened his hand towards his villa.

"That'll do nicely."

Barcelo shrugged off his tailored jacket, which was now ruined, streaked with blood and dirt. Turning to his men, he shouted, "One-on-one. Nobody interferes."

Clenching and unclenching his fists, he moved his bulk into a boxer's crouch and motioned Vartain forward. Circling as he studied his opponent, Barcelo knew you didn't ascend to the head of a biker gang without being able to walk the walk. He forced himself to breathe slowly. His fingers felt numb as fresh adrenalin surged. Barcelo held the advantage of size and muscle but the biker looked mean and wiry, certainly dangerous.

Both men inched closer.

Barcelo cut the air with a big right hand.

Dodging to one side Vartain launched himself forward and planted a heel kick that buckled Barcelo's knee. His hands moved like pistons as he followed his kick with a blistering series of straight punches.

Caught off guard by the speed of the biker's attack, Barcelo nearly went down under the flurry of fists. He felt the cartilage in his nose snap. He clubbed the biker with his forearm as he struggled to stay on his feet. *Shit, the French fucker is fast.*

Barcelo reeled back as the biker continued his assault, driving forward with each punch; his vision started to blur as he tried to land a solid punch of his own. An iron grip suddenly latched on to his throat, fingers digging deep behind his trachea as his legs were knocked from beneath him with a savage roundhouse kick. Vartain followed the Spaniard to the ground and continued to smash at his face mercilessly with his right hand. A cheer came from the Rogues.

In an instant, Barcelo reached up with both hands and wrenched Vartain's head a full one hundred and eighty degrees. The cheering stopped abruptly. The terrible sound of snapping vertebra was unmistakeable.

Slowly, blood streaming from his nose and a gash over his left eye, Barcelo regained his feet. "*Vete ala chingada!*"

One of the Rogues stepped forward, hands outstretched, his eyes on his fallen leader. "It's over. We leave."

Barcelo spat a mouthful of bloody saliva to the ground and gestured at the body. "Take your shit with you."

Less than four hundred yards from the combat zone Danny and Clay watched the fight unfold with muted interest. The gunfire had already begun when they arrived so they had moved quickly to one of the few higher vantage points and watched as the carnage played itself out.

They stayed low and out of sight as the vanquished Rogue Angels passed by, their RVs pockmarked with bullet holes in addition to Danny's graffiti.

Clay gave his brother the thumbs up. "Well, that worked just the way you thought it would. Next?"

Danny glanced at his watch. "We'll give it an hour or so. They'll be on the beer by then."

"Then we can wind them back up."

"Come on. I need you to drive me back for the sewage truck."

"Huh?"

"Time to give the Locos some more shit to deal with."

40

Danny hot-wired the sewage truck as easily as the first time. He was mildly surprised that it hadn't been found and claimed by its owners. This was probably because he'd parked it out of sight; he'd left the vehicle at the rear of what looked like a boatshed on the outskirts of town. The engine protested briefly as he inserted the shim into the ignition and twisted. A lot of newer models could be ruined by such a crude hot-wire hack but the truck was old enough that it lacked sophisticated electronics. The engine rumbled into life.

Danny kept Clay in view as they retraced their journey back to Barcelo's villa. As arranged, once they reached the turn-off Clay sped ahead to make sure that the road was clear.

"I'm in place. No lookouts to be seen," said Clay, his voice tinny through the phone.

"Cool, just keep me informed if anything changes. I'm only one minute behind you," replied Danny.

"You sure this'll work?"

"As long as I get up enough speed, yeah. It should."

"Okay, I'll be ready and waiting."

"You got the spikes out?" asked Danny.

"Doin' it as we speak."

"Thirty seconds out…"

"I can hear you coming. That engine is wailing some!"

The truck tore past Clay as it sped up the hill overlooking the villa.

Danny had noted the position during their surveillance. Timing was of the essence. Five. Four. Three. Two. *Jump!*

Danny leapt from the truck a second before it reached the edge of the overlook. Tucking his head and shoulders he rolled in a fluid motion and was back on his feet as he heard the first crash. The truck soared through the air for a few seconds then began tumbling as the wheels struck the sharp incline. The sound of twisting metal combined with the roaring engine sounded unearthly. The tanker skidded to one side and began to spin sideways down the last quarter of the hillside. The distance between the incline and the rear sundeck of the villa was less than ten feet. The truck crashed across the tiled patio area, wrecking the ornate furniture and large barbecue range as it continued its chaotic descent. A large double swing seat with a striped sunshade was sent spiralling into the swimming pool. One of the freestanding gas bottles attached to the grill was catapulted high into the air and disappeared over the edge of the wooden stairs that led down to the sea. The tanker came to an abrupt halt as it smashed down onto the pool deck. The engine gave a defiant rattle then died.

Within seconds a rabble of startled-looking men appeared at the rear of the house. Hands were pointed first at the ruined truck, then at the top of the hill as they realised where it had come from. Danny stayed low, not willing to make himself a target, just in case they had managed to lay hands on any fresh ammo. Shrill voices cut through the air but no shots were fired.

From a low crouch, Danny threw two hand grenades within a second of each other. The first was aimed at the rear of the tanker. The second bounced off the vehicle and landed with a splash in the far end of the pool.

The Locos threw themselves to the ground as the first explosion ripped through the tanker. Razor-sharp shrapnel and dank sewage filled the air. One man screamed as a piece of spinning metal sheared across his right shoulder. The second grenade sent a wash of raw sewage and water high into the air. The men on the decking turned like a pack of wolves and raced into the villa.

Danny jogged back to Clay's waiting car.

"You get their attention?" asked the Texan, a sly smile beginning to creep across his face.

"You know, I think I did. They'll be with us pronto."

"Alrighty then. My turn. Keep the engine running," said Clay.

"Make them count."

The first of the Locos' pick-up trucks roared through the main gates. Clay had stretched the stinger out across the road thirty feet away. As the lead truck drove over the spikes, all four tyres were instantly shredded. The driver of the truck slammed his feet down on the brakes out of sheer instinct. The second truck skidded sideways in a failed attempt to avoid the tail end of truck one and was quickly joined by the third. The three vehicles slammed into each other, all coming to a sudden stop as the front wheels encountered the spiked anti-vehicle device. The men from the fourth truck disembarked and ran forward yelling, brandishing machetes and baseball bats.

They were sent diving for cover as Clay opened fire with his rifle. The L1A1 Self-Loading Rifle was considered by many to be out of date but it was still very efficient. It had served the British Army for decades. Clay liked the narrow weapon as he found it more accurate than the M4 carbine. He squeezed the trigger and put several single shots into the front grill of the fourth truck. He put another two through the windscreen then targeted the men spilling through the gate. One man emerged from the second truck brandishing a combat knife. Clay didn't hesitate. A single round took the man in the thigh and dropped him backwards into the road. Another of the Locos grabbed his fallen friend by the collar and dragged him back towards the villa.

The remaining Locos crashed into each other as they scrambled back into the confines of the estate grounds. Clay emptied the twenty-round magazine in short controlled bursts, the 7.62mm rounds punching through the bodies of the vehicles with ease. He dropped to one knee and changed the mag. A quick pull with his left hand on the cocking bolt and the weapon was ready to rock and roll again. Clay continued to pepper the vehicles with abandon. One of the Locos lurched from behind the third truck and sprinted for cover through the main gate. Two shots from the SLR encouraged him on his way.

Danny reversed the car to within a couple of feet of his

brother. "Time to vamoose!"

"Shit an' I was just startin' to warm up!" shouted Clay. He emptied the last couple of rounds through the windscreen of the third truck.

"Here. Give them something else to remember us by."

Clay caught the last of the hand grenades, pulled the pin and rolled it along the ground under the first disabled truck. Clay ducked as the vehicle was rocked by the detonation. He turned on his heel and climbed into the waiting car.

"My work here is done," Clay declared.

"Yeah, let them pick the bones out of that for a while. Fancy a beer?"

"Sounds good."

The brothers knocked their knuckles together.

"Happy days," said Clay.

41

Barcelo rested his chin on his fists. He looked at the remainder of his outfit. Less than a dozen men stood before him, only three of whom were left unscathed. His eyes felt gritty and tired. Acid burned from his stomach up into his throat. A slow but relentless throbbing had taken up residence in his head, spreading out from the base of his skull. The fight with the Rogue Angels, although the Locos had ultimately prevailed, had taken its toll. The leader of the bikers had broken his nose and the vision in his left eye was blurred and painful. His knee too was swollen and sore. The bag of ice that he pressed against his damaged leg dripped cold water down his shin. He normally preferred to pace in front of his men but wasn't sure he could trust his knee to bear his weight.

"You did well today." Bruised, tired faces stared back. "But those fucking Brits are too tricky for their own good— hitting us right after a battle. They made us look like a bunch of amateur idiots. That can't happen again." Barcelo leaned back in his seat as a fresh wave of nausea swept over him. "But at the end of the day we're still here and they're gone... for now.

I need a drink, a large one. Who wants to do the honours?"

One of the younger Locos raised his hand. "I'll do it, boss."

"Good man." Barcelo pointed to the array of bottles arranged in an alcove in the wall. "Scotch for me. Ballantine's."

"Boss, I know you don't go a bundle on guns but we need to restock. We haven't got a single bullet left to shoot. If any more shit happens we need something to fight back with," Ortega growled through his teeth.

Barcelo nodded in agreement. "Yeah, we need a restock pronto."

Ortega acted as the spokesman for the rest of the men when he said, "We're all loyal to you, boss. You know that. But we need time to recover. Then we go and put an end to the Brits once and for all."

His boss motioned for him to continue.

"I'll send word to our guy in the north to bring us a double drop of ammo. Should be here by tomorrow morning. You want any more hardware?" asked Ortega.

Barcelo leaned back, his black hair falling over his forehead in thick unruly strands. He was no fan of guns, that was true, but they were a necessary evil. It was proving virtually impossible to maintain the gang's status without them. If the Rogues had been a little better armed, the outcome might have been very different. "Get a rifle for every man in the room. An assault rifle, something reliable."

"AKs?"

"Yeah, Kalashnikovs will be fine. And lots of bullets. I don't want to be caught out again. Let's see how tricky they look when they're riddled with holes."

Ortega nodded once in agreement. He looked up as another two men entered the room. Babi Garcia was followed by a younger man who spoke directly to Barcelo. "The road is clear again. My cousin towed the pick-ups and will put the totalled one through the crusher as soon as he gets back to his yard. He's fixed the tyres on the other trucks as well."

Barcelo grunted his recognition of a task well done and told the man to get himself a drink. Then he turned his attention to Garcia.

"And where the hell have you been? I thought you were supposed to be coming back."

Garcia looked nonplussed at Barcelo's accusatory tone. He helped himself to some of Barcelo's top-shelf Scotch without invitation. He pursed his lips. "I was otherwise occupied. You're not my only employer. I had calls I had to take."

"You see what happened here. That damned biker gang were about to hit me where I sleep. It was pure luck we were on our way to find them when they arrived. Caught them on the hop."

Garcia gesticulated to the gathered men. "Looks like they caught you hopping as well."

Ortega exchanged a look with his boss; Barcelo was well aware of his low opinion of Babi Garcia.

"Well, you're here now," said Barcelo.

Ortega huffed, "Better never than late…"

Garcia flashed him a pretentious smile.

Barcelo continued, "After the bikers were done, those British bastards sucker-punched us. Nearly wrecked the back of my house with a sewage truck. There's shit everywhere. I don't know how in hell I'm going to get it out of there. Then the fuckers ran riot on the men who went after them. Put another couple in the hospital."

"So it wasn't the Rogue Angels who filled your cars with crap after all." Garcia finished his drink and poured a refill. He tilted his head to one side.

"What?" As it dawned on him, Barcelo silently berated himself for not making the simple connection earlier. Had he been played and made to look a fool in front of his men? He had wondered briefly what had spurred the Rogues to directly attack the villa. No matter, they were finished now. "I've just been saying those fucking Brits are next! Well I'm glad you're here now."

Ortega stared at Garcia, his disdain plain for everyone in the room to see. It was bad enough that the younger men coming up through the ranks were a threat to his position without psychos like Babi-fucking-Garcia getting favouritism from Barcelo. "Boss, I will lead the men to—"

"No!" Barcelo's voice cut through the room. "I decide who is doing what."

"Boss—"

"I decide!" He slammed his hands down on his desk. "This is how it's going to be: as soon as we have our guns and ammo we storm into town and make sure everybody knows who is in charge. Us! The Locos! Not those fucking idiots on bikes, not the police and definitely not those arrogant foreign bastards. I want them dead. And I want every single one of our collections made tomorrow. I want the money back here on my desk. If anybody gives you as much as a sideways look, you *make* them pay, make them sorry."

Garcia rattled ice cubes around his glass. "I thought you didn't like guns in the streets."

"I don't like guns being used carelessly. Too many punks waving them around just to look tough and most of them can't even hold a gun properly. I hate that fake gangster shit."

"Okay." Garcia shrugged as he saw the boss's face was getting redder. "So what do we do in the meantime? Meditate? Play poker? I think I have a pack of cards in my car."

Ortega hissed through his wired teeth.

Barcelo had his doubts about the mad dog's mentality but he also knew that mad dogs came in handy when you needed a savage message delivered. "I have a meeting in a few hours. Garcia, you are coming with me."

Ortega stood up sharply, wincing from the jolt of pain in his jaw. "Boss?"

Barcelo held out a placatory hand. "I need to meet the Bosnians to arrange another shipment of girls."

"I can still come with you," said Ortega, giving Garcia a sideways glance.

"No. The Bosnians will have already heard that we lost the last shipment. Even though they've already had their money for the last load, they'll want to be sure we're tight on our end. If you show up looking like that they'll laugh in my face. We need the money."

"Fuck the Bosnians." Ortega fumed at being excluded.

Garcia chuckled. "You ever tried to fuck a Bosnian? Not so easy, my friend."

"Fuck you, Garcia."

"Not so easy to do either you'll find."

"Enough or I'll fuck both of you!" cursed Barcelo.

Garcia turned in a slow and easy pivot, sweeping his gaze around the gang. He tapped the tell-tale bulge under his left armpit. "Again, not so easy I think. I've got the only loaded guns in the room."

"Cut the shit, Babi. I want you and another half-dozen men with me," said Barcelo. "This is not a democracy. I need to meet with them as soon as possible. Even though the cops couldn't pin anything on me linked to the last lot of girls, I need to replace the stock. I can't do that without the Bosnians."

"Yes, boss." Garcia bent in an over-exaggerated bow. "And where are we to meet these fine purveyors of wanton flesh?"

"The waterpark."

Garcia pursed his lips, raising his eyebrows high. "I'll get my Speedos."

42

Adam felt a tingling in his stomach as he approached the villa. He slowed his van to look at the scorch marks on the road just outside the main gates, angry butterflies in the dirt. His mouth felt dry and gummy as a guard stepped out from his sentry box. The man waved him forward as Adam lifted a parcel into view and mouthed, "*Paquete.*"

The boxy van cast a long shadow as Adam headed to the rear of the villa as he had several times before. He tried to look as inconspicuous as possible but felt sure that he would be stopped by one of those urban camo-clad maniacs any moment.

At least he was pretty sure that Barcelo wasn't in the villa. He thought he'd passed him on the way in from the main road. Not in his usual big-assed Mercedes though, but in a more modest vehicle with a second following close behind. Adam counted his teeth with the tip of his tongue. "While the cat's away…"

He made sure the compact cable-splicer unit was safe in his pocket as he slipped out of the van. He had sought out and bought two cars in less than a day, trawling through countless vehicles before he found two that he was satisfied with as instructed by the Gunn brothers. That task, although time consuming, had been relatively easy and allowed him to concentrate on more technical work. If he could hack Barcelo's CCTV network and the computers inside the villa, he would become a proper member of the team. One of the good guys. Maybe he'd get to see some of the action. Maybe then Aunt Sally would treat him like a grown-up. He had already scored with the cars. Maybe he would get the chance to kick some butt. Adam nearly dropped the parcel as he tried the elbow smash his wrestling hero Brock Lesnar used to great effect in his matches.

Pausing at the side door, he tried to look inconspicuous and double checked he wasn't being watched. He placed the parcel between his feet and pretended to press keys on his digital delivery log. His eyes traced the path of the cable that ran vertically down the wall parallel to the doorframe. A thin black cable tacked to the wall by small black pins. Another furtive glance and Adam slipped the cable splicer from his pocket. He flinched as the case dropped, landing on the tiles between his feet.

Beads of moisture dotted his face as he dropped to one knee and made a show of inspecting the parcel. Adam gulped and palmed the case, relieved that it didn't appear damaged. He cast another furtive glance over his shoulder.

His fingers were trembling as he gently tugged on the cable to work in some slack as low to the ground as he could manage. A heat crept into his face as he anticipated the icy hand that would close around his neck. Something felt alive in his stomach, twisting and turning. After opening the clamshell case and feeding one side behind the cable he squeezed it tightly closed. The click of the plastic locking button seemed like a gunshot to his senses. *Done!*

He straightened up with the parcel back in hand and rapped on the door sharply. He was about to repeat the knock when a man answered. The man didn't speak rather just lifted his chin in an impatient gesture.

"*Hola. Paquete,*" said Adam and motioned that he required a signature on his digi-pad.

The man was a mean-looking son of a bitch. His arm was in a sling and when he muttered a low *gracias* Adam could see that his teeth were wired. He knew who this man was. The man that had muscled Aunt Sally for money a couple of weeks ago. The guy that Clay had worked over in the Woo Hoo Club.

"*Gracias, Senor Ortega,*" he replied and began to turn away. He was stopped by a tight grip on his arm.

Ortega took a step towards him. "How do you know my name?"

For a long moment Adam feared he was going to fill his boxer shorts but stammered out a response in perfect Spanish. "You just signed for the parcel. I've gotten very good at deciphering handwriting on this thing."

Ortega's gaze flicked once at the digi-pad then back to Adam's face. He released his grip.

A single thick bead of sweat ran down the side of Adam's face like a tear. "*Te veo.*"

Ortega flashed him more of the wire on his teeth and made a point of answering in English. "See you too."

Adam forced himself not to run back to his van even

though it felt like his legs were telling him to do the opposite. All thoughts of trying an elbow smash were forgotten. He felt a sense of relief as he climbed into the driver's seat. He adjusted his position in the seat as the sweat-soaked shirt clung to his skin. That guy was a scary bastard.

He checked his mirror a dozen times as he left the villa grounds and made his way back towards the main road. Stopping his van at the side of the road, he lifted his iPad from its protective neoprene pouch at the side of his seat and loaded the app that linked to the splicer unit. There were a few seconds of electric snow on the screen but then a familiar menu began to cycle options. Adam watched the various systems within the villa register on his screen. Three separate PCs and the central control of the CCTV system were displayed as mini icons. Adam double-tapped each one in turn. After a few seconds each icon reappeared with a green tick superimposed on top. All four systems were now accessible. He tapped the CCTV icon. The iPad screen then split into six panes, each displaying a different view supplied by a camera.

"I friggin' did it!"

He had another eight deliveries to make on his way back to the depot but could barely contain his excitement about telling the guys. This would be the icing on the cake. He would be one of the team.

43

Clay finished his double helping of fillet steak and potatoes. Dez was living up to his claim of being the best cook on the coast. "Damn that boy can cook."

"Of course, that's why he works at the Woo Hoo," replied Pamela. "People come from miles around for our food. Julie's pretty good in the kitchen as well."

Clay cocked his head to one side. "I don't think Danny's interested in her culinary skills."

"Huh?"

"It seems she and Danny have taken a liking to each other," added Clay.

"Well that's up to them. They're both adults."

"Indeed."

Pamela leaned across the table, resting her elbows on the polished surface. "So, what about you, Clay? When are you going to settle back down? I know you loved Diana but it's been years now."

Clay picked up his mug of coffee and inhaled the aroma before he answered. "It's hard to explain. I still feel kind of guilty at times, you know? She's gone and here I am swanning through life with more money than sense."

"You've nothing to feel guilty about. Diana died in a car crash; tragic, but not your fault, Clay."

"I know that in here," he tapped the side of his head, then pointed to his chest. "But in here I feel wrong somehow. Look, I'm hardly a monk. I've had a few casual partners since Diana but I just can't seem to settle on one long enough to get attached."

Pamela smiled and placed her hand on top of his. Her hand looked like a child's in comparison. "You'll find the right woman sooner or later. Don't give up hope."

"That's just it, Pam, I'm not even hoping. I know I could pick up a wife if I wanted one, even with this face. Lots of women out there would like a Texan millionaire for a husband. But if I do find another, I want her to want me for the right reasons."

"Oh, Clay."

He withdrew his hand and adjusted the cutlery on his plate, flicking at the handle of the fork. "Anyway, all the best girls are already taken."

Danny joined them at the table in the rear of the club. "Hey."

Clay hooked a thumb at his brother. "And anyway, I've got this millstone around my neck."

"You referring to me? A millstone? Cheeky bastard."

"Now, now, boys. Be nice." Pamela wagged a finger.

The brothers grimaced at each other.

"You fed and watered?" asked Danny.

Clay licked his lips. "I was just gonna ask if Dez had any of that upside-down cake that I tried yesterday. That was really good. I could squeeze some of that in."

"I've never met anyone who ate as much as you and still looked so healthy. Most people would be the shape of a walrus but you look like you just stepped out of a wrestling ring." Pamela smiled as she headed to the kitchen. "I'll see what I can do."

"Is Dez still angry?"

Danny nodded in the affirmative. "He's spittin' feathers. Can't blame him though. Old man Torres is like family to him and those biker arseholes did him over something serious. Dez says he's going to be kept in the hospital for a week or so."

"We tested those biker boys and they were found wanting."

"Ay-men to that, big bro." Danny looked at Clay's empty plate. "Ready to make a move?"

Clay glanced furtively in the direction of the kitchen door. "Still waitin' on my cake."

The door to the club opened and Adam bounced over to the table. The look on his face was akin to a lottery winner who'd just been told the good news. "I did it!" he announced triumphantly.

"Finally got laid?"

Adam grinned at Clay. "Nah, man, time for that later. I hacked the villa!"

Clay grinned back. The kid was a lot brighter than he looked. "And it works?"

"Yeah. I checked it before I left. We've got access to all the cameras and we can see anything that he looks at online. Works just like a keystroke logger. Anything they type we can see. The camera feed is—"

"We just need to know it works. Nice work, Adam. You

did good." Danny patted him on the shoulder. "How did you get on with buying those cars?"

"Mission accomplished. Two cars: strong bodies, good engines. Low centres of gravity. They're parked out back. I brought one over before work this morning and I drove the other over just now." Adam struck a hero pose, hands on his hips and chest expanded, enjoying his moment. "So, guys, who's the best?"

Clay smiled despite wanting to keep a lid on Adam's exuberance. "You are, Adam. You are." He tried not to stare as Adam's right eye parted company from his left. Clay couldn't recall Superman ever counting his teeth with the tip of his tongue yet Adam held the heroic pose for another few seconds.

The moment was broken by Pamela's arrival. "One supersized order of upside-down cake."

Clay began to devour the sponge base topped with baked apple sauce. Pamela noticed Adam was now staring at the dessert.

"You want some as well?"

"Yes, please, Mrs Duke." Adam plopped himself down at the table next to Clay.

She looked at Danny. "You?"

Danny shrugged. "May as well. I'll come with you."

"Me too," said Clay.

"No, you stay there and finish your cake," replied Pamela. "Finished."

Pamela turned and looked at the empty bowl. She shook her head in wonder. "You fancy some more?" She was rewarded with a slightly self-conscious grin.

"If it's no trouble."

"Wait here."

Danny and Pamela walked off in the direction of the kitchen. Adam turned his uneven gaze back on Clay. "You looking at my wonky eye?"

Clay shifted in his seat. "No, I—"

"It's okay. Everybody does. They don't know which eye to look at. Kind of freaks the girls out."

"Hey, it's not that bad."

Adam shrugged. "When I was a kid they made me wear a patch over my good eye. The doctors said the other eye would correct itself. I went around nearly blind for a year and a half. All the kids at school used to rip the crap out of me. I've heard every pirate joke there is, every cock-eye joke as well."

Clay gave a fleeting thought to his own formative years. "Yeah, kids can be a bunch of shits, can't they?"

"It's called amblyopia. My eye will never be right. The surgery costs way too much. But that's okay; it doesn't bother me much anymore. At least I'm okay to drive. My depth perception is fine."

"We've got another job for you if you're up for it?" Clay knew it was better to keep the kid occupied.

"Ready and willing. What is it?"

"Would you be able to find out if Barcelo owns any boats?"

"I guess so. I'll have to figure out how to do that. I'm sure Google will have the answer." Adam paused. "Why do you want to know that?"

"Just something that Danny and I have been thinkin' on. If he does, it's another way we can get to him. Hit him where it hurts. Can you handle it?"

"Of course I can. I got your cars and hacked the villa didn't I?"

Clay nodded. The kid was resourceful but he needed to make sure he didn't get caught up in the crossfire. "We need to know if he owns any and where they're berthed. As much detail as possible."

Danny and Pamela arrived back to the table with more dessert. Pamela joined them as they began to eat. Clay leaned over and whispered a few words to Adam.

"Oh yeah. Thanks, Daisy," said Adam.

Pamela thumped Clay on the shoulder. "I've told you about that before. That shit sticks."

Adam's gaze flicked to Clay. "You said she liked it."

Clay winked back at him. "Ah, young man, it's all in the delivery."

"If anybody else calls me Daisy friggin' Duke, I'll deliver my right foot up their arse."

"Classy," laughed Danny.

"Who said that? Emmeline Pankhurst?" Clay questioned.

Adam looked confused. "Who's Emmeline Pankhurst?" he asked. "Was she in the Pussycat Dolls?"

44

Barcelo shifted in the car seat and hit the passenger window with his fist. He felt like killing someone. He had worked way too hard building up his patch to let it all slip away. Rogue Angels, British upstarts and now there were reports that the Colombians were working their way down the coast. It would only be a matter of time before they too arrived in Ultima. That would mean more police on the streets, more problems. He would deal with the Colombians if and when they arrived but first he had to set things straight with the Bosnians. He could not let the fragile business arrangement he had with them be jeopardised. The girls were relatively low risk but brought very good returns. As part of the arrangement he got to keep one out of every twenty girls for free. It was a sweet deal. But the girls had a limited shelf life. They could only bring in top dollar for a year or two before they were used up. Then they tended to get passed down to less particular groups to be pimped out for scrat-money. There was always a need for more girls. It was a lucrative business that needed protecting.

The leader of the Bosnians went by the name of Golok. Barcelo knew he was not a man to be trifled with. While he would never admit to being scared of the man, Barcelo knew that any perceived slight to the Bosnian code of honour would not be forgiven or forgotten easily. The Bosnians operated with a ruthlessness that left no room for doubt. They were dangerous men and now a potential crack in the operation had been opened on Barcelo's watch. The girls that they had lost during the evacuation at the club would cost him. Most of the girls came from Bulgaria, Bosnia and more recently the Czech Republic. In truth, it didn't matter to him where they came from as long as they were young. The younger they were the more profit to be made on them.

The payment was always made in used notes of middle values, nothing higher than a fifty. Barcelo clutched the small sports bag tight in his lap. The cash had come from his personal safe, money he bitterly resented handing away. Normally the revenue generated by the previous shipment was enough to pay for the next.

As annoying as he was, Garcia was right: the Brits had played them for fools. But they would pay the ultimate price. No more warning shots; no more trying to take them alive. They were for the sharks. With a bit of luck, he would be the one to personally end it for them. He had snapped the biker's neck and he would do the same for any other challengers that put his livelihood at risk.

Barcelo raised a hand to his face, which still throbbed in pain from the fight. That guy had kicked like a mule.

"You okay?" Garcia regarded his boss with a look of mild amusement from the driver's seat.

Barcelo grunted a monosyllable in way of reply.

"My face hurts too. It's part of the job. I'll get my payback. Maybe you're getting soft. Maybe you've been behind that big desk of yours for too long."

"Fuck off, Babi!" warned Barcelo. "I'm in no mood for your shit today."

"We could stop off at my place for some pills if you want," offered Garcia as he dropped his hand back to the steering wheel. "A couple of purples and a blue would go down nicely. Take the edge off."

"We've no time for that. The Bosnians do not like to be kept waiting."

"Are the Bosnians as tough as their reputation? I've never had the pleasure."

Barcelo looked at Garcia from the corner of his eye. The sly smile that Garcia wore perturbed him.

"Certainly not men who make idle threats. Not men to go against unless you have a death wish."

"Tougher than your Locos?" asked Garcia.

Barcelo glared at Garcia and bunched his fists. "Just drive the fucking car, Babi, and stop needling me."

"So where exactly is this place we're going to?"

"You know the waterpark they started to build a couple of years ago? Ultimagua, they called it. The developers ran out of money so it never opened. But it's a great place to meet away from prying eyes. I've met the Bosnians there a couple times in the past."

"Ultimagua. Huh." Garcia pronounced the word with undisguised disdain. "No prying eyes?"

Barcelo gave him another sideways glance. "No. The

security there is one old man who checks the place once a week on a Tuesday morning."

"The old guy is a friend of yours?"

Barcelo gave the smallest twitch of a smile. "Do you need to ask?"

45

Adam left the Woo Hoo Club with an almost euphoric sense of achievement. Both Danny and Clay had praised him on a job well done on managing to hack the villa network. They had then checked out the two cars he had bought for them. These too had been on the money. Clay had taken to calling him "quartermaster". He was the Q of the group, just like in the Bond movies. But unlike Q, who always got left behind when real action was needed, Adam was determined to show them he could do much more than just press buttons on a keyboard. After promising Danny that he would find out if Barcelo owned any boats, he mentally parked that errand for later. He had a much better idea.

Sally had arrived at the club for an early drink and Adam's plans had nearly faltered before they had begun. "Where are you off to in such a hurry?"

Pointing a finger to some far-off point, he stammered, "New Blu-ray box set. Er, just nipping out."

"Okay, babes, see you later. When you come back I'll buy you dinner."

Despite feeling a little crappy for spinning Aunt Sally a lie, he had hopped back in his car, a newer model Toyota, and sped back towards Barcelo's villa. He was sure he would turn up some real information that they could use to knock Barcelo off his perch.

The cool evening air whistled through the open windows, tugging at his hair and collar as he pressed down on the accelerator. As he drew closer to the villa he eased back on the speed and allowed the car to creep along using the momentum he had built up. He flicked the headlights off. Gravel crunched under the tyres as he steered the vehicle from the road onto the hillside that overlooked the villa, far enough so he couldn't be seen from the house or the gates.

A nervous laugh escaped his throat as he pulled the lever under his seat and scooted back so he had more legroom. The iPad came out next. His fingers worked like an arachnid's legs and in seconds he had the snooper program loaded. He tapped on the first of the icons. The picture on the screen jumbled into a thousand indistinct pixels for a couple of seconds then cleared to show a view that looked from the villa towards the main gates. The CCTV system had been easy to hack, just nerve-wracking during the few tense seconds it had taken to bite into the camera relay cable. Adam counted his teeth with the tip of his tongue as he watched the man in the gatehouse light up a cigarette. He closed that view and tapped the next icon. This resulted in a view of the pool deck. A large overturned tanker truck filled most of the screen. Adam laughed as he moved to the next icon. Another camera view showed the side of the house where he had made his deliveries.

As he tapped the next icon a stream of code appeared

within a separate window. He scanned the code with a practised eye and entered a series of base instructions. A blinking cursor at the bottom of the screen awaited his command. With a self-satisfied sigh he hit the enter key. The code again streamed down his screen too fast for the eye to follow. Then the screen of his iPad changed to mirror that of the PC he had just hacked into.

Adam was midway through punching the air in celebration when the car door was wrenched open. Hands much stronger than his own fastened themselves around his neck and yanked him out of the vehicle. The iPad clattered between his feet, sliding between the pedals.

Adam twisted on the ground and tried to push the hands away from his throat to no avail. Then a second man twisted his arm into a lock, wrenching his wrist until he felt something give way with a searing snap. He yelled out first in surprise then in agony. Just when he thought it couldn't get any worse the man holding his wrist twisted it even further. Purple spots of light danced across his vision as a boot slammed into his face. Once, twice, then a third time. Adam was barely conscious, the toes of his shoes tracing twin tracks in the dust as the two men dragged him down the hill towards the villa.

"You must think we're really stupid to fall for the same trick again. We've been waiting for you bastards to show up again. Boss said you might try another potshot from up here."

"I told the boss I didn't think anyone would be so dumb." The second man grated the bones of Adam's broken wrist together. "But here you are."

Tears ran down Adam's face as he was dragged through

the gates. He felt a tidal wave of dread wash over him. His breath came in short terrified gulps. He knew that the Locos had killed people in the past. He'd read the news, heard the stories: bodies washing up on the beach; people disappearing, never to be seen again. He tried lurching to one side in an effort to break the grip of his captors. He vomited as his wrist was wrenched again. The two men dropped him face down on the villa driveway as they avoided the contents of his stomach. Then the man to his right snatched up his broken wrist again and stamped down onto the small of his back.

Adam tried screaming for help. His voice was no more than a strangled wheeze. He tried again.

One of the men from the gatehouse ran forward and kicked him in the ribs. "Motherfucker!"

Adam cried, deep wracking sobs, as the men dragged him ever closer to the villa. He had made a terrible mistake coming here on his own.

The tiles on the kitchen floor felt like ice against his rapidly swelling face. He had never been hit before. He never imagined the pain could feel this bad. Curled into the foetal position, he sucked in ragged gasps of air. Rough hands searched him for any concealed weapons. He had none. One of the men tugged his wallet from his pocket and flipped it open. His cell phone was snatched from another pocket.

"Adam Bradshaw." The man read the details from the driver's licence. He pressed the heel of his boot onto Adam's knee. "Hello, Adam." He turned to the other man. "Get Ortega. He'll want to meet our new friend."

* * *

Vincenzo Ortega looked down at the young man curled on the floor. His face had already begun to swell, a puffy purple welt around his left eye and cheek. Blood trickled from his nose. "Who is he?"

The guard handed him a wallet. Ortega glanced down at the contents. Then he squatted at Adam's side, lifting his chin with two stiffened fingers. Speaking in Spanish he asked, "I know you don't I? You're the delivery man. Who sent you here? That big fucking American?"

Adam reached out a placatory hand towards Ortega. "Please. I'm just the parcel delivery guy."

Ortega exchanged another look with the guards. They shook their heads in unison. Ortega slapped Adam's hand away. "You were spying on the house."

"No." Adam's voice jumped an octave.

"Yes." Ortega raised his own chin in a sharp gesture. The guards hauled Adam to his feet. The larger of the two then slipped his arms under Adam's, effectively pinning them behind his back. "Who knows you're here?"

Ortega reached out with his left hand. Adam tried to move away but the guard held him fast. "The men that sent you, the Brit and the American?"

"Please, let me go. I won't say anything."

"The names of the two men?" Ortega's fingers closed around Adam's throat. He squeezed gently at first. "Their names?"

Adam coughed and spluttered as the choke took effect. Ortega released the pressure.

"The big American is called Clay? Yes?" Ortega knew this to be so from their encounter at the club. "What about the other, the Brit? Are there any more men I need to know about?" Ortega snapped his hand forward again, slamming Adam's face with a backhand. "You answer me when I ask you a fucking question!"

A crimson tear rolled down Adam's face. His words came out in a high-pitched tumble. "Clay! Yes. And his brother Danny!"

"Brothers? Are you sure?"

Adam nodded, clearly ashamed. "Yes."

"Who hired them, the Dukes from the Woo Hoo?"

Adam nodded. Another backhander slapped into his face.

"Say it!" Ortega's voice carried as much threat as his fist.

"Yes," answered Adam between panicked sobs. "The Dukes. Larry and Pamela."

"Now, who knows you are here? The brothers sent you?" Ortega scrutinised his captive's face as he waited for an answer. He watched with curious interest as Adam's eyes drifted apart. "You came here of your own accord? No one knows?"

Adam's look of horror confirmed Ortega's suspicion. As Ortega's hand again closed around his throat, Adam's phone rang. It was a rock version of the Spider-Man theme tune. Ortega looked at the second guard. He held up the phone so he could read the display. "Answer it."

Immediately a voice began speaking in English. "Adam, it's Danny. Where are you? Your Aunt Sally's still here. She's waiting for you—"

"I have him!" Ortega's voice cut the air like a cleaver.

46

Danny paused mid action, pouring a glass of sparkling water. "Who is this? Barcelo?"

The man on the phone laughed. "No, not Barcelo. Ortega. Your brother and I know one another. Now listen. I have your fat little errand boy. If you want him back in one piece you better do as I say. I want you and that big brother of yours to come back to the villa. The one you nearly ruined with the sewage truck. You come alone. No weapons or the boy dies. Any tricky shit and I'll mail him back to you in bite-sized pieces."

"How do I know he's still alive? Put him on the line."

The line remained silent for a few seconds before Adam's voice cried, "Danny please help me."

"Hang in there, Adam. You'll be okay."

"I want you at the front gates of the villa in an hour. No guns. No cops. If I see anything that even makes my eye twitch, I will gut fat boy."

"He's just a kid. It's us that you want," said Danny. "We'll be there. I want your word that you won't kill him."

"I give you my word that I will if you're not at the

gates in an hour. No guns, no cops."

"I said we'll be there. Put Adam back on."

Ortega laughed. "You want a final word with the boy. Here."

A piercing scream rang out from the phone.

Then the line went dead.

Seconds later a double chime indicated an incoming picture message. Adam's face was frozen mid scream, his hand pinioned to a kitchen table by a hunting knife. The other men in the picture were laughing.

Clay walked into the kitchen. "Hey, I spotted some Serrano ham earlier and got to thinking about an Italian club sandwich and potato chips. Hey, can you get Cheetos over here?" He saw the expression on Danny's face. "What is it?"

"They've got Adam."

"Crap." Clay didn't have to ask who *they* were. "He still breathin'?"

"Aye, for now." Danny explained Ortega's simple demands.

Clay looked sullen when he viewed the picture. "You know they'll still kill him right after they've slotted us."

Danny nodded in agreement.

"So what we gonna do?"

"Kill every last one of them."

Two streams of laughter cut from the bar. Both were distinctive. Pamela and Sally.

"Shit. I'll have to go and sort Sally out," said Danny. "That won't be easy." He stuck his head out of the kitchen door and beckoned her inside, motioning her to sit down. For long moments she looked at the brothers in expectation. Then she began to wail as Danny explained the Locos had Adam captive.

242   JAMES HILTON

She jumped to her feet, pushing Danny back, and pulled her cell phone from her handbag. "I'm calling the police!"

Danny quickly snatched the phone from her hands. "Sally, we can't do that. We can't risk it. I don't think they were bluffing."

Black mascara-stained tears streaked her face. "Oh-my-god, oh-my-god, oh-my-god."

"Don't worry. We'll bring him back," said Danny.

Sally's voice took on a sharper edge. "You were supposed to keep him away from trouble. He's just a big harmless kid. You're supposed to be the hard men. Why the fuck have they got my Adam?" Danny held out his hands to calm her but she slapped them away. "How the hell did they get hold of him?"

"I don't know. I told him to stay well away from them. I even gave him run-around jobs to keep him occupied." Danny explained the errands to find the cars and the information on any boats. Sally slumped back onto the chair. She began to cry even louder than before. Danny looked at Clay. Both felt ill-equipped to comfort her.

The sound of Sally's upset drew in the others and before long they were surrounded by Larry, Pamela, Dez and Julie. Danny explained the turn of events as quickly as he could.

Pamela wrapped an arm around Sally's juddering shoulders. "I'm so sorry, Sally. I feel this is all my fault; I asked Clay and Danny here. I didn't mean for Adam to get hurt."

Sally threw off her arm and slapped her in the face. "But he did get hurt! Maybe it is your fault; you brought them here. We were managing fine without them."

Pamela recoiled from the shock. She held a hand to her stinging cheek. "Sally…" Then she leant forward and embraced Sally a second time. This time the woman let her. "Don't worry," she soothed. "If Clay and Danny said they'll bring him back, then they'll bring him back."

"Or die trying," offered Clay.

Danny left the women in the kitchen. He had seen this too many times before: stricken families shedding tears because of the actions of violent men. Men like the Locos. Men like the Gunn brothers.

Clay and Larry followed him out of the kitchen. "So what are we going to do?" Larry asked.

Clay shook his head. "You can't come, Larry. We've been through this before."

Larry scowled at his old friend. "Fuck you, Clay. I know that already."

"Hey, easy, old buddy." Clay rested a hand on his shoulder. "You've more than given your pound of flesh. This is our turn."

Larry fell silent and turned to see Dez standing in the doorway. "I can help," the cook offered.

Danny was about to send him back downstairs when he kicked the door shut behind him. "I did my national service. Back at the end of the nineties, just before they stopped it. I was a lance corporal with the 11th Field Artillery. I know my way around a rifle. I'm sick to death of these fuckers getting away with it and I want to help."

Danny looked up at Dez. "Look, man, I appreciate the offer but I don't want to get anybody else involved in this."

The cook stepped forward. "We are *already* involved. The Locos are bad news. You think we like having to look the other way? Keeping our heads down? This is Larry's club and my livelihood. I know I'm just a fucking cook to you but this is how I feed my family. If the Locos take the club, then what? You think I could just trundle on as part of the fixtures and fittings. I can help! One of my best friends, Papa Torres, is lying in hospital with tubes in his nose. I'm sick to death of these gangs."

Danny sat back on the bed and really looked at Dez for the first time. "Actually you're right. You're about the same size and build as me, right?"

Dez cocked his head to one side. "I guess so. Why?"

Danny grinned a shark-like grin. "I've got an idea."

"Uh oh," said Clay. "I hear those rusty wheels a'turning."

47

Ortega pulled his knife free from Adam's hand. Blood immediately welled up from the wound. Adam's face was frozen in a silent scream. He slumped to the ground. One of the guards planted a kick to the side of his head. Adam's face went slack in the way only full unconsciousness can deliver.

Ortega looked down at the prostrate body. He considered slipping his knife between the fat boy's ribs and being done with him. With a cluck of resignation, he sheathed his blade, knowing he might need him to ensure the two brothers played by the rules. Also, Barcelo might want to speak to the boy. The boss liked to get his hands dirty on occasion.

Ortega turned to his men. "We've got an hour. Here is what I want you to do…" Ortega knew there was only a half-dozen or so pistol rounds left in the house. They had searched every cupboard and drawer following the encounter with the bikers. The search had turned up only a few cartridges left for the shotguns. But this was going to be up-close and personal. The men scoured the house and grounds for the other items he had requested.

Ortega kept an eye on Adam who lay motionless on the floor. As an added precaution he had one of the guards tape the boy's injured hands behind his back.

Ortega speed-dialled Barcelo. The call was answered after a single ring.

"Boss, we caught one of the Brits sneaking around the villa. We've got him."

"Is he one of the ones we're looking for?"

"No. It's a fat delivery guy. He was here yesterday with a parcel. He was spying on the house. I caught him and now the two men we want are coming to the villa for the boy. Turns out they're brothers."

"Now? They're coming now?" Barcelo's voice carried an air of rising irritation.

"In an hour, boss. I will have them for you."

"I'm on my way to the waterpark. I need to do this. The Bosnians will deal only with me. I can't put this off, there's too much money at stake."

"Don't worry. You take care of business. I can handle this." Ortega bristled as he heard Garcia's annoying laugh in the background.

Barcelo was silent for a few seconds. "I want them both. Alive if possible, but dead is better than letting them run wild again. And, Ortega…"

"Yes, boss?"

"Don't fuck this up." The call ended.

Ortega pictured Garcia laughing again at his expense. He tucked the cell back in his pocket with slow deliberation. When this was over and done with he would find a way to end it for Babi as well.

The men began to congregate back in the plush kitchen. Makeshift weapons were laid out on the table. Knives, a meat cleaver, two baseball bats and an axe lay beside a single pistol and a pump-action shotgun. One of the older men entered the room carrying four bottles with rags for stoppers. "Barcelona bangers, just in case…"

A couple of the men laughed at his quip.

"Just make damned sure you're outside if you use those," Ortega said. "Now, who is the best shot with a pistol?" The men debated the issue for a few seconds then several hands pointed to a familiar face. Aspanu stepped forward. He had been the first man down at the hands of the big American at the Woo Hoo Club.

"Okay. Aspanu, you take the pistol. You shoot them in the guts if they as much as blink."

"With pleasure. That big American owes me big time." Aspanu picked up the pistol. "Maybe I'll shoot him *before* he blinks."

One of the guards from the gate who had caught Adam stepped up and grabbed the shotgun. "I'll take this."

"The rest of you…" Ortega pointed at the blades and clubs and the remaining men chose their weapons. A couple of the younger Locos slashed the air with their blades, the promise of impending violence thick in the room.

Adam began to stir on the floor. Ortega checked the time. The fat slug of a boy had been out for way too long. Fifteen minutes to go. He tapped at Adam with the toe of his shoe. "Get him up."

Adam woke as rough hands hoisted him from the floor by his hair and collar. He yelled in pain as he was thrust back against the kitchen cupboards.

Ortega picked up Adam's phone. He called the last number in the phone's memory. A deep voice with an unmistakeable American accent answered. "Yeah?"

"You must be Clay. You have five minutes to get here or doughnut boy is dead."

Clay's voice rumbled in response. "You said an hour. We're still a good fifteen minutes out."

"Five!" Ortega killed the call.

One of the younger Locos frowned at his captain, his face slack with confusion.

"If we make them hurry they are more likely to be off balance when they arrive," Ortega explained. "If you let the fish tire themselves out, then they are easier to reel in." Ortega closed his eyes and exhaled wearily as the younger man began winding an imaginary reel and grinning.

Thankfully not all of the men were complete idiots. He looked at Aspanu as an idea sprang to mind. "I've got a new job for you."

48

The Locos stood in a wide semicircle near the front door of the villa. Ortega stood in the centre, holding Adam by the boy's broken wrist. The man holding the shotgun stood to his right. A car crept through the gates. The man with the shotgun lifted the weapon to his shoulder, then held up his palm to stop them and with two extended fingers motioned for them to get out of the vehicle.

Ortega hissed air between his teeth as the big American climbed from the driver's seat. A smaller man followed. They looked nothing like brothers. The American looked like a professional wrestler. Ortega knew from experience that he moved faster than most of them too. The smaller guy looked like nothing much to speak of. Both brothers wore baseball caps pulled low and aviator sunglasses. Ortega smiled. They were about to die and they'd arrived dressed for an afternoon at the sports stadium. Real Madrid would have to wait.

Shotgun shouted out commands in English, following Ortega's earlier instructions. "Walk forward. Hands in the air. Good. Stop!"

The shotgun dropped to hip level. "Now with your left hands lift up your shirts and turn around, slowly."

The Locos watched the brothers do as they were told.

"Now, hands on your head."

Ortega twisted Adam's wrist, which caused him to yell out again. "I'm sorry, Clay. I thought they were going to kill me."

"Don't worry, kid. Just do exactly as they say and you'll be home soon." Clay nodded at Adam but fixed his gaze on Ortega. "We're here now."

"I see that. Part of me didn't think you would come, but I'm so glad you did. We have a score to settle, you and I," said Ortega.

"Speak up, dude. I can't hear you." Clay cupped his hand to his ear. Then he tapped the side of his jaw. "You been drinking too much coffee? You sound a little wired."

Ortega bent Adam's discoloured wrist to a right angle sending him instantly to his knees. The man with the shotgun effected his version of an American accent. "Squeal like a pig, fat boy!"

Adam did squeal as Ortega stepped on his lacerated hand, pinning him to the ground.

"Enough!" warned Clay.

Ortega didn't lift his foot. "Now, what about you two. Brothers, eh? Clay and Danny Gunn. You don't look like brothers. Mama like to put it around, eh? Two little bastards I think."

Ortega locked gazes with Clay. The big guy's face was deeply weathered, a series of scars showing as white lines on his tanned skin.

Ortega let Adam slump fully to the ground and moved towards the brothers. "Big tough cowboy. But what about this one?" he said pointing at Danny. "The runt of the litter I think. Hey, Brit-pig, I think the best part of you ran down your mama's thighs."

"Fuck you!" Clay's voice rumbled like a thundercloud.

Ortega continued undaunted. "Ah, brothers, how sweet. You love each other, yes? Brotherly love? Big brother, little brother."

Ortega clicked his fingers and pointed away from Clay. The shotgun roared once and Adam screamed as the smaller man's stomach erupted in a crimson explosion. His body folded in two and he pitched sideways into the ground.

Clay roared and pivoted towards the gunman. Even as he moved Ortega knew he would not make it. The shotgun was now aligned with Clay's chest.

The gunman began to rack the slide of the shotgun. Then he contorted into a strange sideways curve, his hip jutting out to one side. He looked down as the sides of his shirt began to turn a deep red. A second impact caught him square between the shoulder blades. Even as he began to fall in a tangle of loose limbs, Clay snatched the shotgun from his fingers.

The six Locos scattered in every direction as Clay worked the pump-action. *Chak-chak! Boom!* The closest of the Locos pitched head first into the ground, arms flung out behind him as he caught the full load of lead in the small of his back.

Ortega was first through the front door of the villa. He was mid turn as the remaining five Locos scrambled through behind him in terror. The first collided with Ortega and they both went down hard. Ortega stifled a scream as his face slammed into the unforgiving tiles of the portico. He tasted metallic blood as the wirework in his jaw bit deep into his flesh.

The front door slammed shut as the shotgun roared again.

49

The stock of the rifle nestled snugly against Larry's right cheek. His body lay stretched out on the crest of the hill overlooking the villa grounds. He took several deep breaths as he watched the doors of Clay's car open and the two men climb out.

"Breathe, slow and easy," he whispered into the stock of the rifle. He angled his body slightly to one side and dug the toes of his good leg into the hard-packed dirt. The rifle felt comfortable in his grip. It was the same model as he had trained with as a young soldier a lifetime ago.

The turning sensation in his stomach subsided as he exhaled again, slow and easy. A semicircle of men stood in front of the villa. One of them carried a shotgun. The other men brandished knives and clubs. He smiled. If they had more firearms it was a safe bet they would be flashing them instead of the baseball bats and cleavers. He lined up the man with the shotgun in his sights. There was no scope fitted to the rifle but the "iron sights" would serve just fine at this distance.

Larry had insisted on playing his part in Danny's plan.

He had promised to stay out of sight and only open fire if the situation necessitated it. Pamela had, of course, had a screaming fit when he told her he was going with the brothers. That had been the whole point of asking for their help she had argued: so Larry would not be harmed by the Locos. The heated argument had raged for five volatile minutes before Larry had shouted at her: "What would you do if it was me that they had taken instead of Adam?"

Pamela had cried and argued back some more but Larry had left grim-faced with the rifle locked and loaded.

Clay had dropped him off shortly after turning the car onto the access road that led directly to Barcelo's villa. Larry had jogged the remainder as quietly as possible. He was breathing hard as he reached the long incline that overlooked the villa grounds. Adam's car sat abandoned close by. Bitter bile rose in the back of his throat as he struggled to complete the brisk run. Bent almost double, he traversed the slope and selected his vantage point. Clay had driven slowly to buy him a little time to get into position. He had needed every second of that to reach his spot. He knew that physical fitness was the first thing lost from a soldier's skill set.

Out of habit he licked the tip of his index finger then rubbed the saliva into his right eyebrow. He had picked up the trick many years earlier during his time at sniper school. It allowed the shooter to feel the direction of the wind as he prepared to shoot. It had become an unconscious ritual within him. *Position, acquire target, lick, squeeze.*

The sound of an agonised scream drifted up from the villa. Adam was face down with some guy ramming his foot into his back. Larry shifted his aim to the man punishing Adam. It would be an easy shot to put one in the guy's chest, see who was in charge then, but the plan was no shooting unless necessary. Then the shotgun boomed, a brief tongue of flame and Clay was roaring.

"Jesus Christ!" Larry instantly adjusted his aim and snapped off a shot. The man with the shotgun froze mid action and looked down in disbelief. The 7.62mm round had entered his body just above his waist, ripping through his liver with deadly efficiency as it went. Larry watched the man stagger and he squeezed the trigger again. The second shot was more precise than the first. The round caught him directly between the shoulder blades, centre mass. As the man dropped, Clay snatched the shotgun from his hands.

With a collective howl the Locos scattered and raced for the front doors of the villa. The shotgun boomed again and one of the grey-clad gangsters was pitched off his feet with his arms thrown out behind him.

The Locos raced through the doorway in double time. Clay racked another shot but only succeeded in blasting the doors. Larry realigned and sent a tight three-round burst through the closest of the windows. The chances of hitting a body were slim but it would keep their heads down and allow Clay some breathing room. He sent a second tight burst through another window. As he sighted up on a third he heard the voice behind him.

"You Brit *bastardos* never learn. Keep trying the same tricks over and over." The voice was thickly accented. Larry had lived in Spain long enough to know a Barcelona accent when he heard one. He closed his eyes in self-reproach.

Rookie-fucking-mistake. He'd been so intent on the villa he had not monitored his six.

Larry began to turn to face the new threat as a pistol barked twice.

50

Timo watched Ortega scramble to his feet, his hand pressed to the side of his face. The boss looked like he was in serious pain. As the Locos moved away from the front doors, the windows to the right of the portico exploded and bullets ricocheted from the tiled floor. Ortega covered his head with his good arm and ran deeper into the lobby.

A second window shattered and Timo ducked low to avoid the cascade of falling glass. A large Chinese vase next to the door exploded into a thousand blue-and-white pieces. The other Locos made to follow Ortega, but Timo hesitated. He clutched a fire axe tight with both hands. He had been with Barcelo for many years. As a child he had lived through the dismal latter days of Francoist Spain and decade by decade since he had watched his beloved country become ever more polluted by foreigners. His once great Spain was now barely scraping through each year, seemingly at the brink of financial collapse. He knew that Barcelo was right; they had to take back what was rightfully theirs piece by bloody piece. And these Brits were proving hard to get rid of.

At least the smaller one was down for good, his guts spread across the driveway. But that big American bastard was still very much alive and raising hell.

No, he would not run from this marauding cowboy. Timo would kill him and take another piece of Spain back.

The doors shook again at another blast from the shotgun. The doors swung open and the big man stepped into the house. He worked the pump-action and a spent cartridge was ejected onto the tiles.

Ortega and another Loco sprinted through a door and slammed it behind them. Two other Locos ran for the stairs.

Timo scowled at the big American. He raised the axe high. He would not run and be shot in the back. He would die like a man with his weapon in his hand. He watched as the shotgun was pointed at his chest. He pulled the trigger.

Click.

Empty.

An evil grin spread across Timo's face. He stepped towards the big man, hefting the axe. "*Te mato!* What is your name, before I kill you?"

"What? You weren't paying attention outside? The name's Clay Gunn if you gotta know. You gonna kill me, huh? Then you better get to hackin' instead of yakkin'."

Timo sprang forward with a curse and brought the axe down in a wide sweep aiming for Clay's neck. Clay dropped to one knee and caught the blow on the stock of the shotgun. He twisted the weapon to one side in an effort to wrench the axe from his grip. Springing back, Timo angled the axe head to one side and swung again. The second blow whistled past Clay's head and rebounded off the doorjamb.

Timo again stepped back, beckoning Clay forward. He needed room to swing the axe and did not want to risk it sticking in the wooden door. He timed the next swing as Clay stepped forward. The impact detached the pump-action grip and sent it spinning across the room. Timo dodged as the rest of the ruined shotgun flew towards his head like a javelin. The stock of the weapon grazed the side of his face and clattered to the tiles.

"Now you are mine." Timo moved forward double-slashing with the axe. The first traced a horizontal path at head height, which Clay dropped below as Timo knew he would. Without a pause, Timo whipped the axe around in a tight arc and brought it down towards the top of Clay's exposed head.

But the blade never connected. A heavily muscled arm shot out and caught the axe handle mid swing. Timo locked eyes with Clay. He tried to pull the axe away but it felt like the weapon was embedded deep into a tree trunk.

Clay's voice was like a wolf's growl. "This ain't my first rodeo, chump."

Clay didn't try to wrestle for the weapon but kept it locked out and away from his head. His right hand shot out like a piston and seized Timo by the throat. The Loco enforcer gagged as Clay's fingers dug deep into the soft flesh behind his trachea. Timo tried to pull free to no avail. In desperation he grabbed at Clay's throat in return. The man's corded neck felt like a wooden fence post. Timo was left clawing ineffectively at the air between them as Clay straightened out his right arm.

"Know this before you die"—Clay crushed the soft tissue of Timo's throat between his fingers—"I'm going to kill every last one of you."

Timo dropped to his knees as Clay twisted his neck in a tight circle. He struggled desperately to inhale but the pressure was unbearable and his vision began to narrow and blacken. The cartilage in his throat ruptured as Clay suddenly reversed the rotation of his grip.

The last thing Timo heard was Clay's voice. "I'm going to kill every last one of you motherfuckers!"

51

The man guarding the staircase flinched as he heard the distinctive booms of the shotgun. Mateo wanted to run to the front of the villa and join in the action. Yet he had been given very clear orders by Ortega: *Watch the back of the villa! Guard the staircase that leads from the pool deck to the waterfront, thirty feet below. Do not leave it unguarded.*

Mateo jabbed the point of his knife into the top of the wooden corner post. He gave another cursory glance down the staircase. Nothing but sand and sea and shit down there. Barcelo owned a mid-sized boat but it was presently moored five miles up the coast at La Tortuga Marina.

Mateo was one of the newer members of the Locos. He had joined with his cousin, Kino, a few months earlier. Kino had gotten himself killed just a couple of days ago when he and Babi Garcia had tried to petrol bomb the Woo Hoo Club. Mateo was determined not to end the same way as his cousin.

A couple of hollow pops that could have been more gunfire brought his attention back to the front of the house. Damn it. What was happening? The shotgun rang out another couple of times. *Shit!* All the action was at the front of the villa and he was left guarding an overturned truck and a swimming pool that was filled with more shit than a Greek debt agreement.

Agitated, Mateo slammed the point of his knife deep into the post again. He did not see the arm that snaked between his legs from behind. But he did feel the hand as it closed around his testicles in a vice-like grip. Mateo opened his mouth to scream but the arm that passed around his throat in a blur of motion cut off all sound. He grabbed at the arm that was squeezing his neck like an anaconda. The pain in his groin was horrendous. He needed to breathe! Mateo felt his feet lift from the ground as his unseen assailant hoisted him swiftly into the air. Then he was tumbling head first down the wooden staircase. He thrust out his hands in an instinctive effort to break his fall. Something snapped in his shoulder as his body jack-knifed into the wooden planking. Then his legs passed over his head and he felt something twist free in his lower back. Mateo continued to tumble all the way to the sea. Face down, he was already unconscious as the salt water began to fill his throat.

Danny watched the sentry bounce down the staircase. He knew as the man's legs passed over his head like a scorpion that he wasn't coming back. Danny had approached the rear of the villa as planned by following the rugged coastline and emerging up the dockside walkway.

Dez had bravely volunteered to pair up with Clay and, posing as Danny, attended the meeting demanded by Ortega, in order to give Danny an opportunity to launch a surprise attack from the rear. But as some old soldier once said: *The plan was working great until the first shot was fired.* Clay and Dez had gone in unarmed as demanded. They knew the risks, but knew also that Adam was dead if they did otherwise. It was up to Danny to turn the tables by ambush.

Red flashes of fury erupted in Danny's mind as he heard shotgun blasts. The time for subtlety had passed. Either Clay or Dez could be dead!

He wrenched the sentry's blade free from the corner post and drew his Beretta pistol. He would need precision shots inside the villa. He had an AK47 across his back. The pool deck still reeked from the ruptured sewage truck and was deserted. Moving rapidly to the wide patio doors Danny tried the door handle. The door opened silently and Danny stepped inside.

52

A pistol barked twice. A searing pain cut through Larry's upper thigh and a second impact ripped into his right shoulder. Despite the blood pumping across his chest he struggled to bring the rifle around and aim at his attacker. But the younger man was a lot faster and a boot cracked into the side of Larry's face.

"I know you..." The Loco stamped down on the rifle barrel, pinning it to the ground. "You're that old man from the fucking Woo Hoo! You recognise me? Aspanu Perez?"

Larry struggled to free his weapon. Aspanu responded by grinding his other boot heel into Larry's bleeding shoulder. As he writhed in pain the young Loco sent the rifle clattering away with another kick. "All you Brits think you're so tough. Well you don't look so tough now."

Larry closed his eyes momentarily. He had survived multiple conflicts in some of the most turbulent countries in the world. He had survived a devastating roadside bomb and now he was going to die at the hands of a boy who looked no older than twenty.

Aspanu sneered before he swiped his pistol hard across Larry's face. Larry slumped onto his back as the next blow caught him square between the eyes. As a boxer in the army, he had been hit much harder, but that was nearly two decades earlier and he had been two decades fitter. He felt something sting his eyes, obscuring his vision, and knew it was his own blood. Another blow snapped his teeth together, sending his head bouncing off the hard-packed dirt. He felt the younger man plant a knee in his chest, pinning him to the ground.

Larry felt his attacker shift his weight for a brief moment and he saw that the barrel of the pistol dripped blood. His blood.

"Now, I think it is time for you to die." Aspanu spat in Larry's face and pushed the pistol towards his open mouth.

Larry batted the pistol to one side and in a desperate move swung his knees upward and scissored the boy's neck tight between his legs. Larry's prosthetic right leg folded at the knee, tight against the side of Aspanu's throat. Wrapping his left knee around the prosthetic ankle Larry caught the boy in a "triangle choke". The pistol discharged and Larry felt the heat from the muzzle as a bullet whistled past his face. Larry clamped both of his hands around the younger man's wrist and forced the pistol away from his head. He watched the colour of the boy's face change as the blood supply to his brain was cut off. Larry increased the pressure by drawing his heel towards his buttocks. The titanium prosthetic joint proved far more robust than Aspanu's neck. The pistol bucked twice more. Aspanu stared into Larry's face. His panicked eyes and downturned mouth begged for release but Larry held his grip tight, squeezing until his thighs ached. Aspanu's face turned a darker purple and his tongue jutted from his lips.

Only after the pistol dropped from his lifeless fingers did Larry Duke let him slip free.

With a last effort Larry rolled the corpse onto the hard-packed earth. He flopped back into a foetal position. It took several attempts to wipe the blood from his eyes. His left hand probed the gunshot wounds at his shoulder then at his leg. Both hurt like a son of a bitch.

Shit! He had taken two bullets and had his face rearranged. He cast a glance at Aspanu's lifeless face, which stared back accusingly. He spat out a mouth full of bloody saliva. *Still, things could be worse.*

He hoped the Gunn brothers were faring better.

53

Clay regarded the door with contempt. Two Locos had followed their captain through it. Another two had sprinted up the wide sweeping staircase situated at the far left of the lobby.

Clay tried the handle. Locked. He looked at the door, hinges and lock. It was made of solid wood and it would open towards him. That would make it a real bitch to kick down.

With an angry grunt of resignation, he swung the axe. The blade bit into the wood six inches above the handle. Twisting the blade free he swung again and again, with each impact echoing in the tiled lobby. He heard someone yelling; a warning that the American was nearly through the door.

"That's right, you dickwads. I'm coming for you." Clay knew the danger of assaulting the door. If one of his targets got their hands on another firearm they could easily shoot him through the breach. With his pulse hammering in his temples he continued.

A chunk of wood ripped clear from the door, leaving a tangible hole. Clay slammed the axe down several more times until the gap was large enough. Squatting low for a brief moment, he checked that there was no one ready to impale his arm with a blade on the other side. He pushed his arm through the hole and found the simple lock; no bullet or blade found his flesh. A quick twist and it opened.

Through the door, one of the Locos stood at the far end of a hallway. He held a meat cleaver in his raised hand and visibly flinched when he saw the man he'd have to fight. Clay roared and his voice amplified in the confines of the narrow passage.

The Loco launched the cleaver in an overhand throw. Clay dropped low, almost onto his hands and knees, as the heavy blade cut the air above him. The cleaver flew out into the lobby, and Clay grinned maliciously at the now unarmed gangster. He charged forward, axe thrust out, and covered the length of the passageway in a couple of seconds. The Loco attempted to dodge out of Clay's path but the stout wooden handle rammed into his shoulder, knocking him clean off his feet and into the room at the end of the hallway.

Clay followed and the Loco scooted away like a crab on hot sand. They were in a kitchen, which had a large utility island with an oversized sink and gleaming marble work surfaces. Ortega and his men were waiting for him.

On command, two of the younger Locos rushed Clay, armed with knives. One charged straight for him, knife raised high for a downward stab. The other came in low and fast from Clay's right side.

Using the axe handle again as a stave, Clay skipped to his left and rammed the shaft against the first Loco's downward swing. As the blow was blocked he continued the motion and ploughed the stout handle into the base of his skull. The man pitched forward into the path of the second attacker, his arms grabbing out for support. Clay brought the axe down across the back of his head. Both attackers went down. With a roar of fury Clay brought the axe down in another savage blow. The second Loco looked on aghast as his right arm was severed at the elbow.

Clay wiped a dime-sized spot of blood from his face. "Never had a liking for one armed-bandits."

Three more Locos stood between him and Ortega. More than had been standing outside the villa. Clearly they'd kept reinforcements back. Clay stared at the captain. "You know I'm going to save you for last. Make you watch your butt-monkeys get theirs first. Then I'm gonna axe you some questions."

Wincing, Ortega spat out blood-tinged saliva. He gripped a Bushmaster knife. "I think it is you who will die today." His remaining men fanned out into a loose skirmish line and moved towards their target. "Can you stop three at once?"

"Let's find out."

Clay never got the chance. A rapid series of six shots rang out in the kitchen as Danny burst through the door behind Ortega. The three men went down.

Ortega turned and stared at Danny. "But… you're dead."

"My thoughts exactly." Danny's voice was ice.

The bullet caught Ortega below his right eye. His head snapped back and for a second he stood with his arms outstretched like a child playing monsters. Then he collapsed face down, his knife clattering on the tiles.

"That them all?" asked Danny.

Clay shook his head. "I haven't seen Barcelo. But there's at least two more ass-wipes to get upstairs."

"Let's go and have a wee chit-chat. Maybe they know where the head honcho is hiding."

Danny checked the mag in his Beretta. "Three left."

"That's enough for now."

Danny turned, indicating the AK on his back. "Just in case."

54

Danny ascended the stairs as quickly as possible while keeping the pistol aimed up at any prospective targets.

"Left or right?" asked Clay. The landing showed two doors off to their left and four more to the right.

"I'll clear the left. You watch my six. Don't want any nasty surprises."

"Go."

Danny scooted past the first door and reached for the handle with his left hand—when it turned easily he booted the door so hard it clattered against the interior wall of the bedroom beyond. He swept the room, his sight line and weapon moving in accord. Old habits learned long ago. *Wherever the eyes go, the weapon goes.*

"Clear."

Danny entered the second room. "Clear."

Clay stepped aside as his brother crossed the landing and made for the first of the remaining doors.

Repeating the procedure, the room proved empty of gangsters but was an impressive sight to behold. This was obviously Barcelo's master bedroom. It was large enough to ballroom dance in and the entire ceiling above the massive sleigh-ended bed was taken up by a state-of-the-art plasma screen. Danny had never seen a screen so big outside of a cinema. Beautiful dark wood furniture—obviously antique— filled most of the space and a hot tub big enough for at least six people sat to the left of a balcony that overlooked the pool deck and the open sea beyond.

"Nice pad," Clay remarked as he poked his head into the room.

"Three more doors. They've got to be up here somewhere. Let's see who's behind door number four."

Danny moved to the door opposite but before he could do anything one of the remaining Locos burst out from the end door some twenty feet away.

Clay shouted a warning but Danny was already moving.

The attacker raised a Molotov cocktail; the rag stuffed in the neck of the bottle was alight with an orange flame.

Danny squeezed the pistol trigger twice.

The Loco opened his mouth in a silent scream as two crimson flowers bloomed on his abdomen. He faltered but tried once more to throw the incendiary bomb.

Danny's pistol spat out its final bullet.

The bottle exploded, engulfing the bomber in a fountain of yellow flames. The man fell to the floor, scuttling like a crab in a tight circle, arms and legs thrashing, and a horrendous gurgling sound escaped from his throat.

Danny scowled at the sight. He knew all too well what flames did to fragile flesh. The pistol was empty; he reached for the AK to finish the job.

Clay grunted. "Fuck him. That could have been you down there playing crispy critter. Would have been if you hadn't have capped him."

A perfunctory nod from Danny signalled his agreement and he left the Loco to burn. "Let's see if the other guy is a bit more agreeable."

They found the last of the gang huddled in the far corner of a games room. He had hunkered down behind a pool table, his knife held out in front of his blanched face. Danny racked the slide on his battered Beretta pistol for effect. He moved to one side of the pool table as Clay shadowed him on the opposite side.

"Drop the knife or you get a bullet in the kneecap." Danny dipped the muzzle of the pistol twice to illustrate his instructions.

The surviving Loco stared up at the two armed men, his eyes stark and wide. A film of cold perspiration mottled his face. The knife in his extended hand trembled as they drew closer.

"*Hablas friggin' Inglés?*" Danny repeated the motion with his pistol.

The knife dropped to the floor. The remaining Loco soldier held out his hands in a position of surrender.

"Please. Don't kill me!" The man's voice was shrill and spittle flew from his mouth.

Danny kicked the discarded knife to the other side of the room. "I'm going to ask you some questions and I want answers."

"Promise you won't kill me and I'll tell you anything." The cornered man looked like he would sell his soul for clear passage through the doorway behind his two captors.

"You smell that? That's your buddy out there. Kentucky Fried Chicken could serve him with a side of slaw an' fries.

He got off easy." Clay raised his axe as he looked to Danny. "Just let me chop off one of his feet and he'll be singing like a canary."

The Loco pulled his legs in tight to his buttocks as if that would protect him.

"I promise I won't kill you," said Danny. He then added the caveat, "*If* you tell me what I need to know."

"An Englishman's word is his bond. Yes?"

Danny nodded, the edges of his mouth turned down at the corners. "Yes. An Englishman's word is his bond."

The Loco relaxed slightly, uncurling his legs. He avoided looking at Clay who loomed over him. "What do you want to know?"

"Where's your boss—Barcelo?"

The young man took a long breath before answering. "He has gone to the place to meet with his... his..." He struggled to find the correct word in English. "Men who send girls. I don't know who they are. Boss just calls them 'the contacts'."

"Girls?" Danny's mouth turned down at the corners. "You mean the kids from the club?"

"*Si, los pequenos pollos.*"

Clay raised the axe again, his voice rumbling in his chest. "They're not little chickens. They're kids, someone's daughters, you little fucker."

"Where are they meeting these men?" Danny asked.

Clay's knuckles turned white as he raised the axe. "Answer him."

The Loco flinched visibly then mimicked a swimming gesture. "Waterpark."

"Barcelo is having a meet at a waterpark?" Danny

exchanged a look with Clay. "They're meeting in a park full of tourists?"

"No. The park is…" The Loco waved his hands around in loose circles. "No *terminado*."

"Not finished? You mean it's still being built?" asked Danny. "So no tourists. Just Barcelo's little gang and the men that he's meeting?"

"*Si.*"

"Where is it?"

The Loco gave directions to the park in more broken English. When he was satisfied Danny pointed the Beretta at the man's face.

The Loco threw up his hands. "Please! You promised you would not kill me. An Englishman's promise is his word."

"But I'm not English." Danny shook his head slowly. "I'm Scottish."

Click!

The Loco gasped as he realised the pistol was empty.

Clay brought the axe down into the side of the Loco's head, ripping off half his face. The man's mouth formed a tight O before he collapsed back, shuddering against the wall. A burst of arterial blood spurted in a brief explosion of crimson.

"That's for Dez, you son of a bitch."

Danny gritted his teeth, knowing the answer before he even asked the question. "Dez's dead?"

"Never stood a chance. Asshole with the shotgun took him out as soon as we got out of the car."

"He thought he was killing me." Danny hung his head. The last thing he had wanted was any harm to befall Dez or Larry. "Shit! Larry and Adam."

Both brothers rushed back down the stairs. They found Adam, blood-streaked but very much alive. He had made his way over to Clay's car and was slumped with his back against the driver's side. Both of his ruined hands were cradled in his lap and a dark purple bruise framed his left eye. A dark patch stained his trousers at the crotch. The expression on his face was one of abject shame.

"I'm so sorry. I didn't mean for this to happen. I thought I could help." Adam looked down at his hands then at Dez who lay nearby. "Jesus Christ, they killed Dez. This is all my fault."

Danny took Adam's bruised face in his hands, lifting his chin. "This isn't the time for I told you so, but I told you to stay well away."

"I know, I know." Adam began sobbing again. "I got Dez killed."

Clay knelt at Adam's side. He pointed at the bodies of the first Locos that had been killed. "*They* killed Dez... not you."

Danny and Clay lifted Adam to his feet. He emitted a low whine as he cradled his ruined hands.

"Where's your car?" asked Danny.

Adam raised his blood-covered hand and pawed the air. "Up there on the far side of the hill."

"Okay. You're going to the hospital. Larry can drive you. Time for you both to hightail it," said Danny. "I'll call Larry down."

Clay nodded in agreement. "Larry saved my ass back there. He got that fucker with the shotgun good."

Danny grimaced at Dez's bloody corpse. "Not soon enough though."

"He was a stand-up guy but we should never have brought him along, or Larry."

Danny began to wrap Dez in his jacket. "The best laid plans of mice and men…"

"Ay-men to that." Clay scooped up Dez's limp form and placed him with care across the back seats of the car. He touched two fingers to the cook's cooling forehead. "May the next world be better for you than this one was, my friend."

Danny dialled Larry's number. It was answered after four rings.

Larry's voice was little more than a whisper. "I'm down."

55

Larry held up a blood-stained hand as the car screeched to a halt next to him, throwing up a plume of dust and loose stones. Clay was first out of the vehicle. In a second he was carefully cradling his old friend. "Oh shit, Larry."

Larry hung like a child in Clay's massive arms. "Look at the state of me! I'm bleeding at both ends. What a royal cluster-fuck!"

"Easy there while I check you over, see how bad you're hurt."

"I took one in the shoulder and one in the leg. It could have been worse but the little fucker decided he was going to beat me into paste." Larry gestured towards the body of the Loco.

Danny dropped to one knee next to Larry. He pointed to the corpse. "What happened?"

"Guess he thought an old cripple like me didn't have a leg to stand on." Larry tried to wipe some of his blood from his face but only succeeded in wiping the congealed mess down his neck.

"He thought wrong then."

Larry lay quiet as Clay continued to inspect his body for injuries. Blood had soaked both his shirt and trousers to a dark crimson. Larry winced as he was turned onto his side.

"The wound on your leg looks like a through and through but I can't see an exit wound on your shoulder. The slug must still be inside. Can you move your fingers?" asked Clay.

"Crap… that hurts."

"Yeah you got that right. Lie back down." Clay pressed two fingers to the side of Larry's neck.

Danny yanked open the trunk of the car and pulled out a first-aid kit. Ripping it open, he produced a large square of padded gauze.

Larry winced as Danny pulled his shirt down and pressed the absorbent pad against the hole in his shoulder. The blood that oozed from the wound looked like ink against the paleness of his chest. Danny tied a bandage tight around his upper thigh. Blood immediately soaked through the material.

"Ow…" Larry pulled a face.

Danny gave him a tight-lipped smile in response. "Oh shut up, you old hypochondriac. I've had worse wounds in stapler accidents. Keep that pressed tight against your shoulder. We'll get you to the hospital and you're gonna be okay."

Larry gritted his teeth as Clay lifted him and sat him on the back seat of the car. Dez lay propped half against the opposite door; his limbs had a slackness only death can bring. An acrid smell filled the interior of the car. Larry knew exactly what the smell was. He couldn't bring himself to look at his dead friend for more than a second. Larry glanced at Adam who was curled up on the centre of the seat. He too was blood-streaked, his face as pale as sour milk.

Larry nodded at Adam. "Well, here's another fine mess you've gotten me into."

The Laurel and Hardy reference was lost on the young man but caused Danny's mouth to twitch. "Nobody studies the classics anymore."

The moment of morbid levity was broken by Clay's gruff comment. "We've gotta get these two to the hospital. That takes us in the opposite direction from Barcelo. Another chance missed."

"Fuck Barcelo for now. Larry and Adam come first." Danny gave the two injured men a sympathetic look. "We drop them at the ER then we'll see if we can still catch *el jefe* on the hop."

Larry leaned forward. "This car is an automatic. No stick shift to worry about. I can drive this with one hand. I'll get us to the hospital, you need to catch Barcelo and end this."

Clay did not look convinced.

Larry opened the door with his left hand and swung his legs to the ground. "I can make it, Clay. I lived through getting my leg blown off. A couple more bullets in the hide is fuck all."

"What if you pass out while you're driving?"

"You know for a gorilla-sized arsehole with a face full of scars you're still a worry-wart. I'll be fine. To tell you the truth I'm more worried about what Pam is going to do to me for getting myself shot up again. I can feel her teeth in my arse already."

Clay helped Larry into the driver's seat. "You've been shot. You need to get your stories straight for when the cops are called. This is a shit storm. The police are going to be all over it."

Larry spat out a glob of blood. "Adam, Dez and I were out just driving around when these guys dressed in grey camouflage car-jacked us, took our wallets and watches. They left us for dead and took off to the south. I'll make sure the cops aren't looking anywhere near here. I'll just play the amnesia game."

Danny nodded slowly but his face was grim. "What about Dez? He's got family, right?"

"A girlfriend and her seven-year-old boy. Maria and Lorenzo."

"Shit. I should have never let you guys come with us." Danny rubbed a hand across his jaw.

"We came for Adam. Dez knew the risks. I did too. He was a stand-up guy," replied Larry.

"Yeah, but he died posing as me so I could come at them from behind. His blood is on my hands as much as the Locos'." Danny clenched his fists, his knuckles turning white. "This is why I work alone most of the time. People around me tend to die."

"You weren't getting Adam back alive on your own and remember why you're here in the first place. Barcelo and his Locos were going to keep on coming until they got exactly what they wanted." Larry started the engine. "Adam, come up front with me."

Adam did as Larry asked. He turned to Danny and Clay, then nodded at his vehicle, which was still parked further up the hill. "My keys should still be inside. Go an' get that son of a bitch."

Danny nodded in agreement.

"I'll grab anything useful left in the trunk," said Clay.

Larry watched as Danny sprinted to Adam's car and was relieved to hear the vehicle start on the first turn.

"You sure about this?" asked Clay when he was done transferring what was left of their ordnance.

"Godspeed and the devil's right hand," Larry answered. He waved as the Gunn brothers drove off. The old soldier coughed as bile rose in his throat. "All I have to do now is get us to the hospital."

56

Antoni Barcelo stood motionless, his hands clasped behind his back, his weight resting on his left leg. He watched the three identical black Mercedes SUVs slowly wind their way from the front of the empty waterpark towards the visitors' centre.

The approaching Bosnians were, in Barcelo's eyes, a necessary evil. Spain, like the rest of Europe, was now one big open playing field. No one respected the old boundaries or territories any more. The important thing was to decide who to sit at the table with and who to feed to the fish. Outfits such as the Rogue Angels, though still dangerous in their own right, were not in the same league as the Bosnians. Barcelo had recognised both the very real threat and the opportunity presented by the Balkan mafia. They had first made contact nearly two years previously. The introduction had been anything but subtle. Their leader, Josef Golok, had arrived in Ultima with a small entourage of seven soldiers and promptly visited one of the red light houses that operated under the auspices of the Locos.

Barcelo had received a panicked call from Ali, the house

pimp, to say that eight men were standing in the lobby of the whorehouse staring at him in silence. When Barcelo and a dozen of his men had come to investigate, the Bosnians were still there. They all had the same look. Thickset men, short and stocky, heads shaven—apart from a patch on the top of their heads that a cap would easily cover.

Golok stood nearly a head taller than the rest of his men. His face bore horrific scars that told of a near fatal encounter: a deep slash that ran from his forehead to his chin (this effectively divided his face in two, lending him an almost supernatural look). His right ear was missing. The canal that remained looked like an extra nostril, misplaced on the side of his head.

The deal Golok had proposed was simple: every two months or so they would supply a shipment of girls. Barcelo had the option of keeping them and putting them to work as prostitutes or selling them on to another buyer. Both equalled easy money. Barcelo had agreed to the deal and had profited handsomely ever since.

Yet Barcelo knew that Golok and his Balkan mafia could never be taken for granted. Any perceived slight would surely end in bloodshed. Any weakness in the operation would be cut out like a cancer to protect the main body: the Bosnians.

Now Barcelo watched as the three Mercedes rolled to a stop in front of him. Seven of Golok's men stepped out of the vehicles. The AK74s they carried did little to calm his concerns. The enforcers seldom changed; the same hard faces were present at each of their meetings.

Golok stepped from the middle vehicle. He was dark with a tan that he hadn't sported on their previous meeting.

He accepted Barcelo's outstretched hand, shaking it once. "We speak English, yes? My Spanish is still… crap."

Barcelo gave a slight smile. "And my Bosnian is worse."

Golok nodded at the six men that accompanied the Spaniard. "New faces. Where is Ortega? I know Ortega."

"He is taking care of business. These are some of my other men." Barcelo made a circle in the air with his hand. "Up-and-comers."

Golok looked at each of the Locos in turn.

"Shall we?" Barcelo pointed to the visitors' centre behind him. Golok nodded once in response. Not needing to be told, one of Golok's enforcers remained outside with the vehicles while the other six followed Golok and the seven Locos.

They had used the visitors' centre on previous occasions. The building, much like the rest of the park, was unfinished. Multi-coloured wires hung in tangled clumps from the ceiling where light fittings should have been attached. A table sat at the centre of the room. A set of shot glasses and a large bottle of premium vodka awaited them.

Barcelo and Golok sat facing each other at the table while the rest of the men stood behind their respective leaders. The Bosnian traced a circle in the fine layer of dust on the table top. Two dots for eyes and a downturned mouth. He leaned forward, his gaze never wavering from Barcelo for a second. "What happened with the girls?"

Barcelo attempted nonchalance but could feel a heat creeping under his collar. "Some Brits were causing trouble at one of my clubs. They set off some smoke bombs and the fire alarms. Just being a pain in the ass. They're being dealt with as we speak."

"And the girls?" Golok asked again.

He clucked his tongue against the roof of his mouth. "Some of the little bitches made a run for it. Nothing to worry about. I don't think they will be going to the police any time soon."

"But some were caught by the police, yes?"

Barcelo hesitated. There was no point trying to deceive him; that would only make things worse. "Yes."

Golok interlaced his fingers and rested his chin on his knuckles. The relaxed position he adopted left no doubt who was the power player in the room. "The police will connect the girls to you."

"No. The club is not in my name. Nothing there to link the *pollos* back to me."

"Then they will round up your boys," Golok continued, as if he hadn't heard him. "The one with his name above the club door. Then one of the boys will talk. Mention your name; mention *my* name, perhaps. Then we have problem. Big problem."

Barcelo leaned forward to meet the Bosnian's icy gaze. His voice was just above a whisper. "No way. My men are one hundred per cent loyal. They know the rules. No one talks. No one."

Both men remained motionless, scrutinising the other. Barcelo knew this was the tipping point. If Golok desired it, then every one of the Locos in the room would die. Tense seconds ticked by.

"Okay. I trust." The Bosnian stretched his hands into a prayer position, his hands now resting against the long scar that halved his face. "You bring money for next girls?"

Relieved, Barcelo clicked his fingers and one of the Locos

stepped forward and placed the bag of used notes on the table. One of the Bosnians in turn stepped forward and after glancing inside, picked it up and placed it next to Golok's right hand.

"All is good. But remember, when a finger is poisoned it is best to chop off that finger so the rest of the hand is saved."

The Bosnian had asserted his authority in his play but Barcelo knew this was not the time to push back. "Drink?"

Golok smiled and pointed at the bottle of Belvedere. "I will drink."

Barcelo filled two shot glasses to the brim. "To business as usual."

"To *careful* businessmen," countered Golok.

They both drank.

"Another?"

"Another."

Barcelo refilled the glasses. He could see Babi Garcia from the corner of his eye, standing with his hands on his hips. Golok had asserted his status as top dog with his little speech but Barcelo decided to push back just a little. "Golok, this is my man Garcia. He is helping me with the Brits."

Golok motioned to the seat next to Barcelo. "Sit. Have drink."

Garcia came forward and took a seat, accepting a shot glass from his employer.

The Bosnian took his third glass. "Now, tell me more about these Brits."

57

"You think he'll still be there?" Clay peered over the steering wheel.

Danny grunted his response as he inserted a new magazine into his pistol. "If we miss him at the waterpark I'm coming back for him at the villa. Burn the fucking place to the ground with him inside. One way or another Barcelo's time is done."

"I think you're playing my song there, wee one."

Danny gritted his teeth as thoughts of Barcelo's demise filled his mind. "Dez died in my place and that just doesn't sit with me. I'll gonna kill every last one of them."

"Hey, you're preaching to the converted."

"This whole job's going to shit. Larry and Adam hurt, and Dez gone for good."

Clay stared at his brother. "What's the plan? I feel like we're going in blind on this one."

"We are. The truth is we won't know what we're up against until we get there." The last of the Locos had told them of the boss's rendezvous at the empty waterpark but had no knowledge of the men he was meeting. Names? Unknown. Numbers? Unknown. Capability? Unknown. "I guess we'll find out soon enough."

"I guess so. It's a safe bet the gang that runs the skin train won't exactly be boy scouts," said Clay.

"No, but if they're still there, they're going down as well!"

Clay shrugged, offering no contradiction. "In for a penny, in for a pound."

"A pound of flesh in this case."

"Ay-men to that."

Danny smiled briefly. "Jokes aside, our advantage is they don't know we're coming. Downside to that is there could be fifty guys with Uzis, bored and looking for something to shoot."

"Fuck 'em. Remember the Alamo, that's what I say."

"They all died at the Alamo."

"Yeah, but we took a lot of them with us."

"If I see General Santa Anna I'll be sure to bust a cap in his ass for you."

"That's mighty neighbourly of you, little brother." Clay leaned forward in his seat hunching his shoulders slightly. "I wish we had GPS. I've no idea if we're on the right road."

Danny opened the glove compartment and rifled through the contents. An old crumpled hotel brochure, a ballpoint pen and a pack of gum. Nothing of use. Danny took out his phone. Google Maps returned no usable results.

"I can't find directions on my phone. I guess it's because it never officially opened."

"Great, so I just keep driving and hope for the best?" Clay looked left and right and then raised his open palms. "Should have brought that last yahoo with us to point the way."

Danny gave him another wry smile. "Maybe, but it wasn't me who went all *Game of Thrones* on the guy with an axe."

"Ah, forget him. He had it coming. My only regret is I didn't get to kill him twice."

Danny put away his phone. Technology was great when it worked but he had learned long ago never to rely on it. "And you say I'm cold."

The brothers exchanged a look and smiled despite their earlier mood. Danny raised his eyebrows and gave Clay a "what did I tell you" look. He pointed at a weather-beaten sign ahead:

ULTIMAGUA. SLIDE YOUR WAY TO HAPPINESS.
OPENING SUMMER 2012.

Clay slowed the vehicle as he drew closer to the large billboard. The advertisement displayed a cartoon family racing down a water slide side by side. The grins on their faces looked like slices of watermelon. The script on the sign was repeated in Spanish and English. The paint on the supporting arms was faded to an indistinct blue.

"2012? I guess they missed their grand opening day."

"By quite a few years I reckon."

Clay pointed to the bottom of the sign. "Three clicks north. We're nearly there."

"Well let's go have some fun. Perfect place for wet work."

Clay pressed down hard on the accelerator.

58

Babi Garcia sat to the right of his employer. Barcelo looked much more at ease than he had in the previous week. The big man was now laughing and sharing jokes with the leader of the Bosnian crew. Both men were talking in heavily accented English due to it being the closest thing they had to a shared language. But it wasn't the two bosses that held his interest. It was Golok's men. Garcia recognised a quality in them that a lot of Barcelo's Locos did not possess. The men had shark eyes: flat and emotionless, they never stopped moving.

Barcelo recounted a heavily abridged version of the encounters with the brothers. Facts were twisted to make them seem like troublesome interlopers rather than the very dangerous opponents they were proving to be.

The Bosnian leaned back in his seat, drawing his index finger down the long vertical scar that divided his face. "You like my scar, yes?"

Barcelo was mid gulp, the glass of vodka still on his lips, so Garcia answered for them both. "It is very... distinctive."

Golok smirked. "I was a young man in Sarajevo. I

had seen so many bad things already. Terrible things. The Serbs had killed many of my family, my friends. Some just disappeared, but we knew who had taken them. I fought back alongside my friends, but they just kept coming. They were better armed than us and they were like ants. You killed one and another ten took his place."

Garcia looked directly at the disfiguring scar.

"But do you know what was worse than the Serbs?" Golok said. "The so-called peacekeeping forces that came later. The British, Norwegians and Americans strolled in like they owned our country expecting us to kiss their asses. I was in the market square with my younger sister when Serb mortars began to land. They killed my sister and took this." Golok brushed his fingers past his exposed ear canal.

Garcia sipped slowly on his glass of vodka. He had heard many times of the ethnic cleansing perpetrated during the war. The horrific tales of rape and torture. He stifled a smile; he was sorry he had missed it.

The Bosnian held out his glass to be filled and continued. His eyes closed as he spoke. "One of the mortars landed right at my sister's feet. There wasn't enough left of her to bury. I staggered home covered in what was left of my sister to get my father. On the way I ran into some American soldiers. I went to them with my hands out. They pointed their rifles at me, shouting and cursing. I tried to ask them for help but one of them knocked me down and kicked me. As I was standing up he hit me in the face with a trench shovel, one of the folding kind. Left me for dead. I could hear them laughing as they walked away. Laughing like they were at a baseball game or something. *Stee-rike one.* I lay at the side of the road for I don't know how long. Left for dead. But... I did not die."

"So you're not a big fan of the Yanks then?" Garcia asked. Barcelo kicked his foot under the table.

Golok slowly opened his eyes and ran his index finger down the length of his scar. "They're not at the top of my list, no," he said, nodding at Barcelo and Garcia in turn. "I think we are done here. The next girls will arrive on schedule. Make sure there are no more... incidents."

Barcelo stood up, extending his hand. Golok reciprocated. A couple of the Locos who had stood in silence throughout the meeting nodded at the Bosnians in farewell. They were rewarded with steely glares and tight lips.

59

The shadows cast by the surrounding palm trees stretched out like spectral fingers as the dawn rose. The palms flanked the main gates of the park, which formed an archway comprised of large concrete gateposts and a curving sign overhead. Clay guided the car through the open gates.

"Where do you think he'll be?" asked Clay. The unfinished waterpark stretched out with both unsurfaced tracks and paved walkways cutting paths in various directions.

Danny tapped the Beretta lightly against his knuckles. "Drive straight ahead, we'll see if we can spot any cars. Go slow and easy, there may be lookouts."

Loose gravel crunched beneath the tyres as the vehicle followed the widest of the paths. Directly ahead stood the park's centrepiece: a towering volcano. Skeletal framework towers were dotted around it. Some of the towers had connecting half tubes that formed the planned water slides. Few of these were fully finished. A couple of the towers had stairways that curled their way from the ground to the slide's apex. A wide concrete trench formed a perimeter around the interior portion of the park. A lazy river, Clay guessed. Every waterpark seemed to have one. Other sloping tracks of half pipe cut their way through the park's artificial hills. Some of the channels were only a couple of feet wide while others looked wide enough for large family rafts. Palm trees, still shored up by supporting wooden stanchions until their roots found purchase, stood neglected, fronds the colour of summer straw swaying in the gentle breeze.

As Clay drove deeper into the park they passed another large sign. This showed an artist's map of the park with each of the four main areas highlighted in a different colour. The four main quadrants to the park surrounded the volcano. DINOLAND, CREEPY CAVERNS, PIRATES OF THE MEDITERRANEAN and KAPTAIN KORTEZ'S KIDZONE were coloured red, blue, green and yellow.

The brothers exchanged a glance.

Danny shook his head. "Please don't let me die in friggin' KAPTAIN KORTEZ'S KIDZONE. They'd never let me into heaven."

Clay snorted a laugh. "Yeah right. Like you're gettin' into heaven anyways."

Danny looked like he was about to retort when he stiffened in his seat. "There!"

Three identical black SUVs were parked in front of a single-storey building. There were another couple of vehicles parked further back, partly obscured by the three Mercedes. A familiar cold fire began to burn in the pit of Clay's stomach.

Clay steered the Toyota slowly towards the parked cars. Exhaling sharply through his nose like a boxer, Clay warned, "Knuckle up, we've got a watchman."

The man's head snapped up as he heard the rumble of

the approaching engine. The rifle he carried was pressed tight into his shoulder and he started moving towards the vehicle in a low scuttling gait.

Clay could tell by the man's attire—a smart dark suit and white shirt—that he wasn't one of Barcelo's Locos. Those guys only seemed to wear crappy army surplus.

"Stop the car," said Danny.

Clay pressed down on the brakes. Danny opened the glove box and scooped up the hotel brochure he'd looked at earlier.

The man with the rifle shouted at Danny as he climbed from the car. His voice was heavily accented, something Eastern European. "Private property. Get out!"

"Hey, buddy, can you tell me how to get to…"

The man hesitated for a moment, his face relaxing. "Leave." He hooked his thumb towards the park gates.

"Hey, what's that accent? Russian?" Danny asked. "Sounds sexy."

"Bosnian. Now fuck off." The man raised his gun.

The Beretta that Danny had concealed behind the brochure barked once, punching a hole through the paper. The sound echoed around the empty park. The man's head snapped back. He fell dead to the ground.

"So much for the element of surprise," Clay said. "Everything seems stacked against us on this one."

Danny spoke quickly through clenched teeth. "Friggin' great. Bosnians. That's who ships the girls through to Barcelo. No surprises there I suppose."

"What do you want to do?" asked Clay with grim resolve.

"I can see four vehicles from here. Up to five men per vehicle, that's a possible twenty men. If they are Bosnian, they will be well-armed and not bullet shy. Oh, shit, here they come!"

Six suited men raced from the building in tight formation. Their faces looked as mean as the hardware they carried.

Danny raced forward and snatched up the dead man's weapon. He was almost back inside when the first of the bullets began to rip through the car.

60

As was customary, the Bosnians had begun to leave the meeting first. The unmistakable sound of a single gunshot changed that in an instant. The six Kalashnikov assault rifles snapped into readiness as one. All were pointed at the Locos. Garcia braced, ready for trouble.

Barcelo threw up his hands in surrender. "What is this?"

"One shot." Golok spoke through clenched teeth. "Not my man's weapon."

"I don't know who's out there shooting but it's not my men." As Barcelo spoke the words, he knew. "The Brits!"

Golok's men raced from the building, weapons high, shoulders rounded, bodies bent slightly forward as they moved. Their boss picked up the bag of cash and followed his team outside.

Barcelo turned to Babi Garcia, his face reddening. "Give me your pistol!"

Garcia didn't move. He didn't much feel like giving up his weapon.

"This is no time for your shit, Babi. Give me a fucking gun."

Garcia drew his pistol from his shoulder rig. The Kimber Eclipse was both a beautiful and efficient weapon. He raised the weapon slowly until it pointed at his employer's stomach then smiled.

The Bosnians were already out of the door.

Barcelo held out his hand. "Gun!"

Garcia clucked his tongue against the roof of his mouth but rotated the pistol and handed it over butt first. "I want it back."

His boss grunted an approximation of thanks and lumbered after the Bosnian outfit. The other four Locos followed close behind their boss.

Garcia drew his backup weapon: a compact Kimber Super Carry Ultra HD. Smaller and lighter than the Eclipse he'd given Barcelo, the SCU carried the same .45 ACP rounds. Both were deadly efficient weapons. He followed the Locos out.

The Bosnians had opened fire on a single vehicle; the rear and side windows had already shattered and it bounced wildly as it reversed at top speed. There were two men, both hunched low in the front seats of the fleeing vehicle. The man in the passenger seat was the same one Garcia had fought with outside the Woo Hoo Club. Garcia could see his face, growling like a pit bull in a death match. The illuminated sights of his Kimber lined up with the Brit's head.

One shot. *Boom!*

The passenger-side window exploded and the man's head snapped down and out of sight.

61

Danny cursed as he felt a bullet tug at the hair on the top of his head. He twisted and began to raise his stolen weapon. *Shit*, the sling had caught around something at the bottom of his seat. Danny leaned forward, tugging hard to extricate the assault rifle. The vehicle again bucked as Clay powered over an obstruction. Danny lurched low in his seat. The window next to his head exploded inward and he felt a scalding pain bite across the back of his head.

As Clay finally brought the car back under control and raced forward, Danny, ignoring the pain in his scalp, angled the Kalashnikov horizontally over his shoulder and squeezed the trigger. The distinctive rattle from the AK74 added to the assault on his ears. He knew they would ring with tinnitus for hours, *if* he survived.

Clay wrenched the steering wheel to the left and raced down a side road. "Well, that went well."

Danny reached around to the back of his head; his hand came away red. Clay reached for his brother.

"I'm okay. Hurts like a son of a bitch though."

"Crap. What're we doin'? Stayin' or runnin'?"

Danny scowled at his bloody palm. The old axiom of not biting off more than one can chew sprang to mind. "I think we need to fuck off for now. They've got too many guns and they don't look like half-arsed yahoos. We need to find an advantage."

"Warp drive it is. Hang on to your jockstrap. We'll have to drive past them again." Clay kept the accelerator pedal floored as he swung the now perforated Toyota in a tight circle back towards the park entrance. Danny again pivoted in his seat and opened up with a series of three-round bursts with the AK74 at the Bosnian skirmish line.

The Bosnians scooted for cover but continued to return disciplined fire. The Toyota slewed to one side as one of the back tyres was shredded by bullets.

Danny felt the rear of the damaged car veer as traction was lost. The Toyota skidded wildly as the wheel rim bit into the road surface. Clay struggled to bring the fishtailing vehicle under control, dodging to one side as the driver's window was shattered, tiny squares of glass peppering his face. Then the second rear tyre died with an angry exhalation. Bright sparks flew into the air as the wheel rims cut into the concrete and shale of the road.

"Holy crap! Plan B!" Clay's voice was barely audible above the screeching vehicle and the bullets that continued to shred the car. "Shortcut."

Clay drove through a gap between two of the nearest palm trees. The Toyota cut through the dying foliage, leaving a tell-tale swath behind them. The windscreen spider-webbed as a bullet ripped through the gap between the brothers.

Danny curled up his legs as he rounded his spine,

scooting even lower in his seat. He stamped out with both feet knocking most of the ruined windshield clear. The wind whipped through the gaping hole. Danny swore under his breath. Cutting through the undergrowth was pretty dire as far as escape plans went but was preferable to offering their attackers a clear target.

They breached the side of one of the wide half pipes and suddenly the Toyota was airborne. The car crunched down into the concrete channel nose first with another ungodly squeal of protesting metal. More sparks, black smoke and the sound of shearing bolts, and the rear bumper was jettisoned as the vehicle set off down the steep hill. The Toyota traversed the incline like an out-of-control bobsleigh with a cascade of high-flying sparks in their wake.

Clay looked at his brother, the scars on his face crinkled by a tight smile. "Maybe we should have brought two cars?"

"You think?" Danny's attention was focused to the rear as he watched for pursuers. The Toyota was peeling around a curve in the downhill raft run; the driver-side door buckled inward slightly as the vehicle met the concrete wall at an awkward angle, but kept on moving. The car slewed from side to side as it followed the predetermined path of the raft run. Clay wrestled to hold the steering wheel in place but even with his guidance the vehicle did its own thing. The car rode high on the wall to one side then came down with a shudder only to pitch up tight against the opposite wall. Each impact seemed to dislodge another piece of the vehicle, leaving a sporadic trail of motor parts behind them.

"I'm glad this ain't a rental!"

Danny laughed despite the dire situation. "Yeah, you'd

be shafted for getting your deposit back."

"I hear that!" Clay replied through gritted teeth. "Oh, crap! Hang on."

Danny pivoted and looked out the shattered windscreen. The raft run they were barrelling down split into two paths some forty feet away. When filled with a river of gushing water, a raft would bounce harmlessly against the dividing wall and continue on down one of the two available routes. The Toyota, however, was set in its course, heading directly for the V-shaped stanchion that served as a divider. Clay slammed his foot down on the brake pedal, wrenching the steering wheel hard to the left. The Toyota again fishtailed but the brakes had little effect as the weight and inertia carried the dying vehicle into the unyielding barrier.

The Gunn brothers hunched low in their seats, chins tucked tight into their shoulders. Danny snatched at the seatbelt. Too late. Brakes still squealing, the battered car smashed into the immoveable wedge. The airbag exploded in Clay's face, which he protected by hastily crossing his arms.

The vehicle lifted off the ground and threatened to be catapulted up and over the barrier. Both men were slammed first into the roof then back into their seats with savage force. As the car lurched upwards, Danny, whose side of the car had taken the brunt of the crash, felt his shoulder crack hard against the passenger door as it buckled inwards. The ruined vehicle landed with a sickening crunch and what little remained of the windscreen was sent over both men as a shower of tiny squares of glass. Both the hood and trunk lids now sat open at strange angles. Black smoke escaped from the engine and the smell of burning oil and shredded tyres filled the interior.

Danny looked to his older sibling. Spitting out a square of blood-tinged glass, he asked, "You okay?"

Clay looked dazed but nodded in the affirmative. The Texan gripped the door handle and pushed, but the door moved less than two inches, the frame buckled into a closed position. Clay pivoted and stamped out with both feet. The jammed door opened six inches. He kicked out again, this time with a little more leverage. The door bent outward on his second kick and sprang fully open on his third assault.

Danny climbed through the shattered windscreen, sliding butt first over the crumpled hood, the stolen rifle tucked tight under his arm, pistol in hand. A fierce ringing filled his ears. He leaned forward and slowly shook his head in an effort to regain his wavering equilibrium. Blood seeped from a shallow laceration over his right cheekbone. He could taste the familiar copper tang of blood in his mouth. "Next time, I'm driving…"

Clay raised a finger in protest when the sound of racing engines interrupted. "Crap. They're right on our tail."

Danny passed the AK74 to Clay. "Watch my back."

Clay crouched alongside the smoking wreck of the car as the sound of the approaching engines grew louder and louder. "Hurry!"

Danny began to pull items from the trunk: the shoulder bag he'd loaded earlier in the day and the two rifles. The long-barrelled SLR was wedged, the sling trapped between concertinaed metal. He pulled with all of his strength but it held fast and there was no time to cut it free. He abandoned the weapon. The older model Kalashnikov came free after a single tug.

Danny looked back up the course of the raft run. Debris

was scattered as far up the slope as he could see. Spare ammunition flung from the trunk glinted, taunting him. *Damn it. No time!*

Clay shouted a warning. "We gotta move."

As if to illustrate the urgency of the point, the first black Mercedes burst through the treeline fifty yards up the hill. Even with the necessary weaving between the palm trees the Mercedes would be on them in no time.

Danny's voice was razor sharp. "Run!"

62

Golok and his Bosnians had decimated the old Toyota into Swiss cheese in seconds. But the Brits were tricky to be sure. No sooner had the rear tyres been blown out they surprised their pursuers by tearing through a gap in the treeline and disappearing into one of the wide concrete channels.

Barcelo's face was crimson with rage. The Brits had again ambushed him, causing him untold embarrassment in front of the Bosnians. The look that Golok had given him was half dismissal, half contempt. Barcelo yelled at his men, waving in the direction of the raft run. "Get after them!"

The Locos stared back. They had no guns to fight with.

Golok's team ignored the Spaniards and boarded their Mercedes SUVs as if they had practised the high-speed manoeuvre many times. Within seconds they had followed the damaged Toyota. But where the bullet-riddled car had plunged into the dry water run, the Bosnians stayed on the high ground, following the twisting path of the downhill slide easily. The boxy SUVs dodged the bigger of the standing trees but simply crushed any smaller shrubs under the wide wheels. Within thirty seconds of the Toyota careening into the channel there came an unmistakable sound of a vehicle crashing into something immovable. Barcelo yelled again at his men. "Get down there! Stay up above the slide. If the Brits try to climb out, you kill them!"

At this command the Locos split into two groups. Three followed Barcelo on one side of the channel while the other two followed Babi Garcia at a run on the opposite side.

Leaving the Locos behind them, the Bosnians closed on their target. The plume of black smoke emerging from the channel betrayed their location for all to see.

From the passenger seat of his Mercedes, Golok pointed to the Toyota, which was now little more than scrap. He could see two men. One, the smaller and darker of the two, had his head inside the trunk. A much larger man was crouched down at the side of the vehicle, an AK in his hands. The big man was shouting something. Then both men, now armed, took off at full tilt down the left fork of the channel. Golok's vehicles were on the high ground on the far right of the path.

The second and third SUVs came to a stop and Golok barked new orders to his team. They obeyed without hesitation. The three Bosnians from the second vehicle and two from the third gave pursuit on foot, moving rapidly out of sight through the brittle foliage. Golok's driver swung the sleek vehicle in a wide arc and drove back up the hill.

* * *

Trailing behind, Garcia plus one of the younger Locos vaulted to the far side of the channel. Two more slipped down into the base of the raft run while the two remaining men stayed at their boss's side.

Barcelo was in pain. The fight with the biker had been a savage encounter and his injuries were now beginning to burn with a renewed intensity. As he set off he knew within seconds he would not be able to keep up with his team and certainly not with the rugged Bosnians who had disappeared down the hill in seconds. Each faltering step he took sent a new stab of agony through his knee. Staggering to one side, his joint nearly collapsing beneath him, he cursed loudly. The younger of the two Locos looked back at his boss, unsure of what to do.

Barcelo waved the men away. "Go. Get after them. I'll be fine. I'll circle back and make sure they don't get behind us."

"Yes, boss…" he replied. "Be careful."

Raising the Kimber pistol in front of his face, Barcelo growled his response. "I'll be fine. I'll kill both of those bastards on my own if I have to."

63

Clay ran ahead of his brother, his feet pounding loudly against the concrete of the raft run. Every five seconds or so Danny cast a glance over his shoulder but all he could hear was the echoing retorts from Clay's heavy footsteps. Damn, he was big and strong but he could never be accused of being graceful.

Clay looked back at his brother, his face red and beaded with sweat. "I'm getting sick of running."

Danny weighed their options as they continued to follow the course of the curving raft run. The path snaked one way then another. Some were lazy arcs while others were sharp cambers, each turn designed to send a raft full of soaking patrons twisting and turning unpredictably. But the unpredictable course worked in their favour as the direct line of sight was relatively short. If the enemy couldn't see them, they couldn't shoot them. That worked well if you knew the enemy was behind you. But the chance of running blind into an ambush was also a very real and deadly risk.

"There!" Danny pointed to an overturned wheelbarrow which lay discarded against the wall of a shallow curve.

"Time to get off this hamster wheel."

"Ay-men to that."

Clay vaulted up the wall using the wheelbarrow as an impromptu step. He reached and hauled Danny up as if he weighed nothing. No sooner had they climbed from the channel than the distinctive metallic chatter of the Kalashnikov rifles began to sound again. Danny ducked low and returned fire with a tight three-round burst.

At the same moment Clay recoiled as a round from the Bosnians nipped a sliver of skin from his left forearm. He raised his AK and returned fire, dodging behind the bole of a wide palm tree.

Danny quickly stepped back when he felt a bullet fly uncomfortably close to his face but his right heel wedged against the raised edge of the raft run. For a second he felt weightless as his balance sought to correct itself. He reached out with his free hand, grasping at a nearby tree. The tinder-dry sapling disintegrated in his fist and he pitched backwards into the channel once more. Landing painfully with one knee folded beneath him and the other in the air, his back slammed hard into the unyielding half pipe. Only by keeping his chin tucked tight to his chest was he able to avoid knocking himself unconscious. The impact knocked the air from his lungs and sent an angry pain raging from his folded knee joint. His Beretta pistol, now tucked into his waistband, ground painfully into his hip. As he raised his head a man-shaped blur appeared in the channel.

The *blur* was raising his weapon. Danny fired from his awkward sitting position. The short but deadly burst from his battered AK47 caught the man in the thighs. The

Bosnian, still running full tilt, was pitched into a forward dive as Danny's bullets cut through the muscles of his legs. The man landed heavily on his face and the momentum of his downhill run caused him to continue into an ungraceful forward roll, leaving him sprawled sideways across the base of the channel. Another tight burst from Danny's rifle ripped holes in the man's back.

Danny could hear the exchange of fire from above his position. He knew Clay could hold his own but both men were at a real disadvantage. They were outnumbered and outgunned. Forcing himself to his feet, he snatched up the dead man's weapon. It was another Kalashnikov, an AK74. The same model he'd passed to Clay. It was a safe bet that the rest of the roughnecks were carrying the same. Even if each man had only one magazine, that still amounted to a lot of firepower.

Leaning his older AK47 against the wall of the channel, Danny ejected the 74's magazine to check its payload. He was midway through slamming the mag back into position when another man sprang into view above him.

Time seemed to distort.

Danny turned, palming the magazine into place.

The man angled his weapon down at Danny.

Danny's hand sought the trigger of the 74.

The gunman opened fire.

64

"Come get some!" Clay's furious challenge was drowned by the deafening exchange of bullets. The palm tree had provided scant cover and he had been forced to sprint for the better option of a wide metallic box some fifteen feet away. The dark-green cube stood just short of four feet square and had a series of slanted ventilation slots near the top. A large yellow sign on the side, sun bleached like everything else in the park, warned of lethal electric shock if opened.

"Danger of death, story of my life." Clay hunkered his bulky frame behind the substation. A series of rapid shots sent sparks flying from the unit. Clay angled to the right side of the cube and caught sight of the man chasing him down. No, two men. Another had appeared on the far side of the channel.

Clay flinched as bullets shredded the ground in front of Danny. With a yelp, the younger Gunn brother pitched backwards into the raft run.

Clay squeezed the trigger. The closest of his pursuers dodged behind the same tree Clay had just abandoned. The Texan pivoted and dropped to his knee at the other side of the cube. The second man was turning his weapon down into the raft run. He began to fire.

"Danny!" Clay's AK spat fire and the man doubled over, bullets punching crimson holes through his lower abdomen. The man clamped his finger tight on the trigger of his rifle, spraying a hail of bullets into the channel. Then the eviscerated gunman pitched head first into the water slide.

Clay gave out a loud grunt in satisfaction. But any celebration was momentary as the other gunman unleashed a bullet storm in Clay's direction. The substation shuddered as bullets cut through the exterior and ricocheted off the machinery hidden inside. Dodging again to the opposite side, Clay raised his weapon tight to his shoulder. The man was still behind the palm tree. The dark-silver barrel of his identical AK74 angled out from the bullet-riddled tree trunk.

A story Danny had told him years before sprang into Clay's mind. Would it work again? Worth a shot…

The Texan stooped and snatched up a fist-sized rock. He threw the stone overhand at the man's position. "Grenade!"

The Bosnian sprang from cover, eyes wide, as the rock landed just behind him and Clay opened fire. The man continued sideways as the rattling burst from the Texan's rifle shredded his heart and lungs. He dropped to his knees, his hands forming claws at his chest. The man's mouth worked like a fish on a riverbank and a vomit of frothy blood escaped from his throat.

Clay guessed at the sentiment. "Yeah, and the horse you rode in on!"

After making sure there were no other gunmen in sight,

Clay raced back to the raft run. He peered down, a knot forming in his gut.

Danny stared up at him through the iron sights of his weapon. On seeing Clay's worried expression, he grinned and spoke with his best Sean Connery voice. "Well, you're a shite for shore eyes."

"Dumbass," said Clay, extending his hand to haul his brother out of the channel for a second time.

Danny didn't take it. He paused, blowing out his cheeks. "Good timing though. That ass-wipe had me dead in his sights."

"All part of the service." Clay tipped the brim of an imaginary hat. "If I can't off someone for my little brother…"

"Just a second," said Danny. He trotted over to the two dead men who lay in the concrete curve. Ignoring the dark crimson ribbon that now trickled its way down the slope, he ejected the magazines from the fallen weapons. "The newer model Kalashnikovs are chambered for different ammo than the AK47s but spares for the 74s will come in very handy." He pushed one clip into his pocket and passed up the older model Kalashnikov. He then reached up for Clay's hand.

After accepting the second spare mag for the AK74, Clay raised his chin to his left then to his right. "So, do we backpedal, or keep goin' this-a-way?" He visualised the park map he'd seen on the faded sign near the entrance.

"We're here now," Danny said. "We might as well play."

Clay nodded as he glanced at the blood on his forearm. "Or we could keep going in a straight line. We'd reach the perimeter sooner or later. Climb the fence and be home for margaritas before bedtime."

"That sounds like sensible advice coming from a trouble-making Texan." Danny gave a lopsided smile. "But you know that little thing inside your head that stops you doing or saying things you know you shouldn't. Well, mine doesn't seem to be working at the moment."

"Fine by me. I still have a bullet or two left to use up anyway."

"Good, because I can hear more of those fuckers heading this way," said Danny.

Seconds after the brothers had ducked back behind the substation a group of three Locos broke into view. All three men were brandishing knives, which glinted sparks of orange in the early dawn sun. As they reached the dead Bosnians they skidded to a halt. There was a rapid exchange of heated words, which ended with the tallest of the men stabbing the air with his knife and demanding that they continue.

Behind the bullet-riddled cube, Danny motioned for Clay to stay low. The Locos were out of breath and their heavy footsteps announced their proximity easily. Danny allowed the first man to pass the cube then leaned out slightly from behind his vantage point. As the next two men stepped into view he breathed out slowly, relaxing, and squeezed the trigger three times in quick succession. Even if he missed the heart the hypovolaemic shock would render them as good as dead. But he knew there was no missing at this range. *Crack, crack, crack!*

All three men dropped simultaneously, face down, as the three single shots hit home. Each man bore an identical wound: a neat hole just below his left shoulder blade.

As the three men lay twitching in the dirt the man in the middle of the triangle feebly raised his knife in Danny's direction. There was little chance of it being thrown but another shot from the AK47 removed that chance and a portion of the defiant gangster's cranium. Danny angled the rifle towards the other Locos but the workhorse weapon proved empty. "Never enough bullets."

"When this is over we need to talk." Clay's voice was one of disapproval.

Danny scowled at his brother. "I hope you're not gonna give me any crap about shooting them in the back."

"No. I mean about you showing off. Three goons capped like that wins you a friggin' coconut. Makes me feel... inadequate."

Danny glanced down at the dead bodies that littered the ground. His mouth twitched into a bitter smile. "You promised Dez that we'd kill them all. So let's get to it."

"Again, which way?"

Danny pointed to the park's centrepiece. "Let's head for the volcano."

It was Clay's turn to smile. "Yeah, because nothing bad ever happens in a volcano."

"Move it or lose it, ya big ape."

65

Barcelo leaned against the low wall for support. The expensive suit he wore was now stained with sweat and dust. The pain in his knee was sending nausea-inducing spears through his nervous system. He was sure that something was broken in there. His nose and face throbbed in time with the pounding of his heart. Sweat beaded his face, stinging his eyes.

Swearing, he forced himself to move.

Golok and his men were out there chasing down the Brits. If by chance they doubled back he wanted to be ready, not caught wheezing and walking like an arthritic ape. Using one hand for support, he gripped the top of the wall. He could feel the hammering of his heart against the pistol he had taken from Garcia as he pressed it tight against his chest.

The hatred he felt for the two renegades was unbridled and he knew that today was win or lose everything. Leaning back against the wall for a moment he sucked in deep breaths through his mouth.

A week ago everything had been sweet. The collection business was running smoothly, the protection money from the other businesses and the slow but steady muscling of the foreigners was helping him build his empire nicely. Nothing could be traced back to him directly; all of the procured bars, cafés and clubs were now owned by younger members of his outfit. He had learned that lesson early. If the law ever decided to follow the money trail, as he knew it would, he had built in a series of effective firebreaks. Nothing owned in his name meant that there would be nothing to come back on him.

But since those two troublemakers had arrived—*were there really only two of them?*—everything had turned to donkey shit. The Woo Hoo Club had been the start of it all. Once the Brits were dead and gone he would send his men back a final time and take the business. He had offered them a fair price in the beginning but now they would hand over the deeds while begging for their lives.

But they had to catch the Brits first.

The staccato rattle from automatic weapons made him look up sharply. Not just one burst, but several sporadic exchanges. He hoped that Golok's Bosnians had only kneecapped those bastards; he would love a chance to end them both himself. But he knew the chance of Golok's bloodhounds bringing them back alive was slim. The Bosnians were nothing if not thorough.

Another burst of gunfire, then another. A single choked scream of pain then it was quiet again. *Have they caught them already?*

Then another series of shots. Popping like fireworks. *Crack, crack, crack.*

Several seconds of silence followed. The only sound was that of Golok's Mercedes. The SUV was not in sight but the powerful engine echoed throughout the empty waterpark.

One more shot cut through the air. *Crack!*

Were the Brits dead?

Barcelo flinched as the cell phone in his breast pocket warbled. He closed his eyes as he fumbled for the phone with his free hand. Stupid mistakes like not having your phone on silent would get you killed. When he answered his voice was just above a whisper. He was sure the Brits were at the other side of the park by now, and maybe dead, but saw no sense in tempting fate any further. "Yes?"

Garcia's voice had the same conspiratorial tone. "Three of your men are dead."

A new pain took up residence behind Barcelo's eyes. "Three?"

"The Brits are biting back."

"Are you enjoying this, Babi?" Barcelo's knuckles turned white as he gripped his pistol.

"What's not to enjoy? I would have been one of our three, but I swapped places on the way down the hill. Dumb luck, but I'm still alive and kicking. If it's any consolation three of the Bosnians are down as well."

"That doesn't help at all. Keep after them."

"I've got another plan. I'm going to hit them where they least expect it. I'll see you later."

"Babi… Babi?"

But Garcia had terminated the call.

66

The sound of the Mercedes' engine rumbled ominously as it traced a circular path, avoiding the sunken channels and frameworks of the slides. Danny looked again at the four-storey volcano that served as the centrepiece of the park. The rumbling of the engine provided the momentary illusion of the volcano preparing to erupt. But the faux volcano served another purpose. Many parks housed the essential water pumps, generators and maintenance bays inside and under such constructions. It would provide both cover and an opportunity to strike back effectively.

He and Clay ran at a pace a little faster than jogging speed, cutting through the foliage in a straight line. Danny had abandoned the now empty AK47, instead carrying one of the stolen 74s.

Clay dropped to one knee, weapon held high, as the sound of the Mercedes' engine grew louder again. The vehicle was not in sight but the powerful engine echoed from multiple directions. Danny paused and tilted his head to one side, eyes closed, but he couldn't identify from which direction the rumbling came. The SUV seemed to be circling them like a jungle predator. Tense seconds seemed to elongate as they waited in silence, anticipating gunfire. Then it was quiet again. The vehicle had either moved beyond earshot or the engine had been turned off.

"Keep moving," Danny prompted. This spurred Clay back into motion. He again set off with his loping run. A dark patch of sweat marked out a wide inverted triangle on the back of Clay's shirt.

Danny paused at the base of a set of winding steps. The ascending stairs wound their way around a central structure that resembled a pylon. Steps that were designed to let tourists climb to the apex of the tower in order to ride the attached water slide.

An ornate but weathered signpost opposite the slide declared that they were entering the area of the park known as CREEPY CAVERNS. Some twenty feet away from the open stairs loomed a faux cave entrance. Pointed stalactites gave the sculptured cave the appearance of monstrous yawning jaws. The outer walls had already been tagged with multicoloured graffiti. A large set of eyes, complete with frowning bushy eyebrows peered over the name "Pez".

Clay looked back at his brother. He seemed about to ask why Danny had stopped but Danny waved him into silence.

Someone was speaking. The words were indecipherable but the sentiment was unmistakable. The owner of the voice stood some thirty feet away on the footpath that led to both the caverns and the ride steps.

The man looked almost identical to the other suited gunmen they had already encountered. Thick-necked, severe haircut, hard eyes and an AK held at port arms. In his left hand he held a cell phone. The man was nodding and looking from side to side as he talked. With a final affirmation he ended the call and started towards the steps.

Danny felt sure he knew what the man was going to do: he was heading for the high ground so that he would be in a superior position from which to spot the targets for the remaining soldiers in the Mercedes. It was Warfare 101.

Danny scowled. He wasn't about to let that happen. He eased himself from his position of cover and as the man moved closer Danny lined him up in the sights of his weapon. The gunman was looking upwards to the top of the tower.

The stock of the Kalashnikov was cool against the right side of Danny's face. The distinctive smell of the weapon filled his nose. He stayed close to the structure, motionless, not wanting to give the approaching man any chance to retaliate.

The man stepped closer. Danny aimed between two of the horizontal steps. The gap was a little more than eight inches. More than enough.

Another step closer.

"Danny!" Clay's voice cut through the air as another of the gunmen, grim-faced and determined, sprang from cover from atop the entrance of the cavern and immediately opened fire. Only the rising blur of motion in Clay's peripheral vision prevented Danny from being shredded by the onslaught.

Clay returned a volley as Danny ducked back behind the protection of the stanchion post. The man on the top of the cavern dodged to one side as he switched his aim towards Clay. Both men exchanged a three-round burst, like furious boxers using the jab to test out the other's defences.

Danny couldn't see the first man anymore. Ducking low and making himself as small a target as possible, he scooted back to his left. The gunman had not moved towards the cavern entrance—too much ground to cover. He could have retreated but Danny had seen many of their ilk. These men did not run away. That left one option. The man was trying to flank them and he had moved fast. Danny knew he would hit them from a side-on position. It was a classic pincer movement taught to every soldier during basic battlefield training; engage the enemy from the front and while their attention was held, bite into them from their blind side.

The surrounding bushes and trees were desiccated but were still dense in parts. More than dense enough to conceal a stealthy approach. Danny hefted his rifle. *How many rounds were left? Probably not enough.* Danny moved.

Another flurry of bullets cut the air between the cavern crest and Clay, who had moved up the side of the pathway. Danny risked a glance in Clay's direction. He was working his way backwards in a semi-crouch. Clay hopped over a crop of low bushes and moved behind a seven-foot-high dolmen. The man on the top of the cavern would not be able to see him.

Clay shouted, "Danny, you okay?"

But Danny was gone.

67

Danny moved fast, heading first towards the mouth of the cavern then veering off at an angle to the position that the gunman had occupied moments earlier. By moving towards the opening he moved below the second shooter's line of sight. The shooter would have to stand up and move to the edge of the cavern roof and give up his vantage point. He knew Clay would give him a third eye if that happened.

Tracing a wide V-shaped path, Danny moved to the meagre cover afforded by a palm tree that was leaning at an unhealthy angle. A small mound of earth at its base told of roots that had not fully taken hold in the neglected landscape. A quick glance at the dry soil showed another sign. Less than six feet away, a footprint marked the man's path.

Taking care to keep his balance low and centred, the wiry Scotsman moved to the next tree. Eleven measured steps. Crouching behind the base of the wide palm, he listened. Another rattling exchange of fire from the cavern interrupted the moment of tense silence. The corner of Danny's mouth twitched into a brief smile. He knew Clay would keep the other guy busy. Sure enough, a series of staggered single shots was given in way of response. While not the best marksman ever produced by the Rangers, Clay was aggressive and wily. Yeah, he'd keep the other guy busy.

Click... A sound like a knuckle cracking caused Danny's head to swivel. He moved to the next tree, alert for any telltale warnings. He knew the man that he was stalking was a dangerous foe and had no intention of underestimating the threat. A phrase often repeated by his colour sergeant in his former regiment sprang into his mind. *"Bullshit and bravado kills more soldiers than bullets."*

A slight blur of motion flitted between another tree and one of the supporting legs of the overhead water ride. Danny tracked the motion instantly, moving his weapon as a natural extension of his body. The blur had been moving left to right from his perspective. He sighted some twenty feet to the right. Slowing his breathing, he waited for the man to move in between the next two trees. It would only take the briefest of seconds. A tight three-rounder to the body, aiming for centre mass, then another safety shot to the head. Job done.

But the man did not appear. Keeping the rough bole of the tree pressed against his back, Danny began a slow pivot. *Where the hell was he?*

Keeping the AK raised as he moved, Danny shrugged his pack free from his back. In a continuous serpentine movement, he steadied the weapon in his left hand, slipped his right arm through the shoulder strap, then repeated the motion in mirror image. The backpack landed between his feet. Working left-handed he dropped to one knee and opened the plastic clip with his thumb and forefinger. Inside the bag, he slowly moved his hand in a small circle as if swirling water in a sink.

More bullets and curses were exchanged by Clay and the shooter behind him. Danny's hand closed on the item he sought and he pulled the narrow tube free. Similar to the smokers he had used in the Hot Pink Club, the tube contained an incendiary mix. The body of the item was an empty energy drink can with the top removed. Packed inside was more sugar, ground down to a fine powder, baking soda and a little potassium. Rolled in paper like a cigar at the centre was a sausage-shaped amount of tissue soaked in oven cleaner.

Moving as quickly as possible, Danny placed the improvised firebomb on the ground, retrieved his Zippo lighter and held the flame to the gasoline-soaked shoelace that served as a fuse. A blue flame snaked hungrily along the length of the lace. He knew from experience that he had five or six seconds before the heat ignited the powder inside.

Snap... Another sound over towards his left flank. An overhand throw sent the tube sailing through the air into one of the denser clumps of dried foliage.

A flash of orange-and-white flame exploded out over a four-foot-wide radius, instantly setting the surrounding plants ablaze. The grey smoke that blossomed would soon inform every other gangster in the vicinity of their location but Danny had no intention of sticking around.

The flames sprang up to head height in mere seconds, devouring the dry bushes to either side. Danny ran forward at a crouch, heading straight for the flames. Only when he was close enough to feel the heat on his face did he alter his trajectory. He knew the gunman had three options: he would move to his left, his right or backwards. Almost no one would choose to stay close to the flames for fear of being hemmed in by the fire.

Danny was sure the gunman would not retreat. They weren't wired that way. That gave two options: move left or move right. He had a fifty-fifty chance. Danny moved to his left, fast and low, skirting the very edge of the rapidly expanding wall of fire.

He saw a flash of white through the smoke, immediately followed by the unmistakeable rattle of a Kalashnikov. Danny pitched himself to the ground as rounds tore up the tree he had just passed. Something sharp raked against his ribs as he landed in the dirt. Aiming through the flames, Danny squeezed the trigger. Another burst from the gunman came in way of reply. Ignoring the pain in his chest, Danny scrambled to his feet.

Like a deadly chess match, both men fired, moved, reloaded, fired, moved and reloaded again. Then the shooting stopped. There was the sound of a magazine being flung to the ground, and a curse.

The gunman threw down the empty assault rifle as Danny stepped out into view. The man's right hand snaked to his belt and came back clutching a long triangular blade.

"Serbian?" asked Danny, his voice flat.

"Fuck Serbia." The man tapped his knife to his chest. "Bosnian."

Danny nodded.

The Bosnian managed two rapid steps towards Danny before the bullets ripped through his heart. The man landed face down, silent.

Danny rolled his shoulders. "You say potato, I say pot-ah-toe."

He went through the man's pockets in case he could find any ammo the Bosnian had forgotten about in the heat of battle, but came up empty. He did find a cell phone, and pocketed it. Always useful to have a line of communication with the people trying to kill you...

68

Clay pressed his back tight against one of the three standing stones that served as a temporary refuge. Keeping his weapon high he risked a quick glance at the gunman who had also sought cover. The man atop the cavern still had the advantage of height and a wider field of fire and Clay knew he couldn't remain squeezed between the rocks for much longer. If another shooter succeeded in flanking from the direction they had come he would be dead. It was also just a matter of time before one of the ricochets scored a serious hit and left him bleeding out.

As if on cue, a bullet rebounded from the angled standing stone directly behind him and buzzed through the air perilously close to his face. Dark grey smoke had begun to billow from the bushes and trees on the other side of the pathway. *Danny...* Ribbons of hungry orange flame sprang to life, devouring the foliage in every direction.

"Barbecue time."

Clay gritted his teeth and sprang from concealment. The pathway stretched away from the cavern, curving gently to the right. He knew that he would never make that run. Instead he sprinted towards the cavern entrance. He squeezed the trigger of his weapon, not expecting to score a hit on the elevated gunman but hoping to make him duck for cover. The AK74 thrummed in his hands as the final few bullets in the magazine were spent. "Crap. It was good while it lasted."

A burning pain cut a furrow across the slab of muscle that framed his left shoulder blade. Countless small eruptions of dirt around his feet told of the other bullets that had missed their mark. The gunman raised up to full height on the rocky ledge.

Biting down against the pain, Clay tucked his chin to his chest and threw himself into the darkness of the cavern. He tucked and rolled to dissipate the worst of the landing but managed to crack his head, elbow and hip as he bounced down three concrete steps that he had not anticipated. He landed flat on his back, the wind knocked from his lungs. Groaning, he forced himself to his feet. His elbow throbbed with a strange numbness but it was still preferable to a bullet in the face.

Plumes of the thick grey smoke began to fill the arch of the cavern mouth, obscuring the view of the rest of the park. Clay discarded the spent AK74 and withdrew his pistol from his waistband. The Beretta had definitely seen better days but with nearly a full magazine, it was still functional and deadly. Staying low to avoid the worst of the rapidly spreading smoke, Clay looked at his new surroundings. The main walkway led deeper into a wide circular chamber. The majority of this space was formed by a large hollow in the floor. When filled with water, the hollow would form an oval-shaped entrance to the rest of the water ride. A large rectangular cage stood off to one side, presumably destined to store inflatable rings. The cage stood empty, the bars now resembling a prison cell. At the far end of the chamber, some hundred feet or so away, an archway glowed amber in the dawn light.

Staying to the moulded walkway, Clay began to jog towards the exit. But before he had taken a dozen steps a sharp impact echoed around the empty cavern. Dodging behind the meagre cover provided by one of the false stalagmites, Clay snapped off a shot at the gunman who had dropped from the overhanging roof into the smoke-filled entrance. The man landed flat-footed in a wide simian crouch, rifle in hand.

Clay leaned out from the conical formation and sent a tight volley of four shots at the silhouetted target. A loud curse told him that at least one of the shots had found its mark. Then the Kalashnikov spoke back. A brief ribbon of flame illuminated the gunman as he strafed the cavern with his AK74.

Clay pressed himself low to the ground as chips and splinters from the fibreglass and concrete rocks fell all around him. Brushing the grey dust from his eyes he barely had time to react to the gunman who was in mid-sprint towards his position.

The average human male can cover twenty feet in less than one and a half seconds and Clay could tell that the gunman was in better shape than the average human male.

Clay rolled to his knees and raised the Beretta. He squeezed the trigger and used the four remaining shots left in his pistol.

69

Gregor Mosht had been part of Golok's close team for many years. After the war Golok had offered him a new life—with choices. A life where they took what they needed from the world; no more being told what they could or could not do.

He had killed more men since the conflict had ended than during the civil war. He heard the big man shout, his accent unmistakable: American. He knew that Golok hated Americans with a passion; his disfigured face served as a daily reminder of their conduct. After he had killed the lumbering cowboy he would present his head to the boss as a goodwill trophy.

He glanced to his right. Smoke and flames billowed from the trees. His brow furrowed momentarily. He squeezed off another couple of shots at the rocks.

Then the hulking American was up and running, making a break for the cavern entrance below him. For a big guy, he was faster on his feet than you'd think. As the man disappeared into temporary safety, Gregor smiled as he watched a crimson streak cut a neat line across his back.

Grey smoke begin to sting his eyes and in one fluid motion he vaulted over the edge of the moulded parapet. The impact jolted through his lower legs into his knees but he shrugged off the momentary pain.

He stalked forward into the cavern and a large blur of darkness moved rapidly at the peripheral edge of his vision. A single shot bit into the cavern wall three feet to his left. "Can't shoot for shit," he said to himself.

Striding boldly forward, Gregor followed the blur with a hail of bullets. Chips and sparks flew into the air as the AK74 destroyed the man-made stalactite, which the cowboy was using for cover.

A strobe-like sequence of flashes erupted from the base of the rock. Gregor felt a harsh burning impact bite at the base of his ribs. Roaring in both pain and fury Gregor clamped his trigger finger tight. The magazine spent its load in seconds. Without a moment's hesitation, he raced towards the cowboy. If he couldn't shoot him dead, he would smash his head into the ground.

The American rose from behind the bullet-riddled barricade, pistol in hand. Gregor felt bullets cut the air inches from his face as he sprinted forward at full tilt and slammed into his opponent. The big man still had his pistol but Gregor landed on top of him and managed to send it spinning away with a vicious kick to his wrist. The American raised his left arm above his head as Gregor used the assault rifle as a cudgel, smashing the stock at his face.

Gregor felt a hand clamp onto his neck like a vice as he raised the rifle a fourth time. He tried pulling against the junction between the thumb and forefinger, the weakest point of any grip, but the big man's limb seemed fused to his own. He drove his knee hard into the man's solar plexus but he still grabbed Gregor's throat with the crushing power. The pressure on his neck was immense. Spots of yellow light danced across his vision as the American began to shake him back and forth.

Gregor pitched himself forward in a desperate attempt to break the brutal stranglehold. Both men tumbled over the side of the pathway and landed in the base of the empty pool. The cowboy's grip slipped away as he landed heavily on the back of his head and shoulders. The rifle clattered angrily as it was flung in the opposite direction from the two men.

New and intense pain flashed across the base of Gregor's ribs. He glanced down and even in the dim light of the cavern could see the bloodstain spreading across the white of his shirt.

He needed to end this now.

The American was struggling to his feet, shaking his head as he tried to gain his footing. Gregor surged forward again, knowing not to chance going after the fallen weapon, and drove the heel of his boot sideways into the cowboy's scarred face. This sent the big man down again. Gregor smiled despite the terrible pain in his side and timed his next kick perfectly, which snapped into the cowboy's spinal column, striking the nerve cluster between his shoulder blades. *And if you can't breathe, you can't fight.*

He watched the cowboy jolt on all fours as if he'd been electrocuted. Gregor leapt in and snaked his right arm around the big man's neck. He felt the cowboy's throat tighten against his knotted forearm. In a fluid motion he grabbed his own bicep and pressed down on the back of the cowboy's neck.

He leaned forward. "Time to die, Yankee!"

But the big man was reaching back with his own left arm, prising Gregor's fingers free from the back of his head. In a panic he watched the cowboy twist his whole body to one side, sending him flying headlong in a tight cartwheel.

Gregor slammed against the curved outer wall of the empty pool, the rough edges pressing into his back. Roaring against the pain, he rose to his feet as swiftly as he could.

The American was on him instantly.

A hand that felt like rough leather clamped onto his face and drove his head back into the wall. Gregor bucked and struggled but the cowboy held him at arm's length as he raised his right fist like a prize fighter.

"I'm a Texan, not a goddamned Yankee!"

Gregor screamed into the man's hand as his fist slammed into the gunshot wound on his ribs. Another five piston punches splintered his ribs. Gregor raised his left knee in a vain attempt to ward off the blows. Another sledgehammer body shot sent a shockwave through his abdomen. He began to choke on the vomit that erupted into his throat and mouth.

The hand slipped free from Gregor's face and he struggled to register the final blow as the heel of the cowboy's blood-stained hand smashed into the bridge of his nose with lethal force. There was a brief sensation like boiling water in his nose and the base of his skull. Then he slumped to the ground.

70

Danny checked the number of rounds remaining in the AK's curved magazine. *Shit. There's never enough bullets.*

"Clay, where the hell are you?" he hissed in frustration. He had lost sight of his brother near the cavern entrance. Ducking low to avoid the worst of the smoke and flames he pulled his cell phone from his pocket and pressed speed dial. He knew Clay's phone was set to vibrate so it wouldn't betray his location. He got Clay's answerphone.

I guess I'll just have to follow the explosions.

Danny moved, putting plenty of distance between his back and the approaching sheet of fire. Returning to the stepped tower he pivoted left and right. The gunman from the top of the cavern was gone. He hoped he was dead.

Danny retrieved his backpack, slipped his arms through the straps and rolled his shoulders to make the pack comfortable again.

It seemed unlikely that Clay would have entered the cavern with no way of knowing if there was a clear exit at the other end. The prospect of scaling the outer wall of the cavern was a no go. That would have meant giving the gunman perched up there a perfect shot. That left the pathway that curved around the large standing stones. Danny set off at a brisk jog. The smell of acrid smoke receded as he traversed the narrow pathway although a quick backward glance showed a dense grey cloud that framed the horizon like a dark halo.

A six-foot-high plastic dinosaur greeted him at the next junction. The jovial looking T-Rex held a signpost that spelled out the three options: DINOLAND, PIRATES OF THE MEDITERRANEAN or KAPTAIN KORTEZ'S KIDZONE.

Danny looked again to the large volcano at the centre of the park. He started down the path to Dinoland, careful to keep his weight on the balls of his feet as he ran, moving fast and silent. Every fifty yards or so he paused, crouching behind any available cover while he listened out for any tell-tale sounds that would betray the location of any attackers.

How many men were left? No way to know. *Where were the men from the roving SUV?* No way to know.

He pressed his back to a wall that had been constructed to look like the ribcage of a fallen dinosaur. The wide path he had followed passed through the inside of the lizard's fossilized chest cavity, the ribs on both sides of the path curving inward high above his head. Further down the path the oversized saurian skull was half embedded into the base of the volcano. An accusatory eye socket and knife-sized teeth stared back at him.

He tried Clay's phone again but received no answer and moved on. Keeping the base of the volcano to his left, he headed for a large outcrop of rocks. They would provide good cover while he caught his breath and figured out his next move.

After making sure he had not been observed, Danny moved behind the outcrop and allowed himself a long deep breath. No one would be able to see him back here. After leaning the Kalashnikov against one of the rocks he unslung the backpack and looked inside. There wasn't much left in his bag of tricks. He emptied the contents onto the ground between his feet and slipped the last spare clip for the Beretta pistol into his front left trouser pocket. He looked despondently at his remaining stash. A double coil of electrical wire folded into a figure eight. Red wire, blue wire. Insulating tape, a few clothes pegs, a compact Gerber multi-tool. Handy if you had the time and missing ingredients to rig a trip-wire bomb or two but Danny had no grenades or means to cobble an IED together. Scowling at his meagre supplies, he stuffed the wire and tape back in the bag and pocketed the Gerber.

The smell of smoke reached him. He wondered how far the hungry flames had spread. They would serve to keep both the Locos and the Bosnians off balance. Retrieving his rifle, Danny mumbled to himself, "A little bit of chaos goes a long way."

71

Clay rested one hand on the gunman's chest. Unfocussed eyes stared up at the cavern ceiling. A large patch of crimson stained the lower half of the dead man's shirt and a slow trickle of blood ran from the man's nose. It didn't take a medical genius to know that he was dead.

After wiping the blood from his left hand onto the dead man's jacket, he stood up. He could feel a harsh burn across the back of his shoulder. Reaching around to his back, the tips of his fingers came away covered in blood. Flesh wounds often bled like crazy but rarely proved fatal, as long as they were sanitised and stitched at the earliest possible opportunity.

Clay fished out his cell phone. The display screen lit up briefly then went black. He angled the handset around in the meagre light and scowled at the large crack that split the screen.

"Piece of junk." Clay threw the phone to the far side of the waterless pool. Dropping back to one knee, Clay searched the dead man but there was little of interest: a wallet with a couple of credit cards and a neat fold of banknotes. The driver's license identified the man as Gregor Mosht.

He found the man's phone in an inside jacket pocket. Whereas Clay's broken phone had been the cheapest burner model they could find, Gregor's was the latest smartphone on the market. Clay slipped it into his own pocket. He realised he couldn't use it to call Danny as he didn't have the number of his brother's corresponding burner but maybe he could use it to get them out of there, if they didn't get themselves killed. As an afterthought he realised that he could have perhaps switched SIM cards on the two phones—if he hadn't have thrown his away in anger. Then again, he knew that his fingers weren't built for that kind of dexterity; maybe sat at a table with plenty of light and time he would have managed.

He moved in a fast walk towards the archway of weak orange light at the far end of the cavern. As he reached the portal he paused. He would need to be very careful from here. He was unarmed; both the AK and his Beretta pistol were now empty and discarded.

He looked around, trying to get a fix on where he was. The volcano stood off to his right and he knew that his brother would be there. He moved at a brisk pace, using as much cover as possible, moving from tree to tree, from one outcrop of rocks to the next, ever vigilant for the sounds of danger. He knew if he was caught out in the open with no firearm he was dead.

Directly ahead stood a small rectangular structure. If the park had ever opened it would have probably provided drinks and snacks for throngs of sun-kissed tourists. The shack had been built to resemble a beachfront bar, with walls made from bamboo poles and a weathered tin roof. A stained canvas sheet was tethered over the main serving window.

As he drew closer to the booth he felt an unexpected vibration in his pocket.

Gregor's phone. Pressing his back to the wall of the shack Clay pulled the phone free and swiped the green handset icon. He grunted into the phone in way of greeting. A gruff voice assailed Clay's ear. The words were gibberish to him.

Clay smiled briefly before he answered.

"I'm sorry, Greg is dead and therefore unable to take any calls at the moment, but your call is important to us so if you—"

"*Jebi se!*"

Clay continued in the same mock telesales voice, "I'm sorry I didn't catch that, but your call is important to us. If you would like to converse in English please press one, for French please press two. For Assholean, press three."

After a long silence the man spoke again this time in heavily accented English. "You are the American?"

"Well, I'm *one* of them. There's quite a lot of us in the world you know."

"Gregor is dead?"

"Well now, Chuckles, I think you know the answer to that one already." Clay was sure he could hear teeth grinding.

"Always the same with you Americans. You think you are the heroes, full of your own bullshit and wisecracks. You are not heroes. You never were. You are like spoiled children, lumbering around the world, big-headed and overconfident."

"Well, that explains why I never got your Christmas card last year."

The voice on the phone dropped in tone. "I will piss on you as the crows pick out your eyes."

"I'll let you into a little secret, pal: this ain't my first rodeo."

"I'll be sure to kill you slow."

Clay clicked his fingers. "I get it now. You must be asshole number one, the one that ships those little girls to Barcelo, also known as asshole number two. I'll tell you what, tough guy, when we meet I'll punch a hole in you for every little girl's life you've ruined."

"What do you care?" The man snorted in derision. "They're nothing to you. You think you made a difference by setting a handful of them free from Barcelo's club? That is his loss not mine. There's a million more where they came from."

"Tell you what, comrade, why don't you tell me where you are and I'll mosey on over and we can settle our differences properly?"

"*Jebi se!*"

"I take it from your tone of voice that means you don't want to be Facebook friends?"

The insult was repeated but at a much louder pitch.

Clay was smiling but knew he needed to move again. "Hey, pal, what has a ten-inch dick and hangs up?"

Click.

72

Danny placed his left hand on top of the low wall and vaulted over into the wide concrete square that lay in front of the steel door. The door was painted a dark brown in order to blend in with the base of the faux volcano. Block-style letters spelled out the warning: Solo Empleados! Danny tried the door handle and wasn't surprised to find it was locked. It looked simple enough to pick; the hours he'd spent as a boy jiggling and bumping locks had paid off many times over the years.

He drew the Gerber from his pocket. After unfolding one of the smallest blades he inserted it into the chamber and gave the handle of the multi-tool a sharp tap with the heel of his hand. He tried the handle again but it held fast. Danny repeated the motion a few more times until the cylinder lock clicked open. Danny glanced again at the words stencilled on the door. The Employees Only warning made him chuckle. Hardly the biggest transgression he'd committed today. *I'll risk it*, he thought as he stepped inside. He closed the door behind him as quietly as possible.

The interior was much as he'd expected: unadorned breeze-block walls were painted a dull grey, there was a bare concrete floor and the ceiling was covered in various pipes and conduits. Sturdy black cables, each as thick as his upper arm, snaked their way from floor to ceiling at regular intervals. The rubber outer skin designed to protect the heavy-duty electrical cables looked thick and durable. Danny tapped a cable with his knuckles as he passed. The next door he reached was unlocked and opened with a lazy screech of rusty hinges. He stepped out onto a raised platform, sweeping his pistol left to right. *No immediate danger.* The narrow walkway ended in a two-tier staircase leading into a massive open area that smelled faintly of kerosene. Dust motes swirled lazily in the weak orange light that filtered through a series of grates on the far side of the room.

The room housed some of the industrial machinery designed to pump the many millions of gallons of water around the park every day. Danny had no interest in the power output or cubic capacity of the six cyclopean power generators that towered above his head but they certainly looked impressive. The pipes that spread from each of the machines like metallic arteries were painted in blue, red and yellow. Many of the pipes, each thicker than Danny's upper body, curved and disappeared into the floor of the pumping station. Wide circular hand-wheels adorned many of the pipes at the point they curved downwards. On one side of the room stood a large grey cabinet.

Moving to the power unit, Danny twisted the chrome handle and the door to the main control panel swung open.

With careless abandon he began to flick the many switches inside to their ON positions. After a few seconds of waiting the overhead lights began to flicker and hum. Then one by one the fluorescent ceiling lights awoke. A sound like an industrial vacuum cleaner also sprang from the far end of the room. He flicked the last few switches off again. The third switch silenced the vacuum.

A rapid inspection of the wide room yielded little in the way of reward. No barrels of combustible liquids, no vehicles, no real vantage points. Danny gritted his teeth. A barrel or two of petroleum would have come in real handy. The only two barrels in the room were empty apart from a thick layer of dust and a couple of discarded newspapers.

He spotted a large roller door at the opposite end of the room from the circuit breakers. A looped chain hung from the overhead opening mechanism. Danny uncoupled the chain and began to pull down on the slack; with a metallic squeal the door began to rise. He continued the action until a gap of two and a half feet had opened. Warm air pushed inward against the comparatively cool interior.

Staying close to the doorframe, he risked a quick glance outside. He spotted a ramp on a slight incline that stretched from the roller door down to a wire mesh gate that had been painted the same brown shade as the base of the volcano. Dense and weathered shrubs, the same dark straw colour as almost every other dead plant in the park, lined the ramp on both sides from the door to the gate. The gate stood open, angled slightly inwards towards the main building.

He looked back at the two empty barrels. He knew he would have to move quickly. The remaining gunmen would converge on the processing plant as soon as they realised it was occupied. He wanted to be ready when that happened.

He allowed himself the briefest of smiles. *This might just work.*

73

Clay heard the engine rumble despite the driver creeping forward at a snail's pace. The Mercedes swung into view slow and easy as if the occupants were taking in the sights, but the automatic weapons that protruded from the windows told a very different story.

He stayed hidden behind one of the standing stones. The volcano was now within spitting distance. He would let the vehicle pass him by and continue to look for an access point.

He was sure Danny would be there.

The vehicle rolled to a gentle halt some forty feet from his position as a shrill sound cut through the dawn air. Clay crept towards both the vehicle and the source of the noise. He cocked his head to one side as the loud wail was repeated. He recognised the unmistakeable sound of a grievously injured man.

"*Aaaaargh!*" the howl was long and loud. The next words made Clay puff out his cheeks in relief. "Clay! It's Daniel... I'm down. Help me!"

Clay knew that his younger brother would never use his

formal Christian name. He was up to no good. The armed men vaulted from the SUV, weapons shouldered, and moved as one towards the yelling.

Taking care to stay low and out of their peripheral vision, Clay followed them, matching their pace as best he could while still remaining concealed. He watched as one of the three men pushed a chain-link gate further open with his foot.

"Clay… it's Daniel. I've been shot."

The gunmen moved towards the roller door.

"Aaaaargh!"

The gunmen were almost at the door. One man moved to each side of the open portal while the third remained a few steps behind. The man on the right ducked first and was through the gap in a single fluid motion. The second gunman followed.

Clay heard the sound of retching as the third man entered the volcano.

Then everything happened almost simultaneously.

The shutter door dropped into its closed position.

A thunderous outbreak of gunfire erupted from within.

And two Locos leapt screaming at Clay's exposed back.

Clay barely had time to turn. The closer of the two swung a pickaxe, aiming at the back of his head. Clay felt the side of the blade graze his skull as he launched himself away. The Loco swore as his swing missed and the heavy tool punched deep into a fibreglass stone.

The second Loco slashed his knife, aiming for Clay's throat but he batted the man's wrist away with the edge of his hand as he moved towards the SUV.

Clay scowled as the pickaxe came free with a vigorous

tug. The two Locos exchanged a momentary glance then attacked again. Pickaxe rushed straight at Clay, winding up like a lumberjack, while the knife-man raced in from one side.

The pickaxe was a deadly weapon but was also heavy and unwieldy. The spiked blade whistled past and Clay sprang round and slammed a straight right punch into the Loco's spine. He felt his knuckles sink deep into the man's body and knew it was a good shot. The man yelped in pain as he struggled to stay on his feet while the second Loco slashed at Clay's face but missed. Clay skipped back, keeping his weight on the balls of his feet, his centre of balance low.

Clay knew that the knife-man would have turned and run if the bigger Spaniard wasn't leading the way. *The little bastard wants a free lunch*, he thought; he'd wait until the big guy had pinned him to the ground with the pickaxe then dive and cut Clay's throat. Clay launched into a side-thrust kick to his left arm and the force sent the man tumbling ass first into the dust.

The pickaxe cut a wide arc through the air as Clay feigned a grab at the man's neck. The force of his swing again turned and made the attacker twist on his heel but this time Clay was on him and grabbing the weapon. The Loco tried to knee him twice in the groin but Clay twisted and used his momentum to rake the pick shaft up under the Loco's chin. The thick wooden handle snapped the Loco's jaws shut, smashing his teeth together. The Spaniard fell back against the body of the SUV, the door slammed shut behind him, and his hand moved to his broken jaw out of instinct. Clay brought the spiked blade down in a furious arc. The pickaxe bit through the man's torso and the rusted spike sprang a full nine inches through his back, impaling him and pinning him upright as the blade wedged through the metal of the car door. Both of the man's feet jerked several times as he dangled, then he slumped forward, still held in place. His right hand shook briefly like the tail of a startled rattlesnake.

A flash of silver lanced towards Clay's face. Clay turned, raising his hands so his fingertips touched, his arms forming a triangle in front of his face. The knife spun from the Loco's grip, clattering over the roof of the SUV as Clay grabbed his neck. The man backpedalled, but there was no escaping the grip and his face began to turn purple. The Loco tried to punch at Clay's face but the blows were little more than a cuff. The would-be murderer was turned around so his back pressed against the second protruding spike of the pickaxe and he bucked wildly as he realised his fate. Clay thrust his arms out straight and the spike burst through the Loco in a spray of crimson. The man's hands shot out and grabbed at Clay then back at his own ruined chest.

Clay leaned in close as the man's eyes began to cloud over. "You can pick your friends…"

74

Golok heard the loud wailing of the injured man as the Mercedes SUV moved slowly towards the towering volcano. He had heard the sound many times in his life. Soldiers cried for their mothers when they had a bullet lodged in their guts. These men weren't so brave then.

"Clay! It's Daniel… I'm down. Help me!"

The driver stopped on command. The wailing voice was coming from the inside the building and the three Bosnians exited the SUV, clutching their weapons, and moved towards the raised roller door.

The two enforcers moved ahead of their boss. Golok glanced behind as he advanced and—satisfied that there was no assassin creeping up behind—followed his two soldiers. The two men ducked under the roller door. The first gunman moved to the right, sweeping the darker interior with his weapon. Seconds later the second man repeated the process, moving to the left. Golok drew his pistol from his waistband and entered the building.

It was much larger than Golok expected. Dull fluorescent

lights flickered and hummed high overhead and he closed one eye to allow his vision to quickly adapt to the different lighting conditions. The room smelled of stale air and old chemicals. A large rectangle had been painted onto the floor in a darker shade than the grey of the concrete floor. At one of the corners of the rectangle sat two oil drums. Another wail rang out. Both gunmen took a tentative step towards the source of the din.

Gunfire cut through the room sending sparks flying from the mechanism above the roller door. The door dropped like a guillotine.

Golok's men unleashed a stream of fire and pushed forward, thin trails of smoke drifting from their weapons. The gunman nearest the oil drums glanced inside as he passed by. He started, and gestured for Golok to look. A cell phone lay at the bottom, its screen illuminated. Golok realised it must have once belonged to one of his men—it was the same model he gave to all his people, with a dark-blue plastic protective case. He wondered whether the man was dead.

A voice issued forth, on speakerphone, magnified by the body of the steel drum. "Oops, my bad. Now you're trapped in here with us. I guess we'll just have to kill you all."

Golok reached into the drum and picked out the phone. "Easy to make threats when you run and hide like little bitches."

"Listen here, asshole. I'll be sure to bitch slap you to death when I'm good and ready."

Golok snorted a dismissive laugh. "What is it with you two? The loud-mouthed American was full of shit too."

He motioned his two enforcers forward as he spoke again. "You are English, yes?"

"Fuck that! I'm a Scotsman and proud of it."

"All the same to me. You will die the same, colour of your blood is the same."

"One big difference…"

"Difference?" asked Golok, his eyes searching for a glimpse of the speaker amidst the curving pipes and bulky machinery.

"A big one!"

The gunman to Golok's left pitched backwards, a spray of blood erupting from his ruined throat.

"Englishmen can't shoot for shit."

The other gunman raced forward, his own rifle chattering in response. The bullets cut through the air and a spray of water began to cascade from the ceiling as a bullet ruptured one of the sprinkler heads.

The gunman glanced back at his leader. He nodded at the flick of Golok's fingers, moving to the far right of the room. They moved forward in unison, checking behind each island of pipes and machinery. Golok knew the rogue Scotsman was a dangerous enemy and would not hesitate to slaughter them both without a moment of hesitation. His man nodded silently as Golok motioned with two forked fingers, first to his eyes then in a sweeping circular motion around the room. *Keep watching!*

A single shot rang out but then the room again fell quiet. Golok knew the Scotsman was toying with them now. He rested his pistol across the crook of his left elbow as he scanned the room, then raised the phone to his ear. "No smart remarks? Is that because you realise that you have painted yourself into a corner?"

The voice that responded was barely above a whisper. "No, I was just ruminating a while, you know, chewing a couple of things over. One, you speak pretty good English for a Balkan dickhead. And two, I'm wondering if it's best to kill both of you together or slot your henchman first then take my time with you. Get up close and personal. Find out what language you scream in."

"That's one of the many things I hate about you Brits: your overblown sense of self-importance. The man you just killed was worth ten of you."

"Aye? Is that right? Well, he's dead just the same."

"You all think you still rule the British Empire. Truth is you never ruled anything of worth for long."

"Speaking of rules, here's one for you. Pay more attention to what you're walking in."

Golok glanced down. There was now a layer of murky liquid on the concrete floor. For a split second he thought of gasoline, but the smell from the liquid was still that of stagnant water not fuel. He strode forward onto a raised square of concrete upon which sat a tangle of pipes and hand wheels. In a split second he saw the trap below and shouted out a single word of warning to his enforcer.

A flash of blue and yellow sparks cascaded from the ground as the cable connected with the pooled liquid. The gunman went rigid as the electricity coursed through his body. He tried to launch himself away from the pain but was paralysed. A strangled whimper whistled from his throat, more the escaping of air than a tangible sound.

Golok tumbled over the curving pipe as a lesser shock was conducted through the continuing drizzle from the sprinkler system. The pain was still enough to knock him off his feet. He landed flat on his back, the breath knocked from his lungs. His hands and feet were numb as he struggled to right himself. Turning first onto all fours, he looked around for his pistol, shaking his head in an attempt to clear his vision. The pistol lay some ten feet away. With a pained grunt, Golok forced himself to stand. As he moved to retrieve his weapon he looked over to his man. He lay motionless curled into a semi-foetal position, knees drawn towards his chest; his mouth hung open, tongue lolling to one side like an animal. Golok knew that he was now on his own.

He raced forward and scooped the pistol from the floor.

75

Clay rolled his shoulders as he looked at the two men he had just killed. Like a scene from a slasher movie, both men hung limp and lifeless, impaled. Blood had begun to pool at their feet.

Running a hand through his hair, he slowly exhaled through his nose. He imagined how this would look in a court of law: *Yes, Your Honour, I felt in fear for my life so I whacked them both and left them dangling like human butterflies!*

The roaring of a car engine brought him back from his legal ponderings in short order. The car had been approaching slow and steady while he had been occupied with the Locos. Now it raced straight for him. He recognised the man at the wheel: Barcelo.

Clay leapt to one side and avoided being crushed against the SUV by mere inches.

The rear of the car whipped around as Barcelo wrenched the steering wheel and the tyres struggled to maintain traction on the road. The tailgate of the sedan crashed into Clay with enough force to pitch him off his feet.

Barcelo threw open the car door and leaned out, pistol

in hand. The first shot ejected a brief cascade of sparks from the grill of the Bosnians' SUV, inches from Clay's head. Biting down against the new pain in his left knee and elbow, he forced himself to move. The second shot cut the air between his upper arm and his chest. *Too damned close!*

Gaining momentum, Clay tucked his head and combat-rolled out of the line of fire, coming up onto his feet at the far side of the SUV. He circled away, using the body of the Mercedes as a shield.

Cursing in Spanish, Barcelo shot three more bullets through the open windows of the SUV and heaved himself free from the car as it was blocking most of the road, leaving him no option but to follow on foot.

Using his free hand for support, he inched his way around the side of the Mercedes, pistol extended at the ready. Moving with a pronounced limp Barcelo rounded the hood of the vehicle.

"There you are, you American bastard!" Barcelo shouted and raised the pistol.

Clay spotted the Loco's knife on the ground and snatched it up like he'd won a prize. Now he just had to get close enough to ram it between his ribs.

Barcelo's voice was thick with contempt as he spoke. "Just like an American to bring a knife to a gunfight."

Clay stood to his full height and weighed the distance between them. Maybe fifteen feet or so but Barcelo had a clear advantage. His pistol was level and aimed straight at Clay's heart.

"Drop the blade!" Barcelo flicked the barrel of the Kimber briefly at the knife. "Drop it or I—"

Clay snapped his wrist forward in an overhand throw and the knife catapulted towards Barcelo's neck.

The Kimber spat fire twice as Barcelo recoiled away from the flash of silver.

The bullets hit nothing but air.

Clay raced at him, moving low and fast, and driving him into the side of the Mercedes. The SUV bucked on its suspension as the combined weight of the two men struck.

The Spaniard grabbed at Clay's throat with one hand and tried to bring his pistol round. Both men rolled across the side of the vehicle, struggling to remain upright. Clay seized Barcelo's gun hand and twisted it up and away so the barrel pointed back over the boss's own shoulder. Another two shots rang out, the retort from the weapon hurting both men's ears.

Clay yelled out in pain as Barcelo latched onto his arm with a savage bite. In response, Clay rammed his thumb deep into Barcelo's eye socket, grinding it from side to side in a corkscrew motion. The Spaniard bellowed and released his grip.

Clay used the brief moment to knock the gun hard against the roof of the Mercedes. Once, twice, three times did the trick and it tumbled from Barcelo's numb fingers. Barcelo tried to drive a headbutt into Clay's face but instead received a forearm smash under his chin. Both exchanged punches to the face and body like seasoned heavyweight boxers, yelling out in effort as they launched each blow. Dodging an overhand right, Clay straightened Barcelo by way of a palm heel shot under his chin. The Spaniard reciprocated by grabbing Clay's throat with both of his hands. This time his headbutt scored, opening a shallow gash over the Texan's right eye.

Clay reeled back, sparks of pain flashing across his vision, and in one motion brought both of his arms up on the inside of the chokehold. A rapid series of palm heel thrusts loosened the grip and Clay threw an arm around the back of Barcelo's bull neck. A quick pivot and the Spaniard was pitched off his feet in a winding hip throw. Clay followed him to the ground adding his full weight to the already severe impact.

The leader of the Locos thrashed as Clay straddled him, his knees pressing tight into his ribs. As Clay began to throw his next punch, Barcelo bucked his hips and twisted to one side. Clay was thrown off balance, and Barcelo reached up and gripped his head, one hand on his chin, the other at the nape of his neck, and wrenched his hands in opposite directions. A sound like knuckles cracking and the big Texan fell off him to one side.

With a triumphant roar Barcelo struggled into a kneeling position. He had killed the French biker with the same neck breaker. Barcelo flopped to the ground, laughing out loud at his moment of triumph.

"That hurt!" Clay glared at the Spaniard with pure malevolence.

"*Que chingados?*"

"This ain't my first barn dance, Elvis."

Yelling out something incomprehensible to Clay's ear, Barcelo tried to stand. Clay leapt at him, ramming his fingers deep into his nostrils. Gripping the Spaniard's head like a bowling ball, Clay smashed the back of his skull into the ground. Barcelo shuddered and jerked as fingers were rammed even deeper inside his face. Clay smashed him down again. A splash of blood escaped from his thick black hair.

Clay lifted Barcelo's head to his shoulder then smashed

him down a third time. A brutal cracking sound and a final brief convulsion told him that Barcelo was finished.

Clay stood to full height and rolled his head around in a circle. Nothing felt broken despite Barcelo's best attempt. Looking down at the fallen gangster, thoughts of Dez and the little girls from the club flashed into his mind.

He stamped his boot heel deep into Barcelo's throat. "Yeah, and stay down!"

76

After the first shots had been fired inside the maintenance bay, Danny had quickly deduced that the sprinkler system had deployed. The building hadn't gone up in flames as planned and a cascade of stagnant brown water quickly began to form pools upon the concrete floor, years of dust forming a scum on the expanding surface. He moved under a raised walkway similar to the one he had used to enter the building and noticed it was unaffected by the falling water. Looking to his left he spotted another of the many electrical conduits; the same thick black rubber cables that he had seen earlier snaked from floor to ceiling and a plan was quickly formed.

His actions had taken only a few seconds, but as he wrestled the wires free he feared that a bullet would take him in the back. Using his boot to pull the cable taut along the floor he fired a single shot from his AK74. The 5.45mm round cut through the wire with ease. Raw strands of copper wire poked free. An angry flash of blue and yellow sparks confirmed the wire was live. A handy wooden crate would isolate him from the shock. He sat on it.

He checked his phone. The call to the smartphone he'd placed in the oil drum—the one taken from the Bosnian he'd killed in the woods—was still open.

"No smart remarks? Is that because you realise that you have painted yourself into a corner?"

"No, I was just ruminating a while, you know, chewing a couple of things over."

Danny watched the pair step into view. The enforcer was creeping forward like a jungle cat, his head slowly swivelling side to side as he sought a target. Both gangsters were soaked to the skin. Both were less than twenty feet away. As soon as they moved around the next sub pump they would see him.

At the right moment Danny pressed the free end of the cable into the half-inch of water pooled on the floor.

A dull *whoomp* was followed by another flash of sparks as the electricity supply grounded and both Bosnians were sent sprawling. The leader was on a low podium and sheltered from the worst of the shock, but still emitted a sharp gasp of pain as he tumbled over a mess of pipes and wheels. The remaining gunman bucked and shuddered, the raw current causing every muscle in his body to spasm simultaneously. Spittle flew from his mouth as his body was racked by convulsions. He toppled to one side, twitching in a forced seizure. His hands locked around his rifle, fingers forming rigid claws.

Knowing that the longer the exposure lasted meant a higher chance of a lethal shock, Danny continued to hold the cable to the water for as long as he could after the Bosnian gunman had ceased twitching. Then, after gathering up the slack in the wire, Danny threw the whole tangle onto the dry area under the walkway. He got off the wooden crate, his boots sending out ripples in the pooled water.

He fixed his AK74 on the tangle of pipes over which the Bosnian leader had fallen. As he rounded the corner of the pumping mechanism, the scar-faced Balkan gangster was straightening to his full height, pistol in hand.

"Not dead yet!" His lip curled to one side in a sneer. He slapped his chest with his free hand. "Golok!"

"Danny Gunn, pleased ta kill ya!"

Both men opened fire.

Danny felt a slug bite a chunk of skin from his shoulder as he clamped down on the trigger and emptied the remaining rounds into the Bosnian's chest, knocking him off his feet. The pistol flew from Golok's grip as he was pitched backwards onto a wide drainage grate. With a loud clang of protesting metal, the grate buckled inward, then the ground seemed to open up and swallow him whole.

Danny sprang forward, his rifle aimed into the unexpected chasm. Some eighteen inches below the level of the floor whirled a pool of murky brown water. The grate was around ten feet square and constructed from a much flimsier material than he would have expected; perhaps just one more thing left unfinished in the waterpark.

The brown water sloshed violently in the drainage channel. A hand broke the surface for a second or so then disappeared back into the murky liquid. Unable to see the gangster clearly, Danny peppered the channel with a series of single shots, tracing the pattern of a number five on a dice. One of the shots was sure to find a target. As the rifle went silent, the bolt locking open, Danny discarded the Kalashnikov and drew his Beretta from his waistband.

A strange growling sound came from behind him and he quickly turned.

"What the hell?" Danny realised he had heard the sound before; a dead man's rattle. The last vestiges of air escaping from the electrocuted gunman's lungs. He turned his attention back to the open drain.

Golok burst from the water, screaming as he grabbed at Danny's legs.

After a brief moment of weightlessness, Danny was dragged into the swirling water, yelling out in pain as his back crashed against the edge of the drain. The Beretta pistol bounced from his grip and was instantly swallowed by the water. Then with a grip like an anaconda, Golok dragged him down.

Danny clamped his mouth shut as liquid sloshed over his face. The foul-smelling water was the colour of weak coffee. A hand gripped at his collar and forced his head under the surface. Bubbles rolled up and over his face as he struggled to hold his breath. Danny tried to find the bottom of the channel but was twisted to one side by the Bosnian, and a thumb was gouged into his eye. He thrust out again with his legs and struck against a solid surface. Using the bottom of the channel for leverage, Danny let the Bosnian push him down even further, then with his legs tucked beneath him straightened up with as much power as he could muster.

Breaking the surface amid a huge cascade of water, Danny sucked in a great lungful of air. With barely enough time for one breath he felt Golok's arms encircle his neck. Before he could be dragged under again, Danny pivoted into the grip and backhanded Golok across the face; not the prettiest strike but it did loosen the grip enough for him to turn and face the Bosnian. As Golok brought his hands to his injured face, Danny slipped free and put a little distance between them.

Blood seeped from Golok's nose, a darker red against the dirty brown of the water. "*Jebi se!*"

Danny didn't understand the curse but intuited the sentiment behind it. He rolled his shoulders as he appraised his opponent; the guy looked like a walking nightmare. The scar that divided his face was etched deep into his skin and eyes as hard as flint stared back. Danny realised the Bosnian must be wearing some form of body armour under his shirt and jacket. It had to be top end to stop a full burst from the AK at close range. "Every arsehole wears Kevlar these days."

Golok wagged a finger. "Not Kevlar. Dragon Skin. The best!"

"Figures. Money's no problem, right?"

Golok shrugged, the corners of his mouth turned downwards. He moved a little closer. "I'm going to enjoy killing you."

Danny shrugged back and pointed to the side of Golok's head, indicating the remnants of the Bosnian's ear, which was little more than a nubbin of skin around his exposed ear canal. "You really need to take care of your eyes. If you ever need glasses, you're fucked."

Golok sprang at his throat.

77

Danny wasted no effort in body hits. The Dragon Skin body armour was designed to stop high-velocity rounds. There was little chance of a punch or kick doing any damage.

Golok was incredibly strong. Danny felt himself tugged violently from side to side, his feet skidding along the bottom of the channel. With one hand on his collar and clawed fingers in his face he was forced below the water again. With the Bosnian bearing his full weight down on top of him he could not find the leverage to repeat his previous escape and the water was slowing Danny's movement so that it felt like molasses. Sharp fingernails raked across his face as he tried to break free from the hold and he was crushed tight against the channel wall.

Golok yelled. Danny had bitten down on his thumb, catching it securely between his back teeth in the struggle. In a wild cascade of frothing water Danny broke the surface. Cursing at the top of his lungs, Golak began to rain punches down with his free hand. Danny still held the captured thumb tight between his teeth like a blood-filled Cuban cigar, unwilling to relinquish the advantage. He shook his head from side to side, savaging the Bosnian's hand like a pit bull. As the gangster began to club at his head Danny effected the Crazy Monkey guard, moving his hands as if brushing his hair with his fingers, his forearms providing a constantly moving shield. The blows thumped into his arms with little effect.

Golok raised himself up, his mouth wide in an agonised yell, and brought his fist down like a hammer. Danny shifted to one side, catching the heavy blow on his left arm, and drove the tip of his right elbow up under the Bosnian's chin. His head snapped back and his feet slipped out from below him.

Danny followed immediately with a straight punch to the gangster's jaw. As the Bosnian was knocked backwards, Danny felt the end of the thumb detach from the rest of his hand and he spat the severed digit into the water. Blood filled his mouth. "I wouldn't try hitch-hiking for a while…"

The Bosnian looked down in horror at his hand. Then he scrambled back, his face twisting in a new expression. "Rats!"

Danny too looked down into the murky water. There were dozens of long dark bodies writhing on the surface. Black eyes like miniature marbles fixed on him with malevolent intent.

Several of the creatures had latched onto Golok and were biting him as they climbed up his shirt. Danny felt a sharp nip on the inside of his elbow. Catching the vermin by its tail Danny sent it spinning through the air. Forcing himself to ignore the swarming rodents he surged forward.

The Bosnian was swiping his hands in wild patterns, dislodging the rats and spraying blood in various directions. Danny loathed the creatures but the Bosnian was clearly terrified of them. A water-slicked rodent clambered over his shoulder and nipped at his neck. Danny grabbed the creature and pushed it into the Bosnian's face.

Desperate to escape, Golok went down below the murky water, which was now filled with hungry rodents that twisted and scrambled in every direction. "*Upomoć!*" Golok shouted as he broke the surface, rats still clinging to his chest and arms.

Danny snapped out his right hand in a tight piston motion and an iron-hard fist slammed into Golak's throat, crushing his trachea into his spinal column and splintering the fragile cartilage. A rat tumbled from the man's chest as the blow struck home.

Wasting no time, Danny climbed out of the pool. He knew it could take up to thirty seconds to die of asphyxiation. The Bosnian was clutching both hands to his throat as his legs folded slowly beneath him; he tipped face first into the water, sending out wide ripples in every direction.

Water dripped from Danny, his clothes clinging to every inch of his body. The muscles in his jaw bunched as he watched the Bosnian submerge. He felt no remorse for the dying man but the swarming rats still caused an instinctive sense of revulsion.

After a few seconds Golok floated to the surface. He was face down and motionless. A rat, leathery tail swishing from side to side, mounted the dead man's back. It regarded Danny briefly with its black marble gaze then began gnawing at the soft flesh at the back of Golok's neck.

78

Clay pressed a hand against the back of his neck, rubbing it slowly from side to side. A painful tightness had crept into the surrounding muscles. The wide triangular slabs of his trapezoids were tense and sore, the nerves in his neck raw. A raft of lesser pains seemed to take effect at once. He knew that the heat of combat was wearing off and his adrenalin levels were dipping. The burning sensation returned from the bullet that had creased his upper back.

Bunching his hands into tight fists, Clay flexed the muscles in his arms, chest and legs. Then he fixed his gaze on the roller door.

Skirting the SUV he found Barcelo's Kimber pistol lying on the ground. He ejected the clip to find that only two rounds remained. "There's never enough bullets," he huffed.

With a grunt of determination, he started towards the base of the volcano. As he jogged towards the entry point he stopped focusing on the pain. He knew that he would hurt like a son of a bitch tomorrow and probably for the rest of the week, but tomorrow didn't concern him. Danny did.

Choosing the right side of the portal, he pressed an ear against the corrugated metal. There was no noise from within. That could mean many things.

They could all be dead, Danny included.

They could be deeper within the structure, still stalking each other.

Or the Bosnians could be standing over the body of his dead brother.

He knew there was only one sure-fire way of finding out. He also knew there was a very good chance of being shot dead if his gamble failed to pay off. But Danny was inside and maybe in mortal danger.

"Aw crap!" Clay gripped the bottom of the door, the edge of the metal digging deep into his fingers and palms as he began to pull upwards. A harsh screech of protesting metal answered his exertions. The door raised slowly, inch by inch until he'd created a gap sufficient to roll under.

Clay was about to do so when a very familiar voice brought a smile to his face.

"Stay there, ya big ape. I'm coming out."

Danny scooted beneath the door and nodded at Clay who was giving him the once-over.

"Three questions," said Clay.

"Just three?"

"For starters."

"Fire away."

"One, are they all dead inside?"

"As disco dancin' dodos," Danny replied. He drew a finger across his throat to illustrate the point.

"Two, why the hell are you so wet? Did you stop off at the

wave pool for a quick dip while I was doing all the real work?"

In response, Danny flicked some of the water at Clay and laughed. "Yeah, that's it exactly. I clocked off early and thought, what the hell. Doofus!"

Clay raised his eyebrows.

"If you must know I ended up going all UFC inside a drainage sluice. Tough son of a bitch. Didn't go down easy. I'm sure he was the leader of the Bosnian crew."

"Ah, my 'phone a friend', I think. We had a chit-chat earlier. I'm not sure he really warmed to my telephone manner."

Danny smiled. "That probably accounts for his foul mood. I've heard you on the phone. You could make Gandhi drop the F-bomb."

"I know, it's a talent. But don't be so envious, you can be an irritating little jerk in your own right."

"Bugger off." Danny faked a punch at his brother. "Isn't it time you went to New York and climbed the Empire State Building again?"

Clay thumped his chest gorilla-style. The muscles in the back of his neck sent out a brief flash of pain in way of protest.

"You said three questions," said Danny. "Ask and be done with it."

Clay frowned as he waited for the ache in the base of his skull to subside.

"You okay?" Danny reached out for his brother.

"Yeah, took a couple of knocks is all. Okay. Question three. How did you know it was me lifting the roller door? Could have been one of the bad guys."

Danny shook his head. "In answer to question three of three, I'll give you a two-part answer."

"Please elucidate."

"I will. Item one: who else is strong enough or dumb enough to rip a friggin' steel roller door out of its moorings?"

Clay shrugged.

"Item two: I saw your boots. Nobody else I know has got feet that big, apart from Godzilla. Put two and two together and got you."

"Nobody likes a smart ass." Clay wiped a smear of blood from his eyebrow. "Anyhow, you can't hit me with both King Kong and Godzilla jibes in one conversation. That's just not right."

Exchanging grimaces, Danny nodded at the pistol in Clay's hand. "Nice Kimber. Don't see so many of those around."

"Yeah, nice piece of kit. Spanish Elvis had ideas of shooting me with it."

"Barcelo? How did that work out for him?" asked Danny.

"Elvis left the building. And there won't be a comeback special, that's for sure."

"Another member of the dodo club?"

"Unless they've perfected head transplants and I didn't get the memo." Clay made a popping sound with his pursed lips. "You think there's any more left before we leave?"

"Dunno. I think it's time we blew this popsicle stand anyway. Even out here in the sticks a local might have seen all the smoke and heard the gunfire. I don't want to be here when the emergency services arrive."

"I hear that." Clay gave a mischievous smile. "Do you think it would be acceptable if we *borrowed* a vehicle from this fine collection of fellows?"

Danny cupped a hand to his ear. "I don't hear any objections."

"Alrighty then. Let's mosey."

They made their way to the Mercedes SUV. Danny paused for a moment as he took in the scene of carnage. "Jeez, Clay. What the hell?"

"Shit needed kickin'."

"You don't say." Pointing to the impaled Locos, Danny added, "It's probably best if we lose the hood ornaments."

Without preamble or ceremony Clay gripped the rear of the two dead men by the shoulders. With one sharp tug and a brief screech of metal the two corpses dropped to the ground.

Danny cast a look at Barcelo. "He looks like he's been dropped from a great height without a parachute."

Clay shrugged. "You know what they say, can't make an omelette…"

"Nice, the keys are still in the ignition. At least that worked in our favour."

Clay climbed into the passenger seat. "You can drive."

"I was planning to. Look what happened last time you were behind the wheel."

79

Danny parked the stolen SUV several blocks from the Woo Hoo. When it was found he didn't want any easy connections to be made that would lead back to Larry and Pamela. Both men sat in rare quiet reflection. The engine of the Mercedes cooled slowly, emitting lazy *tink-tink-tink* sounds.

His clothes were still wet and clung to Danny's skin uncomfortably. As he twisted in his seat the leather upholstery squeaked in protest.

Clay broke the easy silence. "Why do we do this? I mean why the hell? We're both easy-going guys, so why do we always end up with blood on our hands?"

Danny gave a short laugh. "What, are you asking if we're closet psychopaths with a hero complex?"

"I'm not sure I want that as a logo on my T-shirt. There were a couple of times back there I didn't know if you were dead or alive." Clay dropped his chin close to his chest. "You're the only person that I really love in this whole damned world. If you were gone I don't know what I would do."

Danny shifted in his seat again. "Agreed, but we're

both still alive and kicking, so let's worry about our fragile mortality another time."

Clay gave a single short nod. "I could kill a beer or ten."

"Yeah, I hear that, big bro'. I think we're gonna need them and probably a new arse apiece after Pamela gets through with us."

"Oh, crap."

"Yeah, we've still got to face the lioness before we get to call this jaunt finished."

Clay grimaced as he recalled their last conversation. "She's going to go ballistic. I don't envy Larry when she catches up with him. I hope he's okay."

"He's a tough old fucker, he'll be all right." Danny looked down at his knuckles, several of which were missing chunks of skin. "It still grieves me that Dez is dead. We should never have agreed to let them help us. He died because they thought he was me."

Clay puffed out his cheeks. "I know. I feel the same."

"Well, we better go back and face the music. Pamela must have heard from the hospital by now. We'll go and check the status quo."

"Wow. Are they playing a gig at the club?"

"They should invent a new dance: the Texas Dipshit. You could lead it."

"The Texas Dipshit. I think I've done that already. You just add beer and a bottle of tequila."

Danny held up a hand as they climbed from the vehicle. "Hey, give me a second. I just want to have a nose in the trunk, see if there's anything worth taking."

Clay nodded. "You can take the boy out of Scotland,

but you can't take Scotland out of the boy."

"Put a sock in it, you big Yeti."

"You're going all out with the monster insults today, ain't ya?"

"If the freakishly big shoe fits…"

"You'll be wearin' it up your ass in a minute."

"Nothing of worth in the trunk space." Danny moved to the rear passenger door. He lifted out a jacket, quickly checked the pockets but again turned up nothing. Wedged behind the passenger seat was a sports bag that took up most of the footwell. Danny lifted the bag onto the seat and pulled on the zipper. "Bingo!"

Clay looked inside. Thick wads of euros, each secured by an elastic band, filled more than half of the bag's capacity. "That'll buy a taco or two."

"Damn right. I'll consider it our severance bonus."

"You keep it, Danny. Spend it wisely on wine and women. I don't need it."

"Coolo mondo. It'll help tide me over during quiet times."

Clay thumped him playfully on the shoulder, almost knocking him back into the SUV. "Since when do you have any quiet times? Look at the shit you've caused since you got here."

Leaving the keys in the ignition and the doors unlocked, the Gunn brothers began the short walk back to the Woo Hoo Club.

They were still a block away when they heard the yelling and smelled the smoke.

80

Babi Garcia gave little more than a fleeting thought to the fates of the Locos and the Bosnians that he had left behind at the waterpark. They were not his people, or his concern. Barcelo paid well and provided some interesting interludes but he would never be his *jefe*. No one would be. Babi was his own boss, his own man and in no need of a gang to do his bidding or to provide him with protection.

He looked around the club. It was past dawn—posters outside had advertised an all-night fiesta with half-price drinks—but it was still half full. The exhausted specimens on display were a perfect example of everything he detested about humanity. Men that thought they were way more handsome and funny than they really were, strutting around like idiotic peacocks. The women were either hags that thought that a face full of heavy make-up and a short skirt would hold back the effects of time, or young girls wearing next to nothing, with their over-exaggerated facial expressions while taking endless selfies.

"I'll wipe those stupid grins off your faces in a minute,"

Babi said under his breath, his voice thick with intent.

The staff seemed a little on edge, a tinge of worry behind their smiles. Babi fixed his gaze on one in particular. She was flitting back and forth behind the bar, mixing drinks and working the cash register with practised hands. Her brown hair, pulled back into a ponytail, seemed to constantly change colour as it caught the glow from the multicoloured lights arranged above the expansive display of bottles behind her. She would do nicely.

Back to business. Work first then play, Babi reminded himself. He moved around the club slowly. The customers were way too preoccupied with their own idiocies to notice what he was doing before their very eyes. In each hand he held a can of lighter fluid and as he traced his way from the front to the rear of the club in a circuitous route, he squeezed the cans in a slow but steady rhythm.

At the rear corner he stepped into the men's toilets. The music was a little less intrusive behind the door. One man stood facing a urinal. He held the pose familiar to drunken men the world over, left hand high on the tiled wall, supporting his weight, as the other directed his stream into the ceramic pan.

The man gave a brief glance over his shoulder as Babi entered the room, then went back to emptying his bladder.

Babi allowed a small pool of lighter fluid to form next to the door. He then walked towards the urinals. Aiming at the man's back, he directed the twin jets of fluid at his back and shoulders.

The man turned as the cold liquid soaked his shirt against his skin. Babi dropped the cans to the floor.

"Hey, what the fuck are you doing?"

Babi kicked him hard between his legs, making him double over. Garcia pulled out a Zippo lighter, sparked a flame, then extended his hand in a casual motion. He smiled as the man's back was engulfed in an instant. The man began to scream as the flames devoured his shirt and started on his flesh. He spun in wild circles, his arms beating with little effect at his back.

Babi watched the burning man fall against the sinks then collapse to the tiled floor.

"*La Flambé Flamenco.*"

Garcia grabbed three toilet rolls from a shelf near the cubicles and rubbed each one into the pool of fluid next to the door. He sparked the lighter again, this time waving it near the floor, and the pool of lighter fluid ignited instantly. Twin lines of fire raced under the door. A few seconds later the yelling and screaming began.

When he walked back into the bar area the patrons of the Woo Hoo Club were doing a very different dance than earlier. Bodies crashed into one another as they tried to escape the flames, which had sprung up all over the club within a few short seconds. Tables and chairs toppled to the ground, spilling drinks and bodies.

Garcia knelt and touched the first of the paper rolls to the flames before throwing it overhand into the middle of the club. The screams intensified as bodies flailed at each other. He set the second roll alight and watched it arc through the air like a miniature comet. A pot-bellied man in an oversize tie-dye shirt yelled out in fear as the ball of fire landed in his arms. He cast it away, losing his glasses as he did so. It landed behind the bar, sending the staff scattering for safety.

The third roll Garcia tossed at the back of a woman who had squeezed into a Lycra dress that looked two sizes too small. She shrieked, spinning a full circle as the burning wad hit the bare skin of her back.

Garcia grinned. A young man appeared in front of him brandishing an unopened bottle of whisky. The man looked to be mid-twenties at most. Not a member of staff. No uniform, no name badge, just some have-a-go hero. With the bottle cocked high at his right shoulder the man ran at Babi, yelling as he rushed forward. The bottle passed within a couple of inches of Garcia's head but failed to make contact.

Garcia swayed back, moving his head away from the bottle's trajectory. Before the young man had time to try another swing, Babi stepped in and with a simple push on the man's shoulder sent him toppling off balance. As the challenger straightened up and moved for another swing, Garcia drew his pistol from his belt and backhanded the weapon across his face. The young man went down to his hands and knees, the bottle rolling across the floor, and Garcia sighted his pistol on a point between the man's shoulder blades.

He was about to squeeze the trigger when a young woman crashed into him from behind. The single shot that exploded from the Kimber missed the man's back but drilled a hole into his forearm just above the wrist. He screamed.

Garcia had wanted to leave the have-a-go hero paralysed for the rest of his days and now some bitch had ruined his fun. Garcia rounded on the woman, to see it was the brown-haired girl that he'd eyed earlier. He grabbed at her, his fingers winding tight into her ponytail, and she yelped sharply as he pushed the Kimber under her chin.

"*Hola, chica.*" Garcia blew her a kiss. "Scream if you want to. You think any of these *pendejos* will come and save you? Look at them run, like the bloated drunken rats they are."

The fire crept closer to the main bar. Garcia pushed his captive towards the rear of the club, not caring to be near the countless bottles of flammable spirits when they went up.

"What is your name, *chica*?"

The woman stared back at the man with a stricken expression. A sharp tug on her hair and a jab with the pistol elicited a gasping answer.

"Julie."

Garcia repeated the name back to her several times like it carried a sour taste. He knocked the Kimber against her chest. "Another English *puta* with her *tetas* on display. You are like mould on bread. Everywhere you go, you spoil the country. Drunken, loud and vulgar. If I had my way I would kill every single one of you."

Julie tried to pull away and for a brief moment almost wriggled free of his grasp. Then his arm coiled around her throat, pulling her tight against his body with the pistol pressed painfully against her spine.

"Try that again and I'll shoot you in the back. If you survive you will spend the rest of your miserable life in a wheelchair. Understand?"

Julie replied with an inarticulate noise and nodded her head.

Garcia scowled at her, anticipating the things he had planned for her flesh. He took another look at the flailing bodies that were struggling to escape through the main doors and smiled. Turning Julie in a tight circle he moved the pistol from her back and fired. A woman at the rear of the crowd was pitched to the ground.

"Parting shot!" Garcia winked and then forced Julie through the staff door and headed towards the rear exit.

81

Danny raced towards the rear doors of the club. The screams from within and the smoke that billowed from the open door left no doubt what was happening.

A man and woman emerged, locked in an embrace. No not an embrace. He had an arm locked tight around her throat. Her face was a mask of fear.

"Julie!"

Danny's voice halted the man in his tracks. He twisted Julie around, bringing the Kimber SCU to the side of her head. "That's close enough, *pendejo*."

Danny took a slow step closer.

"You want this bitch's brains over your shoes? Just keep on coming."

Danny exhaled. He took another slow step, letting the bag drop to the ground. He held his hands out to the side of his body, palms up.

Julie stared into his eyes. Her face was white, her mouth a tight line. The pistol dug hard into the side of her face.

Garcia grunted as he tightened the hold around Julie's

neck. Another man had entered the wide alley at the rear of the club. He stood head and shoulders taller than the Scotsman and held a pistol up and ready.

Garcia flinched as something exploded in the kitchen behind him. An orange fireball filled the doorway, expanding vigorously as it met the outside air.

"You got him, Clay?" Danny asked.

"Dead in my sights."

Garcia flicked his attention from the hulking American back to the closer threat.

"That's my brother, Clay. I should warn you that he was the best shot in his regiment. You shoot the girl, he shoots you. Your one chance is to drop your weapon."

Air hissed between Garcia's teeth. "You think I would trust an Englishman and an American? Maybe *you* should join the Locos."

"Scotsman."

"Texan!"

Garcia shook his head, scowling at Danny. "Last time we met, a young boy got in the way of our fun. Now you bring along Buffalo Bill to fight your battles. I thought you were going to be more of a challenge than that, a worthy opponent, but you're just another pussy *pendejo* that can't finish what he started."

"Listening to you is getting real old, real quick." Danny shifted his weight onto his left foot. "I'll give you three seconds to drop your gun."

"*Chingate!*"

"One…"

Garcia repeated his curse in English, slow and loud. "Go fuck yourself!"

"Two…"

Julie slammed her right hand back between Garcia's legs. She grabbed onto what she found there and squeezed, her knuckles turning white.

Garcia's pistol bucked in his hand as he roared in pain.

Julie dropped to her knees as the flash from the pistol seared across her face.

Spearing forward, Danny leaped over Julie's crouching form, one hand seizing Garcia's gun hand, the other going for his throat.

The pistol barked again, the flash illuminating both faces for a brief instant.

Pulling him close, Danny smashed his nose with a vicious headbutt. Garcia pitched back onto his heels, blood streaming down his lower face. Keeping the pistol angled away from both his own and Julie's body, Danny hit him with his head a second time, the impact sharp and brutal. Julie scrambled to safety, covering her head with her arms.

As both men wrestled for control of the firearm, Clay moved closer. The two men were now locked in a deadly embrace, hands at each other's throats, gripping so tight their knuckles were white. Garcia's pistol was forced high above his head as Danny dropped his weight and surged forward.

Clay sighted on the centre of Garcia's gun hand and squeezed the trigger.

Boom!

Garcia's fingers exploded in a red mist as the .45 ACP round found its target. The Kimber pistol he had been trying to lever towards Danny's head fell to the ground.

Danny let him fall. He gazed down at what was left of

the Spaniard's hand. He'd seen pictures of shark bites that looked prettier. Behind him, orange flames licked around the edges of the doorway like devils' fingers, black smoke filling the void.

"You're finished. Done. No more fire bombs for you, Torchy."

Clay stepped closer, the pistol aimed at the fallen man. "Not to worry. I hear Spanish prisons are just a laugh a minute. Wonder how long you'll get?"

Garcia lurched to his feet, the bloody remnant of his hand cradled against his chest. His voice was ragged as he swayed on unsteady legs. "I don't care how long I get. When I get out I'll slit the throat of everyone that works in this godforsaken club. I'll do the cripple first then come back for his wife—"

"Well ain't you just a ray of golden sunshine." Clay flashed him a grin befitting a rapturous TV evangelist. "If you're happy and you know it clap your—oh!"

"I'll fucking kill them all and then I'll—"

The heel of Danny's boot slammed out in a side-thrust kick, catching Garcia in the centre of his chest. The smoke and flames within the doorway seemed to open momentarily like the claw of a behemoth, then he was gone. An agonised scream echoed from within the inferno.

Clay placed a hand on his brother's shoulder. "Hey, out of the frying pan…"

Danny stepped back from the searing heat and helped Julie to her feet.

"I thought I was going to die," she said, her voice thick with emotion.

"But you didn't." Danny cupped her face in his hands.

"You did really well. A lot of people would have frozen up."

"I did it without thinking. I just kind of panicked."

Danny kissed her as he brushed hair from her face. She would sport the painful burn from the muzzle flash for a week or two. The red stripe across her cheek looked almost like war paint.

"I hope everybody got out of the club okay," said Clay. As he frowned, the lattice of old scars on the side of his face crinkled.

Julie shook her head. "I nearly didn't. I was upstairs when I heard the screaming. Must have gone up really fast. I was only up there a minute or two. I ran back down when I heard the screams. There were flames everywhere."

"Somehow I don't think that was Mr Crispy's first job," replied Clay.

"Wasn't. That was the same fucker who was pitching Molotovs at me the other night. Nearly got me a couple of times," Danny said.

"Live by the scorch, die by the scorch," said Clay. "So he got what was coming to him."

"Not soon enough though." Danny motioned at the smoke and flames.

"Ay-men to that." Clay pushed his tongue under his upper lip. "Pam's gonna have my hide for this."

Danny reached out to both Julie and Clay, a hand on each shoulder. "Let's go round to the front, see what's happening."

Clay tucked the Kimber into his waistband, then covered the weapon with his shirt. Danny picked up the bag of money. As they made their way around the building the noise grew in volume.

A crowd of a few hundred people had gathered in the

street. Many wore expressions of shock, tears cutting streaks through their make-up and smoke-coated faces. Several were coughing and hacking. Many more were waving their smartphones in the air, filming the event.

"Look at these arseholes," spat Danny. "They'll be selling popcorn next."

"This'll all be on the Internet before the fire is out," Julie said, nodding in agreement.

Several men and women made their way towards Julie with their arms outstretched. All wore the same staff T-shirts. One of the girls caught her in an embrace. "Jesus, Julie. We didn't know where you were. We thought you might still be inside."

Julie returned the hugs. "No, thankfully I got out the back way."

The sirens of approaching fire engines elicited a cheer from some of the spectators. Two trucks drove up, the lead driver sounding the horn in an effort to cut a path through the jumble of bodies.

"You okay with these guys?" asked Danny. "We need to go and check on Larry and Pam."

Julie nodded softly, her eyes filling with tears. "I'll be okay here."

"I'll see you later then." Danny dipped his head slightly as he caught the uncertainty in her voice as she withdrew half a step.

Her next words were drowned out by the cheering from the crowd as the first jets of water were released by the fire crew.

82

The smell of hospitals was the same the world over. That slightly disconcerting cocktail of cleaning chemicals, nervous perspiration, relief and sorrow. Clay and Danny sat opposite Pamela in the waiting room. Her face was puffy and streaked by tears.

"So it was all for nothing." Her voice was flat and tired. "Larry is lying in intensive care and the club is gone. I wish we'd never called you."

"Pam, I..." Clay reached for his friend but she shrugged away from his touch. His hand hovered awkwardly in the space between them.

The tense moment was broken as Sally and Phil entered the room at jogging pace. Sally's questions came out in a flood of nervous emotion. "Where's Adam? Is he all right? We've been sick with worry. What the hell is going on?"

Pamela looked up at the new arrivals. "He's okay. Broken arm and some cuts and bruises. He'll live."

"Larry?" Sally's shaped eyebrows moved like caterpillars as she spoke.

"Damn fool managed to get himself shot up again."

Clay stood to his full height. "He saved my life doing so. And Adam's. If it wasn't for Larry we'd all be dead. Give him a break, Pam."

"Don't tell me what to do, Clay. It's my husband in there, getting bullets picked out of his butt."

"I think the bullets went straight through him."

Pamela rounded on Danny, anger flashing in her eyes. "Is that supposed to be funny, Danny? Because it isn't."

Danny held out his hands.

"And what about poor Dez. You had no business taking him with you on your friggin' Rambo adventure. He's dead you know. His family is just down the hall and I can't even look at them."

"I know he's dead," Danny almost shouted. "He died pretending to be me, to give us a fighting chance. But what Clay said is true. If it wasn't for Larry we might all be dead. So count your blessings he's still breathing. I agree, we shouldn't have let them join us but we had no fucking options. Adam's head was on the chopping block. That's why they came. To save their friend."

Pamela began to speak but Danny cut her off. "You knew the risks from the start. Instead of blaming your friends and family just remember who was trying to steal your business out from under your feet. The fucking Locos! That's who deserves your anger, not us."

Pamela cupped her head in her hands. This time she allowed Clay's arm to hug her tight without objection.

"A much wiser man than me once said the night is darkest just before dawn. Larry will pull through and he'll be back on his feet in no time." Clay felt Pamela judder against his chest as she began to cry again.

The door of the waiting room swung open and a male nurse ushered Adam inside. Looking like a survivor from a disaster movie, he shambled in on stiff legs. His face was one big bruise, swollen and misshaped. One arm was cradled in a sling, a thick cast encircling his forearm. His other hand was also bandaged.

He was helped to a seat and Sally fussed around him while Phil looked on with a concerned gaze. Adam stared at the Gunn brothers with unmistakeable admiration. "You both came back. I knew you would. Aunt Sally, you should have seen these guys, they're unbelievable."

Sally tried to quieten her nephew but he continued despite her best efforts. "Did you get them all?"

Danny gave a single stern nod.

Tears spilled down his battered features. The quiet voice that came next was that of vindicated relief. "I knew you would."

The remainder of the day was filled with more questions than answers. Pamela grew increasingly short and terse with the hospital staff as she asked about Larry's condition. He had lost a lot of blood and the trauma from the gunshot wounds had wreaked havoc on his already damaged body. Sometime close to four in the afternoon a doctor whose name badge identified him as Dr Inosanto entered the room with a satisfied smile and gave Pamela the news she was desperate to hear.

After a round of shared embraces Clay decided that the Dukes had earned some private time. "We'll come back after dinner to check on him. Go easy on the old coot, Daisy. He did it all because he loves you."

She smiled up at him.

"That smile's like sunshine after the rain," said Clay as he gently shook her.

"See you later, you big dumb-assed Yank." She stood on her tiptoes and kissed the side of his face. "Thank you."

After a quick goodbye, Sally and Phil led Adam towards the exit. Adam looked over his shoulder, his eyes parting company from each other as he counted his teeth with his tongue. With unabashed admiration he looked at the sutures on Clay's face. "You look like Marv from *Sin City*!" He waved a bandaged hand as he was ushered through the auto doors.

"You ready for something to eat? I know I am." Danny patted the flat muscles of his stomach.

"Damned right," Clay said. "I'm sure there will be a café around here somewhere."

"Good, because I'm about to double their takings in one sitting. I hope they do decent steak and eggs. I could eat half a steer myself."

"I'm thinking about going vegetarian. You know Dad died of a heart attack, probably from all those cheeseburgers he used to eat. Don't want to go the same way." Danny smiled as he took in the expression on his brother's face.

"Two things: one, don't ever expect *me* to stop eating meat. And two, what the hell are our chances of dying from cholesterol? You attract bullets like Brad Pitt attracts women."

"Classy."

"Indeed."

83

One week later

The Woo Hoo had been reduced to a blackened shell. The smell of smoke clung stubbornly to every surface like a bad memory. The windows, doors and framework were missing and the club now resembled an oversized barbecue pit. Odd piles of blackened furniture were piled on the pavement outside, still awaiting removal. The buildings on each side of the club had sustained smoke damage and were closed.

Larry and Pamela huddled together as they surveyed what was left of their club. Larry propped himself on a new set of crutches while Pamela was rarely more than a few inches from his side. It had been that way from the moment the hospital had signed his release.

Behind them stood Danny, Clay and Julie. Jacks sniffed around the piles of charred wood with an occasional disapproving huff. He did not venture inside the remnants of the club, casting dubious looks at the charred building with his good eye.

Danny stepped up to Larry. "How are things going with the insurance company?"

"Ah, you know they never want to pay up. But they will. Pam upped the cover on the place like you said to. We were covered for nearly four times the amount that we were originally. When the money comes through the Woo Hoo will be bigger and better than ever."

"So you are definitely sticking around? That's good."

Larry and Pamela exchanged a look. She brushed a strand of errant hair from her face. "After everything that's happened we couldn't just take the money and run. Besides, this is our home. We've put down roots here."

"The bag of money we found in the car will help tide you over until the insurance pays up."

Larry shook his head. "Nah, Danny. It was good of you to offer but we gave that to Dez's family. They need it a lot more than we do."

"At least it went to a good home."

"It did," agreed Larry and Pam in unison.

"Dez's family are still talking to the police. They need answers that we can't give them," added Pam.

"How are you faring with the cops?" asked Clay.

"It's hard going. They ask the same ten questions over and over. They know that this wasn't a random attack but can't prove it. This is going to go on for a long, long time. They pulled three bodies out of the club. One poor bugger in the toilets and a woman out of the bar." Larry shifted his weight on his crutches. "Oh, and the bonus prize in the kitchen."

"Yeah, he got what was coming to him," said Danny.

"Don't worry about it. Your names will never come

up." Larry lifted his chin in respect to the two mismatched brothers. "You're welcome here any time. Both of you."

Pamela nodded furtively in Julie's direction. "I know someone else that wouldn't be upset if you decided to hang around a while."

"I've already had that conversation. She knows I'm leaving tomorrow." Danny shrugged apologetically.

Larry winced. "That explains the sour looks you keep getting."

"Aye. I don't blame her. I think she's a bit scared of me and what I do. I'm just not what she's looking for."

Pamela scrutinised him with concern. "But what are *you* looking for, Danny?"

"I don't know. I'll send you both a postcard when I find it."

"Well, like Larry said, you and Clay have always got a free place to stay with us if you need one."

"Good to know," said Clay. "And you've got my number if you ever need us again."

Pamela thumped him on the chest. "We need your help like I need an extra layer of fat on my arse."

Clay jostled her playfully. "Oh I don't know; you could stand to carry a little more junk in the trunk."

Danny turned to talk to Julie but she had walked away from the club with Jacks. The dog looked back at the club, balanced on his three good legs, then waddled after Julie. Danny puffed out his cheeks.

"She'll be okay," said Pamela.

Danny knew there was nothing else to say.

Clay shared an embrace with both Larry and Pamela. "We better be going. We ship out first thing in the morning. I just need to go and settle up our hotel bill. I'll keep in touch."

"Make sure that you do," said Larry.

"Hey, you two stay out of trouble," said Danny.

The Dukes smiled back at him. Larry tapped his boot with a crutch. "That should be easy, you killed all the troublemakers in a fifty-mile radius."

Clay nodded in agreement. "Ay-men to that."

On the roof of the Woo Hoo Club, a crow with feathers the same colour as the charred building squawked once. The two sharp taps of its beak upon the tiles were unnoticed by the people below. Seemingly satisfied, the carrion bird launched itself into the air and after another squawk flew out to sea.

ACKNOWLEDGEMENTS

A big thank you as always to my wife Wendy. Writing is so much more than just hammering out words on a laptop. It also takes much narrowing of eyes and rubbing of chin. Wendy endures both on a regular basis.

Thank you also to Team Titan. My tireless editor Miranda Jewess who takes my words and makes them better. Philippa Ward and Lydia Gittins too for their help and support.

My respect goes out to all of our servicemen and women, of land, air and sea, past and present, who wore the uniform and stood when it counted most.

ABOUT THE AUTHOR

James Hilton is the author of *Search and Destroy*, the first novel in the Gunn Brothers series. He is a 4th Dan Blackbelt in Shotokan Karate, and has worked as a martial arts instructor, which has been invaluable in crafting his fight scenes. He is currently planning a YA series. He lives in Carlisle. His brother is bestselling thriller author Matt Hilton.

The
Bartender's
Best Friend

a complete
guide to cocktails,
martinis, and mixed drinks

Mardee Haidin Regan

JOHN WILEY & SONS, INC.

Published by John Wiley & Sons, Inc., Hoboken, New Jersey
Published simultaneously in Canada

For general information on our other products and services or for technical
support, please contact our Customer Care Department within the United
States at (800) 762-2974, outside the United States at (317) 572-3993 or fax
(317) 572-4002.

Wiley also publishes its books in a variety of electronic formats. Some content
that appears in print may not be available in electronic books.

Library of Congress Cataloging-in-Publication Data

Regan, Mardee Haidin.
    The bartender's best friend : a complete guide to cocktails, martinis,
  and mixed drinks / Mardee Haidin Regan.
      p. cm.
    Includes bibliographical references and index.
    ISBN 0-471-22721-8 (cloth)
    1. Cocktails. 2. Bartending. I. Title.

  TX951.R368 2002
  641.8'74—dc21   2002068981

Printed in the United States of America

10   9   8   7   6   5

*This book is for my husband, Gary Regan,
light of my life and this bartender's
very best friend.*

Acknowledgments

Oh my, I'm not very good at remembering everybody who has impressed me, blessed me, or obsessed me. Susan Wyler, my friend and editor, knocked my socks off with her generosity, enthusiasm, and tender loving care—huge thanks for that. Andrea Johnson and the production team were the soul of patience as I dug my way through the manuscript, mucking things up or not, querying too much or not—more thanks to you. Then, too, I heartily thank the sage though curmudgeonly Stephan Wilkinson, who named this book; I heartily thank my husband, Gary Regan, for smilingly withstanding the tumult I create in our lives; and I heartily thank every single person I ever met, just because each moment and each encounter is that important. Now, turn the page, the rest is much more fun and interesting.

Contents

Introduction: About This Book

Cocktails are fashion—they bespeak the era of their creation. Cocktails are an expression of style, and like music, art, architecture, theater, and design, in many ways they reflect the attitude of the nation. Right now cocktail culture is soaring. No matter where you look—in magazines, newspapers, films, and on television—you see people drinking cocktails.

Many of our favorite cocktails reflect our mind-set. Some are based on classic combinations, some are casual and irreverent, often verging on downright silly, and many are the result of any number of incredible new ingredients in the marketplace. You couldn't get root-beer schnapps in the fifties.

Cocktail trends are an aspect of pop culture. Although some drinks hearken to our childhoods, scores of others take their inspiration from foods, films, television, songs, books, and world events. One sizeable group of drinks are alcoholic concoctions that taste like something entirely different—a cookie or a candy bar. Another group of drinks requires a helper—it takes two to drink a Mouth Margarita. And then there are the drinks whose names are X-rated. Don't object. That's the way it is. And they sell like wildfire.

Who is the bartender's best friend? The best tipper at the bar? Probably. But in writing this book, I've tried to be a friend to the bartender by including many cocktails and mixed drinks that are actually ordered at bars nationwide. When someone orders a Manhattan, you might not have to look in this book, but the recipe is here if you need it, and if somebody asks you to fix them a Schnapp, Crackle & Pop , and you're a little bewildered, just turn to "S" and you'll be serving one up in no time.

On a more serious note, the bartender's very best friend can often be an experienced, sober driver or the local taxi service. Why? Because as enjoyable and fun as drinking and serving cocktails, wines, and beers can be, the unimpeachable fact is that alcohol affects our bodies and our minds, impairing our judgment and reaction time. Don't drink and drive, and don't let others drink and drive either. What's ultimately most fashionable is being alive to enjoy another day.

Bartending Basics

Making a cocktail has just four requirements. The first three are easy: You need ingredients—the spirits, the juices, the ice, the sodas, the garnishes. You need equipment—a shaker, a strainer, a spoon. And you need something to serve the drink in, be it the finest lead crystal cocktail glass or a paper cup. The fourth requirement, however, is the tough one. You need to understand how to use these elements, and, ideally, you must acquire a grasp of how they intermingle. And therein lies the rub: You can make drinks or you can master drink-making, the craft of bartending. The choice is yours; the basics are outlined here. Mastering the craft requires thought, effort, and just like getting to Carnegie Hall—practice, practice, practice.

EQUIPMENT

Tools and the methods of using them define the quality of the job performed. And just as a carpenter invests in his saws, a chef in his knives, or a painter in his brushes, a bartender needs to have the right stuff on hand to make the job easier and more professional. Once the proper tools are in place, you're good to go. Here's what's needed:

Barspoon: An ingenious long-handled spoon that has an almost teardrop-shaped bowl and a twisted shaft that makes stirring with one hand very easy. Absolutely essential if you want to do it right.

Bar towels: Two kinds—small, absorbent terrycloth towels that can be used as a bar mat to soak up spillage, splashes, and condensation; tightly woven, flat-weave cotton or linen dishtowels for polishing glasses or grasping wet, chilled wine bottles that are being held in a wine bucket. You'll need several of each.

Blender: A heavy-duty machine capable of rendering ice cubes and other ingredients into slush. Can opt for the 32- or 48-ounce container; I prefer a metal to a plastic base. Essential for frozen drinks.

Boston shaker: The most important tool for cocktail making—a two-part implement consisting of a mixing glass bottom and a taller, slightly wider, flat-bottomed metal cup. In use, the metal half is upended over the mixing glass, overreaches the juncture of the two rims, and allows the bartender to shake with ease and with no spills or leaks. The cups are "broken" apart. If pouring from the metal half, a Hawthorne strainer is used; if pouring from the mixing glass half, a julep strainer is used.

Bottle opener: The standard tool for removing bottle caps, a number of different designs are available, but all deliver the same end result: getting that metal cap off the bottle.

Can opener: The handheld kitchen tool that will remove one end of a can, useful for very thick mixtures, such as coconut cream. A handheld model is sufficient for behind the bar.

Champagne stopper: A winged, spring-loaded gizmo that clamps over the lip of a champagne bottle and helps keep the CO_2 (carbon dioxide) inside the bottle where it belongs.

Cheesecloth: Essential for straining solids from steeped mixtures. Remember, always soak cheesecloth with water and wring out well before using it to strain liquid mixtures; if you don't, you'll lose a considerable amount of the liquid ingredient to absorption by the cheesecloth.

Churchkey: A double-duty device: the rounded end is a bottle opener; the pointed end is for piercing cans of liquids, like tomato juice.

Citrus reamer: A manual device for extracting the juice from halved citrus fruits; some are handheld and must be used over a glass or bowl to collect the juices; others are stationary with a bowl-shaped bottom to collect the juices; still others are large levered devices that sit on the countertop. Electric juicers are also available.

Citrus strippers and zesters: Handy devices that can help cut various widths of citrus zests—from very small, fine curls to $1/4$-inch-wide swaths. In capable hands, a paring knife can be used.

Cocktail napkins and/or coasters: Essential for collecting any condensation or drips when serving a cocktail.

Cocktail picks: Usually small, thin skewers for selecting garnishes for a drink; one end of a cocktail pick might be adorned in some way to make picking it up easier.

Cocktail shaker: The three-part tool made for shaking cocktails. A large bottom cup is topped with a tight-fitting lid and the lid itself has a cap that is fitted with a built-in strainer to prevent all but the tiniest shards of ice from being poured into the drink. Some more stylized cocktail shakers have a capped pour spout—like a teapot with a spout cover—with a built-in strainer.

Corkscrew: Absolutely essential for uncorking a wine bottle. Dozens and dozens of designs exist; choose whatever style makes your life easiest. I personally prefer the Screwpull to all others because it does not require upper-arm strength; the cork is removed by continual turning in one direction.

Cutting boards: Necessary for preparing garnishes and avoiding damage to wooden bartops.

Foil cutter: A handy gizmo for cleanly cutting away the foil or lead capsule that encases the top of a wine bottle.

Funnel: A useful tool for transferring liquids into small-mouthed containers or bottles.

Glass pitcher: An excellent, multipurpose vessel for behind the bar. It will hold water, juices, and mixtures of all kinds for easy pouring when needed.

Grater: A small, handheld device that can be used for whole nutmegs and for producing fine shreds of citrus zest or fresh ginger.

Ice bucket: Absolutely vital for the home bar—a sizeable container to hold fresh ice for use in preparing and serving cocktails.

Ice crusher: An electric device that breaks large cubes into crushed shards of ice. Be warned: they are noisy in operation.

Ice scoop: A stainless-steel tool that makes quick work of filling a shaker, mixing glass, or serving glass with ice.

Ice tongs: A tool that provides a stylish but tedious method for adding ice cubes to a vessel; see Ice scoop.

Jigger: An hourglass-shaped, most likely metal device that usually has a 1-ounce measure on its smaller end and a 1 1/2-ounce measure on the opposite end. However, jiggers are made in many sizes; check yours to know what volume each end measures. I suggest that beginners search out what I call a tippable measure: It looks like a large tablespoon-size measuring spoon that has a metal rod sticking out from the measure's bowl on opposite sides. You can center it over a mixing glass, pour in the desired measure of ingredient, and just rotate the rod to pour the ingredient into the glass, leaving the measure empty and ready to measure the next ingredient. Nifty.

Knives: Sharp extensions of the bartender's hands. Two sizes of knife are usually required: a paring knife for cutting fruit garnishes and a larger-bladed all-purpose knife that can halve a grapefruit or behead a pineapple.

Measuring cups: For the beginning bartender, a 1-cup liquid measuring cup will aid in checking free-poured measures. Large measuring cups are handy for punch-making and as auxiliary pitchers.

Measuring spoons: Usually used for measuring dry ingredients such as spices.

Mixing glass: The workhorse tool at any bar, the 16- to 20-ounce glass vessel that is used for stirring ingredients over ice.

Muddler: Usually a wooden, pestle-shaped implement that has a flat but bulbous end that is used to crush ingredients together, in the bottom of a mixing glass or in a serving glass.

Sip-sticks, stirrers, swizzle sticks, straws: Thin, often tubular, sometimes disposable devices used to mix ingredients for a Highball or for sipping through.

Speed pourers: Marvelously handy, removable pour spouts that fit tightly into the neck of most standard bottles and allow the bartender to pick up the bottle and pour immediately. Also, these pourers make it easy for a bartender to free pour often-used ingredients by using a counting system that is discussed under Bartending Techniques (page 38).

Strainers: Two types of bar strainers are essential at every bar: a Hawthorne strainer (at right) is the one with the curly wire around half of its circumference so that it fits snugly inside the metal half of a Boston shaker. A julep strainer is a shallow-bowled, perforated, short-handled spoon that fits neatly inside a mixing glass.

INGREDIENTS

Spirits

Distilled spirits have been with us since the 1100s when the art of distillation, which had been practiced for centuries at that point, was finally used to distill alcoholic products, such as wine. Initially, because spirits were liquids that could be set on fire, they were known as ardent spirits, from the Latin *adere,* meaning "to burn," but because they were first used as medicines, they became known as the water of life, and this name is still with us today. France produces *eaux-de-vie;* Scandinavia makes *aquavit,* and both of these terms translate to "water of life." Even the Gaelic word *uisga beatha* (Ireland) or *usquebaugh* (Scotland) which was anglicized to "whisk(e)y," means water of life. Here are some definitions for the main categories of distilled spirits, along with some explanations of various specific bottlings, and the most important distillation terms you should know.

Absente: See Absinthe and Absinthe Substitutes.

Absinthe and Absinthe Substitutes: Absinthe was outlawed in many countries during the first couple of decades of the twentieth century, and although its popularity waned, it has recently made a big comeback in countries where it wasn't banned—notably Andorra, the Czech Republic, England, Germany, Japan, and Spain. The reason that absinthe was banned was that it was said to be addictive and hallucinogenic because of one ingredient, wormwood, a bitter herb, that contains thujone, which has a molecular structure that's strikingly similar to THC, the active ingredient in marijuana. In all probability, though, it was the high alcohol content of absinthe—most bottlings verged on almost 70 percent alcohol by volume (abv)—that caused absinthe drinkers to act so strangely.

In the United States, where absinthe was made illegal in 1915, we now use absinthe substitutes—Pernod, Ricard, Herbsaint, and Absente—when absinthe is called for in a drink. These spirits are often consumed after dilution with water, but in the case of Absente, it's best to add sugar, too.

Amer Picon: Hard to find in the United States, this is a French apéritif wine with orange/herbal notes.

American Brandy: Distilled from a fermented mash of grapes, American distillers have a huge advantage over many other brandymakers: the law does not proscribe which grape varieties can be used, and thus, they can employ whichever grape variety takes their fancy. The result is some truly great American brandies that are loaded with complexity, perhaps because they are made from top-notch grapes.

Apple Brandy: Distilled from a fermented mash of apples, apple brandy is usually aged in oak barrels, sometimes for decades, but more usually for about three to five years.

Applejack: A blended apple brandy used in many cocktails.

Armagnac: A grape brandy made in the Gascony region of France, which is divided into three subregions: Ténarèze, Haut-Armagnac, and Bas-Armagnac. Armagnac must be made only from white grapes, Ugni Blanc (also known as Saint-Emilion), Colombard, and Folle Blanche varieties being the most common. Armagnac is usually aged in black oak casks, and the minimum age of the brandy is noted on the bottle using the same terminology as cognac (see box, page 9).

Bourbon: Distilled from a fermented mash that must contain a minimum of 51 percent corn, the other grains used are malted barley and either rye or wheat. Bourbon must be aged in new, charred oak barrels for a minimum of two years, though most bottlings have spent at least four years in the wood. The name, bourbon, comes from the Kentucky county from which whiskey from the area was shipped in the late 1700s. Bourbon can be made legally anywhere in the United States, although, with the exception of one Virginia distillery, at the time of writing it is all made in Kentucky. Bourbon is the only spirit that was born in the United States; all others originated elsewhere.

Small-batch bourbon usually denotes whiskey that has been selected from a small quantity of barrels that has aged into what the distiller thinks is a whiskey that's superior to his regular bottlings. Keep in mind, though, that each distillery has its own criteria for using this term, and it has not been legally defined.

Brandy: Distilled from a fermented mash of fruits, the most common brandies are grape-based, though many made from other fruits are also available.

Brandy de Jerez: A brandy made from a fermented mash of grapes, usually Airén or Palomino varietals, in the Jerez district of Spain. Brandy de Jerez is aged in oak using the solera method, which means that the barrels are stacked on top of each other, usually about 12 barrels high, and newly made brandy is entered into the top layer. Every few months, some brandy is taken from the bottom layer, which contains the oldest brandy, and this is replaced with brandy from the next level up. The procedure is repeated until what started out as young brandy on the top layer has aged its way through the layers and is removed. All the while, newly made brandy is entered at the top layer so that the continuous mingling and aging process can continue. "Solera" bottlings are aged for around one year, "Solera Reserva" brandies must spend two years in oak, and bottles labeled "Solera Gran Reserva" spend upwards of seven years in wood.

> ## Brandies
>
> **Cognacs, Armagnacs, and Calvados use the following designations to denote the minimum age of the brandy in the bottle:**
>
> **VS (Very Special): $2^1/_2$ years**
>
> **VSOP (Very Special Old Pale): $4^1/_2$ years**
>
> **VO (Very Old): $4^1/_2$ years**
>
> **Réserve: $4^1/_2$ years**
>
> **XO (Extra Old): 6 years**
>
> **Napoléon: 6 years**

Cachaça: A style of rum made from sugarcane in Brazil—essential to a true Caipirinha.

Calvados: A brandy distilled from a fermented mash of apples, although a small percentage of pears are also used, made in the Calvados region of Normandy, France. Calvados is aged in oak casks—mainly Limousin—and the minimum age of the brandy is noted on the bottle using the same terminology as Cognac (see box above).

Campari: A bitter apéritif from Italy used in cocktails and mixed drinks such as the Negroni. It is notable for its red color and its affinity to orange flavors.

Canadian Whisky: Usually a blended whisky from Canada, which can be flavored legally with a small percentage of products, such as prune wine and even bourbon.

Cognac: A grape brandy made in the Cognac region of France which is divided into six subregions: Grande Champagne, Petite Champagne, Borderies, Fins Bois, Bons Bois, and Bois Ordinaires. Cognac, by law, must be made only from white grapes, and 90 percent of the grapes must be Ugni Blanc (also known as Saint-Emilion), Folle Blanche, and/or Colombard. Cognac usually is aged in Limousin oak casks for a minimum of 30 months, at which point it can be labeled as a VS (Very Special) bottling. Cognacs aged for longer than this use a variety of other designations (see box, page 9).

Distilled Spirits

From the Latin *dis* or *des,* which implies separation, and *stilla,* meaning "drop," distillation means "to separate, drop by drop." In terms of distilled spirits, this means that a fermented mash, or "soup," of fruits, grains, sugars, or vegetables, is entered into a still and heated. Since the alcohol in the mash evaporates at a lower temperature than the water, the steam that rises contains more alcohol than the original mash. This steam is collected, then condensed, and depending on the method of distillation used, it might have to be redistilled until it contains enough alcohol—40 percent minimum—to be called a distilled spirit.

Continuous stills, invented in the late 1700s or early 1800s, are tall chimney-like pieces of equipment fitted with numerous perforated plates situated at regular intervals in the chimney. Steam is introduced to the bottom of the still, while the fermented mash is poured into the top. The steam evaporates the alcohol from the mash as it descends through the perforated plates, and this steam, now laden with alcohol, can be drawn off and condensed at various levels in the still. If the steam is allowed to reach the top of the still, it can contain as much as 95 percent alcohol, but if it is drawn off at lower levels, it will be weaker. Continuous stills, however, are not used to produce spirits that have less than 40 percent alcohol, so redistillation is unnecessary. Continuous stills are used to produce vodka, and most other varieties of distilled spirits.

Pot stills, usually onion-shaped copper vessels with a long, tapering chimney extending from the top, are used to make specialty spirits, such as single malt scotches and various brandies. In this kind of still, the fermented mash is usually strained of all solids before being entered, in order to prevent scorching. The still is heated, usually by means of a steam jacket, but sometimes coal and/or wood is still used. The vapors rise up the tapered chimney and are condensed. This product of one distillation doesn't contain enough alcohol to be known as a spirit, so it must then be entered into another pot still, and go through the process again.

Dubonnet: French apéritif wines—rouge and blanc—used in drinks such as the Dubonnet Cocktail.

Eaux-de-vie: Distilled from a fermented mash of fruits, eaux-de-vie are rarely aged, and are made in, more or less, every country that produces fruit. Most of the best bottlings come from the United States (mainly from California and Oregon), France, Italy, Germany, and Switzerland.

Fruit Brandies: The most common fruit brandies found behind American bars contain a small amount of true brandy, and are sweetened and flavored to be suitable cocktail ingredients.

Gin: Gin was first made in Holland in the 1500s, and English soldiers who fought alongside the Dutch in the Thirty Years War, brought the spirit home calling it Dutch Courage, because it had been used to prepare them for battle. The word *gin* comes from the French *genièvre,* which means "juniper."

Basically, gin is a flavored vodka, the main flavoring agent being juniper, but other botanicals, such as angelica, caraway, cardamom, cassia, cinnamon, coriander, fennel, ginger, lemon zest, licorice, and orange zest can also be used. Gin producers don't normally reveal their recipes, and even if they list their ingredients, they never tell us what amounts they have used. London Dry Gin is crisp and dry, and the words denote a style, not necessarily where the product was made. Plymouth gin is similar in style to some London Dry Gins, but it must be made in Plymouth, England. Old Tom Gin was a sweetened gin that's no longer on the market. Genever or Hollands Gin is made in Holland and has a malty sweetness not found in other styles. Gins flavored with citrus juice, such as lime and grapefruit, have recently been introduced to the market, and there are even gins available now flavored with cucumbers, mint, and passion fruit.

Grappa: An unaged Italian brandy distilled from grape pomace—the leftover skins, seeds, and other detritus from the winemaking process.

Herbsaint: See Absinthe and Absinthe Substitutes.

Irish Whiskey: Irish whiskey, like scotch, can be divided into two distinct categories—single malts and blended whiskeys—although most Irish whiskey is blended. Single malt Irish whiskey is made in the same way as single malt scotch (see page 15), although peat isn't usually used in the process, and therefore, the smokiness evident in scotch isn't found in the vast majority of Irish whiskeys. Blended Irish whiskey is made by blending together single malts with neutral grain whiskeys, in the same way that blended scotch is made.

Kirsch: An unaged brandy distilled from a fermented mash of cherries.

Marc: An unaged French brandy distilled from grape pomace—the leftovers from the winemaking process. Marc is the French equivalent of Italian grappa.

Mash: A "soup" of fruits, grains, sugars, or sometimes vegetables and water, that is fermented, by the introduction of yeast, to produce alcohol.

Mezcal: A Mexican spirit made from several species of the agave plant, but not the blue agave plant that must be used for tequilas. While tequila must be produced in certain designated areas, mezcal can be made anywhere in Mexico. Mezcal is a much rougher spirit, often tinged with a smoky flavor from roasting the agaves in clay ovens.

Pernod: See Absinthe and Absinthe Substitutes.

Pisco Brandy: True Pisco is a Peruvian grape brandy, made mainly with Quebranta grapes, and aged for short periods in clay vessels. It is essential to a Pisco Sour.

Ricard: See Absinthe and Absinthe Substitutes.

Rum: Distilled from a mash of molasses or sugarcane juice, most of the rum consumed in the United States comes from Puerto Rico. However, rum is produced in and imported from almost every Caribbean nation, and, indeed, almost every sugar-producing country.

Rums imported from Puerto Rico are required by law to be aged in oak for at least one year. Many rums are aged for far longer, developing into complex, dry spirits suitable for sipping.

Rums are available in light (or white), amber, añejo, and dark varieties, but since every rum-producing nation has its own rules and regulations governing these products, it's impossible to know how long each one of them has been aged in oak unless an age statement appears on the label.

Flavored rums have become very popular in the last decade or so. It's easy to find a variety of flavors, banana, citrus, coconut, lemon, lime and mint, orange, pineapple, raspberry, spiced, vanilla, and wild cherry among them.

Rye Whiskey: Made from a fermented mash containing a minimum of 51 percent rye and aged in new charred oak barrels, rye whiskey is making a comeback among whiskey drinkers. Although some people refer to blended Canadian whiskies as "ryes," they are not; look for the words, "straight rye whiskey" on the label.

Scotch Whisky: Made in Scotland from a fermented mash of grains, scotch can be divided into two main categories. Single malt scotch is distilled in pot stills from a fermented mash of malted barley, and must spend a minimum of three years in oak barrels before being bottled. Most bottlings, however, spend far longer than that in the wood, and this is usually reflected by an age statement on the label. Each single malt must be the product of just one distillery, the name of which is found on the label of most bottlings. Complicating matters even more, single malt scotches as a category are often further broken down according to the region in which they are made (see box, page 15). Pure malt scotch, known in Scotland as vatted malt whisky, is made by blending single malts from more than one distillery to achieve a specific flavor profile.

Blended scotch is made by blending single malt scotch with neutral grain whisky, which can be made from a fermented mash of any grain, although corn is usually predominant, and a small amount of malted barley is usually used, as well. The amount of single malt scotch in a blended bottling usually governs its price, so the more expensive blended whiskies tend to be made with a higher percentage of single malt.

The smokiness found in scotch, whether it be single malt or blended, varies from one bottling to the next, but it comes from the barley, which, after germination, is dried over peat fires prior to being introduced to the mash. The amount of time that the malted barley spends over the smoldering peat will govern the amount of smokiness found in the finished product.

Single-Barrel Whisk(e)y: Most whiskeys, even single malt scotches, are made by marrying together whiskeys from a number of barrels. In the case of single-barrel whiskey, this is not the case, and these bottlings contain product from just one barrel that the distiller has decided has matured into a superior spirit.

Single Malt Scotches

Single malt scotches can be made anywhere in Scotland, but generalizations about specific qualities found in whiskies from various regions can be drawn, even though bottlings vary from one distillery to the next.

Islay (EYE-luh) single malts, such as Ardbeg, Bowmore, and Laphroaig, are from an island just off the western coast of Scotland. Islay malts are usually quite peaty and smoky with notes of iodine, and even seaweed sometimes being present.

Lowland single malts, such as Auchentoshan, Bladnoch, Glenkinchie, and Littlemill, are usually lighter in character than other bottlings, and they are seldom described as being overly smoky or peaty.

Campbeltown single malts, such as Glen Scotia, Longrow, and Springbank, from the west coast of Scotland, are known for their brininess, and usually display a certain degree of smokiness, too.

Highland single malts, such as Edradour, Glenmorangie, Knockando, and Oban, vary widely in character, but most often they can be described as being fresh and heathery, with some fruity notes present in certain bottlings.

Speyside single malts, such as Aberlour, The Glenlivet, and The Macallan, come from a sub-region of the Highlands that most aficionados claim produces the best of the best whiskies. Speyside bottlings vary tremendously from one to the next, but virtually all of them are very complex, well-knit whiskies, with hints of smoke and peat.

Sloe Gin: Not every bottling of sloe gin uses gin as its base, but this spirit gets its flavor from the sloe berries found on blackthorn bushes.

Tennessee Whiskey: Distilled from a fermented mash containing a minimum of 51 percent corn, Tennessee whiskey must be made within the state of Tennessee, and it differs from bourbon in that it is filtered through large vats of sugar maple charcoal before it is aged in new charred oak barrels, giving it a sweet sootiness not found in any other whiskeys.

Tequila: Distilled from a fermented mash of blue agave *(Weber tequilana azul),* a member of the amaryllis family that looks like a very large pineapple, tequila is made in Mexico, and must come from the state of Jalisco, or in demarcated regions of the states of Nayarit, Guanajuato, Michoacán, or Tamaulipas.

The two basic varieties of tequila are 100-percent blue agave and *mixto*. By law, *mixto* tequila can be made with as little as 51 percent blue agave, with the rest of the product usually being made up of sugar-based products. One hundred–percent agave tequilas are just what they sound like—made only from the blue agave plant; these are most prized by tequila lovers. Blanco, or "white," tequilas are not aged at all, but *joven abocado,* meaning "young and smoothed," bottlings, usually known as "gold" tequilas, contain a percentage of tequila that spent at least two months in oak. *Reposado,* or "rested," tequilas spend a minimum of two months in barrels before being bottled, and *Añejo,* or "aged," tequilas spend a minimum of 12 months in the wood.

Vodka: This spirit can be made from a fermented mash of almost anything, but it's usually made from grains or potatoes. Whether vodka originated in Poland or Russia is a matter that will be debated for centuries to come. Vodka contains very few, if any, impurities, and therefore, it has little in the way of flavor or aroma. However, individual bottlings do differ, and like any other spirit, some are better than others. As a massive generalization, potato vodkas, made mainly in Poland, although at least one is made in the United States, are a little sweeter than grain-based bottlings.

Flavored vodkas have become very popular in recent years, and some of them are responsible for many of today's newest cocktails and mixed drinks. Almost every flavor under the sun seems to be on the market now; you can choose from apple, berry, bilberry, bison grass, chocolate, cinnamon, citrus, coffee, cranberry, currant, honey, honey pepper, honey and quince, lemon, lime, orange, peach, pear, pepper, raspberry, strawberry, vanilla, wild apple, wild berry, and many more are sure to be on the shelves by the time you read this.

Whisk(e)y: Spelled with the "e" in Ireland and the United States, and without it in Scotland and Canada, whiskey is distilled from a fermented mash of grains. See **Scotch Whisky, Canadian Whisky, Bourbon, Rye Whiskey, Tennessee Whiskey,** and **Irish Whiskey.**

Liqueurs

Liqueurs are sweetened, usually diluted spirits that have been flavored by specific botanicals, fruits, herbs, nuts, spices, and products from almost every food group. Sometimes known as cordials in the United States, liqueurs have been with us since at least the 1300s, when monks, seeking to make medicines, flavored distilled spirits with medicinal herbs, and sweetened them, sometimes with honey, to make them more palatable. Here's a list of the most important liqueurs, along with explanations of what to expect from them:

Alizé: A passion fruit–flavored, brandy-based liqueur.

Alizé Red Passion: A passion fruit– and cranberry juice–flavored, brandy-based liqueur.

Amaretto: An almond-flavored liqueur that originated in Italy.

Anisette: A syrupy aniseed-flavored liqueur.

Apricot Brandy: An apricot-flavored liqueur containing a percentage of real brandy.

Apry: A brand-name apricot-flavored liqueur.

B & B: Bénédictine mixed with brandy—this delicious liqueur was created at New York's "21" Club shortly after the repeal of Prohibition.

Baileys Irish Cream: Made with Irish whiskey and heavy cream, Baileys brand is one of today's most popular liqueurs.

Bénédictine: A French herbal liqueur made by Bénédictine monks since 1510.

Blackberry Brandy: A blackberry-flavored liqueur containing a percentage of real brandy.

Chambord: A French black raspberry–flavored liqueur sweetened with honey and spiced with herbs.

Chartreuse: Made by French Carthusian monks since 1737, this is an herbal liqueur available in both green and yellow bottlings.

Chéri-Suisse: A Swiss chocolate cherry–flavored liqueur.

Cherry Brandy: A cherry-flavored liqueur not to be confused with kirsch, an unsweetened brandy made from cherries.

Cherry Heering: A brand name of cherry brandy made in Denmark.

Cointreau: A top-notch brand-name bottling of triple sec — by far the best triple sec on the market.

Crème de Banane: A sweet banana-flavored liqueur.

Crème de Cacao: A chocolate-flavored liqueur available in both white and dark bottlings — both are similar in flavor to each other.

Crème de Cassis: A black currant–flavored liqueur originating in France, though many bottlings are now made in the United States.

Crème de Framboise: A raspberry-flavored liqueur from France.

Crème de Menthe: A mint-flavored liqueur that comes in both green and white bottlings — both are similar in flavor to each other.

Crème de Noyaux: An almond-flavored liqueur that contributes the pink color to a Pink Squirrel cocktail — substitute amaretto if you can't find this product.

Cuarenta y Tres Licor 43: A fruit- and herb-based Spanish liqueur, the name translates to "forty three," the number of ingredients used in its production.

Curaçao: A sweet, orange-flavored liqueur, sometimes white, sometimes blue, and sometimes red — all bottlings are similar in flavor.

Danziger Goldwasser: A German liqueur with mainly aniseed and caraway flavors and flakes of real gold. This liqueur has been made since 1598, at which time gold was believed to have healing qualities.

Drambuie: A honeyed scotch-based liqueur flavored with various herbs and spices. The name comes from the Gaelic *an dram buidheach,* meaning "the drink that satisfies." The recipe was supposedly given to Captain John Mackinnon by Bonnie Prince Charlie in 1746, when Mackinnon sheltered him on the Isle of Skye after his defeat by the English at the Battle of Culloden.

Forbidden Fruit: A brandy-based liqueur flavored with grape-fruit, oranges, and honey.

Frangelico: An Italian hazelnut liqueur spiced with cinnamon, cardamom, citrus zest, and various other botanicals.

Galliano: An Italian liqueur with predominant vanilla and orange notes; it is essential for a Harvey Wallbanger.

Glayva: A scotch-based liqueur that, like Drambuie, is flavored with honey and herbs.

Grand Marnier: An orange-flavored, cognac-based French liqueur, made since 1871 by the Marnier-Lapostolle family. Much of the aged cognac used to make Grand Marnier comes from the best regions of Cognac, and after being infused with orange peels and sweetened with simple syrup, the liqueur is then returned to barrels for further aging.

Cordon Rouge is the bottling of Grand Marnier most familiar to us, but it is also available in Grande Marnier Cuvée du Centenaire, which was issued to celebrate the 100-year anniversary of the liqueur, and Grand Marnier Cent Cinquantenaire, released to commemorate the 150-year anniversary of Lapostolle's company, which has been pro-ducing liqueurs since 1827. The Grand Marnier Cuvée du Centenaire is made with 10-year-old cognac, and the Grand Marnier Cuvée du Cent-Cinquantenaire uses XO cognacs.

Irish Mist: Based on an ancient formula for Heather Wine, this Irish whiskey–based liqueur is flavored with honey and spiced with herbs.

Jägermeister: A German liqueur, somewhat medicinal in flavor, but very popular in the United States. Jägermeister, literally translated, means "master of the hunt."

Kahlúa: A Mexican coffee-flavored liqueur dating back to the 1930s.

Kümmel: A caraway-flavored liqueur from Holland.

Limoncello: An Italian lemon zest–flavored liqueur that is becoming increasingly popular in the United States. Store it in the freezer.

Mandarine Napoléon: A French cognac-based liqueur with the flavors of tangerine zest.

Maraschino: A cherry liqueur that isn't too sweet, Maraschino is made from Dalmatian cherries. I think this product deserves more attention; it is a basic ingredient in many classic cocktails.

Midori: A honeydew melon–flavored liqueur (*Midori* is Japanese for "green") that is very popular in the United States.

Ouzo: A Greek anise-flavored liqueur.

Peach Brandy: A peach-flavored liqueur containing a percentage of real brandy.

Peach Schnapps: A dryish peach-flavored liqueur.

Peppermint Schnapps: A peppermint-flavored liqueur, usually drier than crème de menthe.

Sambuca: An anise-based Italian liqueur, available in white and black bottlings—black sambuca is usually flavored with lemon zest as well as anise.

Southern Comfort: A fruit-flavored American liqueur with predominantly peach notes. Though everyone seems to think this product contains bourbon, it does not.

Strawberry Brandy: A strawberry-flavored liqueur containing a percentage of real brandy.

Strega: An Italian herbal liqueur made with over 70 botanicals—the word *strega* means "witch."

Tia Maria: A Jamaican liqueur made from a base of rum and flavored with coffee.

Triple Sec: An orange-flavored liqueur used in many mixed drinks, such as the Margarita.

Tuaca: An Italian herbal liqueur with predominant vanilla notes and a hint of oranges.

Wines and wine-based ingredients

Champagne (and other sparkling wines)

Effervescent wines are made in all winemaking countries, but the methods used are based on those that originated in the Champagne region of France in the early 1700s. Most wine aficionados today still recognize champagnes made in the delimited region of northeastern France known as the Champagne district, as the real thing.

French champagne can be made only from three types of grapes—two black and one white—Pinot Noir, Pinot Meunier, and Chardonnay. The grape juice is separated from the black grape skins before they can impart any color to the wine. Further, real champagne (and the best sparkling wines from elsewhere) must be made using the *méthode champenoise,* a stringent, time-consuming process proscribed by French law. The *méthode champenoise* involves adding sugar and yeast to the wine at the time of bottling; this results in a secondary fermentation that creates the bubbles in champagne. After the secondary fermentation is complete, the champagne is disgorged; that is, the sediment created by the yeast is removed by immersing the neck of the bottle in a freezing liquid, and the temporary cap and the sediment that clings to it, are removed. Usually, a little sugar that has been dissolved in mature wine (dosage) is then added to the bottle before it is once again sealed. All that just to get those wonderful little bubbles into the wine and then keep them inside the bottle until it's opened.

STYLES OF FRENCH CHAMPAGNE

Blanc de Blancs: Champagnes made from 100 percent Chardonnay (white) grapes.

Blanc de Noir: Champagnes made from Pinot Noir, and/or Meunier grapes; both varietals are black.

Brut: Literally means "very dry," but in fact these champagnes do bear some sweetness.

Extra Brut: Drier than Brut.

Sec: Literally means "dry," but these champagnes are usually medium-sweet.

Extra Sec: Literally means "extra-dry," but in fact, these champagnes are usually only medium-dry.

Demi-Sec: Literally means "semi-dry," but these champagnes are actually medium-sweet to sweet.

Doux: Literally means "sweet," and these bottlings are very sweet.

Vintage Champagnes: Bottlings containing only wines from the year noted on the label. A champagne is chosen to be a vintage bottling when the wine of one particular year is deemed to be exceptional by the winemaker.

Champagne should be served at a temperature of about 45°F, so be sure to chill it well. Do not shake or agitate the bottle before opening it. Remove the foil that covers the neck, and then loosen the cage by grasping the small wire loop and untwisting it. Hold the bottle at a 45-degree angle and take care that it isn't in a direct line with Grandma's antique mirror or your best friend's head. Firmly grasp the cork with one hand and hold the base of the bottle with the other. Gently twist *the bottle* while holding the cork steady until the cork is released. Don't "pop" the cork; ease the bottle away from it.

Slowly pour the champagne into champagne glasses, ideally flutes, adding small amounts to each glass and allowing the foam to subside before adding more. Swirling is not recommended, but staring at the upward-rising stream of bubbles is a treat.

Dubonnet

An apéritif wine produced in two styles: Dubonnet Rouge and Dubonnet Blanc. Though either product is highly recommendable as an apéritif—serve it over ice with a citrus twist—Dubonnet sometimes replaces vermouth in Martinis, other cocktails, and some mixed drinks.

Lillet

A French apéritif wine that is produced in Blanc and Rouge renditions. Use Lillet as you would Dubonnet, or try substituting it for vermouth in cocktail recipes. Lillet is somewhat fruitier and spicier than Dubonnet.

Madeira

A red wine fortified with grape brandy, Madeira is named for the island where it was born. The aging process for Madeira is unique to the wine industry: The wine is stored in oak casks in buildings built especially for the purpose. Temperatures are kept high—usually between 104° and 114°F—for about six months. The wine then is transferred to cooler cellars where it rests for at least a year and a half. Finally, it matures in a solera system, as does sherry (see page 27). When you hear about the destructive properties of heat on wine maturation, remember that Madeira is the exception; the heat it withstands is intentional. Once open, this hearty wine will last indefinitely without spoiling.

THE STYLES OF MADEIRA AND
HOW TO SERVE THEM

Madeira can be any of five distinct styles. All, except Rainwater, are named after the grape variety used to make them:

Sercial: The driest style, Sercial should be served slightly chilled in a small wine glass.

Verdelho: A medium-dry, highly acidic style, Verdelho should also be served slightly chilled in a small wine glass.

Rainwater: A versatile, lighter style of Madeira that is a pale, light blend of other Madeiras. Rainwater should be served chilled, from the refrigerator, in a small wine glass.

Bual: This Madeira is medium-sweet, perfect for after-dinner sipping. Serve it at room temperature in a small wine glass.

Malmsey: The sweetest Madeira, wonderfully fragrant, full-bodied and rich on the palate. Serve it at room temperature in a small wine glass.

Port

Originally a Portuguese wine that was fortified with local grape brandy, port now is produced almost everywhere that table wines are made. The brandy used to fortify the new wine is unaged and added to the wine at a very high proof. Since this increases the alcohol content, fermentation stops, leaving some of the grape sugars unfermented, thus sweetening the wine. After fortification, the port is stored in oak casks. Inexpensive ports may be aged for as little as one year, but many of the better bottlings are kept in casks for as long as 10 and up to 40 years. Vintage port, the only type that is aged in glass after aging in wood, continues to improve after it is bottled. It should be kept at a constant temperature of about 48°F, and the bottle should be stored on its side.

How to Decant Vintage Port

During their aging process sediment develops in Vintage ports. Though harmless, this "crust" is visually and texturally unattractive; therefore, these ports are decanted before they are enjoyed. Several hours or even a day ahead of time, stand the bottle upright—away from the light and where it won't be disturbed—to allow the sediment to settle. The ritualistic way of decanting a fine Vintage port is very theatrical: Line a funnel with a double or triple layer of dampened cheesecloth. Place the funnel into the neck of a decanter. Next, holding a candle behind the neck of the port bottle, pour the wine into the funnel, checking the neck to see if any sediment can be seen. Once you see sediment, stop pouring. (If you want to modernize the ritual, use a flashlight.) Once opened, don't linger in drinking a vintage port; its charms will dissipate with extended exposure to air.

STYLES OF PORT AND HOW TO SERVE THEM

Ports are made in three colors—white, tawny, and ruby—so they're extremely easy to tell apart. Their qualities, however, are as different as their colors. Two other types are also produced: late-bottled Vintage port and Vintage port; one is a collector's item, the other can be drunk right away.

White port: Some are dry and light-bodied, but most are sweeter and medium-bodied, so each bottling must be tasted to see what style it is. White ports are made from white grapes. Usually offered as an apéritif, white port should be served well chilled, in small wine glasses.

Ruby port: Normally a young wine that has very often spent less than four years in casks (known as "pipes" in the port business). Wines from a variety of pipes are blended together to produce a sweet, medium- to full-bodied port that represents each individual producer's style. Ruby port should be served at room temperature in small wine glasses; it is also the port of choice for cocktail- and drink-making.

Tawny port: When inexpensive, tawny port is invariably nothing more than a blend of white and ruby ports. Aged tawny ports, on the other hand, are truly special. Tawny port starts its life as ruby port, and it is the extended aging period that contributes to both the change of the wine's color—from a deep purple to ruby to a tawny brown—and its change in flavor: The longer the port rests in the pipes, the more its sweetness mellows to a complex, fruity nuttiness, until, at around age 30, some ports bear the distinct flavors of dried fruits while retaining a pleasant dry nuttiness. Aged tawny port should be savored at room temperature in small wine glasses.

Late-Bottled Vintage port: Normally a good-quality port that has aged in wood for over four years but seldom more than six. These are fine wines that are far less expensive than vintage bottlings, but they do not improve in the bottle, and can, therefore, be consumed immediately after purchase. Late-bottled Vintage port should be served at room temperature in small wine glasses.

Vintage port: Bottled after spending only two years in port pipes, these are wines that have been declared by a very strict regulatory board to be of the finest quality. Unlike wood-aged bottlings, Vintage ports continue to age and improve in the bottle and should be kept for at least 10 years or considerably more before opening. Many experts claim that to experience a truly great Vintage port, a minimum of two decades of bottle-aging is necessary. Vintage port should be served at room temperature in small wine glasses.

Punt è Mes

The brand name of an Italian apéritif that is like a bitter, less-sweet version of vermouth.

Saké

Is it a beer or a wine? That's the question. Saké is made from rice, a grain, and therefore, should be classified as a beer since, technically, wines are made from fruits. However, the U.S.

Bureau of Alcohol, Tobacco, and Firearms classifies saké a Japanese wine that is made from "other agricultural products." Go figure. In any case, no matter what it is, saké is good. Specific types of rice are used and then fermented to produce the product that will mature in wood casks into saké. Not all sakes are served warm; many of the finer ones are chilled for serving. Look for an increase in imports of high-end sakés that are made with the care and precision of other fine wines—or beers.

Sherry

A Spanish wine fortified with brandy that can be produced in a delimited area of southern Andalusía that encompasses the towns of Sanlúcar de Barrameda, Puerto de Santa María, and Jerez de la Frontera. Originally known in England as Sherry-Sack, and commonly referred to in Elizabethan times simply as Sack, it is thought that the wine gained its name from the town of Jerez (HAIR-eth), which was eventually corrupted to sherry. The sack part of the name probably originated from the Spanish word *sacar,* meaning "export." It makes great sense that sherry became a widely exported wine since the main reason for fortifying wines with brandy was to stabilize them so they could stand up to long voyages at sea.

The sherry-making process is complex: After the wine ferments completely, a process that takes several months, it is pumped into oak casks that are deliberately not filled all the way full. The winemaker then must wait to see if a thin white layer of airborne yeast, known as flor, will form on its surface.

When the flor forms a thick layer, the wine will become the light, dry, fino style of sherry. If the layer is thinner, the wine will oxidize more than fino because it has greater contact with the air; these wines will darken and become an amontillado. When no film appears at all, the wine is destined to become an oloroso sherry. Over the next one to two years, the wines are watched closely and are checked for alcohol content. Depending on the flor and the experience of the bodega master, unaged grape brandy is added to fortify the wine. Wines that will become olorosos are fortified to a slightly higher alcohol level than those that will become finos. When ready, the wine is transferred to sherry butts—smaller oak casks—and are then shipped to the solera for aging.

The solera aging system is reserved for sherries, Spanish brandies (see page 9), and Madeiras (see page 23). The sherry butts are arranged in tiers—often 10 tiers high—with the oldest sherries on the bottom and the youngest on top. When some of the sherry—never more than half—is drawn off the lowest tier, it is replenished with wine from the tier above it. Thus, by the time a wine reaches the bottom level, it has aged and mingled, always with older sherries in the solera.

STYLES OF SHERRY AND HOW TO SERVE THEM

Fino sherries: Pale, light, and dry, fino sherries should be served chilled, from the refrigerator, in Sherry Copita glasses or on the rocks. They are an excellent apéritif and just right for late afternoon tapas.

Manzanilla sherries: Cousins of finos, Manzanillas are aged in Sanlúcar de Barrameda, a town located on the Mediterranean Sea. They feature an extremely delicate body and a slight saltiness, perhaps due to the location of their aging. Manzanillas should be served chilled, from the refrigerator, in Sherry Copita glasses or on the rocks.

Amontillado sherries: Darker in color and nuttier on the palate than their drier fino cousins, Amontillado sherries should be served chilled, from the refrigerator, in Sherry Copita glasses or on the rocks.

Oloroso sherries: These have a deep amber color, and a nutty, sweet, full body that fills the mouth. Serve them at room temperature in Sherry Copita glasses.

Cream sherries: Actually a style of oloroso sherry, these, too, are sweet, and have a somewhat creamy texture. Cream sherries should be served at room temperature in Sherry Copita glasses.

Pedro Ximénez sherries: The sweetest of all, these should be served at room temperature in Sherry Copita glasses.

Vermouth

A member of the category known as aromatized wines, vermouths are wines that have been flavored with botanical ingredients—herbs, spices, flowers, roots, seeds, and fruits—and are fortified with brandy. Italy produced the first vermouth in the late 1700s; it was red and sweet and came to be referred to as "Italian." The French produced the first dry, pale-colored vermouth a couple of decades later, and it came to be referred to as "French." These days, vermouths are produced in many, many countries; each bottling, though, has its own character and style. Though some inexpensive vermouths are made by merely introducing essences and flavorings to fortified wine, the best bottlings are manufactured using a far more complicated procedure.

Many companies start out with a wine that has been aged, sometimes for as long as 12 months, and most vermouths—even most red, sweet vermouths—are made from white wine. The wine is then fortified, but only slightly, by the addition of mistelle, a mixture of unfermented grape juice and brandy. Botanicals are then introduced to the wine by any of several methods. Sometimes they are infused into the wine at room temperature; sometimes the wine is heated slightly to speed up infusion time; and sometimes herbs are infused into distilled spirits, such as brandy, that are then added to the wine, fortifying it further.

After the wine has been aromatized, it is sometimes returned to oak casks for further aging. Before bottling, it must undergo a technical stabilizing process that filters out any tartrates.

STYLES OF VERMOUTH

Dry Vermouth: Usually made from very light, dry wines, dry vermouths are usually soft, herbal, and crisp. Vital for a Martini.

Sweet Vermouth: Sweeter, of course, than dry vermouth, sweet vermouth also bears a slight bitterness due to the higher percentage of quinine used in production, and the herbal accents are often less forthcoming.

Bianco Vermouth: Clear in color, like dry vermouth, bianco bottlings are slightly sweeter than their dry cousins and somewhat more herbal.

Rosé Vermouth: Similar to bianco vermouth but pale pink in color and dry on the palate.

STORING AND SERVING VERMOUTH

Once opened, store your vermouth in the refrigerator. And if the bottles you have are more than six months old, replace them, because oxidation will have ruined their sprightly appeal. If you don't use vermouth very often, it might be a good idea to buy the smaller 375 ml–size bottles.

Serve vermouths, straight from the bottle, on ice. The French Kiss cocktail—a 50/50 combination of sweet and dry vermouths—can be an excellent apéritif. Also, when cooking, if a bit of wine is called for, vermouth can add more complexity than most table wines.

Wine

Wine is an entire world of its own, and, indeed, it spans the world, produced on every continent except Antarctica. Bartending involves using all four types of wine: sparkling wine, like champagne and Prosecco; aromatized wines, like vermouth and many apéritifs; fortified wines, like port, sherry, and Madeira; and still wines, like your basic reds, whites, and rosés.

Most cocktail recipes that call for still wines should be made with a good dry white, dry red, or dryish rosé. And when your guest or customer requests, say, a white wine, be sure that the wine you're pouring is fresh and tasty and properly presented.

HOW TO SERVE WINE

Though dozens of different sizes and shapes of wine glasses can be found in the market, a good basic wine glass will have a capacity of at least eight ounces, preferably more, and ideally, it will be a stemmed glass. When you pour, do not fill the glass more than halfway full and handle the glass by the stem only.

White wines should be served chilled, not icy cold; red wines should be at cool room temperature—don't keep them next to the radiator.

How to Taste Wine

Tasting wine requires your whole body. Start by looking at the wine; note its color, texture, and clarity. Smell the wine; stick your nose well into the glass and take a deep breath. Next, swirl the wine in the glass and smell it again; new aromas might present themselves. Now, taste the wine; take a mouthful, not just a sip, and swish it around your mouth so that it comes in contact with all of your taste buds. Take note of every quality—its feel, its texture, its flavor, its acidity. Finally, swallow the wine. Does it linger in the mouth? Does it have any effect on your throat? Consider the experience. Did it taste like it smelled? Did it look full-bodied but feel and taste thin in the mouth? Would you like to drink more of it?

Opening a Bottle of Wine

Screw caps—and they're becoming increasingly popular—aside, many people are intimidated by the act of pulling a cork from a wine bottle. They shouldn't be—if they have a good corkscrew and know how to use it. (I'll repeat my personal recommendation, the Screwpull.) First, wipe off the bottle with a clean cloth. Stand it on a flat surface and use a small knife or a foilcutter to remove the top of the plastic or lead capsule that covers the cork. Cut just below the lip of the bottle. Next, position the worm of your corkscrew slightly off-center and begin turning it firmly to burrow the worm into the cork—because the worm is a spiral, starting it off-center will result in its being centered in the cork. Use levers, elbow grease, or whatever mechanism your corkscrew offers to extract the cork from the bottle. Finally—and this is important—use a clean cloth to wipe the interior and exterior lip of the bottle before pouring from it.

Beer

Like wine, beer is an entire world of it own, the product of grains, hops, water, and yeasts that promote fermentation. The category divides into two parts: lagers, which are brewed using yeasts that ferment on the bottom of a tank, and ales, which are brewed using top-fermenting yeasts. Lagers are low in alcohol, light in body, and the most popular style of beer in the United States; styles include light lagers, bocks, pilsners, smoked beers *(rauchbiers)*, and malt liquors. Ales, generally higher in alcohol, heavier in body, and more robust in flavor, include many styles: stout, porter, wheat beers, pale ales, as well as numerous others.

Although beer drinks aren't actually cocktails, a recent trend includes beer in some concoctions, and oftentimes a shot of some liquor or spirituous mixture is dropped into a mug of beer and drunk in combination. The classic Boilermaker, though not a cocktail per se, uses beer as the chaser to the whiskey shot.

Mixers

Mixers require little explanation; most are complete the way you buy them. One exception is simple syrup, which you will see throughout the recipes in this book. I ardently recommend that you make your own—it's very simple—and keep it on hand in the refrigerator; its shelf-life is practically infinite. Having simple syrup on hand and using it in place of granulated sugar and water in recipes ensures a better blending of flavors and a better texture in the drink.

Beef bouillon	Ginger ale
Clamato juice	Ginger beer
Club soda	Grapefruit juice
Coconut cream	Grenadine
Cola (diet and regular)	Half-and-half
Cranberry juice	Heavy cream
Fruit nectars (peach, pear, apricot)	Lemon juice (fresh)

Lime juice (fresh)

Lemon-lime soda
    (diet and regular)

Lime juice cordial,
    such as Rose's

Milk

Mineral water (still)

Orange juice

Pineapple juice

Simple syrup
    (recipe follows)

Tomato juice

Tonic

Whipped cream

Simple Syrup

MAKES 4 CUPS (1 QUART)

> **3 cups water**
>
> **3 cups granulated sugar**

Heat the water in a saucepan set over moderately high heat. When it begins to simmer, add the sugar and stir until it dissolves. Do not let the mixture boil. Remove the pan from the heat and set aside to cool to room temperature. Pour the simple syrup through a funnel into an empty, clean, 1-liter liquor bottle and cap tightly. Store in the refrigerator.

Condiments and flavorings

Allspice (ground)

Angostura bitters

Apples

Bananas

Berries

Black pepper

Candies

Celery seed

Cinnamon (sticks and ground)

Cloves

Cocoa powder (unsweetened)

Cocktail onions

Coffee beans

Cucumbers

Eggs

Falernum syrup

Fresh mint

Grapefruits

Horseradish

Lemons

Limes

Maraschino cherries

Nutmeg

Old Bay Seasoning

Olives (cocktail, anchovy-
stuffed, almond-stuffed)

Orange bitters

Orange flower water

Oranges

Orgeat syrup

Peach bitters

Sugar (granulated, superfine,
and confectioners'; cubes
or lumps)

Peychaud's bitters

Rose flower water

Salt (kosher)

Tabasco sauce

Worcestershire sauce

GLASSWARE

Let's face it: Drinking a Mint Julep out of an antique, sterling silver, ice-coated Julep cup is an experience everyone should have—at least once. But then, sipping a Julep from a plastic cup will do quite nicely, thank you, if you happen to be sitting in a box seat at Churchill Downs on the first Saturday in May, just aching for the Kentucky Derby to begin its run. Indeed, whenever we have the opportunity to drink from fine glassware, we should, it's marvelous, but we can't expect the corner bar to share their finery with us; they use what's appropriate and affordable, and clean (we ardently hope). Don't think about running out to buy a whole wardrobe of cocktail glasses; they're easily collected one or two or six at a time. And depending on your drinking and entertaining habits, you might not need certain special-purpose glasses at all.

Here's a round-up of what's typically stocked at a bar. Whatever glass you use, do yourself a favor: fill the glass with water and then pour it into a measuring cup for liquids so you know the glass's capacity. Then you can adjust your recipe to suit the glass it will be served in. Also, if you are having cocktails near a pool or on the beach, use plastic or paper drinkware. Broken glass is just too dangerous in those locales.

beer glass,
16 to 20 ounces

champagne flute glass,
6 to 9 ounces

beer mug,
12 to 20 ounces

champagne saucer
glass, 6 to 9 ounces

pilsner glass,
10 to 20 ounces

sherry copita glass,
4 to 6 ounces

all-purpose wine
goblet, 8 to 14 ounces

sherry glass,
4 to 6 ounces

white wine glass,
8 to 14 ounces

cocktail glass,
4 to 12 ounces

red wine glass,
8 to 14 ounces

collins glass,
8 to 14 ounces

champagne tulip glass,
6 to 9 ounces

cordial glass,
1 to 3 ounces

highball glass,
8 to 10 ounces

pony glass,
2 to 3 ounces

hurricane glass,
16 to 20 ounces

pousse-café glass,
3 to 4 ounces

Irish coffee glass,
8 to 10 ounces

brandy snifter

jigger glass,
2 to 3 ounces

punch cup,
6 to 8 ounces

rocks (old-fashioned)
glass, 5 to 6 ounces

shot glass,
1 to 3 ounces

large rocks
(double
old-fashioned)
glass, 8 to 10
ounces

sour glass,
4 to 6 ounces

zombie glass,
12 to 20 ounces

Basic Garnishes

Whenever you think that garnishes are just extras or fancy flourishes, take a look at the Gibson, a cocktail that is a Naked Martini until it is defined by its pearl onion garnish. Garnishes are not mere, optional extras. Many, many cocktails don't have specific garnishes; you may add one, of course, if you choose to, but its qualities should complement the drink, not merely fancy it up. When a twist is called for, I am instantly furious if the bartender merely waves a piece of citrus zest over my glass and drops it in. If I want the benefit of the oils from the zest, I must fish it out myself, rub the outside of it around the lip of the glass, and then twist it for its almost invisible little spritz of oils on top of my drink. The difference between a Scotch and Soda with a twist dropped in and one that's properly made is remarkable.

If you know beforehand that you'll be preparing a variety of drinks, it's a good idea to prepare at least the basics—twists, wedges, and wheels—ahead of time. Don't, however, let them dry out once cut. Fold several sheets of paper toweling and soak with cold water. Place on top of the cut fruit and refrigerate until needed.

One last general hint: Wash and dry all fruit that is used with its peel intact for a garnish. You don't know where it's been!

Citrus wedges: Top and tail each fruit. Cut lengthwise into two equal halves. Cut each half into no more than four wedges—there's nothing worse than a citrus wedge with no oomph to it.

Citrus twists: Cut off one end of the fruit to create a flat base. Stand the fruit upright on a cutting board. Working from the top toward the bottom of the fruit and using a paring knife, cut vertical $1/2$-inch-wide strips of peel. You want the colorful outer peel and just enough of the inner white pith to keep the twist sturdy enough to twist without breaking. Continue cutting twists; the remaining fruit can be squeezed for its fresh juice.

Citrus wheels: Top and tail each fruit. Place the fruit on its side and, using a large knife, thinly slice into uniform rounds;

discard the end pieces if they are not attractive. If the wheel will be perched on the lip of the glass, make a single cut from the outer edge to the center of each wheel.

Citrus slices: Though these look like wheels cut in half, that's not the proper way to cut them. Top and tail each fruit. Cut lengthwise into two equal halves. Place each half, cut side down, on a cutting board and cut into uniform slices. If the slice is meant to perch over the rim of the glass, make a single cut from the center of each wheel up to, but not through, the peel.

Fruit spirals: Citrus spirals are essential for all drinks in the Crusta category. Though citrus spirals are most often called for, several fruits lend themselves to spiral cutting—especially apples and pears. Spirals are very pretty, but unless you're a genius with a knife, they might take some practice to master. Using a paring knife or a citrus zester and starting toward the blossom or stem end of the fruit, cut into the peel and keep cutting around the circumference, spiraling round and round toward the opposite end of the fruit. Ideally, you'll end up with a continuous, springy coil of fruit peel. Usually, the entire spiral is used in a cocktail (although some of your mistakes can be attractive hung over the lip of a glass). Remember, practice makes perfect—I suggest using apples for starters and working up to citrus.

BARTENDING TECHNIQUES

Learning to Free Pour

The most important—and liberating—technique worth learning is how to pick up a bottle and free pour a shot of liquor. The method is simple; all it requires is practice and consistency. Here's how to learn how to free pour:

Fill an empty liquor bottle with water; insert a speed pourer into the neck of the bottle. Have ready a $1^1/2$-ounce jigger and an empty mixing glass. Now, pick up the bottle, grasping it so that your thumb or index finger is wrapped over the base of the speed pourer and the others are tightly wrapped around the top of the neck of the bottle. Upend the bottle over the jigger and start silently counting in your head until the jigger is full. Pour out the water and continue the process, finding your own count for pouring $1^1/2$ ounces of liquid. Remember, you must always count at the same speed for your measurement to be consistent.

When you think you have mastered your count, pour your $1^1/2$-ounce measure into the empty mixing glass, and then pour the water from the mixing glass into a jigger to check that your measurement is correct. Once you are confident that you can pour a $1^1/2$-ounce measure by using the counting method, you should be able to pour other measurements—1 ounce, 2 ounces, etc.—simply by adjusting your count appropriately.

Chilling a Glass

If possible, store the glassware you think you'll need in the refrigerator or freezer. If there's no room, glass chilling should be done before you start preparing the cocktail so that there's enough time for it to get cold. I suggest doing this in a sink. Fill the glass with ice and enough water to overflow the glass; let it sit in the sink while you mix the drink. Pick up the glass of ice and water by the stem, if there is one. Jiggle the glass so the water overflows again; pour out the ice and water. Hold the glass upside down and shake to get rid of any remaining drops.

Coating the Rim of a Serving Glass with a Dry Ingredient

I'm more or less "my way or the highway" about this topic since the sugar, salt, cocoa powder, or chocolate sprinkles are ingredients that you consume while sipping your drink. Indeed, a Sidecar without its sugar-coated rim is too tart, and a Chocolate Martini is only half as good and less than half as pretty without its cocoa powder rim. Technique is everything here; see page 40 for detailed instructions for how to do it the right way.

We've all experienced it: You order a Margarita. The bartender moistens the rim of the glass with a wedge of lime and then inverts the glass into a shallow bowl or tray of coarse salt. The salt forms a thickish crust where the glass was moistened. The bartender then prepares the drink, pours it into the glass, and sets it in front of you. Yuk! Where oh where does any recipe for a Margarita include a half-teaspoon or more of salt in the drink? Nowhere. Does no one realize that after running a wedge of lime around the circumference of the glass, both the inside and outside edges are being moistened, and that by then upending the rim in salt, both the inside and outside of the glass's rim will be thickly coated with salt? Pour the liquid in the glass and all that salt on the inside of the glass melts into the drink.

Here is the very best way to coat the rim of a glass for serving. Use it with salt on the rim of Margarita or Salty Dog cocktails, use it with sugar for your Sidecars and Lemon Drops, and use it with cocoa powder for the rim of your Chocolate Martinis.

Please note: Glasses can be rimmed ahead of time; in fact, it gives the coating time to air-dry a bit before use. If you know you'll be serving, say, a Lemon Drop to all guests upon their arrival at a party, prepare the glasses in advance so they're ready to use when you need them.

Using a wedge of fruit or a bit of paper towel dipped in one of the liquid ingredients of the cocktail you're making, moisten the exterior of the rim of the serving glass. Grasp the glass from its base or stem and hold it sideways, parallel to the floor, over a sink or trash basket. Pour the coating ingredient—sugar, salt, cocoa powder, etc.—into a salt shaker or onto a small plate and sprinkle the moistened edge of the glass, rotating it as you go, until lightly but evenly coated with the ingredient, and letting any excess fall into the sink. It's that simple.

DRINK-MAKING TECHNIQUES

Bartending is all about verbs, and verbs provide a type of shorthand for describing the techniques of making a cocktail. The key verbs in bartending are: build, stir, shake, blend, and layer. Three further action verbs can crop up from time to time: float, muddle, and flame. If you listen to bartenders discussing a new recipe, you might hear, "Build, Highball, lemon wedge," or "Shake, strain, cocktail, float." The first of these describes, probably, a Highball, a drink that is made in the glass you will serve it in. The second drink referred to above would involve shaking some of the ingredients together, straining them into a cocktail glass, and then floating another ingredient on top. Here are the techniques that should be mastered by everyone who wants to think of himself or herself as a bartender.

Building

Building a drink most usually refers to making a Highball—a drink that is made in the glass in which it is served. A Highball glass is filled with ice, the liquor is poured in, and the mixer is added on top. If a citrus garnish such as a lemon or lime wedge is to be added, the juice is squeezed into the drink after the mixer. When that's done, the bartender must stir the drink with a sip-stick to combine the ingredients. However, if the drink is, say, a scotch and soda with a twist of lemon peel, the bartender would stir the liquids together first and then rim the edge of the glass with the oils and express the oils over the top. In any case, the sip-stick remains in the glass so the drinker can stir more, if desired, or sip through it.

Stirring

The technique used in classic Martini-making applies to all cocktails that are made from clear ingredients—no eggs, milk, cream, or fruit juices allowed. Basically, if you can see through each ingredient, you will be stirring the drink. The mixing glass should be two-thirds full of ice. The ingredients are poured in and the barspoon is used to stir the ingredients together and, most critically, chill them with the ice for 20 to 30 seconds. The amount of water that is melted during this stirring is vital to the overall balance of the drink. This is the best reason not to use spirits that have been stored in the freezer; the cold temperature of the chilled ingredient will lessen ice meltage during stirring, and the drink's balance will be affected. Though a barspoon can be used like any spoon for stirring, the twisted shaft offers its user an easier and more stylish technique. Place your thumb on one side of the shaft and the first two fingers on the opposite side. Slide your thumb back and forth along the shaft, pushing against the two fingers on the opposite side; the spoon will agitate the ice in an up-and-down movement.

Stirred drinks must be strained into a chilled glass or onto fresh ice in the serving glass. Use a julep strainer, fitted at a slant into the mixing glass, to strain the liquid from the ice.

Shaking

My personal favorite method—I love truly cold cocktails and shaking often produces tiny shards of ice so small that they sneak through the perforations of a strainer. Cocktails are shaken when they contain fruit juices, milk, cream, eggs, horseradish, and other thickish ingredients. You will use either a three-part cocktail shaker or a Boston shaker, the favored choice of most professional bartenders.

To shake a cocktail in a cocktail shaker: Fill the bottom cup two-thirds full of ice. Pour in the ingredients; set the top in place and check that it is tightly closed. Grasp the shaker where the top and bottom parts meet, raise the shaker to the side of your head, curl your index finger over the top to prevent it from flying off, and begin shaking vigorously. Continue shaking for 10 to 20 seconds. Remove the cover and strain the cocktail into the chilled or ice-filled glass.

To shake a cocktail using a Boston shaker: Fill the glass half of the shaker two-thirds full of ice. Add the ingredients. Invert the metal half of the shaker over the glass and rap it firmly on its flat bottom to unite the two parts. Lift up the shaker and invert it, metal cup end down. Grasp the shaker—the bottom in one hand, the top in the other—lift it to the side of your head, and shake vigorously for 10 to 20 seconds. Complete your shaking with the metal cup on the bottom and the glass half on top.

To "break" the metal cone from the glass part, strike the metal half of the shaker with the heel of your hand at the juncture where the cups meet. Lift off the mixing glass and set it aside. Fit a Hawthorne strainer within the mouth of the metal cup. Holding it in place with your index finger, strain the cocktail into the chilled or ice-filled glass.

Blending

An electric blender is required to make frozen drinks. If the amount of ice is not stated in the recipe, fill the container no more than half full. Add the ingredients; cover. Set the container in place and blend, pulsing if necessary, until all of the ingredients are pureed and the ice is crushed. After a few seconds you will hear the noise of the blender change; stop the blender and stir the ingredients. Cover and blend some more. Repeat as needed to prevent lumps.

Muddling

Muddling requires a muddler (see Equipment, page 2) and a sturdy glass; don't use your finest hand-blown crystal for a drink that requires muddling. The ingredients—usually fruit slices, sugar, bitters, and/or water—are placed in the bottom of a glass. The flat end of the wooden muddler is used to press the juices from the fruit or sugar and break it up while mashing it together with any liquid. Muddling brings out the qualities of fruits because it presses oils from the peel as well as juice from the flesh.

Floating

Floating an ingredient is usually the last act before serving the cocktail. Often high-proof rum or a liqueur is floated on a drink that has been stirred or shaken, strained, and poured. Floated ingredients are meant to stand alone on top of the drink; you don't want to mix them in. Pour them gently over the back of a barspoon.

Flaming

First, last, and always, be careful when igniting alcohol. Do it away from bottles of liquor, your face and hair, or hanging party decorations. Sometimes, a floated ingredient, say 151-proof rum, is ignited because its high alcohol content ensures a quick ignition. Sometimes the oil expressed from a citrus peel is ignited for the burst of flavor it produces, for the marvelous aroma that can result, or purely for the pyrotechnical show that results. Remember that smothering a fire is most effective, so the wise bartender will keep a saucer and a moist bar towel handy.

Layering

The classic layered drink is the Pousse-Café, a rainbow-hued sweet drink that calls for a number of liqueurs but requires they be poured one atop the other without mixing. Layering works because different liquids have different specific densities, and as long as you pour the densest liquid as the bottom layer and then top it with a succession of second-densest, third-densest, etc., the ingredients will float perfectly. But there, too, is the problem: Because we have such a profusion of different brands and flavors of liqueurs available today, the specific density of each product differs—one company's crème de menthe will be more or less dense than another's. (Basically, the ones with the highest sugar content will have the highest specific densities.) Thus, though you will find lists of ingredients, usually from densest to least dense, I suggest you judge for yourself based on the thickness of the ingredients you want to use. And though some recipes tell you to layer the specific ingredients they contain, you'll find that often it simply doesn't work or the ingredient will work when it's cold but not at room temperature.

If you do want to layer liqueurs, slowly, gently, and carefully pour each layer over the back of a barspoon so that it glides atop the layer below.

Specific Densities

When layering ingredients for a Pousse-Café, pour the spirit with the highest specific gravity as the bottom layer and top it with successively less dense spirits. Thus, according to this chart, which lists the specific densities of liqueurs in the Marie Brizard line plus a few other brands, you might create a layered drink that is clear, topped with red, topped with blue, and finished with a final layer of clear—white crème de cacao, strawberry liqueur, blue curaçao, and either triple sec or vodka. Remember, heaviest liqueurs on the bottom, lighter ones on top.

Note: These spirits are listed in descending order, from the heaviest to the lightest.

Brand & Bottling	Specific density	Brand & Bottling	Specific density
Matilde Cassis	1.19200	Marie Brizard Amaretto	1.08152
Marie Brizard Dark Crème de Cacao	1.16020	Marie Brizard Blackberry Liqueur	1.08010
Marie Brizard White Crème de Cacao	1.15920	Marie Brizard Peach Liqueur	1.07320
Kahlùa	1.15200	Bénédictine liqueur	1.07250
Marie Brizard Coffee Liqueur	1.14200	Galliano liqueur	1.06500
Marie Brizard Anisette	1.13710	Baileys Irish cream liqueur	1.05480
Marie Brizard Green Crème de Menthe	1.12040	Marie Brizard Watermelon Liqueur	1.05160
Marie Brizard White Crème de Menthe	1.12040	Marie Brizard Mango Passion	1.05400
Matilde Framboise	1.12000	Marie Brizard Poire William	1.04960
Mathilde Poire	1.11700	Marie Brizard Triple Sec	1.03980
Marie Brizard Parfait Amour	1.11630	Cointreau liqueur	1.03850
Mathilde Pêche	1.11600	Mathilde Anisette	1.03000
Marie Brizard Strawberry Liqueur	1.10680	Mathilde Café	1.03000
Marie Brizard Raspberry Liqueur	1.10468	Matilde Triple Sec	1.02500
Marie Brizard Blue Curaçao	1.09990	B & B liqueur	1.02450
Marie Brizard Apricot Liqueur	1.09760	Marie Brizard Grand Orange	1.02450
Tia Maria	1.09400	Mathilde XO Cognac à l'orange	0.98810
Marie Brizard Orange Curaçao	1.09160	SKYY Citrus vodka	0.95720
		SKYY vodka	0.94980

The Home Bar

A home bar can take whatever form suits its bartender or its location. When I was growing up, we had no bar—liquor was stored in a kitchen cabinet, wine was in the garage, and the manual ice crusher sat next to the grater and the measuring cups. Some of my friends' parents had incredible bars back then, though, usually in the basement rec room, often with a real wooden bar, tall bar stools or swivel chairs, and a back bar area to display the liquor bottles, mechanical toys, neon signs, and beer paraphernalia that were highly sought-after. Collectible decanters were all the rage, as were beer steins in a multitude of sizes, and Highball glasses emblazoned with pictures of pretty women—Vargas girls, usually—whose bathing suits disappeared when cold liquids were poured into the glass.

If the bar area was located upstairs, it tended to be much fancier and more sophisticated. Really wonderful Art Deco or Danish Modern cocktail carts were outfitted to contain liquor decanters, tiny ice buckets, special glassware, and often some strikingly beautiful glass stirrers. Sometimes the living room had a wet bar in the corner; glass shelves displayed liquors— often in crystal decanters—and more often than not, a number of bottles of sweet liqueurs. One family I knew had a beer tap that jutted out from the stones of their floor-to-ceiling fire- place—now, that was cool.

Today, though, your home bar is what you make it. If you have a collection of lovely cocktail accoutrements, show them off. If not, your homely collection of Boston shaker, barspoon, and Hawthorne strainer plus your ingredients simply need to be where you can find them at a moment's notice.

STOCKING A HOME BAR

Even if none of your friends drinks gin, you really should keep one bottle on hand if you want to have a properly stocked home bar. If many of your friends drink gin, then think about stocking two or three different brands. Here's a list of everything you should at least consider having in stock if you want to be known as a well-prepared home bartender.

Spirits

Applejack: Optional but desirable.

Blended Whisky: Optional at my house, but maybe not at yours.

Bourbon

Campari: Optional but desirable.

Cognac

Gin

Irish Whiskey

Rum: Light rum is a must; amber, dark, and añejo are optional.

Rye Whiskey (Straight): Optional.

Scotch: Blended scotch is a must; single malt scotch is an option.

Tennessee Whiskey: Could you really have a bar without a bottle of Jack Daniel's or George Dickel?

Tequila: White, aka Blanco, Plata, or silver is a must; Gold, Reposado, and Añejo are optional.

Vodka: Plain vodka is a must. A few flavored vodkas are optional but desirable.

Liqueurs

Consider which cocktails and mixed drinks your crowd likes before deciding on your final list.

Amaretto

Apricot Brandy: Optional.

Baileys Irish Cream: Refrigerate after opening.

Blackberry Brandy: Optional.

Chambord: Optional, but getting more essential every day.

Cherry Brandy

Cointreau or other triple sec

Crème de banane: Optional.

Crème de cacao: White, at least. No, get both.

Crème de cassis

Crème de menthe: Both white and green.

Grand Marnier

Jägermeister

Kahlúa

Maraschino liqueur

Peach schnapps

Pernod: Optional.

Sambuca

Southern Comfort

Wines

Many of these wines are optional, so you should consider what cocktails and mixed drinks you'll be making on a regular basis, and whether or not you'll actually open a bottle of, say, port or sherry if you buy it.

Dry Vermouth: Refrigerate after opening.

Sweet Vermouth: Refrigerate after opening.

Port and/or Sherry: Refrigerate dry sherries after opening.

Dry White Wine: Chardonnay and/or Sauvignon Blanc— refrigerate before opening.

Dry Red Wine: Consider Merlot, Côtes du Rhône, Cabernet Sauvignon, Pinot Noir.

Beer

American lager

Craft-brewed pale ale

Low-calorie beer

Nonalcoholic beer

Stout

Mixers

Bottled water

Club soda

Cola

Diet cola

Ginger ale

Lemon-lime soda

Milk, half-and-half, or heavy cream

Simple syrup

Tonic water

Fruit juices

Cranberry

Grapefruit

Lime

Lemon

Orange

Pineapple

Tomato

Condiments, etc.

Angostura bitters

Celery salt

Cocktail olives: Refrigerate after opening.

Cocktail onions: Refrigerate after opening.

Grenadine

Horseradish: Refrigerate after opening.

Lime juice cordial: Refrigerate after opening.

Maraschino cherries:
Refrigerate after opening.

Peychaud's bitters

Salt and pepper

Sugar: Granulated and
superfine.

Sugar cubes or lumps

Tabasco sauce

Worcestershire sauce

Equipment

Barspoon

Boston shaker or cocktail
shaker

Bottle opener

Churchkey

Citrus reamer

Cocktail stirrers or sip-sticks

Coasters or cocktail napkins

Cutting board

Corkscrew

Hawthorne strainer, if using a
Boston shaker

Ice bucket with tongs

Jigger

Julep strainer

Mixing glass

Paring knife

Straws

THE COCKTAIL PARTY BAR

Some people are partygivers; others can't imagine throwing a
party. Here's my thinking: For a dinner party, holiday meal, or
special celebration where I will serve a meal, my limit is 12 for
a sit-down and maybe up to 20 for a serve-yourself buffet or
barbecue. On the other hand, one of the greatest hosts I ever
met, the very stylish Lee Bailey, taught me a secret many
moons ago: Have a cocktail party—all you need to serve is
nuts. And that's just what he did—with great élan, mixed cocktail nuts in bail-handled shiny paint cans direct from the nut
supplier—at the many parties I attended chez Bailey.

Well, I'm a big copycat. That's just what I do, too. The best
aspect of cocktail parties is that you can invite dozens—hundreds, even—of people, and though you'll run yourself ragged
getting everything ready on party day, you'll be free to enjoy
your guests, your cocktails, and the crowd.

Now, don't get crazy about this party; you can limit its difficulty. Indeed, I hereby give you permission to be different: *You*

do not have to have a full open bar. You can make it, say, a Cosmopolitan party—the only alcoholic drink served will be the Cosmopolitan. You could have a vodka party that features iced vodka, flavored vodkas, and no other liquor. You can have a punch party if you want to do absolutely everything ahead of time. In fact, making a tasty nonalcoholic punch that individual drinkers can spike for themselves is an excellent ploy for a get-together that can include children and adults.

My best tips for large-scale partygiving are these:

- **have large trash cans handy;**
- **have lots and lots of cocktail napkins around;**
- **don't run out of ice;**
- **serve nuts—or equally simple-to-put-out and replenish store-bought snacks;**
- **hire a bartender, if possible;**
- **don't let anyone overdo it;**
- **appoint designated drivers and have a taxi service number handy;**
- **pray for good weather.**

The drinks that follow include classics, old favorites, contemporary favorites, and some popular, trendy drinks that may or may not last. Listings are alphabetical by title, from A to Z, to make finding them easy. Because I know that some of you will be looking for certain kinds of drinks, we have devised special icons to indicate the following categories:

Classic Cocktails   Punches

Nonalcoholic Drinks   Shooters

Participatory Drinks

Drinks A to Z

A.B.C.

Let's start at the very beginning.

> **2 ounces scotch**
> **$^1/_2$ ounce apricot brandy**
> **$^1/_2$ ounce sweet vermouth**

Pour all of the ingredients into a mixing glass two-thirds full of ice cubes. Stir well. Strain into a chilled Cocktail glass.

A-Bomb

The double shot of coffee—from the Kahlúa and the Tia Maria—in this one just explodes in your mouth.

> **$^1/_2$ ounce Kahlúa**
> **$^1/_2$ ounce Baileys Irish cream liqueur**
> **$^1/_2$ ounce vodka**
> **$^1/_2$ ounce Tia Maria**

Pour all of the ingredients into a shaker two-thirds full of ice cubes. Shake well. Strain into a chilled Pony glass.

Abbey Cocktail

A recipe from the 1930s—still going strong.

> **2 ounces gin**
> **1 ounce Lillet Blanc**
> **1 ounce orange juice**
> **2 dashes of orange bitters**

Pour the gin, Lillet, orange juice, and bitters into a shaker two-thirds full of ice cubes. Shake well. Strain into a chilled Cocktail glass.

Absinthe Cocktail

Many travelers to the Czech Republic return to our shores with a bottle of Absinthe, where it still is sold legally. If you haven't been to Prague lately, substitute Absente, Pernod, Ricard, or Herbsaint for the absinthe.

> 2 ounces absinthe or one of its substitutes
>
> 1 ounce cold water
>
> 2 dashes of Angostura bitters

Pour all of the ingredients into a mixing glass two-thirds full of ice cubes. Stir well. Strain into a chilled Cocktail glass.

Absinthe Drip

The ritual of making this drink is well worth the effort.

> 1 sugar cube
>
> 1 $^1/_2$ ounces absinthe, Absente, Herbsaint, or Pernod
>
> Water

Place an absinthe spoon or tea strainer over a wine glass. Place the sugar cube over the perforations. Pour in the absinthe or substitute, letting it drip over the sugar cube. Add water to taste, pouring it slowly over the sugar cube, until the sugar dissolves and the mixture turns cloudy.

Absolut Royal Fuck

> 1 ounce Crown Royal
>
> $^1/_2$ ounce Absolut Kurant
>
> $^1/_2$ ounce peach schnapps
>
> Splash of cranberry juice
>
> Splash of pineapple juice

Pour all of the ingredients into a shaker two-thirds full of ice cubes. Shake well. Strain into a chilled Cocktail glass.

Absolut Sex

Some men have been known to fall asleep immediately after having one of these.

> 1 ounce Absolut Kurant

1 ounce Midori melon liqueur

1 ounce cranberry juice

Splash of lemon-lime soda

Pour the Kurant, melon liqueur, and cranberry juice into a shaker two-thirds full of ice cubes. Shake well. Strain into a chilled Cocktail glass or serve on the rocks. Add the splash of soda on top.

Acapulco Cocktail

This is almost like a rum-based Margarita.

2 ounces light rum

$^1/_2$ ounce triple sec

$^1/_2$ ounce lime juice cordial, such as Rose's

$^1/_2$ ounce simple syrup (page 33)

Pour all of the ingredients into a shaker two-thirds full of ice cubes. Shake well. Strain into a chilled Cocktail glass.

Acid

1 ounce Bacardi 151-proof rum

1 ounce Wild Turkey 101-proof bourbon

Coke or Dr. Pepper soda, for chaser

Pour the rum into a Pony glass; add the bourbon. Drink in one gulp, followed by one of the chasers.

A Day at the Beach

This is the perfect sweet drink for summertime sipping.

1 ounce Malibu rum

$^1/_2$ ounce amaretto

4 ounces orange juice

$^1/_2$ ounce grenadine

Wedge of fresh pineapple and a fresh strawberry, for garnish

Pour the rum, amaretto, and orange juice into a shaker two-thirds full of ice cubes. Shake well. Strain into a chilled Highball glass. Drizzle the grenadine on top. Garnish with the pineapple wedge and strawberry.

Adios Motherfucker (AMF)

$1/2$ ounce vodka

$1/2$ ounce rum

$1/2$ ounce tequila

$1/2$ ounce gin

$1/2$ ounce blue curaçao

1 ounce fresh lemon juice

$1/2$ ounce simple syrup (page 33)

2 ounces lemon-lime soda

Pour all of the ingredients into an ice-filled Collins glass. Stir gently.

Adonis Cocktail

A drink that will turn a 90-pound weakling into Johnny Weismuller? I doubt it, but this is an old recipe that's worth resurrecting.

2 ounces dry sherry

1 ounce sweet vermouth

Dash of orange bitters

Pour all of the ingredients into a mixing glass two-thirds full of ice cubes. Stir well. Strain into a chilled Cocktail glass.

Affinity Cocktail

I have an affinity for this one.

1 ounce scotch

1 ounce sweet vermouth

1 ounce dry vermouth

2 dashes of Angostura bitters

Pour all of the ingredients into a mixing glass two-thirds full of ice cubes. Stir well. Strain into a chilled Cocktail glass.

Afternoon Delight Martini

> 2 ounces vanilla vodka
>
> 1 ounce white chocolate liqueur
>
> 1 ounce Cointreau
>
> Maraschino cherry and a Vanilla Wafer cookie,
>   for garnishes

Pour the vodka, white chocolate liqueur, and Cointreau into a
shaker two-thirds full of ice cubes. Shake well. Strain into a
chilled Cocktail glass. Garnish with the cherry; serve the cookie
alongside.

A Fuzzy Thing

A good drink to have on your way to the forum.

> 2 ounces Absolut Citron
>
> 1 ounce triple sec
>
> 1 ^{1}/$_2$ ounces peach schnapps
>
> 1 ounce orange juice
>
> 1 ounce pineapple juice
>
> 1 ounce grapefruit juice

Pour all of the ingredients into a shaker two-thirds full of ice
cubes. Shake well. Strain into an ice-filled wine goblet.

Agent Orange

If you like brandy, it makes an excellent substitute for
the vodka.

> 1 ounce vodka
>
> ^{1}/$_2$ ounce Grand Marnier
>
> ^{1}/$_4$ ounce triple sec
>
> Splash of orange juice

Pour all of the ingredients into a shaker two-thirds full of ice
cubes. Shake well. Strain into a chilled Highball glass.

Alabama Slammer

A tasty, sweet drink—no matter where you drink it, in Alabama or in the slammer.

> 1 ounce amaretto
> 1 ounce Southern Comfort
> 1 ounce sloe gin
> 1 ounce fresh orange juice

Pour all of the ingredients into a shaker two-thirds full of ice cubes. Shake well. Strain into an ice-filled Rocks glass.

Alaska

They say this drink is favored by gnomes from Nome. Wouldn't Juneau?

> $1^1/_2$ ounces gin
> $1/_2$ ounce yellow Chartreuse

Pour both ingredients into a mixing glass two-thirds full of crushed ice. Stir well. Strain into a chilled Cocktail glass.

Alexander

The paterfamilias of the Brandy Alexander.

> 2 ounces gin
> 1 ounce white crème de cacao
> 1 ounce light cream
> Freshly grated nutmeg, for garnish

Pour the gin, crème de cacao, and cream into a shaker two-thirds full of ice cubes. Shake well. Strain into a chilled Cocktail glass. Sprinkle lightly with the nutmeg.

Alexander Nevsky Martini

He was Prince of Novgorod from 1236 to 1251.

> 2 ounces Stolichnaya Razberi vodka
> 1 ounce Bombay Sapphire gin
> 4 fresh raspberries, for garnish

Pour the vodka and gin into a mixing glass two-thirds full of ice cubes. Stir well. Strain into a chilled Cocktail glass. Add the raspberries.

Alfonso Cocktail

Make this one with dry champagne or sparkling wine.

> 1 sugar cube
>
> 2 dashes of Angostura bitters
>
> $^1/_2$ ounce Dubonnet Rouge
>
> 5 ounces champagne or other sparkling wine

Drop the sugar cube into a Champagne Flute and dash with the bitters. Pour the Dubonnet and champagne into the glass. Don't stir: You'll lose the bubbles.

Algonquin

Named for the hotel on West 43rd Street in Manhattan, not the tribe.

> 2 ounces blended Canadian whisky
>
> $^1/_2$ ounce dry vermouth
>
> 1 ounce pineapple juice

Pour all of the ingredients into a shaker two-thirds full of ice cubes. Shake well. Strain into a chilled Cocktail glass.

Alien Secretion

> $^1/_2$ ounce vodka
>
> $^1/_2$ ounce Midori melon liqueur
>
> $^1/_2$ ounce Malibu rum
>
> Splash of pineapple juice

Pour all of the ingredients into a shaker two-thirds full of ice cubes. Shake well. Strain into a chilled Cocktail glass.

Allies Cocktail

This drink was around in 1930, so it's not a tribute to the victors of WWII.

> 1 ounce gin
> 1 ounce dry vermouth
> 1/4 ounce kümmel

Pour all of the ingredients into a mixing glass two-thirds full of ice cubes. Stir well. Strain into a chilled Cocktail glass.

Alternating Kurant Martini

A drink from the 1990s that stuck around with good reason—it's good. —*From The Purple Martini, Denver, Colorado.*

> 3 ounces Absolut Kurant vodka
> Splash of Chambord raspberry liqueur
> Splash of dry vermouth
> Lemon twist, for garnish

Pour the vodka, Chambord, and vermouth into a mixing glass two-thirds full of ice cubes. Stir well. Strain into a chilled Cocktail glass. Add the lemon twist.

Altoid

Drinking one of these is far more exciting than sucking a mint.

> 1/2 ounce Rumpleminz
> 1/2 ounce vodka
> 1/2 ounce blue curaçao
> 1/4 ounce fresh lemon juice
> 1/4 ounce simple syrup (page 33)

Pour all of the ingredients into a shaker two-thirds full of ice cubes. Shake well. Strain into a chilled Pony glass.

Amaretto Alexander

This is an excellent variation on the original Alexander—
sweeter but very tasty.

> **2 ounces amaretto**
>
> **1 ^{1}/$_2$ ounces white crème de cacao**
>
> **1 ounce light cream**
>
> **Slivered almonds, for garnish**

Pour the amaretto, crème de cacao, and cream into a shaker two-
thirds full of ice cubes. Shake well. Strain into a chilled Cocktail
glass. Sprinkle lightly with the almonds.

Amaretto Sour

> **2 ounces amaretto**
>
> **1 ounce fresh lemon juice**
>
> **Maraschino cherry, for garnish**

Pour the amaretto and lemon juice into a shaker two-thirds full of
ice cubes. Shake well. Strain into a chilled Sour glass. Garnish
with the cherry.

Amer Picon Cocktail

If you're not wildly into bitter ingredients, you might
want to increase the grenadine to suit your palate.

> **2 ounces Amer Picon**
>
> **1 ounce fresh lime juice**
>
> **Splash of grenadine**

Pour all of the ingredients into a shaker two-thirds full of ice
cubes. Shake well. Strain into a chilled Cocktail glass.

American Beauty

Just a little something to fix up before stepping into a tubful of hot water and rose petals.

> $3/4$ ounce brandy
> $3/4$ ounce dry vermouth
>   Dash of white crème de menthe
> $3/4$ ounce orange juice
> $3/4$ ounce grenadine

Pour the brandy, vermouth, crème de menthe, orange juice, and grenadine into a shaker two-thirds full of ice cubes. Shake well. Strain into a chilled Cocktail glass.

American Dream

This shooter might just give you a sugar rush.

> $1/4$ ounce Kahlúa
> $1/4$ ounce amaretto
> $1/4$ ounce Frangelico
> $1/4$ ounce dark crème de cacao

Pour all of the ingredients into a mixing glass two-thirds full of ice cubes. Stir well. Strain into a chilled Pony glass.

American Flag

Think about serving this on the Fourth of July.

> $3/4$ ounce grenadine
> $3/4$ ounce white crème de cacao
> $3/4$ ounce blue curaçao

Pour the grenadine into a sherry glass. Gently float the white crème de cacao on top. Pour the blue curaçao on top to make the third layer.

Americano

If you love Campari, you'll love this cocktail. Cin-cin!

> $1^1/_2$ ounces Campari
> $1^1/_2$ ounces sweet vermouth

Club soda

Orange slice, for garnish

Pour the Campari and vermouth into an ice-filled Highball glass. Stir well. Fill the glass with club soda. Garnish with the orange slice.

An-Apple-A-Day

—*Created by LibationGoddess, Audrey Saunders, New York City, 2000.*

1 ounce Gordon's gin

1 ounce Pucker apple liqueur

$^1/_4$ ounce maraschino liqueur

$^3/_4$ ounce fresh lime juice

$^1/_2$ ounce grapefruit juice

$^1/_2$ ounce simple syrup (page 33)

Maraschino cherry, for garnish

Pour the gin, liqueurs, juices, and simple syrup into a shaker two-thirds full of ice cubes. Shake well. Strain into an ice-filled Highball glass. Add the cherry.

Andalusia

2 ounces dry sherry

$^1/_2$ ounce light rum

$^1/_2$ ounce brandy

Pour all of the ingredients into a mixing glass two-thirds full of ice cubes. Stir well. Strain into a chilled Cocktail glass.

Añejo Highball

—*Created by master mixologist Dale DeGroff, New York City.*

1 $^1/_2$ ounces añejo rum

$^1/_2$ ounce white curaçao

$^1/_2$ ounce fresh lime juice

2 dashes of Angostura bitters

4 to 5 ounces ginger beer

Lime wheel and orange slice, for garnishes

Pour all of the ingredients into an ice-filled Highball or Collins glass. Stir well. Add the garnishes.

Angel's Tit

Believe it or not, this one's been around since at least the 1930s.

> **2 ounces dark crème de cacao**
>
> **Dollop of whipped cream**
>
> **Maraschino cherry, for garnish**

Pour the crème de cacao into a small Pousse-Café glass or Sherry glass. Top with the whipped cream. Garnish with the cherry.

Antifreeze

This drink can also be served as a shooter—it was taught to me by Stuffy Shmitt, a bartender/musician in New York City.

> **$^1/_2$ ounce vodka**
>
> **$^1/_2$ ounce blue curaçao**
>
> **$^1/_2$ ounce Bacardi 151-proof rum**
>
> **$^1/_2$ ounce peppermint schnapps**

Pour all of the ingredients into a mixing glass two-thirds full of ice cubes. Stir well. Strain into a chilled Rocks glass.

Apocalypse

Now!

> **1 ounce white crème de menthe**
>
> **1 ounce peppermint schnapps**
>
> **$^3/_4$ ounce vodka**
>
> **$^3/_4$ ounce Southern Comfort**
>
> **$^1/_2$ ounce Kahlúa**
>
> **$^1/_2$ ounce bourbon**
>
> **2 to 4 ounces hot chocolate**
>
> **Whipped cream, for garnish**

Pour the crème de menthe, schnapps, vodka, Southern Comfort, Kahlúa, and bourbon into a large coffee mug. Fill with the hot chocolate. Garnish with the whipped cream.

Apple & Cinnamon Joy

This is a great variation on the Apple Martini.

1 ounce apple schnapps

$^1/_4$ ounce Goldschlager

Pour the schnapps into a Pony glass. Drizzle the Goldschlager on top. Stir twice.

Apple Blossom

1 ounce brandy

2 ounces apple juice

$^1/_4$ ounce fresh lemon juice

Splash of vodka

Pour all of the ingredients into a shaker two-thirds full of ice cubes. Shake well. Strain into an ice-filled Rocks glass.

Apple Brandy Cocktail

You can use applejack if you have no apple brandy.

2 ounces apple brandy

$^1/_2$ ounce fresh lemon juice

$^1/_2$ ounce grenadine

Pour all of the ingredients into a shaker two-thirds full of ice cubes. Shake well. Strain into a chilled Cocktail glass.

Apple Martini

Without a doubt, *the* hottest drink of 2000.

1 ounce vodka

1 ounce sour apple schnapps

1 ounce apple juice

Thin slices of Granny Smith apple, for garnish

Pour all of the ingredients into a shaker two-thirds full of ice cubes. Shake well. Strain into a chilled Cocktail glass. Garnish with the apple slices.

Apple Pie Cocktail

There are no apple flavors in this drink, but this is how it has been made for over 70 years.

> 1 ounce light rum
>
> 1 ounce sweet vermouth
>
> $^1/_4$ ounce apricot brandy
>
> $^1/_4$ ounce fresh lemon juice
>
> 2 dashes of grenadine

Pour all of the ingredients into a shaker two-thirds full of ice cubes. Shake well. Strain into a chilled Cocktail glass.

Apple Pie Shooter

Two people are required to prepare this drink.

> 2 ounces apple juice
>
> 1 ounce vodka
>
> Whipped cream in a can
>
> Cinnamon sugar in a salt or pepper shaker

The drinker should sit in a chair with head back, mouth open. The helper pours the apple juice and then the vodka into the drinker's mouth. The drinker must hold the liquids in the mouth—no swallowing or choking allowed. Helper adds a healthy shot of whipped cream and a light sprinkling of the cinnamon sugar. Drinker sits up, swishes the ingredients together, and swallows.

Apple Sidecar

—Adapted from a recipe by Ryan Magarian, Restaurant Zoe, Seattle, Washington.

> Superfine sugar and a tangerine wedge, for rimming the glass
>
> $1^1/_2$ ounces vodka
>
> $^1/_2$ ounce Clear Creek apple brandy
>
> 1 ounce fresh lemon juice
>
> 1 ounce simple syrup (page 33)
>
> $^1/_2$ ounce fresh tangerine juice

Prepare the glass. Pour all of the ingredients into a shaker two-thirds full of ice cubes. Shake well. Strain into the sugar-rimmed Cocktail glass.

Appleberry Punch ☕

MAKES 20 FOUR-OUNCE SERVINGS

> 1 quart unsweetened apple cider
>
> 1 quart cranberry juice
>
> 5 whole cloves
>
> 2 small (3-inch) cinnamon sticks, broken
>
> 1 teaspoon freshly grated nutmeg
>
> 1 large block of ice, for serving
>
> 8 ounces Van Gogh Wild Appel vodka
>
> 20 orange wheels, for garnish

Pour the apple cider and cranberry juice into a nonreactive large pot set over high heat. Add the cloves, cinnamon sticks, and nutmeg and bring the mixture to a boil. Reduce the heat to low, cover, and simmer for 20 minutes.

Strain the mixture through a double layer of dampened cheesecloth; discard the solids. Set aside to cool to room temperature, about 1^1/$_2$ hours.

Cover and refrigerate for at least 2 hours, and up to 5 days.

Place the block of ice into a punch bowl. Add the chilled punch and the apple vodka. Float the orange wheels on top.

Applejack

> 1 ounce Jack Daniel's Tennessee whiskey
>
> 2 ounces applejack
>
> ^{3}/$_4$ ounce fresh lemon juice
>
> ^{1}/$_4$ ounce simple syrup (page 33)
>
> 1 ounce club soda

Fill a Rocks glass with ice. Add all of the ingredients. Stir well.

Applejack Cobbler

Crushed ice is a wonderful thing. Remember, it's the basis of all Cobblers, no matter what liquor you choose.

2 $^1/_2$ ounces applejack

$^1/_2$ ounce simple syrup (page 33)

Paper-thin apple or pear slices, for garnish

Pour the applejack and simple syrup into a wine goblet filled with crushed ice. Stir just to distribute. Layer the apple slices on top.

Applejack Collins

2 ounces applejack

$^1/_2$ ounce fresh lemon juice

$^1/_2$ ounce simple syrup (page 33)

5 to 6 ounces club soda

Paper-thin apple or pear slices, for garnish

Pour the applejack, lemon juice, and simple syrup into a shaker two-thirds full of ice cubes. Shake well. Strain into an ice-filled Collins glass; add the club soda. Stir to distribute. Garnish with the apple slices.

Applejack Flip

Applejack makes one of the most flavorful Flips, and the nutmeg garnish highlights the fruit notes in the spirit.

2 $^1/_2$ ounces applejack

1 $^1/_2$ ounces simple syrup (page 33)

1 egg

Freshly grated nutmeg, for garnish

Pour the applejack and simple syrup into a shaker two-thirds full of ice cubes; add the egg. Shake very well. Strain into a chilled wine goblet. Dust with the nutmeg.

Applejack Rickey

Rickeys were named for Colonel Joe Rickey, a pre-Prohibition political lobbyist.

> $2^1/_2$ ounces applejack
>
> 1 ounce fresh lime juice
>
> 5 to 6 ounces club soda
>
> Lime wedge, for garnish

Pour the applejack and lime juice into an ice-filled Highball glass. Add the club soda; stir briefly. Garnish with the lime wedge.

Apples & Oranges Martini

> $1^1/_2$ ounces Van Gogh Wild Appel vodka
>
> 1 ounce triple sec
>
> $^1/_2$ ounce orange juice
>
> $^1/_2$ ounce apple juice
>
> Apple slice and orange slice, for garnishes

Pour the vodka, triple sec, and both juices into a shaker two-thirds full of ice cubes. Shake well. Strain into a chilled Cocktail glass. Garnish with the apple and orange slices.

Apricot Cooler

> $2^1/_2$ ounces apricot brandy
>
> 6 to 7 ounces lemon-lime soda
>
> Lemon twist, for garnish

Pour the apricot brandy and lemon-lime soda into an ice-filled Collins glass. Stir to distribute. Garnish with the lemon twist.

Apricot Fizz

2 ounces apricot brandy

1 ounce fresh lemon juice

$^1/_2$ ounce simple syrup (page 33)

5 to 6 ounces club soda

Wedge of fresh or dried apricot, for garnish

Pour the apricot brandy, lemon juice, and simple syrup into a shaker two-thirds full of ice cubes. Shake well; strain into a chilled wine goblet. Pour in the club soda; stir to distribute. Garnish with the apricot.

Apricot Martini

This drink is wonderfully dry. If you want a sweeter version, add more apricot brandy.

2 ounces vodka

$^1/_2$ ounce apricot brandy

Pour both ingredients into a mixing glass two-thirds full of ice cubes. Stir well. Strain into a chilled Cocktail glass.

Apricot Rickey

$2^1/_2$ ounces apricot brandy

1 ounce fresh lime juice

5 to 6 ounces club soda

Lime wedge, for garnish

Pour the apricot brandy and lime juice into an ice-filled Highball glass. Pour in the club soda, stir to distribute. Garnish with the lime wedge.

Apricot Sour

One of the most popular cocktails from the swinging 1970s.

2 ounces apricot brandy

$^3/_4$ ounce fresh lemon juice

$^1/_2$ ounce simple syrup (page 33)

Orange wheel and maraschino cherry, for garnish

Pour the apricot brandy, lemon juice, and simple syrup into a shaker two-thirds full of ice cubes; shake well. Strain into a chilled Sour glass. Add the orange and cherry garnishes.

Apricot Vesper Martini

$1^1/2$ ounces gin

$1^1/2$ ounces vodka

$3/4$ ounce apricot brandy

Pour all of the ingredients into a shaker two-thirds full of ice cubes. Shake well. Strain into a chilled Cocktail glass.

Arabesque

—Created at La Griglia, Houston, Texas.

5 strawberries, hulled

1 ounce citrus vodka

1 ounce Campari

1 ounce champagne or other sparkling wine

In a blender, combine the strawberries, vodka, and Campari with a few ice cubes. Pour into a Champagne Flute and top with the champagne.

Arawak Cocktail

—Created at Trotters, Port of Spain, Trinidad.

2 ounces blended whisky

$1/2$ ounce dry vermouth

$1/4$ ounce pineapple juice

Dash of tamarind juice

2 dashes of Angostura bitters

Pineapple cube, for garnish

Pour all of the ingredients into a shaker two-thirds full of ice cubes. Shake well. Strain into a chilled Cocktail glass. Add the pineapple garnish.

Arbor Martini

2 $^1/_2$ ounces Stolichnaya Vanil vodka

$^1/_4$ ounce Stolichnaya Persik vodka

Thin slice of vanilla bean, for garnish

Pour both vodkas into a mixing glass two-thirds full of ice cubes. Stir well. Strain into a chilled Cocktail glass. Add the vanilla bean.

Artillery Punch 🍵

MAKES 24 SIX-OUNCE SERVINGS

1 750ml-bottle rye whiskey

1 750ml-bottle red wine

1 quart chilled strong tea

12 ounces dark rum

6 ounces gin

6 ounces brandy

1 ounce Bénédictine

12 ounces orange juice

8 ounces fresh lemon juice

6 ounces simple syrup (page 33)

1 large block of ice

Lemon wheels, for garnish

Pour all of the ingredients, except for the ice and lemon wheels, into a large pot or bowl. Stir well, cover, and refrigerate for at least 4 hours.

Place the block of ice in the center of a punch bowl. Pour in the punch; float the lemon wheels on top.

Astor Martini

—*From Astor Place, South Beach, Florida.*

4 ounces Ketel One vodka

1 ounce Campari

2 ounces grapefruit juice

Pour all of the ingredients into a shaker two-thirds full of ice cubes. Shake well. Strain into a chilled, very large, Cocktail glass.

Attaboy

—From the Savoy Hotel, London.

> **2 ounces gin**
>
> **1 ounce sweet vermouth**
>
> **$^1/_4$ ounce grenadine**

Pour all of the ingredients into a mixing glass two-thirds full of ice cubes. Stir well. Strain into a chilled Cocktail glass.

Aviation Cocktail

You may drink this if you're a passenger but never when piloting a plane.

> **2 ounces gin**
>
> **$^1/_2$ ounce maraschino liqueur**
>
> **$^1/_2$ ounce fresh lemon juice**

Pour all of the ingredients into a shaker two-thirds full of ice cubes. Shake well. Strain into a chilled Cocktail glass.

AWOL

—Created by Lane Zellman, New Orleans, 1993.

> **$^1/_2$ ounce Midori melon liqueur**
>
> **$^1/_2$ ounce chilled pineapple juice**
>
> **$^1/_2$ ounce vodka**
>
> **$^1/_2$ ounce 151-proof rum**

Layer all of the ingredients in a Pousse-Café glass. Carefully ignite the rum and allow it to burn for only 7 to 10 seconds. Extinguish the flame by blowing it out or covering the top with the stem of another glass. Drink slowly in one luxurious swallow.

B & B

—Created at The "21" Club, New York City, shortly after the repeal of Prohibition.

> **1 ounce brandy**
>
> **$^3/_4$ ounce Bénédictine**

Pour both ingredients into a brandy snifter. Swirl to blend.

Bacardi Cocktail

Much like a Daiquiri, but this one gets its rosy color from the grenadine.

> 2 ounces Bacardi light rum
> 1 ounce fresh lime juice
> $1/2$ ounce grenadine

Pour all of the ingredients into a shaker two-thirds full of ice cubes. Shake well. Strain into a chilled Cocktail glass.

Bacardi Cocktail

Watch what you're pouring when you make a Bacardi Cocktail—in 1936 a New York bar owner was taken to court for using a rum other than Bacardi. Bacardi won the case, and the New York State Supreme Court upheld the decision.

Bahama Mama

A favorite tropical drink on Paradise Island.

> $1/4$ ounce Kahlúa
> $1/2$ ounce dark rum
> $1/2$ ounce coconut liqueur
> $1/2$ ounce Bacardi 151-proof rum
> 1 ounce fresh lemon juice
> 4 ounces pineapple juice

Pour all of the ingredients into a shaker two-thirds full of ice cubes. Shake well. Strain into an ice-filled Collins glass.

Baileys Comet Martini

> $1^1/4$ ounces Van Gogh Wild Appel vodka
> $1^1/4$ ounces Baileys Irish cream liqueur

Pour both ingredients into a shaker two-thirds full of ice cubes. Shake well. Strain into a chilled Cocktail glass.

Bald Pussy

$3/4$ ounce Midori melon liqueur

$1/2$ ounce lime vodka

$1/2$ ounce vodka

$1/2$ ounce triple sec

$3/4$ ounce blueberry schnapps

Splash of fresh lime juice

Splash of lemon-lime soda

Fill a Collins glass with ice. Pour in all of the ingredients and stir to distribute.

Baltimore Bracer Cocktail

2 ounces brandy

$3/4$ ounce anisette

1 egg white

Pour all of the ingredients into a shaker two-thirds full of ice cubes. Shake very well. Strain into a chilled Cocktail glass.

Bamboo Cocktail

Drink this as an apéritif and your meal is bound to be outstanding.

2 ounces dry sherry

2 ounces dry vermouth

2 dashes of Angostura bitters

Pour all of the ingredients into a mixing glass two-thirds full of ice cubes. Stir well. Strain into a chilled Cocktail glass.

Banana Cream Pie

1 ounce crème de banane

1 ounce white crème de cacao

1 ounce vodka

1 ounce half-and-half

Pour all of the ingredients into a shaker two-thirds full of ice cubes. Shake well. Strain into a chilled Cocktail glass.

Banana Daiquiri

When using fresh bananas in cocktails such as this, riper is always better.

1 $1/2$ ounces light rum

$1/2$ ounce simple syrup (page 33)

1 small ripe banana, cut up

1 $1/2$ ounces fresh lime juice

Place 1 cup of ice cubes in a blender. Add all of the ingredients. Blend at low speed to break up the ice. Raise the speed to high and blend until thick. Pour the drink into a wine goblet or other large glass.

Banana Split Martini

—Adapted from a recipe by Christie Hartmann and Gage Tschyevkosky, Wolfgang Puck's Grand Café, Denver, Colorado.

Strawberry and chocolate syrups, for drizzling inside the glass

2 ounces Grey Goose vodka

2 ounces Godiva White Chocolate liqueur

1 ounce crème de banane

Banana slice and a strawberry pirouette cookie, for garnishes

Drizzle a large, chilled Cocktail glass with a bit of the strawberry and chocolate syrups. Pour the vodka, chocolate liqueur, and crème de banane into a shaker two-thirds full of ice cubes. Shake well. Strain into the Cocktail glass. Add the garnishes.

Banana-Rum Martini

If you like sweet drinks, you'll love this one.

2 ounces dark rum

$1/2$ ounce crème de banane

Pour both ingredients into a mixing glass two-thirds full of ice cubes. Stir well. Strain into a chilled Cocktail glass.

Banff Cocktail

When in Canada. . . . For a drier version of this drink, try
using Cointreau instead of curaçao.

2 ounces blended Canadian whisky

$^{1}/_{2}$ ounce curaçao

$^{1}/_{2}$ ounce cherry brandy

Dash of Angostura bitters

Pour all of the ingredients into a mixing glass two-thirds full of
ice cubes. Stir well. Strain into a chilled Cocktail glass.

Banshee

1 ounce crème de banane

1 ounce white crème de cacao

1 ounce heavy cream

Pour all of the ingredients into a shaker two-thirds full of ice
cubes. Shake well. Strain into a chilled Cocktail glass.

Barbie Shot

A pink drink that makes you feel like a living doll.
Where's Ken?

1 ounce Malibu rum

1 ounce vodka

1 ounce cranberry juice

1 ounce orange juice

Pour all of the ingredients into a shaker two-thirds full of ice
cubes. Shake well. Strain into a chilled Cocktail glass.

Barney on Acid

$^{1}/_{2}$ ounce blue curaçao

$^{1}/_{2}$ ounce Jägermeister

Splash of cranberry juice

Pour all of the ingredients into a mixing glass two-thirds full of
ice cubes. Stir well. Strain into a Pony glass.

Baron Cocktail

This drink originally called for more sweet vermouth, but these ratios work very well.

2 ounces gin

1 ounce dry vermouth

$^1/_4$ ounce curaçao

2 dashes of sweet vermouth

Pour all of the ingredients into a mixing glass two-thirds full of ice cubes. Stir well. Strain into a chilled Cocktail glass.

Batida Mango

Batidas are Brazil's answer to frozen fruit daiquiries.

2 ounces cachaça

$^1/_2$ ripe mango, cut into chunks

1 teaspoon sugar

In a blender, combine the cachaça, mango, sugar, and 1 cup of ice cubes. Blend well. Pour into a chilled wine goblet.

Bay Breeze

It's a common mistake to make this drink with vodka, but rum was the original base spirit.

2 ounces light rum

3 ounces cranberry juice

1 ounce pineapple juice

Pour all of the ingredients into a Highball glass filled with ice cubes. Stir briefly.

Beach Blanket Bingo ⊘

4 ounces cranberry juice

4 ounces grapefruit juice

Splash of club soda

Splash of lime juice

Pour all of the ingredients into an ice-filled Collins glass; stir to chill.

Beachcomber

A drink favored by "Trader Vic" Bergeron.

> **Superfine sugar and a lime wedge, for rimming the glass**
> **2 ounces light rum**
> **$^1/_4$ ounce maraschino liqueur**
> **$^1/_4$ ounce cherry brandy**
> **$^1/_2$ ounce fresh lime juice**

Use the sugar and lime wedge to coat the exterior rim of a Cocktail glass. Pour all of the remaining ingredients into a shaker two-thirds full of ice cubes. Shake well. Strain into the sugar-rimmed glass.

Beadlestone Cocktail

> **2 ounces scotch**
> **1 ounce dry vermouth**
> **Dash of Angostura bitters**

Pour all of the ingredients into a mixing glass two-thirds full of ice cubes. Stir well. Strain into a chilled Cocktail glass.

Beam Me Up Scotty

> **$^1/_2$ ounce Kahlúa**
> **$^1/_2$ ounce crème de banane**
> **$^1/_2$ ounce Baileys Irish cream liqueur**

Layer in order in a Pony glass.

Beauty Spot Cocktail

> **1 ounce gin**
> **$^1/_2$ ounce dry vermouth**
> **$^1/_2$ ounce sweet vermouth**
> **$^1/_4$ ounce orange juice**
> **1 egg white**
> **Dash of grenadine**

Pour the gin, both vermouths, and orange juice into a shaker two-thirds full of ice cubes; add the egg white. Shake very well. Strain into a chilled Cocktail glass. Drop the grenadine on top.

Bellini

When in Venice, do as everyone does: Go to Harry's Bar and sip on one or two of these classic cocktails.

MAKES 4 TO 6 DRINKS

1 to 2 ripe white peaches, washed and stoned—leave the peel on—flesh cut into cubes

$\frac{1}{4}$ to $\frac{1}{2}$ ounce fresh lemon juice

$\frac{1}{4}$ ounce simple syrup (page 33)

1 750-ml bottle Prosecco

In a blender, combine the peach cubes, lemon juice, and simple syrup; blend well. Spoon about $\frac{1}{4}$ cup of the puree into each chilled Champagne Flute. Gently pour in the sparkling wine. If you have to stir, do so gently.

Bellini Martini

If you don't have peach nectar on hand, leave it out, the schnapps will do the job.

2 ounces vodka

$\frac{3}{4}$ ounce peach schnapps

$\frac{3}{4}$ ounce peach nectar

Lemon twist, for garnish

Pour the vodka, schnapps, and nectar into a shaker two-thirds full of ice cubes. Shake well. Strain into a chilled Cocktail glass. Add the lemon twist.

Belmont Cocktail

This drink is named for the New York racetrack where the Belmont Stakes, the third leg of the Triple Crown, is run every year.

2 ounces gin

$\frac{1}{2}$ ounce half-and-half

Splash of grenadine

Pour all of the ingredients into a shaker two-thirds full of ice cubes. Shake well. Strain into a chilled Cocktail glass.

Bénédictine Chapel Martini

—*From The Purple Martini, Denver, Colorado.*

> **3 ounces gin**
> **Splash of Bénédictine**
> **Splash of sweet vermouth**
> **Splash of dry vermouth**

Pour all of the ingredients into a mixing glass two-thirds full of ice cubes. Stir well. Strain into a chilled Cocktail glass.

Bennett Cocktail

It's possible that this was named for James Gordon Bennett, a newspaper baron who used to announce his arrival in a restaurant by yanking the tablecloths from all the tables he passed. A fun date, no?

> **2 ounces gin**
> **$^1/_2$ ounce fresh lime juice**
> **$^1/_4$ ounce simple syrup (page 33)**
> **Dash of orange bitters**

Pour all of the ingredients into a shaker two-thirds full of ice cubes. Shake well. Strain into a chilled Cocktail glass.

Bermuda Rose Cocktail

Drink this only if wearing dark pink shorts.

> **2 ounces gin**
> **$^1/_2$ ounce apricot brandy**
> **$^1/_2$ ounce sweet vermouth**
> **Dash of grenadine**

Pour all of the ingredients into a mixing glass two-thirds full of ice cubes. Stir well. Strain into a chilled Cocktail glass.

B

Betsy Ross

Something to sip while sewing or on Independence Day.

> 3 ounces brandy
>
> 1 ounce ruby port
>
> $^1/_2$ ounce curaçao
>
> Dash of Angostura bitters

Pour all of the ingredients into a mixing glass two-thirds full of ice cubes. Stir well. Strain into a chilled Cocktail glass.

Between the Sheets

If you know where or how this drink's name originated, please let me know—it's a mystery to me, but the drink was popular in London during the 1920s.

> 1 ounce brandy
>
> 1 ounce light rum
>
> 1 ounce triple sec
>
> $^1/_2$ ounce fresh lemon juice
>
> $^1/_2$ ounce simple syrup (page 33)

Pour all of the ingredients into a shaker two-thirds full of ice cubes. Shake well. Strain into a chilled Cocktail glass.

B-52

Layer this beautifully in three stripes or drink it as a shooter.

> $^3/_4$ ounce Kahlúa
>
> $^3/_4$ ounce Baileys Irish cream liqueur
>
> $^3/_4$ ounce Grand Marnier

Pour the Kahlúa into a Pousse-Café glass. Float the Irish cream liqueur on top, and gently pour the Grand Marnier on top of that.

Bicycle Built for Two Punch

MAKES 8 TO 10 ICE-FILLED SERVINGS

> 10 ounces brandy
>
> 10 ounces ruby port
>
> 5 ounces Cointreau

6 ounces orange juice

5 ounces fresh lemon juice

12 ounces ginger ale

2 lemons, cut into thin wheels

1 orange, cut into thin wheels

Combine all of the ingredients in a large pitcher. Stir well and refrigerate. Pour into ice-filled, sugar-rimmed Collins glasses.

Big Pine Key Cocktail

—Adapted from a recipe by Robert (Bobbo) Semmes, a cocktail aficionado from South Carolina.

1 ^{1}/2 ounces gin

1 ounce Cointreau

^{3}/4 ounce fresh lime juice

Orange twist, for garnish

Pour the gin, Cointreau, and lime juice into a shaker two-thirds full of ice cubes. Shake well. Strain into a chilled Cocktail glass. Add the orange twist garnish.

Bijou Cocktail

This one's a jewel.

1 ^{1}/2 ounces gin

^{1}/2 ounce sweet vermouth

^{1}/4 ounce green Chartreuse

2 dashes of orange bitters

Pour all of the ingredients into a mixing glass two-thirds full of ice cubes. Stir well. Strain into a chilled Cocktail glass.

Bishop Punch

Here's a drink that's called a punch but is made in individual servings—like a Planter's Punch. Go figure.

> 1 ounce fresh lemon juice
>
> 1 ounce orange juice
>
> $^1/_2$ ounce simple syrup (page 33)
>
> 4 ounces red wine
>
> Orange slice, for garnish

Pour the citrus juices and simple syrup into a shaker two-thirds full of ice cubes. Shake well. Strain into a chilled wine goblet. Pour in the wine; stir briefly. Add the orange slice.

Bistro Sidecar

—Adapted from a recipe by Chef Kathy Casey, Kathy Casey Food Studios, Seattle, Washington.

> Superfine sugar and a lemon wedge, for rimming the glass
>
> 1 $^1/_2$ ounces brandy
>
> $^1/_2$ ounce Tuaca
>
> $^1/_2$ ounce Frangelico
>
> $^1/_4$ ounce fresh lemon juice
>
> $^1/_4$ ounce simple syrup (page 33)
>
> $^1/_2$ ounce fresh tangerine juice
>
> Roasted hazelnut, for garnish

Prepare the glass. Pour all of the liquid ingredients into a shaker two-thirds full of ice cubes. Shake well. Strain into the sugar-rimmed Cocktail glass. Drop the hazelnut into the drink.

Bitter-Sweet

The bitters really bring this drink together, and if you are a fan of Angostura, feel free to add an extra dash or two.

> 1 ounce sweet vermouth
>
> 1 ounce dry vermouth
>
> 2 dashes of Angostura bitters
>
> Lemon twist, for garnish

Pour both vermouths and the bitters into a mixing glass two-thirds full of ice cubes. Stir well. Strain into a chilled Cocktail glass. Garnish with the lemon twist.

Black & Tan

Though traditionally the stout and amber ale are mixed together in the glass, a more recent trend is to layer the stout on top of the ale. I'm going traditional on this; you can do what you want.

8 ounces Irish stout

8 ounces amber ale

Carefully pour the stout and the ale into a 16-ounce beer glass.

Black & White Cocktail

3 ^{1}/$_2$ ounces chilled strong coffee

1 ^{1}/$_2$ ounces brandy

^{1}/$_2$ ounce white crème de cacao

Dollop of whipped cream

Chocolate sprinkles, for garnish

Pour the coffee, brandy, and crème de cacao into a chilled Champagne Flute. Top with the whipped cream and a sprinkle of chocolate sprinkles.

Black Devil

Black olives are seldom used in mixed drinks, but they taste wonderful after sipping this dry rum Martini.

2 ounces light rum

^{1}/$_2$ ounce dry vermouth

1 brined black olive, pitted, for garnish

Pour the rum and vermouth into a mixing glass two-thirds full of ice cubes. Stir well. Strain into a chilled Cocktail glass. Add the olive.

Black Feather

"He stuck a feather in his cap . . ." —*Adapted from a recipe by Robert Hess (aka DrinkBoy), Seattle, Washington.*

> **2 ounces brandy**
>
> **1 ounce dry vermouth**
>
> **$^1/_2$ ounce Cointreau**
>
> **Angostura bitters to taste**
>
> **Orange twist, for garnish**

Pour all of the ingredients into a mixing glass two-thirds full of ice cubes. Stir well. Strain into a chilled Cocktail glass. Add the twist.

Black Martini

> **2 ounces vodka**
>
> **1 ounce Chambord raspberry liqueur**
>
> **$^1/_2$ ounce blue curaçao**

Pour all of the ingredients into a mixing glass two-thirds full of ice cubes. Stir well. Strain into a chilled Cocktail glass.

Black Opal Martini

—*From The Purple Martini, Denver, Colorado.*

> **3 ounces Smirnoff Black vodka**
>
> **Splash of Opal Nera black sambuca**
>
> **3 coffee beans, for garnish**

Pour the vodka and sambuca into a mixing glass two-thirds full of ice cubes. Stir well. Strain into a chilled Cocktail glass. Garnish with the coffee beans.

Black Russian

Use less Kahlúa for a drier drink. Yum.

> **2 ounces vodka**
>
> **1 $^1/_2$ ounces Kahlúa**

Pour the vodka and Kahlúa into an ice-filled Rocks glass. Stir to distribute.

Black Stockings Martini

  2 ounces Van Gogh Dutch Chocolate vodka

  $^3/_4$ ounce Chambord raspberry liqueur

  $^3/_4$ ounce Godiva White Chocolate liqueur

  Lemon twist, for garnish

Pour the vodka, Chambord, and chocolate liqueur into a shaker two-thirds full of ice cubes. Shake well. Strain into a chilled Cocktail glass. Garnish with the twist.

Black Stripe

This is a very old drink, probably first served in the 1700s when sugar, molasses, and Caribbean rum were available ingredients in the newly settled America.

  2 teaspoons dark molasses

  1 ounce hot water

  2 ounces dark rum

  Lemon twist, for garnish

Pour the molasses and hot water into an Irish Coffee glass; stir well to dissolve the molasses. Pour in the rum; stir well. Garnish with the twist.

Black Velvet

A stately drink that is said to have been created after the death of Prince Albert, Queen Victoria's consort.

  8 ounces chilled Irish stout

  8 ounces chilled not-too-dry champagne or
      other sparkling wine

Carefully pour the stout and champagne into a chilled 16-ounce beer glass.

B

Black Velveteen

This is a less expensive version of the Black Velvet and it works very well indeed.

> **8 ounces chilled Irish stout**
>
> **8 ounces chilled hard cider**

Carefully pour the stout and cider into a chilled 16-ounce beer glass.

Black Widow

> **1^1/2 ounces citrus vodka**
>
> **1^1/2 ounces black sambuca**

Pour both ingredients into a mixing glass two-thirds full of ice cubes. Stir well. Strain into a chilled Cocktail glass.

Blackthorne

> **2 ounces Irish whiskey**
>
> **^{3}/4 ounce sweet vermouth**
>
> **2 dashes of Pernod**
>
> **2 dashes of Angostura bitters**
>
> **Lemon twist, for garnish**

Pour the whiskey, vermouth, Pernod, and bitters into a mixing glass two-thirds full of ice cubes. Stir well. Strain into a chilled Cocktail glass. Add the twist.

Blarney Stone

Named for the famous "wishing stone" at Blarney Castle which is believed to have been broken from the Scottish Stone of Scone. Scottish kings were crowned over the stone because it was believed to have special powers. This drink has special powers of its own.

> **2 ounces Irish whiskey**
>
> **^{1}/4 ounce white curaçao**
>
> **^{1}/4 ounce absinthe substitute, such as Absente, Pernod, Herbsaint, or Ricard**

Dash of maraschino liqueur

Lemon twist, for garnish

Pour the whiskey, curaçao, absinthe substitute, and maraschino liqueur into a mixing glass two-thirds full of ice cubes. Stir well. Strain into a chilled Cocktail glass. Add the twist.

Blood and Sand

You should try this drink even if you don't care for scotch—it's a rich, fruity treat.

1 ounce blended scotch whisky

1 ounce orange juice

1 ounce cherry brandy

1 ounce sweet vermouth

Pour all of the ingredients into a shaker two-thirds full of ice cubes. Shake well. Strain into a chilled Cocktail glass.

Blood Orange

—*Created by John Simmons, Petaluma, New York City, 1995.*

2 ounces Stolichnaya Ohranj vodka

1 ^{1}/$_2$ ounces Campari

Blood orange slice or wedge, for garnish

Pour the vodka and Campari into a mixing glass two-thirds full of ice cubes. Stir well. Strain into a chilled Cocktail glass. Add the blood orange garnish.

Bloodhound Cocktail

2 ounces gin

^{1}/$_2$ ounce dry vermouth

^{1}/$_2$ ounce sweet vermouth

^{1}/$_4$ ounce strawberry liqueur

Pour all of the ingredients into a mixing glass two-thirds full of ice cubes. Stir well. Strain into a chilled Cocktail glass.

Bloody Bull

2 ounces vodka

2 ounces tomato juice

2 ounces beef bouillon

$^1/_4$ ounce fresh lemon juice

Pinch of ground black pepper

Pinch of celery salt

3 dashes of Worcestershire sauce

Dash of hot sauce

Lemon wedge, for garnish

Pour the vodka, tomato juice, beef bouillon, and lemon juice into a shaker two-thirds full of ice cubes. Add the pepper, celery salt, Worcestershire, and hot sauce. Shake well. Strain into an ice-filled Highball glass. Add the lemon wedge.

Bloody Caesar

2 ounces vodka

4 ounces Clamato juice

$^1/_4$ ounce fresh lemon juice

Pinch of ground black pepper

Pinch of celery salt

Dash of hot sauce (optional)

Lemon wedge, for garnish

Pour the vodka, Clamato juice, and lemon juice into a shaker two-thirds full of ice cubes. Add the pepper, celery salt, and hot sauce. Shake well. Strain into an ice-filled Highball glass. Add the lemon wedge.

Bloody Maria

See **Bloody Mary**; substitute tequila for the vodka.

Bloody Mary

This classic drink has a long history that began in Paris and moved to New York City, where it was renamed The Red Snapper, then went back to its original moniker. It has been greatly improved over the years and has become universally popular. Note that this one uses lemon juice, which produces a much better cocktail than lime juice.

2 ounces vodka

4 ounces tomato juice

$^1/_2$ ounce lemon juice

$^1/_4$ teaspoon black pepper

Pinch of salt

$^1/_4$ teaspoon ground cumin

2 dashes of Worcestershire sauce

2 dashes of hot sauce

Lemon wedge, for garnish

Pour the vodka, tomato juice, and lemon juice into a shaker two-thirds full of ice cubes; add the pepper, salt, cumin, Worcestershire, and hot sauce. Shake well. Strain into an ice-filled Highball glass. Add the lemon wedge.

Blow Job

This shot should be drunk without using your hands. Pick up the Pony glass between your lips and tilt your head back.

$^1/_2$ ounce butterscotch schnapps

$^1/_2$ ounce Irish cream liqueur

Whipped cream

In a Pony glass, layer the butterscotch schnapps with the Irish cream. Spray the whipped cream on top, mounding it about 2 inches high.

BLT

2 ounces Bacardi Limón rum

6 to 8 ounces iced tea

Pour the rum into an ice-filled Collins glass. Fill with iced tea. Stir well.

Blue Apples in Hawaii Martini

1 $^1/_2$ ounces Van Gogh Wild Appel vodka

$^3/_4$ ounce blue curaçao

1 $^1/_2$ ounces pineapple juice

Pour all of the ingredients into a shaker two-thirds full of ice cubes. Shake well. Strain into a chilled Cocktail glass.

Blue Blazer

This Blazer dates to before 1862—must be threadbare by now. If you try this at home, be verrrry careful.

2 ounces scotch whisky

1 $^1/_2$ ounces hot water

$^1/_2$ ounce simple syrup (page 33)

Lemon twist, for garnish

Pour the scotch and the hot water into an Irish Coffee glass or a metal tankard and ignite it carefully with a match. Carefully pour the flaming liquid into a second Irish Coffee glass or metal tankard and repeat this process, pouring it back and forth between the glasses three or four times. Add the simple syrup; stir briefly. Add the twist.

Blue Cosmopolitan

This works well with lime juice instead of grapefruit juice—try both versions.

Lime wedge and superfine sugar, for rimming the glass

2 ounces citrus vodka

1 ounce blue curaçao

$^1/_2$ ounce grapefruit juice

$^1/_2$ ounce simple syrup (page 33)

Use the lime wedge and sugar to coat the exterior rim of a Cocktail glass. Pour all of the remaining ingredients into a mixing glass two-thirds full of ice cubes. Stir well. Strain into the sugar-rimmed Cocktail glass.

Blue-Eyed Blonde

This is a favorite shooter among Trinidadians.

  $1/2$ ounce Frangelico
  $1/2$ ounce crème de banane
  $1/2$ ounce blue curaçao

Layer in the order given into a Pousse-Café or Pony glass.

Blue Kamikaze

  2 ounces vodka
  $3/4$ ounce blue curaçao
  $3/4$ ounce fresh lime juice

Pour all of the ingredients into a shaker two-thirds full of ice cubes. Shake well. Strain into a chilled Cocktail glass.

Blue Martini

  2 ounces gin
  $1/2$ ounce blue curaçao

Pour both ingredients into a mixing glass two-thirds full of ice cubes. Stir well. Strain into a chilled Cocktail glass.

Blue Train Cocktail

Could this be named for the gorgeous turn-of-the-century restaurant in Paris?

  2 ounces gin
  $1/2$ ounce blue curaçao
  $1/2$ ounce fresh lemon juice

Pour all of the ingredients into a shaker two-thirds full of ice cubes. Shake well. Strain into a chilled Cocktail glass.

Blueberry Daiquiri

1 1/2 ounces blueberry schnapps or liqueur

1 1/2 ounces light rum

3/4 ounce fresh lime juice

Pour all of the ingredients into a shaker two-thirds full of ice cubes. Shake well. Strain into a chilled Cocktail glass.

B9 Martini

—From Butterfield 9, Washington, D.C.

1 1/2 ounces Grey Goose orange-flavored vodka

1/2 ounce peach schnapps

Chilled champagne or other sparkling wine

Pour the vodka and peach schnapps into a mixing glass two-thirds full of ice cubes. Stir well. Strain into a chilled Cocktail glass. Add a splash of the champagne.

Bobbo's Bride Straight-Up

—Adapted from a recipe by Laurel Semmes, somewhere in South Carolina.

1 ounce gin

1 ounce vodka

1/2 ounce peach schnapps

1/2 ounce Campari

Peach slice, for garnish.

Pour the gin, vodka, schnapps, and Campari into a mixing glass two-thirds full of ice cubes. Stir well. Strain into a chilled Cocktail glass. Add the peach slice.

Bobby Burns

This cocktail is probably named for the eighteenth-century Scottish poet, Robert Burns, whose works include the incomprehensible lyrics to "Auld Lang Syne."

2 ounces blended Scotch whisky

1 ounce sweet vermouth

1/4 ounce Bénédictine

Pour all of the ingredients into a mixing glass two-thirds full of ice cubes. Stir well. Strain into a chilled Cocktail glass.

Bocce Ball

2 ounces amaretto

4 ounces orange juice

Orange wheel, for garnish

Pour the amaretto and orange juice into an ice-filled Highball glass. Stir briefly; add the orange wheel.

Boilermaker

This is a shooter followed by a chaser.

2 ounces whiskey

10 ounces beer

Pour each ingredient into its own glass. Toss back the whiskey and chase it with the beer.

Bolero

2 ounces dark rum

$^1/_2$ ounce brandy

$^1/_2$ ounce fresh lime juice

$^1/_2$ ounce orange juice

$^1/_2$ ounce simple syrup (page 33)

Pour all of the ingredients into a shaker two-thirds full of ice cubes. Shake well. Strain into a chilled Cocktail glass.

Bolo's Pomegranate Sangria

—Created by Chef Bobby Flay, Bolo, New York City.

MAKES ABOUT 8 SIX-OUNCE SERVINGS

- 1 750-ml bottle dry red wine
- 8 ounces American brandy
- 8 ounces simple syrup (page 33)
- 4 ounces orange juice
- 6 ounces pomegranate molasses or pomegranate juice
- 2 oranges, sliced into thin wheels
- 3 green apples, cored and cut into thin slices
- 2 lemons, sliced into thin wheels

Combine all of the ingredients in a large pot or bowl. Stir to blend. Cover and let sit, refrigerated, for at least 2 hours and up to 2 days. Serve in ice-filled wine goblets.

Bolo's White Peach Sangria

—Created by Chef Bobby Flay, Bolo, New York City.

MAKES ABOUT 8 SIX-OUNCE SERVINGS

- 1 750-ml bottle Pinot Grigio
- 8 ounces American brandy
- 8 ounces simple syrup (page 33)
- 4 ounces orange juice
- 6 ounces white peach puree
- 4 peaches, pitted and sliced
- 3 green apples, cored and cut into thin slices
- 2 lemons, sliced into thin wheels

Combine all of the ingredients in a large pot or bowl. Stir to blend. Cover and let sit, refrigerated, for at least 2 hours and up to 2 days. Serve in ice-filled wine goblets.

Bosom Caresser

The racy name of this drink dates to the late 1800s.

>   2 ounces brandy
>   1 ounce white curaçao
>   Dash of grenadine
>   1 egg yolk

Pour all of the ingredients into a shaker two-thirds full of ice cubes. Shake very well. Strain into a chilled Cocktail glass.

Boston Cocktail

>   1 1/2 ounces gin
>   1 1/2 ounces apricot brandy
>   1/4 ounce fresh lemon juice
>   Splash of grenadine

Pour all of the ingredients into a shaker two-thirds full of ice cubes. Shake well. Strain into a chilled Cocktail glass.

Bourbon & Branch

The recipe that answers the question: "What is 'branch water' anyway?"

>   2 1/2 ounces bourbon
>   4 to 5 ounces still spring water

Pour the bourbon and water into an ice-filled Highball glass. Stir briefly.

Bourbon Cobbler

If you make this drink when blueberries are plentiful, use them as a garnish—they marry very well to the bourbon.

>   2 1/2 ounces bourbon
>   1/2 ounce simple syrup (page 33)
>   Fresh fruit in season, for garnish

Pour the bourbon and simple syrup into a wine goblet filled with crushed ice. Stir briefly. Add the garnish of choice.

Bourbon Crusta

Superfine sugar and a wedge of lemon,
for rimming the glass

Lemon peel spiral (see technique, page 38)

2 ounces bourbon

$^1/_2$ ounce white curaçao

$^1/_2$ ounce fresh lemon juice

Rim a Sour glass using the sugar and lemon wedge. Place the lemon peel spiral into the glass so that it lines almost the entire interior.

Pour the bourbon, curaçao, and lemon juice into a shaker two-thirds full of ice cubes. Shake well. Strain into the glass.

Bourbon Daisy

2 $^1/_2$ ounces bourbon

1 ounce fresh lemon juice

$^1/_2$ ounce grenadine

Lemon twist, for garnish

Pour the bourbon, lemon juice, and grenadine into a shaker two-thirds full of ice cubes. Shake well. Strain into a crushed-ice-filled Highball glass. Add the twist.

Bourbon Fix

2 $^1/_2$ ounces bourbon

1 ounce fresh lemon juice

$^1/_2$ ounce pineapple juice

Fresh fruit in season, for garnish

Pour the bourbon, lemon juice, and pineapple juice into a shaker two-thirds full of ice cubes. Shake well; strain into a crushed ice–filled Highball glass. Add the garnish of choice.

Bourbon Fizz

2 ounces bourbon

1 ounce fresh lemon juice

$^1/_2$ ounce simple syrup (page 33)

5 to 6 ounces club soda

Fresh fruit in season, for garnish

Pour the bourbon, lemon juice, and simple syrup into a shaker two-thirds full of ice cubes. Shake well. Strain into a chilled wine goblet. Add the club soda; stir briefly. Add the garnish of choice.

Bourbon Milk Punch

Milk punches are very popular in New Orleans, "The Big Easy."

2 ounces bourbon

$^1/_2$ ounce dark crème de cacao

4 ounces milk

Dash of vanilla extract

Dash of ground cinnamon

Freshly grated nutmeg, for garnish

Pour the bourbon, crème de cacao, milk, and vanilla into a shaker two-thirds full of ice cubes; add the cinnamon. Shake well. Strain into an ice-filled Rocks glass. Sprinkle with the nutmeg.

Bourbon Old-Fashioned

1 sugar cube

3 dashes of Angostura bitters

1 orange slice

1 lemon wedge

1 maraschino cherry

$2^1/_2$ ounces bourbon

In a Double Old-Fashioned glass, muddle the sugar cube, bitters, orange slice, lemon wedge, and maraschino cherry. Fill the glass with ice cubes. Add the bourbon; stir well.

Bourbon Rickey

2 ^{1}/2 ounces bourbon

1 ounce fresh lime juice

5 to 6 ounces club soda

Lime wedge, for garnish

Pour the bourbon and lime juice into an ice-filled Highball glass. Add the club soda; stir briefly. Add the lime wedge.

Bourbon Sling

2^1/2 ounces bourbon

^{1}/2 ounce Southern Comfort

^{1}/2 ounce fresh lemon juice

5 to 6 ounces club soda

Lemon wedge, for garnish

Pour the bourbon, Southern Comfort, and lemon juice into a shaker two-thirds full of ice cubes. Shake well. Strain the drink into an ice-filled Collins glass. Add the club soda; stir briefly. Add the lemon wedge.

Bourbon Smash

At first glance you might be tempted to think that this is a Mint Julep, but the methods for making Smashes and Juleps are different from each other.

6 fresh mint leaves

^{3}/4 ounce simple syrup (page 33)

2 ^{1}/2 ounces bourbon

Mint sprig, for garnish

Place the mint leaves in the bottom of a Double Old-Fashioned glass; add the simple syrup and muddle well with a muddler or the back of a sturdy spoon. Fill the glass with crushed ice. Add the bourbon; stir briefly. Add the mint sprig.

Bourbon Sour

2 ounces bourbon

$^3/_4$ ounce fresh lemon juice

$^1/_2$ ounce simple syrup (page 33)

Orange wheel and maraschino cherry, for garnish

Pour the bourbon, lemon juice, and simple syrup into a shaker two-thirds full of ice cubes. Shake well. Strain the drink into a chilled Sour glass. Add the orange and cherry garnishes.

Bourbon Stinger

2 ounces bourbon

$^1/_2$ ounce white crème de menthe

Pour both ingredients into a shaker two-thirds full of ice cubes. Shake well. Strain into a crushed ice–filled wine goblet.

Bourbon Swizzle

2 ounces bourbon

$^1/_2$ ounce fresh lemon juice

$^1/_2$ ounce apricot brandy

5 to 6 ounces ginger ale

Lemon wheel, for garnish

Pour the bourbon, lemon juice, and apricot brandy into a shaker two-thirds full of ice cubes. Shake well. Strain the mixture into an ice-filled Collins glass. Add the ginger ale; stir briefly. Add the lemon wheel and a swizzle stick.

Brain Damage

1 ounce Jägermeister

$^3/_4$ ounce gin

$^1/_2$ ounce vodka

Pour all of the ingredients into a mixing glass two-thirds full of ice cubes. Stir well. Strain into a chilled Pony glass.

Brain Hemorrhage

Prepared properly, this drink looks like an internal organ. Check with your neurosurgeon before drinking.

> **2 ounces peach schnapps**
> **$^1/_2$ ounce Baileys Irish cream liqueur**
> **Splash of grenadine**

Pour the peach schnapps into a Sherry or Pony glass. Slowly pour in the Irish cream; do not mix—the cream will clump together and settle at the bottom of the schnapps all by itself. Pour the grenadine on top.

Brain Tumor

Another awful-looking drink that tastes good to those with a sweet tooth.

> **2 ounces Baileys Irish cream liqueur**
> **$^1/_2$ ounce Chambord raspberry liqueur**

Pour the Irish cream into an ice-filled Pony glass. Carefully drizzle the Chambord over the top so that it resembles veins of blood.

Brainstorm

Here's what is basically a Bobby Burns cocktail with the same ingredients but in different proportions.

> **2 ounces scotch**
> **$^1/_2$ ounce Bénédictine**
> **$^1/_4$ ounce sweet vermouth**

Pour all of the ingredients into a mixing glass two-thirds full of ice cubes. Stir well. Strain into a chilled Cocktail glass.

Brandied Egg Nog

MAKES 8 SIX-OUNCE SERVINGS

4 eggs

6 ounces brandy

2 ounces Grand Marnier

1 teaspoon vanilla extract

$^1/_2$ teaspoon ground cinnamon

$^1/_2$ teaspoon ground allspice

$^1/_4$ teaspoon ground cloves

1 quart whole milk

Freshly grated nutmeg, for garnish

Break the eggs into a bowl and whisk until frothy. Add the brandy, Grand Marnier, vanilla, cinnamon, allspice, and cloves. Slowly whisk in the milk until the egg nog is thoroughly mixed. Ladle or pour into Irish Coffee glasses; add a sprinkle of nutmeg to each serving.

Brandied Hazelnut Martini

Served after dinner, this cocktail could be dessert.

2 ounces brandy

$^1/_2$ ounce Frangelico

Pour the brandy and Frangelico into a mixing glass two-thirds full of ice cubes. Stir well. Strain into a chilled Cocktail glass.

Brandy Alexander

It's possible that this drink popped up on the other side of the Atlantic while Americans were suffering through the dry days of Prohibition.

2 ounces brandy

1 ounce dark crème de cacao

1 ounce heavy cream

Freshly grated nutmeg, for garnish

Pour the brandy, crème de cacao, and heavy cream into a shaker two-thirds full of ice cubes. Shake well. Strain into a chilled Cocktail glass. Sprinkle the nutmeg on top.

Brandy Blazer

1 orange wheel

1 lemon wedge

1 maraschino cherry

2 ounces brandy

$^1/_2$ ounce simple syrup (page 33)

Lemon twist, for garnish

Muddle the orange wheel, lemon wedge, and maraschino cherry in a mixing glass. Add the brandy and simple syrup; stir briefly. Carefully ignite the mixture with a match. Stir with a barspoon until the flame is extinguished. Strain into an Irish Coffee glass. Add the twist.

Brandy Cobbler

2 $^1/_2$ ounces brandy

$^1/_2$ ounce simple syrup (page 33)

Fresh fruit in season, for garnish

Pour the brandy and simple syrup into a wine goblet filled with crushed ice. Stir briefly. Add the garnish of choice.

Brandy Cooler

2 $^1/_2$ ounces brandy

6 to 7 ounces club soda

Lemon twist, for garnish

Pour the brandy and club soda into an ice-filled Collins glass. Stir briefly. Add the twist.

Brandy Crusta

The original Crusta, this drink has been around since the mid-1800s.

> Superfine sugar and a lemon wedge, for rimming the glass
>
> Lemon peel spiral (see technique, page 38)
>
> 2 ounces brandy
>
> $1/2$ ounce white curaçao
>
> $1/2$ ounce fresh lemon juice

Rim a Sour glass using the sugar and lemon wedge. Place the lemon peel spiral into the glass so that it lines almost the entire interior.

Pour the brandy, curaçao, and lemon juice into a shaker two-thirds full of ice cubes. Shake well. Strain into the glass.

Brandy Daisy

> $2 1/2$ ounces brandy
>
> 1 ounce fresh lemon juice
>
> $1/2$ ounce grenadine
>
> Lemon twist, for garnish

Pour the brandy, lemon juice, and grenadine into a shaker two-thirds full of ice cubes. Shake well. Strain into a crushed ice–filled Highball glass. Add the twist.

Brandy Fizz

> 2 ounces brandy
>
> 1 ounce fresh lemon juice
>
> $1/2$ ounce simple syrup (page 33)
>
> 5 to 6 ounces club soda
>
> Fresh fruit in season, for garnish

Pour the brandy, lemon juice, and simple syrup into a shaker two-thirds full of ice cubes. Shake well. Strain into a chilled wine goblet. Pour in the club soda; stir briefly. Add the garnish of choice.

B

Brandy Flip

Brandy Flips, which date to the eighteenth century, were probably the first style of Flip to gain popularity. In order to be a true Flip, a drink must be made with a base spirit, wine (usually a fortified wine such as port) or beer, a raw egg, and simple syrup. Flips are served straight up in a wine goblet or beer glass and are garnished with nutmeg.

2 $^1/_2$ ounces brandy

$^3/_4$ ounce simple syrup (page 33)

1 egg

Freshly grated nutmeg, for garnish

Pour the brandy and simple syrup into a shaker two-thirds full of ice cubes; add the egg. Shake very well. Strain into a chilled wine goblet. Sprinkle with the nutmeg.

Brandy Milk Punch

If you've never had a milk punch, run, don't walk—they are delicious.

2 ounces brandy

1 ounce white crème de cacao

4 ounces milk

Freshly grated nutmeg, for garnish

Pour the brandy, crème de cacao, and milk into a shaker two-thirds full of ice cubes. Shake well. Strain the mixture into an ice-filled Collins glass. Sprinkle the nutmeg on top.

Brandy Sling

2 $^1/_2$ ounces brandy

$^1/_2$ ounce Grand Marnier

$^1/_2$ ounce fresh lemon juice

5 to 6 ounces club soda

Lemon wedge, for garnish

Pour the brandy, Grand Marnier, and lemon juice into a shaker two-thirds full of ice cubes. Shake well. Strain into an ice-filled Collins glass. Add the club soda; stir briefly. Add the garnish.

Brandy Smash

The Brandy Smash is the original Smash.

> **6 fresh mint leaves**
> **$3/4$ ounce simple syrup (page 33)**
> **$2^1/2$ ounces brandy**
> **Mint sprig, for garnish**

Place the mint leaves in the bottom of a Rocks glass; add the simple syrup and muddle well with a muddler or the back of a sturdy spoon. Fill the glass with crushed ice. Pour on the brandy; stir briefly. Add the mint sprig.

Brandy Sour

> **2 ounces brandy**
> **$3/4$ ounce fresh lemon juice**
> **$1/2$ ounce simple syrup (page 33)**
> **Orange wheel and maraschino cherry, for garnish**

Pour the brandy, lemon juice, and simple syrup into a shaker two-thirds full of ice cubes. Shake well. Strain the drink into a chilled Sour glass. Add the orange and cherry garnishes.

Brass Monkey

"It would freeze the tail off a brass monkey."
—Before the Mast, *by C. A. Abbey, 1857*

> **4 ounces orange juice**
> **1 ounce vodka**
> **$3/4$ ounce light rum**
> **Splash of Galliano**

Pour the orange juice, vodka, and rum into an ice-filled Collins glass; stir to blend. Float the Galliano on top.

Brave Bull

This drink was immensely popular during the 1970s, perhaps because the combination of tequila and Kahlúa is a match made in heaven.

> **2 ounces white tequila**
>
> **$^1/_2$ ounce Kahlúa**

Pour the tequila and Kahlúa into an ice-filled Rocks glass; stir briefly.

Brazil Cocktail

> **1 $^1/_2$ ounces dry sherry**
>
> **1 ounce dry vermouth**
>
> **Dash of Pernod**
>
> **Dash of Angostura bitters**

Pour all of the ingredients into a mixing glass two-thirds full of ice cubes. Stir well. Strain into a chilled Cocktail glass.

Bronx Cocktail

This drink was reportedly created at the old Waldorf-Astoria when the hotel was on the site where the Empire State Building now stands. The bartender who first made it, Johnnie Solon, had visited the Bronx Zoo just prior to inventing this cocktail. He said he had heard that his customers saw strange animals after having too many drinks, so it seemed appropriate to him.

> **2 ounces gin**
>
> **1 ounce orange juice**
>
> **$^1/_4$ ounce dry vermouth**
>
> **$^1/_4$ ounce sweet vermouth**

Pour all of the ingredients into a shaker two-thirds full of ice cubes. Shake well. Strain into a chilled Cocktail glass. Hang a plastic monkey off the edge.

Bronx Cocktail, Dry

    2 ounces gin
    1 ounce orange juice
    $^1/_2$ ounce dry vermouth

Pour all of the ingredients into a shaker two-thirds full of ice cubes. Shake well. Strain into a chilled Cocktail glass. Hang a plastic monkey off the edge.

Brooke Shields

    1 ounce orange juice
    $^1/_2$ ounce fresh lemon juice
    $^1/_4$ ounce fresh lime juice
    6 ounces ginger ale
    Dash of grenadine
    Maraschino cherry, for garnish

Pour all of the citrus juices into a shaker two-thirds full of ice cubes. Shake well. Strain into an ice-filled Collins glass. Add the ginger ale and grenadine; stir briefly. Add the garnish.

Brown Cow Special

    3 ounces Kahlúa
    10 to 12 ounces milk
    Splash of chocolate syrup

Combine the Kahlúa and milk in a Hurricane glass half-filled with ice. Stir well. Drizzle the chocolate syrup on top.

Bruise

    2 ounces Absolut Mandrin vodka
    $^1/_2$ ounce Chambord raspberry liqueur
    $^1/_2$ ounce blue curaçao
    2 ounces pineapple juice
    Splash of lemon-lime soda

Build in an ice-filled Highball glass. Stir well.

Brunch Punch

Preparing brunch tends to be a busy time for the host, so serving a premade punch is an excellent idea.

MAKES ABOUT 24 SIX-OUNCE SERVINGS

8 ounces vodka

8 ounces peach schnapps

4 ounces Chambord raspberry liqueur

$^1/_2$ gallon orange juice

2 liters ginger ale or lemon-lime soda

1 block of ice

Chill all of the ingredients ahead of time. Mix together in a large punch bowl and add the ice.

Bubble Gum Shooter

$^1/_2$ ounce vodka

$^1/_2$ ounce crème de banane

$^1/_2$ ounce peach schnapps

$^1/_2$ ounce orange juice

Layer the ingredients in a Pony glass.

Buck's Fizz

Named for the Buck's Club, London.

2 ounces orange juice

4 ounces champagne or other sparkling wine

Dash of grenadine

Orange slice, for garnish

Pour the orange juice into a Champagne Flute; carefully add the champagne or sparkling wine. Drizzle the grenadine on top. Add the orange slice.

Bullfrog

Here's a tall drink for warm-weather sipping.

2 ounces vodka

1 ounce triple sec

$^1/_2$ ounce fresh lemon juice

4 ounces club soda

Lemon wedge, for garnish

Pour the vodka, triple sec, and lemon juice into a shaker two-thirds full of ice cubes. Shake well. Strain into an ice-filled Collins glass. Pour in the club soda; stir briefly. Add the lemon wedge.

Bullshot

I like to substitute celery seed for the celery salt in this drink, but its flavor takes a few seconds to come through.

2 ounces vodka

4 ounces beef bouillon

$^1/_4$ ounce fresh lemon juice

Pinch of ground black pepper

Pinch of celery salt

3 dashes of Worcestershire sauce

Dash of hot sauce

Lemon wedge, for garnish

Pour the vodka, beef bouillon, and lemon juice into a shaker two-thirds full of ice cubes; add the pepper, celery salt, Worcestershire sauce, and hot sauce. Shake well. Strain into an ice-filled Highball glass. Add the lemon wedge.

Buttered Toffee

Something for just before bedtime?

>1 ounce Kahlúa
>
>1 ounce Baileys Irish cream liqueur
>
>1 ounce amaretto
>
>3 ounces half-and-half

Pour the Kahlúa, Irish cream, and amaretto into a wine goblet filled with ice. Add the half-and-half and stir well.

Butterfinger

One of my favorite candy bars, this liquid version makes an appealing adult snack.

>2 ounces butterscotch schnapps
>
>1^1/$_2$ ounces Baileys Irish cream liqueur
>
>6 ounces milk
>
>Splash of chocolate syrup

Pour the schnapps, Irish cream, and milk into a shaker two-thirds full of ice cubes. Shake well. Strain into an ice-filled Collins glass. Drizzle some chocolate syrup on top.

Buttery Nipple

Nary a clue as to how this got its name.

>^{3}/$_4$ ounce butterscotch schnapps
>
>^{3}/$_4$ ounce Baileys Irish cream liqueur

Pour the schnapps into a Pony glass. Layer the Irish cream on top.

Cabaret

This drink used to contain a sweet-vermouth type of wine known as Caperitif, but it's no longer available.

>2 ounces gin
>
>^{1}/$_2$ ounce sweet vermouth
>
>Dash of absinthe substitute, such as Absente, Herbsaint, Pernod, or Ricard
>
>Dash of Angostura bitters
>
>Lemon twist, for garnish

Pour the gin, vermouth, absinthe substitute, and bitters into a mixing glass two-thirds full of ice cubes. Stir well. Strain into a chilled Cocktail glass. Add the lemon wedge.

Café Brûlot

I'll never forget my first Café Brûlot. It was at Commander's Palace in New Orleans way back when Emeril Lagasse was chef there.

MAKES 2 DRINKS

> 3 lemon twists
>
> 3 orange twists
>
> 4 whole cloves
>
> 1 cinnamon stick (about 2 inches long)
>
> 1^1/$_2$ ounces brandy
>
> 1 ounce white curaçao
>
> 1^1/$_2$ cups strong, hot coffee

Place the citrus twists, cloves, cinnamon stick, brandy, and curaçao in a nonreactive large saucepan over moderately low heat. Cook until warm but not too hot. Carefully ignite the liquid with a match and allow it to flame for about 10 seconds. Pour in the hot coffee and stir well until the flames subside. Divide the mixture between 2 Irish Coffee glasses.

Caipirinha

Brazil has become famous for its national drink that's made with cachaça (KUH-shah-suh). If you can't find cachaça, use an inexpensive light rum. Alternately, try a Caipiroska (recipe follows).

> ^{1}/$_2$ lime, cut into 4 to 6 wedges
>
> 1 tablespoon granulated sugar
>
> 2 ounces cachaça

Place the lime wedges and sugar in a heavy Rocks glass and muddle thoroughly to release all of the juice from the limes. Fill the glass with crushed ice. Add the cachaça; stir thoroughly.

Caipiroska

1/2 lime, cut into 4 to 6 wedges

1 tablespoon granulated sugar

2 ounces vodka

Place the lime wedges and simple syrup in a heavy Rocks glass and muddle them thoroughly to release all of the juice from the limes. Fill the glass with crushed ice. Add the vodka; stir thoroughly.

Cajun Martini

2 1/2 ounces pepper vodka

1/2 ounce dry vermouth

Slice of jalapeño pepper, for garnish

Pour the vodka and vermouth into a mixing glass two-thirds full of ice cubes. Stir well. Strain into a chilled Cocktail glass. Add the jalapeño.

Cajun Moon Martini

—*From The Purple Martini, Denver, Colorado.*

3 ounces Absolut Peppar vodka

Splash of the juice from a jar of pearl onions

Pearl onion, for garnish

Pour the vodka and onion juice into a mixing glass two-thirds full of ice cubes. Stir well. Strain into a chilled Cocktail glass. Add the pearl onion.

Calm Before the Storm

This is a variation on the Dark and Stormy.

2 ounces Gosling's Dark Seal rum

1/2 ounce ginger vodka

1/2 ounce fresh lime juice

2 to 3 ounces ginger beer

Pour the rum, vodka, and lime juice into a shaker two-thirds full of ice. Shake well. Strain into an ice-filled Highball glass. Add the ginger beer.

Campari & Grapefruit Juice

2 ounces Campari

4 ounces grapefruit juice

Pour both ingredients into an ice-filled Highball glass; stir briefly.

Campari & Orange Juice

2 ounces Campari

4 ounces orange juice

Pour both ingredients into an ice-filled Highball glass; stir briefly.

Campari Royale

2 ounces Campari

1 ounce Grand Marnier

3 ounces orange juice

Orange wheel, for garnish

Pour the Campari, Grand Marnier, and orange juice into an ice-filled Highball glass; stir briefly. Add the orange wheel.

Campari Special

2 ounces Campari

1 ounce Grand Marnier

Orange twist, for garnish

Pour the Campari and Grand Marnier into a mixing glass two-thirds full of ice cubes. Stir well. Strain into a chilled Cocktail glass. Add the twist.

C

Canadian Egg Nog

MAKES 8 SIX-OUNCE SERVINGS

  4 eggs

  6 ounces blended Canadian whisky

  2 ounces Yukon Jack liqueur

  1 teaspoon vanilla extract

  $1/2$ teaspoon ground cinnamon

  $1/2$ teaspoon ground allspice

  $1/4$ teaspoon ground cloves

  4 cups whole milk

  Freshly grated nutmeg, for garnish

Break the eggs into a large bowl and whisk until frothy. Add the whisky, liqueur, vanilla, cinnamon, allspice, and cloves. Whisk to combine. Slowly add the milk, whisking all the time, until the egg nog is thoroughly mixed. Serve in Irish Coffee glasses; garnish with the nutmeg.

Canadian Julep

  1 ounce simple syrup (page 33)

  3 ounces blended Canadian whisky

  3 large mint sprigs, for garnish

Pour the simple syrup into a crushed ice–filled Julep cup; stir well. Add the whisky; stir until a film of ice forms on the exterior of the Julep cup. Add the mint sprigs.

Canaletto

I learned how to make this in Venice in the late 1990s and find that the sweetness of the Prosecco works magic here.

MAKES 3 TO 4 DRINKS

  1 cup fresh raspberries

  2 to 3 ice cubes

  $1/4$ ounce fresh lemon juice

$^1/_4$ ounce simple syrup (page 33)

Chilled Prosecco or other sparkling wine

Puree the raspberries, ice cubes, lemon juice, and simple syrup in a blender. Divide the mixture equally among 3 or 4 Champagne Flutes. Carefully top each drink with Prosecco, slowly stirring the ingredients together. (You might have to do this in stages, waiting for the Prosecco to settle each time.)

Candy Apple

Personally, I would have named this the Caramel Apple.

2 ounces amaretto

1 ounce butterscotch schnapps

6 to 8 ounces apple juice

Pour all of the ingredients into an ice-filled Collins glass; stir well.

Canteen

—Adapted from a recipe by Joey Guerra, the Canteen restaurant, New York City.

2 ounces light rum

2 ounces Southern Comfort

$^1/_4$ ounce amaretto

$^1/_4$ ounce fresh lime juice

Dash of simple syrup (page 33)

Pour all of the ingredients into a shaker two-thirds full of ice cubes. Shake well. Strain into a chilled Cocktail glass.

Cape Codder

This could be the drink that put cranberry juice on the map behind bars.

2 $^1/_2$ ounces vodka

4 to 6 ounces cranberry juice

Lime wedge, for garnish

Pour the vodka and cranberry juice into an ice-filled Highball glass. Stir briefly; add the lime wedge.

C

Caramel Apple Martini

2¹/₄ ounces Van Gogh Wild Appel vodka

1 ounce butterscotch schnapps

Pour both ingredients into a mixing glass two-thirds full of ice cubes. Stir well. Strain into a chilled Cocktail glass.

Carbonated Piston Slinger

—Adapted from a recipe by Dr. Cocktail (Ted Haigh), high priest of cocktail history.

1¹/₂ ounces 151-proof Demerara rum

¹/₂ ounce sloe gin

¹/₂ ounce fresh lime juice

Club soda

Lime wedge and a maraschino cherry, for garnishes

Build in an ice-filled Hurricane glass. Fill with soda water and stir well. Add the garnishes.

Cardinal

1¹/₂ ounces añejo rum

¹/₂ ounce maraschino liqueur

Dash of triple sec

Dash of grenadine

Pour all of the ingredients into a mixing glass two-thirds full of ice cubes. Stir well. Strain into a chilled Cocktail glass.

Cardinal Punch

If you're serving this to the Monsignor, you can rename the recipe.

MAKES ABOUT 20 SIX-OUNCE SERVINGS

6 ounces dark rum

4 ounces fresh lemon juice

3 ounces simple syrup (page 33)

2 750-ml bottles dry red wine

1 750-ml bottle champagne or other sparkling wine

8 ounces sweet vermouth

8 ounces brandy

1 large block of ice

Orange wheels, for garnish

Pour 2 ounces of the rum, all of the lemon juice, and all of the simple syrup into a shaker two-thirds full of ice cubes; shake well. Strain into a large punch bowl. Pour in the remaining 4 ounces of rum, the red wine, champagne, vermouth, and brandy; stir well. Add the ice and let chill, stirring from time to time, for at least 30 minutes. Ladle into punch cups; garnish each serving with an orange wheel.

Caribbean Cooler

2 ^{1}/$_2$ ounces light rum

4 ounces ginger beer

Lemon twist, for garnish

Pour the rum and ginger beer into an ice-filled Collins glass; stir briefly. Add the twist.

Caribbean Cosmopolitan

2 ^{1}/$_2$ ounces citrus vodka

^{1}/$_2$ ounce Cointreau

^{1}/$_4$ ounce pineapple juice

^{1}/$_4$ ounce cranberry juice

Maraschino cherry, for garnish

Pour all of the ingredients into a shaker two-thirds full of ice cubes. Shake well. Strain into a chilled Cocktail glass. Add the cherry.

Caribbean Martini

1 ^{1}/$_2$ ounces Stolichnaya Vanil vodka

^{3}/$_4$ ounce Malibu rum

Splash of pineapple juice

Pour all of the ingredients into a shaker two-thirds full of ice cubes. Shake well. Strain into a chilled Cocktail glass.

Caribbean Millionaire

1 ounce dark rum

1 ounce crème de banane

$^1/_2$ ounce apricot brandy

$^1/_2$ ounce fresh lemon juice

Dash of sloe gin

Sliced banana, for garnish

Pour the rum, crème de banane, apricot brandy, lemon juice, and sloe gin into a shaker two-thirds full of ice cubes. Shake well. Strain into an ice-filled Collins glass. Garnish with the banana.

Caribbean Punch

If serving this in a family situation, omit the rums and spike individual servings for the adults.

MAKES 25 TO 30 SIX-OUNCE SERVINGS

1 pineapple, peeled and cored

8 ounces fresh lemon juice

3 ounces simple syrup (page 33)

1 teaspoon freshly grated nutmeg

1 teaspoon ground cinnamon

1 teaspoon ground allspice

1 750-ml bottle light rum

1 750-ml bottle spiced rum

32 ounces pineapple juice

48 ounces orange juice

12 ounces ginger ale

Thinly slice half of the peeled, cored pineapple and set aside. Cut the remaining pineapple half into 1-inch cubes. Place the cubes in a blender and add 4 ounces of the lemon juice, the simple syrup, nutmeg, cinnamon, and allspice. Blend on high speed; pour the mixture into a large punch bowl.

Add the remaining 4 ounces lemon juice, both rums, the pineapple juice, the orange juice, and the ginger ale. Stir well. Add 1 large block of ice. Float the reserved sliced pineapple on top.

Carrot Cake

But where's the cream cheese icing?

>   1 ounce Baileys Irish cream liqueur
>
>   1 ounce butterscotch schnapps
>
> $^1/_4$ ounce Goldschlager or cinnamon schnapps

Pour all of the ingredients into a shaker two-thirds full of ice cubes. Shake well. Strain into a chilled Pony glass.

Carrot Top

See also **Lemon Top**.

>   12 ounces amber ale
>
>   2 ounces ginger beer

Pour the ale into a pint glass and top with the soda.

Caruso

Named for the late opera tenor Enrico Caruso, this drink used to be made with equal amounts of all three ingredients. It works far better this way; it's a drink that will make you sing.

>   2 ounces gin
>
> $^1/_2$ ounce dry vermouth
>
>   Dash of green crème de menthe

Pour all of the ingredients into a mixing glass two-thirds full of ice cubes. Stir well. Strain into a chilled Cocktail glass.

Casablanca

Ah, Rick. Ah, Ilsa. Ah, Victor Lazlo. Ah, Sam.

>   2 $^1/_2$ ounces light rum
>
> $^1/_2$ ounce triple sec
>
> $^1/_2$ ounce maraschino liqueur
>
> $^1/_2$ ounce fresh lime juice

Pour all of the ingredients into a shaker two-thirds full of ice cubes. Shake well. Strain into a chilled Cocktail glass.

Casino Cocktail

$2 \frac{1}{2}$ ounces gin

$\frac{1}{2}$ ounce maraschino liqueur

1 ounce fresh lemon juice

Dash of orange bitters

Pour all of the ingredients into a shaker two-thirds full of ice cubes. Shake well. Strain into a chilled Cocktail glass.

Century Sour

—Created by King Cocktail Dale DeGroff, New York City, 1998.

1 ounce Alizé passion fruit liqueur

1 ounce Apry apricot liqueur

$\frac{3}{4}$ ounce fresh lemon juice

Lemon twist, for garnish

Pour the Alizé, Apry, and lemon juice into a shaker two-thirds full of ice cubes. Shake well. Strain into a chilled Cocktail glass. Add the lemon twist.

CEO Cocktail

Just for big shots.

—Adapted from a recipe by Dr. Cocktail (Ted Haigh).

2 ounces brandy

1 ounce Lillet Blanc

$\frac{1}{2}$ ounce Chambord or crème de cassis

2 dashes of orange bitters

Lemon twist, for garnish

Pour the brandy, Lillet, Chambord, and orange bitters into a shaker two-thirds full of ice cubes. Shake well. Strain into a chilled Cocktail glass. Add the lemon twist.

Chambord French Martini

—Adapted from a recipe from Asia de Cuba, New York City.

1 ounce vodka

$\frac{1}{2}$ ounce Chambord raspberry liqueur

2 ounces pineapple juice

Pour all of the ingredients into a shaker two-thirds full of ice cubes. Shake well. Strain into a chilled Cocktail glass.

Chambord Royale

> 1 ounce Chambord raspberry liqueur
>
> 1 ounce vodka
>
> 1 ounce pineapple juice
>
> $^1/_2$ ounce cranberry juice

Pour all of the ingredients into a shaker two-thirds full of ice cubes. Shake well. Strain into a chilled Cocktail glass.

Champagne Cobbler

C'est magnifique!

> 4 ounces champagne or other sparkling wine
>
> 1 ounce Grand Marnier
>
> Fresh fruit in season, for garnish

Pour the champagne and Grand Marnier into a wine goblet filled with crushed ice; stir briefly. Add the garnish of choice.

Champagne Cocktail

One of the all-time favorites, this drink has been made this way for around 150 years.

> 1 sugar lump
>
> 2 to 3 dashes Angostura bitters
>
> 5 ounces champagne or other sparkling wine
>
> Lemon twist, for garnish

Put the sugar lump and the bitters into a Champagne Flute; carefully add the champagne. Add the twist.

Champagne Fizz

1 ounce gin

1 ounce fresh lemon juice

Dash of simple syrup (page 33)

4 ounces chilled champagne or other sparkling wine

Pour the gin, lemon juice, and simple syrup into a shaker two-thirds full of ice cubes; shake well. Strain into a chilled Champagne Flute. Carefully pour in the champagne.

Champagne Punch Royale

The night they invented champagne? Ah, yes, I remember it well.

MAKES ABOUT 24 SIX-OUNCE SERVINGS

1 large block or ring of ice with raspberries frozen in it

4 ounces chilled brandy

4 ounces chilled Chambord raspberry liqueur

4 ounces chilled triple sec

3 750-ml bottles chilled champagne or other sparkling wine

16 to 20 ounces chilled club soda

Fresh raspberries, for garnish

Place the ice in the center of a large punch bowl; add the brandy, Chambord, triple sec, champagne, and club soda. Stir briefly. Float the raspberries on top.

Chanticleer Cocktail

This drink was apparently created, prior to 1917, to celebrate the opening of a Manhattan restaurant of the same name. FYI—"chanticleer" is another word for rooster. You might want to serve it alongside some hard-cooked quail's eggs.

1 ounce gin

1 ounce dry vermouth

$^{1}/_{2}$ ounce triple sec

Orange twist, for garnish

Pour the gin, vermouth, and triple sec into a mixing glass two-thirds full of ice cubes. Stir well. Strain into a chilled Cocktail glass. Add the twist.

Charger 🍸

> **8 ounces club soda**
>
> **2 dashes Angostura bitters**
>
> **Lime wedge, for garnish**

Pour the club soda and bitters into an ice-filled Collins glass. Stir briefly; add the lime wedge.

Charles Cocktail

This is basically a Rob Roy made with brandy. What I want to know is who it's named for. The Prince? The river? Ray? Nick and Nora?

> **2 ounces brandy**
>
> **1 ounce sweet vermouth**
>
> **Dash of orange bitters**

Pour all of the ingredients into a mixing glass two-thirds full of ice cubes. Stir well. Strain into a chilled Cocktail glass.

Charlie Chaplin

If you order this, be prepared to be called "The Little Tramp."

> **1 ounce apricot brandy**
>
> **1 ounce sloe gin**
>
> **1 ounce fresh lime juice**

Pour all of the ingredients into a shaker two-thirds full of ice cubes. Shake well. Strain into a chilled Cocktail glass.

Cherries Jubilee Martini

—From The Purple Martini, Denver, Colorado.

> **3 ounces Ketel One vodka**
>
> **Splash of amaretto**
>
> **Maraschino cherry, for garnish**

Pour the vodka and amaretto into a mixing glass two-thirds full of ice cubes. Stir well. Strain into a chilled Cocktail glass. Add the cherry.

Cherry Blossom Cocktail

A spring drink to be sure.

> **1 ^{1}/$_2$ ounces brandy**
>
> **1 ounce cherry brandy**
>
> **^{1}/$_2$ ounce triple sec**

Pour all of the ingredients into a mixing glass two-thirds full of ice cubes. Stir well. Strain into a chilled Cocktail glass.

Cherry Brandy Rickey

A grown-up version of the Shirley Temple?

> **2 ^{1}/$_2$ ounces cherry brandy**
>
> **1 ounce fresh lime juice**
>
> **6 to 8 ounces club soda**
>
> **Lime wedge, for garnish**

Pour the cherry brandy and lime juice into an ice-filled Highball or Collins glass. Pour in the club soda; stir briefly. Add the lime wedge.

Cherry Kiss Martini

—Created by Jim Hewes, the Round Robin Bar at the Willard Inter-Continental hotel, Washington, D.C.

> **1 Cocktail glass, chilled in the freezer**
>
> **^{1}/$_4$ ounce Godiva Chocolate liqueur**
>
> **Maraschino cherry with stem, for garnish**
>
> **2 ounces Ketel One vodka, chilled in the freezer**

Pour the Godiva Chocolate liqueur into the frozen Cocktail glass and swirl it around to coat the glass. Add the cherry to the glass and pour in the vodka.

Chi Chi

The vodka-based variation on the classic Piña Colada. If you're not fond of rum, give this one a try.

> 2 $^1/_2$ ounces vodka
>
> 6 ounces pineapple juice
>
> 2 ounces coconut cream, such as Coco Lopez
>
> Pineapple spear and a chunk of fresh coconut, for garnish

Pour the vodka, pineapple juice, and coconut cream into a blender two-thirds full of ice cubes; blend thoroughly. Pour the mixture into a large wine goblet; add the garnishes.

Chocolate Almond

> $^1/_2$ ounce amaretto
>
> $^1/_2$ ounce dark crème de cacao
>
> $^1/_2$ ounce Baileys Irish cream liqueur

Pour all of the ingredients into a shaker two-thirds full of ice cubes. Shake well. Strain into a chilled Pony glass.

Chocolate Cake Shooter

And what do you think this tastes like?

> $^3/_4$ ounce citrus vodka
>
> $^3/_4$ ounce Frangelico
>
> Lemon wedge
>
> Superfine sugar

Combine the vodka and Frangelico in a Pony glass. Heavily coat the lemon wedge with the sugar. Drink the shot in one, and immediately suck on the sugar-coated lemon wedge.

Chocolate Cream Martini

1 ounce Baileys Irish cream liqueur

1 ounce white crème de cacao

1 ounce vodka

Pour all of the ingredients into a shaker two-thirds full of ice cubes. Shake well. Strain into a chilled Cocktail glass or an ice-filled Rocks glass.

Chocolate Martini

A massive success! This was a runaway hit in the late 1990s, and it was reportedly created in Miami.

Unsweetened cocoa powder and white crème de cacao, for rimming the glass

2 ounces vodka

1 ounce white crème de cacao

Hershey's Hug or chocolate chips, for garnish

Prepare the glass. Pour the vodka and crème de cacao into a mixing glass two-thirds full of ice cubes. Stir well. Place the Hug or chocolate chips in the bottom of the cocoa-rimmed Cocktail glass. Strain the Martini into the glass.

Chocolate Peppermint

2 ounces Godiva chocolate liqueur

$^1/_2$ ounce peppermint schnapps

Pour both ingredients into a mixing glass two-thirds full of ice cubes. Stir well. Strain into a chilled Cocktail glass.

Chocolate-Covered Martini

1 maraschino cherry

$1^1/_2$ ounces vodka

$^1/_2$ ounce Godiva chocolate liqueur

$^1/_2$ ounce vanilla schnapps

Place the cherry in the bottom of a chilled Cocktail glass. Pour the vodka, Godiva liqueur, and schnapps into a mixing glass two-thirds full of ice cubes. Stir well. Strain into the Cocktail glass.

Chocolate-Raspberry Martini

> 1 ounce Kahlúa
>
> 1 ounce Chambord raspberry liqueur
>
> 2 ounces heavy cream
>
> **Chocolate shavings, for garnish**

Fill a Cocktail glass with crushed ice. Pour in the Kahlúa and Chambord. Top with the heavy cream. Sprinkle with the chocolate shavings.

Choirboy ✪

A bad choirboy might add a tot of rum.

> 3 ounces grape juice
>
> 1 ounce fresh lemon juice
>
> 1 ounce fresh pineapple juice
>
> **Pineapple spear, for garnish**

Pour the juices into a shaker two-thirds full of ice cubes. Shake well. Strain into a chilled wine goblet. Add the pineapple spear.

Christina Martini

—From Villa Christina, Atlanta, Georgia.

> 3 ounces Tanqueray Sterling vodka
>
> **Splash of Amaretto di Saronno**
>
> **Splash of blue curaçao**

Pour the vodka, amaretto, and curaçao into a mixing glass two-thirds full of ice cubes. Stir well. Strain into a chilled Cocktail glass.

Cider-Cranberry Rum Punch

Without the rum, this makes a good nonalcoholic punch.

MAKES ABOUT 25 SIX-OUNCE SERVINGS

$^1/_2$ gallon unsweetened apple cider

48 ounces cranberry juice

10 whole cloves

4 small (3-inch) cinnamon sticks, broken

1 teaspoon freshly grated nutmeg

1 teaspoon ground allspice

$^1/_2$ teaspoon ground cardamom

1 large block of ice, for serving

1 750-ml bottle dark rum, bourbon, or brandy

Lemon slices, for garnish

At least 4 hours or up to 1 week before the party, pour the apple cider and cranberry juice into a large, nonreactive stockpot. Set the pot over high heat, add all of the spices, and bring the mixture to a boil. Reduce the heat to low, cover, and simmer for 30 minutes.

Strain the mixture through a strainer lined with a double layer of dampened cheesecloth; discard the solids. Set aside to cool to room temperature, about 2 hours.

Pour the punch back into the bottles that held the cranberry and apple juices and refrigerate.

About 30 minutes before your guests arrive, place the block of ice into the punch bowl. Add the chilled punch. You can add the liquor at this point, or set the bottle next to the punch bowl so guests can decide for themselves. Float the lemon slices on top of the punch.

Cinco de Mayo

Created to celebrate the May 5, 1862, victory of the
Mexican Army over the French at the Battle of Puebla.

$2^1/2$ ounces añejo or white tequila

1 ounce fresh lime juice

$1/2$ ounce grenadine

Pour all of the ingredients into a shaker two-thirds full of ice
cubes. Shake well. Strain into a chilled Cocktail glass.

Cinderella

3 ounces orange juice

3 ounces peach nectar

Dash of grenadine

Splash of club soda

Pour the orange juice, peach nectar, and grenadine into an ice-
filled Collins glass. Stir briefly; top with the club soda.

Cinnamon Cream Martini

2 ounces Stolichnaya Vanil vodka

$1/2$ ounce Goldschlager

Pour both ingredients into a mixing glass two-thirds full of ice
cubes. Stir well. Strain into a chilled Cocktail glass.

Claridge Cocktail

Could this be named after the famous London hotel?
Maybe. But we know that it was served at London's
Savoy Hotel, circa 1930.

$1^1/2$ ounces gin

$1^1/2$ ounces dry vermouth

$3/4$ ounce Cointreau

$3/4$ ounce apricot brandy

Pour all of the ingredients into a mixing glass two-thirds full of
ice cubes. Stir well. Strain into a chilled Cocktail glass.

Classic Cocktail

Like a Sidecar but with maraschino liqueur added—
it's mighty tasty.

> **Superfine sugar and a lemon wedge, for rimming the glass**
> **1 $^1/_2$ ounces brandy**
> **$^1/_2$ ounce triple sec**
> **$^1/_2$ ounce maraschino liqueur**
> **$^1/_2$ ounce fresh lemon juice**

Prepare the glass. Pour all of the ingredients into a shaker
two-thirds full of ice cubes. Shake well. Strain into the sugar-
rimmed Cocktail glass.

Climax

> **$^1/_2$ ounce amaretto**
> **$^1/_2$ ounce white crème de cacao**
> **$^1/_2$ ounce triple sec**
> **$^1/_2$ ounce vodka**
> **$^1/_2$ ounce crème de banane**
> **1 ounce half-and-half**

Pour all of the ingredients into a shaker two-thirds full of ice
cubes. Shake well. Strain into a chilled Cocktail glass.

Clover Club Cocktail

Reportedly created prior to Prohibition at the
Philadelphia club of the same name, the original
recipe contained raspberry syrup, not grenadine.

> **2 ounces gin**
> **$^1/_2$ ounce fresh lemon juice**
> **$^1/_2$ ounce grenadine**
> **1 egg white**

Pour all of the ingredients into a shaker two-thirds full of ice
cubes. Shake very well. Strain into a chilled Cocktail glass.

Coco Loco

A drink for fans of Harry Nilsson.

> 1 whole coconut
> 1 ounce white tequila
> 1 ounce light rum
> 1 ounce gin
> $^1/_2$ ounce grenadine
> Lime slice, for garnish

Cut a 3-inch hole in the top of the coconut; leave the coconut water inside. Add the tequila, rum, gin, grenadine, and several ice cubes. Stir well. Garnish with the slice of lime (you put the lime in the coconut!); serve with a long straw.

(If you prefer to drink this in a glass, drill 2 holes in the coconut and drain the water into a mixing glass over several ice cubes. Add the tequila, rum, gin, and grenadine; stir well. Strain into a wine goblet or Highball glass and add the lime.)

Coconut Cream Pie

And what does this one taste like?

> 1 ounce vanilla schnapps
> 1 ounce Malibu rum
> 3 ounces heavy cream

Pour all of the ingredients into a shaker two-thirds full of ice cubes. Shake well. Strain into a chilled Cocktail glass.

Coconut-Banana Freeze

> 2 ripe bananas, cut up
> 3 ounces dark rum
> 2 ounces canned coconut cream, such as Coco Lopez
> 2 dashes of Angostura bitters

Combine all of the ingredients in a blender and add 1 cup of ice cubes. Puree until frozen. Spoon into a Hurricane glass.

Cognac Coulis

MAKES 2 FIVE-OUNCE DRINKS

> 2 ripe kiwi fruits, peeled and sliced
>
> 6 large ripe strawberries, hulled
>
> 5 large ice cubes
>
> 3 ounces cognac
>
> 1 ounce Grand Marnier

Reserve 2 slices of the kiwi for garnish. Place the remaining kiwi, the strawberries, ice cubes, and cognac in a blender; puree until smooth. Divide the mixture between 2 Cocktail glasses. Drizzle half of the Grand Marnier over each drink; garnish each with a slice of kiwi.

Colorado Bulldog

Believe it or not, Kahlúa and cola are great partners for people with a sweet tooth.

> 1 ounce vodka
>
> 1 ounce Kahlúa
>
> 2 ounces milk
>
> Splash of cola

Pour the vodka, Kahlúa, and milk into a shaker two-thirds full of ice cubes. Shake well. Strain into an ice-filled Rocks glass. Add the splash of cola.

Continental

Although it's a very small amount, the crème de menthe in this drink shines right through. Be careful not to add more than the amount called for; the mint can dominate all of the other flavors.

> 2 ounces light rum
>
> $1/4$ ounce green crème de menthe
>
> $1/2$ ounce fresh lime juice
>
> Dash of simple syrup (page 33)
>
> Lemon twist, for garnish

Pour the rum, crème de menthe, lime juice, and simple syrup into a shaker two-thirds full of ice cubes. Shake well. Strain into a chilled Cocktail glass. Add the twist.

Cooperstown Cocktail

Named for the home of the Baseball Hall of Fame.

> 1 ounce gin
>
> 1 ounce sweet vermouth
>
> 1 ounce dry vermouth
>
> Mint sprig, for garnish

Pour the gin and both vermouths into a mixing glass two-thirds full of ice cubes. Stir well. Strain into a chilled Cocktail glass. Add the mint sprig.

Coppertone Punch

MAKES 6 SEVEN-OUNCE SERVINGS

> 8 ounces Midori melon liqueur
>
> 8 ounces Malibu rum
>
> 8 ounces crème de banane
>
> 8 ounces pineapple juice
>
> 1 block of ice
>
> Pineapple rings, for garnish

Combine the Midori, Malibu, crème de banane, and pineapple juice in a large pitcher. Cover and chill for at least 1 hour. Place the block of ice in a punch bowl. Add the chilled punch. Float the pineapple rings on top.

Cornell Cocktail

Said to be most popular at Cornell's renowned School of Hotel Administration.

> 2 ounces gin
>
> $^1/_2$ ounce maraschino liqueur
>
> $^1/_2$ ounce fresh lemon juice
>
> 1 egg white

Pour all of the ingredients into a shaker two-thirds full of ice cubes. Shake very well. Strain into a chilled Cocktail glass.

Coronation

1 ounce gin

1 ounce dry vermouth

1 ounce Dubonnet Blanc

Pour all of the ingredients into a mixing glass two-thirds full of ice cubes. Stir well. Strain into a chilled Cocktail glass.

Corpse Reviver #1 🍸

Corpse Revivers were popular in Victorian England and were actually a category of drinks with nothing in common except that all were strong and all were a spirituous way to, well, revive your spirits.

2 ounces brandy

1 ounce sweet vermouth

1 ounce applejack

Pour all of the ingredients into a mixing glass two-thirds full of ice cubes. Stir well. Strain into a chilled Cocktail glass.

Corpse Reviver #2

Completely different from the previous recipe, but, no doubt, sure to revive you.

1 ounce gin

1 ounce triple sec

1 ounce Lillet Blanc

1 ounce fresh lemon juice

Dash of absinthe substitute, such as Absente, Pernod, Herbsaint, or Ricard

Pour all of the ingredients into a shaker two-thirds full of ice cubes. Shake well. Strain into a chilled Cocktail glass.

Corpse Reviver #3

Are you feeling better yet?

1 ounce cognac

1 ounce Campari

1 ounce triple sec

$^1/_2$ ounce fresh lemon juice

Pour all of the ingredients into a shaker two-thirds full of ice cubes. Shake well. Strain into a chilled Cocktail glass.

Corpse Reviver #4

This Corpse Reviver, like some others that were popular in the 1800s, actually fits into two categories: It's a Pousse Café since it is a layered drink, and it's also a Shooter, since it is meant to be consumed in one go.

$^3/_4$ ounce Frangelico

$^3/_4$ ounce maraschino liqueur

$^3/_4$ ounce green Chartreuse

Pour the ingredients, in the order given, over the back of a spoon into a Pousse Café glass, floating one on top of the other.

Cosmopolitan

For my money, *the* hottest drink in the USA, the drink that became a classic overnight during the 1990s.

2 ounces citrus vodka

1 ounce Cointreau

$^1/_2$ ounce cranberry juice

$^1/_2$ ounce fresh lime juice

Pour all of the ingredients into a shaker two-thirds full of ice cubes. Shake well. Strain into a chilled Cocktail glass.

Cottage Cheese

For my money, *the* most disgusting drink imaginable.

1 ounce Irish cream

1 ounce lime juice cordial, such as Rose's

Pour the Irish cream into the mouth of the drinker, who must hold the Irish cream without swallowing it. Add the lime juice cordial and swish the ingredients to combine them. Swallow before it's too late.

Cough Drop

Feeling better?

> 1 ounce blackberry brandy
>
> 1 ounce peppermint schnapps

Build in a Pony glass.

Cranberry Frog

Here's a drink for the kiddies; the grown-up version follows.

> 4 ounces orange juice
>
> 4 ounces cranberry juice

Pour both ingredients into an ice-filled Hurricane glass. Stir to chill.

Cranberry Toad

> 2 ounces vodka
>
> 4 ounces orange juice
>
> 4 ounces cranberry juice

Pour all of the ingredients into an ice-filled Hurricane glass. Stir to chill.

Cranny Apple Martini

Van Gogh Wild Appel vodka is a marvelous new ingredient, and it shows its stuff clearly here.

> $1^1/2$ ounces Van Gogh Wild Appel vodka
>
> 1 ounce pineapple juice
>
> $1/2$ ounce cranberry juice
>
> $1/2$ ounce apple juice
>
> Apple peel spiral, for garnish

Pour the vodka and 3 juices into a shaker two-thirds full of ice cubes. Shake well. Strain into a chilled Cocktail glass. Hang the apple spiral off the lip of the glass.

Crantini

Pretty as a picture.

> 1 ^{1}/$_2$ ounces vodka
>
> ^{1}/$_2$ ounce triple sec
>
> ^{1}/$_2$ ounce dry vermouth
>
> 3 ounces cranberry juice

Pour all of the ingredients into a mixing glass two-thirds full of ice cubes. Stir well. Strain into a chilled Cocktail glass.

Creamsicle

Takes you back, doesn't it? This one's for the daytime.

> 1 ^{1}/$_2$ ounce vanilla schnapps
>
> 1 ^{1}/$_2$ ounces milk
>
> 3 ounces orange juice

Pour all of the ingredients into a shaker two-thirds full of ice cubes. Shake well. Strain into an ice-filled Rocks glass.

Creamsicle Martini

And this one's for the nighttime.

> 1 ounces Stolichnaya Vanil vodka
>
> ^{1}/$_2$ ounce Cointreau
>
> 1 ounce orange juice
>
> ^{1}/$_2$ ounce simple syrup (page 33)

Pour all of the ingredients into a shaker two-thirds full of ice cubes. Shake well. Strain into a chilled Cocktail glass.

Crème de Menthe Frappé

> 2 ounces green crème de menthe
>
> 3 straws, each cut to measure about 3 inches long

Fill a chilled Sour glass or Champagne Saucer glass with crushed ice until it forms a dome that rises in the center of the glass. Drizzle the crème de menthe over the ice. Sip from the straws.

Creole

A Southern relative of the Bullshot.

 2 ounces light rum
 2 ounces beef bouillon
 $1/2$ ounce fresh lemon juice
 2 dashes of hot sauce
 Pinch of salt
 Pinch of ground black pepper

Pour the rum, bouillon, and lemon juice into a shaker two-thirds full of ice cubes; add the hot sauce, salt, and pepper. Shake well. Strain into an ice-filled Rocks glass.

Crimson Cosmo

—Adapted from Luna Park, San Francisco, California.

 4 ounces fresh pomegranate juice
 3 ounces vodka
 2 ounces Cointreau
 Pomegranate seeds, for garnish (optional)

Pour all of the ingredients into a mixing glass two-thirds full of ice. Shake vigorously. Strain into a very large chilled Cocktail glass. Garnish with several pomegranate seeds, if desired.

Crimson Martini

A recent addition to many Martini menus, this drink is extremely popular with Campari lovers.

 2 ounces gin
 $1/2$ ounce dry vermouth
 $1/4$ ounce Campari
 Orange wheel, for garnish

Pour the gin, vermouth, and Campari into a mixing glass two-thirds full of ice cubes. Stir well. Strain into a chilled Cocktail glass. Add the orange wheel.

Cuba Libre

The trick to a great Cuba Libre lies in the lime juice.
Remember, it's not just a simple rum and cola with a
lime wedge garnish, it's more, much more. This recipe is
terrific.

>   2 $^1/_2$ ounces light rum
>
>   1 ounce fresh lime juice
>
>   3 ounces cola
>
>   Lime wedge, for garnish

Pour the rum and lime juice into a shaker two-thirds full of ice
cubes. Shake well and strain into an ice-filled Collins glass. Add
the cola; stir briefly. Add the lime wedge.

Cuban Cocktail

Many cocktails made their way to the United States from
Cuba during Prohibition. This is merely a sweet Daiquiri,
which also originated in Cuba.

>   2 ounces light rum
>
> $^1/_2$ ounce fresh lime juice
>
> $^1/_2$ ounce simple syrup (page 33)

Pour all of the ingredients into a shaker two-thirds full of ice
cubes. Shake well. Strain into a chilled Cocktail glass.

Curious Comfort

>   1 $^1/_2$ ounces blue curaçao
>
>   1 ounce Southern Comfort
>
>   2 $^1/_2$ ounces pineapple juice

Pour all of the ingredients into a shaker two-thirds full of ice
cubes. Shake well. Strain into an ice-filled Rocks glass.

Curtis Cocktail

2 ounces gin

$^1/_2$ ounce triple sec

$^1/_2$ ounce sweet vermouth

Dash of orange bitters

Pour all of the ingredients into a mixing glass two-thirds full of ice cubes. Stir well. Strain into a chilled Cocktail glass.

Daiquiri

The Daiquiri dates to the late 1800s, when the Spanish-American War was raging in Cuba. Reportedly, two Americans, who were working in Cuba at the time, created the drink by mixing the local light rum with sugar and fresh lime juice. They needed to drink the lime juice for their health, and the sugar and the local rum helped it go down nicely. Perhaps they were merely making a drink that pleased them, or maybe they thought that the combination of alcohol, fresh lime juice, and sugar would keep the mosquitoes away.

2 ounces light rum

1 ounce fresh lime juice

$^1/_2$ ounce simple syrup (page 33)

Lime wedge, for garnish

Pour the rum, lime juice, and simple syrup into a shaker two-thirds full of ice cubes. Shake well. Strain into a crushed ice–filled Rocks glass. Squeeze the lime wedge on top.

Dark and Stormy

This is a very popular drink in Bermuda, and one of the few Highballs that calls for a specific brand of liquor. The Dark and Stormy is enormously refreshing when escaping the heat is the goal of the day.

2 $^1/_2$ ounces Gosling's Black seal rum

5 ounces ginger beer

Lime wedge, for garnish

Pour the rum and ginger beer into an ice-filled Highball glass. Stir briefly; add the lime wedge.

Darth Vader ⊘

Named for the anti-hero in the Star Wars movies, this drink is completely delicious.

> **1 ounce fresh lime juice**
>
> **$^1/_2$ ounce simple syrup (page 33)**
>
> **Splash of grenadine**
>
> **6 ounces ginger beer**

Pour the lime juice, simple syrup, and grenadine into a shaker two-thirds full of ice cubes. Shake well. Strain into an ice-filled Collins glass; add the ginger beer. Stir briefly.

Deadly Sin

—Adapted from a recipe by Rafael Ballesteros, somewhere in Spain.

> **2 ounces scotch or bourbon**
>
> **$^1/_3$ ounce sweet vermouth**
>
> **$^1/_4$ ounce maraschino liqueur**
>
> **Dash of orange bitters**
>
> **Orange twist, for garnish**

Pour all of the ingredients into a mixing glass two-thirds full of ice cubes. Stir well. Strain into a chilled Cocktail glass. Add the orange twist garnish.

Death in the Afternoon

Named for one of Ernest Hemingway's novels, no doubt he drank it during his years in Paris.

> **1 ounce Pernod**
>
> **5 ounces champagne or other sparkling wine**

Pour the Pernod into a Champagne Flute. Add the champagne.

D

Deauville Cocktail

    1 ounce brandy

    1 ounce applejack

    1 ounce triple sec

    1 ounce fresh lemon juice

Pour all of the ingredients into a shaker two-thirds full of ice cubes. Shake well. Strain into a chilled Cocktail glass.

Debonair Cocktail

A wonderful cocktail that's made with single malt scotch.

    2 ounces Oban or Springbank single malt scotch

    1 ounce Original Canton Delicate Ginger liqueur

    Lemon twist, for garnish

Pour the scotch and ginger liqueur into a mixing glass two-thirds full of ice cubes. Stir well. Strain into a chilled Cocktail glass. Add the twist.

Delmonico

Reportedly created at Delmonico's bar in New York City, sometime prior to 1917.

    1 ^{1}/2 ounces gin

    1 ^{1}/2 ounces dry vermouth

    Dash of orange bitters

    2 orange twists, for garnish

Pour all of the ingredients into a mixing glass two-thirds full of ice cubes. Stir well. Strain into a chilled Cocktail glass. Add the twists.

Dempsey Cocktail

Named for Jack Dempsey, the famed boxer who won the heavyweight boxing title in 1919.

    1 ^{1}/2 ounces gin

    1 ^{1}/2 ounces applejack

$^1/_4$ ounce absinthe substitute, such as Absente, Pernod, Herbsaint, or Ricard

$^1/_4$ ounce grenadine

Pour all of the ingredients into a mixing glass two-thirds full of ice cubes. Stir well. Strain into a chilled Cocktail glass.

Diplomat

An oh, so tactful cocktail.

1 $^1/_2$ ounces dry vermouth

$^1/_2$ ounce sweet vermouth

Dash of maraschino liqueur

Lemon twist and a maraschino cherry, for garnishes

Pour both vermouths and the maraschino liqueur into a mixing glass two-thirds full of ice cubes. Stir well. Strain into a chilled Cocktail glass. Add the twist and cherry.

Dirty Bloody Martini

2 ounces pepper vodka

1 ounce dry vermouth

2 ounces Clamato or tomato juice

$^1/_2$ ounce olive juice (from a jar of olives)

3 olives, for garnish

Pour the vodka, vermouth, Clamato or tomato juice, and the olive juice into a shaker two-thirds full of ice cubes. Shake well. Strain into a chilled Cocktail glass. Garnish with the olives.

Dirty Girl Scout

Did she fall in the mud?

1 ounce Baileys Irish cream liqueur

1 ounce Kahlúa

1 ounce vodka

Dash of white crème de menthe

Pour all of the ingredients into a shaker two-thirds full of ice cubes. Shake well. Strain into an ice-filled Rocks glass.

D

Dirty Martini

Feel free to play with the proportions here but don't get carried away with the olive juice—too much can be just plain awful.

> 2 ^{1}/$_2$ ounces gin or vodka
>
> ^{1}/$_4$ ounce dry vermouth
>
> ^{1}/$_4$ ounce olive juice (straight out of the jar)
>
> Stuffed green olive, for garnish

Pour the gin, vermouth, and olive juice into a mixing glass two-thirds full of ice cubes. Stir well. Strain into a chilled Cocktail glass. Add the olive.

Dirty Mother

> 2 ounces Kahlúa
>
> 1 ounce light cream

Pour the ingredients into a shaker two-thirds full of ice cubes. Shake well. Strain into an ice-filled Rocks glass.

Doctor's Highball

—Adapted from a recipe by Dr. Cocktail (Ted Haigh), eminent cocktail historian.

> 2 ounces applejack or calvados
>
> 1 teaspoon superfine sugar
>
> Club soda
>
> 4 dashes of peach bitters
>
> Green apple slice, for garnish

Pour the applejack and sugar into an ice-filled Highball glass. Fill with the club soda; add the bitters. Stir briefly. Add the apple slice.

Dog's Nose

This drink dates back to the days of Charles Dickens.

> 12 ounces porter or stout
>
> 2 teaspoons brown sugar
>
> 2 ounces gin
>
> Freshly grated nutmeg, for garnish

Pour the porter or stout into a large sturdy glass and heat it in a microwave for about 1 minute. Add the brown sugar and gin and stir lightly. Grate the nutmeg on top.

Double Standard Sour

> 1 ounce blended Canadian whisky
>
> 1 ounce gin
>
> $^1/_2$ ounce fresh lemon juice
>
> Dash of simple syrup (page 33)
>
> Dash of grenadine
>
> Maraschino cherry and a lemon twist, for garnish

Pour the whisky, gin, lemon juice, simple syrup, and grenadine into a shaker two-thirds full of ice cubes. Shake well. Strain into a chilled Sour glass. Add the garnishes.

Down Under Martini

—From The Purple Martini, Denver, Colorado.

> 3 ounces gin
>
> Splash of Pernod
>
> Dash of Angostura bitters

Pour all of the ingredients into a mixing glass two-thirds full of ice cubes. Stir well. Strain into a chilled Cocktail glass.

D

Dreamsicle

Another blast from the past.

> 1 ounce amaretto
>
> $^1/_2$ ounce vanilla vodka or vanilla schnapps
>
> $^1/_2$ ounce triple sec
>
> 2 ounces orange juice
>
> 2 ounces heavy cream

Pour all of the ingredients into a shaker two-thirds full of ice cubes. Shake well. Strain into an ice-filled Rocks glass.

Dreamy Dorini Smoking Martini

—Adapted from a recipe by LibationGoddess, Audrey Saunders, 2001.

$^1/_2$ ounce Laphroaig 10-year-old scotch

2 ounces Grey Goose vodka

2 to 3 drops of Pernod

Lemon twist, for garnish

Pour the scotch, vodka, and Pernod into a shaker two-thirds full of ice cubes. Shake well. Strain into a chilled Cocktail glass. Add the twist.

Dr. Pepper

Who knew that this combination of ingredients could possibly combine to taste so remarkably like Dr. Pepper?

7 ounces beer

7 ounces cola

1 ounce amaretto

Pour the beer and cola into a large beer mug. Pour the amaretto into a shot glass. Drop the shot glass into the mug and drink immediately.

Dubliner

—From the Ardent Spirits e-letter: Volume 1, Issue 2, March 1999.

2 ounces Bushmill's Malt Irish whiskey

$^1/_2$ ounce sweet vermouth

$^1/_2$ ounce Grand Marnier

Green maraschino cherry, for garnish

Pour all of the ingredients into a mixing glass two-thirds full of ice cubes. Stir well. Strain into a chilled Cocktail glass. Add the cherry.

Dubonnet Cocktail

Especially yummy before dinner.

> 1^1/$_2$ ounces Dubonnet Rouge
>
> 1^1/$_2$ ounces gin
>
> Lemon twist, for garnish

Pour the Dubonnet and gin into a mixing glass two-thirds full of ice cubes. Stir well. Strain into a chilled Cocktail glass. Add the twist.

Dubonnet Manhattan

A great variation on the Manhattan.

> 2 ounces bourbon
>
> 1 ounce Dubonnet Rouge
>
> 2 dashes of orange bitters
>
> Orange wheel, for garnish

Pour the bourbon, Dubonnet, and bitters into a mixing glass two-thirds full of ice cubes. Stir well. Strain into a chilled Cocktail glass. Add the orange wheel.

Duplex

Originally made, prior to World War I, with orange bitters, this version calls for maraschino liqueur instead.

> 1^1/$_2$ ounces sweet vermouth
>
> 1^1/$_2$ ounces dry vermouth
>
> 1/$_4$ ounce maraschino liqueur

Pour all of the ingredients into a mixing glass two-thirds full of ice cubes. Stir well. Strain into a chilled Cocktail glass.

Dying Bastard

Maybe he deserves to.

> 1 ounce brandy
>
> 1 ounce gin
>
> 1 ounce rum
>
> 1 ounce ginger ale
>
> 1/2 ounce fresh lime juice
>
> Dash of Angostura bitters

Pour all of the ingredients into an ice-filled Highball glass. Stir well.

East India Cocktail

A cocktail that also makes a great party punch.

> 1 1/2 ounces brandy
>
> 1/2 ounce orange juice
>
> 1/2 ounce pineapple juice
>
> 2 dashes of Angostura bitters

Pour all of the ingredients into a shaker two-thirds full of ice cubes. Shake well. Strain into a chilled Cocktail glass.

Eight Seconds

An estimate of how long it takes to get over this?

> 1/2 ounce Jägermeister
>
> 1/2 ounce Goldschlager
>
> 1/2 ounce Hot Damn cinnamon schnapps
>
> 1/2 ounce Rumpleminz

Pour all of the ingredients into a mixing glass two-thirds full of ice cubes. Stir well. Strain into a chilled Pony glass.

El Diablo

A Spanish devil of a drink.

> 2 ounces tequila
>
> 3/4 ounce crème de cassis

3 to 5 ounces ginger ale

Lime wedge, for garnish

Pour the tequila and cassis into an ice-filled Highball glass; stir well. Add the ginger ale to taste. Squeeze the lime wedge over the drink and drop it in.

El Floridita

Named for the Havana bar that Papa Hemingway frequented.

$1^1/_2$ ounces light rum

$^1/_2$ ounce sweet vermouth

$^1/_2$ ounce fresh lime juice

Dash of white crème de cacao

Dash of grenadine

Pour all of the ingredients into a shaker two-thirds full of ice cubes. Shake well. Strain into a chilled Cocktail glass.

El Niño

1 ounce vodka

1 ounce peach schnapps

$^1/_2$ ounce blue curaçao

3 ounces pineapple juice

3 ounces orange juice

Splash of club soda

Pour the vodka, schnapps, curaçao, and fruit juices into a shaker two-thirds full of ice cubes. Shake well. Strain into an ice-filled Collins glass. Top with the club soda.

El Presidente

2 ounces light rum

$^1/_2$ ounce fresh lime juice

$^1/_2$ ounce pineapple juice

Dash of grenadine

Pour all of the ingredients into a shaker two-thirds full of ice cubes. Shake well. Strain into an ice-filled Rocks glass.

E

Emerald Isle Cocktail

A good drink to serve on March 17, Saint Patrick's Day.

> 2 ounces gin
>
> $1/4$ ounce green crème de menthe
>
> 3 dashes of Angostura bitters

Pour all of the ingredients into a mixing glass two-thirds full of ice cubes. Stir well. Strain into a chilled Cocktail glass.

English Rose Cocktail

This cocktail, named for its color, can be served over crushed ice in a small wine goblet if desired.

> Superfine sugar and a lemon wedge,
>   for rimming the glass
>
> $1^1/2$ ounces gin
>
> $3/4$ ounce dry vermouth
>
> $3/4$ ounce apricot brandy
>
> $1/4$ ounce fresh lemon juice
>
> 2 dashes of grenadine

Prepare the glass. Pour all of the ingredients into a shaker two-thirds full of ice cubes. Shake well. Strain into the sugar-rimmed Cocktail glass.

Everybody's Irish

The greenish tint of this drink makes it ideal for sipping on Saint Patrick's Day.

> 2 ounces Irish whiskey
>
> $1/4$ ounce green Chartreuse
>
> $1/4$ ounce green crème de menthe

Pour all of the ingredients into a mixing glass two-thirds full of ice cubes. Stir well. Strain into a chilled Cocktail glass.

E

Eve's Seduction Apple Martini

—Adapted from a recipe by Matt Knepper, Fifth Floor Bar, Hotel Palomar, San Francisco, California.

> $1^1/_2$ ounces Van Gogh Wild Appel vodka
>
> $^1/_4$ ounce amaretto
>
> $^1/_4$ ounce fresh lemon juice
>
> $^1/_4$ ounce fresh lime juice
>
> $^1/_4$ ounce simple syrup (page 33)
>
> Chilled champagne or other sparkling wine

Pour the vodka, amaretto, lemon juice, lime juice, and simple syrup into a shaker two-thirds full of ice. Shake well. Strain into a chilled Champagne Flute and top with the champagne.

Eyes Wide Shut Martini

Named for Stanley Kubrick's last film. We'll miss him.

> $^1/_2$ ounce Southern Comfort
>
> $^1/_2$ ounce Crown Royal
>
> $^1/_2$ ounce amaretto
>
> $^1/_2$ ounce orange juice
>
> $^1/_2$ ounce pineapple juice
>
> $^1/_2$ ounce cranberry juice
>
> Splash of grenadine

Pour all of the ingredients into a shaker two-thirds full of ice cubes. Shake well. Strain into a chilled Cocktail glass.

Fallen Angel

A pick-me-up for when you've been naughty.

> 2 ounces gin
>
> $^1/_4$ ounce white crème de menthe
>
> $^1/_2$ ounce fresh lemon juice
>
> 2 dashes of Angostura Bitters

Pour all of the ingredients into a shaker two-thirds full of ice cubes. Shake well. Strain into a chilled Cocktail glass.

F

Faux Bellini ⊕

MAKES 4 DRINKS

> 1 ripe white peach, pitted but not peeled,
>   and cut into 1-inch cubes
> $^1/_4$ ounce fresh lemon juice
> $^1/_4$ ounce simple syrup (page 33)
> 16 ounces nonalcoholic sparkling wine or apple juice

Combine the peach cubes, lemon juice, and simple syrup in a
blender; puree. Divide the puree among 4 chilled Champagne
Flutes. Gently pour in the sparkling wine; stir gently to combine.

Fernandito

This drink was created in Puerto Rico in the late 1990s.

> 1 $^1/_2$ ounces spiced rum
> $^1/_2$ ounce cranberry juice
> $^1/_2$ ounce fresh orange juice
> $^1/_2$ ounce fresh lime juice
> Lime wedge, for garnish

Pour all of the ingredients into a shaker two-thirds full of ice
cubes. Shake well. Strain into a chilled Cocktail glass. Add the
lime wedge.

Ferrari

The nuttiness of the amaretto adds bite to the herbal
qualities of the vermouth here. It's a drink that will get
your engine started.

> 1 $^1/_2$ ounces dry vermouth
> $^1/_2$ ounce amaretto

Pour both ingredients into a mixing glass two-thirds full of ice
cubes. Stir well. Strain into a chilled Cocktail glass.

F

Fifth Avenue

A very Saks-y classic Pousse-Café that was created in the 1920s.

> **¹/₂ ounce white crème de cacao**
> **¹/₂ ounce apricot brandy**
> **¹/₂ ounce heavy cream**

Pour the ingredients, in the order given, over the back of a spoon into a Pousse-Café glass, floating one on top of the other.

50/50 Martini

Historically, this drink represents the dry gin Martini as it was served at the beginning of the twentieth century.

> **1 ¹/₂ ounces gin**
> **1 ¹/₂ ounces dry vermouth**
> **2 dashes of orange bitters**

Pour all of the ingredients into a mixing glass two-thirds full of ice cubes. Stir well. Strain into a chilled Cocktail glass.

'57 Chevy

Love those tail fins.

> **1 ¹/₂ ounces Southern Comfort**
> **¹/₂ ounce vodka**
> **¹/₂ ounce Grand Marnier**
> **1 ounce pineapple juice**

Pour all of the ingredients into a shaker two-thirds full of ice cubes. Shake well. Strain into a chilled Cocktail glass.

F

Fine and Dandy

What to order when the bartender asks, "How are you today?"

>2 ounces blended Canadian whisky
>
>$^1/_2$ ounce Dubonnet Rouge
>
>$^1/_2$ ounce triple sec
>
>Lemon twist, for garnish

Pour the whisky, Dubonnet, and triple sec into a mixing glass two-thirds full of ice cubes. Stir well. Strain into a chilled Cocktail glass. Add the twist.

Fino Martini

One of the earliest variations on the classic Martini, this drink dates to the 1930s.

>2 $^1/_2$ ounces gin
>
>$^1/_4$ ounce fino sherry

Pour both ingredients into a mixing glass two-thirds full of ice cubes. Stir well. Strain into a chilled Cocktail glass.

Fireball Shooter

This drink is a hot one—you might need the next drink to put the fire out.

>$^3/_4$ ounce cinnamon schnapps
>
>$^3/_4$ ounce Bacardi 151-proof rum

Pour both ingredients into a mixing glass two-thirds full of ice cubes. Stir well. Strain into a chilled Pony glass.

Fireman's Sour

This is a close cousin of the Bacardi Cocktail, but you can use whatever rum you like when you make it.

>2 ounces light rum
>
>$^1/_2$ ounce fresh lime juice
>
>$^1/_4$ ounce grenadine
>
>Maraschino cherry, for garnish

Pour the rum, lime juice, and grenadine into a shaker two-thirds full of ice cubes. Shake well. Strain into a chilled Cocktail glass. Add the cherry.

Fish House Punch

This one was born in Philadelphia a long time ago, and it's said that George Washington himself tasted it.

MAKES ABOUT 24 SIX-OUNCE SERVINGS

> 1 large block of ice, for serving
>
> 8 ounces chilled simple syrup (page 33)
>
> 2 ounces ice water
>
> 10 ounces chilled fresh lime juice
>
> 10 ounces chilled fresh lemon juice
>
> 2 750-ml bottles chilled dark rum
>
> 18 ounces chilled brandy
>
> 12 ounces chilled peach brandy

Place the large block of ice in the center of a large punch bowl. Pour in all of the ingredients and stir well.

Flame of Love Martini

Created for singer/actor Dean Martin by Pepe at Chasen's, Los Angeles, California.

> $^1/_4$ ounce dry sherry
>
> 2 orange twists
>
> 3 ounces gin or vodka

Coat a chilled Martini glass with the sherry and discard the excess. Flame one of the twists over the glass. Stir the liquor over ice until very cold; strain into the glass. Flame the second twist over the drink.

F

Flamingo Cocktail

An excellent cocktail for Pink Floyd fans.

> **2 ounces gin**
> **$1/2$ ounce apricot brandy**
> **$1/2$ ounce fresh lime juice**
> **Dash of grenadine**

Pour all of the ingredients into a shaker two-thirds full of ice cubes. Shake well. Strain into a chilled Cocktail glass. Decorate with a pink flamingo.

Flirtini

What those girls on *Sex and the City* sip on.

> **3 to 4 fresh raspberries**
> **$1^1/2$ ounces Stolichnaya Razberi vodka**
> **$1/2$ ounce Cointreau**
> **Splash of fresh lime juice**
> **Splash of pineapple juice**
> **Splash of cranberry juice**
> **Brut champagne or other dry sparkling wine**
> **Mint sprig, for garnish**

Muddle the raspberries in the bottom of a chilled Champagne Flute. Pour the vodka, Cointreau, and fruit juices into a shaker two-thirds full of ice cubes. Shake well. Strain into the Champagne Flute. Top with the champagne; add the mint sprig.

Florida Cocktail

A good four o'clock cocktail before leaving for an Early Bird dinner.

> **$1^1/2$ ounces gin**
> **$1/2$ ounce triple sec**
> **$1/2$ ounce fresh orange juice**
> **$1/2$ ounce fresh lime juice**

Pour all of the ingredients into a shaker two-thirds full of ice cubes. Shake well. Strain into a chilled Cocktail glass.

Flying Dutchman

2 ounces gin

$^1/_2$ ounce triple sec

Pour both ingredients into a mixing glass two-thirds full of ice cubes. Stir well. Strain into an ice-filled Rocks glass.

Flying Scotsman

Named for the famous British steam train that, in 1928, became the first nonstop train from London to Edinburgh.

1$^1/_2$ ounces blended scotch

1 ounce sweet vermouth

$^1/_4$ ounce simple syrup (page 33)

$^1/_4$ ounce Angostura bitters

Pour all of the ingredients into a mixing glass two-thirds full of ice cubes. Stir well. Strain into a chilled Cocktail glass.

Folly Martini

2$^1/_2$ ounces Stolichnaya Kafya vodka

$^1/_4$ ounce sambuca

3 coffee beans, for garnish

Pour the vodka and sambuca into a mixing glass two-thirds full of ice cubes. Stir well. Strain into a chilled Cocktail glass. Add the coffee beans.

Fontainebleu Sidecar

F

Superfine sugar and a lemon wedge, for rimming the glass

2 ounces bourbon

$^1/_2$ ounce triple sec

$^3/_4$ ounce fresh lemon juice

Dash of Grand Marnier

Prepare the glass. Pour the bourbon, triple sec, and lemon juice into a shaker two-thirds full of ice cubes. Shake well. Strain into the sugar-rimmed Cocktail glass. Float the Grand Marnier on top.

Freddy Fudpucker

This is a variation on the popular Harvey Wallbanger, but the tequila, which substitutes for the vodka, adds complexity that vodka just can't deliver.

> **2 ounces white tequila**
>
> **3 ounces orange juice**
>
> **$^1/_2$ ounce Galliano**

Pour the tequila and orange juice into an ice-filled Highball glass; stir briefly. Carefully pour the Galliano over the back of a spoon so that it floats on top of the drink.

Freddy Kruger

This drink is simply a NIGHTMARE!

> **$^1/_2$ ounce Jägermeister**
>
> **$^1/_2$ ounce sambuca**
>
> **$^1/_2$ ounce vodka**

Pour all of the ingredients into a mixing glass two-thirds full of ice cubes. Stir well. Strain into a chilled Pony glass.

French Champagne Cocktail

> **1 sugar cube**
>
> **2 dashes of Angostura bitters**
>
> **$^1/_2$ ounce crème de cassis**
>
> **5 ounces chilled champagne**

Drop the sugar cube into the bottom of a chilled Champagne Flute. Add the bitters; add the cassis. Gently pour in the champagne.

French Connection

You can play with the ratios of Grand Marnier to cognac to achieve sweeter or drier versions of this drink.

> **2 ounces cognac**
>
> **1 ounce Grand Marnier**

Pour both ingredients into an ice-filled Rocks glass. Stir well to chill.

French Kiss

Don't knock it till you've tried it.

> **2 ounces sweet vermouth**
>
> **2 ounces dry vermouth**
>
> **Lemon twist, for garnish**

Pour both vermouths into an ice-filled Rocks glass; stir briefly. Add the twist.

French Rose Cocktail

> **1 $^1/_2$ ounces gin**
>
> **$^1/_4$ ounce dry vermouth**
>
> **$^1/_2$ ounce cherry brandy**

Pour all of the ingredients into a mixing glass two-thirds full of ice cubes. Stir well. Strain into a chilled Cocktail glass.

French 75

Here's the rule to remember: The French 75 uses gin, the French 76 uses brandy.

> **2 ounces gin**
>
> **$^1/_2$ ounce fresh lime juice**
>
> **$^1/_4$ ounce simple syrup (page 33)**
>
> **4 ounces chilled champagne**

Pour the gin, lime juice, and simple syrup into a shaker two-thirds full of ice cubes. Shake well. Strain the mixture into a crushed-ice-filled wine goblet; top with the champagne.

French 76

> **2 ounces brandy**
>
> **$^1/_2$ ounce fresh lemon juice**
>
> **$^1/_4$ ounce simple syrup (page 33)**
>
> **4 ounces chilled champagne**

Pour the brandy, lime juice, and simple syrup into a shaker two-thirds full of ice cubes. Shake well. Strain the mixture into a crushed ice–filled wine goblet; top with the champagne.

F

Frozen Banana Daiquiri

> 2 ounces light, gold, or dark rum
> 1 ounce fresh lime juice
> 1 ripe banana, cut into chunks

Pour all of the ingredients into a blender containing 1 cup of ice cubes. Blend well. Pour into a chilled wine goblet.

Frozen Daiquiri

> 2 ^{1}/$_2$ ounces light rum
> 1 ounce fresh lime juice
> ^{1}/$_2$ ounce simple syrup (page 33)

Pour all of the ingredients into a blender containing 1 cup of ice cubes. Blend well. Pour into a chilled wine goblet.

Frozen Margarita

Repeat after me: "I will always use fresh lime juice in my Margaritas. Nothing else will do."

> 3 ounces white tequila
> 2 ounces triple sec
> 1 ounce fresh lime juice

Pour all of the ingredients into a blender containing 1 cup of ice cubes. Blend well. Pour into a chilled wine goblet.

Frozen Matador

> 2 ounces white tequila
> 1 ounce pineapple juice
> 1 ounce fresh lime juice

Pour all of the ingredients into a blender containing 1 cup of ice cubes. Blend well. Pour into a chilled wine goblet.

Frozen Peach Daiquiri

> 2 ounces light rum
> 1 ounce fresh lime juice
> 1 ripe peach, stoned and cut into 8 wedges

Place all of the ingredients into a blender containing 1 cup of ice cubes. Blend well. Pour into a chilled wine goblet.

Frozen Peach Margarita

2 ounces white tequila

1 ounce fresh lime juice

1 ripe peach, stoned and cut into 8 wedges

Place all of the ingredients into a blender containing 1 cup of ice cubes. Blend well. Pour into a chilled wine goblet.

Frozen Piña Colada

2 ounces light or dark rum

2 ounces pineapple juice

2 ounces cream of coconut

Place all of the ingredients into a blender containing 1 cup of ice cubes. Blend well. Pour into a chilled wine goblet.

Frozen Strawberry Daiquiri

2 ounces light rum

1 ounce fresh lime juice

8 ripe strawberries, hulled and halved

Place all of the ingredients into a blender containing 1 cup of ice cubes. Blend well. Pour into a chilled wine goblet.

Frozen Strawberry Margarita

F

2 ounces white tequila

1 ounce fresh lime juice

8 ripe strawberries, hulled and halved

Place all of the ingredients into a blender containing 1 cup of ice cubes. Blend well. Pour into a chilled wine goblet.

Fuddy-Duddy Fruit Punch

Make this punch and let adults spike it if they please.

MAKES ABOUT 32 SIX-OUNCE SERVINGS

- 2 quarts grapefruit juice
- 1 quart orange juice
- 1 quart tangerine juice
- 12 ounces cranberry juice
- 4 ounces fresh lime juice
- 4 ounces fresh lemon juice
- 6 ounces simple syrup (page 33)
- 2 ounces grenadine
- 1 ounce orgeat syrup
- 1 large block of ice, for serving

Pour all of the liquid ingredients into a nonreactive large pan or bowl; stir well. Cover and refrigerate until chilled, at least 4 hours.

Place the ice in the center of a large punch bowl. Add the punch.

Full Monte

—Created by LibationGoddess, Audrey Saunders, New York City, circa 2000.

- ¹/₄ ounce vodka
- ¹/₄ ounce gin
- ¹/₄ ounce light rum
- ¹/₄ ounce tequila
- ¹/₄ ounce maraschino liqueur
- ¹/₂ ounce fresh lemon juice
- ¹/₂ ounce simple syrup (page 33)
- 2 dashes of Angostura bitters
- Champagne or other sparkling wine

Pour the vodka, gin, rum, tequila, maraschino liqueur, lemon juice, simple syrup, and bitters into a shaker two-thirds full of ice cubes. Shake well. Strain into a chilled Champagne Flute. Top with the champagne.

Fuzzy Navel

My sister's favorite.

> 2 ounces vodka
>
> 1 ounce peach schnapps
>
> 3 to 4 ounces fresh orange juice

Pour all of the ingredients into an ice-filled Highball glass; stir briefly.

Gauguin

Named for Paul Gauguin, one of the leading French painters of the Post-Impressionist period, and the man who asked in 1898, "Where do we come from? What are we? Where are we going?"

> 2 ounces light rum
>
> $1/2$ ounce triple sec
>
> 1 ounce passion fruit syrup
>
> 1 ounce fresh lemon juice
>
> 1 ounce fresh lime juice

Pour all of the ingredients into a blender containing 1 cup of ice cubes. Blend well. Pour into a chilled wine goblet.

Georgia Peach

> 2 ounces peach schnapps
>
> 4 ounces fresh orange juice
>
> 4 ounces cranberry juice

Build in an ice-filled Collins glass. Stir well.

G

German Chocolate Cake

Guess what this tastes like?

> 1 ounce Malibu rum
>
> 1 ounce crème de cacao
>
> $^1/_2$ ounce Frangelico
>
> $^1/_2$ ounce heavy cream
>
> Shredded coconut, for garnish

Pour all of the ingredients into a shaker two-thirds full of ice cubes. Shake well. Strain into a chilled Cocktail glass. Garnish with the coconut.

Gibson

Named for Charles Dana Gibson, magazine illustrator and the creator of the Gibson Girl of the late 1800s.

> 3 ounces gin
>
> $^1/_2$ ounce dry vermouth
>
> 3 pearl onions, for garnish

Pour the gin and the vermouth into a mixing glass two-thirds full of ice cubes. Stir well. Strain into a chilled Cocktail glass. Add the onions.

Gilligan's Island

A recipe that calls for the same ingredients as Sex on the Beach, but in different proportions.

> 1 ounce vodka
>
> 1 ounce peach schnapps
>
> 3 ounces orange juice
>
> 3 ounces cranberry juice

Pour all of the ingredients into a shaker two-thirds full of ice cubes. Shake well. Strain into an ice-filled Collins glass.

Gimlet

The Gin Gimlet was the first-ever Gimlet and is sometimes referred to merely as a Gimlet, the "Gin" being understood by many experienced bartenders. The drink is thought to have been created in order to entice British sailors to drink lime juice to ward off scurvy.

> 2 1/2 ounces gin
>
> 1/2 ounce lime juice cordial, such as Rose's
>
> Lime wedge, for garnish

Pour the gin and lime juice cordial into an ice-filled Rocks glass; stir briefly. Add the lime wedge.

Gin & Bitter Lemon

> 2 ounces gin
>
> 3/4 ounce fresh lemon juice
>
> 3/4 ounce simple syrup (page 33)
>
> 4 ounces tonic water

Build in an ice-filled Highball glass. Stir to chill.

Gin & It

The "It" in the Gin & It refers to the sweet vermouth that often is referred to as "Italian," since Italy was the birthplace of sweet vermouth.

> 3 ounces gin
>
> 1/2 ounce sweet vermouth

Pour the gin and the vermouth into a mixing glass two-thirds full of ice cubes. Stir well. Strain into a chilled Cocktail glass.

Gin & Sin

> 2 ounces gin
>
> 1 ounce orange juice
>
> 1/2 ounce fresh lemon juice
>
> 2 dashes of grenadine

Pour all of the ingredients into a shaker two-thirds full of ice cubes. Shake well. Strain into a chilled Cocktail glass.

G

Gin & Tonic

> 2 $^1/_2$ ounces gin
>
> 4 ounces tonic water
>
> **Lime wedge, for garnish**

Pour the gin and the tonic water into an ice-filled Highball glass. Stir briefly. Squeeze the lime and drop it in.

Gin Bloody Mary

This is an idiosyncratic drink that gin lovers really enjoy, although far more people like to stick to Bloody Marys made with vodka (page 88).

> 2 ounces gin
>
> 4 ounces tomato juice
>
> $^1/_2$ ounce fresh lemon juice
>
> $^1/_4$ teaspoon black pepper
>
> **Pinch of salt**
>
> $^1/_4$ teaspoon ground cinnamon
>
> 2 dashes of Worcestershire sauce
>
> **Lemon wedge, for garnish**

Pour the gin, tomato juice, and lemon juice into a shaker two-thirds full of ice cubes. Add the pepper, salt, cinnamon, and Worcestershire. Shake well. Strain into an ice-filled Highball glass. Add the lemon wedge.

Gin Buck

This is probably the original Buck.

> 1 lemon wedge
>
> 2 ounces gin
>
> 5 ounces ginger ale

Squeeze the lemon wedge into a Highball glass and drop it into the glass. Fill the glass with ice cubes. Add the gin and ginger ale. Stir briefly.

G

Gin Crusta

Superfine sugar and a lemon wedge, for rimming the glass

Lemon peel spiral (see technique, page 38)

2 ounces gin

$^1/_2$ ounce curaçao

$^1/_4$ ounce fresh lemon juice

Rim a Sour glass using the lemon wedge and sugar. Place the lemon peel spiral into the glass so that it lines almost the entire interior.

Pour the gin, curaçao, and lemon juice into a shaker two-thirds full of crushed ice. Shake well; strain into the glass.

Gin Daisy

This Daisy is considered to be the classic.

$2^1/_2$ ounces gin

1 ounce fresh lemon juice

$^1/_2$ ounce grenadine

Lemon twist, for garnish

Pour the gin, lemon juice, and grenadine into a shaker two-thirds full of crushed ice. Shake well. Strain into a crushed ice–filled Highball glass. Add the twist.

Gin Fix

This Fix is considered to be the classic.

$2^1/_2$ ounces gin

1 ounce fresh lemon juice

$^1/_2$ ounce pineapple juice

Fresh fruit in season, for garnish

Pour the gin, lemon juice, and pineapple juice into a shaker two-thirds full of crushed ice. Shake well. Strain into a crushed ice–filled Highball glass. Add the garnish of choice.

G

Gin Fizz

2 ounces gin

1 ounce fresh lemon juice

$^1/_2$ ounce simple syrup (page 33)

5 to 6 ounces club soda

Fresh fruit in season, for garnish

Pour the gin, lemon juice, and simple syrup into a shaker two-thirds full with ice cubes. Shake well; strain into a chilled wine goblet. Add the club soda; stir briefly. Add the garnish of choice.

Gin Rickey

2 $^1/_2$ ounces gin

1 ounce fresh lime juice

5 to 6 ounces club soda

Lime wedge, for garnish

Pour the gin and lime juice into an ice-filled Highball glass. Add the club soda, stir briefly. Add the lime wedge.

Gin Sais Quoi?

—Adapted from a recipe by Dr. Cocktail (Ted Haigh).

1 $^1/_2$ ounces gin

$^1/_2$ ounce ouzo

1 ounce fresh lemon juice

$^1/_4$ ounce black currant syrup or grenadine

2 dashes of orange bitters

Lemon twist, for garnish

Pour the gin, ouzo, lemon juice, syrup or grenadine, and bitters into a shaker two-thirds full of ice cubes. Shake well. Strain into a chilled Cocktail glass. Garnish with the twist.

G

Gin Sling

Although the Singapore Sling is based on gin, this refreshing drink is completely different from it.

> 2 ^{1}/$_2$ ounces gin
>
> ^{1}/$_2$ ounce triple sec
>
> ^{1}/$_2$ ounce fresh lemon juice
>
> 5 to 6 ounces club soda
>
> Lemon wedge, for garnish

Pour the gin, triple sec, and lemon juice into a shaker two-thirds full of ice cubes; shake well. Strain the drink into an ice-filled Collins glass. Add the club soda; stir briefly. Add the lemon wedge.

Gin Smash

Hmmm—gin and mint. Give it a try.

> 6 fresh mint leaves
>
> ^{3}/$_4$ ounce simple syrup (page 33)
>
> 2 ^{1}/$_2$ ounces gin
>
> Mint sprig, for garnish

Place the mint leaves in the bottom of a Rocks glass. Add the simple syrup and muddle well. Fill the glass with crushed ice. Add the gin; stir briefly. Garnish with the mint sprig.

Gin Sour

> 2 ounces gin
>
> ^{3}/$_4$ ounce fresh lemon juice
>
> ^{1}/$_2$ ounce simple syrup (page 33)
>
> Orange wheel and maraschino cherry, for garnish

Pour the gin, lemon juice, and simple syrup into a shaker two-thirds full of ice cubes. Shake well. Strain the drink into a chilled Sour glass. Add the garnishes.

G

Gin Swizzle

2 ounces gin
$^1/_2$ ounce fresh lime juice
$^1/_2$ ounce triple sec
5 to 6 ounces ginger ale
Lemon wheel, for garnish

Pour the gin, lime juice, and triple sec into a shaker two-thirds full of ice cubes; shake well. Strain the mixture into an ice-filled Collins glass. Add the ginger ale; stir briefly. Add the garnish and a swizzle stick.

Ginger Beer Shandy

See also **Shandy Gaff**.

8 ounces ginger beer
8 ounces amber ale

Carefully pour the ginger beer and the ale into a 16-ounce beer glass.

Ginger Julep

Created at the Red Star Tavern and Road House, Portland, Oregon.

Leaves from 4 fresh mint sprigs
1 ounce simple syrup (page 33)
$^1/_2$ ounce fresh lime juice
2 ounces chilled champagne
2 ounces ginger beer

Place the mint leaves, simple syrup, and lime juice in a shaker; muddle well. Add ice and shake well. Strain into a chilled Champagne Flute. Add the champagne and ginger beer.

Gingered Peach ✪

3 ounces peach nectar
8 ounces ginger beer

Pour both ingredients into an ice-filled wine goblet.

G

Girl Scout Cookie

1¹/₂ ounces peppermint schnapps

1¹/₂ ounces Kahlúa

3 ounces half-and-half

Pour all of the ingredients into a shaker two-thirds full of ice cubes. Shake well. Strain into a chilled Cocktail glass.

Glad Tidings Glögg

Flaming this Swedish drink provides quite a show, but be very careful while lighting it.

MAKES 6 SIX-OUNCE SERVINGS

1 750-ml bottle brandy

4 ounces simple syrup (page 33)

8 whole cloves

¹/₂ cup raisins

¹/₂ cup blanched almonds

8 ounces ruby port

Place the brandy, simple syrup, cloves, raisins, and almonds into a large saucepan set over moderately low heat. Cook until warm. Ignite the liquid with a match, and allow it to flame for about 15 seconds. Add the port and stir constantly with a long-handled wooden spoon until the flames subside. Ladle into Irish Coffee glasses, making sure that each glass contains some of the raisins and almonds.

Glenkinchie Clincher

Created for a reception for singer Tony Bennett in London.

2 ounces Glenkinchie single malt scotch

¹/₄ ounce amaretto

¹/₄ ounce triple sec

Maraschino cherry, for garnish

G

Pour the scotch, amaretto, and triple sec into a mixing glass two-thirds full of ice cubes. Stir well. Strain into a chilled Cocktail glass. Add the cherry.

Godchild

Part I of the drink trilogy.

> 1 ounce vodka
>
> 1 ounce amaretto
>
> 1 ounce heavy cream

Build in an ice-filled Rocks glass; stir briefly.

Godfather

Part II of the trilogy.

> 2 ounces scotch
>
> 1 ounce amaretto

Build in an ice-filled Rocks glass; stir briefly.

Godmother

Part III of the trilogy.

> 2 ounces vodka
>
> 1 ounce amaretto

Build in an ice-filled Rocks glass; stir briefly.

Godiva White Polar Bear

> 1 ^{1}/$_2$ ounces Godiva White Chocolate liqueur
>
> 1 ^{1}/$_2$ ounces peppermint schnapps

Build in an ice-filled Rocks glass; stir briefly.

Going Dutch Martini

> 2 ounces Van Gogh Wild Appel vodka
>
> 2 ounces cranberry juice
>
> Granny Smith apple slice, for garnish

Pour the vodka and cranberry juice into a shaker two-thirds full of ice cubes. Shake well. Strain into a chilled Cocktail glass. Garnish with the apple slice.

G

Golden Cadillac

Almost 50 years old and still going.

> 2 ounces white crème de cacao
> $3/4$ ounce Galliano
> 1 ounce light cream

Pour all of the ingredients into a shaker two-thirds full of ice cubes. Shake well. Strain into a chilled Cocktail glass.

Golden Cadillac with Whitewall Tires

> $1^1/2$ ounces Stolichnaya Vanil vodka
> $1^1/2$ ounces Godiva White Chocolate liqueur
> $1^1/2$ ounces white crème de cacao
> $1/2$ ounce Galliano
> 1 ounce heavy cream

Pour all of the ingredients into a shaker two-thirds full of ice cubes. Shake well. Strain into a chilled Cocktail glass.

Golden Dawn Cocktail

> 1 ounce gin
> 1 ounce apricot brandy
> 1 ounce calvados or applejack

Pour all of the ingredients into a mixing glass two-thirds full of ice cubes. Stir well. Strain into a chilled Cocktail glass.

Golden Delicious Martini

This is a wonderful variation on the Apple Martini.

> 2 ounces Wild Appel vodka
> $1/2$ ounce Goldschlager

Pour both ingredients into a mixing glass two-thirds full of ice cubes. Stir well. Strain into a chilled Cocktail glass.

G

Golden Dream

    2 ounces Galliano
    $^1/_2$ ounce triple sec
    1 ounce orange juice
    1 ounce light cream

Pour all of the ingredients into a shaker two-thirds full of ice cubes. Shake well. Strain into a chilled Cocktail glass.

Goldfish Martini

This was the signature drink at a Manhattan speakeasy during Prohibition.

    2 ounces gin
    1 ounce dry vermouth
    $^1/_4$ ounce goldwasser liqueur

Pour all of the ingredients into a mixing glass two-thirds full of ice cubes. Stir well. Strain into a chilled Cocktail glass.

Gorilla Tits

Who knows? Who cares?

    $^1/_2$ ounce dark rum
    $^1/_2$ ounce bourbon
    $^1/_2$ ounce Kahlúa

Build in an ice-filled Rocks glass. Stir with a sip-stick.

Gotham

Adapted from a recipe created by David Wondrich, a cyber cocktail guy, in 2001 for the debut issue of New York's *Gotham* magazine.

    2 ounces cognac
    1 ounce Noilly Prat dry vermouth
    $^1/_2$ ounce crème de cassis
    2 dashes of fresh lemon juice
    Lemon twist, for garnish

G

Pour all of the ingredients into a shaker two-thirds full of ice cubes. Shake well. Strain into a chilled Cocktail glass. Add the twist.

Gotham Martini

—From the Four Seasons Hotel, New York City.

> **3 ounces Absolut vodka**
> **$^1/_2$ ounce blackberry brandy**
> **$^1/_2$ ounce black sambuca**
> **3 blackberries, for garnish**

Pour the vodka, blackberry brandy, and sambuca into a mixing glass two-thirds full of ice cubes. Stir well. Strain into a chilled Cocktail glass. Add the blackberries.

Grape Kool Crush

Grown-up grape Kool-Aid.

> **1 $^1/_2$ ounces blue curaçao**
> **$^1/_2$ ounce vodka**
> **1 ounce cranberry juice**
> **1 ounce grape juice**
> **$^1/_2$ ounce cola**
> **Splash of pineapple juice**

Pour all of the ingredients into a shaker two-thirds full of ice cubes. Shake well. Strain into an ice-filled Collins glass.

Grapefruit Fizz ✪

> **6 ounces fresh grapefruit juice**
> **3 ounces lemon-lime soda**
> **Dash of Angostura bitters**

Build in an ice-filled Collins glass; stir briefly.

G

Grasshopper ☖

Very popular during the 1970s, this drink is poised to make a comeback.

> 1 $\frac{1}{2}$ ounces green crème de menthe
>
> 1 $\frac{1}{2}$ ounces white crème de cacao
>
> $\frac{3}{4}$ ounce light cream

Pour all of the ingredients into a shaker two-thirds full of ice cubes. Shake well. Strain into a chilled Cocktail glass.

Green Devil

The Green Devil is a variation on the Gin Gimlet, but the flavor of the crème de menthe makes it altogether different.

> 2 ounces gin
>
> $\frac{1}{2}$ ounce lime juice cordial, such as Rose's
>
> $\frac{1}{4}$ ounce green crème de menthe

Pour all of the ingredients into a mixing glass two-thirds full of ice cubes. Stir well. Strain into an ice-filled Rocks glass.

Greyhound

A cooling drink for the dog days of summer.

> 2 $\frac{1}{2}$ ounces vodka
>
> 4 ounces grapefruit juice

Build in an ice-filled Highball glass; stir briefly.

Grog

> 2 $\frac{1}{2}$ ounces dark rum
>
> 2 $\frac{1}{2}$ ounces spring water
>
> 2 dashes of Angostura bitters

Pour all of the ingredients into a mixing glass two-thirds full of ice cubes. Stir well. Strain into an ice-filled Rocks glass.

G

Guilty Pleasure Martini

1 1/2 ounces Van Gogh Wild Appel vodka

1/2 ounce Kahlùa

1/4 ounce butterscotch schnapps

Granny Smith apple wedge, for garnish

Pour the vodka, Kahlùa, and schnapps into a shaker two-thirds full of ice cubes. Shake well. Strain into a chilled Cocktail glass. Garnish with the apple wedge.

Guinness Shandy

8 ounces Guinness stout

8 ounces lemon-lime soda

Mix together in a beer mug.

Gypsy

This drink dates back to the 1930s, but the garnish is a recent addition.

1 1/2 ounces gin

1 1/2 ounces sweet vermouth

Maraschino cherry, for garnish

Pour the gin and vermouth into a mixing glass two-thirds full of ice cubes. Stir well. Strain into a chilled Cocktail glass. Garnish with the cherry.

Harry Denton Martini

Named for one of San Francisco's best-loved bon vivants.

1 1/4 ounces Bombay Sapphire gin

1/2 ounce green Chartreuse

Pour both ingredients into a shaker two-thirds full of ice cubes. Shake well. Strain into a chilled Cocktail glass.

H

Harvard Cocktail

Go Pforzheimer!

>   1 1/2 ounces brandy
>   1 1/2 ounces sweet vermouth
>   1/4 ounce simple syrup (page 33)
>   1/4 ounce Angostura bitters

Pour all of the ingredients into a shaker two-thirds full of ice cubes. Shake well. Strain into a chilled Cocktail glass.

Harvey Wallbanger

Walk carefully after having one of these; look out for walls.

>   2 ounces vodka
>   6 ounces orange juice
>   1/2 ounce Galliano

Pour the vodka and the orange juice into an ice-filled Highball glass; stir briefly. Float the Galliano on top of the drink.

Havana Cocktail

>   2 ounces light rum
>   1 ounce pineapple juice
>   1 ounce fresh lemon juice

Pour all of the ingredients into a shaker two-thirds full of ice cubes. Shake well. Strain into a chilled Cocktail glass.

Hawaiian Cocktail

>   2 ounces gin
>   1/2 ounce triple sec
>   1/2 ounce pineapple juice
>   2 dashes of Angostura bitters

Pour all of the ingredients into a shaker two-thirds full of ice cubes. Shake well. Strain into a chilled Cocktail glass.

Hemingway Daiquiri

Just what Papa ordered.

   $1^1/_2$ ounces light rum

   $3/_4$ ounce maraschino liqueur

   1 ounce fresh lime juice

   1 ounce grapefruit juice

Pour all of the ingredients into a blender and add 4 to 6 ice cubes. Start slowly and increase the speed, blending until frozen. Strain into a very large Cocktail glass.

Hennessy Martini

A mixture of cognac and lemon juice was favored by the French during the late 1700s, but this drink dates back only to the 1990s when the Hennessy cognac people promoted it heavily.

   2 ounces Hennessy cognac

   $1/_4$ ounce fresh lemon juice

Pour both ingredients into a mixing glass two-thirds full of ice cubes. Stir well. Strain into a chilled Cocktail glass.

Highland Fling

   $2^1/_2$ ounces scotch

   $3/_4$ ounce sweet vermouth

   2 dashes of orange bitters

Pour all of the ingredients into a mixing glass two-thirds full of ice cubes. Stir well. Strain into a chilled Cocktail glass.

H

Hogmanay Cocktail

Hogmanay is the Scottish word for New Year's Eve cele-
brations, the origins of which date back to the pagan
practice of sun and fire worship in the deep midwinter.
If you want to celebrate New Year in grand fashion,
Scotland is the place to be.

>   2 $^1/_2$ ounces scotch
>
> $^1/_4$ ounce absinthe substitute, such as Absente, Herbsaint,
>   Pernod, or Ricard

Pour both ingredients into a mixing glass two-thirds full of ice
cubes. Stir well. Strain into a chilled Cocktail glass.

Hogmanay Egg Nog

Serve this on New Year's Day.

MAKES 8 SIX-OUNCE SERVINGS

>   4 eggs
>
>   6 ounces scotch
>
>   2 ounces Drambuie
>
>   1 teaspoon vanilla extract
>
> $^1/_2$ teaspoon ground cinnamon
>
> $^1/_2$ teaspoon ground allspice
>
>   1 quart whole milk
>
>   Freshly grated nutmeg, for garnish

Break the eggs into a large bowl and whisk until frothy. Add
the scotch, Drambuie, vanilla, cinnamon, and allspice; whisk
to combine. Slowly add the milk, whisking until thoroughly
mixed. Ladle into Irish Coffee glasses; sprinkle on the nutmeg.

Hole-in-One

>   2 ounces scotch
>
>   1 ounce dry vermouth
>
> $^1/_4$ ounce fresh lemon juice
>
>   Dash of orange bitters

Pour all of the ingredients into a shaker two-thirds full of ice
cubes. Shake well. Strain into a chilled Cocktail glass.

Hop, Skip, and Go Naked Punch 🍵

MAKES ABOUT 16 SIX-OUNCE SERVINGS

> 6 ounces Bacardi 151-proof rum
>
> 6 ounces peach schnapps
>
> 1 can (6 ounces) frozen limeade concentrate
>
> 1 can (6 ounces) frozen lemonade concentrate
>
> 2 liters lemon-lime soda
>
> Club soda, if desired

Combine all of the ingredients in a large punch bowl and stir to blend. Add extra club soda, if desired. Serve over ice.

Hop Toad

Believe it or not, this drink has graced cocktail menus since the early 1900s, but the bitters are a recent addition.

> $1^1/2$ ounces dark rum
>
> 1 ounce apricot brandy
>
> $1/2$ ounce fresh lime juice
>
> 2 dashes of Angostura Bitters

Pour all of the ingredients into a shaker two-thirds full of ice cubes. Shake well. Strain into a chilled Cocktail glass.

Horse's Neck

This was originally a nonalcoholic drink, but the whiskey made its way into it sometime around, or just after, Prohibition.

> Lemon peel spiral (see technique, page 38)
>
> $2^1/2$ ounces bourbon
>
> 4 to 5 ounces ginger ale

Place the lemon peel spiral into a Collins glass; fill the glass with ice cubes. Pour the bourbon and ginger ale into the glass; stir briefly.

Hot Apple Pie

And this one tastes like . . . ?

> **3/4 ounce Irish cream**
> **3/4 ounce Goldschlager**
> **Ground cinnamon**

Layer the Irish cream and Goldschlager in a Pony glass. Dust the top with cinnamon. Ignite with a match (this might be difficult). After the fire goes out, make sure the glass is not too hot; you don't want to burn your lips.

Hot Buttered Rum

Americans have been enjoying Hot Buttered Rum for over 150 years.

> **2 ounces dark rum**
> **1/2 ounce simple syrup (page 33)**
> **3 whole cloves**
> **1 cinnamon stick (about 3 inches long)**
> **4 to 5 ounces boiling water**
> **2 teaspoons unsalted butter**
> **Freshly grated nutmeg, for garnish**

Pour the rum and simple syrup into an Irish Coffee glass. Add the cloves and cinnamon stick. Add the boiling water to almost fill the glass. Add the butter; stir briefly. Sprinkle with the nutmeg.

Hot Honeyed Mulled Wine

Prepare this drink just prior to party time so the aroma will greet guests as they walk in the door.

MAKES 6 SIX-OUNCE SERVINGS

> **8 whole cloves**
> **1 teaspoon freshly grated nutmeg**
> **1 teaspoon ground allspice**
> **1 cinnamon stick (about 3 inches long)**
> **2 ounces honey**
> **12 ounces hot water**

1 750-ml bottle dry red wine

6 lemon twists

Place the cloves, nutmeg, allspice, and cinnamon stick into a large saucepan; add the honey and hot water. Bring the mixture to a boil over high heat. Reduce the heat to low and simmer for 10 minutes.

Strain the mixture through a sieve lined with a double layer of dampened cheesecloth and return it to the pan. Pour in the wine and warm over moderate heat until hot. Divide among 6 Irish Coffee glasses; add a lemon twist to each serving.

Hot Spiced Halloween Cider Punch

MAKES 8 SIX-OUNCE SERVINGS

8 whole cloves

1 teaspoon freshly grated nutmeg

1 teaspoon ground allspice

$^1/_2$ teaspoon ground mace

2 cinnamon sticks (each 3 inches long)

12 ounces hot water

36 ounces hard cider

4 ounces applejack

8 apple slices, for garnish

Place the cloves, nutmeg, allspice, mace, and cinnamon sticks into a large saucepan; add the hot water. Bring the mixture to a boil over high heat. Reduce the heat to low and simmer for 10 minutes.

Strain the mixture through a sieve lined with a double layer of dampened cheesecloth and return it to the pot. Pour in the hard cider and warm over moderate heat until hot. Divide among 8 Irish Coffee glasses; add $^1/_2$ ounce of the applejack and an apple slice to each serving.

H

Hot Spiked Chocolate

Brandy and hot chocolate create a marriage made in heaven, and if you use Mexican chocolate, which is flavored with almonds and cinnamon, you'll think you're attending the wedding reception. Phone your neighbors.

MAKES 6 SERVINGS

48 ounces prepared hot chocolate

6 ounces brandy

3 ounces dark crème de cacao

Whipped cream

Freshly grated nutmeg, for garnish

Prepare the hot chocolate and pour it into a large bowl. Add the brandy and crème de cacao; stir to blend. Ladle into 6 mugs. Top each serving with whipped cream and a sprinkling of nutmeg.

Hot Toddy

Toddies have been popular among Americans since the 1700s, and at that time, the drink wasn't always heated.

1 ^{1}/$_2$ ounces bourbon, rum, or brandy

2 whole cloves

Pinch of ground mace

Pinch of ground cinnamon

4 to 5 ounces boiling water

Lemon twist and cinnamon sugar, for garnishes

Pour the spirit into an Irish Coffee glass; stir in the cloves, mace, and cinnamon. Add boiling water to almost fill the glass. Add the twist and a sprinkle of cinnamon sugar.

Hudson Bay

1 ounce gin

^{1}/$_2$ ounce cherry brandy

^{1}/$_4$ ounce Bacardi 151-proof rum

$^1/_2$ ounce fresh orange juice

$^1/_4$ ounce fresh lime juice

Pour all of the ingredients into a shaker two-thirds full of ice cubes. Shake well. Strain into a chilled Cocktail glass.

Hurricane

Batten down the hatches, this drink was created at Pat O'Brien's restaurant in New Orleans, Louisiana, circa 1945.

1 ounce light rum

1 ounce dark rum

$^1/_2$ ounce passion fruit juice

$^1/_2$ ounce fresh lime juice

$^1/_4$ ounce simple syrup (page 33)

Pour all of the ingredients into a shaker two-thirds full of ice cubes. Shake well. Strain into a chilled Cocktail glass.

Ideal Cocktail

2 ounces gin

1 ounce dry vermouth

$^1/_2$ ounce grapefruit juice

Pour all of the ingredients into a shaker two-thirds full of ice cubes. Shake well. Strain into a chilled Cocktail glass.

Imperial Cocktail

$1^1/_2$ ounces gin

$^3/_4$ ounce dry vermouth

Dash of maraschino liqueur

Maraschino cherry, for garnish

Pour the gin, vermouth, and maraschino liqueur into a mixing glass two-thirds full of ice cubes. Stir well. Strain into a chilled Cocktail glass. Add the cherry.

In & Out Martini

The name of this Martini comes from the method used
to make it.

> 2 ^{1}/$_2$ ounces gin
>
> Splash of dry vermouth

Pour the gin into a mixing glass two-thirds full of ice cubes. Stir
well. Pour the vermouth into a chilled Cocktail glass; swirl to coat
the entire interior of the glass. Pour out any excess. Strain the
gin into the glass.

Income Tax Cocktail

This is an ideal cocktail to serve on April 15, August 15,
or whatever day you finally file your taxes.

> 1 ^{1}/$_2$ ounces gin
>
> ^{3}/$_4$ ounce dry vermouth
>
> ^{3}/$_4$ ounce sweet vermouth
>
> 1 ounce orange juice
>
> 2 dashes of Angostura bitters

Pour all of the ingredients into a shaker two-thirds full of ice
cubes. Shake well. Strain into a chilled Cocktail glass.

International Cocktail

—*Created by King Cocktail Dale DeGroff, New York City.*

> 2 ounces Gentleman Jack Rare Tennessee whiskey
>
> 1 ounce Dry Sack sherry
>
> 2 dashes of Angostura bitters
>
> Orange twist, for garnish

Pour the whiskey, sherry, and bitters into a shaker two-thirds full
of ice cubes. Shake well. Strain into a chilled Cocktail glass.
Flame the orange twist.

Irish Champagne Cocktail

1 sugar cube

2 to 3 dashes of Angostura bitters

1 ounce Irish whiskey

5 ounces champagne or other sparkling wine

Lemon twist, for garnish

Drop the sugar cube into the bottom of a Champagne Flute; sprinkle with the bitters. Pour in the whiskey. Carefully pour in the champagne. Add the twist.

Irish Cherry

Serve this with a chocolate dessert.

2 ounces Irish cream liqueur

$^1/_2$ ounce cherry brandy

Pour both ingredients into a shaker two-thirds full of ice cubes. Shake well. Strain into a chilled Cocktail glass.

Irish Chocolate Martini

1 $^1/_2$ ounces Baileys Irish cream liqueur

1 $^1/_2$ ounces white crème de cacao

1 $^1/_2$ ounces vodka

Pour all of the ingredients into a shaker two-thirds full of ice cubes. Shake well. Strain into a chilled Cocktail glass.

Irish Chocolate Smooch

2 ounces Van Gogh Dutch Chocolate vodka

$^3/_4$ ounce Baileys Irish cream liqueur

$^1/_2$ ounce green crème de menthe

$^1/_2$ ounce white crème de cacao

Orange wheel, for garnish

Pour the chocolate vodka, Irish cream, crème de menthe, and crème de cacao into a shaker two-thirds full of ice cubes. Shake well. Strain into a chilled Cocktail glass. Add the orange wheel.

Irish Cinnamon Martini

1 1/2 ounces Baileys Irish cream liqueur

1 1/2 ounces Stolichnaya Zinamon vodka

Pour both ingredients into a shaker two-thirds full of ice cubes. Shake well. Strain into a chilled Cocktail glass.

Irish Cobbler

2 1/2 ounces Irish whiskey

1/2 ounce simple syrup (page 33)

Fresh fruit in season, for garnish

Pour the whiskey and simple syrup into a crushed-ice-filled wine goblet; stir briefly. Add the garnish of choice.

Irish Coffee

When in San Francisco, have one of these at The Buena Vista.

1 1/2 ounces Irish whiskey

1/2 ounce simple syrup (page 33)

4 ounces hot coffee

Dollop of whipped cream

Dash of green crème de menthe

Pour the whiskey, simple syrup, and coffee into an Irish Coffee glass; stir briefly. Spoon the whipped cream onto the coffee so that it floats on top. Drizzle the crème de menthe over the cream.

Irish Coffee Cocktail #1

1 1/2 ounces Baileys Irish cream liqueur

1 1/2 ounces Stolichnaya Kafya vodka

Dollop of whipped cream

Pour the Irish cream and vodka into a shaker two-thirds full of ice cubes. Shake well. Strain into a chilled Cocktail glass. Float the whipped cream on top.

Irish Coffee Cocktail #2

> 3 ounces chilled espresso coffee
>
> 2 ounces Irish whiskey
>
> Dollop of whipped cream

Pour the espresso and whiskey into a shaker two-thirds full of ice cubes. Shake well. Strain into a chilled Cocktail glass. Float the whipped cream on top.

Irish Coffee Martini

> $1^1/_2$ ounces Baileys Irish cream liqueur
>
> $1^1/_2$ ounces Stolichnaya Kafya vodka

Pour both ingredients into a shaker two-thirds full of ice cubes. Shake well. Strain into a chilled Cocktail glass.

Irish Collins

> 2 ounces Irish whiskey
>
> $^1/_2$ ounce fresh lemon juice
>
> $^1/_2$ ounce simple syrup (page 33)
>
> 5 to 6 ounces club soda
>
> Fresh fruit in season, for garnish

Pour the whiskey, lemon juice, and simple syrup into a shaker two-thirds full of ice cubes. Shake well. Strain into an ice-filled Collins glass. Add the club soda; stir briefly. Add the garnish of choice.

Irish Cooler

> $2^1/_2$ ounces Irish whiskey
>
> 6 to 7 ounces ginger ale
>
> Lemon twist, for garnish

Pour the whiskey and ginger ale into an ice-filled Collins glass; stir briefly. Add the garnish.

Irish Fizz

If you substitute lime juice for the lemon juice in
this recipe, the resultant drink will be considerably more
tart.

> 2 ounces Irish whiskey
>
> 1 ounce fresh lemon juice
>
> $1/2$ ounce simple syrup (page 33)
>
> 5 to 6 ounces club soda
>
> Fresh fruit in season, for garnish

Pour the whiskey, lemon juice, and simple syrup into a shaker
two-thirds full of ice cubes. Shake well; strain into a chilled wine
goblet. Add the club soda; stir briefly. Add the garnish
of choice.

Irish Julep

> 1 ounce simple syrup (page 33)
>
> 3 ounces Irish whiskey
>
> 3 large mint sprigs, for garnish

Pour the simple syrup into a crushed-ice-filled Julep cup;
stir well. Add the whiskey; stir until a film of ice forms on the
exterior of the Julep cup. Add the mint sprigs.

Irish Old-Fashioned

> 3 dashes of Angostura bitters
>
> 1 orange slice
>
> 1 lemon wedge
>
> 1 maraschino cherry
>
> 1 sugar cube
>
> $2 1/2$ ounces Irish whiskey

In a Double Old-Fashioned glass, muddle the bitters, orange slice,
lemon wedge, and maraschino cherry into the sugar cube. Fill the
glass with ice cubes and add the whiskey; stir well.

Irish Peach Martini

> 1 ^{1}/$_2$ ounces Baileys Irish cream liqueur
>
> 1 ^{1}/$_2$ ounces Stolichnaya Persik (peach) vodka

Pour both ingredients into a shaker two-thirds full of ice cubes. Shake well. Strain into a chilled Cocktail glass.

Irish Raspberry Martini

> 1 ^{1}/$_2$ ounces Baileys Irish cream liqueur
>
> 1 ^{1}/$_2$ ounces Stolichnaya Razberi vodka

Pour both ingredients into a shaker two-thirds full of ice cubes. Shake well. Strain into a chilled Cocktail glass.

Irish Rickey

> 2 ^{1}/$_2$ ounces Irish whiskey
>
> 1 ounce fresh lime juice
>
> 5 to 6 ounces club soda
>
> Lime wedge, for garnish

Pour the whiskey and lime juice into an ice-filled Highball glass. Add the club soda; stir briefly. Add the lime wedge.

Irish Sangaree

With just a touch of honey from the Irish Mist liqueur, and the aroma from the nutmeg garnish, this is a complex potion.

> 2 ounces Irish whiskey
>
> ^{1}/$_2$ ounce ruby port
>
> ^{1}/$_2$ ounce Irish Mist liqueur
>
> Freshly grated nutmeg, for garnish

Pour the whiskey, port, and Irish Mist into a mixing glass two-thirds full of ice cubes. Stir well. Strain into a chilled wine goblet. Sprinkle with the nutmeg.

Irish Sling

2 $1/2$ ounces Irish whiskey

$1/2$ ounce cherry brandy

$1/2$ ounce fresh lemon juice

5 to 6 ounces club soda

Lemon wedge, for garnish

Pour the whiskey, cherry brandy, and lemon juice into a shaker two-thirds full of ice cubes; shake well. Strain the drink into an ice-filled Collins glass. Add the club soda; stir briefly. Add the lemon wedge.

Irish Strawberry Martini

1 $1/2$ ounces Baileys Irish cream liqueur

1 $1/2$ ounces Stolichnaya Strasberi vodka

Pour both ingredients into a shaker two-thirds full of ice cubes. Shake well. Strain into a chilled Cocktail glass.

Irish Vanilla Martini

1 $1/2$ ounces Baileys Irish cream liqueur

1 $1/2$ ounces Stolichnaya Vanil vodka

Pour both ingredients into a shaker two-thirds full of ice cubes. Shake well. Strain into a chilled Cocktail glass.

Irresistible Manhattan

I'm not sure who created this drink, but the amaretto works just perfectly with both the whisky and the vermouth in this recipe.

1 $1/2$ ounces blended Canadian whisky

1 ounce sweet vermouth

1 ounce amaretto

$1/4$ ounce maraschino cherry juice (straight from the jar)

Dash of Angostura bitters

Pour all of the ingredients into a mixing glass two-thirds full of ice cubes. Stir well. Strain into a chilled Cocktail glass.

Is Paris Burning?

Named for the 1966 film starring Jean-Paul Belmondo, Gert Fröbe, Orson Welles, and Leslie Caron, the combination of these two ingredients is a classic.

> **2 ounces cognac**
>
> **1 ounce Chambord raspberry liqueur**

Pour both ingredients into a mixing glass two-thirds full of ice cubes. Stir well. Strain into a chilled Cocktail glass.

Island Breeze

MAKES 2 EIGHT-OUNCE DRINKS

> **2 ripe bananas, peeled and roughly chopped**
>
> **3 ounces dark rum**
>
> **3 ounces canned coconut cream**
>
> **2 dashes of Angostura bitters**

Place all of the ingredients into a blender containing 1 cup of ice cubes. Blend well. Pour into 2 chilled wine goblets.

Italian Champagne Cocktail

Even if you are not a fan of the bitter herbal flavors of Campari, you might enjoy this variation on the Champagne Cocktail since the sugar will counteract the bitterness somewhat.

> **1 sugar cube**
>
> **1 ounce Campari**
>
> **5 ounces Prosecco, champagne, or other sparkling wine**
>
> **Orange twist, for garnish**

Drop the sugar cube into the bottom of a Champagne Flute; add the Campari. Carefully pour in the Prosecco. Add the twist.

Italian Coffee

Amaretto is an equally Italian substitute for the
Frangelico in this recipe.

1 $^1/_2$ ounces Frangelico

4 ounces hot coffee

Dollop of whipped cream

Pour the Frangelico and coffee into an Irish Coffee glass; stir
briefly. Spoon the whipped cream onto the coffee so that it floats
on top.

Italian Stallion Martini

—From Villa Christina, Atlanta, Georgia.

3 ounces Tanqueray Sterling vodka

Splash of Galliano

Splash of Frangelico

Pour all of the ingredients into a mixing glass two-thirds full of
ice cubes. Stir well. Strain into a chilled Cocktail glass.

Ivory Coast Martini

—From The Purple Martini, Denver, Colorado.

3 ounces gin

Splash of white crème de cacao

Splash of dry vermouth

Pour all of the ingredients into a mixing glass two-thirds full of
ice cubes. Stir well. Strain into a chilled Cocktail glass.

Jack & Coke

2 ounces Jack Daniel's Tennessee whiskey

4 ounces Coca-Cola

Build in an ice-filled Highball glass. Stir briefly.

Jack Rose

Created prior to 1920, and reportedly named for its
color, which was compared to a Jacqueminot rose.

2 $^1/_2$ ounces applejack

$^1/_2$ ounce fresh lemon juice

$^1/_4$ ounce grenadine

Pour all of the ingredients into a shaker two-thirds full of ice cubes. Shake well. Strain into a chilled Cocktail glass.

Jack Rose Royale

3 ounces applejack

$^1/_2$ ounce Chambord

$^1/_2$ ounce fresh lemon juice

Pour all of the ingredients into a shaker two-thirds full of ice cubes. Shake well. Strain into a chilled Cocktail glass.

Jade

2 ounces light rum

$^1/_2$ ounce curaçao

$^1/_2$ ounce green crème de menthe

$^1/_2$ ounce fresh lime juice

Pour all of the ingredients into a shaker two-thirds full of ice cubes. Shake well. Strain into a chilled Cocktail glass.

Jägermonster

1 $^1/_2$ ounces Jägermeister

1 $^1/_2$ ounces grenadine

5 ounces orange juice

Pour all of the ingredients into a shaker two-thirds full of ice cubes. Shake well. Strain into an ice-filled Hurricane glass.

Jamaican Coffee

1 $^1/_2$ ounces Tia Maria

4 ounces hot coffee

Dollop of whipped cream

Pour the Tia Maria and coffee into an Irish Coffee glass; stir briefly. Float the whipped cream on top.

Jamaican Martini

2 ounces dark rum

$^1/_2$ ounce Tia Maria

Pour both ingredients into a mixing glass two-thirds full of ice cubes. Stir well. Strain into a chilled Cocktail glass.

Jamaican Quaalude

1 ounce Malibu rum

1 ounce Frangelico

1 ounce Baileys Irish cream liqueur

1 ounce milk

Pour all of the ingredients into a shaker two-thirds full of ice cubes. Shake well. Strain into an ice-filled Rocks glass.

Jamaican Ten Speed

—*Created by Roger Gobbler, Café Terra Cotta, Tucson, Arizona.*

1 ounce vodka

$^3/_4$ ounce melon liqueur

$^1/_4$ ounce crème de banana

$^1/_4$ ounce Malibu rum

$^1/_2$ ounce half-and-half

Pour all of the ingredients into a shaker two-thirds full of ice cubes. Shake well. Strain into a chilled Cocktail glass.

James Joyce

A variation on the Oriental Cocktail, this was named for the Irish writer because of its Irish whiskey base. As James Joyce noted, "Christopher Columbus, as everyone knows, is honoured by posterity because he was the last to discover America."

1 $^1/_2$ ounces Irish whiskey

$^3/_4$ ounce sweet vermouth

$^3/_4$ ounce triple sec

$^1/_2$ ounce fresh lime juice

Pour all of the ingredients into a shaker two-thirds full of ice cubes. Shake well. Strain into a chilled Cocktail glass.

Japanese Cocktail

   1 ^{1}/$_2$ ounces brandy

   ^{1}/$_2$ ounce orgeat syrup

   Dash of Angostura bitters

Pour the brandy, orgeat syrup, and bitters into a shaker two-thirds full of ice cubes. Shake well. Strain into a chilled Cocktail glass.

Jell-O Shots

   1 package Jell-O flavor of choice

   8 ounces boiling water

   8 ounces vodka

Dissolve the Jell-O in the boiling water; stir very well. Add the vodka and stir well. Pour the mixture into a shallow pan, ice-cube trays, tiny disposable cups, or whatever you choose. Chill until set.

Jersey Lightning

So-called because applejack originated in New Jersey.

   2 ounces applejack

   1 ounce sweet vermouth

   1 ounce fresh lime juice

   ^{1}/$_2$ ounce simple syrup (page 33)

Pour all of the ingredients into a shaker two-thirds full of ice cubes. Shake well. Strain into a chilled Cocktail glass.

Jock Collins

This drink is sometimes called a Scotch Collins, and although it isn't as popular as the Tom Collins, it is a marvelous drink to serve to scotch lovers.

> **2 ounces scotch**
> **$^1/_2$ ounce fresh lemon juice**
> **$^1/_2$ ounce simple syrup (page 33)**
> **5 to 6 ounces club soda**
> **Fresh fruit in season, for garnish**

Pour the scotch, lemon juice, and simple syrup into a shaker two-thirds full of ice cubes. Shake well. Strain into an ice-filled Collins glass. Add the club soda; stir briefly. Add the garnish of choice.

Jockey Club Cocktail

This pre-Prohibition cocktail was named for the American Jockey Club and was served at the Waldorf-Astoria bar in New York. The original recipe, though, called for just gin and orange bitters. This is a twenty first–century variation.

> **2 ounces gin**
> **$^3/_4$ ounce amaretto**
> **Dash of Angostura bitters**
> **Dash of orange bitters**

Pour all of the ingredients into a shaker two-thirds full of ice cubes. Shake well. Strain into a chilled Cocktail glass.

John Collins

aka Bourbon Collins.

> **2 ounces bourbon**
> **$^1/_2$ ounce fresh lemon juice**
> **$^1/_2$ ounce simple syrup (page 33)**
> **5 to 6 ounces club soda**
> **Fresh fruit in season, for garnish**

Pour the bourbon, lemon juice, and simple syrup into a shaker two-thirds full of ice cubes. Shake well. Strain into an ice-filled

Collins glass. Add the club soda; stir briefly. Add the garnish of choice.

Journalist Cocktail

This drink appears in a Prohibition-era British cocktail book, so it might have been named for the hard-drinking newspapermen of Fleet Street.

  2 ounces gin

  $1/4$ ounce dry vermouth

  $1/4$ ounce sweet vermouth

  $1/4$ ounce triple sec

  $1/4$ ounce fresh lemon juice

  2 dashes of orange bitters

Pour all of the ingredients into a shaker two-thirds full of ice cubes. Shake well. Strain into a chilled Cocktail glass.

Junior Mint

  $1\,1/2$ ounces white crème de cacao

  $1\,1/2$ ounces white crème de menthe

  $1/2$ ounce Malibu rum

  1 Junior Mint, for garnish

Pour the crème de cacao, crème de menthe, and rum into an ice-filled Rocks glass; stir briefly. Pierce the Junior Mint with a sip-stick and add it to the drink.

Kahlúa & Cream

  2 ounces Kahlúa

  1 ounce heavy cream

Pour both ingredients into an ice-filled Rocks glass. Stir, if desired.

K

Kamikaze

This drink started out as a shooter but has turned more respectable; it's now a sipping cocktail.

2 ounces vodka

^{1}/$_2$ ounce triple sec

^{1}/$_4$ ounce fresh lime juice

Pour all of the ingredients into a shaker two-thirds full of ice cubes. Shake well. Strain into a chilled Cocktail glass.

Kentucky Black Hawk

2 ^{1}/$_2$ ounces bourbon

^{1}/$_4$ ounce sloe gin

^{1}/$_2$ ounce fresh lemon juice

^{1}/$_2$ ounce simple syrup (page 33)

Pour all of the ingredients into a shaker two-thirds full of ice cubes. Shake well. Strain into a chilled Cocktail glass.

Kentucky Champagne Cocktail

1 sugar cube

2 to 3 dashes Peychaud's bitters

1 ounce bourbon

5 ounces champagne or other sparkling wine

Lemon twist, for garnish

Drop the sugar cube into the bottom of a Champagne Flute; add the bitters and bourbon. Carefully pour in the champagne. Add the twist.

Kentucky Colonel

Notable Kentucky Colonels include Lyndon B. Johnson; Winston Churchill; America's first man to orbit the earth, John Glenn; and Mardee Haidin Regan. Honest.

2 ^{1}/$_2$ ounces bourbon

^{1}/$_2$ ounce Bénédictine

Lemon twist, for garnish

Pour the bourbon and Bénédictine into a mixing glass two-thirds full of ice cubes. Stir well. Strain into a chilled Cocktail glass. Add the twist.

Kentucky Cowhand

> 2 ounces bourbon
> $^1/_4$ ounce Southern Comfort
> $^1/_4$ ounce light cream

Pour all of the ingredients into a shaker two-thirds full of ice cubes. Shake well. Strain into a chilled Cocktail glass.

Kentucky Distillery Punch

This punch packs a wallop—feel free to dilute it with more club soda or some ginger ale.

MAKES ABOUT 24 SIX-OUNCE SERVINGS

> 1 750-ml bottle bourbon
> 1 750-ml bottle dark rum
> 1 750-ml bottle brandy
> 6 ounces simple syrup (page 33)
> 1 cup fresh lemon juice
> 2 ounces grenadine
> 1 large block of ice
> 16 ounces ginger ale

Pour the bourbon, rum, brandy, simple syrup, lemon juice, and grenadine into a nonreactive large pan or bowl; stir well. Cover and refrigerate until chilled, at least 4 hours.

Place the ice in the center of a large punch bowl; add the punch. Pour in the ginger ale.

Kentucky Longshot

Created by the late Bartender Emeritus Max Allen, Jr. of Louisville's Seelbach Hotel as the signature drink for the 1998 Breeder's Cup race.

- 1 $1/2$ ounces bourbon
- $1/2$ ounce Original Canton Delicate Ginger liqueur
- $1/2$ ounce peach brandy
- 1 dash each of Peychaud's bitters and Angostura bitters
- 3 strips candied ginger, for garnish

Pour the ingredients into a mixing glass two-thirds full of ice cubes. Stir well. Strain into a chilled Cocktail glass. Add the candied ginger.

Kentucky Sidecar

- Superfine sugar and a lemon wedge, for rimming the glass
- 2 $1/2$ ounces bourbon
- $1/2$ ounce triple sec
- $1/2$ ounce fresh lemon juice

Prepare the glass. Pour all of the ingredients into a shaker two-thirds full of ice cubes. Shake well. Strain into the sugar-rimmed Cocktail glass.

Kentucky Stinger

- 1 $1/2$ ounces bourbon
- $1/4$ ounce Southern Comfort
- $1/4$ ounce white crème de menthe

Pour all of the ingredients into a shaker two-thirds full of ice cubes. Shake well. Strain into a crushed-ice-filled wine goblet.

Keoki Coffee

- 1 ounce brandy
- 1 ounce Kahlúa
- 4 ounces hot coffee
- Dollop of whipped cream

Pour the brandy, Kahlúa, and coffee into an Irish Coffee glass; stir briefly. Spoon the whipped cream onto the coffee so that it floats on top.

Key Lime Pie Martini

And this one would taste like . . . ?

>1 ounce Licor 43 (aka Quarenta y Tres)
>
>$^1/_2$ ounce vodka
>
>$^1/_2$ ounce lime juice cordial, such as Rose's
>
>$^3/_4$ ounce heavy cream

Pour all of the ingredients into a shaker two-thirds full of ice cubes. Shake well. Strain into a chilled Cocktail glass.

KGB

A top secret recipe.

>1$^1/_2$ ounces gin
>
>$^1/_2$ ounce Kirschwasser
>
>$^1/_4$ ounce apricot brandy
>
>$^1/_2$ ounce fresh lemon juice
>
>$^1/_2$ ounce simple syrup (page 33)
>
>Lemon twist, for garnish

Pour the gin, Kirschwasser, apricot brandy, lemon juice, and simple syrup into a shaker two-thirds full of ice cubes. Shake well. Strain into a chilled Cocktail glass. Garnish with the lemon twist.

King Alphonse

Possibly named for the thirteenth-century Spanish king who conquered the city of Jerez in 1264 and owned vineyards in the area.

>2 ounces Kahlúa
>
>Large dollop of whipped cream

Pour the Kahlúa into an ice-filled Rocks glass. Spoon the whipped cream onto the drink so that it floats on top.

Kir

Named for Canon Felix Kir, Mayor of Dijon from 1945 to 1965, in the Burgundy region of France. Burgundy produces wonderful black currants, and this is where crème de cassis originated.

> **5 ounces chilled dry white wine**
> **$^1/_4$ ounce crème de cassis**
> **Lemon twist, for garnish**

Pour the wine and cassis into a wine glass; stir briefly. Add the twist.

Kir Martini

> **2 $^1/_2$ ounces gin**
> **$^1/_2$ ounce dry vermouth**
> **$^1/_4$ ounce crème de cassis**

Pour all of the ingredients into a mixing glass two-thirds full of ice cubes. Stir well. Strain into a chilled Cocktail glass.

Kir Royale

> **5 ounces chilled champagne or other sparkling wine**
> **$^1/_4$ ounce crème de cassis**
> **Lemon twist, for garnish**

Pour the champagne and cassis into a Champagne Flute; stir briefly. Add the twist.

Knickerbocker Cocktail

A great Martini variation from the 1930s.

> **2 ounces gin**
> **$^1/_2$ ounce dry vermouth**
> **$^1/_4$ ounce sweet vermouth**
> **Lemon twist, for garnish**

Pour the gin and both vermouths into a mixing glass two-thirds full of ice cubes. Stir well. Strain into a chilled Cocktail glass. Add the twist.

Knockout Cocktail

The teaspoon of crème de menthe is the "knockout" drop in this cocktail. Use just a drop if you find that it dominates the drink too much.

1 ounce gin

1 ounce dry vermouth

$1/4$ ounce absinthe substitute, such as Absente, Herbsaint, Pernod, or Ricard

Dash of white crème de menthe

Pour all of the ingredients into a mixing glass two-thirds full of ice cubes. Stir well. Strain into a chilled Cocktail glass.

Kretchma

2 ounces vodka

1 ounce white crème de cacao

$3/4$ ounce fresh lemon juice

$1/4$ ounce grenadine

Pour all of the ingredients into a shaker two-thirds full of ice cubes. Shake well. Strain into a chilled Cocktail glass.

Kurant Collins

2 ounces Absolut Kurant vodka

1 ounce fresh lemon juice

$1/2$ ounce simple syrup (page 33)

3 ounces club soda

Pour the vodka, lemon juice, and simple syrup into a shaker two-thirds full of ice cubes. Shake well. Strain into an ice-filled Collins glass. Add the club soda; stir briefly.

K

La Jolla Cocktail

2 ounces brandy

$^1/_2$ ounce crème de banane

$^1/_2$ ounce orange juice

$^1/_2$ ounce fresh lemon juice

Pour all of the ingredients into a shaker two-thirds full of ice cubes. Shake well. Strain into a chilled Cocktail glass.

Lager & Lime

1 to 2 ounces lime juice cordial, such as Rose's

12 ounces chilled lager

Pour both ingredients into 16-ounce beer glass.

Lark Creek Inn Tequila Infusion

Absolutely fabulous—and totally addictive.
—*Created by Bradley Ogden, Lark Creek Inn, Larkspur, California, 1995.*

1 serrano chile

1 pineapple, peeled and cut into 1-inch chunks

1 tarragon sprig

1 750-ml bottle reposado tequila

Cut the top and tail from the chile and discard them. Slice the chile lengthwise down the center; discard the seeds. Place the chile into a large glass container; add the pineapple chunks and the tarragon. Pour in the tequila, cover, and set aside in a cool, dark place to rest for 48 to 60 hours.

Strain the mixture through a sieve lined with a double layer of dampened cheesecloth; discard the solids. Return the tequila to the bottle and chill it in the refrigerator or freezer for at least 12 hours. Serve neat, in a Margarita or however you want.

Leap Year

—Created on February 29, 1928, at London's Savoy Hotel.

> 2 ounces gin
>
> $1/2$ ounce sweet vermouth
>
> $1/2$ ounce Grand Marnier
>
> $1/4$ ounce fresh lemon juice
>
> Lemon twist, for garnish

Pour the gin, vermouth, Grand Marnier, and lemon juice into a shaker two-thirds full of ice cubes. Shake well. Strain into a chilled Cocktail glass. Add the twist.

Leg Spreader

> $1^1/2$ ounces Midori melon liqueur
>
> $1^1/2$ ounces coconut rum
>
> 6 to 8 ounces pineapple juice
>
> 2 splashes lemon-lime soda

Pour the Midori, rum, and pineapple juice into a shaker two-thirds full of ice cubes. Shake well. Strain into an ice-filled Hurricane glass. Top with the soda.

Lemon Drop

As guests of a Christmas Day celebration at my house will tell you, this is a great drink served straight up or on the rocks. Don't drink it as a shooter unless you want to fall asleep before Christmas dinner is served.

> Superfine sugar and a lemon wedge,
>   for rimming the glass
>
> 2 ounces citrus vodka
>
> $1/2$ ounce triple sec
>
> $1/2$ ounce fresh lemon juice

Prepare the glass. Pour the vodka, triple sec, and lemon juice into a shaker two-thirds full of ice cubes. Shake well. Strain into the sugar-rimmed Cocktail glass.

L

Lemon Kiss Cocktail

1 1/2 ounces limoncello

1 1/2 ounces vodka

Lemon twist, as garnish

Pour the limoncello and vodka into a mixing glass two-thirds full of ice cubes. Stir well. Strain into a chilled Cocktail glass. Add the twist.

Lemon Wedge Highball

1 1/2 ounces gin

1 ounce limoncello

4 ounces tonic water

Build in an ice-filled Highball glass. Stir with a sip-stick.

Lemon Wedge Martini

1 1/2 ounces limoncello

1 1/2 ounces gin

Lemon twist, as garnish

Pour the limoncello and gin into a mixing glass two-thirds full of ice cubes. Stir well. Strain into a chilled Cocktail glass. Garnish with the twist.

Lemonade Parade

2 ounces fresh lemon juice

1/2 ounce simple syrup (page 33)

6 to 8 ounces cold water

Paper-thin lemon slices, for garnish

Pour the lemon juice and simple syrup into an ice-filled Collins glass. Add the cold water; stir briefly. Add the lemon slices.

Lemon-Ginger Fizz

A safe way to slake your thirst.

> 1 ounce fresh lemon juice
>
> 1 ounce fresh lime juice
>
> 2 ounces ginger beer
>
> 4 ounces club soda

Build in an ice-filled Collins glass; stir briefly.

Lemon-Top

Compare this one to the **Carrot Top**.

> 12 ounces amber ale
>
> 2 ounces lemon-lime soda

Pour the ale into a beer glass and top with the soda.

Licorice Martini

> 2 ounces Kahlúa
>
> $^1/_2$ ounce sambuca

Pour both ingredients into a mixing glass two-thirds full of ice cubes. Stir well. Strain into a chilled Cocktail glass.

Limeade Parade

> 2 ounces fresh lime juice
>
> $^1/_2$ ounce simple syrup (page 33)
>
> 6 to 8 ounces cold water
>
> Paper-thin lime slices, for garnish

Pour the lime juice and simple syrup into an ice-filled Collins glass. Add the cold water; stir briefly. Add the lime slices.

L

Liquid Cocaine #1

Liquid Cocaine is fun to order just because of the reaction you get from some bartenders and waitpeople.

> **1 ounce Southern Comfort**
>
> **1 ounce dark rum**
>
> **1 ounce amaretto**
>
> **1 ounce pineapple juice**
>
> **Dash of grenadine**

Pour all of the ingredients into a shaker two-thirds full of ice cubes. Shake well. Strain into a chilled Cocktail glass.

Liquid Cocaine #2

> **$^1/_2$ ounce peppermint schnapps**
>
> **$^1/_2$ ounce Jägermeister**
>
> **$^1/_2$ ounce cinnamon schnapps**

Pour the ingredients into a mixing glass two-thirds full of ice cubes. Stir well. Strain into a chilled Pony glass.

Liquid Cocaine #3

> **$^1/_2$ ounce peppermint schnapps**
>
> **$^1/_2$ ounce Jägermeister**
>
> **$^1/_2$ ounce cinnamon schnapps**
>
> **$^1/_2$ ounce dark rum**

Pour the ingredients into a mixing glass two-thirds full of ice cubes. Stir well. Strain into a chilled Pony glass.

Liquid Cocaine #4

> **$^1/_2$ ounce Southern Comfort**
>
> **$^1/_2$ ounce dark rum**
>
> **$^1/_2$ ounce amaretto**
>
> **$^1/_2$ ounce pineapple juice**

Pour the ingredients into a shaker two-thirds full of ice cubes. Shake well. Strain into a chilled Pony glass.

Liquid Heroin

Another "drug drink."

> 2 ounces Jägermeister
> $1/2$ ounce peppermint schnapps

Pour the ingredients into a mixing glass two-thirds full of ice cubes. Stir well. Strain into a chilled Cocktail glass.

Liquid Joy

This does not taste like dishwashing detergent, I promise. —*Created by Ryan Damm at Harvard University, circa 2000.*

> 2 ounces light rum
> 3 ounces pineapple juice
> 3 ounces ginger ale

Build in an ice-filled Highball glass. Stir with a sip-stick.

Long Beach Iced Tea

> $1/2$ ounce vodka
> $1/2$ ounce gin
> $1/2$ ounce light rum
> $1/2$ ounce tequila
> $1/2$ ounce triple sec
> $1/2$ ounce fresh lemon juice
> $1 1/2$ ounces cranberry juice
> Lemon wedge, for garnish

Pour the vodka, gin, rum, tequila, triple sec, and both juices into a shaker two-thirds full of ice cubes. Shake well. Strain into an ice-filled Highball glass. Add the lemon wedge.

L

Long Island Iced Tea

$^1/_2$ ounce vodka

$^1/_2$ ounce gin

$^1/_2$ ounce light rum

$^1/_2$ ounce tequila

$^1/_2$ ounce triple sec

$^1/_2$ ounce fresh lemon juice

Cola

Lemon wedge, for garnish

Pour the vodka, gin, rum, tequila, triple sec, and lemon juice into a shaker two-thirds full of ice cubes. Shake well. Strain into an ice-filled Collins glass. Top with the cola. Add the lemon wedge.

Long Kiss Goodnight Martini

1 ounce vodka

1 ounce Stolichnaya Vanil vodka

$^1/_2$ ounce white crème de cacao

White chocolate curl, for garnish

Pour both vodkas and the crème de cacao into a mixing glass two-thirds full of ice cubes. Stir well. Strain into a chilled Cocktail glass. Hang a white chocolate curl off the edge of the glass.

Louisville Cocktail

This is a variation on the Manhattan, with a touch of Bénédictine—feel free to increase or decrease the liqueur to suit your taste. It's just the drink for Derby Day when you've tired of Mint Juleps.

2 ounces bourbon

$^1/_2$ ounce sweet vermouth

$^1/_2$ ounce Bénédictine

Pour all of the ingredients into a mixing glass two-thirds full of ice cubes. Stir well. Strain into a chilled Cocktail glass.

Love Potion

- 1 ounce orange vodka
- $^{1}/_{2}$ ounce Chambord raspberry liqueur
- $^{1}/_{2}$ ounce cranberry juice

Pour all of the ingredients into a mixing glass two-thirds full of ice cubes. Stir well. Strain into a chilled Pony glass.

Lynchburg Lemonade

Lynchburg, Tennessee, where Jack Daniel's is made, is a dry town. Whiskey, whiskey everywhere—but not a drop to drink.

- 1 $^{1}/_{2}$ ounces Jack Daniel's Tennessee whiskey
- 1 $^{1}/_{2}$ ounces triple sec
- 1 ounce fresh lemon juice
- $^{1}/_{2}$ ounce simple syrup (page 33)
- 4 ounces lemon-lime soda

Pour all of the ingredients into an ice-filled 16-ounce Mason jar. Stir to blend.

Madeira Cobbler

Madeira was a favorite wine of our Founding Fathers. It has been said that "Washington's taste for Madeira wine shows up with mind-numbing regularity." He spent over $6,000 on alcoholic beverages between September 1775 and March 1776.

- 3 ounces Madeira
- $^{1}/_{2}$ ounce simple syrup (page 33)
- Fresh fruit in season, for garnish

Pour the Madeira and simple syrup into a wine goblet filled with crushed ice; stir briefly. Add the garnish of choice.

M

Madras

> 2 ounces vodka
>
> 2 ounces orange juice
>
> 1 1/2 ounces cranberry juice

Build in an ice-filled Highball glass; stir briefly.

Mai Tai

Vic Bergeron, better known to most people as Trader Vic, created the Mai Tai in the 1940s. Bergeron wrote that after he first made the drink, he ". . . gave two of them to Ham and Carrie Guild, friends from Tahiti, who were there that night. Carrie took one sip and said, *'Mai Tai—Roa Ae*.' In Tahitian this means 'Out of This World—The Best.' Well, that was that. I named the drink 'Mai Tai.'"

> 1 1/2 ounces dark rum
>
> 1 ounce light rum
>
> 1 ounce triple sec
>
> 1/2 ounce apricot brandy
>
> 1 ounce fresh lime juice
>
> 1 ounce simple syrup (page 33)
>
> Dash of orgeat syrup

Pour all of the ingredients into a shaker two-thirds full of ice cubes. Shake well. Strain into a large, ice-filled wine goblet.

Maiden's Blush Cocktail

The grenadine provides the blush in this drink that dates back to the 1930s.

> 2 ounces gin
>
> 1/2 ounce white curaçao
>
> 1/2 ounce fresh lemon juice
>
> Dash of grenadine

Pour all of the ingredients into a shaker two-thirds full of ice cubes. Shake well. Strain into a chilled Cocktail glass.

M

Maiden's Prayer

   1 ounce gin

   1 ounce triple sec

   $^1/_2$ ounce fresh lemon juice

   $^1/_2$ ounce orange juice

Pour all of the ingredients into a shaker two-thirds full of ice cubes. Shake well. Strain into a chilled Cocktail glass.

Malibu Bay Breeze

   2 ounces Malibu rum

   2 ounces cranberry juice

   2 ounces pineapple juice

Pour all of the ingredients into an ice-filled Highball glass; stir briefly.

Malibu Sunrise

   2 ounces Malibu rum

   4 to 6 ounces orange juice

   1 ounce grenadine

Pour the rum and orange juice into an ice-filled Highball glass; stir briefly. Quickly pour the grenadine down the side of the glass so it sinks to the bottom and then spirals up of its own volition.

Mamie Taylor

What you'd get if Mamie Eisenhower married Zachary Taylor. In fact, Margaret Taylor, Zachary's wife, was nick-named "Mamie."

   2 ounces scotch

   5 ounces ginger ale

   1 ounce fresh lemon juice

Build in a Highball glass three-quarters full of crushed ice. Stir briefly.

M

Man o' War

One of the greatest horses there ever was, Man o' War (1917–1947) ran 21 races, winning all but one when he finished second to a horse named Upset in 1919 at Saratoga. His defeat was so unbelievable that the jockeys of both Man o' War and Upset were denied racing licenses by The Jockey Club the following year due to suspicions of race fixing.

- **2 ounces bourbon**
- **1 ounce white curaçao**
- **$^1/_2$ ounce sweet vermouth**
- **$^1/_2$ ounce fresh lime juice**

Pour all of the ingredients into a shaker two-thirds full of ice cubes. Shake well. Strain into a chilled Cocktail glass.

Mandrintini #1

—Created by Peter George, Trotters, Port of Spain, Trinidad.

- **$2^1/_2$ ounces Absolut Mandrin vodka**
- **$^3/_4$ ounce orange juice**
- **$^3/_4$ ounce cranberry juice**

Pour all of the ingredients into a shaker two-thirds full of ice cubes. Shake well. Strain into a chilled Cocktail glass.

Mandrintini #2

- **$2^1/_2$ ounces Absolut Mandrin vodka**
- **$^3/_4$ ounce orange juice**
- **$^3/_4$ ounce Cointreau**

Pour all of the ingredients into a shaker two-thirds full of ice cubes. Shake well. Strain into a chilled Cocktail glass.

Manhattan

Created in the late 1700s, the Manhattan was one of the first popular drinks to use vermouth. It has spawned many children, the Rob Roy and the Preakness Cocktail among them.

2 $^1/_2$ ounces rye, bourbon, or blended whiskey

$^3/_4$ ounce sweet vermouth

2 dashes of Angostura bitters

Maraschino cherry, for garnish

Pour the whiskey, vermouth, and bitters into a mixing glass two-thirds full of ice cubes. Stir well. Strain into a chilled Cocktail glass. Add the cherry.

Manhattan, Dry

2 $^1/_2$ ounces rye, bourbon, or blended whiskey

$^3/_4$ ounce dry vermouth

2 dashes of Angostura bitters

Lemon twist, for garnish

Pour the whiskey, vermouth, and bitters into a mixing glass two-thirds full of ice cubes. Stir well. Strain into a chilled Cocktail glass. Add the twist.

Manhattan, Perfect

2 $^1/_2$ ounces rye, bourbon, or blended whiskey

$^1/_2$ ounce sweet vermouth

$^1/_2$ ounce dry vermouth

2 dashes of Angostura bitters

Maraschino cherry and a lemon twist, for garnish

Pour the whiskey, both vermouths, and the bitters into a mixing glass two-thirds full of ice cubes. Stir well. Strain into a chilled Cocktail glass. Add the garnishes.

Manila Fizz

2 ounces gin

Dash of simple syrup (page 33)

1 egg

3 ounces root beer

Pour the gin and simple syrup into a shaker two-thirds full of ice cubes; add the egg. Shake very well. Strain into a Collins glass three-quarters full of crushed ice. Add the root beer; stir.

Mansion Martini

—From the Mansion on Turtle Creek, Dallas, Texas.

> Splash of tequila
>
> 3 ounces Bombay Sapphire gin or Stolichnaya Cristall vodka
>
> 2 jalapeño-stuffed olives, for garnish

Rinse a chilled Cocktail glass with the tequila; pour out any excess. Pour the gin or vodka into a mixing glass two-thirds full of ice cubes. Stir well. Strain into the Cocktail glass. Add the olives.

Maraschino Martini

> 2 $^1/_2$ ounces gin
>
> $^1/_4$ ounce dry vermouth
>
> $^1/_4$ ounce maraschino liqueur
>
> Dash of Peychaud's bitters
>
> Maraschino cherry, for garnish

Pour the gin, vermouth, maraschino liqueur, and bitters into a mixing glass two-thirds full of ice cubes. Stir well. Strain into a chilled Cocktail glass. Add the cherry.

Mardeeni

A delicious drink, if I do say so myself.

> Granulated sugar and 1 teaspoon finely grated orange zest, for rimming the glass
>
> 3 ounces orange-flavored vodka
>
> Splash of Lillet Blanc
>
> Orange twist, for garnish

Stir the sugar and the orange zest together and use it to rim a chilled Cocktail glass. Pour the vodka and Lillet into a mixing glass two-thirds full of ice. Stir well. Strain into the glass. Add the twist.

Margarita

Margarita Sames, a socialite from San Antonio, Texas, claims to have created this drink in the 1940s, when she threw extravagant parties at her ranch. It's said that she first made the drink for Nicky Hilton of the hotel Hiltons, and her husband not only named the drink for her, he also had a set of glasses made that were etched with her name.

>   **Kosher salt and a lime wedge, for rimming the glass**
>
>   **3 ounces white tequila**
>
>   **2 ounces Cointreau or triple sec**
>
>   **1 ounce fresh lime juice**

Prepare the glass. Pour all of the ingredients into a shaker two-thirds full of ice cubes. Shake well. Strain into the salt-rimmed Cocktail glass.

Maria Sta Note
—Adapted from a recipe from Joseph Bastianich, co-owner, Esca, New York City.

>   **1 sugar cube**
>
>   **Dash of grappa**
>
>   **Dash of limoncello**
>
>   **Chilled Prosecco**

Place the sugar cube into a Champagne Flute and soak it with the grappa. Add the limoncello. Top with the Prosecco.

Marin-i-tini
—Adapted from a recipe by Manne Hinojosa, Walnut Creek Yacht Club, Walnut Creek, California.

>   **1 $^1/_2$ ounces Pearl Vodka**
>
>   **$^1/_2$ ounce Cointreau**
>
>   **$^1/_2$ ounce peach schnapps**
>
>   **$^1/_2$ ounce fresh lime juice**
>
>   **$^1/_4$ ounce blue curaçao**
>
>   **Lime twist, for garnish**

Pour the vodka, Cointreau, schnapps, and lime juice into a shaker two-thirds full of ice cubes. Shake well. Strain into a chilled Cocktail glass. Gently pour the blue curaçao down the side of the glass so that it rests on the bottom. Add the twist.

M

Marmalade Martini

This is jammin'.

>2 ounces gin
>
>1/4 ounce dry vermouth
>
>1 teaspoon orange marmalade

Pour all of the ingredients into a shaker two-thirds full of ice cubes. Shake well. Strain into a chilled Cocktail glass.

Martinez

Arguably, the predecessor of the Martini, this drink dates back to the 1880s, and it's been suggested that it came about as a gin-based variation of the Manhattan.

>2 ounces gin
>
>1/2 ounce sweet vermouth
>
>1/4 ounce maraschino liqueur
>
>1/2 ounce simple syrup (page 33)

Pour all of the ingredients into a mixing glass two-thirds full of ice cubes. Stir well. Strain into a chilled Cocktail glass.

Martini

The Martini has been around for about 100 years. It slowly evolved from a drink made with equal parts of gin and dry vermouth, with orange bitters as an additional ingredient that didn't disappear until the 1940s, to a drink that sometimes barely sees the vermouth bottle. This is a cocktail that everyone wants to be made "their" way, so be prepared to go through some strange rituals when making this one. One writer in the 1960s suggested that, by placing a light bulb close to a bottle of dry vermouth and putting a bottle of gin on the other side, enough vermouth would be "radiated" into the gin to make the perfect dry Martini.

Martini, Dry 🍸

>3 ounces gin
>
>1/2 ounce dry vermouth
>
>Lemon twist or cocktail olive, for garnish

Pour the gin and vermouth into a mixing glass two-thirds full of ice cubes. Stir well. Strain into a chilled Cocktail glass. Add the garnish.

Martini, Extra Dry

> 3 ounces gin
> $1/4$ ounce dry vermouth
> Lemon twist or cocktail olive, for garnish

Pour the gin and vermouth into a mixing glass two-thirds full of ice cubes. Stir well. Strain into a chilled Cocktail glass. Add the garnish.

Martini, Medium

> $2\,1/2$ ounces gin
> $3/4$ ounce dry vermouth
> Lemon twist or cocktail olive, for garnish

Pour the gin and vermouth into a mixing glass two-thirds full of ice cubes. Stir well. Strain into a chilled Cocktail glass. Add the garnish.

Martini, Sweet

> $2\,1/2$ ounces gin
> $1/4$ ounce sweet vermouth
> Lemon twist, for garnish

Pour the gin and vermouth into a mixing glass two-thirds full of ice cubes. Stir well. Strain into a chilled Cocktail glass. Add the twist.

Martini Jo

—*Created by Chef Jean Joho, Brasserie Jo, Chicago, Illinois.*

> $3\,1/2$ ounces Skyy vodka
> $1/2$ ounce Lillet Rouge
> Orange twist, for garnish

Pour the vodka and Lillet into a mixing glass two-thirds full of ice cubes. Stir well. Strain into a chilled Cocktail glass. Add the twist.

Mary Pickford

Named for the popular silent-screen movie actress, who played in 238 films between 1908 and 1942.

> **2 ounces light rum**
>
> **1 ounce pineapple juice**
>
> **Dash of maraschino liqueur**
>
> **Dash of grenadine**

Pour all of the ingredients into a shaker two-thirds full of ice cubes. Shake well. Strain into a chilled Cocktail glass.

Maurice

Chevalier anyone? This is a variation on the pre-Prohibition drink, the Bronx Cocktail, that appeared in Europe during the 1920s.

> **2 ounces gin**
>
> **$1/4$ ounce dry vermouth**
>
> **$1/4$ ounce sweet vermouth**
>
> **$1/4$ ounce absinthe substitute, such as Absente, Pernod, Herbsaint, or Ricard**
>
> **1 ounce fresh orange juice**

Pour all of the ingredients into a shaker two-thirds full of ice cubes. Shake well. Strain into a chilled Cocktail glass.

Melon Ball

> **$1^1/2$ ounces Midori melon liqueur**
>
> **1 ounce vodka**
>
> **2 ounces pineapple juice**

Pour all of the ingredients into a shaker two-thirds full of ice cubes. Shake well. Strain into an ice-filled Rocks glass.

Merry Widow

Created at the Waldorf-Astoria to celebrate the 1907 Broadway opening of Franz Lehar's operetta of the same name. The show was so popular that unauthorized products, including a line of corsets, called themselves "Merry Widow" to cash in on the craze.

1 ^{1}/$_2$ ounces Dubonnet Rouge

1 ^{1}/$_2$ ounces dry vermouth

Pour both ingredients into a mixing glass two-thirds full of ice cubes. Stir well. Strain into a chilled Cocktail glass.

Metropolitan

A variation on the Cosmopolitan that is oh, so fine.
—Created by Chuck Coggins at Marion's Continental Restaurant and Lounge in downtown Manhattan.

2 ^{1}/$_2$ ounces Absolut Kurant vodka

^{1}/$_2$ ounce lime juice cordial, such as Rose's

^{1}/$_2$ ounce fresh lime juice

^{1}/$_2$ ounce cranberry juice

Lime wedge, for garnish

Pour the vodka, lime cordial, lime juice, and cranberry juice into a shaker two-thirds full of ice cubes. Shake well. Strain into a chilled Cocktail glass. Add the lime wedge.

Mexican Coffee

1 ^{1}/$_2$ ounces Kahlúa

4 ounces hot coffee

Dollop of whipped cream

Pour the Kahlúa and coffee into an Irish Coffee glass; stir briefly. Spoon the whipped cream onto the coffee so that it floats on top.

Michel Martini

2 ^{1}/$_2$ ounces Stolichnaya Vanil vodka

^{1}/$_4$ ounce Stolichnaya Zinamon vodka

3 coffee beans

Pour both vodkas into a mixing glass two-thirds full of ice cubes. Stir well. Strain into a chilled Cocktail glass. Add the coffee beans.

M

Midnight Special Cocktail

Probably named for the song of the same name, which has no known composer; Leadbelly's arrangement is usually cited as being the best.

> 2 ounces gin
>
> 1 ounce apricot nectar
>
> 2 dashes of Angostura bitters

Pour all of the ingredients into a shaker two-thirds full of ice cubes. Shake well. Strain into a chilled Cocktail glass.

Midori Green Russian

> 1 $^1/_2$ ounces Midori melon liqueur
>
> 1 $^1/_2$ ounces vodka
>
> 2 to 4 ounces heavy cream

Build in an ice-filled Rocks glass. Stir briefly.

Midsummer Dream

> 5 fresh strawberries, hulled
>
> 2 ounces vodka
>
> 1 ounce Kirschwasser
>
> $^1/_2$ ounce strawberry liqueur
>
> 2 to 6 ounces Schweppes Russian or other light raspberry soda

Puree the strawberries in a blender. Scrape the puree into a shaker two-thirds full of ice. Add the vodka, Kirschwasser, and strawberry liqueur. Shake well. Strain into a chilled wine goblet. Top with the raspberry soda to taste.

Mikhail's Martini

> 2 ounces Stolichnaya Kafya vodka
>
> $^1/_4$ ounce Stolichnaya Vanil vodka
>
> 3 or 5 coffee beans, for garnish

Pour both vodkas into a mixing glass two-thirds full of ice cubes. Stir well. Strain into a chilled Cocktail glass. Add the coffee beans.

Milky Way Martini

Referring to the galaxy or the candy bar?

> 2 ounces Stolichnaya Vanil vodka
>
> 2 ounces Godiva chocolate liqueur
>
> 1 ounce Baileys Irish cream liqueur

Pour all of the ingredients into a mixing glass two-thirds full of ice cubes. Stir well. Strain into a chilled Cocktail glass.

Millennium Manhattan

> 2 ounces bourbon
>
> 1 ounce sweet vermouth
>
> $^1/_2$ ounce peach schnapps
>
> 3 dashes of Angostura bitters
>
> Maraschino cherry, as garnish

Pour the bourbon, vermouth, schnapps, and bitters into a mixing glass two-thirds full of ice cubes. Stir well. Strain into a chilled Cocktail glass. Add the cherry.

Millionaire Cocktail #1

In the early twentieth century there was a Millionaire Cocktail made with gin, dry vermouth, and grenadine. The ingredients in this version were detailed in a 1930s cocktail book. Millionaire Cocktails #2 and #3 have been omitted intentionally; see Millionaire Cocktail #4.

> 1 $^1/_2$ ounces dark rum
>
> $^1/_2$ ounce sloe gin
>
> $^1/_2$ ounce apricot brandy
>
> $^1/_2$ ounce fresh lime juice

Pour all of the ingredients into a shaker two-thirds full of ice cubes. Shake well. Strain into a chilled Cocktail glass.

M

Millionaire Cocktail #4

Adapted from a recipe by Dr. Cocktail (Ted Haigh).

>2 ounces Myers's rum
>
>1 ounce sloe gin
>
>1 ounce apricot brandy
>
>1 ounce fresh lime juice

Pour all of the ingredients into a shaker two-thirds full of ice cubes. Shake well. Strain into a chilled Cocktail glass.

Millionaire's Margarita

—Adapted from a recipe by well-known beverage consultant Steve Olsen, New York City.

>2 ounces El Tesoro de Don Felipe Paradiso Añejo tequila
>
>$1/2$ ounce Grand Marnier Cuvée du Centenaire
>
>$1^1/2$ ounces fresh lime juice
>
>Lime wheel or orange wedge, for garnish

Pour the tequila, Grand Marnier, and lime juice into a shaker two-thirds full of ice cubes. Shake well. Strain into a chilled Cocktail glass or ice-filled Rocks glass. Add the garnish.

Mimosa

Many people forget to put the triple sec in this drink— don't be one of them.

>$1/2$ ounce triple sec
>
>1 ounce fresh orange juice
>
>4 ounces champagne or other sparkling wine
>
>Orange wheel, for garnish

Pour the triple sec, orange juice, and champagne into a Champagne Flute. Stir briefly. Add the orange wheel.

Mind Eraser

A sister to the shooter, this cocktail looks like a Pousse-Café but is drunk in one gulp through a straw.

>$1/2$ ounce Kahlúa
>
>$1/2$ ounce vodka
>
>$1/2$ ounce club soda

Pour the ingredients, in the order given, over the back of a spoon into a Pousse-Café glass, floating one on top of the other. Place a short straw in the glass and drink from the bottom up in one go.

Minnesota Manhattan

—*Created by Jaqui Smith, Grange Hall, New York City.*

> 2 ^{1}/$_2$ ounces Stolichnaya Okhotnichya vodka
>
> 1 ounce sweet vermouth
>
> 2 dashes of Angostura bitters
>
> Maraschino cherry, as garnish

Pour the vodka, vermouth, and bitters into a mixing glass two-thirds full of ice cubes. Stir well. Strain into a chilled Cocktail glass. Add the cherry.

Mint Julep #1

A drink for the first Saturday in May, when the Kentucky Derby is run in Louisville, Kentucky, the Mint Julep dates back to at least the early 1800s. In 1806, *Webster's Dictionary* defined julep as "a kind of liquid medicine," but three years prior to that, an Englishman described it as, "A dram of spirituous liquor that has mint in it, taken by Virginians of a morning."

It's likely that the Mint Julep was originally made with brandy and/or peach brandy, but bourbon is now the accepted base liquor.

> 3 ounces bourbon
>
> 1 ounce simple syrup (page 33)
>
> Bouquet of fresh mint

Fill a Julep Cup or Highball glass with crushed ice. Add the liquids, stir, add more ice, and stir again until ice forms on the outside of the cup. Add the bouquet of mint. Serve with 3 or 4 short straws.

M

Mint Julep #2

Bouquet of fresh mint

1 ounce simple syrup (page 33)

3 ounces bourbon

Take 5 or 6 leaves from the bouquet of mint and muddle them with the simple syrup in the bottom of a Julep Cup or Highball glass. Fill the glass with crushed ice, add the bourbon, stir, add more ice, and stir again until ice forms on the outside of the vessel. Add the remaining mint as a garnish. Serve with 3 or 4 short straws.

Mint Julep #3
(made ahead of time)

MAKES ABOUT 12 DRINKS

10 ounces simple syrup (page 33)

8 ounces hot water

Bouquet of fresh mint

1 quart bourbon

Bring the simple syrup and hot water to a boil in a small saucepan. Add the mint and stir briefly. Remove the pan from the heat, cover, and set aside to cool to room temperature, about 1 hour.

Add the mixture to the bourbon. When you build the individual drinks, you will need more fresh mint for garnishes. Build the drinks as described in recipes #1 and #2.

Mint Martini

—*From Boulevard restaurant, San Francisco, California.*

1 1/2 ounces vodka

Splash of green crème de menthe

Miniature candy cane, for garnish

Pour the vodka and crème de menthe into a mixing glass two-thirds full of ice cubes. Stir well. Strain into a chilled Cocktail glass. Add the candy cane.

Minttini

2 ounces vodka

1 ounce white crème de menthe

$^1/_2$ ounce dry vermouth

Pour all of the ingredients into a mixing glass two-thirds full of ice cubes. Stir well. Strain into a chilled Cocktail glass.

Mithering Bastard

1 $^1/_2$ ounces scotch

$^1/_2$ ounce triple sec

1 ounce orange juice

Build in an ice-filled Rocks glass. Stir well.

Mocha Martini

2 $^1/_2$ ounces vodka

1 ounce white or dark crème de cacao

$^1/_2$ ounce Kahlúa

Pour all of the ingredients into a mixing glass two-thirds full of ice cubes. Stir well. Strain into a chilled Cocktail glass.

Modern Cocktail

This drink was "modern" in the 1920s, and the original recipe called for a dash of orange bitters, too.

2 ounces scotch

$^1/_2$ ounce dark rum

2 dashes of absinthe substitute, such as Absente, Pernod, Herbsaint, or Ricard

Dash of fresh lemon juice

Maraschino cherry, for garnish

Pour the scotch, rum, absinthe substitute, and lemon juice into a shaker two-thirds full of ice cubes. Shake well. Strain into a chilled Cocktail glass. Add the cherry.

M

Mojito

A Cuban drink that probably made its way to the United States during the 1920s when Americans went to Havana to get a legal drink during Prohibition. The Mojito has become incredibly popular in the past few years, and deservedly so. Hemingway sipped Mojitos at La Bodeguita in Havana, and I've been told that a piece of cardboard hangs behind the bar there, inscribed with the following words, written by him: "My Mojito in La Bodeguita, My Daiquiri in El Floridita."

> **6 to 8 fresh mint leaves**
>
> **$^3/_4$ ounce simple syrup (page 33)**
>
> **$^1/_2$ lime, cut into several wedges**
>
> **2 ounces light rum**
>
> **2 ounces club soda**
>
> **Lime wedge, for garnish**

Place the mint leaves, simple syrup, and lime wedges in the bottom of a Highball glass; muddle well. Fill the glass with crushed ice. Add the rum and club soda; stir briefly. Add the lime wedge.

Monkey Gland Cocktail #1

A popular drink in Europe in the 1920s, this is the American version that calls for Bénédictine. The next recipe is the original formula.

> **2 $^1/_2$ ounces gin**
>
> **$^1/_2$ ounce fresh orange juice**
>
> **$^1/_2$ ounce Bénédictine**
>
> **Splash of grenadine**

Pour all of the ingredients into a mixing glass two-thirds full of ice cubes. Stir well. Strain into a chilled Cocktail glass.

Monkey Gland Cocktail #2

> **2 $^1/_2$ ounces gin**
>
> **$^1/_2$ ounce fresh orange juice**
>
> **$^1/_2$ ounce absinthe substitute, such as Absente, Pernod, Ricard, or Herbsaint**
>
> **Splash of grenadine**

M

Pour all of the ingredients into a mixing glass two-thirds full of ice cubes. Stir well. Strain into a chilled Cocktail glass.

Monk's Coffee

Named for the Carthusian monks who first concocted Chartreuse in the 1700s.

1 ^{1}/$_2$ ounces green Chartreuse

4 ounces hot coffee

Dollop of whipped cream

Pour the Chartreuse and coffee into an Irish Coffee glass; stir briefly. Float the whipped cream on top.

Morning Glory Fizz

2 ounces vodka

^{1}/$_2$ ounce white crème de cacao

1 ounce light cream

4 ounces club soda

Freshly grated nutmeg, for garnish

Pour the vodka, crème de cacao, and cream into a shaker two-thirds full of ice cubes. Shake well. Strain into an ice-filled Collins glass. Add the club soda; stir well. Sprinkle with the nutmeg.

Moscow Mule

Created during the 1940s at the Cock and Bull in Los Angeles, this was the drink that first got Americans drinking vodka on a regular basis. It was originally served in small copper tankards.

2 ounces vodka

1 ounce fresh lime juice

4 to 6 ounces ginger beer

Lime wedge, for garnish

Pour the vodka, lime juice, and ginger beer into an ice-filled Highball glass. Stir briefly. Add the lime wedge.

M

Mouth Margarita

This is a fun drink to make—I've even heard of a bar in New Jersey where they spin you around in a dentist's chair to properly mix the cocktail.

> 3/4 ounce white tequila
> 1/2 ounce triple sec
> 1/4 ounce fresh lime juice

Pour all three ingredients into the drinker's mouth. Grasp his or her head and shake vigorously (but not too vigorously). When well blended, the drinker may swallow.

Mud Puddle Masterpiece

Bravo, Maestro!

> 1 3/4 ounces Van Gogh Dutch Chocolate vodka
> 3/4 ounce Godiva Chocolate liqueur
> 1/2 ounce Frangelico
> 1/2 ounce Baileys Irish cream liqueur
> Chocolate shavings, for garnish

Pour the vodka and three liqueurs into a shaker two-thirds full of ice cubes. Shake well. Strain into a chilled Cocktail glass. Sprinkle with the chocolate shavings.

Mudslide

> 1 ounce Kahlúa
> 1 ounce vodka
> 1 ounce Baileys Irish cream liqueur

Pour all of the ingredients into a shaker two-thirds full of ice cubes. Shake well. Strain into a chilled Cocktail glass.

Naked Girl Scout

> 3/4 ounce Godiva chocolate liqueur
> 3/4 ounce peppermint schnapps

Pour both ingredients into a mixing glass two-thirds full of ice cubes. Stir well. Strain into a chilled Pony glass.

Naked Martini

"Remember: conservatism is not desirable where gin and pleasure are concerned." —*Isaac Stern*

>   3 ounces gin
>
>   Lemon twist or cocktail olive, for garnish

Pour the gin into a mixing glass two-thirds full of ice cubes. Stir well. Strain into a chilled Cocktail glass. Add the garnish.

Navy Grog

Named for eighteenth-century British Admiral Vernon Gordon, who ordered that rations of rum and water be served to sailors as a restorative. Gordon was known as "Old Grog," because his coat was made from a coarse cloth known as grogram.

> $^1/_2$ ounce light rum
>
> $^1/_2$ ounce amber or gold rum
>
> $^1/_2$ ounce dark rum
>
> $^1/_2$ ounce Grand Marnier
>
>   1 ounce grapefruit juice
>
>   1 ounce orange juice
>
>   1 ounce pineapple juice

Pour all of the ingredients into a shaker two-thirds full of ice cubes. Shake well. Strain into an ice-filled Collins glass.

Grog

Mark your calendar for Black Tot Day—July 31st. The date marks the anniversary of the end of free daily rum for British soldiers, who had their rations taken away from them in 1970, over 200 years after the tradition was started by Admiral Edward Vernon, a British naval officer. Because Vernon wore a coat made of grogram, a coarse cloth, his nickname was "Old Grog," and the rations of rum and water he prescribed for the sailors became known as Grog.

N

Negroni 🍸

This variation on the Americano is said to have been the creation of Count Negroni in the late 1800s. Apparently everyone at the Count's local bar was drinking Americanos, and he didn't want to be seen drinking such a common potion. Many people now drink Negronis made with vodka in place of the gin.

> **1 ounce gin**
>
> **1 ounce sweet vermouth**
>
> **1 ounce Campari**
>
> **Orange wheel, for garnish**

Pour the gin, vermouth, and Campari into an ice-filled Rocks glass. Stir briefly. Add the orange wheel.

Nelson's Blood

> **1 ounce ruby port**
>
> **Chilled champagne or other sparkling wine**

Build in a Champagne Flute.

New Orleans Cocktail

Absinthe was very popular in New Orleans before it was made illegal in 1912. In fact, there's still a bar on Bourbon Street called The Old Absinthe House.

> **2 ounces bourbon**
>
> **$^1/_2$ ounce absinthe substitute, such as Absente, Pernod, Herbsaint, or Ricard**
>
> **$^1/_2$ ounce simple syrup (page 33)**
>
> **$^1/_2$ ounce fresh lemon juice**

Pour all of the ingredients into a shaker two-thirds full of ice cubes. Shake well. Strain into a chilled Cocktail glass.

New Orleans Milk Punch

>   2 ounces bourbon
>
> $^1/_2$ to 1 ounce dark crème de cacao
>
>   3 to 5 ounces milk

Pour all of the ingredients into a shaker two-thirds full of ice cubes. Shake well. Strain into an ice-filled Rocks or Highball glass. Sprinkle with nutmeg or cinnamon, if desired.

New Orleans Pink Gin

The Pink Gin is a British drink, but when made with Peychaud's bitters, a product made in New Orleans, and served chilled, it becomes all-American.

>   3 dashes of Peychaud's bitters
>
> $2^1/_2$ ounces Plymouth gin

Pour both ingredients into a mixing glass two-thirds full of ice cubes. Stir well. Strain into a chilled Cocktail glass.

New York Cocktail

If I can make it there . . .

>   2 ounces blended Canadian whisky
>
> $^1/_2$ ounce fresh lemon juice
>
> $^1/_2$ ounce simple syrup (page 33)
>
>   Dash of grenadine
>
>   Lemon twist, for garnish

Pour the whisky, lemon juice, simple syrup, and grenadine into a shaker two-thirds full of ice cubes. Shake well. Strain into a chilled Cocktail glass. Add the twist.

Ninja

A drink that sneaks up on you.

> $^1/_2$ ounce dark crème de cacao
>
> $^1/_2$ ounce Midori melon liqueur
>
> $^1/_2$ ounce Frangelico

Layer in order into a Pony glass.

Norman's Watermelon Martini

Created by master bartender Norman Bukofzer, New York City.

>   2 1/2 ounces gin
>   1/4 ounce Marie Brizard watermelon liqueur
>   Juice of a lime wedge
>   Lemon twist, for garnish

Pour the gin, liqueur, and lime juice into a mixing glass two-thirds full of ice cubes. Stir well. Strain into a chilled Cocktail glass. Add the twist.

Nut & Berry Martini

>   2 ounces Chambord raspberry liqueur
>   2 ounces Frangelico

Pour both ingredients into a mixing glass two-thirds full of ice cubes. Stir well. Strain into a chilled Cocktail glass.

Nutty Martini

—From The Purple Martini, Denver, Colorado.

>   3 ounces vodka
>   Splash of Frangelico

Pour both ingredients into a mixing glass two-thirds full of ice cubes. Stir well. Strain into a chilled Cocktail glass.

Nyquil

And this would taste like . . . ? Say goodnight, Gracie.

>   3/4 ounce vodka
>   1/4 ounce Jägermeister
>   2 drops of green food coloring

Pour all of the ingredients into a shaker two-thirds full of ice cubes. Shake well. Strain into a chilled Pony glass.

Oatmeal Cookie

>   1 ounce Baileys Irish cream liqueur
>   1 ounce Jägermeister

1 ounce butterscotch schnapps

$^1/_2$ ounce cinnamon schnapps

6 to 8 golden raisins, for garnish

Pour the Irish cream, Jägermeister, and both schnapps into a shaker two-thirds full of ice cubes. Shake well. Strain into a chilled Cocktail glass or an ice-filled Highball glass. Thread the raisins on a cocktail pick and garnish with it.

Oktoberfest Punch

Oktoberfest is usually celebrated by beer drinkers, so this must be for the people who aren't fond of ale or lager. The German festival began in 1810, when Crown Prince Ludwig of Bavaria married Princess Therese of Saxon-Hildburghausen. The festivities lasted for five full days and ended with a horse race held on a green named "Theresienwiese" (Theresa's green) in honor of the bride. Over the following years the horse race was repeated every October, and Oktoberfest was born.

MAKES ABOUT 24 SIX-OUNCE SERVINGS

1 750-ml bottle dry red wine

2 750-ml bottles dry white wine

3 ounces sweet vermouth

3 ounces dry vermouth

8 ounces applejack

8 ounces citrus vodka

8 ounces peach schnapps

8 ounces cranberry juice

2 ounces simple syrup (page 33)

1 large block of ice

Orange and lemon wheels, for garnish

Pour all of the wines, vermouths, applejack, citrus vodka, peach schnapps, cranberry juice, and simple syrup into a large pan or bowl. Cover and refrigerate for at least 4 hours. Place the block of ice in the center of a large punch bowl. Pour in the punch; add the garnishes.

O

Old-Fashioned

This classic cocktail has changed greatly over the years: The original probably was made with rye whiskey, but many people now prefer blended Canadian whisky. Muddling the fruit with the bitters and sugar is essential, although there was no fruit save for a twist of lemon in the original nineteenth-century recipes for this drink.

> **3 dashes of Angostura bitters**
> **1 orange slice**
> **1 lemon wedge**
> **1 maraschino cherry**
> **1 sugar cube**
> **2 ^{1}/$_2$ ounces blended Canadian whisky**

In a Double Old-Fashioned glass, muddle the bitters, orange slice, lemon wedge, and maraschino cherry into the sugar cube. Fill the glass with ice cubes. Add the whisky; stir well.

Old San Juan Cocktail

> **1 ^{1}/$_2$ ounces amber rum**
> **^{1}/$_2$ ounce cranberry juice**
> **1 ounce fresh lime juice**
> **Lime wedge, for garnish**

Pour the rum, cranberry juice, and lime juice into a mixing glass two-thirds full of ice cubes. Shake well. Strain into a chilled Cocktail glass. Add the lime wedge.

Olympic Cocktail

> **1 ^{1}/$_2$ ounces brandy**
> **^{1}/$_2$ ounce triple sec**
> **^{1}/$_2$ ounce fresh orange juice**

Pour all of the ingredients into a shaker two-thirds full of ice cubes. Shake well. Strain into a chilled Cocktail glass.

O

Olympic Gold Martini

—*Created by Michael R. Vezzoni, The Four Seasons Hotel, Seattle, Washington.*

> 1 ounce Bombay Sapphire gin
>
> 1 $^1/_2$ ounces Absolut Citron vodka
>
> Splash of Original Canton Delicate Ginger liqueur
>
> Dash of Martel Cordon Bleu cognac
>
> Lemon twist, for garnish

Pour the gin, vodka, ginger liqueur, and cognac into a mixing glass two-thirds full of ice cubes. Stir well. Strain into a chilled Cocktail glass. Add the lemon twist.

1-900-FUK-MEUP

One internet poll cited this as the most-requested cocktail among its respondents. Hmmmm, I think they just like to say the words.

> $^1/_2$ ounce Absolut Kurant vodka
>
> $^1/_4$ ounce Grand Marnier
>
> $^1/_4$ ounce Chambord raspberry liqueur
>
> $^1/_4$ ounce Midori melon liqueur
>
> $^1/_4$ ounce Malibu rum
>
> $^1/_4$ ounce amaretto
>
> $^1/_2$ ounce cranberry juice
>
> $^1/_4$ ounce pineapple juice

Pour all of the ingredients into a shaker two-thirds full of ice cubes. Shake well. Strain into a chilled Cocktail glass.

O

Opal Cocktail

One 1930s recipe for this drink calls for orange-flower water instead of the orange bitters; you might want to give that variation a try.

- 1 ^{1}/$_2$ ounces gin
- ^{1}/$_2$ ounce triple sec
- 1 ounce orange juice
- 2 dashes of orange bitters

Pour all of the ingredients into a shaker two-thirds full of ice cubes. Shake well. Strain into a chilled Cocktail glass.

Opening Cocktail

This is a sweet variation on the Manhattan, using Canadian whisky instead of bourbon.

- 2 ounces blended Canadian whisky
- ^{1}/$_4$ ounce sweet vermouth
- 2 dashes of grenadine
- 2 dashes of Angostura bitters

Pour all of the ingredients into a mixing glass two-thirds full of ice cubes. Stir well. Strain into a chilled Cocktail glass.

Opera Cocktail

"Going to the opera, like getting drunk, is a sin that carries its own punishment with it." —*Hannah More (1745–1833), British writer, reformer, philanthropist*

- 2 ounces gin
- ^{1}/$_2$ ounce Dubonnet Rouge
- ^{1}/$_2$ ounce maraschino liqueur

Pour all of the ingredients into a mixing glass two-thirds full of ice cubes. Stir well. Strain into a chilled Cocktail glass.

O

Orange Blossom Cocktail

2 ounces gin

2 ounces orange juice

Orange wheel, for garnish

Pour the gin and orange juice into a shaker two-thirds full of ice cubes. Shake well. Strain into a chilled Cocktail glass. Add the orange wheel.

Orange Grove Cocktail

A variation on the Orange Blossom. Just the thing when picking oranges?

1 ounce gin

1 ounce dry vermouth

1 ounce orange juice

2 dashes of orange bitters

Pour all of the ingredients into a shaker two-thirds full of ice cubes. Shake well. Strain into a chilled Cocktail glass.

Orange Mandarin Martini

—*From The Purple Martini, Denver, Colorado.*

3 ounces Stolichnaya Ohranj vodka

Splash of Grand Marnier

Orange slice, for garnish

Pour the vodka and Grand Marnier into a mixing glass two-thirds full of ice cubes. Stir well. Strain into a chilled Cocktail glass. Add the orange slice.

Orangeade Parade ⊘

4 ounces fresh orange juice

$1/4$ ounce grenadine

2 ounces club soda

Build in an ice-filled Collins glass; stir briefly.

O

Oreo Cookie

According to the Oreo website, the cookie, which debuted in 1912, could have been named in any of the following ways:

- Some say the name came about because it just seemed like a nice, melodic combination of sounds with just a few catch letters and it was easy to pronounce.
- Others attest that the name is based on the French word for gold (*or*), a color used on early package designs.
- There's a tale that the name comes from the Greek word for mountain (*oreo*) and that the name was applied because the first test version was, if you can imagine this, hill shaped.
- Legend also has it that the Oreo was named by taking the "RE" out of cream and sandwiching it between the two "O"s from the word chocolate . . . just like the cookie.

> **$^1/_2$ ounce Kahlúa**
> **$^1/_2$ ounce white crème de cacao**
> **$^1/_2$ ounce Baileys Irish cream liqueur**
> **Splash of vodka**

Layer all of the ingredients in a Pony glass.

Oriental Cocktail

> **$1^1/_2$ ounces bourbon**
> **$^1/_2$ ounce sweet vermouth**
> **$^1/_2$ ounce triple sec**
> **$^1/_2$ ounce fresh lime juice**

Pour all of the ingredients into a shaker two-thirds full of ice cubes. Shake well. Strain into a chilled Cocktail glass.

Pacific Rim #1

The gin version, created by Ginger DiLello, Philadelphia Fish and Company, Philadelphia.

3 ounces vodka

$^1/_2$ ounce Original Canton Delicate Ginger liqueur

Strip of crystallized ginger

Pour all of the ingredients into a mixing glass two-thirds full of ice cubes. Stir well. Strain into a chilled Cocktail glass. Add the ginger garnish.

Pacific Rim #2

The vodka version, also created by Ginger DiLello, Philadelphia Fish and Company, Philadelphia.

2 ounces gin

1 ounce Original Canton Delicate Ginger liqueur

Strip of crystallized ginger

Stir and strain into a chilled Martini glass. Add the crystallized ginger garnish.

Paddy Cocktail

A variation on the Manhattan, this one stars Irish whiskey.

1 $^1/_2$ ounces Irish whiskey

1 ounce sweet vermouth

2 dashes of Angostura bitters

Pour all of the ingredients into a mixing glass two-thirds full of ice cubes. Stir well. Strain into a chilled Cocktail glass.

Palmer Cocktail

There was a drink with this name in the 1930s made with whiskey, lemon juice, and bitters. This version's far more interesting.

2 $^1/_2$ ounces gin

$^1/_2$ ounce sweet vermouth

$^1/_2$ ounce maraschino liqueur

$^1/_2$ ounce fresh lemon juice

Pour all of the ingredients into a shaker two-thirds full of ice cubes. Shake well. Strain into a chilled Cocktail glass.

P

Pan Galactic Gargle Blaster

What does this name mean?

> $1/2$ ounce vodka
>
> $1/2$ ounce triple sec
>
> $1/2$ ounce Yukon Jack liqueur
>
> $1/2$ ounce peach schnapps
>
> $1/2$ ounce Jack Daniel's Tennessee whiskey
>
> $1/2$ ounce fresh lime juice
>
> $1/2$ ounce cranberry juice
>
> Lemon-lime soda

Build in an ice-filled Collins glass, filling it with the soda. Stir with a long straw.

Panama Cocktail

This was the predecessor to the Brandy Alexander.

> 1 ounce brandy
>
> 1 ounce white crème de cacao
>
> 1 ounce light cream

Pour all of the ingredients into a shaker two-thirds full of ice cubes. Shake well. Strain into a chilled Cocktail glass.

Paradise Cocktail

Paradise comes from the Persian word, *pardes*, meaning a "pleasure-ground" or "king's garden."

> 2 ounces gin
>
> 1 ounce apricot brandy
>
> 1 ounce orange juice
>
> Dash of lemon juice

Pour all of the ingredients into a shaker two-thirds full of ice cubes. Shake well. Strain into a chilled Cocktail glass.

Paris Is Burning

Named for Jennie Livingston's universally acclaimed documentary about Harlem's drag queen balls. The film won many awards, including the Grand Jury Prize at the

P
T

Sundance Film Festival, and the 1990 San Francisco International Lesbian & Gay Film Festival Audience Award for Best Documentary.

> **2 ounces cognac**
> **$1/2$ ounce Chambord raspberry liqueur**
> **Lemon twist, for garnish**

Pour the cognac and Chambord into a Brandy Snifter. Heat in a microwave for 20 seconds on high power. Garnish with the twist.

Parisian Cocktail

This formula dates back to London in the 1920s.

> **1 ounce gin**
> **1 ounce dry vermouth**
> **1 ounce crème de cassis**

Pour all of the ingredients into a mixing glass two-thirds full of ice cubes. Stir well. Strain into a chilled Cocktail glass.

PB&J

The first patent for peanut butter was submitted in 1895 by the Kellogg brothers, who eventually discarded the product, and Joseph Lambert, one of their former employees, started selling the machines they had used to grind the peanuts.

In 1904 at the Universal Exposition, a businessman named C. H. Summer introduced peanut butter to the American nation at large, and four years later, Krema Products started selling peanut butter. Krema is the oldest peanut butter company still in operation.

> **$1/2$ ounce vodka**
> **$1/2$ ounce Chambord raspberry liqueur**
> **$1/2$ ounce Frangelico**

Pour all of the ingredients into a mixing glass two-thirds full of ice cubes. Stir well. Strain into a chilled Pony glass.

P

Peach and Lemon Champagne Punch ☕

MAKES 30 TO 40 SIX-OUNCE PUNCH CUPS

> 16 ounces chilled simple syrup (page 33)
>
> 1 750-ml bottle chilled citrus vodka or rum
>
> 1 750-ml bottle chilled dry sherry
>
> 8 ounces chilled peach schnapps
>
> 4 ounces maraschino liqueur
>
> 4 750-ml bottles chilled champagne or sparkling wine
>
> 1 liter chilled lemon-lime soda
>
> 1 large block of ice
>
> 6 peaches, stoned and sliced, for garnish

Stir all of the liquids together in a large punch bowl. Add the block of ice; garnish with the peach slices.

Peach Brandy Julep

It's very probable that peach brandy was the base of America's earliest Juleps.

> 3 ounces peach brandy
>
> 2 dashes of Angostura bitters
>
> 3 large mint sprigs, for garnish

Pour the peach brandy and the bitters into a crushed-ice-filled Julep Cup. Stir until a film of ice appears on the exterior of the cup. Add the mint garnish.

Peaches & Cream Martini

> 1 1/2 ounces Baileys Irish cream liqueur
>
> 1 1/2 ounces peach schnapps

Pour both ingredients into a shaker two-thirds full of ice cubes. Shake well. Strain into a chilled Cocktail glass

P

Peachy Keen

Isn't it just?

- 2 ounces dark rum
- 2 ounces peach nectar
- 2 ounces orange juice

Pour all of the ingredients into an ice-filled Collins glass; stir briefly.

Pear Martini

- 2 ounces vodka
- 1 ounce pear brandy
- Pear slice, for garnish

Pour all of the ingredients into a mixing glass two-thirds full of ice cubes. Stir well. Strain into a chilled Cocktail glass. Garnish with the pear slice.

Peg o' My Heart

We know that this drink was served prior to 1920, so it was probably named for a wildly popular song, written in 1913.

- 2 ounces dark rum
- 1 ounce fresh lime juice
- $^1/_2$ ounce grenadine

Pour all of the ingredients into a shaker two-thirds full of ice cubes. Shake well. Strain into a chilled Cocktail glass.

P

Pegu Club Cocktail

This drink was created at the Pegu Club in Burma, sometime prior to 1930.

2 ounces gin

$^1/_2$ ounce white curaçao

$^1/_2$ ounce fresh lime juice

2 dashes of Angostura bitters

2 dashes of orange bitters

Pour all of the ingredients into a shaker two-thirds full of ice cubes. Shake well. Strain into a chilled Cocktail glass.

Peppermint Martini

2 ounces Kahlúa

$^1/_2$ ounce peppermint schnapps

Pour all of the ingredients into a mixing glass two-thirds full of ice cubes. Stir well. Strain into a chilled Cocktail glass.

Peppermint Patty

1 ounce peppermint schnapps

$^1/_2$ ounce (1 squirt) chocolate syrup

Pour the schnapps into the drinker's mouth. Squirt in the chocolate syrup. Shake the drinker's head to mix the ingredients. Allow the drinker to swallow.

Perfection Cocktail

Was this created for little ole me?

2 ounces brandy

$^1/_4$ ounce sweet vermouth

$^1/_4$ ounce dry vermouth

$^1/_4$ ounce triple sec

Pour all of the ingredients into a mixing glass two-thirds full of ice cubes. Stir well. Strain into a chilled Cocktail glass.

P

Pernod Frappé

2 ounces Pernod

3 straws, each cut to measure about 3 inches long

Fill a chilled Cocktail glass with crushed ice until it forms a dome that rises in the center of the glass. Drizzle the Pernod into the glass. Add the straws.

Phantasm Fizz

—Adapted from a recipe by cocktail historian Dr. Cocktail (Ted Haigh), who sees phantasms with great regularity.

1 $^1/_2$ ounces Kirschwasser

$^1/_2$ ounce Parfait Amour liqueur

Chilled champagne

Dash of orange bitters

Stemless maraschino cherry, for garnish

Combine all of the ingredients in a Champagne Flute and stir lightly. Garnish with the cherry.

Phoebe Snow Cocktail

This drink was not named for the popular singer from the 1960s; it's been around since the early 1900s, and was probably named for a fictional character used to promote a railroad that boasted that its trains were fueled by anthracite, the highest grade, and cleanest burning, form of coal.

1 $^1/_2$ ounces Dubonnet Rouge

1 $^1/_2$ ounces brandy

Dash of absinthe substitute, such as Absente, Pernod, Herbsaint, or Ricard

Pour all of the ingredients into a mixing glass two-thirds full of ice cubes. Stir well. Strain into a chilled Cocktail glass.

Pierce Brosnan

Oh, to be a Bond girl. —*Adapted from a recipe created for Pierce Brosnan by Salvatore Calabrese, The Lanesborough Hotel, London.*

> 1 $1/2$ ounces vodka, straight from the freezer
>
> $1/2$ ounce chilled champagne
>
> $1/4$ ounce absinthe substitute, such as Pernod, Ricard, Herbsaint, or Absente
>
> 1 sugar cube

Pour the vodka into a well-chilled Martini glass, add the champagne and stir briefly (don't shake!). Place the sugar cube onto a bar spoon or teaspoon, soak it with the absinthe substitute, and ignite it with a match. Drop the flaming sugar cube into the drink.

Pierced Navel

This is simply a Woo Woo without the vodka.

> 2 ounces peach schnapps
>
> 4 ounces cranberry juice

Pour both ingredients into an ice-filled Highball glass; stir briefly.

Pimm's Cup

Pimm's Cup was invented by James Pimm, a restaurateur in London who opened his first restaurant in 1823. The gin-based drink, flavored with fruit liqueurs and herbs, was Pimm's original recipe, but at one time you could get Pimm's #2 Cup, made with scotch, #3 with brandy, #4 with rum, #5 with rye, and #6 with vodka. He started bottling his gin-based drink, flavored with fruit liqueurs and herbs, circa 1859.

> 4 ounces Pimm's Cup #1
>
> 8 ounces ginger ale, club soda, ginger beer, or lemon-lime soda
>
> Cucumber spear, for garnish

Pour the Pimm's and the soda into an ice-filled 20-ounce beer tankard; stir briefly. Add the cucumber spear.

P

Piña Colada

Created in 1954 by bartender Ramón "Monchito" Marrero at the Caribe Hilton Hotel, San Juan, Puerto Rico.

> **2 ounces light rum**
>
> **6 ounces pineapple juice**
>
> **2 ounces coconut cream, such as Coco Lopez**
>
> **Pineapple spear, for garnish**

Pour the rum, pineapple juice, and coconut cream into a shaker two-thirds full of ice cubes. Shake well. Strain into an ice-filled wine goblet. Add the garnish.

Pineapple-Cherry Cooler

> **2 ounces gin**
>
> **$^1/_2$ ounce cherry brandy**
>
> **4 ounces pineapple juice**

Build in an ice-filled Highball glass; stir briefly.

Pink Gin #1

A this-side-of-the-pond version of the British classic.

> **2 ounces Plymouth Gin**
>
> **3 dashes of Angostura bitters**

Pour both ingredients into a mixing glass two-thirds full of ice cubes. Stir well. Strain into a chilled Cocktail glass.

Pink Gin #2

Reportedly created as a medicinal tonic for nineteenth-century British naval officers.

> **3 dashes of Angostura bitters**
>
> **$2^1/_2$ ounces gin**

Coat the interior of a small wine goblet with the bitters and discard the excess. Add the gin.

Pink Gin #3

3 dashes of Angostura bitters
2 1/2 ounces gin

Pour both ingredients into a mixing glass two-thirds full of ice cubes. Stir well. Strain into a chilled Cocktail glass.

Pink Gin # 4

3 dashes Peychaud's bitters
2 1/2 ounces gin

Pour both ingredients into a mixing glass two-thirds full of ice cubes. Stir well. Strain into a chilled Cocktail glass.

Pink Grapefruit

6 ounces fresh grapefruit juice
1/2 ounce grenadine
2 dashes of Peychaud's bitters

Build in an ice-filled Collins glass; stir briefly.

Pink Lady

The original 1930 recipe for this drink didn't call for heavy cream, so this version is a revised formula.

2 ounces gin
1/2 ounce heavy cream
2 dashes of grenadine
1 egg white

Pour all of the ingredients into a shaker two-thirds full of ice cubes. Shake very well. Strain into a chilled Cocktail glass.

P

Pink Lemonade

—Created by Bryna O' Shea, San Francisco, California.

> **2 ounces Bacardi Limón rum**
>
> **$1/2$ ounce triple sec**
>
> **$1/2$ ounce fresh lemon juice**
>
> **$1/2$ ounce cranberry juice**
>
> **$1/2$ slice lemon, for garnish**

Pour the rum, triple sec, and both juices into a shaker two-thirds full of ice cubes. Shake well. Strain into a chilled Cocktail glass. Add the lemon slice.

Pink Squirrel

If you can't find crème de noyaux, use amaretto instead.

> **2 ounces crème de noyaux**
>
> **1 ounce white crème de cacao**
>
> **1 ounce light cream**

Pour all of the ingredients into a shaker two-thirds full of ice cubes. Shake well. Strain into a chilled Cocktail glass.

Pisco Sour

There is no substitute for Pisco brandy; you'll have to seek it out. The bitters in this drink are often dashed on top instead of being mixed with the other ingredients. Try it both ways.

> **2 ounces Pisco brandy**
>
> **$3/4$ ounce fresh lemon juice**
>
> **$1/2$ ounce simple syrup (page 33)**
>
> **1 egg white**
>
> **2 dashes of Angostura bitters**

Pour all of the ingredients into a shaker two-thirds full of ice cubes. Shake very well. Strain into a chilled Cocktail glass.

Planter's Punch

2 ounces dark rum

2 ounces fresh grapefruit juice

1 ounce pineapple juice

1 ounce fresh lime juice

$^1/_2$ ounce simple syrup (page 33)

1 ounce club soda

Pineapple spear, for garnish

Pour the rum, fruit juices, and simple syrup into a shaker two-thirds full of ice cubes. Shake well. Pour into an ice-filled Collins glass. Pour in the club soda; stir briefly. Add the pineapple spear.

PMS Special

2 ounces Bacardi 151-proof rum

2 ounces fresh grapefruit juice

1 baby aspirin, for accompaniment

Pour the rum and grapefruit juice into a shaker two-thirds full of ice cubes. Shake well. Strain into a chilled Cocktail glass. Take the baby aspirin with the first sip.

Pompier Cocktail

Based on the Pompier Highball, the gin is an additional ingredient.

2 $^1/_2$ ounces dry vermouth

$^1/_2$ ounce gin

$^1/_2$ ounce crème de cassis

Lemon twist, for garnish

Pour the vermouth, gin, and cassis into a mixing glass two-thirds full of ice cubes. Stir well. Strain into a chilled Cocktail glass. Add the twist.

P

Pompier Highball

1 1/2 ounces dry vermouth

1/2 ounce crème de cassis

Club soda

Lemon twist, for garnish

Pour the vermouth and cassis into a mixing glass two-thirds full of ice cubes. Stir well. Strain into an ice-filled Highball glass. Top with the club soda. Add the twist.

Pony's Neck ✪

1 lemon peel spiral (see technique, page 38)

6 to 8 ounces ginger ale

Dash of Angostura bitters

Place the lemon peel spiral into a Collins glass; fill the glass with ice cubes. Pour the ginger ale and bitters into the glass; stir briefly.

Port & Brandy

When your tummy feels bad, this is the best remedy.

1 1/2 ounces ruby port

1 1/2 ounces brandy

Pour the port and brandy into a small wine goblet; stir briefly.

Port & Brandy Cobbler

1 1/2 ounces ruby port

1 1/2 ounces brandy

1/2 ounce simple syrup (page 33)

Fresh fruit in season, for garnish

Pour the port, brandy, and simple syrup into a wine goblet filled with crushed ice. Stir briefly. Add the garnish of choice.

P

Port Wine Sangaree

2 ounces ruby port

$^1/_2$ ounce simple syrup (page 33)

Freshly grated nutmeg, for garnish

Pour the port and simple syrup into a mixing glass two-thirds full of ice cubes; stir well. Strain into a chilled wine goblet. Sprinkle with the nutmeg.

Porto Champagne Cocktail

1 sugar cube

2 to 3 dashes Angostura bitters

1 ounce ruby port

5 ounces champagne

Lemon twist, for garnish

Drop the sugar cube into the bottom of a Champagne Flute; sprinkle with the bitters. Add the port; carefully pour in the champagne. Add the twist.

Pousse-Café

The Pousse-Café is actually a category of drinks, not a specific one. This one's good for starters. *Pousse-Café* translates to "push the coffee."

$^1/_2$ ounce grenadine

$^1/_2$ ounce green crème de menthe

$^1/_2$ ounce light rum

Pour the ingredients, in the order given, over the back of a spoon into a Pousse Café glass, floating one on top of the other.

Prairie Oyster

Some say this cures hangovers. I say that only vegetable soup cures hangovers. Oyster lovers should give this one a try anyway.

1 egg

$^1/_4$ ounce fresh lemon juice

Dash of hot sauce

Salt and pepper

Break the egg into a large Rocks glass; add the lemon juice, hot sauce, and salt and pepper to taste. Drink in one go.

Preakness Cocktail

In 1873, the year after a horse named Preakness won the very first race to be held at the Pimlico racetrack, Governor Oden Bowie of Maryland, a horseman and racing entrepreneur, named the then new race for three-year-olds after the horse. The word *Preakness* comes from the language of the Minisi, a northern New Jersey tribe of Native Americans, who called their area *Pra-qua-les*, meaning quail woods. The name just evolved into Preakness.

2 ounces blended Canadian whisky

1 ounce sweet vermouth

2 dashes of Bénédictine

Dash of Angostura bitters

Lemon twist, for garnish

Pour the whisky, vermouth, Bénédictine, and bitters into a mixing glass two-thirds full of ice cubes. Stir well. Strain into a chilled Cocktail glass. Add the twist.

Presbyterian

For my money, it's tasty no matter what your religion.

2 $^1/_2$ ounces blended Canadian whisky

2 ounces ginger ale

2 ounces club soda

Lemon twist, for garnish

Pour the whisky, ginger ale, and club soda into an ice-filled Highball glass; stir briefly. Add the twist.

P

Prince of Wales Champagne Cocktail

Bonnie Prince Charlie? David? Charles? William?

- 1 sugar cube
- 2 to 3 dashes of Angostura bitters
- $1/2$ ounce Drambuie
- 5 ounces champagne or other sparkling wine
- Lemon twist, for garnish

Drop the sugar cube into the bottom of a Champagne Flute; sprinkle with the bitters. Add the Drambuie; carefully pour in the champagne. Add the twist.

Princeton Cocktail

Named for the university, which was founded in 1746, an early version of a drink with this name calls for sweetened gin with orange bitters and club soda, and yet another calls for gin, port, and orange bitters. This recipe is the twenty first–century version.

- $1^1/2$ ounces gin
- $1/2$ ounce dry vermouth
- $1/2$ ounce fresh lime juice
- $1/2$ ounce simple syrup (page 33)

Pour all of the ingredients into a shaker two-thirds full of ice cubes. Shake well. Strain into a chilled Cocktail glass.

Purple Haze

- 2 ounces vodka
- 2 ounces blackberry schnapps
- 2 ounces fresh orange juice

Pour all of the ingredients into a shaker two-thirds full of ice cubes. Shake well. Strain into a chilled Cocktail glass.

P

Purple Hooter #1

   $^1/_2$ ounce vodka

   $^1/_2$ ounce Chambord raspberry liqueur

   $^1/_2$ ounce triple sec

   $^1/_2$ ounce fresh lime juice

Pour all of the ingredients into a shaker two-thirds full of ice cubes. Shake well. Strain into an empty Rocks glass to serve as a shooter. Can also be served in a chilled Cocktail glass or an ice-filled Rocks glass.

Purple Hooter # 2

   1 ounce vodka

   1 ounce Chambord

   1 ounce cranberry juice

Pour the ingredients into a shaker two-thirds full of ice cubes. Shake well. Strain into an empty Rocks glass to serve as a shooter. Can also be served in a chilled Cocktail glass or an ice-filled Rocks glass.

Purple Penis

This drink is popular with bartenders far and wide. Many of them suggest that when it is ordered, the barkeep should pretend not to hear. The object? To make the drinker shout out its name even louder.

   2 ounces vodka

   $1^1/_2$ ounces blue curaçao

   $1^1/_2$ ounces Chambord raspberry liqueur

   2 ounces cranberry juice

   1 ounce fresh lemon juice

   1 ounce simple syrup (page 33)

Pour all of the ingredients into a shaker two-thirds full of ice cubes. Shake well. Strain into a chilled Collins glass.

P

Pussyfoot

A nonalcoholic drink named for a Prohibition activist known as "Pussyfoot" Johnson.

> **6 ounces orange juice**
>
> **1 ounce fresh lime juice**
>
> **1 ounce fresh lemon juice**
>
> **1 egg yolk**

Pour all of the ingredients into a shaker two-thirds full of ice cubes. Shake very well. Strain into an ice-filled wine goblet.

Ramos Gin Fizz

The Ramos Gin Fizz originated in the Big Easy but making one isn't so easy at all. Your upper body must be in good shape because this drink requires shaking for a full 3 minutes—no cheating allowed.

> **2 ounces gin**
>
> **$^1/_4$ ounce fresh lime juice**
>
> **$^1/_4$ ounce fresh lemon juice**
>
> **$^1/_2$ ounce simple syrup (page 33)**
>
> **4 drops of orange flower water**
>
> **1 egg white**
>
> **1 ounce light cream**
>
> **2 ounces club soda**

Pour the gin, citrus juices, simple syrup, orange flower water, egg white, and cream into a shaker two-thirds full of ice cubes. Shake very well for at least 3 minutes. Strain into a chilled wine goblet. Add the club soda; stir briefly.

Raspberry Cream Cocktail

> **1 $^1/_2$ ounces Baileys Irish cream liqueur**
>
> **1 $^1/_2$ ounces Stolichnaya Razberi vodka**

Pour both ingredients into a mixing glass two-thirds full of ice cubes. Stir well. Strain into a chilled Cocktail glass or an ice-filled Rocks glass.

P

Raspberry Gimlet

1 $^{1}/_{2}$ ounces Van Gogh Raspberry vodka

$^{1}/_{2}$ ounce fresh lime juice

$^{1}/_{2}$ ounce lime cordial, such as Rose's

Pour all of the ingredients into a shaker two-thirds full of ice cubes. Shake well. Strain into a chilled Cocktail glass.

Razzle-Dazzle Martini

1 $^{1}/_{2}$ ounces Van Gogh Raspberry vodka

$^{3}/_{4}$ ounce Chambord raspberry liqueur

$^{1}/_{2}$ ounce Godiva White chocolate liqueur

Pour all of the ingredients into a shaker two-thirds full of ice cubes. Shake well. Strain into a chilled Cocktail glass.

Red Death

$^{1}/_{2}$ ounce vodka

$^{1}/_{2}$ ounce sloe gin

$^{1}/_{2}$ ounce Southern Comfort

$^{1}/_{2}$ ounce triple sec

2 $^{1}/_{2}$ ounces orange juice

Build in an ice-filled Highball glass. Stir with a sip-stick.

"Some people like to see things through rose colored glasses. I, myself, prefer Martini glasses."
—*Michel Roux, Chairman and C.E.O., Crillon Importers Ltd.*

Red Snapper

In 1934, when Vincent Astor hired Fernand "Pete" Petiot as a bartender at New York's St. Regis Hotel, Astor wasn't keen on the name of Petiot's signature drink, The Bloody Mary, and changed it to The Red Snapper. The original name remained its popular moniker, though.

> **2 ounces tomato juice**
>
> **2 ounces vodka**
>
> **Dash of Worcestershire sauce**
>
> **Pinch of salt**
>
> **Pinch of cayenne pepper**
>
> **Dash of fresh lemon juice**

Pour all of the ingredients into a shaker two-thirds full of ice cubes. Shake well. Strain into an ice-filled Highball glass.

Red Wine Cooler

> **4 ounces dry red wine**
>
> **4 ounces lemon-lime soda**
>
> **Lemon twist, for garnish**

Pour the wine and soda into an ice-filled Collins glass. Stir briefly; add the twist.

Redheaded Whore

> **1 1/2 ounces brandy**
>
> **1 1/2 ounces sloe gin**
>
> **1/2 ounce peach schnapps**

Pour all of the ingredients into a mixing glass two-thirds full of ice cubes. Stir well. Strain into a chilled Cocktail glass or an ice-filled Rocks glass.

Remsen Cooler

The original cooler, this drink is often erroneously made with gin. Remsen used to be a brand name of scotch— the true base of this drink.

2 ^{1}/$_2$ ounces scotch

6 to 7 ounces club soda

Lemon twist, for garnish

Pour the scotch and club soda into an ice-filled Collins glass. Stir briefly. Add the twist.

Ritz of New York

—Created by Dale DeGroff, New York City.

1 ounce cognac

^{1}/$_2$ ounce triple sec

2 splashes of maraschino liqueur

^{1}/$_2$ ounce fresh lemon juice

2 ^{1}/$_2$ to 3 ounces chilled dry champagne or other sparkling wine

Strip of orange peel, for flaming

Pour the cognac, triple sec, maraschino liqueur, and lemon juice into a mixing glass two-thirds full of ice cubes. Stir well. Strain into a chilled Champagne Flute. Add the champagne. Flame the orange peel over the drink and discard.

Riveredge Cocktail

—Adapted from a recipe by James Beard.

MAKES 4 DRINKS

Grated zest of 1 orange

2 ounces orange juice

6 ounces gin

2 ounces dry vermouth

Pour all of the ingredients into a blender filled with 4 to 6 ice cubes. Blend until the ice is broken up and the ingredients are well combined. (This is not meant to be a frozen drink.) Divide among 4 chilled Cocktail glasses.

Rob Roy

This drink was created at the Waldorf-Astoria Hotel, New York, and named for the 1913 Broadway musical of the same name.

> 2 $^1/_2$ ounces scotch
> $^1/_2$ ounce sweet vermouth
> **Maraschino cherry, for garnish**

Pour the scotch and vermouth into a mixing glass two-thirds full of ice cubes. Stir well. Strain into a chilled Cocktail glass. Add the cherry.

Rob Roy, Dry

> 2 $^1/_2$ ounces scotch
> $^1/_2$ ounce dry vermouth
> **Lemon twist, for garnish**

Pour the scotch and vermouth into a mixing glass two-thirds full of ice cubes. Stir well. Strain into a chilled Cocktail glass. Add the twist.

Rob Roy, Perfect

> 2 $^1/_2$ ounces scotch
> $^1/_4$ ounce sweet vermouth
> $^1/_4$ ounce dry vermouth
> **Lemon twist, for garnish**

Pour the scotch and both vermouths into a mixing glass two-thirds full of ice cubes. Stir well. Strain into a chilled Cocktail glass. Add the twist.

Robotussin

It's sure to kill a cough—automatically.

> 1 $^1/_2$ ounces cherry brandy
> 1 $^1/_2$ ounces root beer schnapps

Pour both ingredients into a mixing glass two-thirds full of ice cubes. Stir well. Strain into a chilled Pony glass or Cocktail glass.

Rolls Royce Cocktail

A drink from the U.K., circa 1930.

>   2 ^{1}/$_2$ ounces gin
> ^{1}/$_4$ ounce sweet vermouth
> ^{1}/$_4$ ounce dry vermouth
>   Dash of Bénédictine

Pour all of the ingredients into a mixing glass two-thirds full of ice cubes. Stir well. Strain into a chilled Cocktail glass.

Rooster Tail

Was it the origin of the word *cocktail*?

>   Salt and a lime wedge, for rimming the glass
>   1 ^{1}/$_2$ ounces tequila
>   1 ^{1}/$_2$ ounces fresh orange juice
>   1 ^{1}/$_2$ ounces tomato juice

Prepare the glass. Pour all of the ingredients into a shaker two-thirds full of ice cubes. Shake well. Strain into the salt-rimmed, ice-filled Highball glass.

Rosebud

"'Rosebud.' The most famous word in the history of cinema. It explains everything, and nothing. Who, for that matter, actually heard Charles Foster Kane say it before he died?" — Roger Ebert

>   2 ounces red or pink grapefruit juice
>   2 ounces citrus vodka
> ^{1}/$_2$ ounce triple sec
>   1 ounce lime juice cordial, such as Rose's

Pour the grapefruit juice into an ice-filled Collins glass. Pour the vodka, triple sec, and lime juice cordial into a shaker two-thirds full of ice. Shake well. Strain into the Collins glass so the mixture floats on the grapefruit juice.

Royal Champagne Cocktail

$1/2$ ounce brandy

5 ounces champagne or other sparkling wine

Orange twist, for garnish

Pour the brandy and champagne into a Champagne Flute. Add the twist.

Royal Mimosa

$1/4$ ounce brandy

$1/4$ ounce Grand Marnier

1 ounce orange juice

4 ounces champagne or other sparkling wine

Orange wheel, for garnish

Pour the brandy, Grand Marnier, orange juice, and champagne into a Champagne Flute. Stir briefly. Add the orange wheel.

Ruby Martini

A gem of a cocktail.

$2^1/2$ ounces gin

$1/4$ ounce dry vermouth

$1/4$ ounce cherry brandy

Pour all of the ingredients into a mixing glass two-thirds full of ice cubes. Stir well. Strain into a chilled Cocktail glass.

Rum Cobbler

$2^1/2$ ounces dark rum

$1/2$ ounce simple syrup (page 33)

Fresh fruit in season, for garnish

Pour the rum and simple syrup into a wine goblet filled with crushed ice. Stir briefly. Add the garnish of choice.

Rum Collins

2 ounces dark rum

$1/2$ ounce fresh lemon juice

$^1/_2$ ounce simple syrup (page 33)

5 to 6 ounces club soda

Fresh fruit in season, for garnish

Pour the rum, lemon juice, and simple syrup into a shaker two-thirds full of ice cubes. Shake well. Strain into an ice-filled Collins glass. Add the club soda; stir briefly. Add the garnish of choice.

Rum Cooler

2 $^1/_2$ ounces dark rum

6 to 7 ounces ginger ale

Lemon twist, for garnish

Pour the rum and ginger ale into an ice-filled Collins glass. Stir briefly. Add the twist.

Rum Crusta

Lemon wedge and superfine sugar, for rimming the glass

Lemon peel spiral (see technique, page 38)

2 ounces dark rum

$^1/_2$ ounce curaçao

$^1/_2$ ounce fresh lemon juice

Rim a Sour glass using the lemon wedge and sugar. Place the lemon peel spiral into the glass so that it almost lines the entire interior. Pour the rum, curaçao, and lemon juice into a shaker two-thirds full of crushed ice. Shake well; strain into the glass.

Rum Daisy

2 $^1/_2$ ounces light rum

1 ounce fresh lemon juice

$^1/_2$ ounce grenadine

Lemon twist, for garnish

Pour the rum, lemon juice, and grenadine into a shaker two-thirds full of ice cubes. Shake well. Strain into a crushed ice–filled Highball glass. Add the twist.

Rum Fix

2 1/2 ounces light rum

1 ounce fresh lemon juice

1/2 ounce pineapple juice

Fresh fruit in season, for garnish

Pour the rum, lemon juice, and pineapple juice into a shaker two-thirds full of ice cubes. Shake well. Strain into a crushed ice–filled Highball glass. Add the garnish of choice.

Rum Fizz

This drink can be made with lemon juice instead of lime juice if you so desire.

2 ounces dark rum

1 ounce fresh lime juice

1/2 ounce simple syrup (page 33)

5 to 6 ounces club soda

Fresh fruit in season, for garnish

Pour the rum, lime juice, and simple syrup into a shaker two-thirds full of ice cubes. Shake well. Strain into a chilled wine goblet. Add the club soda; stir briefly. Add the garnish of choice.

Rum Julep

1 ounce simple syrup (page 33)

3 ounces dark rum

3 large mint sprigs, for garnish

Pour the simple syrup into a crushed ice–filled Julep Cup; stir well. Add the rum; stir until a film of ice forms on the exterior of the Julep Cup. Add the mint garnish.

Rum Rickey

2 1/2 ounces light rum

1 ounce fresh lime juice

5 to 6 ounces club soda

Lime wedge, for garnish

Pour the rum and lime juice into an ice-filled Highball glass. Add the club soda; stir briefly. Add the lime wedge.

Rum Runner

2 ounces Bacardi 151-proof rum

1 $^1/_2$ ounces blackberry brandy

1 ounce crème de banane

$^1/_2$ ounce fresh lime juice

Splash of grenadine

Lime wedge, for garnish

Pour the rum, brandy, crème de banane, lime juice, and grenadine into a blender. Add 4 to 6 ice cubes; blend until frozen. Pour into a wine goblet. Add the lime wedge.

Rum Sangaree

2 ounces dark rum

$^1/_2$ ounce ruby port

$^1/_2$ ounce triple sec

Freshly grated nutmeg, for garnish

Pour the rum, port, and triple sec into a mixing glass two-thirds full of ice cubes; stir well. Strain into a crushed ice–filled wine goblet. Sprinkle with the nutmeg.

Rum Sling

2 $^1/_2$ ounces light rum

$^1/_2$ ounce simple syrup (page 33)

$^1/_2$ ounce fresh lemon juice

5 to 6 ounces club soda

Lemon wedge, for garnish

Pour the rum, simple syrup, and lemon juice into a shaker two-thirds full of ice cubes; shake well. Strain into an ice-filled Collins glass. Add the club soda; stir briefly. Add the lemon wedge.

Rum Sour

2 ounces light rum

3/4 ounce fresh lemon juice

1/2 ounce simple syrup (page 33)

Orange wheel and maraschino cherry, for garnishes

Pour the rum, lemon juice, and simple syrup into a shaker two-thirds full of ice cubes; shake well. Strain into a chilled Sour glass. Add the garnishes.

Rum Swizzle

2 ounces dark rum

1/2 ounce fresh lemon juice

1/2 ounce triple sec

5 to 6 ounces ginger ale

Lemon wheel, for garnish

Pour the rum, lemon juice, and triple sec into a shaker two-thirds full of ice cubes; shake well. Strain into an ice-filled Collins glass. Add the ginger ale; stir briefly. Add the lemon wheel and a swizzle stick.

Russian Quaalude

This drink caught on in the late 1980s.

1 ounce vodka

1 ounce Baileys Irish cream liqueur

1 ounce Frangelico

Pour all of the ingredients into a shaker two-thirds full of ice cubes. Shake well. Strain into a Pony glass. It's also good sipped from an ice-filled Rocks glass.

Russian Walnut Martini

—*Adapted from 2087 An American Bistro, Thousand Oaks, California.*

2 ounces Stolichnaya vodka

1 ounce Nocello Walnut liqueur

1/2 ounce dark crème de cacao

Pour all of the ingredients into a mixing glass two-thirds full of ice cubes. Stir well. Strain into a chilled Cocktail glass.

Rusty Nail

"The latest [cocktail made with a liqueur], the Rusty Nail, is also one of the most mellow—a simple libation of Scotch on the rocks with a float of Drambuie."
—Thomas Mario, *Playboy*, April 1968

2 ounces scotch

1/2 ounce Drambuie

Lemon twist, for garnish

Pour the scotch and Drambuie into an ice-filled Rocks glass. Stir briefly. Add the twist.

Rye & Ginger

Though this drink is usually built with blended Canadian whisky, it really should contain straight rye whiskey.

2 1/2 ounces rye whiskey

4 ounces ginger ale

Build in an ice-filled Highball glass. Stir briefly.

Safe Sex on the Beach ⊘

3 ounces cranberry juice

3 ounces grapefruit juice

2 ounces peach nectar

Build in an ice-filled Collins glass. Stir.

Saketini

2 1/2 ounces gin or vodka

1/4 ounce saké

Anchovy-stuffed olive

Pour the gin or vodka and saké into a mixing glass two-thirds full of ice cubes. Stir well. Strain into a chilled Cocktail glass. Garnish with the olive.

Salt & Pepper Martini

Salt and a lime wedge, for rimming the glass

2 ^{1}/$_2$ ounces pepper vodka

^{1}/$_4$ ounce dry vermouth

Pinch of salt

Prepare the glass. Pour the vodka and vermouth into a mixing glass two-thirds full of ice cubes. Add a pinch of salt. Stir well. Strain into the salt-rimmed Cocktail glass.

Salty Chihuahua

Inspired by the Salty Dog, this one is especially for small-dog lovers.

Salt and a lime wedge, for rimming the glass

2 ^{1}/$_2$ ounces tequila

4 ounces grapefruit juice

Prepare the glass. Pour both ingredients into the ice-filled, prepared Highball glass. Stir briefly.

Salty Dog

If you don't salt the rim of the glass, it's a Greyhound.

Salt and a lime wedge, for rimming the glass

2 ^{1}/$_2$ ounces vodka

4 ounces grapefruit juice

Prepare the glass. Pour both ingredients into the ice-filled, salt-rimmed Highball glass. Stir briefly.

San Francisco Cocktail

1 ^{1}/$_2$ ounces sloe gin

^{1}/$_2$ ounce sweet vermouth

^{1}/$_2$ ounce dry vermouth

2 dashes of Angostura bitters

Pour all of the ingredients into a mixing glass two-thirds full of ice cubes. Stir well. Strain into a chilled Cocktail glass.

Sangria

Usually made with red wine, the name of this punch probably comes from the Spanish *sangre*, meaning "blood."

MAKES ABOUT 14 SIX-OUNCE SERVINGS

1 1/2 750-ml bottles dry red wine

1/2 750-ml bottle white wine

6 ounces brandy

6 ounces triple sec

6 ounces simple syrup (page 33)

6 ounces fresh orange juice

6 ounces cranberry juice

Diced apples and pears plus orange and lemon wheels, for garnishes

Pour all of the liquids into a large bowl; stir well. Cover and refrigerate until chilled, at least 4 hours. Pour the sangria into a large pitcher. Add the garnishes and stir to mix in.

Satan's Whiskers

1/2 ounce gin

1/2 ounce dry vermouth

1/2 ounce sweet vermouth

1/2 ounce Grand Marnier

1/2 ounce fresh orange juice

Dash of orange bitters

Pour all of the ingredients into a shaker two-thirds full of ice cubes. Shake well. Strain into a chilled Cocktail glass or an ice-filled Rocks glass.

Sazerac

The Sazerac was created in New Orleans in the mid-1800s and originally contained brandy as a base liquor. Rye whiskey became the base later in that century, and bourbon replaced rye, probably right after Prohibition.

Dash of absinthe substitute, such as Absente, Pernod, Herbsaint, or Ricard

2 ounces bourbon

$^1/_2$ ounce simple syrup (page 33)

2 dashes of Peychaud bitters

Lemon twist, for garnish

Coat the interior of a Rocks glass with the absinthe substitute. Fill the glass with crushed ice. Pour the bourbon, simple syrup, and bitters into a mixing glass two-thirds full of ice cubes. Stir well. Strain into the glass. Add the twist.

Schnapp, Crackle, & Pop

1 ounce Van Gogh Wild Appel vodka

$^1/_2$ ounce cinnamon schnapps

4 to 5 ounces champagne or other sparkling wine

Pour all of the ingredients into a chilled Champagne Flute.

Schnapp It Up Punch

MAKES ABOUT 8 EIGHT-OUNCE SERVINGS

8 ounces peach schnapps

8 ounces wildberry schnapps

8 ounces vodka

32 ounces cranberry juice

Combine all of the ingredients in a punch bowl. Add ice cubes and stir to chill.

Scofflaw Cocktail

A French creation from the 1920s when "scofflaw" was a brand-new word.

> 2 ounces dry vermouth
>
> 1 ounce fresh lemon juice
>
> $^1/_2$ ounce grenadine
>
> Dash of orange bitters or triple sec

Pour all of the ingredients into a shaker two-thirds full of ice cubes. Shake well. Strain into a chilled Cocktail glass or an ice-filled Rocks glass.

Scorpion

Can you say, "Tiki Bar"?

> 2 ounces dark rum
>
> $^1/_2$ ounce brandy
>
> $^1/_2$ ounce dry vermouth
>
> $^1/_4$ ounce gin
>
> 1 ounce orange juice
>
> 1 ounce fresh lemon juice
>
> Dash of orgeat syrup
>
> Mint sprig, for garnish

Pour all of the liquids into a shaker two-thirds full of ice cubes. Shake well. Strain into a large, ice-filled wine goblet. Add the mint sprig.

Scotch and Soda

> 2 $^1/_2$ ounces scotch
>
> 5 ounces club soda

Build in an ice-filled Highball glass; stir briefly.

Scotch & Ginger Ale

> 2 $^1/_2$ ounces scotch
>
> 5 ounces ginger ale

Build in an ice-filled Highball glass; stir briefly.

Scotch Buck

1 lemon wedge

2 ounces scotch

5 ounces ginger ale

Squeeze the lemon wedge into a Highball glass and drop it into the glass. Fill the glass with ice cubes. Add the scotch and ginger ale. Stir briefly.

Scotch Cobbler

2 ^{1}/$_2$ ounces scotch

^{1}/$_2$ ounce simple syrup (page 33)

Fresh fruit in season, for garnish

Pour the scotch and simple syrup into a wine goblet filled with crushed ice. Stir briefly. Add the garnish of choice.

Scotch Cooler

2 ^{1}/$_2$ ounces scotch

6 to 7 ounces ginger ale

Lemon twist, for garnish

Pour the scotch and ginger ale into an ice-filled Collins glass. Stir briefly. Add the twist.

Scotch Fizz

2 ounces scotch

1 ounce fresh lemon juice

^{1}/$_2$ ounce simple syrup (page 33)

5 to 6 ounces club soda

Fresh fruit in season, for garnish

Pour the scotch, lemon juice, and simple syrup into a shaker two-thirds full of ice cubes. Shake well. Strain into a chilled wine goblet. Add the club soda; stir briefly. Add the garnish of choice.

Scotch Mist

This drink is in the style of a Frappé, although most drinks in that category contain just one ingredient.

2 ounces scotch

$^1/_2$ ounce Drambuie

Fill a Sour glass with crushed ice; add the scotch and Drambuie.

Scotch Nut

2 ounces scotch

$^1/_2$ ounce amaretto

Pour both ingredients into a mixing glass two-thirds full of ice cubes. Stir well. Strain into a chilled Cocktail glass.

Scotch Old-Fashioned

3 dashes of Angostura bitters

1 orange slice

1 lemon wedge

1 maraschino cherry

1 sugar cube

2 $^1/_2$ ounces scotch

In a Double Old-Fashioned glass, muddle the bitters, orange slice, lemon wedge, and maraschino cherry into the sugar cube. Fill the glass with ice cubes. Add the scotch; stir well.

Scotch Sling

2 $^1/_2$ ounces scotch

$^1/_2$ ounce apricot brandy

$^1/_2$ ounce fresh lemon juice

5 to 6 ounces club soda

Lemon wedge, for garnish

Pour the scotch, apricot brandy, and lemon juice into a shaker two-thirds full of ice cubes; shake well. Strain the drink into an ice-filled Collins glass. Add the club soda; stir briefly. Add the lemon wedge.

Scotch Smash

6 fresh mint leaves
3/4 ounce simple syrup (page 33)
2 1/2 ounces scotch
Mint sprig, for garnish

Place the mint leaves in the bottom of a large Rocks glass; add the simple syrup and muddle well. Fill the glass with crushed ice. Add the scotch; stir briefly. Add the mint garnish.

Scotch Sour

2 ounces scotch
3/4 ounce fresh lemon juice
1/2 ounce simple syrup (page 33)
Orange wheel and a maraschino cherry, for garnishes

Pour the scotch, lemon juice, and simple syrup into a shaker two-thirds full of ice cubes; shake well. Strain the drink into a chilled Sour glass. Add the garnishes.

Scotch Stinger

2 ounces scotch
1/2 ounce white crème de menthe

Pour both ingredients into a shaker two-thirds full of ice cubes. Shake well. Strain into a crushed ice–filled wine goblet.

Scotch Swizzle

2 ounces scotch
1/2 ounce fresh lemon juice
1/2 ounce triple sec
5 to 6 ounces ginger ale
Lemon wheel, for garnish

Pour the scotch, lemon juice, and triple sec into a shaker two-thirds full of ice cubes; shake well. Strain the mixture into an ice-filled Collins glass. Add the ginger ale; stir briefly. Add the lemon wheel and a swizzle stick.

Scottish Sidecar

Please note: no sugar rim on this Sidecar.

> 2 $^1/_2$ ounces scotch
> $^1/_2$ ounce triple sec
> 1 ounce orange juice

Pour all of the ingredients into a shaker two-thirds full of ice cubes. Shake well. Strain into a chilled Cocktail glass.

Screaming Banana Banshee

> $^1/_2$ ounce crème de banane
> $^1/_2$ ounce vodka
> $^1/_2$ ounce white crème de cacao
> 1 $^1/_2$ ounces heavy cream

Pour all of the ingredients into a shaker two-thirds full of ice cubes. Shake well. Strain into a chilled Cocktail glass.

Screwdriver

Garnish with a screwdriver.

> 2 $^1/_2$ ounces vodka
> 4 ounces orange juice

Build in an ice-filled Highball glass; stir briefly.

Seabreeze

> 2 ounces vodka
> 2 ounces grapefruit juice
> 1 $^1/_2$ ounces cranberry juice
> Lime wedge, for garnish

Pour the vodka and both juices into an ice-filled Highball glass. Stir briefly. Add the lime wedge.

S

Seelbach Cocktail

Created at Louisville's Seelbach Hotel in Kentucky, around 1917, when a bartender reportedly spilled champagne into a Manhattan Cocktail.

 1 ounce bourbon

 1/2 ounce triple sec

 7 dashes of Angostura bitters

 7 dashes of Peychaud's bitters

 Chilled champagne

 Orange twist, for garnish

Build in a Champagne Flute. Add the garnish.

7 & 7

 2 1/2 ounces Seagram's 7 whiskey

 4 ounces 7 UP

 Lemon twist, for garnish

Pour the whiskey and 7 UP into an ice-filled Highball glass. Stir briefly. Add the twist.

Sex on the Beach

Peach schnapps, OJ, CJ, vodka, and Sex on the Beach—yum.

 2 ounces vodka

 1 ounce peach schnapps

 2 ounces orange juice

 1 1/2 ounces cranberry juice

Build in an ice-filled Highball glass; stir briefly.

Sex with the Bartender Martini

Enough said.

 3/4 ounce Bacardi Limón rum

 3/4 ounce triple sec

 3/4 ounce fresh lime juice

 1/2 ounce grenadine

Pour all of the ingredients into a shaker two-thirds full of ice cubes. Shake well. Strain into a chilled Cocktail glass.

Shagadelic Shooter

—Adapted from 2087 An American Bistro, Thousand Oaks, California.

> **2 ounces white tequila**
> **$^1/_2$ ounce blue curaçao**
> **$^1/_2$ ounce fresh lemon juice**
> **Maraschino cherry, for garnish**

Pour the tequila, curaçao, and lemon juice into a shaker two-thirds full of ice cubes. Shake well. Strain into a Pony glass. Garnish with the cherry.

Shandy Gaff

A drink that dates back to at least the 1880s.

> **8 ounces lemon-lime soda**
> **8 ounces amber ale**

Carefully pour the soda and ale into a 16-ounce beer glass.

Shark Bite

Shades of *Jaws*.

> **$^3/_4$ ounce spiced rum, such as Captain Morgan's**
> **$^3/_4$ ounce light rum**
> **$^1/_2$ ounce blue curaçao**
> **1 ounce fresh lime juice**
> **$^1/_2$ ounce simple syrup (page 33)**
> **3 drops of grenadine, for garnish**

Pour the rums, curaçao, lime juice, and simple syrup into a shaker two-thirds full of ice cubes. Shake well. Strain into a chilled Cocktail glass. Garnish with the drops of grenadine.

Sherry Sangaree

2 ounces dry sherry

$^1/_2$ ounce simple syrup (page 33)

Freshly grated nutmeg, for garnish

Pour the sherry and simple syrup into a mixing glass two-thirds full of ice cubes; stir well. Strain into a chilled wine goblet. Sprinkle with the nutmeg.

Shirley Temple ⊕

Shirley Temple made almost 50 movies between 1932 and 1943. In the late 1960s, she ran for Congress, and although she lost the election, as Shirley Temple Black she went on to have a successful career with the United Nations and the State Department.

1 ounce orange juice

$^1/_2$ ounce fresh lemon juice

Splash of fresh lime juice

6 ounces lemon-lime soda

Dash of grenadine

Maraschino cherry, for garnish

Pour the citrus juices into a shaker two-thirds full of ice cubes. Shake well. Strain into an ice-filled Collins glass. Add the soda and the grenadine; stir briefly. Add the cherry.

Sidecar 🍸

Reportedly created in Paris during World War I, this classic cocktail was named for a customer at the bar where it was invented, who was driven to and from the bar in the sidecar of a motorcycle.

Superfine sugar and a lemon wedge, for rimming the glass

2 ounces cognac or brandy

$^1/_2$ ounce Cointreau

$^1/_2$ ounce fresh lemon juice

Prepare the glass. Pour all of the ingredients into a shaker two-thirds full of ice cubes. Shake well. Strain into the sugar-rimmed Cocktail glass.

Silver Bullet

There are many different versions of the Silver Bullet, although gin seems to be the base for all of them. This scotch-laced formula dates back to the early 1960s.

> $2^1/_2$ ounces gin
>
> 2 dashes of scotch
>
> Lemon twist, for garnish

Pour the gin and scotch into a mixing glass two-thirds full of ice cubes. Stir well. Strain into a chilled Cocktail glass. Add the twist.

Singapore Sling #1

Created at the Raffles Hotel in Singapore, circa 1915, there are many versions of the Singapore Sling, but the original formula seems to be lost to history. This recipe is one that's commonly used in American bars, and the one that follows is based on the formula used today at the Raffles Hotel.

> 2 ounces gin
>
> $^1/_2$ ounce Bénédictine
>
> $^1/_2$ ounce cherry brandy
>
> 1 ounce fresh lemon juice
>
> $^1/_2$ ounce simple syrup (page 33)
>
> 2 to 3 ounces club soda
>
> Lemon twist, for garnish

Pour the gin, Bénédictine, cherry brandy, lemon juice, and simple syrup into a shaker two-thirds full of ice cubes. Shake well. Strain into an ice-filled Collins glass. Pour in the club soda. Add the twist.

Singapore Sling #2

2 ounces gin

$^1/_2$ ounce Bénédictine

$^1/_2$ ounce triple sec

1 ounce cherry brandy

3 ounces pineapple juice

1 ounce fresh lime juice

2 dashes of Angostura bitters

Club soda

Pour the gin, Bénédictine, triple sec, cherry brandy, pineapple and lime juices, and the bitters into a shaker two-thirds full of ice cubes. Shake well. Strain into an ice-filled Collins glass. Pour in the club soda to taste. Garnish at will.

Singapore Sling #3

This version of the Singapore Sling works well for people who don't like the medicinal notes of Bénédictine.

2 $^1/_2$ ounces gin

1 ounce cherry brandy

$^1/_2$ ounce lemon juice

$^1/_2$ ounce simple syrup (page 33)

1 to 2 dashes of Angostura bitters

Club soda

Pour the gin, cherry brandy, lemon juice, simple syrup, and bitters into a shaker two-thirds full of ice cubes. Shake well. Strain into an ice-filled Collins glass. Top with the club soda. Garnish at will.

Single Malt Scotch Martini

—*Created by master bartender Norman Bukofzer, New York City.*

3 ounces single malt scotch

$^1/_2$ ounce fino sherry

Lemon twist, for garnish

Pour the scotch and sherry into a mixing glass two-thirds full of ice cubes. Stir well. Strain into a chilled Cocktail glass. Add the twist.

Skyy Diver Martini

—From the Cruise Room in the Oxford Hotel, Denver, Colorado.

3 ounces Skyy vodka

Splash of Rumpleminz peppermint schnapps

Pour both ingredients into a mixing glass two-thirds full of ice cubes. Stir well. Strain into a chilled Cocktail glass.

Slippery Nipple

^{1}/$_2$ ounce Baileys Irish cream liqueur

^{1}/$_2$ ounce Kahlúa

^{1}/$_2$ ounce butterscotch schnapps

Layer in order in a Pony glass.

Sloe Comfortable Screw

The simple version.

^{3}/$_4$ ounce sloe gin

^{3}/$_4$ ounce Southern Comfort

^{3}/$_4$ ounce vodka

3 to 5 ounces orange juice

Pour all of the ingredients into a shaker two-thirds full of ice cubes. Shake well. Strain into an ice-filled Highball glass.

Sloe Comfortable Screw Against the Wall with Satin Pillows

The party version.

^{1}/$_2$ ounce sloe gin

^{1}/$_2$ ounce Southern Comfort

^{1}/$_2$ ounce vodka

^{1}/$_2$ ounce Galliano

^{1}/$_2$ ounce Frangelico

3 to 5 ounces orange juice

Pour all of the ingredients into a shaker two-thirds full of ice cubes. Shake well. Strain into an ice-filled Highball glass.

Sloe Gin Fizz

What everybody used to order the minute they reached legal drinking age.

> 2 ounces sloe gin
>
> 1 ounce fresh lemon juice
>
> $1/2$ ounce simple syrup (page 33)
>
> 5 to 6 ounces club soda
>
> Fresh fruit in season, for garnish

Pour the sloe gin, lemon juice, and simple syrup into a shaker two-thirds full of ice cubes. Shake well. Strain into a chilled wine goblet. Add the club soda; stir briefly. Add the garnish of choice.

Sloe Gin Rickey

> 2 ounces sloe gin
>
> 1 ounce fresh lime juice
>
> 5 to 6 ounces club soda
>
> Lime wedge, for garnish

Pour the sloe gin and lime juice into an ice-filled Highball glass. Add the club soda, stir briefly. Add the lime wedge.

Smurf Piss

Don't ask.

> $1/2$ ounce light rum
>
> $1/2$ ounce blueberry schnapps
>
> $1/2$ ounce blue curaçao
>
> $1/2$ ounce fresh lemon juice
>
> Lemon-lime soda

Pour the rum, schnapps, curaçao, and lemon juice into a shaker two-thirds full of ice cubes. Shake well. Strain into an ice-filled Highball glass. Top with the soda. Stir with a sip-stick.

Snake Bite #1

This drink is very popular in the U.K., and it really packs a punch.

8 ounces hard cider

8 ounces amber ale

Carefully pour the cider and ale into a 16-ounce beer glass.

Snake Bite #2

8 ounces hard cider

8 ounces brown ale

Carefully pour the cider and ale into a 16-ounce beer glass.

Snake Bite #3

This version of the Snake Bite is American, and made its debut in the early 1970s.

2 ounces blended Canadian whisky

$^1/_2$ ounce white crème de menthe

Pour both ingredients into a mixing glass two-thirds full of ice cubes. Stir well. Strain into a chilled Pony glass.

Snickertini Martini

$1^1/_2$ ounces Van Gogh Dutch Chocolate vodka

$^3/_4$ ounce Frangelico

$^3/_4$ ounce Godiva chocolate liqueur

Orange wheel, for garnish

Pour all of the ingredients into a shaker two-thirds full of ice cubes. Shake well. Strain into a chilled Cocktail glass. Garnish with the orange wheel.

Sol y Sombre

The Sol y Sombre is a Spanish creation—play with the ratios to vary the level of sweetness.

$1^1/_2$ ounces brandy

$1^1/_2$ ounce anisette

Pour both ingredients into a mixing glass two-thirds full of ice cubes. Stir well. Strain into a snifter.

Sombrero

>2 ounces Kahlúa
>
>1 1/2 ounces light cream

Pour both ingredients into a shaker two-thirds full of ice cubes. Shake well. Strain into an ice-filled Rocks glass.

Soul Kiss Cocktail

The Soul Kiss Cocktail was served at London's Savoy Hotel in the 1920s, where they also had a variation on the drink that contained no whisky.

>2 ounces blended Canadian whisky
>
>1/4 ounce dry vermouth
>
>1/4 ounce Dubonnet Rouge
>
>1/2 ounce orange juice

Pour all of the ingredients into a shaker two-thirds full of ice cubes. Shake well. Strain into a chilled Cocktail glass.

South Beach Martini

Deco, palm trees, hot sand, yes.

>1 1/2 ounces orange vodka
>
>1 1/2 ounces citrus vodka
>
>1/2 ounce Cointreau
>
>1/2 ounce fresh lime juice
>
>Orange twist, for garnish

Pour the orange and citrus vodkas, the Cointreau, and lime juice into a shaker two-thirds full of ice cubes. Shake well. Strain into a chilled Cocktail glass. Garnish with the orange twist.

Southern Comfort Manhattan

This drink is a fairly sweet variation on the Manhattan— it was very popular in the late 1970s.

>2 1/2 ounces Southern Comfort
>
>1/2 ounce sweet vermouth
>
>2 dashes of Angostura bitters
>
>Maraschino cherry, for garnish

Pour the Southern Comfort, vermouth, and bitters into a mixing glass two-thirds full of ice cubes. Stir well. Strain into a chilled Cocktail glass. Add the cherry.

Southern Comfort Sidecar

Superfine sugar and a lemon wedge, for rimming the glass

2 ounces Southern Comfort

$1/4$ ounce triple sec

$1/2$ ounce fresh lemon juice

Prepare the glass. Pour all of the ingredients into a shaker two-thirds full of ice cubes. Shake well. Strain into a the sugar-rimmed Cocktail glass.

Southern Comfort Sour

2 ounces Southern Comfort

$3/4$ ounce fresh lemon juice

Orange wheel and a maraschino cherry, for garnishes

Pour the Southern Comfort and lemon juice into a shaker two-thirds full of ice cubes; shake well. Strain the drink into a chilled Sour glass. Add the garnishes.

Southern Godfather

$2 1/2$ ounces bourbon

$1/4$ ounce amaretto

$1/4$ ounce Southern Comfort

Build in an ice-filled Rocks glass; stir briefly.

Southern Screw

2 ounces vodka

2 ounces Southern Comfort

6 ounces orange juice

Build in an ice-filled Collins glass. Stir to distribute.

Southside Cocktail

The Southside has been around for decades, but it has made quite a comeback in recent years.

> 2 ounces gin
>
> 1 ounce fresh lemon juice
>
> $^1/_2$ ounce simple syrup (page 33)
>
> 2 mint sprigs, for garnish

Pour the gin, lemon juice, and simple syrup into a shaker two-thirds full of ice cubes. Shake well. Strain into a chilled Cocktail glass. Add the mint sprigs.

Spiced Cider

Spike individual servings at will.

MAKES ABOUT **8** SIX-OUNCE SERVINGS

> 1 quart unsweetened apple cider
>
> 4 whole cloves
>
> 1 cinnamon stick (about 3 inches long), broken
>
> $^1/_2$ teaspoon freshly grated nutmeg
>
> 12 ounces pear nectar
>
> 1 large block of ice
>
> Apple and pear slices, for garnishes

Pour the apple cider into a large saucepan set over high heat. Add the cloves, cinnamon, and nutmeg and bring the mixture to a boil. Reduce the heat to low, cover, and simmer for 20 minutes.

Strain the mixture through a sieve lined with a double layer of dampened cheesecloth; discard the solids. Set aside to cool to room temperature. Pour in the pear nectar. Cover and refrigerate until chilled.

Place the block of ice into a punch bowl. Add the chilled punch. Add the garnishes.

Spiced Cranberry-Citrus Punch

- 1 quart cranberry juice
- 16 ounces orange juice
- 16 ounces tangerine juice
- 5 whole cloves
- 2 cinnamon sticks (each about 3 inches long), broken
- 1 teaspoon freshly grated nutmeg
- 1 large block of ice, for serving
- Mandarin orange segments, for garnish

Pour the juices into a large saucepan set over high heat. Add the cloves, cinnamon sticks, and nutmeg and bring the mixture to a boil. Reduce the heat to low, cover, and simmer for 20 minutes.

Strain the mixture through a sieve lined with a double layer of dampened cheesecloth; discard the solids. Set aside to cool to room temperature. Cover and refrigerate until chilled.

Place the block of ice into a punch bowl. Add the chilled punch. Add the garnishes.

> "Cider was very cheap; but a few shillings a barrel. It was supplied in large amounts to students at college, and even very little children drank it. President John Adams was an early and earnest wisher for temperance reform; but to the end of his life he drank a large tankard of hard cider every morning when he first got up. It was free in every farmhouse to all travelers and tramps."
> —Home Life in Colonial Days, *by Alice Morse Earle, 1898*

Spiced Hard Cider–Pear Punch

MAKES ABOUT 8 SIX-OUNCE SERVINGS

> 5 whole cloves
>
> 2 cinnamon sticks (each about 3 inches long), broken
>
> 1 teaspoon freshly grated nutmeg
>
> 8 ounces hot water
>
> 1 quart hard cider
>
> 4 ounces applejack
>
> 4 ounces brandy
>
> 4 ounces pear brandy
>
> 1 large block of ice, for serving
>
> Apple and pear slices, for garnishes

Place the cloves, cinnamon sticks, nutmeg, and hot water in a glass bowl, cover, and microwave on high for 2 minutes. Set aside to cool to room temperature.

Strain the mixture through a sieve lined with a double layer of dampened cheesecloth; discard the solids.

Pour in the cider, applejack, and both brandies; stir well. Cover and refrigerate until chilled.

Place the block of ice into a punch bowl. Add the chilled punch. Add the garnishes.

Spiced Rum & Chocolate Martini

> 2 ounces Captain Morgan's spiced rum
>
> $^1/_2$ ounce Godiva chocolate liqueur
>
> Maraschino cherry, for garnish

Pour the rum and chocolate liqueur into a mixing glass two-thirds full of ice cubes. Stir well. Strain into a chilled Cocktail glass. Add the cherry.

Spiced Rum Daiquiri

2 ounces spiced rum, such as Captain Morgan's

1 ounce fresh lime juice

$^1/_2$ ounce simple syrup (page 33)

Lime wedge, for garnish

Pour the rum, lime juice, and simple syrup into a shaker two-thirds full of ice cubes. Shake well. Strain into a crushed ice–filled Rocks glass. Add the lime wedge.

Spiced Rum Piña Colada

2 ounces spiced rum, such as Captain Morgan's

6 ounces pineapple juice

$1^1/_2$ ounces coconut cream, such as Coco Lopez

Pineapple spear, for garnish

Pour the rum, pineapple juice, and coconut cream into a shaker two-thirds full of ice cubes. Shake well. Strain into an ice-filled wine goblet. Add the pineapple spear.

Spiced Tea-for-Ten Punch

MAKES 10 SERVINGS

1 teaspoon grated fresh ginger

$^1/_2$ teaspoon ground allspice

6 ounces orange juice

8 ounces hot water

24 ounces brewed strong, hot tea

10 orange twists, for garnish

Combine the ginger, allspice, orange juice, and hot water in a glass bowl, cover, and microwave on high for 2 minutes. Set aside to steep for 10 minutes.

Strain the mixture through a sieve lined with a double layer of dampened cheesecloth; discard the solids. Pour about 1 ounce of the orange juice mixture into each teacup. Add the hot tea and an orange twist to each.

Spicy Martini

This is a very spicy potion, indeed—you can use less Tabasco if you wish.

> **3 ounces gin**
>
> **³/₄ ounce dry vermouth**
>
> **15 drops of Tabasco sauce**

Pour all of the ingredients into a mixing glass two-thirds full of ice cubes. Stir well. Strain into a chilled Cocktail glass.

Spiked Tea Punch ☕

MAKES 10 TO 12 SIX-OUNCE SERVINGS

> **5 whole cloves**
>
> **2 star anise**
>
> **3 cinnamon sticks (each about 3 inches long), broken**
>
> **1 teaspoon freshly grated nutmeg**
>
> **1 teaspoon grated fresh ginger**
>
> **8 ounces hot water**
>
> **1 quart strong tea, chilled**
>
> **4 ounces Drambuie**
>
> **4 ounces scotch**
>
> **4 ounces Original Canton Delicate Ginger liqueur**
>
> **1 large block of ice**

Combine the cloves, star anise, cinnamon sticks, nutmeg, ginger, and hot water in a glass bowl. Cover and microwave on high for 2 minutes. Set aside to cool to room temperature.

Strain the mixture through a sieve lined with a double layer of dampened cheesecloth; discard the solids.

Pour in the tea, Drambuie, scotch, and ginger liqueur; stir well. Cover and refrigerate until chilled.

Place the block of ice into a punch bowl. Add the chilled punch.

Starlight

—Created by Tony Abou-Ganim, Bellagio, Las Vegas, Nevada.

> 1 ¹/₄ ounces Campari
>
> ¹/₄ ounce Cointreau
>
> ¹/₂ ounce fresh lemon juice
>
> ¹/₂ ounce orange juice
>
> ¹/₄ ounce simple syrup (page 33)
>
> Club soda
>
> ¹/₂ ounce brandy
>
> Lemon wheel and a lime wheel, for garnishes

Pour the Campari, Cointreau, lemon juice, orange juice, and simple syrup into a shaker two-thirds full of ice cubes. Shake well. Strain into a Collins glass half-filled with ice. Add club soda to almost fill the glass; float the brandy on top. Garnish with the citrus wheels.

Stiletto

The flavors in this cocktail come together beautifully.
This drink can also be served over ice in a Rocks glass.

> 2 ¹/₂ ounces bourbon
>
> ¹/₄ ounce amaretto
>
> ¹/₄ ounce fresh lime juice

Pour all of the ingredients into a shaker two-thirds full of ice cubes. Shake well. Strain into a chilled Cocktail glass.

Stinger

This is the one drink that's traditionally shaken, even though it contains no dairy products or fruit juices.

> 2 ¹/₂ ounces brandy
>
> ¹/₂ ounce white crème de menthe

Pour both ingredients into a shaker two-thirds full of ice cubes. Shake well. Strain into a crushed ice–filled wine goblet.

Stirrup Cup

1 ounce brandy

1 ounce cherry brandy

$3/4$ ounce fresh lime juice

$1/2$ ounce simple syrup (page 33)

Pour all of the ingredients into a shaker two-thirds full of ice cubes. Shake well. Strain into an ice-filled Rocks glass.

Stout Sangaree

The classic Sangaree.

10 ounces stout

2 ounces ruby port

Freshly grated nutmeg, for garnish

Pour the stout and port into a large wine goblet; sprinkle with the nutmeg.

Strawberries & Cream Cocktail

$1^1/2$ ounces Baileys Irish cream liqueur

$1^1/2$ ounces Stolichnaya Strasberi vodka

Pour both ingredients into a shaker two-thirds full of ice cubes. Shake well. Strain into an ice-filled Rocks glass.

Suffering Bastard

1 ounce gin

1 ounce light rum

$1/2$ ounce lemon juice

Dash of Angostura bitters

1 ounce ginger ale

Build in an ice-filled Highball glass. Stir with a sip-stick.

Summer Martini

2 $^1/_2$ ounces Stolichnaya Kafya vodka

$^1/_4$ ounce Stolichnaya Razberi vodka

Fresh raspberry, for garnish

Pour both vodkas into a mixing glass two-thirds full of ice cubes. Stir well. Strain into a chilled Cocktail glass. Add the raspberry.

Sunsplash

—*Created by Tony Abou-Ganim, Bellagio, Las Vegas, Nevada.*

2 $^1/_2$ ounces Stolichnaya Ohranj vodka

$^1/_2$ ounce Cointreau

1 ounce fresh lemon juice

1 ounce orange juice

$^1/_2$ ounce cranberry juice

$^1/_2$ ounce simple syrup (page 33)

Orange slice and lemon twist, for garnish

Pour the vodka, Cointreau, juices, and simple syrup into a shaker two-thirds full of ice cubes. Shake well. Strain into a chilled Cocktail glass. Garnish with the orange slice and lemon twist.

Surfer on Acid

Here's the classic drink to be born from the Jägermeister craze of the 1990s.

$^3/_4$ ounce coconut rum

$^1/_2$ ounce Jägermeister

1 ounce pineapple juice

Pour all of the ingredients into a shaker two-thirds full of ice cubes. Shake well. Strain into a chilled Pony glass.

Swedish Coffee

This drink is based on an old Swedish tradition.

Place a sterilized coin in the bottom of an Irish Coffee glass. Fill with hot coffee until the coin disappears. Fill with vodka until the coin reappears. Sweeten to taste.

Sweet Radish Martini

—From The Purple Martini, Denver, Colorado.

> **3 ounces Boodles gin**
> **Splash of Drambuie**
> **Pearl onion, for garnish**

Pour the gin and Drambuie into a mixing glass two-thirds full of ice cubes. Stir well. Strain into a chilled Cocktail glass. Add the pearl onion.

Take Courage Martini

—From Villa Christina, Atlanta, Georgia.

> **3 ounces Tanqueray Sterling vodka**
> **Splash of Tia Maria**
> **Splash of Grand Marnier**
> **Coffee bean, for garnish**

Pour the vodka, Tia Maria, and Grand Marnier into a mixing glass two-thirds full of ice cubes. Stir well. Strain into a chilled Cocktail glass. Add the coffee bean.

Tart Gin Cooler

The Tart Gin Cooler, created in the 1990s, is a wonderfully refreshing drink.

> **2 ounces gin**
> **2 ounces fresh pink grapefruit juice**
> **3 ounces tonic water**
> **2 dashes of Peychaud's Bitters**

Build in an ice-filled Collins glass. Stir with a straw.

T-Bone

> **1 ^{1}/$_2$ ounces bourbon**
> **^{1}/$_2$ ounce A-1 steak sauce**

Layer both ingredients in a Pony glass.

Tangerine Martini

—From the Morton's of Chicago Martini Club.

> 3 ounces Tanqueray Sterling vodka
>
> $1/2$ ounce Mandarine Napoléon
>
> Orange slice, for garnish

Pour the vodka and Mandarine into a mixing glass two-thirds full of ice cubes. Stir well. Strain into a chilled Cocktail glass. Add the orange slice.

Tea Tini

—Adapted from a recipe from the Peninsula Grill, Charleston, South Carolina.

> Superfine sugar and a lemon wedge, for rimming the glass
>
> $1^3/4$ ounces Stolichnaya Ohranj vodka
>
> 1 ounce sweet iced tea
>
> $1/4$ ounce fresh lemon juice
>
> Lemon wedge, for garnish

Prepare the glass. Pour the vodka, tea, and lemon juice into a shaker two-thirds full of ice cubes. Shake well. Strain into the sugar-rimmed Cocktail glass. Add the lemon wedge.

> "The little rum we had was a great service but our nights were particularly distressing. I generally served a teaspoon or two to each person and it was joyful tidings when they heard my intentions."
>
> *—Captain William Bligh, 1789, after being set adrift with 18 sailors from HMS Bounty, and not sighting land for over six weeks*

Tea Toddies ☕

1 gallon brewed tea

$^1/_2$ vanilla bean, split, halved, and bruised

4 small (3-inch) cinnamon sticks, broken

12 whole cloves

12 whole allspice berries

Zest of 2 oranges

Zest of 2 lemons

Bourbon, brandy, or dark rum, for spiking

24 lemon twists, for garnish

Combine the tea, all of the spices, and the citrus zests in a large saucepan set over high heat. Bring almost to a boil; immediately reduce the heat to low, cover, and steep, stirring occasionally, for 20 minutes. Do not allow the mixture to boil.

Strain the mixture into thermal carafes or keep it hot on the coffeemaker.

Serve into individual mugs, adding 1 $^1/_2$ ounces bourbon, brandy, or dark rum to each mug, if desired. Garnish each serving with a lemon twist.

Tequila Collins

2 ounces tequila

$^1/_2$ ounce fresh lime juice

$^1/_2$ ounce simple syrup (page 33)

5 to 6 ounces club soda

Fresh fruit in season, for garnish

Pour the tequila, lime juice, and simple syrup into a shaker two-thirds full of ice cubes. Shake well. Strain into an ice-filled Collins glass. Pour in the club soda; stir briefly. Add the garnish of choice.

Tequila Conquistador

>   2 ounces white tequila
>
>   2 ounces fresh grapefruit juice
>
>   4 ounces tonic water

Build in an ice-filled Collins glass. Stir with a sip-stick or straw.

Tequila Cooler

>   2 $^1/_2$ ounces tequila
>
>   6 to 7 ounces lemon-lime soda
>
>   **Lemon twist, for garnish**

Pour the tequila and the lemon-lime soda into an ice-filled
Collins glass. Stir briefly. Add the twist.

Tequila Fix

>   2 $^1/_2$ ounces tequila
>
>   1 ounce fresh lime juice
>
> $^1/_2$ ounce pineapple juice
>
>   **Fresh fruit in season, for garnish**

Pour the tequila, lime juice, and pineapple juice into a shaker
two-thirds full of crushed ice. Shake well. Strain into a crushed
ice–filled Highball glass. Add the garnish of choice.

Tequila Fizz

>   2 ounces tequila
>
>   1 ounce fresh lime juice
>
> $^1/_2$ ounce simple syrup (page 33)
>
>   5 to 6 ounces club soda
>
>   **Fresh fruit in season, for garnish**

Pour the tequila, lime juice, and simple syrup into a shaker two-
thirds full of ice cubes. Shake well; strain into a chilled wine goblet. Add the club soda; stir briefly. Add the garnish of choice.

Tequila Gimlet

2 1/2 ounces tequila
1/2 ounce lime juice cordial, such as Rose's
Lime wedge, for garnish

Pour the tequila and lime cordial into an ice-filled Rocks glass; stir briefly. Add the lime wedge.

Tequila Martini, Dry

3 ounces white tequila
1/2 ounce dry vermouth
Lemon twist or cocktail olive, for garnish

Pour the tequila and vermouth into a mixing glass two-thirds full of ice cubes. Stir well. Strain into a chilled Cocktail glass. Add the garnish of choice.

Tequila Martini, Extra Dry

3 ounces white tequila
1/4 ounce dry vermouth
Lime wedge, for garnish

Pour the tequila and vermouth into a mixing glass two-thirds full of ice cubes. Stir well. Strain into a chilled Cocktail glass. Add the lime wedge.

Tequila Martini, Medium

2 1/2 ounces white tequila
3/4 ounce dry vermouth
Lime wedge, for garnish

Pour the tequila and vermouth into a mixing glass two-thirds full of ice cubes. Stir well. Strain into a chilled Cocktail glass. Add the lime wedge.

Tequila Martini, Sweet

2 $^1/_2$ ounces añejo tequila

$^1/_4$ ounce sweet vermouth

Maraschino cherry, for garnish

Pour the tequila and vermouth into a mixing glass two-thirds full of ice cubes. Stir well. Strain into a chilled Cocktail glass. Add the cherry.

Tequila Mary

2 ounces tequila

4 ounces tomato juice

$^1/_2$ ounce fresh lime juice

$^1/_4$ teaspoon black pepper

Pinch of salt

$^1/_4$ teaspoon cayenne pepper

3 dashes of hot sauce

3 dashes of Worcestershire sauce

Lime wedge, for garnish

Pour the tequila, tomato juice, and lime juice into a shaker two-thirds full of ice cubes; add the pepper, salt, cayenne, hot sauce, and Worcestershire. Shake well. Strain into an ice-filled Highball glass. Add the lime wedge.

Tequila Mockingbird

2 $^1/_2$ ounces white tequila

$^1/_2$ teaspoon white crème de menthe

$^1/_2$ ounce fresh lime juice

Pour all of the ingredients into a shaker two-thirds full of ice cubes. Shake well. Strain into a chilled Cocktail glass.

Tequila Neat

As easy as 1, 2, 3.

1 lime wedge
Pinch of salt
2 ounces tequila

Rub the lime wedge onto the back of your hand where the thumb meets the forefinger.

Sprinkle the salt onto the damp area of your hand.

Lick the salt from your hand, knock the tequila straight back, and then bite down on the lime wedge.

Tequila Punch #1

2 ounces white tequila
2 ounces fresh orange juice
2 ounces pineapple juice
$1/2$ ounce fresh lime juice
2 to 3 ounces club soda

Pour the tequila and all of the fruit juices into a shaker two-thirds full of ice cubes. Shake well. Strain into an ice-filled Collins glass. Add the club soda.

Tequila Punch #2

2 ounces white tequila
3 ounces pineapple juice
$1/2$ ounce fresh lemon juice
$1/4$ ounce grenadine

Pour all of the ingredients into a shaker two-thirds full of ice cubes. Shake well. Strain into an ice-filled Rocks glass.

Tequila Sidecar

Superfine sugar and a lime wedge, for rimming the glass
$2^1/2$ ounces white tequila
$1/2$ ounce triple sec
$1/2$ ounce fresh lime juice

Prepare the glass. Pour all of the ingredients into a shaker two-thirds full of ice cubes. Shake well. Strain into the sugar-rimmed Cocktail glass.

Tequila Sour

2 ounces white tequila

$^3/_4$ ounce fresh lime juice

$^1/_2$ ounce simple syrup (page 33)

Lime wedge, for garnish

Pour the tequila, lime juice, and simple syrup into a shaker two-thirds full of ice cubes. Shake well. Strain into a chilled Sour glass. Add the lime wedge.

Tequila Stinger

2 ounces white tequila

$^1/_2$ ounce white crème de menthe

Pour both ingredients into a shaker two-thirds full of ice cubes. Shake well. Strain into a crushed ice–filled wine goblet.

Tequila Sunrise

2 $^1/_2$ ounces white tequila

4 ounces fresh orange juice

$^1/_4$ ounce grenadine

Pour the tequila and orange juice into an ice-filled Highball glass; stir briefly. Pour the grenadine directly into the center of the drink.

Tequila Woo Woo

If you're not familiar already, get to know this drink.

2 ounces white tequila

$^1/_2$ ounce peach schnapps

4 ounces cranberry juice

Build in an ice-filled Highball glass; stir briefly.

Tequila-Papaya Freeze

MAKES 2 DRINKS

    2 ounces white tequila

    1 ripe papaya, peeled, pitted, and cubed

    1 ounce fresh lime juice

    1 ounce grenadine

    $1/2$ ounce lime juice cordial, such as Rose's

Blend all of the ingredients with 4 to 6 ice cubes. Divide between 2 large wine goblets.

Tequini

    $1^1/2$ ounces tequila

    $1/2$ ounce dry vermouth

    Dash of Angostura bitters

    Lemon twist and a lime twist, for garnishes

Pour the tequila, vermouth, and bitters into a mixing glass two-thirds full of ice cubes. Stir well. Strain into a chilled Cocktail glass. Add both twists.

Test Tube Baby

    1 ounce vodka

    $1/2$ ounce sambuca

    Heavy cream

Pour the vodka and sambuca into a Pony glass. Dip a sip-stick into a container of cream and place your finger over the top to hold the liquid inside. Dip the stick into the bottom of the glass and release your finger to let the cream flow out.

Thames Champagne Cocktail

    1 sugar cube

    $1/2$ ounce Pimm's Cup #1

    5 ounces champagne or other sparkling wine

Drop the sugar cube into the bottom of a chilled Champagne Flute. Add the Pimm's; add the champagne.

The Other B & B

1 $^1/_2$ ounces Baileys Irish cream liqueur

1 $^1/_2$ ounces brandy or cognac

Pour both ingredients into a shaker two-thirds full of ice cubes. Shake well. Strain into a chilled Cocktail glass.

The Social

—Created by King Cocktail Dale DeGroff, New York City, 1998.

2 ounces Jack Daniel's Tennessee whiskey

$^3/_4$ ounce fresh lemon juice

$^1/_2$ ounce Cherry Heering

$^1/_2$ ounce simple syrup (page 33)

Maraschino cherry and a lemon twist, for garnishes

Pour the Jack Daniel's, lemon juice, Cherry Heering, and simple syrup into a shaker two-thirds full of ice cubes. Shake well. Strain into a chilled Cocktail glass. Add the cherry and twist.

Third Rail Cocktail

There used to be two versions of this drink, but this formula is the one that withstood the test of time.

1 ounce dark rum

1 ounce applejack

1 ounce brandy

2 dashes of absinthe substitute, such as Absente, Pernod, Herbsaint, or Ricard

Pour all of the ingredients into a mixing glass two-thirds full of ice cubes. Stir well. Strain into a chilled Cocktail glass.

360-Degree Martini

A drink that will have you going in circles.

> Old Bay seasoning and a lime wedge, for rimming the glass
>
> 1 ounce pepper vodka
>
> 3/4 ounce lemon vodka
>
> 3/4 ounce lime vodka
>
> 1/2 ounce dry vermouth
>
> Splash of Worcestershire sauce

Prepare the glass. Pour all of the ingredients into a mixing glass two-thirds full of ice cubes. Stir well. Strain into the Old Bay–rimmed Cocktail glass.

Three Wise Men

> 1/2 ounce Jack Daniel's Tennessee whiskey
>
> 1/2 ounce Jim Beam bourbon
>
> 1/2 ounce Johnnie Walker scotch

Pour all of the ingredients into a mixing glass two-thirds full of ice cubes. Stir well. Strain into a Pony glass.

Three Wise Men Go Hunting

> 1/2 ounce Jack Daniel's Tennessee whiskey
>
> 1/2 ounce Jim Beam bourbon
>
> 1/2 ounce Johnnie Walker scotch
>
> 1/2 ounce Wild Turkey bourbon

Pour all of the ingredients into a mixing glass two-thirds full of ice cubes. Stir well. Strain into a Pony glass.

Tidal Wave

The original Tidal Wave was created at Pedro's, an Upper East Side Manhattan bar, in the early 1970s.

    1 ounce dark rum
    1 ounce brandy
    1/2 ounce vodka
    1/2 ounce tequila
    2 ounces pineapple juice
    1 ounce fresh lime juice
    1/4 ounce grenadine

Pour all of the ingredients into a shaker two-thirds full of ice cubes. Shake well. Strain into a large, ice-filled wine goblet.

Tipperary Cocktail

    1 1/2 ounces Irish whiskey
    1/2 ounce sweet vermouth
    1/2 ounce green Chartreuse

Pour all of the ingredients into a mixing glass two-thirds full of ice cubes. Stir well. Strain into a chilled Cocktail glass. Sing while you drink it.

Toasted Almond

    1 ounce amaretto
    1 ounce Kahlúa
    1 1/2 ounces light cream

Pour all of the ingredients into a shaker two-thirds full of ice cubes. Shake well. Strain into an ice-filled Rocks glass.

Tom & Jerry

This drink was supposedly created by a nineteenth-century bartender, Jerry Thomas, and it's said that he refused to make it until after the first snowfall of the year.

MAKES ABOUT 24 SIX-OUNCE SERVINGS

12 eggs, separated

1 $^1/_2$ cups sugar

1 teaspoon baking soda

16 ounces dark rum

16 ounces brandy

$^1/_2$ gallon plus 1 cup milk, scalded

Freshly grated nutmeg, for garnish

In a mixing bowl, combine the egg yolks, 1 $^1/_4$ cups of the sugar, and the baking soda. Whisk until creamy and thick.

In another mixing bowl, beat the egg whites until frothy. Sprinkle on the remaining $^1/_4$ cup sugar and continue beating until soft peaks form. Fold the egg whites into the egg yolk mixture to lighten it. Gradually whisk in the rum and brandy.

To serve: Divide the drink among 24 Tom & Jerry cups or punch cups. Add some of the hot milk to each cup. Dust each serving with nutmeg.

Tom Collins

Early recipes for this drink called for Old Tom, a sweetened gin that's no longer made. "This is a long drink, to be consumed slowly with reverence and meditation."
—The Fine Art of Mixing Drinks, *by David Embury, 1958.*

2 ounces gin

$^1/_2$ ounce fresh lemon juice

$^1/_2$ ounce simple syrup (page 33)

5 to 6 ounces club soda

Fresh fruit in season, for garnish

Pour the gin, lemon juice, and simple syrup into a shaker two-thirds full of ice cubes. Shake well. Strain into an ice-filled Collins glass. Pour in the club soda; stir briefly. Add the garnish of choice.

Tomate

This is a simple drink that you'll usually see being served in France or in French bistros in the United States.

> **2 $^1/_2$ ounces absinthe substitute, such as Absente, Pernod, Herbsaint, or Ricard**
>
> **$^1/_4$ ounce grenadine**

Build in an ice-filled Rocks glass; stir briefly.

Tonic & Lime ✪

> **$^1/_2$ ounce lime juice cordial, such as Rose's**
>
> **6 to 8 ounces tonic water**
>
> **Lime wedge, for garnish**

Pour the lime juice cordial and tonic water into an ice-filled Collins glass. Stir briefly. Add the lime wedge.

Tonic Bracer ✪

> **6 to 8 ounces tonic water**
>
> **2 dashes of Angostura bitters**
>
> **Lime wedge, for garnish**

Pour the tonic and bitters into an ice-filled Collins glass. Stir briefly. Add the garnish.

Trilby Cocktail

This drink was named after George du Maurier's *Trilby*, which was later seen on the big screen as *Svengali*, but the drink wasn't the only object to adopt the name — along with the Trilby hat, there used to be ice cream, shoes, sausages, cigars, and cigarettes named for Trilby.

> **2 ounces gin**
>
> **1 ounce sweet vermouth**
>
> **2 dashes of orange bitters**

Pour all of the ingredients into a mixing glass two-thirds full of ice cubes. Stir well. Strain into a chilled Cocktail glass.

Trinity Cocktail

1 ounce gin

1 ounce sweet vermouth

1 ounce dry vermouth

Pour all of the ingredients into a mixing glass two-thirds full of ice cubes. Stir well. Strain into a chilled Cocktail glass.

Tropical Cocktail

A drink with this name that dates back to the 1930s called for entirely different ingredients than these—this is a more up-to-date formula.

2 ounces dark rum

1 ounce pineapple juice

$^{1}/_{2}$ ounce fresh lime juice

Dash of grenadine

Pour all of the ingredients into a shaker two-thirds full of ice cubes. Shake well. Strain into a chilled Cocktail glass.

Tweety Bird

Where's Sylvester?

$1^{1}/_{2}$ ounces light rum

$^{1}/_{2}$ ounce Galliano

$^{1}/_{2}$ ounce Grand Marnier

1 ounce fresh lemon juice

Pour all of the ingredients into a shaker two-thirds full of ice cubes. Shake well. Strain into a chilled Cocktail glass.

Ugly

2 ounces tomato juice

6 ounces beer

Salt

Pour the beer into a beer mug. Pour the tomato juice down the side of the glass so it sits on the bottom. Sprinkle salt on top. When the beer foam is about to spill over, chug the drink and then scream, "Ugly!"

Valentino

This is a variation on the Negroni. See also **Vodka Valentino**.

>   2 $^1/_2$ ounces gin
> $^1/_2$ ounce Campari
> $^1/_2$ ounce sweet vermouth
>   Orange twist, as garnish

Pour the gin, Campari, and vermouth into a mixing glass two-thirds full of ice cubes. Stir well. Strain into a chilled Cocktail glass. Add the twist.

Vanilla Coke

>   1 $^1/_2$ ounces Stolichnaya Vanil vodka
>   4 ounces Coca-Cola

Build in an ice-filled Highball glass. Stir with a sip-stick.

Vanilla Cream

>   1 $^1/_2$ ounces Baileys Irish cream liqueur
>   1 $^1/_2$ ounces Stolichnaya Vanil vodka

Pour both ingredients into a shaker two-thirds full of ice cubes. Shake well. Strain into an ice-filled Rocks glass or a chilled Cocktail glass.

Velvet Hammer

>   2 ounces vodka
> $^3/_4$ ounce white crème de cacao
> $^3/_4$ ounce heavy cream

Pour all of the ingredients into a shaker two-thirds full of ice cubes. Shake well. Strain into a chilled Cocktail glass.

Velvet Peach

—Adapted from a recipe by cocktail historian Dr. Cocktail (Ted Haigh), who is, himself, a peach.

>   2 ounces white rum
>   1 ounce Tuaca
>   1 ounce fresh lime juice
>   2 dashes of peach bitters

Pour all of the ingredients into a shaker two-thirds full of ice cubes. Shake well. Strain into a chilled Cocktail glass.

Venetian

>   3/4 ounce Van Gogh Wild Appel vodka
>   3/4 ounce Baileys Irish cream liqueur
>   3/4 ounce Frangelico

Pour all of the ingredients into a shaker two-thirds full of ice cubes. Shake well. Strain into a chilled Cocktail glass.

Vermouth Cassis

This drink is also known as the Pompier Highball.

>   2 1/2 ounces dry vermouth
>   1/2 ounce crème de cassis
>   4 to 6 ounces club soda
>   Lemon twist, for garnish

Pour the vermouth and cassis into an ice-filled Collins glass. Add club soda to fill the glass; stir briefly. Add the twist.

Vermouth Cocktail

>   1 1/2 ounces sweet vermouth
>   1 1/2 ounces dry vermouth
>   2 dashes of Angostura bitters
>   Maraschino cherry, for garnish

Pour both vermouths and the bitters into a mixing glass two-thirds full of ice cubes. Stir well. Strain into a chilled Cocktail glass. Add the cherry.

Vesper Martini

One of the few clear drinks that should be shaken, this Martini variation uses both gin and vodka and was ordered in *Casino Royale,* the only film in which David Niven, the late British actor, played James Bond. Ursula Andress played Vesper Lynd in the movie, and the drink is named for her character.

2 ounces gin

1 $^1/_4$ ounces vodka

$^1/_2$ ounce Lillet Blanc

Lemon twist, for garnish

Pour the gin, vodka, and Lillet into a shaker two-thirds full of ice cubes. *Shake* well. Strain into a chilled Cocktail glass. Add the twist.

Vincent's Dutch Swirl Martini

$^3/_4$ ounce Van Gogh Dutch Chocolate vodka

$^3/_4$ ounce Van Gogh Vanilla vodka

$^1/_2$ ounce Kahlúa

$^1/_2$ ounce Godiva White chocolate liqueur

$^1/_4$ ounce amaretto

Chocolate shavings, for garnish

Pour the chocolate and vanilla vodkas, the Kahlúa, white chocolate liqueur, and amaretto into a shaker two-thirds full of ice cubes. Shake well. Strain into a chilled Cocktail glass. Sprinkle with the chocolate shavings.

Virgin Blackberry Colada ◍

7 ounces pineapple juice

2 $^1/_2$ ounces coconut cream, such as Coco Lopez

10 to 12 blackberries

Pineapple spear, for garnish

Place the pineapple juice, coconut cream, and blackberries into a blender containing 1 cup of ice cubes. Blend well. Pour into a chilled wine goblet. Add the pineapple spear.

Virgin Caesar ☉

    6 ounces Clamato juice
    $1/2$ ounce fresh lemon juice
    Pinch of ground black pepper
    Pinch of celery salt
    Dash of hot sauce
    Dash of Worcestershire sauce
    Lemon wedge, for garnish

Pour the Clamato juice and lemon juice into a shaker two-thirds
full of ice cubes; add the pepper, celery salt, hot sauce, and
Worcestershire. Shake well. Strain into an ice-filled Highball
glass. Add the lemon wedge.

Virgin Mary ☉

    6 ounces tomato juice
    $1/2$ ounce fresh lemon juice
    $1/4$ teaspoon black pepper
    Pinch of salt
    $1/4$ teaspoon celery seed
    $1/4$ teaspoon ground cumin
    2 dashes of Worcestershire sauce
    2 dashes of hot sauce
    Lemon wedge, for garnish

Pour the tomato juice and lime juice into a shaker two-thirds full
of ice cubes; add the pepper, salt, celery seed, cumin,
Worcestershire, and hot sauce. Shake well. Strain into an ice-
filled Highball glass. Add the lemon wedge.

Virgin Peach Colada ☉

    7 ounces pineapple juice
    $2 1/2$ ounces coconut cream, such as Coco Lopez
    1 ripe peach, stoned, cut into pieces
    Pineapple spear, for garnish

Place the pineapple juice, coconut cream, and peach into a blender containing 1 cup of ice cubes. Blend well. Pour into a chilled wine goblet; add the pineapple spear.

Virgin Peach Daiquiri 🍸

> 2 ounces fresh lime juice
>
> 1 ounce simple syrup (page 33)
>
> 1 ripe peach, stoned, cut into 6 pieces

Place all of the ingredients into a blender containing 1 cup of ice cubes. Blend well. Pour into a chilled wine goblet.

Virgin Piña Colada 🍸

> 7 ounces pineapple juice
>
> 2 ounces orange juice
>
> 2 $1/2$ ounces coconut cream, such as Coco Lopez
>
> 1 cup pineapple chunks
>
> Pineapple spear, for garnish

Place the pineapple juice, orange juice, coconut cream, and pineapple chunks into a blender containing 1 cup of ice cubes. Blend well. Pour into a chilled wine goblet; add the pineapple spear.

Virgin Planter's Punch 🍸

> 2 ounces grapefruit juice
>
> 2 ounces pineapple juice
>
> 1 ounce tangerine juice
>
> 1 ounce fresh lime juice
>
> $1/2$ ounce simple syrup (page 33)
>
> 1 ounce club soda
>
> Pineapple spear, for garnish

Pour the fruit juices and simple syrup into a shaker two-thirds full of ice cubes. Shake well. Pour into an ice-filled Collins glass; add the club soda and stir briefly. Add the garnish.

Virgin Raspberry Colada

> 7 ounces pineapple juice
>
> 2 $1/2$ ounces coconut cream, such as Coco Lopez
>
> 1 cup raspberries
>
> Pineapple chunk and a raspberry, for garnish

Place the pineapple juice, coconut cream, and raspberries into a blender containing 1 cup of ice cubes. Blend well. Pour into a chilled wine goblet; add the garnishes.

Virgin Strawberry Daiquiri

> 1 $1/2$ ounces fresh lime juice
>
> 1 ounce simple syrup (page 33)
>
> 1 cup ripe strawberries, hulled and halved
>
> Ripe strawberry, for garnish

Place the lime juice, simple syrup, and halved strawberries into a blender containing 1 cup of ice cubes. Blend well. Pour into a chilled wine goblet; add the strawberry.

Virgin Strawberry-Banana Daiquiri

> 2 ounces fresh lime juice
>
> 1 ounce simple syrup (page 33)
>
> 5 strawberries, hulled
>
> 1 ripe banana, cut into 1-inch pieces

Place all of the ingredients into a blender containing 1 cup of ice cubes. Blend well. Pour into a chilled wine goblet.

Vodka & Tonic

> 2 $1/2$ ounces vodka
>
> 4 ounces tonic water
>
> Lime wedge, for garnish

Pour the vodka and tonic into an ice-filled Highball glass. Add the lime wedge.

Vodka Buck

 1 lemon wedge

 2 ounces vodka

 5 ounces ginger ale

Squeeze the lemon into a Highball glass; drop it into the glass. Fill glass with ice cubes. Add the vodka and ginger ale; stir.

Vodka Collins

 2 ounces vodka

 $^1/_2$ ounce fresh lemon juice

 $^1/_2$ ounce simple syrup (page 33)

 5 to 6 ounces club soda

 Fresh fruit in season, for garnish

Pour the vodka, lemon juice, and simple syrup into a shaker two-thirds full of ice cubes. Shake well. Strain into an ice-filled Collins glass. Add the club soda; stir briefly. Add the garnish of choice.

Vodka Cooler

 2 $^1/_2$ ounces vodka

 6 to 7 ounces lemon-lime soda

 Lime wedge, for garnish

Pour the vodka and lemon-lime soda into an ice-filled Collins glass. Stir briefly. Add the lime wedge.

Vodka Crusta

 Superfine sugar and a lemon wedge, for rimming the glass

 Lemon peel spiral (see technique, page 38)

 2 ounces vodka

 $^1/_2$ ounce white curaçao

 $^1/_2$ ounce fresh lemon juice

Prepare the glass. Place the lemon peel spiral into the sugar-rimmed Sour glass so that it almost lines the entire interior. Pour the vodka, curaçao, and lemon juice into a shaker two-thirds full of ice cubes. Shake well. Strain into the glass.

Vodka Daisy

> 2 $^{1}/_{2}$ ounces vodka
>
> 1 ounce fresh lemon juice
>
> $^{1}/_{2}$ ounce grenadine
>
> Lemon twist, for garnish

Pour the vodka, lemon juice, and grenadine into a shaker two-thirds full of ice cubes. Shake well. Strain into a crushed ice–filled Highball glass. Add the twist.

Vodka Fix

> 2 $^{1}/_{2}$ ounces vodka
>
> 1 ounce fresh lemon juice
>
> $^{1}/_{2}$ ounce pineapple juice
>
> Fresh fruit in season, for garnish

Pour the vodka, lemon juice, and pineapple juice into a shaker two-thirds full of ice cubes. Shake well. Strain into a crushed ice–filled Highball glass. Add the garnish of choice.

Vodka Fizz

> 2 ounces vodka
>
> 1 ounce fresh lime juice
>
> $^{1}/_{2}$ ounce simple syrup (page 33)
>
> 5 to 6 ounces club soda
>
> Fresh fruit in season, for garnish

Pour the vodka, lime juice, and simple syrup into a shaker two-thirds full of ice cubes. Shake well; strain into a chilled wine goblet. Add the club soda; stir briefly. Add the garnish of choice.

Vodka Gibson

The vodka version of the gin-based classic.

> 3 ounces vodka
>
> $^{1}/_{2}$ ounce dry vermouth
>
> 3 pearl onions, for garnish

Pour the vodka and vermouth into a mixing glass two-thirds full of ice cubes. Stir well. Strain into a chilled Cocktail glass. Add the onions.

Vodka Gimlet

2 $^{1}/_{2}$ ounces vodka

$^{1}/_{2}$ ounce lime juice cordial, such as Rose's

Lime wedge, for garnish

Pour the vodka and lime cordial into an ice-filled Rocks glass; stir briefly. Add the lime wedge.

Vodka Martini, Dry

3 ounces vodka

$^{1}/_{2}$ ounce dry vermouth

Lemon twist or cocktail olive, for garnish

Pour the vodka and vermouth into a mixing glass two-thirds full of ice cubes. Stir well. Strain into a chilled Cocktail glass. Add the garnish.

Vodka Martini, Extra Dry

3 ounces vodka

$^{1}/_{4}$ ounce dry vermouth

Lemon twist or cocktail olive, for garnish

Pour the vodka and vermouth into a mixing glass two-thirds full of ice cubes. Stir well. Strain into a chilled Cocktail glass. Add the garnish.

Vodka Martini, Medium

2 $^{1}/_{2}$ ounces vodka

$^{3}/_{4}$ ounce dry vermouth

Lemon twist or cocktail olive, for garnish

Pour the vodka and vermouth into a mixing glass two-thirds full of ice cubes. Stir well. Strain into a chilled Cocktail glass. Add the garnish.

V

Vodka Martini, Sweet

2 1/2 ounces vodka

1/4 ounce sweet vermouth

Lemon twist, for garnish

Pour the vodka and vermouth into a mixing glass two-thirds full of ice cubes. Stir well. Strain into a chilled Cocktail glass. Add the twist.

Vodka Rickey

2 1/2 ounces vodka

1 ounce fresh lime juice

5 to 6 ounces club soda

Lime wedge, for garnish

Pour the vodka and lime juice into an ice-filled Highball glass. Add the club soda; stir briefly. Add the lime wedge.

Vodka Sling

2 1/2 ounces vodka

1/2 ounce cherry brandy

1/2 ounce fresh lemon juice

5 to 6 ounces club soda

Lemon wedge, for garnish

Pour the vodka, cherry brandy, and lemon juice into a shaker two-thirds full of ice cubes. Shake well. Strain into an ice-filled Collins glass. Add the club soda; stir briefly. Add the lemon wedge.

Vodka Sour

2 ounces vodka

3/4 ounce fresh lemon juice

1/2 ounce simple syrup (page 33)

Orange wheel and a maraschino cherry, for garnishes

Pour the vodka, lemon juice, and simple syrup into a shaker two-thirds full of ice cubes. Shake well. Strain into a chilled Sour glass. Add the garnishes.

Vodka Valentino

The vodka version of the gin-based Valentino.

> **2 ounces vodka**
>
> **¹/₂ ounce Campari**
>
> **¹/₂ ounce sweet vermouth**
>
> **Orange twist, for garnish**

Pour the vodka, Campari, and vermouth into a mixing glass two-thirds full of ice cubes. Stir well. Strain into a chilled Cocktail glass. Add the twist.

Vulcan Mind Probe

Or is it a Mind Melt? Or Mind Meld?

> **³/₄ ounce Bacardi 151-proof rum**
>
> **³/₄ ounce ouzo**

Layer in a Pony glass.

Ward Eight

The Ward Eight was created at Boston's Lock-Ober Café, " . . . the place where Caruso cooked his own sweet-breads; where John F. Kennedy habitually ordered the lobster stew, drank the broth and gave the meat to the waiter; where a dying man came for his last lunch; and where, when regular customers pass away, their plates are turned over and their chairs are cocked against the table." —*http://www.locke-ober.com/*

> **2 ounces bourbon**
>
> **1 ounce orange juice**
>
> **1 ounce fresh lemon juice**
>
> **Dash of grenadine**

Pour all of the ingredients into a shaker two-thirds full of ice cubes. Shake well. Strain into a chilled Cocktail glass.

W

Whisky Buck

1 lemon wedge

2 ounces blended Canadian whisky

5 ounces ginger ale

Squeeze the lemon wedge into a Highball glass and drop it into the glass. Fill the glass with ice cubes. Add the whisky and ginger ale. Stir briefly.

Whisky Cobbler

2 $^1/_2$ ounces blended Canadian whisky

$^1/_2$ ounce simple syrup (page 33)

Fresh fruit in season, for garnish

Pour the whisky and simple syrup into a wine goblet filled with crushed ice. Stir briefly. Add the garnish of choice.

Whisky Collins

2 ounces blended Canadian whisky

$^1/_2$ ounce fresh lemon juice

$^1/_2$ ounce simple syrup (page 33)

5 to 6 ounces club soda

Fresh fruit in season, for garnish

Pour the whisky, lemon juice, and simple syrup into a shaker two-thirds full of ice cubes. Shake well. Strain into an ice-filled Collins glass. Add the club soda; stir briefly. Add the garnish of choice.

Whisky Cooler

2 $^1/_2$ ounces blended Canadian whisky

6 to 7 ounces ginger ale

Lemon twist, for garnish

Pour the whisky and ginger ale into an ice-filled Collins glass. Stir briefly; add the twist.

W

Whisky Crusta

Superfine sugar and a lemon wedge, for rimming the glass

Lemon peel spiral (see technique, page 38)

2 ounces blended Canadian whisky

$^1/_2$ ounce white curaçao

$^1/_2$ ounce fresh lemon juice

Prepare the glass. Place the lemon peel spiral into the sugar-rimmed Sour glass so that it almost lines the entire interior. Pour the whisky, curaçao, and lemon juice into a shaker two-thirds full of ice cubes. Shake well. Strain into the glass.

Whisky Daisy

2 $^1/_2$ ounces blended Canadian whisky

1 ounce fresh lemon juice

$^1/_2$ ounce grenadine

Lemon twist, for garnish

Pour the whisky, lemon juice, and grenadine into a shaker two-thirds full of ice cubes. Shake well. Strain into a crushed ice–filled Highball glass. Add the twist.

Whisky Fix

2 $^1/_2$ ounces blended Canadian whisky

1 ounce fresh lemon juice

$^1/_2$ ounce pineapple juice

Fresh fruit in season, for garnish

Pour the whisky, lemon juice, and pineapple juice into a shaker two-thirds full of ice cubes. Shake well. Strain into a crushed ice–filled Highball glass. Add the garnish of choice.

W

Whisky Fizz

2 ounces blended Canadian whisky

1 ounce fresh lemon juice

$1/2$ ounce simple syrup (page 33)

5 to 6 ounces club soda

Fresh fruit in season, for garnish

Pour the whisky, lemon juice, and simple syrup into a shaker two-thirds full of ice cubes. Shake well. Strain into a chilled wine goblet. Add the club soda; stir briefly. Add the garnish of choice.

Whisky Mac

A Scottish antidote for a cold winter night.

2 ounces scotch

1 ounce green ginger wine

Build in an ice-filled Rocks glass.

Whisky Rickey

$2\,1/2$ ounces blended Canadian whisky

1 ounce fresh lime juice

5 to 6 ounces club soda

Lime wedge, for garnish

Pour the whisky and lime juice into an ice-filled Highball glass. Add the club soda; stir briefly. Add the lime wedge.

Whisky Sangaree

2 ounces blended Canadian whisky

$1/2$ ounce ruby port

$1/2$ ounce Yukon Jack liqueur

Freshly grated nutmeg, for garnish

Pour the whisky, port, and Yukon Jack into a mixing glass two-thirds full of ice cubes; stir well. Strain into a chilled wine goblet. Sprinkle with the nutmeg.

Whisky Sling

2 ¹/₂ ounces blended Canadian whisky

¹/₂ ounce simple syrup (page 33)

¹/₂ ounce fresh lemon juice

5 to 6 ounces club soda

Lemon wedge, for garnish

Pour the whisky, simple syrup, and lemon juice into a shaker two-thirds full of ice cubes. Shake well. Strain the drink into an ice-filled Collins glass. Add the club soda; stir briefly. Add the lemon wedge.

Whisky Smash

6 fresh mint leaves

³/₄ ounce simple syrup (page 33)

2 ¹/₂ ounces blended Canadian whisky

Mint sprig, for garnish

Place the mint leaves in the bottom of a large Rocks glass; add the simple syrup and muddle well. Fill the glass with crushed ice. Add the whisky; stir briefly. Add the mint garnish.

Whisky Sour

Some of us like to substitute bourbon for the Canadian whisky.

2 ounces blended Canadian whisky

³/₄ ounce fresh lemon juice

¹/₂ ounce simple syrup (page 33)

Orange wheel and a maraschino cherry, for garnishes

Pour the whisky, lemon juice, and simple syrup into a shaker two-thirds full of ice cubes. Shake well. Strain into a chilled Sour glass. Add the garnishes.

W

Whisky Swizzle

2 ounces blended Canadian whisky

$^1/_2$ ounce fresh lemon juice

$^1/_2$ ounce simple syrup (page 33)

5 to 6 ounces ginger ale

Lemon wheel, for garnish

Pour the whisky, lemon juice, and simple syrup into a shaker two-thirds full of ice cubes. Shake well. Strain into an ice-filled Collins glass. Add the ginger ale; stir briefly. Add the lemon wheel and a swizzle stick.

White Iced Tea

$^1/_2$ ounce vodka

$^1/_2$ ounce gin

$^1/_2$ ounce light rum

$^1/_2$ ounce tequila

$^1/_2$ ounce triple sec

$^1/_2$ ounce lemon juice

Lemon-lime soda

Lemon wedge, for garnish

Pour the vodka, gin, rum, tequila, triple sec, and lemon juice into a shaker two-thirds full of ice cubes. Shake well. Strain into an ice-filled Collins glass. Top with the soda. Add the lemon wedge.

White Lady Cocktail

2 $^1/_2$ ounces gin

1 ounce light cream

1 egg white

$^1/_2$ ounce simple syrup (page 33)

Pour all of the ingredients into a shaker two-thirds full of ice cubes. Shake very well. Strain into a chilled Cocktail glass.

White Rabbit

$1^1/_2$ ounces Stolichnaya Vanil vodka

$1^1/_2$ ounces vanilla schnapps or liqueur

$1^1/_2$ ounces heavy cream or milk

Build in an ice-filled Highball glass. Stir with a sip-stick.

White Russian

"Listen, Maude, I'm sorry if your stepmother is a nympho, but I don't see what it has to do with—do you have any Kahlúa." —From The Big Lebowski, the movie in which Jeff Bridges, as "The Dude," drinks more White Russians than you might think possible.

2 ounces vodka

1 ounce Kahlúa

1 ounce light cream

Pour all of the ingredients into a shaker two-thirds full of ice cubes. Shake well. Strain into an ice-filled Rocks glass.

White Spider

Though it's actually a Vodka Stinger, this drink is better known by this creepier name. Shake this; don't stir it.

2 ounces vodka

$^1/_2$ ounce white crème de menthe

Pour both ingredients into a shaker two-thirds full of ice cubes. Shake well. Strain into an ice-filled Rocks glass or a crushed ice–filled wine goblet.

White Wine Spritzer

6 ounces white wine

1 to 2 ounces club soda

Lemon twist, for garnish

Pour the wine and club soda into an ice-filled Collins glass. Stir briefly; add the twist.

W

Widow's Dream Cocktail

More like a widow's nightmare if you ask me.

1 ¹/₂ ounces Bénédictine

1 egg

Dollop of whipped cream

Pour the Bénédictine into a shaker two-thirds full of ice cubes; add the egg. Shake very well. Strain into a chilled Cocktail glass. Top with the whipped cream.

Widow's Kiss #1

The Widow's Kiss is a Prohibition-era drink created in Europe while Americans were enduring the Great Drought.

1 ounce calvados

¹/₂ ounce yellow Chartreuse

¹/₂ ounce Bénédictine

Dash of Angostura bitters

Pour all of the ingredients into a mixing glass two-thirds full of ice cubes. Stir well. Strain into a chilled Cocktail glass.

Widow's Kiss #2

1 ¹/₂ ounces brandy

¹/₂ ounce yellow Chartreuse

¹/₂ ounce Bénédictine

2 dashes of Angostura bitters

Pour all of the ingredients into a mixing glass two-thirds full of ice cubes. Stir well. Strain into a chilled Cocktail glass.

Windex

Because it looks like what?

2 ounces vodka

¹/₂ ounce blue curaçao

¹/₂ ounce triple sec

Pour all of the ingredients into a mixing glass two-thirds full of ice cubes. Stir well. Strain into a chilled Cocktail glass or chilled spray bottle.

Witch's Tit

2 ounces Kahlúa

Dollop of whipped cream

$^1/_2$ maraschino cherry, for garnish

Pour the liqueur into a Pousse-Café glass. Top with the cream; add the garnish.

Woo Woo

2 ounces vodka

$^1/_2$ ounce peach schnapps

4 ounces cranberry juice

Build in an ice-filled Highball glass; stir briefly.

XYZ Cocktail

2 ounces light rum

1 ounce triple sec

1 ounce fresh lemon juice

Pour all of the ingredients into a shaker two-thirds full of ice cubes. Shake well. Strain into a chilled Cocktail glass.

Yale Cocktail

This cocktail has changed because its original recipe included crème Yvette, a violet-flavored liqueur, but it's no longer available.

$2^1/_2$ ounces gin

$^1/_4$ ounce dry vermouth

$^1/_4$ ounce blue curaçao

Dash of Angostura bitters

Pour all of the ingredients into a mixing glass two-thirds full of ice cubes. Stir well. Strain into a chilled Cocktail glass.

Y

Yellowbird

A Caribbean drink that will take you to sandy shores.

> 2 ounces light rum
> $^1/_2$ ounce Galliano
> $^1/_2$ ounce triple sec
> $^1/_2$ ounce fresh lime juice

Pour all of the ingredients into a shaker two-thirds full of ice cubes. Shake well. Strain into a chilled Cocktail glass.

Yumyum Martini

> 2$^1/_2$ ounces Stolichnaya Kafya vodka
> $^1/_4$ ounce Stolichnaya Zinamon vodka
> Short cinnamon stick, for garnish

Pour both vodkas into a mixing glass two-thirds full of ice cubes. Stir well. Strain into a chilled Cocktail glass. Add the cinnamon stick.

Zaza Cocktail

The Zaza Cocktail was named for a nineteenth-century Broadway play, not for the character in *La Cage aux Folles*.

> 1$^1/_2$ ounces gin
> 1$^1/_2$ ounces Dubonnet Rouge
> Orange twist, for garnish

Pour the gin and Dubonnet into a mixing glass two-thirds full of ice cubes. Stir well. Strain into a chilled Cocktail glass. Add the twist.

Zipperhead

The term *zipperhead* originated at IBM, where it was used to describe people with closed minds.

> 1 ounce vodka
> 1 ounce Chambord raspberry liqueur
> 1 ounce lemon-lime soda

Layer in an ice-filled Rocks glass. Sip through a straw.

Zombie

The king of all Tiki Bar drinks, the Zombie was created
by Donn the Beachcomber, originator of the Tiki
Bar–themed restaurant in the United States. It made its
debut at the Hurricane Bar at the 1939 World's Fair.

> 2 ounces añejo rum
>
> 1 ounce dark rum
>
> 1 ounce light rum
>
> $^1/_2$ ounce applejack
>
> 1 ounce fresh lime juice
>
> $^1/_2$ ounce pineapple juice
>
> $^1/_2$ ounce papaya nectar
>
> $^1/_2$ ounce simple syrup (page 33)
>
> $^1/_2$ ounce 151-proof Demerara rum
>
> Pineapple spear, maraschino cherry, and a mint sprig,
> for garnishes

Pour the first 3 rums, the applejack, lime juice, pineapple
juice, papaya nectar, and simple syrup into a shaker two-thirds
full of ice cubes. Shake well. Strain into an ice-filled Zombie
or Hurricane glass. Float the 151-proof rum on top. Add the
garnishes.

Zorbatini

> 2 ounces vodka
>
> $^1/_2$ ounce ouzo
>
> Green olive, for garnish

Pour the vodka and ouzo into a mixing glass two-thirds full of ice
cubes. Stir well. Strain into a chilled Cocktail glass. Garnish with
the olive.

Z

The Professional Bartender: How to Be the Best

Aaah, the life of a bartender: Holding court behind two feet of shining mahogany every night; shaking and stirring while customers watch in wonder at the delectable nectars that cascade from the shaker into sleek cocktail glasses; being the fountain of knowledge, the baroness of bar lore, the princess of trivia, and the sage whose knowledge knows no bounds; constantly attending swank parties where multimillionaires proudly introduce you as their bartender; unclogging the toilet in the ladies' room. So who said it would always be glamorous?

I married a bartender. I've been a bartender, but never for very long and never at a place that forced me to do my homework or make an effort to develop a style for myself. I've rarely met a bartender I didn't like: I've met bad bartenders, and I've been privileged to sit across from the best, and I've noted that all of them—the good, the bad, and the middling—exhibit that gene that makes them yearn for a good Boston shaker and an audience to play to—and I give good audience, no doubt about it.

The role of a professional bartender is much more complex than most people think. And though it sometimes remains a job one seeks out while looking for that Broadway break or finishing that MBA, bartending is a craft that can—and should—garner praise and recognition equal to that of a well-respected and talented chef. But before you get that good, you need to acquire knowledge, style, and most of all, experience.

THE QUALITIES OF A GOOD PROFESSIONAL BARTENDER

Not just any Regular Joe off the street can become a good professional bartender—at least not without a good deal of work. However, there are some general qualities and recommendations that apply to the job, whether it's at a high-end restaurant or at a beach bar where sandals and bikinis are standard attire.

Be punctual: In fact, be more than punctual: Get to work early. If you are the opening bartender, you will be setting up for the entire day's business—restocking everything from liquor to bottled beers to wines, ingredients, paper goods, cleaning supplies; counting banks or floats (the money that you start with at the beginning of your shift); cutting fruit garnishes; polishing bottles and glasses; and doing whatever else is necessary at that particular place of business.

Be organized: Without getting overly picky about the order in which things are done, doesn't it make sense to restock items that need to chill and to get any messy tasks out of the way first? You bet. If you have chores to do in the basement or stock room—lugging huge buckets of ice to chill ingredients and use for serving, for example—do those things before you start cutting fruit garnishes and fanning out a tall stack of cocktail napkins. (Indeed, many opening bartenders arrive at work wearing grungy clothes because they know that the early part of their work is messy. They change into work clothes once those chores are out of the way.) As a rule, do anything and everything that requires your being away from the bar first. After that, get behind your bar and set it up to work for you.

Be physically strong: Unless barbacks do all of the heavy lifting—keg changing, ice hauling, and restocking—a certain amount of strength is necessary to do the job well.

Be honest: A bartender's pay is usually the combination of a low hourly wage and all the tips that he or she can make. Stories of bartender thievery are legion, but if you are good at your job, you shouldn't need to supplement your income by cheating the management and owners.

Be hard-working: Although it's not necessary to be a perpetual motion machine, there's always something that can be done behind the bar—polishing or washing glasses, straightening bottles, getting rid of all that superfluous matter that continually gathers.

Be tactful and diplomatic: Though it depends on the bar itself, bartenders generally keep the party rolling by trading quips, introducing one customer to the next, and having a good time while they work. But since the business involves serving beverage alcohol, sooner or later a customer will get out of control. A good bartender will cut a customer off before they become belligerent and will make sure that they know they can come back another time. Alternatively, a bartender has the power to "eighty-six"—permanently bar a customer—from the premises. When this becomes necessary, be sure that all of the staff and management are aware of the circumstances and the identity of the eighty-sixed former patron.

Be personable: Ideally, a bartender must get along well with the floor staff, the kitchen staff, the managers, and every single customer who walks through the door. He or she knows when to talk to people, when to keep his mouth shut, which customers have had enough drinks, who is becoming a nuisance to other customers, and who is merely trying to be friendly and break into the local scene.

Be well-groomed: Since the bartender is often the first person a customer sees upon entering a restaurant or bar, he or she should be presentable at all times. Many places have a uniform or dress code that must be followed. Just be sure that your hands and nails are clean and tidy at all times. Wash your hands after handling sticky ingredients or dusty bottles.

Be a gymnast: It is absolutely vital that a bartender be able to vault over the bar—one handed—in order to handle any situation on the opposite side. Nah, just kidding.

Be able to prioritize: Don't think this won't happen to you. It's the middle of a busy shift: What are you going to do first? Deliver food to your bar customers, serve the waitpeople, prepare a couple of drinks for the customers who just walked in, or answer the telephone? You need to be able to handle it all, without losing your cool or your temper. Most people don't understand just how complicated and stressful it can be to work behind a bar.

Be sober at work: Let's face it, some people want to be bartenders because they love to drink and hang out in bars.

However, there is no such thing as a good professional bartender who is tipsy, or worse, drunk while on the job. Wait until your shift is over to imbibe.

Be a good manager: At many restaurants, the man or woman behind the mahogany needs be able to take control of the entire restaurant at the drop of a hat. It's often the case that at the exact moment that the manager pops out to the bank, the deep-fryer will catch fire, a table of three will try to walk out on their check, and a busperson will spill coffee on a haughty customer's white linen suit. Someone must take charge of the situation, and the fact is, when a problem arises, the entire staff and the majority of customers will often run straight to the bartender—even if the manager is standing right there.

Bartenders are authority figures. "The bar is the pilot house of the restaurant," says Dale DeGroff, former head bartender and beverage manager at New York's Rainbow Room, "and the bartender is captain of the ship. Some people say that if there isn't a priest around, a bartender can marry people—that's authority for you."

Thus, given all the above, the ideal bartender is punctual, presentable, fairly strong, trustworthy, and able to read minds, judge characters, set the atmosphere, take control, make decisions, deal with troublemakers, command respect, and remain sober for eight hours at a stretch. Strangely enough, the majority of restaurateurs believe that knowing how to mix drinks is way down on the list of priorities when it comes to hiring a bartender. I don't agree.

BEHIND THE PROFESSIONAL BAR

You need to be able to make drinks—confidently, properly, and, ideally, quickly. That's where the layout of the bar is key to your success. Unfortunately, however, every bar layout is different. Naturally, some aspects are constant.

Most bars will have a number of stainless-steel sinks; usually at least two are used for glass washing, some are used as tubs to contain ice for serving, and some are used as tubs for chilling wine, bottled beers, and other ingredients that need to be kept cold.

Most bars will have a soda gun, a push-button nozzle that dispenses cola, lemon-lime soda, tonic, club soda, and usually water, ginger ale, or another ingredient.

Virtually every bar will have at least one cash register; many will have a service area at one end where the bartender serves the waitstaff's drink orders.

Most bars will have beer engines that dispense one or more draft beers; many will also have commercial espresso machines that are plumbed into the water system.

A number of refrigerated cabinets are the norm behind most bars; often there are display shelves for backup bottles of high-volume, popular liquor brands; drawers usually provide a haven for supplies of cocktail napkins, sip-sticks, straws, and other necessities.

At sink level it's important to have plenty of storage and work space; blenders might await use there, certainly whole fruit like bananas or pineapples will be kept there for use when needed.

Most bars will have what's called a speed rack, a long metal trough affixed at sink level that holds the most-often-used ingredients—so-called well liquors—that are poured when customers don't specify a brand name. Speed racks can be arranged in whatever order is most useful to that individual bar; for an all-around bar, the lineup from left to right is usually vodka, gin, tequila, rum, triple sec, blended whisky, scotch, bourbon, brandy, and then sweet and dry vermouths. Each of these bottles, as well as all of the most often-requested brands should be fitted with speed pourers, each facing with the open end of the spout to the left when looking at the bottle's front label. Any bottles that are visible to the public should be placed with front labels facing out; labels and bottles facing every which way are the sign of a sloppy bartender.

Plastic bottles with different colored pour spouts are excellent containers for juices and simple syrup; color-code them so you

Wine Bottle Volumes

$^1/_2$ standard wine bottle: 375 ml

Standard wine/liquor bottle: 750 ml

Magnum: 1.5 liters

Double Magnum: 3 liters

Rehoboam: approximately 4.5 liters

Jeroboam: 4.5 liters

Imperial: approximately 6 liters

Methuselah: approximately 6 liters

Salmanazar: approximately 9 liters

Balthazar: approximately 12 liters

Nebuchadnezzar: approximately 14 liters

How Many Drinks are in the Bottle?

One 750-ml bottle of wine = a little over five 5-ounce glasses of wine.

One 750-ml bottle of liquor = seventeen $1^1/_2$-ounce shots.

One liter bottle of liquor = $22^1/_2$ $1^1/_2$-ounce shots.

One liter of soda or juice = seven 12-ounce Highball glasses, each filled with ice and one shot of liquor.

know what's inside at a glance. These might also be kept in the speed rack.

Most bars span the area from the customer's side to four or five inches from the bartender's side and then step down an inch or so. In that space sits a rubber bar mat that looks like Dr. Scholl invented its stubby rubber surface. This bar mat is where a bartender lines up the glassware for the specific order being prepared. The mat provides a flat area directly in front of the customer and the bar mat sops up any liquids that are splashed outside the glasses.

However the brand-name liquors are displayed—usually in multileveled shelves on the back bar—their arrangement should be sensible, that is, all vodkas together, all gins together, etc. Bottles that are not frequently poured will not be fitted with speed pourers. When using them, the bartender can do one of several things: insert a speed pourer spout, free pour, or use a jigger for measuring. When finished using any ingredient, every item behind the bar should be returned to its normal location so that other bartenders will find it where it's supposed to be.

And now we come to making the drinks. For specific techniques, refer to Bartending Techniques (page 38) and Drink-Making Techniques (page 40) . There you'll learn everything you need to know to handle the experience effectively. Efficiency is the keyword in drink making. If you are ambidextrous, you are extremely lucky. For those of us who are not capable of functioning equally well with our right and left hands, learning to use both hands is a most worthwhile expenditure of time. Practice is key. Making a Highball by pouring the liquor with one hand and simultaneously operating the soda gun with the other is a must. When one hand frees up, it can next grab a sip-stick or garnish or place a cocktail napkin in front of a customer. Go out and watch a few good bartenders; you'll be surprised at the efficiency of their movements.

When you have a busy bar with a number of customers clamoring for your attention, the best, most practical way to cope is to keep your head down and work as quickly as possible on the order at hand. Glance up only to serve and accept payment. Then make eye contact with the next customer and keep going. Getting flustered doesn't help; keeping a cool head does.

Should You Attend Bartending School?

Gee, I don't know. Certainly some of them are excellent for conveying the basics of cocktail-making in a functioning bar or restaurant. I've spoken to graduates who glowed about the course they took, but like everything else, bartending schools are sure to run the gamut from really good to poor. I know one person who paid good money to attend a bartending school, and he showed me his "textbook" after completing the classes. I am not exaggerating when I say that more than 65 percent of the information in the "manual" was downright incorrect—even some of the classic drink recipes. If I were seriously considering a bartending school, I would ask for the names of former students and phone them to ask about the course and their opinion of its worth. If the school is not willing to furnish the names of satisfied graduates, I'd look for another.

Frankly, my best advice for people who are serious about the subject is to get your basic training in whatever way is possible. Then go out and beg for a job—as a barback, as a trainee, in any position that affords the opportunity to watch the accomplished and learn the moves and processes. In this case, experience is the best teacher. Practicing with a bottle of water and a few simple tools can make a huge difference to the budding bartender. In addition, start reading cocktail books— especially old ones to see how it was done and compare it to how it's done now. All of the recipes included here need not be memorized, but anyone serious about learning the craft of bartending should acquaint himself or herself with the classic recipes and classic ingredients while keeping up with what's going on right now.

Experimentation and practice, in this case at least, make perfect.

A Bartender's Glossary

Absinthe substitute: Any of several clear, anise-flavored liquors—Absente, Herbsaint, Pernod, and Ricard, among them—that are used to replace the true absinthe, which has been outlawed in the United States but is still legal in several European countries. Absinthe substitutes become an opaque shade of yellow-green when water is added to them.

Ale: A group of beers that are made using a strain of yeast that ferments at the top of a vat. A number of styles of ale exist, amber ales, barley wines, bitter ales, cream ales, India pale ales, lambics, porters, Scotch ales, stouts, Trappist ales, and wheat beers, among them.

Apéritif: A single beverage or combination of ingredients that usually include an alcoholic component that are drunk before dinner as an appetite stimulant.

Armagnac: A French grape-based aged brandy made in Gascony.

Aromatized wines: Wines that are flavored by any of several methods with herbs, spices, and other botanical ingredients. Vermouth is a prime example, as are several apéritifs, Dubonnet and Lillet, among them.

Barspoon: A long-handled spoon with a twisted shaft that is used to stir cocktail ingredients during their preparation.

Beer: Generally, this term refers to alcoholic beverages made by fermenting cooked grains, hops, and yeast. Lagers and ales are styles of beer.

Bitters: An alcoholic-based infusion of a base spirit and, usually, a number of herbs, spices, other botanicals, and other flavorings that are produced as proprietary brands by a few producers. Cocktail bitters, such as Angostura and Peychaud's, are used in very small quantities to add complexity to a drink mixture.

Blended whisk(e)y: A spirit made by combining one or more flavorful whisk(e)ys with flavorless neutral whisk(e)y to produce a particular flavor profile.

Boston shaker: A cocktail-shaking tool comprised of two parts: a metal cone and a 16- to 20-ounce mixing glass. The two parts fit snugly together to allow shaking, while the glass portion alone is used for stirring ingredients together.

Botanicals: A collective term describing the fresh and dried herbs, fruits, spices, and other components used to flavor some usually aromatic liquors, beers, and wines.

Bourbon: Any whiskey made in the United States, distilled from a fermented mash of grains that contains at least 51 percent corn and aged in new oak barrels for a minimum of two years.

Brandy: A spirit distilled from fermented grape or other fruit juice.

Buck: A Highball made of a base spirit, the juice of a squeezed lemon wedge, and ginger ale.

Calvados: An aged brandy made in a specific geographical area of Normandy, France, from a fermented mash of apples although a small percentage of pears is usually included.

Champagne: A sparkling wine made according to the *méthode champenoise* in a specific geographical area of the Champagne district of northeastern France.

Chaser: A beverage that immediately follows the drinking of another, as in a Boilermaker.

Churchkey: A tool that has a rounded bottle opener at one end and a V-shaped piercing can opener at the end. Generally, the V-shaped end is used to open cans of liquid, such as tomato juice or beef bouillon.

Cobbler: A cocktail made from of a base spirit or wine and simple syrup, which is poured into a wine goblet full of crushed ice and then stirred together.

Cocktail: A combination of ingredients that have been shaken or stirred with ice and strained into a chilled or ice-filled glass.

Collins: A mixed drink made from a base spirit, lemon juice, simple syrup, and club soda that is served in an ice-filled Collins glass with a fresh fruit garnish.

Cooler: A drink made of a base spirit, wine, or liqueur topped with a sweet carbonated beverage that is served in a Collins glass with a lemon twist garnish.

Cordial: Also known as a liqueur, a bottled beverage made from liquor, one or more sweetening agents, and other flavorings.

Crusta: A mixed drink made from a base spirit, lemon juice, and maraschino liqueur that is strained into a sugar-rimmed Sour glass that is lined with a lemon peel spiral.

Daisy: A mixed drink made from a base spirit, lemon juice, and grenadine that is served over crushed ice in a Highball glass and has a lemon twist garnish.

Dash: An inexact, small measure shaken from the bottle that should equal about $1/16$ teaspoon.

Digestif: A single beverage or combination of ingredients that usually have an alcoholic component and are drunk after dinner to stimulate digestion.

Eaux-de-vie: The French name for colorless brandies distilled from fermented fruit juices.

Fermentation: When yeast is introduced to sugar, or simple starches, in a mash, or "soup" of fruits, grains, sugars, or vegetables, it feeds on the sugar and produces heat, carbon dioxide, and beverage alcohol, and this process is known as fermentation.

Fix: A mixed drink made from a base spirit, lemon juice, and pineapple juice that is served over crushed ice in a Highball glass with fresh fruit for garnish.

Fizz: A mixed drink made from a base spirit, lime or lemon juice, simple syrup, and club soda that is served straight up in a wine goblet with fresh fruit for garnish.

Flip: A mixed drink made from a base wine, spirit, or beer, a whole raw egg, and simple syrup that is served straight up in a wine goblet or beer glass with grated nutmeg as a garnish.

Fortified wine: A wine that has had brandy added to it, such as Madeira, port, or sherry.

Frappé: A drink composed solely of a base liqueur or spirit that is served over crushed ice in a Saucer Champagne glass or a Sour glass.

Garnish: An ingredient, usually fruit or vegetable, that is added to a mixed drink or cocktail just before serving.

Gin: A spirit usually made from a fermented mash of grains that is flavored at some step in its manufacture with juniper and other botanical ingredients.

Hawthorne strainer: A bar tool with a spring coil that is used to strain liquids from the metal half of a Boston shaker.

Highball: The simplest form of a mixed drink that comprises just two ingredients, such as scotch and soda or vodka and tonic, which are poured directly into a Highball glass for serving.

Irish whiskey: A spirit made in Ireland that is distilled from a fermented mash of grains.

Jigger: 1) A liquid measurement equal to $1^1/_2$ fluid ounces; 2) a metal or glass tool used by a bartender to measure 1 fluid ounce or $1^1/_2$ fluid ounces of an ingredient.

Julep strainer: A perforated bar tool that is used to strain ingredients that have been stirred together and chilled in a mixing glass.

Lager: A style of beer made with a bottom-fermenting yeast.

Liqueur: Also sometimes known as a cordial, a bottled beverage made from liquor, one or more sweetening agents, and other flavorings.

Madeira: A wine fortified with brandy, produced on the island of Madeira.

Mash: The word used to describe the fruits, fruit juices, or cooked grains that are fermented with yeast to produce wine or beer or the mixture that will be distilled into spirits.

Mixed drink: A combination of two or more liquid ingredients, at least one of them containing alcohol. A Highball is one type of mixed drink.

Mixing glass: A 16- to 20-ounce glass designed for stirring together the ingredients for cocktails; also the glass half of a Boston shaker.

Muddling: The process in which a bartender uses a usually wooden pestle to crush together ingredients, such as wedges of fruit, sugar cubes, and bitters, and express their flavorful components.

Neat: Spirits served straight from the bottle without being chilled or mixed with other ingredients.

Perfect: A term that usually describes a cocktail that contains equal parts of both sweet and dry vermouths.

Pony: 1) A 1-fluid-ounce measure of liquid; 2) a serving glass usually used for serving spirits neat or for shooters.

Port: A Portuguese wine that is fortified with brandy and is produced in the Douro region of Portugal.

Proof: In the United States, the alcohol content of a beverage expressed by degree and based on 200 degrees equaling 100 percent. Therefore, 80-proof vodka is 40 percent alcohol by volume. Other countries use different scales and because of the confusion this presents, bottlings of current products express the alcohol content as the percentage by volume.

Rickey: A cocktail made from a base spirit, fresh lime juice, and club soda that is served over ice in a Highball glass, with a wedge of lime for garnish.

Rum: A spirit distilled from a fermented mash of molasses or sugarcane juice.

Rye whiskey: An aged spirit distilled from a fermented grain mash containing a minimum of 51 percent rye grain.

Sangaree: A cocktail made from a base wine, spirit, or beer plus a sweetening agent and garnished with grated nutmeg.

Scotch: An aged spirit that is distilled in Scotland from a fermented mash of grains.

Shaker: A bar tool that creates a sure seal and is fitted with a built-in strainer that is used to shake together the ingredients for cocktails.

Sherry: A wine fortified with brandy, made in a specific geographical area of Spain that surrounds the city of Jerez.

Shooter: A cocktail meant to be downed in a single gulp.

Shot: A $1^1/_2$-ounce measure of an ingredient.

Simple syrup: A solution of sugar dissolved in water that is used to sweeten cocktails. Recipe on page 33.

Single malt scotch: A type of whisky produced by a single distillery in Scotland from a fermented mash of malted barley and aged for at least three years in oak barrels.

Sling: A mixed drink made from a base spirit, citrus juice, simple syrup or a liqueur, and club soda that is served over ice in a Collins glass and usually garnished with fresh fruits.

Smash: A mixed drink made from a base spirit, simple syrup, and crushed mint leaves that is served over crushed ice in a Rocks glass and is garnished with a mint sprig.

Sour: A mixed drink composed of a base spirit, lemon juice, and simple syrup that is served straight up in a Sour glass or over ice in a Rocks glass.

Sparkling wine: Wine, such as champagne or Prosecco, that is carbonated by a secondary fermentation that takes place within the bottle.

Spirit: An alcoholic beverage, such as brandy, gin, rum, or vodka, that is made by distilling a fermented mash of grains or fruits to a potency of at least 40 percent alcohol by volume.

Splash: An inexact, small measure that should equal about $1/_8$ teaspoon.

Straight up: A drink when served without ice.

Straight whiskey: A spirit that is distilled from a fermented mash of grains and is aged in oak barrels to mature and develop flavor.

Swizzle: A cocktail made with a base spirit, citrus juice, simple syrup or a liqueur, and a carbonated beverage that is served in a Collins glass with a swizzle stick for stirring.

Tennessee whiskey: A spirit made in Tennessee that is distilled from a fermented mash of grains that is filtered through sugar-maple charcoal before aging.

Tequila: A liquor made in specific geographical areas of Mexico from a fermented mash of the *Tequilana Weber* variety of blue agave.

Toddy: A drink made from a base spirit, hot water, and various spices that is usually served in an Irish Coffee glass.

Vermouth: A wine slightly fortified with spirits and flavored by various aromatic botanicals.

Vodka: A spirit distilled from a fermented mash of grains, vegetables, and/or sugar.

Whisk(e)y: A liquor, such as scotch, bourbon, or rye, distilled from a fermented mash of grains that is aged in oak barrels. When the word is spelled without the *e,* it refers to products of Scotland and Canada, while those spelled with the *e* are made in Ireland, or the United States.

Zest: The colorful outer layer of citrus fruit peels where the essential oils are located.

Bibliography

Angostura Bitters Complete Mixing Guide. New York: J. W. Wupperman, 1913.

An Anthology of Cocktails together with Selected Observations by a Distinguished Gathering and Diverse Thoughts for Great Occasions. London: Booth's Distilleries, Ltd., no date.

Arthur, Stanley Clisby. *Famous New Orleans Drinks & how to mix 'em*. Gretna, Louisiana: Pelican Publishing Company, 1989.

Baker, Charles H., Jr. *The Gentleman's Companion*. New York: Crown Publishers, 1946.

——. *The South American Gentleman's Companion*. New York: Crown Publishers, 1951.

Beebe, Lucius. *The Stork Club Bar Book*. New York/Toronto: Rinehart & Company, 1946.

Berry, Jeff, and Annene Kaye. *Beachbum Berry's Grog Log*. San Jose: SLG Publishing, 1998.

Broom, Dave. *Spirits & Cocktails*. London: Carlton, 1998.

Brown, Charles. *The Gun Club Drink Book*. New York: Charles Scribner's Sons, 1939.

Brown, Gordon. *Classic Spirits of the World*. New York: Abbeville Press, 1996.

Brown, John Hull. *Early American Beverages*. New York: Bonanza Books, 1966.

Cotton, Leo, ed. *Old Mr. Boston De Luxe Official Bartender's Guide*. Boston: Berke Brothers Distilleries, Inc., 1949.

——. *Old Mr. Boston De Luxe Official Bartender's Guide*. Boston: Mr. Boston Distiller Inc., 1966.

Craddock, Harry. *The Savoy Cocktail Book*. New York: Richard R. Smith, Inc., 1930.

Crockett, Albert Stevens. *The Old Waldorf-Astoria Bar Book*. New York: A. S. Crockett, 1935.

DeVoto, Bernard. *The Hour*. Cambridge, Massachusetts: The Riverside Press, 1948.

Dickens, Cedric. *Drinking with Dickens*. Goring-on-Thames (England): Elvendon Press, 1980.

Duffy, Patrick Gavin. *The Official Mixer's Guide*. New York: Alta Publications, Inc., 1934.

Earle, Alice Morse. *Customs and Fashions in Old New England*. New York: Charles Scribner's Sons, 1913.

Edmunds, Lowell. *Martini, Straight Up: The Classic American Cocktail*. Baltimore and London: The John Hopkins University Press, 1998.

Embury, David A. *The Fine Art of Mixing Drinks*. New revised ed. New York: Doubleday & Company, 1958.

Emmons, Bob. *The Book of Tequila: A Complete Guide*. Chicago and La Salle: Open Court Publishing Company, 1997.

Gaige, Crosby. *Crosby Gaige's Cocktail Guide and Ladies' Companion*. New York: M. Barrows & Company, Inc., 1945.

Grimes, William. *Straight Up or On the Rocks—The Story of the American Cocktail*. New York: North Point Press, 2001.

Grossman, Harold J., revised by Harriet Lembeck. *Grossman's Guide to Wines, Beers, and Spirits. Sixth revised ed.* New York: Charles Scribner's Sons, 1977.

Haimo, Oscar. *Cocktail and Wine Digest*. New York: The International Cocktail, Wine, and Spirits Digest, Inc., 1955.

Harwell, Richard Barksdale. *The Mint Julep*. Charlottesville: University Press of Virginia, 1985.

Hastings, Derek. *Spirits & Liqueurs of the World*. Constance Gordon Wiener, consulting ed. London: Footnote Productions, Ltd., 1984.

Kappeler, George J. *Modern American Drinks: How to Mix and Serve All Kinds of Cups and Drinks*. New York: The Merriam Company, 1895.

Mario, Thomas. *Playboy's Host & Bar Book*. Chicago: Playboy Press, 1971.

Murray, Jim. *The Complete Guide to Whiskey*. Chicago: Triumph Books, 1997.

Ray, Cyril. *Cognac*. London: Peter Davis, Ltd., 1973.

Sardi, Vincent, with George Shea. *Sardi's Bar Guide*. New York: Ballantine Books, 1988.

Saucier, Ted. *Ted Saucier's Bottoms Up*. New York: The Greystone Press, 1951.

Terrington, William. *Cooling Cups and Dainty Drinks*. London: Routledge and Sons, 1869.

Thomas, Jerry. *How to Mix Drinks or The Bon Vivant's Companion*. New York: Dick & Fitzgerald, 1862.

———. *The Bar-Tender's Guide or How to Mix all Kinds of Plain and Fancy Drinks*. New York: Fitzgerald Publishing Corporation, 1887.

United Kingdom Bartender's Guild, comp. *The U.K.B.G. Guide to Drinks*. London: United Kingdom Bartender's Guild, 1955.

Vermeire, Robert. *Cocktails How to Mix Them*. London: Herbert Jenkins Limited, no date.

Index

C

L

T